The ABDUCTORS

The ABDUCTORS

STUART CLOETE

TRIDENT PRESS

New York 1966

Library of Congress Catalog Card Number: 66-15655

Published simultaneously in the United States and
Canada by Trident Press, a division of Simon & Schuster, Inc.,
630 Fifth Avenue, New York, N.Y. 10020

Printed in the United States of America

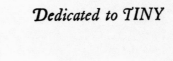
Dedicated to TINY

The ABDUCTORS

PART ONE

KIDNAP

KIDNAPPER. A child stealer, orig[inally] one who sold the children he stole to the plantations in North America.

Eric Partridge
Dictionary of Slang and Unconventional English

1 : The Governess

Lavinia Lenton looked at her husband. How handsome he was. Sometimes she thought he looked very like pictures of the late Prince Consort. So it was really not surprising that the girl should have made advances to him. But how many men would have told their wives? How few there were who would not have taken advantage of such an opportunity!

Sitting on a low brown velvet-covered chair, she raised her dark blue cashmere dress to show a little more of the white accordion pleats of the taffeta petticoat that hid her feet. Through the open window came the slow clip-clop of a carriage horse on the drive beyond the rhododendrons. A blackbird began to sing. Although it was autumn the day had a springlike feeling. Sharp enough for fires but not really cold.

"The girl will have to go," her husband said. One hand was in the pocket of his sponge-bag black and white check trousers, the other played with the gold watch chain that ran across his gray waistcoat.

"Yes," she said. "Yes, of course." She did not think she had ever been so angry. That a girl, a governess to her children, should do this under her roof. Taking her wages and eating her food. That she should dare. . . . Her breast, compressed by her corsets, rose and fell.

She felt her husband's eyes on her. He was looking at her in that way. That was the girl's fault, too. Bringing it out in him. . . .

Edward Lenton thought his wife made quite a picture sitting there. Quite a picture, with the sunlight coming in through the window, shining in the gold of her hair, flowing over her tight, white, high-necked blouse, her blue skirt with its white frilled petticoat that concealed all but the patent leather toe of one shoe. He wondered what she was really like under all those clothes. Even her nightdresses were high-necked, long-sleeved. But very few men ever saw their wives. Of course, she had never seen him either. He said: "Don't say anything about it till the end of the month. Then pay her and give her a month's wages instead of notice."

"Not say anything, Edward?" Lavinia rose from her chair in one graceful motion, sweeping her skirt round her in a wave of indignation. "I have never been so insulted, never been so angry. I intend to tell that young woman what I think of her sluttish behavior. Now—at once!"

"You will not do anything of the kind, my dear. I forbid it. There will be no words of any kind. And when you give her her notice there

[3]

is to be no discussion. You will pay her and you will give her a month's wages in lieu of notice. That is all. And a character of course." He smiled sardonically.

"You can imagine what that will be." Mrs. Lenton sank back into her chair.

"What you write is your business, Lavinia, but there will be no vulgar recriminations. You are thirty-three years old, and it is time you realized that there are good and bad women in the world. That we were unfortunate enough to employ a girl who turned out to be a 'wrong 'un' is just a piece of bad luck. She cannot be changed and I do not propose to have a girl of that moral character bandying words with my wife. Purity is easily contaminated, my dear. Those who touch pitch are defiled. So you will have as little conversation with her as possible. . . ." He smiled at her, half bowed, and went out of the room.

Mrs. Lenton looked at the heavy mahogany door as it closed with a soft, decisive click. In half an hour her life had changed. Evil had come into it, had crept in like a snake beneath the door. Evil disguised as a girl of eighteen, straight from a country parsonage. It was hard to believe but, as Edward said, still waters often ran deep. There was no doubt about that. But what a shock it would be for Ellen's father. What a shock it had been to her and poor Edward! She could imagine how taken aback he must have been when the girl had held his hand pressed into her bosom. She had not even been fully clothed. In a dressing gown and nightdress, he said. She must have been waiting for him in the passage that led to the bathroom. His hand pressed into the warm softness of that hussy's bosom! She felt herself blushing at the thought. And fancy a girl wanting, asking, for the indignities that were the price of marriage. A man's hands. A man. How right Edward always was! There certainly were good women and bad ones. She thought about the Bible. Jezebel, Delilah. . . .

The gilt clock on the mantelpiece chimed nine. Above the clock was a steel engraving of the Queen—Victoria Regina. On either side of it was a pair of blue Sèvres candlesticks. Between these major pieces, small bronze animals—horses, elephants, two cocks, a dog, and a cow—wandered haphazardly on an olive green velvet field. The white marble mantelpiece was carved, sculptured with acanthus leaves and Grecian, Wedgwoodlike urns over the arching hearth. Brass fire irons shone like gold in the firelight beneath it.

Like the mantelpiece, the occasional tables were covered with olive green velvet from which hung little blobs like velvet marbles, or the seed pods of the great plane trees in Berkeley Square. Their town house looked out on them. At the planes and the fountain. The green grass behind the high railings. The never-ending stream of carriages that went past. She often thought about London. The season. Soon her daughter Evangeline would be coming out. Another two years.

Mrs. Lenton's eyes were drawn back to the mantelpiece. At eight-thirty she had known nothing. Now this. All her thirty-three years the clock had been ticking away. All the sixteen years of her marriage, all the lives of her two children, her three miscarriages and two stillbirths, and only now had she noticed it, really noticed it, because time and age had become a new dimension when Edward said she was old enough to know the facts of life.

There must be no scenes, no words. Edward was right. But she was going to say what was on her mind. Silence was too much to expect. With a swish of petticoats she went over to the bellpull. The wires jangled and she heard the bell ring in the basement. A moment later a footman came in.

"You rang, Madam?"

"Send May to me, Charles."

"Yes, Madam."

Her husband had caught her only partly dressed. When he had knocked at her door and said: "I've got to see you at once," she had told Parker to hurry with her blouse and tie up her hair with a ribbon. She looked at herself now in the long glass. Thirty-three, he had said. As if she did not know it. Every woman knew when she was thirty. When the twenties were over. But she did not look it. Not now, with her hair tied with a ribbon like a girl, her eyes bright and her color high with anger.

She would send May to fetch her. This was women's business. For a moment she felt a revulsion against all men, even her husband. She would see Ellen in the boudoir. That was the place for this kind of business, not here. She made a *moue* of disgust. When it was over, she'd have Nestor saddled and go for a gallop in the park. Blow the cobwebs away. The nastiness of it.

The schoolroom at Mortal was on the third floor with only servants' rooms above it. The nursery wing, with its day and night nurseries, bathroom, sitting room, governess' and nurses' rooms. The windows were all barred against accidents—children could lean out too far and fall. The rooms looked like comfortable prisons done up in white paint and cretonne. But the generations of children who had been raised there had never known anything else except when they went downstairs. If they thought about it at all, they must have thought grownups did not fall out of windows, and left it at that.

But the view between the bars, framed by the white-painted iron, was beautiful—over the park with its great solitary oaks and groups of beeches, with its herd of fallow deer, strolling pheasants, occasional lolloping hare and the rabbits that lived among the rhododendrons, leaving their shelter in the early morning and evening, a living border of white, hopping scuts (there was never any shooting near the house). A joy to the watching children, generation after generation of them.

In the sunlight that flooded the rooms, two fair-haired girls bent over the table sucking their pencils. Eva, the elder, was fifteen, tall for her age, slim, with gray-blue eyes. Betty, her little sister, was only five. An angelic, lovely child, painstakingly making pothooks and hangers in a copybook. Eva was wrestling with fractions. On the other side of the table their governess stared out of the window, watching the white clouds drifting over the blue sky. She was fair too. She might have been her pupils' elder sister. English, all of them. Pink and white and gold. Fresh as posies.

"I think I've got it right now," Eva said.

"Bring it here, darling."

The girl came over with her exercise book. Ellen Pickford put her arm round the child. What nice children they were—so friendly, loving, and easy to manage.

"You've got it right this time, dear," she smiled. "Now try the next one."

When Eva sat down again, Ellen resumed her study of the clouds. A flock of tumbler pigeons flashed wings as they turned and fell through the sunshine. How peaceful it all was! A great house set like a jewel in the estate that surrounded it like a casket. Woodland, open fields, plough, and farms.

But something had happened today that upset her. Something she had feared for almost a month, but had put no name to. It had been just a feeling she had had. The way Mr. Lenton had looked at her. On two occasions he had taken her hand. Once, finding her alone, he had put his arm round her waist. You're a pretty thing, he'd said. She had blushed crimson all the way down her neck. No man had ever said anything like that to her, or had tried to touch her. But it could not mean anything. Not from Mr. Lenton, married to a beautiful woman and the father of the children she was teaching. Her employer.

But today he had kissed her; seized her from behind, turning her to him, pressing his body into hers. He had kissed her fiercely, savagely, on the lips, hurting her. "No!" she'd said. "No, Mr. Lenton!"

He said: "It had better be yes, my girl. And I'll have more than kisses from you."

What had he meant? What could he mean? She could not think clearly any more. She could only watch the drifting clouds and the pigeons. They were back, wheeling and falling again.

A governess was in a curious position—neither guest nor servant, something in between. She ate with the family if they were alone. Though she knew they liked her, she had discovered that the servants resented waiting on governesses. They gave no tips. They were ladies—gentry—but without the means necessary to uphold their social position. No better than servants, but they put on airs, with their educated voices and fancy manners.

One thing Ellen found hard to understand was the number of governesses there had been at Mortal. Only one had stayed a long time—Muriel—and she had left when Eva was twelve. She had stayed four years, coming as a nursery governess when Eva was eight. She still spoke of her. Then, in the last three years, there had been four girls—all young, all pretty, according to Eva, but none of them had made much impression on her. She barely remembered their names. One had been called Lavinia, like their mother; another Charlotte, the others Emma and Francesca. But why had they not stayed? It was a nice house. Mrs. Lenton was most kind. She had been so pleased to see her.

"I do hope you'll stay, Miss Pickford," she had said. "We have been so unfortunate with our governesses lately. Girls just don't seem able to stand a quiet country life now. It is quiet, you know. . . ."

"I am a country girl, Mrs. Lenton," she had replied. "I'm sure I shall be happy here; it is so beautiful."

"It is beautiful, isn't it, my dear?" Mrs. Lenton had gone on. "I was brought up here, educated in your schoolroom. . . ."

Evangeline was having trouble with her arithmetic because she was upset. Coming down the passage to the schoolroom wing, she had seen her father kiss Miss Pickford, heard her say: "No! NO!" and her father say something she did not understand about "more than kisses." Had he hurt her? She had wanted to ask, to cry out. She loved Ellen Pickford but this was some grownup business that was beyond her. Out of her reach. So she had dropped back, holding on to the banisters, and gone downstairs again and out into the garden. She did not want to meet her father or see Ellen till she had stopped crying. He must have hurt her to make her cry. But why?

She looked up under her lashes at her governess. There were still traces of tears on her face. She was biting her lower lip as if she was trying to keep it from trembling. She looked as if the slightest thing might start her off again. Tears came into her own eyes. It was terrible not to understand or be able to help.

There was a knock on the schoolroom door.

"Come in!" Ellen said. She wondered who it was. No one ever disturbed the children's lessons.

It was May.

"Yes?" she said.

"It's Madam, Miss. She says you're to come."

"Now? At once?"

"Yes, Miss."

Ellen looked at the two girls who were staring at her over their books. How pretty they were, how sweet! Betty was just a baby and it was hard to believe that Evangeline was fifteen, almost a woman. Still harder to believe she was only three years older than this child. A woman. A woman indeed, with its awful implications. Mrs. Lenton had sent for her. Should she take this opportunity to tell her? How did one say a thing like that? Say: "Your husband kissed me. Tried to touch me. Told me I had better let him. . . ." Would she believe her?

"Go on with your lessons," she said to the girls, and got up to follow the maid down the stairs to the first floor.

The girl opened the door of Mrs. Lenton's sitting room. A small, cozy room with a coal fire bright in the grate. This was where she gave her orders to the housekeeper and the cook, kept her accounts, and wrote her letters—part boudoir, part study. Intimate, filled with old furniture, hand-painted china, old pictures—cabinet photographs in blue velvet and silver frames, watercolors of country houses and Scottish moors. Cozy. Cozy was the word. Thick-carpeted, the steel fire irons bright with emery. Ellen had never been in this room before.

Mrs. Lenton sat in an armchair, staring at her as if she was a stranger; her hair was tied with a wide black ribbon and she was twisting a lace-edged handkerchief between her fingers. She must have come straight in here from her bedroom. She had not even said "Good morning."

"I sent for you, Miss Pickford, as soon as my husband told me of your disgraceful behavior."

"My what, Mrs. Lenton?"

"Madam," Mrs. Lenton said. "When a girl who is supposed to be a lady behaves like a slut, she loses her social privileges."

"But what have I done—Madam?" This was terrible. What had she done? What had he said? It was he who had. . . . Oh, now she saw it.

"Slut?" she said. "What do you mean, Mrs. Lenton?"

"I mean that a girl who offers herself to her mistress' husband is a slut. Imagine my feelings. Imagine what would have happened had Mr. Lenton not been an honorable man and demanded your immediate discharge. You would have lived here under my roof as his paramour.

"It is now the twenty-fourth. You will leave at the end of the month, the thirty-first. I shall pay you a month's wages in lieu of notice. This delay is merely to save talk. There must be no scandal. You will continue to dine with us, when we are alone, as usual. You may go now," she said. "And of course I can give you no character. You could not expect me to recommend you to anyone, could you?"

Ellen went out of the room. On the landing of the second floor, she passed Mr. Lenton. "So you're leaving us, my dear," he said. "What a pity! You could have been so comfortable and happy here." He smiled sadly at her. She brushed past him. Raising her skirts, she ran up the stairs.

And she had been wondering how she was going to tell Mrs. Lenton. She began to laugh. She was laughing and crying as she burst into the schoolroom. Flinging herself into her chair and sinking her head into her arms on the table, she burst into racking sobs. The children ran to her side to comfort her.

"Don't cry! Please don't cry!" Evangeline said.

"No I mustn't, must I, darling? I must be brave." But how was one to be brave when the world had come to an end?

Downstairs Edward Lenton picked up a letter he had written to read it over, to savor it. It was, in its way, a masterpiece.

Dear Mrs. Caramine,

We have been forced to discharge the children's governess who turned out to be rather a hussy, as so many of these pretty little country girls do, once they lose their shyness. She is eighteen, the daughter of a country parson. As my wife has refused to give her a character, she may be at a loss when she reaches London. I therefore commend her to you. With your vast acquaintance I am sure you can find her a situation and thus put my mind at rest. I will put her on the 2:20 on Thursday, the 31st. She will be wearing a gray dress, a long blue cloak, and a small black straw bonnet trimmed with cherries. I am confident she will do you credit.

I remain

Yours sincerely,
Edward Lenton

A beautiful letter. He really ought to go in for politics. He had a talent for it, for arranging things, for negotiation and intrigue. The thirty-first. She would still come down to dinner at 8:30 when the girls were in bed. That had been a concession to that fool Hawley, who had foisted her onto them. To change it now would mean talk in the servants' hall, and that was where most scandals began. Her father was Hawley's friend. That is to say, as much a friend as a penniless vicar could be to a great landowner.

"I won't have her treated as a servant, Edward," he had said. "Got to dine with you."

And dine she had and did. Except when they had people to stay for the shooting and the hunting; or tennis and garden parties in the summer. She always wore a miserable little blue muslin thing she must have made for herself. How he would have loved to dress her!

A week today. Another seven nights of it, of seeing her there, silent, still as a mouse, eating nothing, her eyes cast down, her eyelashes resting on her cheeks. How had she dared refuse him? A miserable little creature who should have been flattered by his attentions, as the others had been. Four of them. One had lasted a long time. Muriel had been his mistress for four years. She had not wanted to leave. But he had made her go before it began to show. He'd said: "You'll go to London to have the baby. I'll come and see you. A little flat," he had said. "You give notice. Say you are needed at home. I'll put you on the train and have you met."

"You'll come to see me?" she'd said.

"Of course, my darling."

"And the baby?"

"We'll get someone in the country to take care of it. Good air. Milk."

And she had gone. Really, old Carmine ought to be very grateful to him. But never, it seemed to him, had he wanted a girl more than Ellen. She was so young, so undeveloped, thin-armed, long-legged as a boy, so childlike. And this little chit had defied him. In a way he liked that, too. It showed she had blood. The vicar was a Pickford, the younger son of a younger son, and her mother had been a cousin of some kind. All the others had been too easy. They had come like dogs when he called them. When he said: "Leave your door unlocked tonight," they had been waiting for him.

At dinner, while he talked about the shooting and the neighbors to his wife, his eyes devoured Ellen. They peeled the blue muslin off her like a skin, and cut her into edible morsels as if she was a roast pheasant, the taste of her sharpened by the red currant jelly of her refusal.

When Mrs. Caramine received Edward Lenton's letter, she threw it over to Ada Prettyman. "Have her met," she said.

"Who by, Carrie?"

"Shaw-Kimble. You can't beat her for that kind of job. This girl's a lady. It will take a lady to catch a lady. They trust each other, you know. That's what makes Shaw-Kimble so valuable. And this is something rather special. Do you want to know the story? Give me the letter back."

She re-read it and said: "She's a virgin. She refused Edward Lenton and so he got his wife to sack her. He expects us to keep her for him. Probably thinks we should be grateful and do his dirty work for nothing. But he'll pay, my dear. I can get five hundred guineas any time for a girl like that, so why should I make him a present of her? Besides, there's always a risk. It's not like an Irish servant girl, or a girl her mother sells in the street. She may be poor but still have connections."

Suddenly she laughed. "I'm going to write to Delphine. This is going to be interesting."

To Delphine, who was in Boulogne with her relatives, she simply wrote:

"Hold yourself in readiness, with usual references.

Caramine."

Just two lines.

2 : The End of the World

In spite of its being the end of the world as far as Ellen was concerned, life continued at Mortal as before. Morning prayers, grace before and after meals upstairs in the children's sitting room and downstairs in the dining room at night. Through it all—the routine that had become a habit—she moved in a dream. Giving the girls their lessons, bathing Betty, putting them to bed, kissing them good night. Seeing they cleaned their teeth and said their prayers. Doing their hair. Cutting Betty's nails—all twenty of them. The number twenty struck her as strange. She had never thought of it before. Her mind fastened onto things like that. She prayed, kneeling beside her bed at night. She read her Bible—a whole chapter of the New Testament—before she blew out her candle. Things she had hardly noticed before became important: the smell of hot paint from the water cans the chambermaids brought upstairs for the baths; the hip bath itself—the tub brown outside, like the water can, and white inside; the songs of the black-birds and thrushes in the garden; the sound of distant shots as the shooting party brought down the driven birds. Cocks only. Beautiful green-headed, ring-necked, long-tailed pheasants, raised by Mr. Joliffe to be killed. She'd seen them when she first came, spotted chicks running in and out of the coops that held the hens that had hatched them imprisoned.

But thank God for the party—there had been only three dinners *en famille* before they came. Bachelors, soldiers alone, and married couples. She remembered Colonel Hawley saying that the shooting at Mortal was famous.

The brake and carriages had gone to the station to meet the trains. The ladies had all brought their maids. Most of the men had their valets, loaders, and dogs—flat- and curly coated retrievers, field spaniels. She had seen the leather gun cases and ammunition in boxes carried in. She had caught glimpses of women in their beautiful dresses and long white gloves, the men in tails and white ties as they went in to dinner. The women bright as birds, as pheasants. There were flowers everywhere—carnations and orchids, and great mop-headed yellow chrysanthemums in pots from the greenhouse.

The place was full of strange servants carrying clothes they had pressed, fetching things, bringing things to the spare bedrooms. Neat French maids, knowing valets. The housemaids were overworked carrying bathwater, emptying perfumed baths.

Ellen had always loved the children, but now her affection increased. She had hoped to see them grow up. Hoped to see them presented, married. What a lot of hopes she had had! She still could not believe she was really going, that it had really happened. That *it* which she never defined in her mind. It was Mr. Lenton's holding her in his arms, his hand on her breast. It was what he had said. The look in his eyes—a kind of mad look that had been followed by fury. It was Mrs. Lenton's saying: "I am Madam." It was the look on May's face, as if she guessed something. But one could not talk to servants. That was almost the worst of it. No one to talk to. She could not write to her father about it, so she just wrote as usual: about the shooting party, about three hundred brace of pheasants the first day with ten guns, about the gun dogs, about the house full of flowers, about the children.

She had told the children nothing. She had not the heart to. As if they, too, sensed something, they became even more affectionate. Night was even harder to bear. And the days passed and the white nights, winding themselves up like a string on a spool that got shorter and shorter. Days, hours, even minutes, began to count. She could not think of the future. She could not even think of the present because, without a future, there was no present.

Then the day came. She packed secretly. The children were sent out on an expedition with May. There were no goodbyes, no good wishes. Just an envelope, containing a five-pound note and a third-class ticket to London, brought to her on a small silver tray by Henry, the second footman, with a message that the trap was ready. He took down her valise and little trunk. The groom who was driving touched his cap and they were off, the wheels spinning on the gravel of the drive, crunching it like rolled bread crumbs.

In the distance, as they drove through the park, she saw the children with May. Very small, like dolls on a green carpet.

The groom had turned to her and said: "Don't cry, Miss." He had put his hand on her knee. A groom. A man. But why not? She was not even a governess now. She was nothing. To him she was just a pretty girl crying. She knew he would have liked to take her in his arms. And if he had, what could she have done? She had no home, no job, no protector. No position of any kind. This drive was the knife that cut her off from everything she had ever known, a severing of an umbilical cord. The warm security of the womb had gone. Like a baby, she must face the world. But a baby was not alone. It had parents, it had love. Home? Of course she had a home, but she was too proud to return to it. Too tenderhearted to face her father and hurt him, too ashamed to face the squire, who would certainly believe the Lentons' story rather than her own.

Poignant described these last days. Poignant. Events, emotions, objects, all assumed a new dimension. A great oak standing alone, still clothed in its brown autumn foliage as it waited for winter nakedness, assumed a new dimension, became more than a tree. The little station at Mortal Major was more than a station: it was a turning point in her life. Last time she had been here it had been ablaze with flowers, symbolic, it had seemed to her, of her own happiness, almost as if it had been specially decorated for her. Now the flowers were dead, waiting to be pulled out. Only a few Michaelmas daisies were still in their purple bloom. Brave, she thought them. Brave flowers. She must be brave, too. A brave girl . . . but she did not feel brave.

The train came puffing in. She saw a porter put her little trunk in the van. She turned the grimy brass handle of a third-class carriage and thought: "It will dirty my gloves." There was only one old lady in the carriage. Somebody's grandmother. Had she been visiting a married son or daughter? Did she live up the line? Was she going to London to shop? She was obviously county, as they said. But a lot of county people traveled third class, leaving the first to the parvenus—the new rich—who had bought places in the country and were posing as squires.

She thought of Mac, the Scottish deerhound. He was the only dog in the house. He would tolerate no rival, Eva said. They'd tried other dogs but he simply would not have them. "He did not kill them, but he would have, Miss Ellen," Eva said. "Oh yes, indeed, if we had not given them away!" Mac had come up to the nursery floor twice in the last week—something he had never done before—as if he felt something was up. She loved horses and dogs, but had kept away from the stables because she knew that was no place for a governess with all those men about. Kept away till the last few days, and then she'd gone because nothing mattered now.

There were two fox terriers in the stables—good ratters—and four or five cats. And the horses, of course. She loved the smell of horses and the stable sounds—the bang of wooden buckets on the cobbles, the stamp of hooves, the neighing that went on when it was time to feed, the horses' heads out of their boxes, their eyes excited, their ears cocked.

She'd hunted at home. There had always been someone ready to mount Miss Pickford, the parson's daughter. She'd even brought her old habit, just in case. She'd gone into Nestor's box several times. He was Mrs. Lenton's hunter, a beautiful black thoroughbred. She'd gone to pat him, and cry with her face in the horse's mane. Mr. Blackburn had caught her there, standing up to her knees in the clean wheat-straw bedding. Crying a little, whispering and talking to the horse, that had turned toward her and was nuzzling her waist with its soft mousy nose.

"Like horses, Miss?" he'd said, pretending to see nothing strange about her. "They know, Miss. They know who loves them, they do." He'd slapped the strong quarters. "Eh boy?" he said. "Know your friends, don't you? Come when you like, Miss," he said. "The boys'll give you no trouble." She thought of horses and dogs, and her friends at home. Anything to stop thinking about *it*.

Her mind went back to little things that happened long ago. Long, long ago. Six months, but in another life now. She remembered Mr. Lenton standing to watch her as she had raised her skirts to go upstairs. She remembered something one of the maids had said—was it May?—about that Muriel. If only she had spoken to her she might have learnt something. Always "ifs." But what had she known of the world or people? What, indeed, did she know now?

The old lady said: "Would you like to look at a paper, my dear? The

Morning Post and the *Times*—I always take them both." Then she had gone on to talk of the Suez Canal that had been completed fifteen years ago. About how she had once met Ferdinand de Lesseps and had been through the Canal when she went to visit a son in the Indian Civil Service. "A hot country, my dear. India is very hot, and curry did not agree with me.

"Chlorodyne," she went on. "Dr. Collis Brown's Chlorodyne is something you must always have with you if you go to India, my dear."

Go to India! Well, where she was going was even further than India. Nowhere was the most distant place in the world. But she was glad of the old lady's gossip: the Crimean War, the Mutiny, Florence Nightingale, the wonders of the Crystal Palace. The dear Queen, who had never recovered from dear Albert's death. "I was the same, my dear, when I lost my husband. I never recovered." She talked of Gladstone's Land Act that pleased neither the landlords nor the peasants in Ireland. Oh yes! She had a daughter there. And then those awful Fenians who, only two years ago, had murdered dear Lord Cavendish and Mr. Burke in Phoenix Park. "In a park, my dear, in broad daylight, with flowers and children playing. . . ."

The countryside went by. Fields, woods, farms, houses. The telegraph poles slicing England into chunks. The train passed a pack of foxhounds with the huntsmen and whips in pink, going back to their kennels. Even dogs. Hounds had homes.

The old lady's voice went on: *Chupatties,* rice, my bearer, *syce* . . . the Viceroy's ball—such uniforms, my dear. Pomp . . . ceremony. . . . Lancers, polo, pig-sticking. . . . It was all just an accompaniment to the flicking telegraph poles and the noise of the train going over the ties. They seemed to say: "What are you going to do now, Ellen. . . . What are you going to do now . . . ?" There was no need to answer the old lady. Just say: "Yes. Yes, of course. How wonderful!" and so on.

And then the country began to merge into town. The grass was not so green. There were more houses, streets, factories. "We're nearly there," the old lady said. "It won't be long now."

That was the worst of it. It wouldn't be long. Ellen thought of the last time she had been in London, of the drive from Victoria Station to Paddington. How excited she had been! London, the greatest capital in the world. What a success she was going to be! How lucky she was to be going as a governess to such nice people—relatives of the squire. Two sweet girls.

"Sweet girls, my dear," Colonel Hawley had said when he had interviewed her for them at the Hall. Her father had driven her to the station in the trap.

"My dear vicar," the Colonel had said, "I'm sure she'll be happy there. Nice people, lovely place—Mortal. Splendid shooting." As if shooting would be an attraction to her. As if a governess, not quite a servant and certainly not one of the family even if she was a lady, had anything to do with the real life of a great house. Though of course she had not known that then. As the vicar's daughter, she had visited all the houses in the vicinity as a guest. The county girls had been her friends since childhood. But when you were paid it was different. She had decided to be a governess to help her father. His stipend was very small. But at least this way she would cost him nothing. And the world—how she wanted to see the world! A bird wanting to try her wings.

Her head ached. Her eyes stung as unshed tears turned to acid in the atmosphere of smoke and soot. She found it even hard to breathe. The whole station under its glass roof was yellowish with a kind of sulphurous fog. The gaslights flared, each in a nimbus of brighter yellow, like rows of winter suns illuminating nothing. Engines, like exhausted dragons, puffed white clouds of steam and smoke that hung over them and then sank, turned into sooty moisture.

A porter walked along the train banging the carriage doors. People, expecting to be met, pushed past her. Others hurried on alone or in pairs. A child cried. Someone trod on a dog's foot. The platform was almost empty now. It was no use standing here. She must make up her mind. Get her little trunk out of the van, get a porter, go to a hotel she had been told about in South Kensington, and look for work. Advertisements. An agency. But what would she tell them? She had no character. No one to vouch for her. She could not ask the Colonel for more help after she had disgraced him. For that was what he would think when he got their letter. And Papa. What could she tell Papa? What would he think? He was so innocent. He knew nothing of lies, nothing more evil than a country girl having to get married in a hurry. She wished she could have arrived earlier in the day. It would be quite dark in an hour. But they had said it would be inconvenient to send her to the station before three. Mr. and Mrs. Lenton had become *they* now. They had ceased to be people.

Mrs. Shaw-Kimble recognized the girl at once from the description Mrs. Caramine had given her. Slim, gray eyes, fair hair, wearing a long blue traveling coat over a gray dress and a black straw bonnet trimmed with black cherries. She was carrying a small valise and looked distraught, as she made an ineffectual gesture to stop a passing porter.

Mrs. Shaw-Kimble went up to her, motherly as a hen. "Miss Denham," she said, "I am so glad you could come. I have no idea what I should have done if you had not been able to manage it. So kind," she gushed. "So kind," enveloping the girl in her arms and kissing her. "Like a daughter," she said. "You know I lost my dear daughter only last year. Just before Christmas. That's why,"—she paused to wipe a tear away—"the children . . ." she ended vaguely.

"Denham?" Ellen said. "My name is Pickford. I am Ellen Pickford."

Mrs. Shaw-Kimble looked about her. No one else was left on the platform. "There's no one else," she said. "No other young lady. Oh dear!" She dabbed at her eyes with her small, black-edged handkerchief. "What shall I do? Can't you come to me, my dear? Just for the night? I must have someone to leave the children with—my grandchildren, of course, Miss . . . ?"

"Pickford," Ellen said again. "Ellen Pickford."

"Miss Pickford. You see my friend, Lady Morecomb, said she was sending her niece down—a Miss Denham—to help me. Hetty Denham. Just for the night. She said she would put her on this train but I must promise to meet her. London is so dangerous for young girls." She looked about once more. "And who is meeting you, my dear? I don't see anybody."

"No one is meeting me. I was going to a hotel, to look around till I found something to do." Tears filled Ellen's eyes. "My box," she said. "I have a box in the van."

"We'll get it," Mrs. Shaw-Kimble said. "God must have sent you to me, my dear. Now I can go to my poor sister's bedside. Her deathbed, I'm afraid. Come, my dear," she said. "Come Ellen." She raised her umbrella to call a porter.

They looked like a mother and daughter with forty years between them. The last child of an aging woman, partridge-plump now, grayhaired, but with an air of authority, of knowing her own mind, of being somebody.

Mrs. Shaw-Kimble turned to the girl. "You're very pretty," she said. "Much prettier than Hetty Denham, I'm sure." She smiled up at the girl, who was six inches taller than she. Slim. A real beauty. No wonder old Carmine had been excited.

"By the way," she said, "you don't even know my name, do you dear? I thought you were Hetty so I never introduced myself, did I? She was expecting me to meet her, you see. My name is Mrs. Green. Sophia

Green. We'll put the box in a cab, my dear. It can follow the brougham."

She led Ellen to the waiting carriage. A liveried footman opened the door. The inside was upholstered in dark blue morocco leather that smelt beautiful. Ellen wondered what the children she was to take care of for the night were like. She loved children. She thought of the two sweet girls she had left, and wondered what their mother would tell them. She wished she had been allowed to say goodbye. How lucky she was to have met such a nice woman!

"I hope your sister is not as ill as you think, Mrs. Green," she said.

"Sister?" Mrs. Shaw-Kimble opened her eyes which had been closed. These adventures always tired her. She was getting too old for them but she could not have lived without the money. Not in any style. She had been thinking about the other girls she had met at various railway stations—they must run to more than a hundred over the years—and of her association with Carmine. Cards. She'd been up to her ears in debt when Carmine had called on her and made her a proposition.

"Sister?" she said again. "How kind you are to worry, Ellen. I don't know. I don't know at all. But," she added, folding her black-gloved hands in her lap, "it might be a happy release. She is in great pain. If God calls her . . . If God . . ." She waved the black-kid sausages of her fingers in the air with a gesture of resignation, said "God" again, and relapsed into silence. This girl was a beauty. She often thought about the girls she met. What did they do to them? She supposed men got what they wanted from them, got what they paid for. But that was none of her business.

The big Cleveland bay trotted solemnly along. It was really dusk now, almost dark. Lighting-up time. The carriage pulled up while the footman got down from the box to light the candles in the lamps.

Ellen watched a lamplighter with his long stick lighting the street lamps. They flared up but offered neither warmth nor comfort. Evenly spaced along the pavement, they spilled their light as if it was liquid onto the fog that was clouding the streets with a yellow, evil-smelling muslin veil.

She saw girls standing by the lights. Such pretty girls. She wondered what they were doing. Why did they not go home? They all looked as if they were waiting for someone. But how could that be? Why could they not choose some better place to meet their friends? She was still thinking about it when the carriage stopped and the footman opened the door. She saw steps in front of her. A big house. No. 23. But 23 what? She had no idea. Street, Crescent, Road, Square? She thought it must be Square, because there was an iron railing enclosing large trees. But it could have been Gardens.

The man who had run all the way from Paddington behind the cab to earn a possible sixpence, helped the cabby down with Ellen's little trunk. A rough man, with torn clothes, broken boots, and a dirty red handkerchief tied round his neck.

3 : The Madam

Mrs. Green led Ellen up the white Bath-bricked stairs and opened the door with her latchkey. They went in, with the footman behind them carrying the small valise. The hall was dark, medium-sized, paneled with mahogany, the floor a great chessboard of white and black marble squares. There were no pictures on the walls, no chest for carriage rugs, no hatrack on which coats could be hung. It was anonymous, and out of its anonymity rose a red-carpeted staircase, curving gracefully upward in a series of ellipses, getting smaller and smaller till they terminated below the glass dome, from which hung the chandelier that illuminated the ascent.

Ellen heard the cabman put down her box on the marble, and the front door bang. Mrs. Green and she, with the footman behind, had reached the first landing. She looked down just as the cabman looked up. He had a round face like a red plum pudding, with currant eyes.

"Rum place this," he said. "No bloody catch on the door. 'Ow do you get out, mate? That's wot I wants to know."

He had hardly finished speaking when someone appeared, pushed money into his hand, and opened the door for him.

Neither Mrs. Green nor the footman had paused. They were a dozen steps ahead. Picking up her skirts, Ellen ran up to join them as they turned down a short passage and through a green-baize-covered door. A moment later Mrs. Green was pulling the chintz curtains over the windows of a pretty bedroom, while the footman lit the gas. It was a pretty room. The bed, curtains, the slipcovers of the two armchairs were white and green, splashed with giant red and pink roses. The carpet was dark red, the eiderdown rose pink.

"What a pretty room!" Ellen said.

"It's yours, my dear. And I think you should rest. Go to bed. Lie down, anyway, and I'll send you up some tea."

"The children?" Ellen asked.

"I'll take you to them after tea. Oh, here it is. They must have heard us. Come in," Mrs. Green almost chirped, as a servant came into the room with a tea tray. "Have a nice tea, dear, and a rest," Mrs. Green said. "Help Miss Pickford off with her bonnet and cloak, Harris." She looked at the blue and gold enamel watch that hung from the bosom of her dark green bodice. "Why, it's six already," she said. "I'll be back in an hour. You'll be rested and feel better then." She went out without closing the door.

Harris relieved Ellen of her clothes. She was a big woman of forty or more, with strong hands that were almost like a man's, and big feet. She moved the tea tray, lifted up the silver cover of the muffin dish, looked at Ellen for a moment—stared really—and left the room.

Ellen poured herself a cup of tea, ate a muffin that was dripping with butter and, feeling much better, sat back in one of the armchairs.

She felt something was wrong. She could not decide what it was, but there was something. Where were the children? Why had Mrs. Green needed her, needed anyone in fact, in a big house like this that was full of servants? What had the cabby meant when he had said there was no handle on the front door? Door? Why had Mrs. Green not shut the bedroom door when she went out? The woman had, the servant.

Ellen sprang up and tried the handle. It turned in her hand but did not open. She went to the window and pulled back the curtains. It was barred. Of course nursery windows were generally barred, but this was not a nursery. She was a prisoner. And no one knew where she was. But why? In God's name, why?

Mrs. Caramine was small, sharp, dark, a little Manchester terrier of a woman, with the neat legs of the breed. Beautiful legs they were, and always had been. They had been the making or undoing of her, according to the point of view. By the time Bentham, the Lancer who had first kept her, had died, her legs were well known in London. Like hock bottles upside down, nicked into the prettiest ankles in the world. So there were plenty of takers even before poor Bentham was under the sod, and she had been able to pick and choose. In those days she'd still liked men, liked their hands on her, and their lips. Liked all of it. And many were the satin slippers ruined with Mumm and Pommery by her lovers' loving cups. Her toes were pretty, the "This little pig went to market" kind of toes, like a baby's, that men pulled and nibbled as if they were sweetmeats. High insteps, beautiful knees and thighs.

There had been a time when fivers fell like autumn leaves on her Aubusson carpet. What a lovely carpet that had been! Buff, with garlands of pink roses. Fivers just to look at her legs, by God, and more—a lot more—to touch. What a bloody work of art I was then, she thought, a bloody shepherdess—warm, smoother than silk to touch. Spilled milk, that's what those years were, but not much of it. More like spilled champagne and cognac, with the cigar smoke wreathed about her, living, boiling snakes of it. Havana. The best. Always the best for Carrie Caramine. That was the way it had begun. That was the way it had gone on.

Fifty was her stated age, but she was more—five years more at least—but pretty still by gas and candlelight. From a distance she looked as she had always looked. So many women put on weight, but she had seen to that. Careful as a jockey. The simile made her laugh because it was all upside down, like so much in life.

She wore her dyed black hair in ringlets, like the Empress Eugénie when Winterhalter had painted her. Her eyes were still immense, dark brown pools, but dead now—like wet stones. The eyes of a woman who has seen too many naked men and naked girls: unsurprisable. Once the trout of passion had risen in those pools. The eyes had flashed, rippled with light and hidden laughter. How she had teased them! She had always made it last. Slow to begin, because afterward it was all emptiness till next time. The art of a courtesan, of a kept woman, was to inflame and to hold. A gentleman's generosity was a variable, dependent upon his needs. Her needs, too. Hers for money—played against his lust. With an unspoken bargain always struck. There was, in fact, not very much difference between a bedroom and a counting house.

She lit a cigar and sipped her brandy and soda. The first cigar had been for a bet—a monkey—and she'd won it. But how sick she had been! She always told the girls that the first cigar was worse than the first man. There was a certain similarity here, too. Now both were a comfort to her. An occasional man, and a cigar every night after dinner. She rearranged her bronze and green shot-taffeta dress. She favored shot silk. Her hand crept up to her tiny, tightly laced waist. Fat! What silly cows they were to let themselves get fat. It wasn't just a woman's face that was her fortune, it was the whole of her. But they forgot it. They just looked at their faces in the glass. It might be the first thing a man noticed, but it wasn't what he remembered. Figure, walk, style, clothes. Even the way you took them off. Bentham had taught her how to undress. "Christ," he said one day, "it's like watching someone peel a banana. Don't hurry. Don't stand still. Move, smile, bend. Let them fall so that you stand like a flower in its petals. Don't pick them up. Let your maid do that." He'd been a good teacher, trained her like a bloody spaniel. Told her things about men, about the way they thought and didn't think, about what they wanted. Unusual, too, some of their wants were. She hadn't believed him then, but now she could have told him a thing or two.

She liked this hour by herself before business began. She liked to think, to remember. She often thought about good women. She'd had some good girls through her hands, but once they were broken in it was over. When they lost their pride, they were done. Not like some of the common little vixens who acted so quiet and suddenly played up.

Mrs. Caramine thought of the two letters she had written. One began:

Dear Mr. Lenton,

I am sorry your governess turned out so badly but these things happen, and the cloud may after all have a silver lining. If you happen to be in London in about ten days we might discuss the matter.

In the meantime a young French lady, very highly recommended and qualified, has asked me to put an advertisement in the *Times* to say that she is looking for a position as governess to a nice family. Her name is Delphine Le Grand. She is dark, vivacious, very pretty. And discreet, though only twenty-five. I'm sure she would fit into your household to perfection and I think when the advertisement appears you might be able to persuade Mrs. Lenton to employ her. Her references are excellent, and French is so important in the education of a young lady of fashion today. . . .

She went on about the weather—rather foggy and cold—some social gossip, and concluded:

Your sincere friend,
Carrie Caramine

She added a P.S.:

I trust Delphine's appearance will not prejudice you against her, as her manners and dress are very quiet. She is a Protestant, coming of a good Huguenot family, so that there will be no difficulty on this score. She speaks excellent English and is a most accomplished teacher of young girls and children. Looking forward to seeing you shortly. I am glad to say I have been able to help the young lady you mentioned to find a satisfactory position.

The other letter contained a postal order made out to the *London Times* and the advertisement that would appear in the "wanted" column:

Young French lady, good appearance, highly recommended, seeks position as governess in a nice family. Country preferred. Box 1781.

She thought of the other girl Edward had sent her. Another governess, whom he had seduced and made pregnant. "In foal," was the way he'd put it. She'd taken care of Muriel, sent her to the country to have the baby. A boy. That had been good news to give him. It had hit him hard because he wanted a son. "My by-blow, a boy!"

"Son and heir," she'd said. "But you can't have your cake and eat it, Mr. Lenton. You married an heiress, an only child, and they're not good breeders as a rule. The stock's running out, you know. That's what makes 'em rich. I remember you told me Mrs. Lenton had no uncles—just an aunt—and her father was an only son. A lot of money and a lot of children don't go together very often, do they?"

The boy was at school now. She was paying for it. Not out of the goodness of her heart, but because she wanted to show him to Lenton one day. And Muriel had married.

It had taken a long time but it was all *en train* at last. Fate had played into her hands. It always did if you had patience and waited long enough. Forty years it had taken. That was when it had begun.

That was a day she would never forget—an afternoon. Her mother was out and Uncle Jack had let himself into their little flat with his latchkey. There had been a number of uncles in her life, one of them her father. She remembered him vaguely. A tall, thin, quiet, rather sad man with reddish muttonchop whiskers. Then when she was about six he had stopped coming, and another uncle had come in his place.

John Lenton—Uncle Jack to her—had hung up his hat and ulster and said: "Where's your mother, Carrie?" She had been fourteen then. It was her birthday and her mother had gone out early. "Things to do, darling," she'd said. "Shopping. And I'll bring back the cake."

"When do you expect her back, sweetheart?"

"Not for a couple of hours, Uncle Jack. She has only just left."

"Damn it," he said. "I haven't much time."

Quite often he was short of time in the afternoon, and then her mother sent her out with a note to some friends who had a little girl, and she would play dolls with her or they would read.

"A couple of hours, eh? Come here, darling."

She went over to him. He was looking at her in a queer way. Later she was to know that way very well. She'd had on her silk tartan party dress, hunting Stuart, mostly red. It had a tight bodice and the skirt was pleated almost like a real kilt. He had pulled her onto his knee and kissed her. Then, holding her with one hand, he had pulled her drawers off and had her. There, on the big sofa. She had struggled and screamed. But it was no use. He was too strong. Savage. He'd said: "By God, I came here for it and I'll have it! I'm keeping you both, aren't I?" She had not known what he meant. She was in hysterics with pain and fright as he panted over her.

That was when her mother had come in. He had stood up and she had fallen to the floor. She lay there, half sitting up, staring at them.

Her mother, her eyes flashing, had gone for him and ripped him across the cheek with her nails. "You beast!" she said. "After all I've put up with from you!"

He hit her, knocking her down with the flat of his hand. "You'd better get used to it, Lily. I'll have the two of you now. You're getting old, my dear. You're not a girl any more. Thirty, if you're a day. I was looking for a new one and here she was all the time, ready to hand." He mopped the blood from his face with a white silk handkerchief. Her mother lay on the sofa sobbing.

He went over to the little fireplace and stood with his back to it. "You can cook for us, Lily, and maid her. I like this flat. It's convenient." Then he had laughed. "By God," he said "this will amuse the chaps. Mother and daughter. Glad you were out, my girl. I'll send a check to-morrow." And he had gone, banging the door behind him.

John Charles Lenton. Edward Lenton's father.

Her mother had got up and gone to the bedroom to tidy herself. Then she had said: "I'll go and get the cake now." That was all. Nothing else. Nothing about what had happened. Those were the last words her mother had spoken. An hour later a policeman and some people had brought her back, dead.

"Flung 'erself under a bus, she did, pore soul, and so pretty too."

After that there'd been a lot of coming and going. She did not remember what had happened. She had not gone out. She'd eaten some cold sausages and bread. A neighbor had taken her in. She'd been ill. Very ill. She did not know who'd seen to the funeral. The next thing she remembered was Bentham coming. She was still staying with the people in the next flat. The Smiths. She often wondered what had happened to them.

Bentham was a kind of uncle too, but not a real one like the others. He just came to talk to her mother and never stayed long. When he was there she was never sent away. Maisie Smith had said: "You'd better go with him, dear." And she had gone.

Six years she'd lived with him. More pet than mistress, he had set her up in a little house in St. John's Wood, an area famous for such establishments and laughingly known as "the grove of the Evangelist."

If she had ever loved a man, it was Captain George Fitzpatrick Bentham of the Household Cavalry. He had never forced her. He had taught her to ride and drive, turning her into a first-class horsewoman and whip. She was one of a crowd of them—Cyprians, anonymous, pretty horse breakers as they were called—who drove in the Park and rode in Rotten Row from five to seven, and met socially almost every day at the Achilles Statue—symbolic, perhaps, of their virile lords and masters—to talk and compare jewels, furs, clothes, horses, and equipages. The flower of their kind. Gorgeous as tropical birds. When Bentham had died, she had mourned him for a week, bought a trousseau of widow's weeds that suited her dark hair and milk-white skin, and turned to his friends. Not to one of them—to almost all of them. They all came to her bed. She became quite famous. She had taken the name of Caramine, her mother's name. But they called her Carmine—her favorite color.

Then Mother Hopkins had called on her. She kept the best house in London, and wanted her in it. "It's not good for a girl to live by herself the way you do, dearie," she'd said. Very motherly, Ma Hopkins was.

She'd refused, of course.

But a month later she'd returned the call. Ma Hopkins had given her an idea. A house of her own. But she'd remain free.

"I want to choose, Ma, not be chosen," she said. "I only sleep with my friends."

"Then why did you come?"

"I want to learn the business, and I'll help you part time. I am good at figures."

"Figures, dear? If you're good at figures come tomorrow."

Three years at Ma Hopkins', including two business trips to Paris to inspect fresh batches of French girls. In Paris she'd learnt a lot. There were things Ma Hopkins would not have. No cruelty, no whips, no perversions. But that was what men paid the most for. And she had her own clients. Bentham's friends and their friends. Soon she knew the business inside out. All she had to do was lease a house, furnish it, get three or four topnotchers, and she was in. She had never looked back.

Mrs. Caramine stubbed out her cigar and rang the bell.

"Post these," she said to the footman. Forty years had been a long time to wait, but the minute she heard the name—and that was twelve years ago—she had begun to plot. The parent had eaten sour grapes and Edward's teeth were to be set on edge by one means or another. How she had spoiled him! How she had nursed him along! She knew about his wife, Lavinia, and about the two girls. He had shown her pictures of them.

Old Shaw-Kimble must have slept it off by now. She called it resting. "I must have my little rest, Carrie," she always said, and was shown into the bedroom that had been prepared for her, with two carafes on the washstand—one of water and one of gin. Old fool. Useful. Indispensable almost, but she must never find that out.

She decided to go and look at the girl again. She went upstairs to the room next to Ellen's and put her eye to the peephole. It was invisible from the other side, a tiny black hole in the moss rose pattern of the wallpaper that was kept plugged when not in use. It gave directly onto the bed. That was something she had learned in Paris. That there were men who would pay to look. Voyeurs. Particularly old men who had to be excited.

The girl had not undressed. She probably wouldn't. She had been crying. But she was certainly a beauty. A beauty, a lady, and a virgin. A combination that would cost Edward Lenton five hundred guineas when he came to London. Always guineas. What did they say? "Look after the pennies and the pounds will take care of themselves." Well, that was a good philosophy, but a shilling on every pound was a better one. Besides, it was more professional. "To services rendered . . . so many guineas." That was the way she sent out her bills.

She looked again. The girl had pulled the curtains and was looking out through the bars at the sky.

Ash blonde, slim, willowy, a beautiful mover with pretty hands and small feet. She'd let her stew in her own juice for a couple of days and then she'd talk to her. She might be sensible. Anyway, patience would be necessary. No brutality. Not yet, anyway.

She went downstairs again. It was time to get Fanny Shaw-Kimble up and send her home.

When Mrs. Shaw-Kimble had left Ellen she had gone straight to her room. She called it "my room." She always went there after these "expeditions." She called them expeditions. There were the two carafes on the big marble washstand. She took the tumbler off one of them and smelled it. The wrong one, of course. She took the glass off the other, poured in two fingers of gin, added some water and gulped it down. That was better. These expeditions took it out of her. Thank God she had not had to be disguised this time. Sometimes she met trains dressed as a nun; that was when Carrie got news from Liverpool that some Irish girls were on their way to London.

But it went against her conscience to dress as a nun, a bride of Christ, and bring girls here. Her mind went back again to men and women and what they did. Here the trail of her thought became confused. She thought of romance, of love. But that wasn't it, not in this place. Once she had met one of the girls she had brought here on the stairs. She had not known her. She was wearing a low-cut evening dress, very low. Her lovely shoulders were bare. Her hair was loose down her back, long black hair. She had big gray Irish eyes put in, as they said, "with a sooty finger." The girl had stared at her. She had recognized her, stood frozen for a moment, and then had spat in her face. A big gob of spit from a girl in a white evening gown. She had never forgotten it. What hatred there had been in that face! She had told Carrie. Carrie said she would be punished, no more than that, but the way she had said it. . . . There was no doubt about Carrie Caramine being a bad woman, evil. She was afraid of her but had to do what she told her. Money. Money was the root of all evil. Evil was the root of all money. She lay down on the bed and dozed. She had not even taken off her bonnet. Mrs. Green, always Mrs. Green, when she was not a nun.

Soon that woman would send for her and she'd go. Go the way the girls went when Carrie called them—in fear of punishment, in fear of getting her money cut off. She did not want to sleep, but she did. The gin had relaxed her.

"Well," Mrs. Caramine said when she came in, "you did a good job, Fanny. You always do. I know I can count on you."

Of course she could. She supplied servants, the carriage, the money that paid for them. Carrie Caramine held her like a rabbit in a net.

"She's a beauty, Fanny." Mrs. Caramine licked her lips. She had a small, very pink tongue. What was she thinking of? Fanny Shaw-Kimble did not want to know what she was thinking of. She wanted to get out, to get home, back to her house in Bolton Gardens, with the Colonel's tiger skins and his guns and trophies. If only she could stop playing whist for high stakes. If only. . . .

4 : The Trap

In her room Ellen was making further discoveries. Behind the chintz curtains, folding padded shutters were recessed into the wall. The bed was bolted to the floor. In the drawer of the table there was a card on which, written in a copperplate hand, it stated: *Should you wish to go to the bathroom or need anything, please ring the bell.*

This really brought it home to her, to be taken to the bathroom like a child. She crossed the room and rang the bell.

A few minutes later the door opened—she had heard no steps on the stairs—and Harris came in. This time she took a closer look at her. She wore a black maid's uniform with a white starched cape and apron, but with her enormous feet and hands and the width of her shoulders she looked more than ever like a man disguised as a woman.

"Well?" she said.

"I want to go to the bathroom."

"Come along, then." She pointed to a door down the passage and followed close on her heels.

When Ellen came out she was there like a sentry between her and the stairs. She said: "Go back to your room." Again she followed her, leaving the door ajar. It was evident that it only opened from the outside.

"What's your name?" she asked.

"Ellen. Ellen Pickford."

"Ellen, eh?" No Miss Ellen, no nothing, just a big wooden face, quite immobile and small, hard gray eyes.

"Well you're trapped, Ellen. You know that, don't you? Caught like a bloody mouse in a trap. How did she do it? Old Fanny, I mean. The kids and her sick sister again?"

"Mrs. Green brought me and I want to get out. I've got a little money, Harris. Five pounds. I'll give it to you."

The woman laughed. "A fiver, kid? You don't know what you're worth to the Madam. A lady, pretty as a picture, and a virgin I'll bet."

Ellen felt herself blushing. Virgin. She'd never heard the word except when her father spoke it from the lectern. There were virgins in the Bible, wise virgins who filled their lamps, but she did not really know what it meant.

"Virgin?" she said.

"Never had a man," the woman said.

"Oh! How dare you!"

"Well, you will, ducks, before long. Look, dearie, that's where you are—in a knocking shop. A whore house. You're here for men and if you've any sense you'll take it quiet. Lying down, or any way they want it." She laughed again. "If you don't, I'll hold you for them. Many's the one I've held, and don't think there's a way out or that anyone can hear you scream. There's been lots of screams from this here room, and others too. Thick walls, thick carpet, shutters to the window. And besides, who'd care? No one in this house. So think it over, Miss. Just take it lying down, that's my advice, ducks." She went into peals of rough laughter as if she'd made a joke, and went out.

God, Ellen thought. God would help. She knelt by the bed to pray.

What had happened here, here in this room? What did Harris mean? Screams. A whore house. Something else she did not know about, only that it was wicked. No one had ever told her anything. If her mother had lived. . . . But she knew from the way other girls talked that their mothers didn't tell them anything, even when they got married. It wasn't nice.

She thought about her father, about how he'd worry when his letters weren't answered. She saw him—dear, sweet, gentle, pink-faced from his country life—pushing his white hair out of his eyes as he puttered about in the garden. What would they tell him? They. The Lentons. Why had Mrs. Lenton refused to listen to her? A slut, she'd said, a slut. . . . Only God could help her now. But she knew she'd not have been able to tell Mrs. Lenton anything. She'd have been too ashamed—about how he had touched her breast and pinched her, pulled her to him. How hard he'd been, how strong. How did a girl ever resist a man if she was alone with him?

It was extraordinary and horrible to think of the prayers at Mortal. Of how, before breakfast, the whole staff had filed into the big drawing room and, led by Mr. James and the others in order of seniority, had knelt at the gold, brocade-covered chairs, while Mr. Lenton read from the prayer book and the Bible, and led them in the Lord's Prayer. She had knelt near him and Mrs. Lenton and the children. Looking back on it now, she knew she had felt him staring at her even then. How could a man do that? How was such hypocrisy possible? The prayers had been so familiar. Accustomed to them all her life, she had looked forward to them. They had brought her home and her father nearer to her. She knew that in the vicarage he was conducting prayers too, with old Jane, the cook-general, and Jack, the outside man—groom, gardener, and anything else that was needed about the vicarage.

She lay down fully dressed on the bed. Outside she could hear people whistling for cabs. Free people, servants calling cabs for people who were going home after dinner. And then Harris was back.

"Undress," she said. "The Madam says you're to undress."

"I won't undress."

"Do you want me to undress you?" Harris took hold of her arm.

It was no good. "Unhook me," Ellen said.

The woman unhooked her dress, all the little black hooks and eyes that May had done up for her this morning. May crying, and saying: "It didn't ought ter be allowed. Someone ought ter tell 'er."

"Tell who? Tell her what?"

But the girl had refused to say any more except that she was well out of it. May was pretty, fresh as an apple. Roses and cream, plump. But her voice had been vicious.

Ellen looked for her valise. It was gone.

"Where's my valise?" she said. "It's got my night things in it."

"I took it," Harris said, "and I'll take them too."

She pulled off Ellen's chemise. She knew the Madam was watching. She'd said: "Take off her clothes. I want to see what she's like."

Back at the peephole, Carrie Caramine was more than satisfied with what she saw. There was no doubt the girl was lovely. A milk-white skin tipped with gold, small firm breasts and rounded buttocks, long slim legs, fine ankles. Perfection. This was a piece of goods indeed.

She saw Harris snatch off the chemise and march off with her clothes.

Nakedness. Naked and ashamed. That was the beginning of the treatment. . . .

At Mortal, Lavinia was sitting alone in her boudoir. A crystal lamp, its silk shade fringed with glass beads, illuminated the room with a warm, soft glow. The coal fire burned brightly, the flames burning blue before they turned yellow, the coals bright red.

She was thinking about "The Doll's House," a play Mr. Ibsen had written six years ago. What a scandal it had caused! How furious Edward had been to find her reading it! "Where did you get it, Lavinia?" he'd shouted. "That filthy man. A Jew. . . ."

"I don't think Mr. Hendrik Ibsen is a Jew. He's Swedish. Quite famous, too."

"Infamous. And if he's Swedish, he's a Swedish Jew. Determined to undermine the established order of things, like them all."

He had stamped out, banging the door behind him. One of his rages. He was given to rages. In a child they were called tantrums, in a man rages. There was no real difference except that men were dangerous and children weren't. But he could stand none of these new ideas about women. Women were chattels, subject to fathers, husbands, brothers—to men always. They always had been and always would be.

But Mr. Ibsen didn't think so or he would not have written the play. Mr. Longbeach didn't think so or he would not have lent it to her. How glad she was Edward had not asked her where she had got it. Not that she would have told him. And there was no name on the flyleaf. Let him guess if he wanted to.

What was it Nora said in the play? "You have always been so kind to me. But our home has been nothing but a playroom. I have been your doll, just as at home I was Papa's doll child. . . ." And here the children have been my dolls. . . . That was the way it went as far as she could remember. But that he had written it at all meant something. And that Mr. Longbeach had bought it and lent it to her meant something. It meant that he thought she was a person. Someone real. Not a doll. In America things were better, she had heard. She wished she could talk to Mr. Longbeach about it, but they could never talk. She knew he felt for her position. He knew she understood his feelings. But the gap was too big. He was just a country lawyer, a man of business. Age had separated them. They had met as children. She had not been more than ten or twelve to his fifteen. He had shown her his rabbits. Her mother had gone to see his mother about something to do with the village—town, really—but they called it the village. And he'd said: "Come and see my rabbits." Ferrets, too. She hadn't liked the ferrets. Nasty, sneaky things. But she'd asked him for a rabbit, a white rabbit with a black nose and ears.

Then she'd grown up, been presented to the Queen, married Edward. Her parents had been dead by then. Her mother had died in childbirth and her father, her dear Papa, had been killed in the hunting season that followed her mother's death. On purpose, some people said. Put his horse at an impossible stone wall and they'd both been killed. Man and horse. Perhaps that was a good way for a man to die. Perhaps, but it had left her alone. A young girl, a great heiress, and her aunt had got her married as quickly as she could. Presented and married. All in a kind of whirling dream of diamond tiaras, pearl necklaces, ostrich feathers, waltzes, champagne, four-in-hands, rides in the park with a groom behind her, and Edward, the dashing officer of Her Majesty's Foot Guards, clamoring for her hand. There had been others, too. But he had been the best looking, the most charming, and—though she had only found this out later—the poorest. Out of the schoolroom almost, into bed. Knowing nothing. No one had ever told her anything. Certainly not Aunt Evangeline.

That had been sixteen years ago, when she was seventeen. She could still remember the brutality of it. The terror. Edward's polite contempt for her by day, and the other thing by night. Then she found it was usual. That was what men did to women. How they did it. It was something women had to put up with. The children compensated them for it. But did they? Did they? Two daughters, two stillborn children, three miscarriages—and all he wanted was a son. One of the dead babies had been a son—how he had gone on about it, as if it was his loss, not hers. He did not love his daughters. They were girls. They would become women, get married, and he'd lose his name. He wanted a Lenton heir to his name and to her property—Mortal.

But over the years he had become her master. She did what he wanted and never thought of her own desires. But something was stirring in her. It was as if the carefully trained plant of her life was sending up a new shoot from its root stock. Something wild, undisciplined, and free.

And what about that girl? Had she been right? Why had Edward sent her in by the afternoon train? She would get to London in the dark. And . . . and there was something funny about it. The servants were acting queerly too, as if they had a secret of some kind. And the girls. Edward had not even let them say goodbye to her. They had cried all day. They had sobbed themselves to sleep. They said they loved her. "Where's Miss Ellen? Where's Pinky? Why did she go? She loved us. Why didn't she say goodbye?"

And Edward. Edward had been so gay at dinner, almost boyish. "Good riddance," he'd said. And then he'd said he had to go to London on the seventh. Ellen was in London. She wondered if he would see her. Perhaps he could find her, give her something. She'd give him a character to give her, something noncommittal. If she'd been really bad, the girls could not have loved her.

It was so comfortable here, so warm and cosy. It was terrible to think about the girl. Where was she? What was she doing? She had told her she could not go home. She had asked her not to write to her father or Colonel Hawley, but she'd have to do something about them because when there was no news of Ellen they would certainly make inquiries. Something, but what? She began to cry softly. Life was really very difficult when you knew the "facts," as Edward called them.

In the days that followed Ellen's departure, Mortal was strangely quiet. Ellen, retiring as she had been, had left a gap in the great establishment. There was a housekeeper, Mrs. Fawcett; a butler, Mr. James —no one knew if it was his Christian or surname; two footmen, Charles and Henry; a boots known as "the boy." Six upper-housemaids; four chambermaids; a cook, Mrs. Hunt; four kitchen and scullery maids. And the outside staff: a head gardener, Mr. Jenkins, with six under-gardeners; a head groom, Mr. Blackburn; a second horseman, Jack; five grooms and strappers, and three boys. There was also Joliffe, the head keeper, and four under-keepers; a bailiff, Fairchild, and the staff of the home farm. All the "misters" and "missuses"—to their subordinates and equals—fixed stars about whom the other employees circled in varying degrees of terror. Each was a tyrant, a dictator, an arbiter of morals and manners whose word could mean increased wages or the sack.

Not that Ellen had made friends with anyone. Her position forbade it. A governess led a lonely life—neither fish, fowl nor good red herring, as the saying went. But she had been nice to everyone. Kind, considerate, giving the indoor servants no trouble and a "Good morning" to all she met. They recognized a lady and were sorry for her. Nothing, they knew, was worse than a lady without money, a dependant with no future. Governesses seldom married, but were often seduced.

They had a good guess at what had happened between her and the Master. They knew about the other governesses. Servants had little to occupy their minds and each was a kind of detective, with the kitchen as a clearinghouse for the information they acquired. The state of the sheets, a long hair in a man's bedroom, the lingering scent of a perfume, a greasy mark from a man's hair on a lady's pillow, a hairpin swept up—all were clues.

And the Master. He was a one, all right. A bastard for his greens. He'd almost had May once, but she'd been too quick for him. But he was not hated, or had not been till now. That Muriel, for instance, had only got what she asked for.

This was different, though. Miss Ellen was so young, so gentle, so nice. There was something else they did not understand—why the Master was so gay. If the bird had slipped through his fingers, he should not have been so happy. "Cock-a-hoop. Like a bloody tomcat," Charles said.

Then May, whose job it was to do the Master's study, found Mrs. Caramine's letter. Piecing together letters found torn up in paper baskets was a popular servants' hobby, the earliest form of those picture puzzles that were just beginning to appear. May was the staff expert. All letters that looked interesting were brought to her. She had the trick of it and could read writing well. It took some of the girls all their time to read print.

When she had it all pieced together and stuck with gum arabic on a bit of brown paper, she read it carefully several times. So they were going to get a pretty French governess next. He was to persuade Madam to employ her. He was going to London shortly. As far as the servants were concerned, gentlemen only went to London for one thing. And Caramine? Who the hell was Carrie Caramine? She certainly had never stayed at Mortal.

May used a lot of bad language when she was alone or with the other girls. Mrs. Fawcett had had her on the mat for it.

"I can't help it, Mrs. Fawcett," she'd said. "It's my Dad. He was a soldier—a Horse soldier—the Eighteenth. I've heard it all my life. It's a 'abit," she said, "a bad 'abit, and I got licked for it, too, when I was a kid and said: 'Where's my bloody bread and milk?' My Ma licked me with the back of a 'air brush."

"Well, you're too big to lick now—more's the pity," the housekeeper said. "But it's got to stop."

"Yes Ma'am," May said, giving a bob.

"So don't let it occur again, my girl. Not at least in my hearing," Mrs. Fawcett said with a smile. She was fond of May but manners were manners. Then she'd said: "But it's funny about horses. A foul mouth and blood horses do seem to go together."

"They like it, Mrs. Fawcett."

"Who likes it?"

"The 'orses. Used to it, they are. It's friendly-like."

"Well, don't let me hear any more of it. And people aren't horses."

"No Ma'am," May had said. So now she was more careful, but it still came out when she was excited.

Mrs. Caramine. Charles would know, or would find out from Mr. James. Mr. James knew everything and everybody. He had worked in London.

Two days later in the basement passage Charles had caught her round the waist. "Give us a kiss, May."

"Kiss, you clumsy idiot! What for?"

"For me news."

"News?"

"Mrs. Caramine. I know who she is."

May kissed him. She liked to kiss him. They were courting in a manner of speaking. Walking out.

"Well?" she said.

"Old Jimmy told me, May. They call her Carmine in town. Carrie Carmine, and she runs a fancy whore house in Chelsea."

"Whore house! You mean. . . ."

"Yes, that's what I mean. A queer place, too, according to Jimmy. Kids and things. Things you'd not believe, and I couldn't tell you."

"But why's she writing to the Master and sending a French governess up 'ere?"

"To save him going to London, silly. That's why. So he can get it on the premises. Just fancy that! A French whore at Mortal—oh my!"

Well, that was part of it, but there must be more. May wondered if she'd ever find out.

There were four worlds at Mortal, as there were in most big country houses in England.

The underworld—the poorly lit basement where the servants ate and spent any spare time they had.

The world of the gentry—dining room, big and little drawing rooms, library, study, gun room, bedrooms, lavatories—one to each floor—and Madam's boudoir.

The children's world—day and night nurseries with barred windows, the schoolroom, the governess' bedroom.

Above that, cold in winter and hot in summer, were the attics where the servants slept. All but the housekeeper, butler, and cook, who had bedrooms in the children's wing. So in the daytime the children were insulated by the spare and master bedrooms below them, as if childhood was contagious.

With Ellen gone, the little girls were lonely. "A holiday," their mother said. "No lessons—isn't that lovely?"

They said: "Yes Mama," but they were bored. Meals with Miss Ellen had been fun.

And there was no satisfying Betty, the five-year-old.

"Why'd she go, Eva? Why'd she not say goodbye? I loved her, Eva. I loved her. She smelled so nice."

Evangeline said what her mother had told her to say.

"She was bad, Betty. She was not a good girl." By this time the holiday myth had been exploded.

"She was good! Good!" Betty sobbed. "And I want her. She cuddled me. I want to be cuddled," and she climbed onto her sister's knee.

Evangeline did not think Ellen was bad. Much nicer than Miss Muriel. The others she hardly remembered, only that they had all been rather pretty. But time had merged them into a composite, a rather petulant young woman who said: "Don't do that! Don't do this! Go and wash your hands! Stand still and let me comb your hair. . . ." A young woman who gave them lessons, dressed them up to spend an hour after tea with their mother in the drawing room, and got them ready for church on Sunday.

They had come, stayed a while, and gone. Only Miss Muriel had stayed a long time and Evangeline had not liked her. There had been something about her that reminded her of a cat. Not a nice cat like the tortoiseshell at the stables that was always having kittens, but a sleek, smug cat, like the one in the story, that had just eaten the canary.

And now they were going to have a French governess. Mama had told them so and said she was on the way. She had heard Mama and Papa arguing about it, and had stood outside the door to listen.

"I don't like it, Edward," Mama had said.

"It will be good for them. They'll get a good accent. Her references seem perfect. You're just prejudiced against the French."

"Well, I've written to her and told her to come, but I still don't like it. And I'm worried about Ellen. Where is she? What will she do with no character?"

"Do, my dear? Do what people of that kind always do, Lavinia. She was a wrong 'un."

"I still can't believe it."

"You must. I told you, didn't I? Imagine a woman like that taking care of our children!"

"But what will she do, Edward?" Mrs. Lenton returned to the attack. "It's no good telling me that she'll do what people of that kind always do. What *do* they do? You said I was old enough to know the facts of life. I'm married, I'm thirty-three, as you so kindly pointed out."

"Well, if you insist, but don't say I didn't warn you. I've tried to keep everything unpleasant away from you. There are unpleasant things in life, Lavinia, things that concern no pure woman. Pitch, my dear. Contamination."

"I insist. It's my right to know."

"Very well, then. She'll end on the streets."

"On the streets? In London?"

"Yes dear. You see, you don't know anything."

"Well, it's not my fault if I was never told. No one tells women anything. No one explains. What do they do on the streets?"

"They pick up men and go home with them."

"Strangers, Edward?"

"Of course they're strangers. They go to bed with them, sleep with them, and the men pay them for their services."

"How dreadful! How really awful! Are you sure, Edward?"

"My dear, there have always been women like that." He was becoming irritated. "It's in the Bible. Whores, harlots, the daughters of the horse leech."

"So that's what it meant. I always wondered."

"Yes, my dear, and they are a necessary evil. Prostitutes are the only protection of pure women. If there weren't any tarts, men would go around raping everyone."

Lavinia stood up. "Stop, Edward! I don't want to hear any more!"

"Well, I warned you." Edward Lenton watched his wife sweep out of the room, her skirt held high in her hand as if to avoid the contamination he had talked about.

How silly good women were, and what a waste of beauty! Of course there were some fast women who were ladies. That had been Ellen's attraction—that she had been a lady. It was not easy to get a lady for a mistress. In the last year there had been two society divorces, but on the whole good women were icicles who only married because everyone got married.

Still, he had no complaints except his lack of an heir. If what Carmine had said was true, and Muriel had thrown a colt foal, it proved he could get boys and Lavinia was to blame. It would be dead by now, in some baby farm in the slums. But he had no real complaints. Nothing in life was perfect and Lavinia's fortune had been immense. There were his visits to Carmine in London to look forward to. She knew his taste. Especially the next one. He'd teach that little bitch something, show her who was master. A milk and water miss who had dared to refuse him. And then the French girl who was coming. He had always been partial to French girls.

Lavinia was still upset at the way the children pined for Ellen. They refused to accept the fact that she had gone for good. Eva kept saying she did not want to learn French, asking why Miss Ellen had not said goodbye to them and would not believe she had done anything wrong. "She couldn't, Mama, she was so good. What did she say when you spoke to her . . . ?"

That was the trouble. Ellen had tried to say something and she had refused to listen. Was it possible that she had been afraid to hear what it was . . . ? She knew without actually putting it into words in her mind, that Edward was unfaithful to her, and she accepted it—again, almost unconsciously. Men were like that. But suppose, just suppose . . . ?

And Betty. Little Betty was worse than her sister with her whining. Whenever she saw her all she did was to hang onto her skirts and cry: "I want Pinky, I want Pinky. I love Pinky."

How could a girl so evil, so despicable, inspire such affection? Children were supposed to be good judges of character. Of course Ellen had to be replaced, but it would not be easy with the children in this mood. And she did not like the idea of a French girl—however well recommended—at Mortal. Of course Edward was right. She was prejudiced. She had been to Paris and had not liked what she had seen there.

Couples courting openly in the parks and gardens. There was an immodesty about them that offended her. A boldness, a coquetry.

Still, it was done now. Delphine Le Grand was on her way and she would try to like her. But what was she going to tell people? Except for Muriel, none of her governesses had stayed very long. A governess generally stayed with a family for years and years, often till their charges were presented at court or even married. It would mean more talk and she hated talk.

Then there was Mr. Longbeach. He might think they had been unjust. They had not heard the girl's side. Ellen had said: "But, Mrs. Lenton . . ." and she had been so angry she had not let her go on. Mr. Longbeach would find out, of course. He would find some way to question her. Although he had never married, he was interested in women's rights. In the Married Woman's Property Act, in the woman and child labor laws. As a young man he had met William Stead, who was now the editor of the *Pall Mall Gazette*. A crusader who had exposed a number of scandals: the scandal of the Dilke divorce, the weakness of the Navy. They said it was his leaders that had forced the government to try and rescue Chinese Gordon in the Sudan.

Many people, Edward among them, considered Stead a muckraker, a man who would do anything to sell his paper. But to many others like Mr. Longbeach, he was an inspiration. He saw Mr. Stead whenever he went to London. She wondered if she would ever meet him. She doubted it as, since her marriage, she did not even see much of the Longbeaches. It had been different in her father's time. Then old Mr. Longbeach had been a constant visitor at Mortal. The two men had got on. Her father had said there was no better blood in England than that of its yeomen, though it had been a long time since a Longbeach had farmed. John was the fourth lawyer in a direct line who had handled the affairs of the estate.

It occurred to her that it was rather silly the way she was worrying about what he would think or say about Ellen. It was curious, too, how now that the girl had gone, she was so worried about her. Only eighteen and no references. If only I had given her a reference, she thought. Then, if a prospective mistress had written to her, she could have explained Ellen's leaving in some way.

It was just that the whole thing had been such a shock to her. She had been so overcome with rage that she had not really been quite sane. I am not a cruel woman, she thought. Not vindictive.

She had definitely made up her mind to give Edward a letter of recommendation to take to London when he went, in the hope that he might run across Ellen, a lost needle in the London haystack. To her, London consisted of Mayfair and Belgravia, and people did continually meet people they knew there. Though she had had glimpses of it, she really knew nothing about the rest of London—the vast smoky, seething, sweating, stinking mass of its side streets, courts, alleys, and tenements. England, as Disraeli had said not so long ago, was two countries: two peoples, neither of whom knew anything about the other.

But the fact remained that Lavinia Lenton knew, for the first time in her life, that she was overcome with doubts. Something in the structure of her life had given way.

5 : The Encounter

When Delphine Le Grand got Mrs. Caramine's letter, she made her preparations. She wrote to a friend in Brussels to say she hoped before very long to bring her a nice present. It might take six months and she would be unable to give the exact date, but it would be very kind if she would be so amiable as to have everything prepared. Then she packed her bag and trunk and took the Folkestone boat.

She was a beautiful girl, but no one would have known it. Her large brown eyes were disguised by steel-rimmed glasses. Her long hair, that she could sit on, was pulled back from her face and drawn up into a great shapeless bun on which perched an old nondescript black felt hat. Her figure was masked by a black coat and skirt that only fitted where it touched. Her gloves, shoes and reticule were all old. She was twenty-five but looked thirty at least. To see her, one would have taken her for an upper servant, a housekeeper, or perhaps a governess.

The daughter of a small Parisian shopkeeper, she had by a series of accidents, such as her father's winning a national lottery, received an excellent education, and gone from a convent school to the Sorbonne. Her diploma was in her bag. For six months she had taught children in a bourgeois family in Neuilly. Then she had fallen in with a man who had said that with her looks she should be in the theater. Flattered by his compliments, she had gone to live with him and found herself wearing more spangles than clothes on the stage of a *café chantant*. It was here she had made her first contacts with the half-world and the underworld. Both had enchanted her. She was a born adventuress. For a while she played the badger game, enticing the café customers to her home where they would be surprised in bed by her friend, Armand.

"My God, my husband! He should have been in Nîmes"—or Arles—or Avignon. He was a Provençal.

She also came in contact with the police and made many useful friends among them. Then a well-known procuress approached her.

"You are wasting yourself," she said. "With your education, your diploma, you should be a governess."

"*Gouvernante?* My God, I've been one! It bores me."

"I have a proposition that will not bore you, Mademoiselle. I understand you speak English?"

"I know some English," she said.

"Very well, *ma chère*. You will go to England and get employment as a governess. I will see that you get it. I have friends there," she said vaguely. "Then you will bring me young virgins. There is no danger. Once you have inspired confidence in your employers, it will all go by itself."

This was the fifth trip she had made for Madame Fifi who, for reasons known only to her and the police, had moved to Brussels.

Mrs. Caramine was, as usual, glad to see her. "Did you have a good trip, my dear?"

"Very good, Madame. The sea was calm. I had no adventures, which is not surprising considering my appearance."

"It is very good. Just what is needed. Miss Delphine Le Grand." Caramine laughed. "What were the others?"

"Denise Fichet, Louise Mabrouck, Hortense Dauphin, Marie Goudon," she ticked off her other aliases on her fingers.

"Your room is ready, dear, and you can be pretty again for a day or so. Would you like to work here for a night or two and make a little extra?"

"I will come into the salon, Madame, and see what is offered." They both laughed.

By God, thought Mrs. Caramine, it's going to work. It's all set up. And the timing was perfect. He was coming to London tomorrow. He would see Delphine in all her beauty, undisguised. She would go up to Gloucestershire alone and be settled in by the time he was back. And the girl was ready for him. It was wonderful what a few days' nakedness would do for a proud, shy girl. All she had was a diaphanous lace dressing gown that Harris gave her when she took her to the bathroom.

There had been only one scene but Harris had roughed her up a little and now she was as quiet as a lamb. Too quiet, if anything.

Upstairs, when Harris brought Ellen back, she did not go out of the room. She stood like a grenadier with her back to the window.

"Virgin," she said. "Never seen a man. Not a naked man. Well, they're different, my dear, as you'll soon see. It's the difference that brings them 'ere. Costs 'em a lot of brass, that difference does. Got to put it somewhere. Like an umbrella. You don't carry an umbrella around all the time, do you? But it's women that's the cause of it, the root of all evil. Soft, weak, asking for it. Laying there, clothed in their nakedness. The curse of Eve, that's what it is, with the lot of you. A bloody lot of temptresses." She was ranting now, spittle forming in little bubbles on her thick lips. Enormous, black-silhouetted against the light, her peroxided hair a gold helmet on her head. "Punish them, God said to me. And I'm his servant. Many's the one I've held while they got it. Girls like you, and younger, but women all. Me, that's between the two. A 'frerdite, that's what the doctor said. Very rare. Never to bear a child nor make one. But I've held 'em. I likes to hold 'em, to feel 'em squirm, to hear 'em scream.

"Little bitches," she went on. "But they're doomed, the lot of 'em. A few years here and then downhill. We take care of 'em here. Valuable, like good 'orses. That's what man does with a good 'orse. Takes care of 'im, rides 'im, and then when he's tired of 'im and he's no more good, he sells 'im. She sells 'em to the Frenchies or the Dagoes, or they go from house to house, worse each time, till they end on the docks, taking sailors and niggers, thirty or more a day, for a bob a throw. But here it's a fiver for an hour and ten quid for the night. An' that's what you offered me—a fiver! A bloody insult, that was. She'll make thousands out of you, the Madam will, before you're done—worn out like a 'orse and ready for the knackers." She wiped her face with her hand and sat down, exhausted. "Bitch!" she spat. "You bloody pure little bitch! But we'll set you down right on your back where you belong. Any nonsense an' I'll take you over my knee and spank you like a kid. I'd like that, I would." She opened her great palms and stared at them. "Something you'd remember," she said. "I'd've done it before this but the Madam said 'no' about you. 'Not a mark on 'er, Harris. Too valuable a tit for that.' But we'll see. My time will come, Miss. God will see to that."

Luncheon at Mortal was early. Twelve o'clock. The master was going to town and had to catch his train. Even so small a change in the routine caused a certain excitement among the servants. Everything had to be done an hour earlier. The maids got up at five instead of six to clean the grates and do the rooms.

Edward Lenton bowed his head over his folded hands as he said

Grace. He was smiling, but the damask tablecloth had no eyes to watch him, as he said: "Make us truly thankful, O Lord, for what we are about to receive. In Jesus' name, Amen."

Lord make us truly thankful, he thought, as he ate his mutton chops and Melton Mowbray pie. It was followed by a ripe Stilton. Just right. The claret was excellent—seventy-five had been a good year. There would be time for coffee. He did not like to rush things. Not anything. Again he smiled. You never had to hurry at Carrie Caramine's.

He said: "Bring the coffee, James. The carriage is ready, I suppose?"

"Everything in order, sir. You have plenty of time." The butler served the coffee and went out. Edward was alone with his wife.

Lavinia said: "You'll try, won't you Edward?"

"Try what, my dear?"

"Ellen's letter. I know it sounds silly in such a big place, but you might just see her."

"A needle in a haystack, Lavinia, but if I do . . . and there is such a thing as coincidence." He almost laughed. "But if I do run into her, of course I will."

"I didn't say much, Edward. I just said she had been with us six months and that the children loved her and were sorry when she had to leave. And it's all true. They are inconsolable. And I worry about her. Perhaps we were too hasty." She paused and said: "How long will you be away?"

"I don't know, my dear. A week I should say. I have a lot to do. Loose ends. Odd jobs that should have been dealt with long ago." Regrettably, he wasn't as young as he had been, and a week would be about all he could stand.

In the train he had a first-class compartment to himself. Now he was free and could let himself dream. Soon he would see Ellen. He wondered what Lavinia would think if she knew. He chuckled. He'd have her with a letter from Lavinia in his pocket. He wondered how often he had looked at her. He wondered how she'd strip, what she was like under that awful blue muslin evening dress that had showed just the beginning of her breasts, the faint bulge of them swelling into invisible fullness. Soon he'd know, soon he'd cup them in his hands. The silly little fool! What a good time they could have had! She would have had good clothes—nothing that would call attention to her, but nice ones—and nice underclothes. He might even have set her up in a little flat. He knew his father had always kept a woman in London. He remembered hearing that one of them had killed herself.

In London he went straight to Hart's. It had been his father's club too, and his grandfather's. It was supposed to have been founded by Beau Brummel. Probably a lie. But it was comfortable and he had a lot of friends there, chiefly other country gentlemen like himself. He had a bath, changed and told the bemedaled commissionaire to get him a hansom.

"Twenty-three Coak Street," he said. Old Carmine would give him dinner. He wanted to go there before things started up. They did not get lively till midnight, though usually men began coming at ten. For old customers she was open twenty-four hours a day, but from ten till four in the morning were the busy hours. By midnight it would all be over, he thought. Over for today, that is. For what we are about to receive, he thought again, and laughed out loud. What an idea to have had at luncheon with his wife, with the butler and footmen standing by.

The hansom had a good horse, half-bred, fast and hot-tempered. The drive did not take long. He just saw the horse's quarters moving in front of the apron and dashboard, its ears cocked and laid back alternately. He did not see the gas-lit streets or the people going about their business, or the girls standing waiting for love with a "Are you feeling friendly?" or a "Hullo darling, what about coming home with me?" The words ready, concealed like a half-masticated mouthful behind their lips. Once they had known love, all of them. Now they existed on its parody.

At No. 23 the door was opened by the portly butler. Two footmen, enormous men with cauliflower ears, pugs poorly disguised in their uniform, stood in the main hall.

"Madam is expecting you, sir," the butler said, and ushered Edward into Mrs. Caramine's private suite.

Carrie Caramine, Mrs. Prettyman, and Delphine were in the small sitting room when Edward Lenton was shown in.

"Evening Carrie," he said. "Mrs. Prettyman." He bowed over her hand. But who was the other? Lovely. A tall, dark girl with good eyes, black hair, and a beautiful figure.

"Glad you could manage to drop by, Mr. Lenton," Mrs. Caramine said.

"Delighted Ma'am. Always try to when I'm in London, as you know."

"I know." She gave him a deep, long look from her splendid eyes. "Everything is ready for you, or will be by ten."

She saw him looking at Delphine. They were, in fact, looking at each other. A man-and-woman look, as if they both saw a bed with the sheets drawn back. Well, if they wanted to, why not? Delphine had said she might if she saw anyone she fancied, and she fancied him all right. Which was a good thing, considering the circumstances.

"And who . . . ?" Lenton was saying as he went toward her.

Mrs. Caramine interposed herself between them. "This is a surprise for you, a bonus as it were. Just fancy that, Mr. Lenton. Two surprises in one evening! I really do spoil you, don't I?"

"You always have. But you haven't introduced us."

"Miss Delphine Le Grand, your new governess, Mr. Lenton."

"My God!" he said. "She'll never do. Not with those looks. Not a raving beauty."

"*Merci*, Monsieur," Delphine said. "But I shall be no problem, shall I, Madame?" She turned to Mrs. Caramine.

"You'll be surprised, Mr. Lenton, when you see her at Mortal. Glasses, downright dowdy, a real governess."

Delphine laughed. "I was on the stage," she said.

"An ornament to the boards, I'm sure." Lenton took her hand. She made no attempt to withdraw it. It was smooth, long-fingered, almost boneless.

Mrs. Caramine said: "Come along, Ada, we've got things to do," and went out. In the hall she said: "Let them get to know each other. They look as if they are going to get on."

Ada Prettyman smiled sourly. "I think you'd better knock on the door when you come back, Carrie."

Mrs. Caramine laughed. "I'll be a little while. I'm going to see the girl upstairs."

"How is she shaping up?"

"Pretty well, I think. Harris frightened her and she spends a lot of time praying. Not much to eat, no clothes, nothing to do. It works, my dear. It always works."

She paused, her hand on the mahogany stair rail. "If it doesn't, there's always Harris." She went up slowly.

Ellen had been dozing. When she woke, a small dark woman with enormous eyes, whom she had not seen come in, was sitting in one of the chintz-covered armchairs. Dressed in black silk, a rope of pearls round her neck, mitts on her folded, beringed hands, she sat motionless. She was very small, with a tiny waist.

She said: "I am Mrs. Caramine and I want to talk to you." Her voice was soft. She seemed to be a lady. Almost a lady.

Clasping her lacy negligee to her body, Ellen said: "Oh, Mrs. Caramine, what am I doing here? I don't understand it. Please let me go!"

"That's what I came to talk about, my dear. I am afraid you will never go. So you might as well make up your mind about that. You are too valuable to me." Her voice hardened. "You can have it soft and comfortable, with good food and lovely clothes, or you can have it the other way. And that's the way Harris would like it. I expect she told you. My dear, this is the best whore house in London. It is patronized by the best people. The police leave us alone. It's no crime to run a brothel, but they can be a nuisance. Once a girl is a whore, my dear, there's no going back. Nowhere else to go, is there? Home? Do you think people want girls back afterward? Work? What work could you do, and who'd employ you even if you could get out, which is impossible? So just be sensible, Ellen. Do what you're told. And once you're used to it, you'll be happy enough. What's happiness anyway?" With that cryptic remark, Mrs. Caramine got up and went out, her skirts rustling, leaving a wave of tuberose perfume behind her.

Now only God was left. Ellen knelt by the bed to pray again. Good food, good clothes, if she did what they said. Never! She'd never do it. God would help her. Dishonor. She'd been brought up to think death preferable to dishonor though she had not, till now, really known what dishonor was. But how did one die? How did one kill oneself? She was a prisoner. This was a life sentence if she could not escape. And her keeper Harris was a madwoman, a religious maniac. She had heard her father speak of them. A 'frredite. What was that? A sect of some kind?

Alone in the sitting room, her hand still in his, Delphine stared into Edward Lenton's eyes, her moist lips parting. "How fortunate it is, Monsieur," she said, "that we are destined to be friends."

He pulled her to him and bent over to kiss her, forcing her neck back, her belly into his.

Fortunate, by God! This was a luscious fruit, indeed. Desire mounted. She was drawing him back to the sofa. She was as eager as he. This was no whore pretending. He had made a conquest, but he must control himself. There was bigger game waiting for him. Better fish to fry. He let go of her and said: "We must wait."

"Wait?" she laughed at him. "Oh, Monsieur," she asked, "are you saving your love for another?" She shook her finger at him. "But I am not *jaloux*. I understand. Madame told me there was someone waiting for Monsieur. Not that it surprises me—a man so attractive. But, as

Monsieur says, we have time. Months of time, is it not so? When I instruct Monsieur's young daughters."

Now she turned her back on him. A lovely back, as white as milk. The dark maroon velvet of her gown was cut very low over the shoulders. The dress had a suspicion of a bustle that was part train. "A drink?" she said, pouring out some brandy. "To fortify Monsieur?" She gave him a glass and raised her own. "To love, Monsieur, *l'amour!* Is that not what we women are made for, to give pleasure?" She lowered her eyes. The long black lashes lay on her cheek. A moment of mock modesty.

There was a knock on the door.

"Come in!" Lenton said.

Mrs. Caramine looked at them, smiled and said: "Well, I expect you are right. And there'll be plenty of time in the country. Delphine goes up tomorrow. It would be a pity to tire yourself when we have taken so much trouble for your entertainment. If you will come with me, I'll take you up."

On the second floor she led him into her office.

"Now we can talk business," she said. "First, she is a beauty. More beautiful than you ever guessed. Next, she is a virgin and a lady. You know my price for that, Mr. Lenton. Five hundred guineas and the use of her for a week. Only you must not hurt her. I want no marks on her. Harris will go up with you. Harris!" she called.

"Yes, Madam."

The woman came into the room. In her hands she had four padded, white kid straps with silver buckles.

"You see," Mrs. Caramine said, "if you have too much trouble, Harris will tie her up or hold her."

"She'll fight?" Lenton said. "By God, I'd like a struggle with the little bitch."

"I have no idea, Mr. Lenton. With a virgin anything is possible. Take him up, Harris."

He followed Harris up the stairs through the thick green-baize padded door. She pointed. "In there," she said.

When the door opened and Ellen saw Mr. Lenton, she forgot her fear of him. A face she knew! Her old employer had come to save her!

She pulled her negligee tighter about her. "Oh Mr. Lenton, thank God you've come! I prayed someone would come."

He stood smoking his cigar in the doorway, with Harris behind him. Something was wrong. He didn't say anything. He just looked. Then he said: "Harris, take that rag off her."

"NO!" Ellen screamed, "no!" as, with one pull that tore the peignoir, Harris ripped it off.

Ellen tried to cover herself with her hands.

Lenton laughed. "Save you?" he said. "I sent you here. I arranged it. I wanted you and you turned me down. No one of your class ever turns me down. I wanted you and I'm going to have you."

Harris showed her the straps. Harris did more than that. Going to the bed, she slipped them on the white painted standards of the head and tail boards. "Shall I tie her, sir? Or hold her?"

"Neither," Lenton said. "You can go out. I'll call you if I need you."

"I'll be at the door, sir."

She'd be there, he knew, listening. Ready. An abominable woman.

When the door was closed he sat down to look at his cowering prize while he finished his cigar. It was too good to waste and he had time. All the time in the world. This was a living picture, much better than any of the little paintings he had in his collection. Andromeda to his dragon, and no Perseus to rescue her. All the time in the world to contemplate this delicious *tableau vivant* of shocked modesty.

Later, she'd come to him naked, to curl up on his knee when he called her, like a pet dog to its master. Later, much later, more men would have her. But he was going to be the first, and they'd only get her when he had finished with her.

When his cigar had burned down he put it out and began to undress. His frogged velvet smoking jacket, his black tie. He undid the first collar stud and put it on the windowsill. He slipped his suspenders off his shoulders so that they hung in loops on either side of his hips. His evening shoes were set side by side, his socks on top of them. He drew off his trousers, his silk underpants, his white shirt, the high stiff collar still attached to a bone-backed stud, his undervest.

Mr. Lenton was naked. Fascinated with horror, Ellen was unable to take her eyes off his muscular body. The difference, Harris had said. There it was—erect, enormous. He came toward her.

A naked man, naked as Adam before the fall, approaching a naked woman to perform a primal act. An act of love, of reproduction. Male and female, He created them. Different, Harris had said. Love. Like an animal, like a bull. She had seen a bull with a cow once. She'd seen a stallion. But she'd never thought of men that way.

He gripped her arms. His eyes were glazed, unfocused. On her back, she still tried to hide herself with her hands. He pulled them away. "It's no good trying to hide your charms, Ellen. I'm going to see them, have them, use them." Then he was on her.

Suddenly she knew what to do. She was being dishonored. It was agony. Her flesh was being torn with his thrusts. Death was better than this, a thousand times better. I'll die, she thought. Just let myself die. And she went slack in his arms.

For a moment Lenton thought she had fainted. But her cheeks were still pink as she lay there, a doll stuffed with sawdust. "Move, you bitch!" he said, slapping her face. But she gave no sign of life. She was not there. Not Ellen Pickford. Ellen Pickford was standing in a corner of the chintz room, watching a naked man rape an ash-blonde girl—a disgusting, inhuman spectacle.

When he got up the doll still lay there, her legs apart, her breasts hardly moving as she breathed. Ellen Pickford watched the man dress. It struck her this was a curious way to learn how a man put on his clothes. She heard him say: "God damn it!" She heard him knock on the door to have it opened. She watched him go out.

Now she was alone with the doll.

As he went downstairs, Lenton made up his mind. He'd not tell Carrie what a fiasco it had been, not give her the laugh on him. Hearing the sound of a piano and a girl singing from the big drawing room he went in, looking as contented and smug as he could.

The evening was in full swing. Someone had wound up the big musical box. A Viennese waltz. He seized the girl nearest to him, a plump little blonde in black, and swung her into it.

The men were in full evening dress, dinner or smoking jackets. One, an older man, was even wearing decorations. He must have come from some function—a regimental dinner or an ambassador's party. The girls were in full fig. Beautiful dresses of green, white, yellow, pink, and red. Only his little one wore black. It looked like a garden, the flowers swaying in the wind of the music. The girls held their long dresses up in their left, long white-gloved hands. Champagne corks popped. It was like a gay, young people's party anywhere, except that the dresses were cut so low that some of the girls' nipples kept popping out and none of them was wearing underclothes.

6 : Two Letters

Mrs. Caramine had wired in Delphine's name the time of her arrival at Mortal Major. The carriage, with its two bay horses and liveried coachman and footman, was waiting for her at the station. As they drove up the drive between the rhododendrons, now a flowerless, sculptured mass of dark green, Delphine congratulated herself. At least she would be comfortable here and, as a lover, the man she had met in London would prove admirable, she was sure. Handsome, rich, and susceptible. Mrs. Caramine had described his habits in great detail, and with this knowledge of him and his tastes, she would be able to twist him round her little finger, as the saying went.

The house was even more splendid than it had looked from a distance. The butler led her upstairs to a boudoir where her new mistress was waiting. A good-looking, fair woman in her thirties. But cold. That could be seen at once. Quite without the sensuality necessary to hold a man. No wonder he needed other company.

Mrs. Lenton was, to her surprise, delighted with her new employee. There would be no nonsense with Edward here. If there had been any nonsense anyway. More and more she was questioning it. Not Edward exactly. He might have misunderstood. If anything, this woman was too dowdy.

"I will show you my diploma from the Sorbonne, Madame," Delphine was fiddling with her reticule. How eager to please she seemed! Her only good feature was her eyes, half hidden behind those hideous spectacles.

"Do you always wear spectacles, Delphine?"

"But yes, Madame. Unfortunately as a child I studied too hard. A bad light, Madame. I come of a poor family, but I think I am what you call blue-stocking in English. A student by nature."

She presented the document. It certified that Marie Thérèse Duclos had passed a number of subjects—Mrs. Lenton did not even read what they were—with honors.

"The name, Madame, may surprise you. But I have had misfortunes. I can no longer bear to be called Marie Thérèse. I was once married, Madame, though you, seeing me today, may find it hard to believe. That name brings him back to me. Marie Thérèse was his, his alone. His name was Le Grand. I was, as Madame can see, née Duclos. As for Delphine, it is a pretty name. I think I found it in a book. Madame is satisfied, I hope. Should Madame wish, she can make inquiries. I will furnish the necessary addresses. People who know me. The Mairie, the Préfecture of Police, and Madame has my other references. Those dealing with the dear little girls it has been my pleasure to instruct."

"Of course, my dear. I am satisfied." Really, she felt sorry for her.

A poor home, her eyes ruined with study, a dear husband whom she had adored.

"Come, Mademoiselle," she said. "I will take you to your room and introduce you to the children."

The children were waiting to meet her, half in excitement, half in fear.

"This is Mademoiselle," their mother said. "Evangeline is the older." Evangeline made a bob. "Betty is my baby."

"I'm not a baby," Betty said.

"You'll always be a baby to me."

Mrs. Lenton led Delphine to her room.

"What a lovely room!" she said. "And what charming children. So like Madame, blonde and beautiful."

Really, the girl was embarrassing the way she gushed. "Thank you, Delphine," she said. "Now I will leave you to unpack."

Alone, Delphine opened her bag and trunk and put her clothes away. The children were beautiful as angels. Madame Fifi would be ravished, enchanted, with them. Everything had gone very well. The diploma was always a problem. The letters of recommendation nothing at all. She wrote them herself in a disguised hand. How were her employers to know that there was no one but a caretaker at the *Château de Fontbaq* in Brittany, where any letters from England to the Duchess—who was in her dotage and lived in Paris—were posted back to Mrs. Caramine. The Comtesse de Briac, the other reference, had been dead for years, and there the *concierge* performed the same service.

She decided to have a sponge bath and get off these abominable clothes, even if it was only for half an hour.

Downstairs, Mrs. Lenton was feeling more and more sorry for the girl. Her new sympathy for Ellen now overflowed onto Delphine. Girl. Woman, she supposed, since she had been married. What a lonely life a governess led . . . why had she never thought of it before? Perhaps if she'd seen more of Ellen. . . .

An idea struck her. She would take up some flowers—a vase of white carnations from the greenhouse. They would make her feel more at home. She picked the vase off one of the tables in the drawing room, went upstairs, knocked on the door, went in without pausing, and stood petrified by what she saw.

Mademoiselle Le Grand had disappeared. Instead, the most beautiful creature she had ever seen, had turned, naked, from the washstand to face her. Her eyes without glasses were beautiful, her black hair hung like a mane to her waist. Her figure was Greek, like the statues in the museums—the only nude females Lavinia had ever seen.

"What . . . what are you doing?" she said. What a silly remark! The girl was obviously washing. She had a wet face cloth in her hand. "I brought you some flowers," she said, putting the vase on the table.

"Oh, Madame will forgive me. It is not my fault," the girl said.

"That I looked the way I did when I arrived. It is because I am too pretty. A pretty girl cannot work in a respectable manner, so . . ." She made a gesture with her hand, as much at ease as if she had been fully dressed. "A disguise, Madame."

"Of course," Lavinia said. She had to say something.

"You see, Madame, all girls wish to be beautiful, but for a poor girl beauty is a curse."

Mrs. Lenton said: "Yes," and went out, downstairs to her bedroom. When she got there she collapsed into a chair. Her knees would no longer support her.

This was the first naked woman she had ever seen. She was like a marble statue in Paris, Rome or Florence, but alive, warm, palpitating. She knew she must palpitate. Part of her shock came from the desire she had only just suppressed to touch her. For a fleeting instant she knew what men must feel for the flesh of a woman. Edward must never know this, must never find out about the girl. How upset he would be! Because it was he who had really insisted on a French governess for the girls.

Suddenly an idea occurred to her. She rang the bell. May answered it.

"Send Parker to me, May."

"Parker is out, Madam. She did not think you would need her in the afternoon."

"Very well, you can maid me. Can you undress me, May?" She had never dressed or undressed without the help of a maid. Anyway, it was all but impossible to lace one's own stays.

"Yes, Madam."

At last she was in her chemise. She sat down to have her silk stockings removed.

"You may go now, May. Come back when I ring."

The girl went out.

Lavinia was going to do the most daring thing she had ever done in her life—look at herself naked in front of the long glass. The only time she was ever naked was in her bath. Dressing and undressing was done most discreetly, a kind of expert fumbling by a maid trained to the work. She had seen bits of herself, of course—her legs, her belly, her bosom—but piecemeal. Or whole, distorted by the water of her bath.

Now she locked the door, pulled off her chemise, went to the mirror, and stood there entranced. She was a statue, too. White, tipped with gold on her belly and under her arms when she raised them. She felt her breasts, weighing them in her hands as if they were fruit. Delphine would have to go if she showed signs of upsetting Edward, but she had taught her something.

Dry-mouthed with astonishment, she stared at this woman who faced her in the mirror, the woman who had had two children, had miscarriages and stillbirths, who was thirty-three years old, but was still as slim as a boy, narrow-waisted and with gently rounded hips.

The sight delighted her. What would happen if she let Edward see her? She knew what would happen. He would be disgusted. Nice women never showed their bodies, never showed love or passion. She had almost felt it, sometimes. Enough to know what it might have been, and then hidden the shameful thought away. Other women. Did Edward really go to other women? Her friends told her their husbands did. She had said: "How can you stand it?"

"What can a woman do, darling? Men are made like that, and if they have others at least they leave us alone."

And she had known in her heart that her husband was no different from the others. But there were so many things in life one knew, and at the same time did not know. More now than ever.

There was no one in the basement except May. She sat there twiddling her thumbs, waiting for Madam's ring. In the afternoon only one maid was on duty. They took it in turns. She was thinking about Madam, how beautiful she was, how kind, how nice. She was thinking about the Master and the letter she had pieced together, when the master bedroom bell, fastened to the end of a curled spring, jangled on the bellboard. She went upstairs.

Madam was in a lace dressing gown. She had laid out on the bed the clothes she wished to put on—chemise, corset, knickers, camisole, petticoats, and an oyster-white cashmere costume.

To her surprise, her mistress pulled off her dressing gown and stood there naked.

"Oh!" May gasped. "Oh!"

"Oh what?"

"Madam is so beautiful!"

Upstairs in the servants' quarters, the girls had little modesty in their shared bedrooms. May was used to naked women, but country girls, plump and rather coarse. As she dressed her mistress, her mind was racing. She'd do it. She'd take the chance. At last she said:

"I'd like to show Madam a letter. Perhaps Madam can explain it. But I'm afraid."

"Afraid of what?"

"Of what Madam will say."

"Why, May?"

"Because I found it all torn up and stuck it together."

"You should not read other people's letters."

"I know, Madam. I never do," May lied. "But I saw some words that worried me. I can't get it out of my head."

"Very well then, go and get it."

"Madam will not be angry?"

"I won't be, I promise."

The girl ran up to her room. Five minutes later she was back, a piece of brown paper in her hand.

Lavinia glanced at it. For a moment she thought she was going to faint.

"All right May," she said. "You may leave it with me, and thank you for letting me have it."

What a day it had been! She must calm herself. She must think. She sat down and picked up the letter. Some pieces were missing but enough remained. Enough. My God! she thought.

Dear Mr. Lenton . . . Your governess turned out so badly . . . cloud after all may have a silver lining. We might discuss the matter . . . young French lady highly recommended . . . Le Grand. Dark, vivacious, and discreet. . . . Fit into your household . . . persuade Mrs. Lenton . . . French is so important in the education of a young lady. . . . Your sincere friend, Carrie Caramine. . . .
P.S. Looking forward to seeing you shortly.

Carrie Caramine. The woman was notorious. She had heard of her from her friends. She kept the most famous brothel in London. So that was where Edward went. And he had introduced a French prostitute into the house as a governess. Now she was sure about Ellen. He'd turned it all round. She had refused his attentions. Now that she thought about it, she remembered the way he had looked at her. And Muriel? Muriel, who had stayed for four years. And all on her money. Women. Horses that he abused and rode to a standstill. It was hard to believe that she had lived with so evil a man.

Tomorrow she would go and see her lawyers in Mortal Major. But there was one more thing she was going to do now. Two things. Two firsts. After all, there had to be a first time for everything.

She sat back and closed her eyes. She must think. One phrase stood out: "cloud after all may have a silver lining." What could that mean? "Looking forward to seeing you shortly." Ellen had reached London at dusk. Edward had said it would be inconvenient to send her by an earlier train. Where had she gone in London? Bits of gossip came back to her about girls alone. Suppose . . . just suppose that woman had got hold of her. That Edward . . . And she'd given him a letter to give her in case he saw her. Needle in a haystack indeed. She was sure—almost sure. And what could she tell that dear old vicar, and George Hawley? What in God's name would she tell them? She was astonished to find herself swearing.

By some accident Edward had left his keys on the chest of drawers. And she was going to do it. Accident? Perhaps because he was so excited about going to London. There were no accidents. Things fitted into each other like May's pieced-up letter. There were gaps, but one could guess them. If I had not seen that girl naked, she thought, I should never have undressed like that. If I had not been so pleased with what I saw, I'd never have let May see me. If May hadn't thought I was beautiful, she'd never have shown me the letter.

And now for a drink. She had never drunk brandy before. She poured two fingers into a glass, gulped and choked. Dreadful stuff! But she felt courage flowing into her veins. Dutch courage. She went into her husband's dressing room and got the keys.

The third one she tried fitted the locked drawer of his desk. She found his checkbook, several checks with entries to Mrs. Caramine. They coincided with his London visits. She found accounts from her "for services rendered" that ran into hundreds of pounds when she totaled them up. And then, finally, she found a thick manila envelope. She opened it and spread the contents on the desk. Twelve small oil paintings of naked women, and six of men and women making what she supposed must be various forms of pagan love. Pornography. She had heard the word and now she was seeing it. Today had been a surfeit of nakedness, horror, deception. She put the pictures back in the envelope, added Mrs. Caramine's bills and the list of checks with their dates and numbers she had made.

Tomorrow she would give them to her lawyers to keep. She was sure Messrs. Longbeach & Longbeach had never had a more curious collection confided to them for safekeeping.

The carriage was ordered for nine. By ten it was bowling through the cobbled streets of Mortal Major.

This was not going to be an easy thing to do, not a thing a lady would ever expect to do. Such subjects were never discussed by them. They were in purdah. Even among themselves, matters of sex and marital relations were only whispered about, hinted at with pursed lips and arching eyebrows between intimate friends. A woman who was divorced, and there was only one cause for divorce—being found in the bed of a man who was not her husband—simply disappeared from the social scene. She slipped from the *monde* to the *demi-monde,* like a pawn in a game of chess, in one move, and disappeared from the board. This half-world of adventuresses, divorced, and kept women was a kind of limbo.

Lavinia remembered her friend, Margaret Salton, saying that she had seen Dorothy Damion driving in her victoria in London one day. Dorothy had been divorced by her husband, Sir Charles, some years ago. The corespondent had been in the Guards. He had married her, but of course had had to send in his papers, and every house in London was closed to them. She wondered what they felt now. She would have given anything to know. A woman who did that must really love a man. She did not know anyone who loved her husband in that way. Bits of poetry came back to her. Byron, Charles Algernon Swinburne, the Song of Solomon in the Bible. Sights she had glimpsed of common people in each other's arms, once a couple lying entwined in a hedge-row, of the way some people, even in the middle class, looked at each other, as if they had some secret.

And then there was what she had forced Edward to tell her about street women and prostitutes. She was sure none of her friends really knew about them. They knew something, vaguely, the way they knew about drunken mothers, and children starving in the East End. But it was not real to them. They might as well have been in China.

Actresses, dancers. Young men took them out. Stage door Johnnies. Gay little dinners in private rooms. Wild oats. All words from which it was not possible to construct a complete picture, only a nebulous image of debauchery, vice, and passion.

Old Mr. Longbeach—James Henry Ponsonby Longbeach—was looking over a mortgage and thinking of the improvidence of his clients, when Mrs. Lenton was shown into his tiny office.

A series of deed boxes, with names in gold letters, lined one wall. Calf-bound legal books lined another. His desk was piled with papers tied into bundles with pink tape. The two Windsor chairs and the bench under the window also bore their load of papers. Papers every which way. And dust—Lavinia thought she had never seen so much dust. Nor had she, not since the last time she had been here.

"Mrs. Lenton," Mr. Longbeach said, "what a delightful surprise!" It was a surprise all right, and he did not look delighted, but he was a courtly old man. "And where is Edward?" He looked toward the door as if he expected to see her husband in the passage. Then, suddenly becoming businesslike, he said: "What can I do for you, Lavinia?"

He had been her father's lawyer. He had held this grown and lovely woman on his knee, and given her golden twisted sticks of barley sugar to suck. Made you think, by God. Time. . . . *Tempus fugit.* . . . And it did, too. The years slipped by as if they were greased with butter. A lovely creature. But what did she want? And why was she alone?

Lavinia looked at the pink-faced, white-haired, blue-eyed old man, at his white bushy eyebrows, at his nose and chin and potbelly. He looked like Mr. Punch. She sank into the only available chair, an ancient maroon-covered armchair whose horsehair and wool entrails were protruding in several places.

"I have a lot to ask you, Mr. Longbeach, and I think I should like your son to be present."

"Young Jack? Of course." He picked up a little silver bell from his desk and rang it. A clerk came in.

"Tell Mr. Jack I want him."

John Longbeach was a good-looking young man a few years older than she. When they had shaken hands and she'd asked him how he was—it was funny to be so formal with a man she had known all her life and whom she had been thinking about so recently—his father said: "Take the papers off that chair and stand them in the corner. Don't disturb them, boy." To Lavinia he said: "That's the first thing a lawyer learns. Never disturb papers. Let 'em lie and you never lose anything. Never."

"Now Lavinia," he went on, "what's this all about and why are you alone?"

"I want some questions answered. What is my income? Not exactly but in round figures?"

"Your father's estate brings in about a hundred thousand pounds a year, I should say. But of course your husband . . ." He paused and went on: "Your husband has control of it."

"If my father had died before I was married and I was over twenty-one, it would have been mine to do as I liked with?"

"Exactly."

"But now I have not a penny, Mr. Longbeach, have I?"

"You are a very rich woman, Lavinia."

"But my husband controls my fortune? I have to ask him for anything I want?"

"I'm sure he refuses you nothing. But the whole thing was a mistake . . . we were never consulted . . . your aunt. . . ."

"Very nice of him, isn't it, Mr. Longbeach, when he spends my money on women in London, in brothels. . . ."

"My dear Lavinia, who told you all this? Aren't you making a mountain out of a molehill? A few little peccadillos. Men . . ." the old man went on vaguely.

There it was again, this man business. "But I do know." She held up the manila envelope. "Here are receipts for 'services rendered'—professional services—from Mrs. Caramine who keeps the most famous—or should I say infamous?—brothel in London. I'm going to leave them here for you to keep for me."

Mr. Longbeach looked embarrassed. "Of course I'll keep them. But are you really sure?"

"I'm sure. And here is Exhibit B, as I think you call it in a court of law. Works of art. Beautifully painted on ivory. What do you think of this one?" She handed one to John who, so far, had not spoken. "There are eighteen of them. They cost nearly two thousand pounds. Do you think my husband should spend my money buying pictures of this nature?" She passed them one by one to John, who looked at them and passed them on to his father.

John Longbeach was looking at his father. The governor'll blow up in a minute, he thought, like a turkey cock, a balloon. A good thing she had me in. He had never seen her in this mood. She was "a good plucked 'un," though. Never heard of a woman taking the bit between her teeth like this before. It took courage to discuss these things, to bring pictures like that. He'd have another look at them when she'd gone. They were calculated to excite people. That was the legal definition of pornography.

"If I behaved like that"—she looked at the old man with wide, quite cold, gray eyes—"he'd divorce me, wouldn't he?"

"My dear Lavinia, I don't know how you can discuss things like this."

"But he would, wouldn't he?" she insisted. "If he caught me in bed with a man, or if I went off for a weekend with a man. And he's had dozens. Orgies. They say Mrs. Caramine spares no pains."

"My dear," old Longbeach said again, "I wish . . ."

"You wish I had not come, not brought it up. I'm not supposed to know, am I? None of us are. Not ladies, that is. Men, of course, are different." She turned to the younger man.

"I want my money. I want freedom."

"Your husband has control of your fortune, I'm afraid," John said. "There's a bill under discussion now in Parliament called 'The Married Woman's Property Act' but till it's passed—if it's ever passed—a woman's money belongs to her husband, to do what he likes with—gambling, women, horses."

"And divorce," Lavinia said. "Could I divorce him?"

"Madam," the old man said, "it is almost impossible for a woman to divorce a man, and adultery on his part is no ground for divorce."

"So I've made my bed and I must lie in it?" Lavinia asked.

"That's about it, Mrs. Lenton," John said.

"So I have no control over my money and he can sleep with any woman he fancies, buy as many dirty pictures as he likes, and expect his marital rights at home?"

"I'm afraid so, Mrs. Lenton," John said. How lovely she was in her indignant anger! No tears, no raised voice. Cool as a cucumber. Then, to his surprise, she smiled.

"You're wrong, Mr. Longbeach. I'll have my way."

"How?" both men asked together.

"Blackmail," she said.

"What?"

"Yes. The receipted bills and the catalogue for the pictures describing them in great detail. They are all in the envelope I am going to give you. Most illuminating. Quite an education to a woman brought up as I have been. And I'll send copies of them to the committees of all his clubs—The Guards, Hart's, White's, Bucks, the Albemarle."

"They'll only laugh," John said.

"Not if I say I'm going to send copies to their wives. I have the lists of members. I can find the addresses in Burke's Peerage and Debrett, and so on. Not when I say I can prove that he introduced one of Mrs. Caramine's whores into my house as a French governess for my children. The other things, the way the world is today, may be laughable to men. But not that! That would break him." She got up. She said: "Please take care of the papers and pretty pictures," shook hands with them both and went out.

"By God, she'll do it too!" John said.

"What a woman! And I used to hold her on my knee and give her barley sugar," his father said, as if this explained everything. Then he added: "We should have given her a glass of sherry and a biscuit, John."

That was the way the old boy's mind worked, John thought. But this wasn't the end of it. Not by a long chalk.

In the carriage on the way home Lavinia congratulated herself on the way she had carried things off. Only Delphine remained to be dealt with. And Edward, of course, on his return. It had been a good idea to get John in. She wondered if she could persuade him to go to London and look for Ellen.

As she went into the house, she met Delphine coming out with the girls. "Now," Delphine said, "say it." The children said: *"Bonjour, Maman."* Delphine said: *"Bonjour,* Madame."

It was impossible to believe that this dowdy creature in glasses was the girl she had seen washing herself yesterday.

"Good morning, girls," she said. "Go and play in the garden for a few minutes. I want to talk to Mademoiselle."

Delphine followed her into the house. In the hall Lavinia turned to face her and said: "About yesterday—I understand your explanation. We shall say no more about it."

"Merci, Madame. Is that all?"

"That is all, Mademoiselle."

Delphine joined the children in the garden. How well it had gone off! What a good thing she had such quick wits! *"Une belle promenade,"* she said, and they set off down the drive.

On the way home Lavinia had decided to let nature take its course with Edward and Delphine. The phrase amused her. She smiled wryly. Let him sleep with her as long as they were careful. And they would be. Look at Muriel—four years of it right under her nose. It would just be another nail in his coffin when the time for exposure came.

She thought about her interview with her lawyers and was astounded at the way she had carried it off. She really was growing up. Learning the facts of life. She smiled bitterly. She wanted to cry, but that would have to be postponed.

She was interested in the change in John—young Mr. Longbeach, she corrected herself mentally. Though he had hardly spoken, she had seen how angry he had been. She had also seen him as a man for the first time, and not just as the family solicitor. That must be what growing up really was, no matter what your age. Seeing people as people. As men and women, and with a realization of what went on between them. Of love, of good and evil. Women brought up as she had been really did live in a kind of Garden of Eden before the Fall—so innocent that they were incapable of recognizing evil even when they saw it. Well, all that was over now. The Doll's House. It occurred to her that if she was just seeing John Longbeach as a man, he must have seen her as a woman when he lent it to her.

Three days later Edward came back. The prodigal's return, Lavinia thought. She had never seen him looking so tired. She waited till they were alone in the drawing room after dinner. And then she said: "And how is Mrs. Caramine, Edward? You had a good time in the whore house, I hope?"

He sprang up. "What nonsense is this?"

"Nonsense, Edward? I have copies of all the bills. 'Services rendered.' Service indeed!"

He stood speechless in front of her. What a week! What a homecoming! How frightful the French girl looked! Was she really the one he had seen in Carrie's room, wearing a dark red evening dress?

"My keys," he spluttered. "You dared to open my desk."

"Oh yes, dear, I dared. I had a brandy first."

"You—drinking brandy!"

"Nasty stuff, but with a good effect. And I did enjoy the pictures, Edward."

"Christ!" he said.

"Please don't swear," Lavinia said. "They are in safekeeping now. The pictures, I mean, and they won't bother you any more. Things like that do bother men, don't they, Edward? Make them feel uncomfortable. You see, I really am learning the facts of life. And I want a check for two thousand pounds tomorrow. It's my money, you know. And of course from now on the door of my room will be locked. You understand why, I presume? No more chance of an heir, Edward. That was all you did it for, wasn't it? The fun was in London. A lot of things are clear now. Ellen, for instance. You didn't see her by any chance at Mrs. Caramine's, I suppose?" She saw from his face she had hit the mark, gave him a look of contempt and swept out of the room.

She must get hold of John Longbeach. He must get Ellen out. But when she sent for him he was away. In London, they said.

7 : The Lawyer

Two days after Edward Lenton's departure from London, Mrs. Caramine received a letter from him stating that his wife had guessed Ellen was at No. 22, that she had found her Services Rendered accounts, and that she had better get the girl out of the house.

What a fool the man was to write such an unguarded letter! But what fools most men were! She had a safe full of similar stuff. She had lists giving times, dates, and the girls they had asked for, from some of the richest and most influential men in England. They might come in handy one day. She hoped she would not need them, but they gave a sense of security.

As for Ellen, she had made five hundred guineas out of her in a week, and she knew a man who would pay another five hundred, landed on the Continent. She would send for his agent and get her away today, on the night boat to Calais. There was plenty of time.

The girl was useless, quite useless. She didn't fight. She showed nothing, apparently felt nothing. Edward Lenton had not said a word about it, but she had watched them. What a disappointment for the poor man! How his pride had been hurt! It had been the same the whole week. She had never seen anything like it. No wonder he looked so tired. She laughed. Hoist by his own petard, she thought, with another bigger one to come, and his wife playing up. Good women were the devil sometimes. No sense of humor, no ability to compromise. Got on their high horses and locked the bedroom door. Well, he'd have Delphine for a while anyway. She sent for Little Tom, one of her runners.

"Go and fetch Fritzie," she said.

As a cover, Baron Fritz von Holtz ran a flower shop in Mayfair, but was authorized to inspect and pay for any parcels of girls—*colis,* they called them, using the French term—that were sent to the Continent. Half down, and half on the receipt of a telegram announcing safe delivery.

No one could have looked less like a trafficker in women than Baron Friedrich Wilhelm Wolfgang von Holtz, a German aristocrat, one of the Death's Head Hussars who, having cheated at cards and killed his accuser, had fled Germany and found asylum in England. The German authorities had been glad to let him go. Penniless, with nothing but his looks and title, he had been very successful in obtaining girls for export abroad, and was as good a judge of woman flesh today as he had been of horse flesh in the past. Tall, not yet forty, slim, distinguished-looking, with a sword cut over his left cheek, he looked exactly what he was: a German ex-cavalry officer whose manner and outward behavior were impeccable. If a man had called him Fritzie in Germany, he would have challenged him, but in this abominable country he was only able to hate him. The feelings of dislike between him and Caramine were mutual, but they respected each other.

He clicked his heels and bowed over her hand.

"*Gnadige Frau,*" he said.

"Fritzie, how nice to see you again! I have a bargain for you. But first a glass of wine."

With a glass of Madeira in his hand, his monocle fast in his left eye, the Baron said: "Where? How old? What is wrong with her? How much?"

Mrs. Caramine smiled at him sweetly. "Last things first, so that you can get used to the shock. Five hundred guineas. She is here. Eighteen. She is almost a virgin. She was till last week. One man only. Blonde, docile—and why do I want to get rid of her?"

"Yes, why?"

"Because she is of good family. That always puts the price up, doesn't it, Fritzie?"

He winced. This *verdamt* old woman, a whore, an old Madam, to speak like that to a Baron of sixteen quarterings.

Mrs. Caramine went on in her soft voice: "Of good family," she repeated, "and they have an idea where she is."

"Frau Caramine, you know the law. There is no law that can take her from your house, not even if they see her at the window. My God," he said, "I have had children of thirteen and their mothers beating with their fists upon the door. . . . If she is so wonderful, why not keep her? That is what I ask."

"I know the law, Fritzie. I stay within it. To be safer still, I pay the police. As a final measure, I have friends in very high places and do them special favors, but I do not like a scandal. With a well-bred girl there can be a hell of a stink, Fritzie. You see, it is one of them. Not just a common girl. As long as they don't know things, they don't care. They know, of course, but they sweep it under the carpet of their conscience. But if they get angry, there can be trouble. The woman who is causing all this trouble is a good woman, a wife. The wife, in fact, of the man who used her."

"Five hundred pounds, you said?"

"Guineas, Fritzie. Five hundred and twenty-five pounds. Two hundred and twelve pounds ten now, and two hundred and twelve tomorrow, when she's safe in Paris."

"Let me see her."

Mrs. Caramine led the way upstairs and into Ellen's room. Ellen was lying on the bed, quite naked, with her hands behind her head, staring at the ceiling with unseeing eyes. She never moved when they came in.

"Straps, I see," the Baron said. "You needed straps, and you said she was docile?"

"They were not used. Just props." Mrs. Caramine said. "They have a moral value, that is why I told Harris to leave them."

"She is bruised. Look at her thighs. Hurt."

"She is not hurt. Come, Ellen, get up!" She took the girl's arms and pulled her to her feet. "Lovely," she said. "Slim, blonde, young, quiet. What the hell do you want, Fritzie? What more? Turn around." She spun Ellen on her heels. "Look at that back, that croup, those calves. Look at her long hair, like silk." Mrs. Caramine ran her fingers through it. She could see he was delighted, but he'd never say so.

"We will go downstairs," he said.

In her office he got out his checkbook.

"Two hundred and twelve pounds ten," Mrs. Caramine said. "To cash, please."

He dipped the pen into the silver inkpot.

"Another glass of wine, Baron?"

"*Bitte,*" he said. They drank to their bargain.

When the Baron had gone, Mrs. Caramine sent for Harris. "Get her dressed," she said. "You're taking her to Calais tonight."

"Yes, Madam," Harris said, but she did not move.

"What is it?"

"She is a wicked girl, Madam. She should be punished. She is lazy. She just lies there. Sloth is an abomination before the Lord. You should have let me see to her, Madam."

"And mark her, you fool? Do you think I'd have got five hundred quid for her—guineas—if she had a mark on her hide? And by God, woman, they'll know what to do with her over there. Besides, they're after her."

"Who is?"

"How the hell do I know? But someone got wind of it, of her being here. Now go and get her dressed and off. You've lots of time. Tell one of the boys to get you a cab, a four-wheeler, and pull down the blinds."

Harris left the room muttering about the Lord. ". . . When I was lazy they used to lick me. A hiding always works. . . . It's a sinful thing but it's God's will. He put the whores in Babylon. . . ."

Upstairs, she brought Ellen's clothes. "Put them on," she said. "You're going home." She always told them that. When they got to the coast she said the sea air would do them good. With luck the Channel crossing upset them. It was generally choppy, and she herself was a splendid sailor. At Ostende or Antwerp or Calais or Boulogne or Dieppe, they were met by a couple who explained to the authorities that the girl was their English niece who had come to learn French. There was never any trouble. The girls she brought were always broken in. They were exhausted, seasick, dazed. For weeks or months they had been out of the world, as much out of it as if they had been in a convent. Brides of lust, of the devil himself. Besides, they were all afraid of Harris—and rightly—for she was the sword of Gabriel, the avenger.

The couple signed a receipt: "*Colis* arrived in good order, undamaged in any way," and with this in her reticule Harris went to a hotel to rest and eat. These were her little holidays. She visited a few brothels where she was known—both government *maisons tolérées* and private establishments. She went to some cabarets and *cafés chantants,* where she looked at the girl performers professionally. Sinners all. What right had they to be free?

And after a day or two she went home. There were no problems, no papers, no passports—only the customs to pass through. Gold was gold. An English sovereign was good in France; a French Louis acceptable in England.

As usual, when she had made a good deal with Fritzie, Mrs. Caramine thanked God for Napoleon Bonaparte. He had clamped down on the French trade in women, the internal trade that is, with his Code. No girl of under twenty-one could be in a brothel. She had to sign papers to register and God knew what all. That was how the trade in English girls had come about. The age of consent was thirteen. It had just been raised from twelve. But half of them didn't know how old they were. Not the kinds picked up in the streets, stolen, or sold by their mothers. No one asked questions at the ports. No one cared. In a way her whole business depended on the hypocrisy of the age. People, nice people, nice women, pretended there were no prostitutes, though God knows what they made of the girls standing under the lampposts in the streets. As for girls being shipped abroad like cattle, that was so unbelievable as to be impossible. So by tacit consent it became possible.

The French supply of adult girls could not fill the demand, and besides there were men who wanted young girls—twelve, thirteen, children, even babies of four or five. They were stolen or bought from baby farmers, who raised them for the purpose. A boy put out to nurse generally died. But a girl baby, if she looked as if she might turn out pretty, was pampered like a lamb for slaughter. And slaughter it was. Few of the children lived more than a year or two in the special brothels that catered to men who wanted this kind of pleasure.

Sometimes Mrs. Caramine thought of putting "By Appointment to certain Kings in Europe" on her notepaper. One of them spent a lot of money on English girls, several thousand a year it was said. And she had supplied some of his wants through Fritzie, who had some very high connections in the courts of Europe.

The worst places for a girl to go were Germany and Austria. There were some houses there where they tortured them to death. The Near East and the Argentine were bad, too. So even in this profession there was no place like home, if they could manage to remain there.

At Mortal Major Lavinia had gone to see John Longbeach again.

"Why did you come back, Mrs. Lenton?" he asked.

"There seemed to be some unfinished business."

"What is it?"

"I want you to go to London for me. And don't worry about money. I got it from him."

"I knew you would," he said.

"I did. Two thousand pounds. Find Ellen. I'm sure she's in that place —Caramine's—and get her out. Buy her out if you must."

"Go to a brothel in London, Mrs. Lenton? Me, a respectable solicitor?"

"Well, I can't go, can I? And I expect you've been in one."

"Why should you think that?"

"You're a man. You're not poor, and you're not married, Mr. Longbeach. You see how fast I'm learning about life?"

"I've been to them," he said. "I've even been to Carrie Caramine's when I was at Oxford."

"You see?" Lavinia said, quite unshocked.

"And I'll do it for you," he said. "My God, Mrs. Lenton"—the lawyer was lost in the man—"I hate this business! I hate women being chattels. Enslaved in brothels and chattels in marriage."

"I felt you were on my side."

"You upset the governor. Those pictures you brought."

"You had another look at them?"

He laughed. "You're very perspicacious."

"Well," Lavinia said, "even I looked at them for a long time, and I'm not a man. There is no doubt, once you get used to the idea, they are beautifully painted."

"Yes," he said.

Mrs. Lenton rose. "The sooner the better," she said.

"Tomorrow, Mrs. Lenton."

Their eyes met. This was a new kind of man to Mrs. Lenton. An upper middle-class man, a businessman. He suddenly seemed to her to be an improvement on the aristocracy. At least he worked for his money. He had neither inherited it nor married it. It occurred to her that he had been in her mind a lot lately.

John Longbeach looked around the main hall at No. 23. It was beautifully furnished, with heavy mahogany chairs, some large pictures of goddesses dressed in wisps of chiffon and reclining on woolly clouds. The curtains were blue velvet, the carpet a thick-piled blue and red. When the butler had opened the door, he said: "Is Mrs. Caramine at home?" and put a card in the silver salver the butler presented to him.

He did not have to wait long.

"Madam will see you. Please come this way."

He followed the butler up a flight of stairs. The place hadn't changed much since he had been here. The pictures seemed to be the same, and so did the furniture. How shy he had been then. . . .

The butler flung open a door.

"Mr. Longbeach, Madam," he said.

The small, neat woman in the armchair rose to greet him. She had not changed much either.

"Mr. Longbeach," she said. "I am glad to welcome you. You were here once before."

"You have a wonderful memory, Madam."

"I have a wonderful filing system. That was why you had to wait a little." She laughed. "I only see old friends, and any client of ours is a friend. Would you like to see the girls, Mr. Longbeach? Some of them are dressed, though we seldom entertain in the morning." She moved toward the bell.

"I'm afraid not, Mrs. Caramine, unless you have a particular girl."

"A type? A redhead? Blonde? Dark? I can offer most kinds."

"A girl called Ellen. A new arrival, I believe."

"Oh Mr. Longbeach, what a pity! You have arrived too late. She decided to go abroad—the Continent. Wanted to learn French, I believe. I'm sure she'll be very successful in Paris. Or was it Brussels?"

"So the bird has flown the coop, Mrs. Caramine?"

"If you like to put it that way. But you are a lawyer as I see from your card, and you know as well as I do, even if she had been here and I had acknowledged it, you could not have got her out."

"I think I could, Mrs. Caramine," Longbeach said, and produced his checkbook. "A thousand pounds?" he said.

Mrs. Caramine rose gracefully from her chair and held out her hand. "Goodbye, Mr. Longbeach," she said. "What a pity you came too late. A pity for both of us."

John Longbeach took the evening train home and found his father waiting for him. The old man was in a rage.

"What's all this gallivanting up to town, boy?" he said. Almost forty was still a boy to him.

"Business, not pleasure, governor."

"What kind of business? Lavinia Lenton's business, I suppose? Damn it, boy, keep clear of her. She's one of these modern women. God knows where she gets it from, bred the way she is. Properly brought up, presented, and married in her first season, straight out of the schoolroom. A cuckoo in the nest. Nigger in the woodpile, I believe the expression is. A throwback of some kind. But she's dangerous, boy. Beautiful, intelligent, and determined."

"Rich too, governor."

"Rich? Of course she's rich, but Edward's got control of her fortune, thank God. Got his head screwed on right, Edward has."

"She's put the screw on him," John said. "Got a couple of thousand out of him as soon as he came home."

"Blackmail," the old man said. "That's what we're coming to. A man blackmailed by his wife. And I won't have you mixed up in it. We're a firm of country solicitors. We administer estates, raise mortgages, buy and sell property, arrange marriage settlements."

"Then you didn't approve of her coming to us?"

"Of course not. He's no worse than any of the others. Better than most in some ways. You don't understand our clients, their views about women and things."

"Quite frankly, I don't. And less today than ever."

"Have a glass of port, John."

He watched his father get out the cut glass decanter and two glasses from the sideboard. The old boy always calmed down if you gave him his head. Let him blow off steam. The trouble was he belonged to the past. He could not face change. He'd been born in 1810, and frightened by tales of Napoleon by his nurse. He remembered the excitement after the Battle of Waterloo. His father had taken him to London and he'd seen the troops march past in triumph. Bands, colors, flags. Cavalry, Guards, Highlanders their pipes screeching. His father had held him up to see the Duke. Wellington, the Iron Duke. What could you do with a man like that, a man who'd been a schoolboy when the first railroad was laid? Who'd gone on his honeymoon in a curricle? That had been with Emma, his first wife. She'd died giving birth to a stillborn child. Then he'd married John's mother, a country girl, a squire's daughter. His sweet mother, plump as a partridge now, and with about as much brains.

Dizzy had said there were two Englands—that of the rich and that of the poor. Two worlds on this little island. But there was a third world coming into being—a powerful middle class. Men who'd climbed up from the gutter and made money, and who were marrying the daughters of gentlemen in poor circumstances. Buying them, really. Racing fillies to be harnessed to drays. But the stock they got was good solid stuff with its feet on the ground. And there were rich Colonials now. Take that chap Rhodes. Diamonds in Africa. Jews. You saw Jews everywhere. He doubted if the governor had even met a Jew except a moneylender, when one of his clients' sons got into their clutches. And women. Florence Nightingale had shown what a woman could do in the Crimea. She'd lighted a fire that could not be put out. These were exciting times.

"Dad," he said—John hardly ever called his father Dad—"sit down."

The old man sat down and held his glass up to the light; it shone ruby red, blood red and bright, as the prisms caught fire.

"I'm going on with this, Dad. Lavinia is right. Women aren't chattels, governor. They're people. They have rights. Their bodies and their money are their own."

His father did not answer him. He knew why. He knew the boy had slipped through his fingers.

The talk at dinner that night was desultory. By God, the old man thought, staring at his son, the boy's a radical. He'll be for universal franchise and compulsory education next. Well, he'd not live to see it, and he was glad. He'd had the best of it—two good wives, and a good son till tonight. Friends. Shooting, hunting. What splendid horses he had had! Timber . . . He was dreaming. In his mind he was jumping a five-bar gate on Orator, a chestnut, the best hunter he'd ever had.

The room was lit with candles in silver candelabra. Old Longbeach would not have gas. Stinking stuff; dangerous too. All right in the streets, but not in a house. The mahogany furniture glowed. The white tablecloth caught the light of the candles and threw it upward into the two men's faces.

Mrs. Longbeach, in evening dress, looked from one to the other of her men—her dear husband and her beloved son. She understood neither of them. The parlormaid, rustling with starch, served them in silence. Course after course. Barley broth, roast lamb, a Queen's pudding, Stilton and Cheddar.

In the morning John Longbeach sent for Blue Bird, a gray Irish mare he'd hunted for one season, and rode over to Mortal. Rode instead of driving the dogcart. He cut a good figure on a horse and the mare was a pretty thing. Still young, and dappled like a child's rocking horse. He wanted Lavinia to see him. He knew he was falling in love with her. Nothing could be more absurd. A married woman with two children, and a great heiress. Nothing could ever come of it. But he felt young and strong and well. A man riding a pretty horse to see a pretty woman.

He cantered up the grass strips that held the drive in their green arms. He saw a cock pheasant running and rode into the rhododendrons to see if he could flush him. The bird went up, cak-caking into the high cover of the mixed woods.

He was near the house now. He wondered what she would be wearing. He had never thought of a woman's clothes before.

At the stables he gave the mare to a groom.

"Shall I put her up, sir?" the man asked.

"I don't think so. Just slack her girths and water her. I shan't be long."

"Some feed, sir?" The man had her bridle in his hand. "Irish, isn't she, sir?"

"She's Irish. And not much feed. Just a handful of oats."

The man led the horse to the water trough, her banged tail switching. Knows we're talking about her, he thought. Horses and women, they always knew.

As Longbeach went in, he met Mr. Lenton.

"Ah John!" he said, "want to see me?"

Very condescending, damn him, John thought. This was a moment he had foreseen and was ready for.

"No, Mr. Lenton," he said. "I came to see Mrs. Lenton."

"On business, I presume?"

"Of course."

"Well, she has no business. I make all the decisions."

"Perhaps we should see her together and let her confirm it, Mr. Lenton?"

"Of course, if you insist."

"I am a solicitor, Mr. Lenton. I have news for her."

"Give it to me."

"I'm afraid I can't."

Mr. Lenton led the way into the morning room. Lavinia was standing by a table arranging flowers. She had a vase of white chrysanthemums in her hand. She put it down.

"How do you do, Mr. Longbeach," she said. "You have news for me?"

"Yes, Mrs. Lenton." John looked from her to her husband.

"You may give it to me in front of Mr. Lenton."

"I should hope so," Edward Lenton said.

"It's bad news," John said. "Ellen Pickford was at Mrs. Caramine's, but she's gone. I was too late."

"Gone?" Lavinia said.

"To the Continent."

"But how? Why?"

"Mrs. Caramine got wind of something," John said. Lavinia turned to face her husband as John went on: "She sent her away."

"Where to?"

"To Europe. France, I should say. Sold her." He could stand no more beating about the bush. "Sold her, like a horse or a dog."

Edward laughed. "You see, Lavinia," he said, "you should let sleeping dogs lie. If she's gone to France, you'll never find her."

"I'm not so sure, Mr. Lenton," John said.

"A needle in a haystack," Edward said. Lavinia remembered his using the sentence before, when he had known where she was. When he had gone to see her with her letter in his pocket. Seen, indeed. What a euphemism . . . seen, had, raped, enjoyed, felt, touched. The whole gamut of sexuality passed through her mind. Words she did not really understand, whose meaning one could only guess at, as she wondered where she had learnt them. But Edward was right about the haystack. How she loathed him!

"Well, what can we do now, Mr. Longbeach?" she asked.

"Detectives, Mrs. Lenton. I've already written to Paris. Detectives," he said, "are like magnets, Mr. Lenton. They find needles in haystacks. But"—he looked back at Lavinia—"I shall need money. Quite a lot of it."

"You shall have it, Mr. Longbeach. Come," Lavinia said and, taking his arm—she had never before, except at a dance or dinner, taken any man's arm, and then both were wearing white kid gloves—she led him past her husband and out of the house toward the stables.

8 : The Package

When Mrs. Lenton went back to the house from the stables, where she had stood watching the lawyer ride off, her husband was waiting for her.

"Come into the library," he said. She followed him, smiling at his temper. Once she would have been intimidated, frightened. This was the master of the house, master of his wife, of his men and maid servants, oxen and asses—all the things it said in the Bible a man should not covet if they belonged to his neighbor. The really funny thing was that in justice, if not in law, everything belonged to her. More particularly, herself. A woman belonged to herself. This was a revolutionary idea.

Watching her husband's back—he still had a military carriage from his years in the army—she thought of John Longbeach. The feel of his hand in hers. Of course they had shaken hands at meeting, but this had been different. When she had been holding his arm, his left hand had come over in front of his body and had deliberately squeezed hers in a gesture of reassurance. No one had ever reassured her like this before.

In the library her husband turned to face her and closed the door.

"Now Madam," he said, "I demand an explanation. What is that counterjumper doing in my house with my wife?" He underlined each *my*. It was his habit. *My* house. *My* wife. *My* children. *My* horses, *my* servants. But he used greater emphasis than usual, which made his assertions even more ridiculous.

She laughed at him, went to a shelf, pulled out a copy of *Paradise Lost*. Her father had loved Milton and had often read it aloud to her in this room.

She opened the calf binding to show her grandfather's bookplate, her family coat of arms: four scallop shells showing that her ancestors had fought in the Crusades, two separate castles, and a stag's head. Those were the quarterings. The crest mounted on the helmet was a hooded hawk. About the shield the mantlings fell in graceful folds. Under them in clear dark letters was her grandfather's name—Sir James Blackstone Mortalland, Bart. She had been a Mortalland. Mortal Major had been named after her family.

She put the book into her husband's hand.

"Your house?" she asked, smiling at him. "Your wife? Now still, after this? I am beginning to think you must be mad, Edward."

"My God!" he shouted, gripping her wrist.

"Let go, Edward." Her voice was dry. "Who do you think I am? Muriel? Ellen? May? One of Caramine's young ladies?"

His hand fell and he threw the book on the floor. "We'll see who's master here, Lavinia. You cannot defy the law."

"I seem to have," she said.

"Not for long. And I'll break open your door."

"For the heir, Edward? What a gentleman you are! But I suppose rape can become a habit."

"God damn it! We'll see, woman," he said, going out and slamming the door behind him.

She picked poor Milton off the carpet and put him back in his place. There were six thousand books in the library, the accumulation of centuries, all leather-bound—in calf, morocco, vellum.

How curious it was that it had taken her so long to discover what kind of man her husband really was under the polished lacquer of his outward behavior.

The lunch gong sounded. She went into the dining room and sat down. Her husband came in and seated himself without a word.

She looked at him dispassionately. A medium-sized man in his forties, conventionally good looking. His dark brown hair had a slight wave. He wore mutton chop whiskers. His mouth was hard without being firm, the lips sensual, and his complexion clear, sunburnt, and reddish from the open air, but flushed now with anger. He had gray eyes, bushy eyebrows. His ears were faunlike, like those of a satyr. His hands were muscular, with a lot of hair on them that ran down over their backs onto his fingers. His body under his clothes—the gray Harris tweed Norfolk jacket he was wearing—was hairy too. She remembered how it felt. Esau was a hairy man, she thought, and found herself wondering if John Longbeach was hairy.

Neither of them spoke. Charles served them. The butler poured the wine. At the end of the meal Edward said grace again, got up with a "Please excuse me," and went out. He had not waited for coffee.

Upstairs Edward Lenton was changing, putting on riding clothes: trousers strapped under the instep to prevent their working up, a stock, and a long-skirted hacking jacket. By God, he'd show her. He'd show that damn young pup of a lawyer, too.

He went into the stable yard by the side entrance to avoid any chance of an encounter with his wife.

He called Blackburn. "Have Nestor saddled up."

"Nestor, sir?" The head groom was taken aback. "Does Madam know, sir? Madam does not like anyone else to ride him."

"Saddle him."

The man turned away and called one of the stablemen. A moment later the two of them went into one of the loose boxes carrying a saddle and double bridle.

Nestor was a black thoroughbred hunter Lavinia had insisted on buying from a man who could not handle him. She was a fine horse-woman with wonderful hands, and Nestor had a very soft mouth. She had had no difficulty with him from the first, had hunted him for two seasons and hacked him whenever she felt like a ride. She did not hunt regularly and took great care never to be in at the kill. Generally well up in front, at the end she would fall back.

The groom led the horse out. Fresh as paint, shiny as jet, fifteen-two, beautifully made, without a white hair on him. The boy held his head while Edward mounted.

"Be careful of his mouth, sir," the head groom said.

"Careful be damned! Think I can't ride him?"

The two men stood side by side watching the master trot out of the yard. "The Madam won't like it," the boy said, and went back to muck out Nestor's box.

Edward did not ride fast. He was turning things over in his mind. Thwarted, by God! So they thought they could thwart him. A conspiracy, that's what it was. His wife disloyal, his lawyer taking her side. Well, they'd soon see.

When he reached Longbeach's office he tied his horse to a ring in the wall and went in, strode past the clerks, right into the old man's office.

"Longbeach," he said, "I want those papers."

"What papers?" Mr. Longbeach said. He did not like this kind of behavior.

"The ones my wife gave you to keep."

"How do you know she brought them here? And how do you know if she did that I would give them to you? They may be at the bank. They might be anywhere."

"They're here." Edward Lenton struck the desk with the buckhorn handle of his riding crop. "And give them to me. You'll give them to me because that is the law. My wife has nothing and you know it. No money, no papers, nothing. When a woman marries she . . ."

"Sit down, Mr. Lenton. Don't shout. Don't hit the desk, and don't presume to instruct me in the law. But," he went on, "unfortunately you are right. They are legally yours, and I will give them to you." He went over to the safe and unlocked it.

The manila envelope was gone.

"They're gone, Mr. Lenton," he said. "Someone has taken them."

"Someone—that jackanapes of a son of yours must have them. He was over to see my wife today. Tell him to keep his nose out of my affairs and hand them over."

"You will please refrain from insulting my son, Mr. Lenton. But I will send for him and see if he can throw any light on the matter."

When John came in his father said: "Mr. Lenton is here."

"So I see, sir."

"He wants his wife's papers. They have gone. They are not in the safe. Do you know where they are?"

"Oh yes. I expected something like this so I removed them."

"You what?" his father said.

"I took them."

Edward sprang to his feet. "Go and get them," he said.

"I'm keeping them, Mr. Lenton. I am acting for your wife."

"Hand them over at once and I'll say no more about the matter."

"I said I was keeping them. If you want them, Mr. Lenton, you might get them by suing. I would suggest your going down the High Street to our colleagues, Springfield and Brewster, a very excellent firm specializing in criminal procedure and auctioneering. You could give them all your business for, though they have no experience in handling estates, they would do a creditable job I am sure. But to ensure the return of the little parcel you want, you will have to accuse me of theft."

"The theft of what?"

"Of twelve nude paintings of women and six paintings of couples copulating in somewhat unusual poses—all on ivory. Valuable works of art worth, according to the receipt, some two thousand pounds. The remaining contents consist of receipts for services rendered from a very well-known brothel. That, Mr. Lenton, is my legal advice, for which there will be no charge. We shall, in fact, say no more about it unless you wish to proceed with the action—a criminal action for theft. Should you do so, I will arrange for the newspaper coverage, Mr. William Stead of the *Pall Mall Gazette* being a personal friend. The accused would, of course, be your wife, which presents certain complications as you are responsible for her torts. Having won your case, you could proceed against me for receiving stolen goods."

Out of the corner of his eye, John could see his father smiling. Edward could not contain himself.

"You dare!" he shouted. "My own lawyers."

"You are a newcomer here, Mr. Lenton," John said. "We have served Mrs. Lenton's family for four generations as lawyers, and perhaps for another ten in other capacities before we rose in the world. This is Mortal Major, Mr. Lenton."

Almost smashing the buckhorn handle of his crop on the desk, Edward Lenton stormed out of the office. What was the world coming to? Counterjumpers, tradesmen, jackanapes! God damn them! He'd get justice somehow. But he knew the young bastard had him.

When her husband left the house riding her hunter, Lavinia knew that the battle was really on. She must work fast. She sent for May.

"May," she said, "do you like me?"

"Like you, Madam?" The girl's eyes were round as gooseberries.

"Do you like me enough to live with me, sleep in my room?"

"I love you Ma'am," the girl blubbered.

"Very well. You'll be my second maid. It'll save Parker waiting up for me sometimes, particularly when we are in London."

"London?" the girl sobbed. "You'll take me to London?"

"In the season. Just for a couple of months or so."

"Oh Ma'am!"

"Now, as you all know, things are not going well in this house. Servants always know. But as my maid I trust you to be discreet."

"What's 'discreet,' Ma'am?"

"Keep your mouth shut."

"Mum's the word, Ma'am."

"Very well. Get one of the other girls to help you move a spare bed into my room, and bring down your things."

The girl curtsied and went out almost at a run. To live with Madam, sleep in the same room, help her dress and undress. Go to town, to London. . . .

Edward Lenton had never been so angry. A violent, cruel man, his temper and hidden desires were cloaked under a mask of manners and convention—a wicked light under the bushel of Victorian custom. Christ! God damn it! He'd teach the bitch! What bitch? Lavinia, Ellen, the bloody lot. He'd find out from Carmine where Ellen had been sent. He'd follow her. You could do things in Europe that even Carmine would not put up with.

He drove his spurs into Nestor. Maddened, the beast sprang into a wild gallop. He pulled on the curb, almost breaking the horse's jaw. He lashed it with the doubled thong of his crop. Blood from Nestor's bleeding lips flecked the white foam that curded his chest. "Come on, you bastard! Faster . . . faster. . . ."

When he dismounted at the stables, the horse stood with trembling knees, its head down, mouth almost in the gravel, its roweled flanks bleeding, its sleek black body scarred with welts.

The boy who took care of him ran up. "Christ!" he said. "Christ! The bloody bastard!" He was crying. The other men and boys stood round, gasping. "Foundered, that's what he is!"

"Get him into his box, boy," the head groom said. "Give him a bottle of beer and a hot bran mash. Bandage his legs and strap him."

"He's done, sir," the boy said. "Foundered."

"And he's not the first, as we all know," the head groom said. "But he was Madam's horse. She'll take it hard. And I've had enough of it. I've got a bit of money saved, and I'm handing in my notice."

"Take me with you, sir," the boy said.

"I may, Jimmy boy. I may, if I get another job." He strode off.

"I want to see the master," he said to Charles who was in the kitchen.

"He's having a bath."

"Then I'll wait. By God, I'll wait till doomsday! That poor bloody horse."

"Well Blackburn, you wanted to see me?" Edward said an hour later.

They were in the gun room. The blued barrels and chased locks of the assorted guns and rifles shone behind the glass cabinets that kept them free of dust.

"Yes sir."

"What about?" Edward knew what it was about. That damn horse of Lavinia's was a kind of pet in the stables.

"Nestor, sir. He's foundered. He'll never hunt again."

"Then sell him. Sell him to the knackers."

"I'd rather shoot him, sir."

"Then shoot him."

"And there's one more thing, sir."

"What is it now?"

"My notice, sir. I want to give you my notice. I'll go at the end of the month."

He'd had to take Madam's horse. She seldom rode any of the others. What a bastard the man was . . . the Master. . . . Blackburn spat and went to see Nestor in his box. He looked a bit better. Jimmy had strapped him, rugged him up, and bandaged his legs and tail. When he went in the boy was leaning over the horse's neck, crying as if his heart would break. Quite a boy, that Jimmy was.

"Look at that, sir," he said to Blackburn, raising the dark-blue, yellow-piped and initialed rug that covered the black's flanks and back. "Look at the way he ripped him, sir."

Blackburn patted the boy's shoulder. "Bloody bastard," he said. "And I don't know how I'll tell the Mistress."

In the Mortal Stables there were six thoroughbred and three-quarter-bred hunters, four carriage horses—two pairs of Cleveland bays that could be driven as a team in the coach, one ladies' hack, and two children's ponies—a Shetland and a New Forest pony with a bit of blood. The old pony who pulled the lawn mower and the three pensioned-off hunters did not count—except for apples and carrots on Sundays. That was a routine between church in the morning and Sunday lunch. The house party always went round to the stables with baskets of horse goodies, to be met with cocked ears and whinnies as the proud heads peered out of their boxes into the yard, as if they had clocks and calendars hung over their mangers.

The three old pensioners had belonged to Colonel Mortaland. Castor and Pollux the grays—white with age now—came from Ireland. Rose was a strawberry-roan mare, also Irish, that had dropped some useful foals. Colonel Mortaland had always been partial to grays and roans. Grays, perhaps because he had started his soldiering as a cornet in the Scots Grays. Roans, because he said he had never seen a bad one. He had been a big man, who rode sixteen stone and bought Irish horses because the best weight carriers came from there. Big, solid chaps that could leap and had the hearts of lions. Like himself. Like Ajax, who tried the impossible wall because his master had asked it of him, and died of it with him.

But none of them would last long now. All over twenty now, and few horses went much beyond that. The day would soon come when the Mistress would tell him to lead them out into the paddock, blindfold them, and put them down with a twelve bore. A terrible day that would be for them all, but better than sending them to the knackers. The Mistress had never been able to understand people selling old horses, to be worked to near death and then sold to be shipped to France or Belgium for slaughter. Old friends and faithful servants betrayed. She'd have them buried in the paddock where so many Mortal horses lay. She'd not let the kennels have them for the hounds. Not the Squire's horses, not her old friends. They'd lie beside Ajax and the horses that had been put down for a hundred years or more, in the field where the brood mares ran with their foals. The Mistress said she wanted them where she could walk over their graves and think about them. And her father no doubt, and how he had not been able to live on in the world alone.

Before she had bought Nestor, Lavinia had hunted her father's grays, who had carried her like a feather on their broad, strong backs. Very pretty she had looked, too. Slim, blonde, top-hatted in her black habit, riding these wise old boys who knew every field and every jump for miles around, and galloped steadily, following the hounds on their own line more or less, but giving in to her when their inclination and her own coincided.

All this was in Blackburn's mind as he walked back to the stable yard. He was going to go, and he'd take the boy with him. A kid that could cry over a horse was his cup of tea all right. Good hands and heart were what made a horseman. But he had not told the young Madam. He could not bring himself to do it.

At last Lavinia pulled herself together enough to go to the stables. She had seen her husband ride in, and had not needed to be told about Nestor.

Blackburn met her in the yard. He'd known she would come.

"Madam," he said, "oh, Madam." His eyes were moist. This hard, leather-faced man's lips were trembling. "Never seen the likes of it, man and boy. More'n forty years with horseflesh, and never seen the likes of it."

Lavinia patted his shoulder as if he was a horse himself.

"I've given me notice, Madam."

"Don't do that, Blackburn. I need friends here."

What a thing for a great lady to say! He'd never thought of the gentry needing friends, with people in and out of the house all the time—weekends, shooting and hunt parties, balls. By God, he thought, they're not so different from the likes of us after all.

They were at the long row of boxes now. He unbolted the door with Nestor's name on it. The horse looked up, his great eyes still rolling, saw his mistress, and whinnied. He was rugged, the surcingle loose about his belly, his four legs bandaged. He came tottering toward her with bent knees, and pushed his mousy, bran-covered nose into her breast.

The boy was sitting on a packing case in the corner, sniffling.

"Broke up, the boy is," Blackburn said. "Loved that horse, he did."

"The bastard!" the boy kept muttering. "The bloody bastard! Me baby. Me pore black baby."

"The Master said sell him to the knackers for the hounds," Blackburn said. "I said: 'Let me shoot him, sir.' We don't want no strangers' hands on 'im."

"Stay, Blackburn, and we won't sell him and we won't shoot him."

"What'll we do, Madam?"

"Send off a boy for the vet at once. We'll patch him up. Strip him off, Blackburn. I want to see how badly he's hurt."

"No sight for a lady, Ma'am."

"Strip him."

The boy took off the surcingle and the rug.

"I washed off the blood and dressed him, Ma'am—a solution of Jeyes."

Lavinia ran her hands over the horse's flanks. He flinched but stood still.

"Take off the bandages."

The boy knelt down, undid the tapes, and rolled them up like puttees.

Lavinia ran her hands down his legs from knee to pastern.

"I'll send over some brandy, Blackburn," she said. "Mash for a day or two, a bit of brandy in it tonight, to make him sleep. Rub his legs with Elliman's. Hot and cold bandages alternately, every hour. Is that all right, Blackburn?"

"You should have been a vet, Madam. It's what we've been doing. All except the brandy."

"Glad you agree. I don't think he's sprung a tendon. If he has, we'll have him fired. His wind may be broken, but we shan't know for a week or so till we can get him out. He looks all right behind."

"He's all right behind, Madam."

"I'll sleep in the box," the boy said.

"Rug him again." Lavinia stroked the horse's nose. "We'll shame him, Nestor. If I can't hunt you, I'll ride you to the meet with all those white spur marks you'll have when hair grows in."

"Black as jet," Blackburn said. "Not a white hair on him, not a saddle gall. And now this. You mean it, Madam? You'll ride him to the meet where they'll all see it? Why, by tomorrow the whole county will know."

And they'll know about May sleeping in my room, too, Lavinia thought.

"Yes Blackburn, they'll soon know most of it and guess the rest."

She must see Parker now, she thought, as a groom clattered out of the yard to get the vet. "Like a bloody pet, he was," she heard a groom say. "A dog or a kitten."

Parker was not surprised at being sent for. Well-trained servants were surprised at nothing, or if they were they never showed it. She'd been Miss Lavinia's mother's maid. She'd dressed her for her presentation at court. How lovely she had looked in her tiara, with white ostrich plumes in her hair, great ropes of pearls and a white satin dress with a long train that had to be kicked away when she backed out of the Queen's presence. She had dressed her for her wedding, too. An heirloom veil of Brussels lace and white silk this time, grosgrain. When her ladyship had died, she had come to her, to her baby. My Miss Lavinia.

"Parker," Lavinia said, pointing to the second bed, "May is coming to sleep here. I want you to train her. It'll save you work and late nights in London waiting up for me, and there are other reasons. I expect you know that."

"Yes, Madam."

"You know, Parker, it's not considered the thing to do to gossip with servants."

"I know, Madam."

"I think we might know more if we did."

"The servants know everything, Madam. I tried to tell your Aunt. . . ."

"Tell her what?"

Parker's temper got the better of her. "That he was no good. Not the man for you. That it was your money he wanted."

"Well dear," her mistress said, "I've made my bed and I must lie in it.

But I'll lie alone." She took the older woman in her arms. "You've been like a mother to me," she said. They were both crying.

"You're too young for it, Vinny."

"For what?"

"To sleep alone, Miss Lavinia. Too young," she said. "Excuse me, Madam." And she went out with her apron over her eyes.

At dinner that night, in black lace over a pale salmon-pink evening dress and wearing her jewels, Lavinia broke the news to her husband. In front of the servants—the butler and two footmen.

"I've moved May into my room, Edward," she said. "Parker's getting old and is going to train May, and I thought I'd be nervous sleeping alone."

"You'd better have Mac sleep there, too," Edward said sarcastically.

"I think I will. Thank you for the idea." Mac stood thirty inches at the shoulder and weighed over a hundred pounds.

They went on talking about the shooting party that was going to take place in ten days. It was the last one of the year.

"Clean out all the cocks," Edward said. "We should get a hundred brace with five good guns."

By God, he was looking forward to it! He wanted to kill something. To see a rocketing pheasant close its wings and come thudding down, to be picked up by the retrievers. He liked the smell of the powder, the feel of the explosion of a shell against his shoulder. Action, that was what he liked. He always regretted missing the Crimea.

A killer, Lavinia thought, that's what he is. He wished I was the horse today. He'd have liked to thrash me, spur me, break me. She shuddered as she thought of Ellen.

"Cold, dear?" Edward asked, and told Charles to ask Parker for a wrap.

"A little cold, Edward. A cold shiver as if someone had walked over my grave."

9 : The Parson Inquires

There had been two letters for Ellen from her father. And now one had come for Mrs. Lenton:

Dear Mrs. Lenton, he wrote, I have not heard from my daughter, Ellen, for more than a fortnight and I am somewhat distressed at her unusual silence. She has always been a good and dutiful daughter and knows how much I look forward to her news. Since her dear mother passed away, she is all I have so I trust you will forgive my writing to you. How is she? Not seriously ill, I trust. One day I hope to have the opportunity of meeting you and Mr. Lenton, and in the meantime I take this opportunity of thanking you both for your kindness to my daughter. Yours sincerely,

C. V. Pickford.

Mrs. Lenton had no idea how to answer him, so she wrote to her cousin, Colonel Hawley, asking him to break the news, and also decided to wire the vicar and ask him to come down the following week.

So in the end it was the squire, Colonel Hawley, who heard from Mrs. Lenton. Not the parson. She wrote enclosing the vicar's letter. She said:

I do not know how to write to him. You will have to break the news. I thought, as you know, we had a treasure in Ellen. The girls adored her. Pretty, gentle, and unassuming. And then what do we find? That we have been nourishing a viper in our bosom, at least that is what I thought at the time. Even then, though I had Edward's word for it, I found it hard to believe that a girl like Ellen—so quiet, so ladylike—should approach my husband like *that,* waylaying him, telling him she loved him, forcing herself upon him. He told me to give her notice, which is what I did, and now her father writes in despair that he has no news of her. So please go and see him. Tell him something—I can only tell you that I know that a dreadful mistake has been made and that Edward lied to me.

The letter arrived at breakfast time. It was on top of the *Times,* unfolded and ironed by the butler to remove the crease. The Colonel liked the smell of the warm paper and printer's ink. Beside the letters was an ivory paper knife to cut their vellum throats.

According to habit, the Colonel put the letters and paper to one side and had his breakfast. Porridge with golden syrup. He lifted the lids of the silver dishes on the side table, each kept warm with a little spirit lamp. Bacon and eggs, kippers, kedgeree, kidneys on toast, haddock. . . . He helped himself to bacon and eggs and a couple of kidneys. Then he had toast and honey, his own honey. He preferred it to marmalade, though that, too, was homemade.

Mrs. Hawley, a tall, rather desiccated woman with a Norman nose that in late middle age resembled the beak of an eagle, had not spoken to her husband. He did not like conversation at breakfast. She had read her own letters before she began to eat. One each from her two married daughters and one from her son in the Hussars, saying that life was becoming more expensive every day, but that he was practicing great economy and eking out an existence on the thousand a year they allowed him. The solution, he supposed, would be a rich wife.

Well, she thought, perhaps that would be the best solution. After all, it was time he settled down. She heard her husband slitting open his letters and then suddenly say: "Ha!" He was annoyed at something. He only said "Ha!" when he was annoyed. He wiped his red face with his table napkin, still leaving some yolk of egg on his moustache.

"What is it, dear?" she said.

"That girl. Ellen. I don't believe a damn word of it. And nor does Lavinia. It's him, Lenton, who's at the bottom of it."

"What don't you believe, George?"

"Here," he said. "Take a look at it." He threw Lavinia's letter over to her.

Euphemia Hawley read it slowly and then said: "George, I agree with you. Ellen's not at all like that. Nothing fast about her."

"I don't trust Edward," her husband said. "He only married Lavinia for her money. I tried to put a stop to it, as you know. You remember, don't you?"

"Yes, dear."

"It was always women with him. Woman-mad. Servants, anyone. Anything with a skirt that had a pretty face. We should never have let Ellen go to Mortal. But when Lavinia wrote I thought it was such a good opportunity for her."

"What are you going to do, George?"

"My duty. I'm going to see her father and then I'm going down to Mortal to have it out. By God," he said, banging the table, "I'm responsible for it. Whatever happened."

He rang the bell that stood beside his place. A footman came in.

"You rang, sir?"

"Yes, John. Tell Perkins to saddle Jack and bring him round."

"You're riding over to the vicarage?"

"As soon as I've changed, my dear."

The Colonel got up, kissed his wife's forehead and went out of the room.

She stared at the closed door. George was a good man. A good husband and father. A good squire. And this was part of it. Breaking bad news. But generally it was to his tenants, to the villagers. Now it was to one of his own kind, a friend. She was sure he was right. Edward Lenton had a finger in this pie. A detestable man.

Jack was a bay, three-quarter-bred hunter that had cost the Colonel two hundred guineas at Tattersalls. Seven years old, with a beautiful temperament and a mouth like silk. The Colonel leaned forward and patted his neck. "A bloody fine kettle of fish this is, my boy," he said.

The horse laid an ear back to listen to him. The Squire always talked to his horses. More sense than people, lots of 'em. And they didn't answer back. No bloody nonsense with horses.

But that girl. Where was she? In London, alone. A pretty, silly, sweet young thing. He loved her like his own daughters. But he felt better now. He always did on the back of a good horse.

He rode cross-country, taking the hedges and fences as they came. He walked him over the ploughed land and cantered over the grasslands. No hurry. Just a nice ride. He didn't want him to sweat. Nice and easy, comfortable as an armchair, with his beautiful shoulders and long, sloping pasterns. From the top of a rise he saw the village and the church. The vicarage and the dark patch of the old yews near the graveyard. He jumped another fence and trotted up the road.

He had not yet decided what he would say to Charles. Poor Charles. By God, he thought, a hundred years ago I'd have called Lenton out.

The Reverend Charles Vernon Pickford had been surprised at not receiving his weekly letter from Ellen. She wrote every Sunday. The letters arrived on Wednesday. This broke the week up nicely—his church service on Sunday and the letter on Wednesday. Of course, she might be ill. He went on expecting a letter or a postcard. Another Wednesday passed without news. By then he had become really anxious and wrote to Mrs. Lenton.

He had written the letter on his best crested notepaper—saved for special occasions—and, having posted it, sat back to wait for an answer. Now he would hear something. Mrs. Lenton would certainly write and there might be something from dear Ellen in the meantime.

Parson Pickford, as his parishioners called him, was proud of his old stone church. Fourteenth century, but with foundations even older than that. Much older. Saxon. And judging from the circular grove of great yews, it had probably served as a center for some ancient pre-Christian cult. These dark trees were enormous and sinister. He had the feeling that terrible things had happened here and, though this was hard to believe, that they continued to exercise some mystic power over the village people. Some young people came here in the light of the full moon to plight their troth. At certain seasons of the year they cut yew twigs and hung them over their beds. All in all, their influence was evil. Even a consecrated church within twenty yards of them was not enough to control their emanations.

He had thought a lot about evil in his life. Evil was the enemy of Christ. There was no real wickedness in the village, but the countryside —and particularly the yew trees—had an aura of something, a vestigial underlay as it were, of sexuality, of fertility rites and phallic worship, which appeared to cling to the green fertile fields and woods and lie hidden in the deep recesses of the simple minds of his people. The impossibility of getting the yews felled, for one thing. One example. Some folk songs and gestures. Curious sayings and unexplained festivals. The horn dance at Michaelmas, when the young men danced in masks with horns tied to their heads.

People, in this backwater, still believed in fairies. At least one old woman was said to be a witch. There were remains here of the old religion that had existed all over Europe before its conversion to Christianity. The worship of the devil, the old horned god—hairy, goatlike, and concupiscent.

Charles Pickford was making a study of these things. Writing a book about them. About the things he had discovered. Some of such indecency that he had written of them in Latin, thus disguising them from vulgar eyes. Young country girls had confessed to him, trusting him with obscene secrets. Yet he could not condemn them as wicked. Misguided only, and subject to forces that even he was bound to acknowledge had a certain reality. It was these impalpable forces that he fought in a country parish that was a hundred, even two hundred, years behind the times.

Colonel Hawley tied up his horse and went to look for the parson. He found him in the garden, tying some brown and gold chrysanthemums to a stake.

"Well, Charles?" he said.

"Well, Squire, what brings you here?"

"Bad news, I'm afraid. I've had a letter from Lavinia Lenton."

"About Ellen? Why didn't she write to me?"

"Thought I'd better break the news, I expect."

"She's not . . . not dead?"

"No, Charles."

"Thank God for that."

"She's disappeared, old boy. Something has gone very wrong."

"I've been worried, Squire. No news, and then a telegram from Mrs. Lenton asking me to come down for a couple of days. I'll spend a night in London on the way with Canon White. Johnnie White. We took Holy Orders together." He paused, and then said: "Excuse me, Squire.

I think I'd like to go into the church for a bit. I want to thank God, Charles. I want to thank Him. You see I was afraid she was dead. I'll pray for her. Whatever happens, she's under God's protection."

They shook hands. Damn it, if the old fool had let him help him, this would never have happened. A hundred a year would have made all the difference, and they'd never notice it. He'd talked to Euphemia about it, and she'd agreed. But Charles was too bloody proud. Poor as a church mouse, and wouldn't let a friend help him.

He watched the black-clad figure go through the yews and into the church. To thank God Ellen was not dead. Poor Charles! There might be worse things than death for a pretty girl alone in the world.

His talk with Charles had been bad enough, but he did not envy Lavinia's interview with him. How would she tell him her husband had tried to seduce his daughter and had then maligned her? Had her thrown out into the street? Nor could he blame Livvy. Naturally, she had believed Edward. Then she had found something out. What had she found out? You learnt a lot about people soldiering, and more still as a squire with two hundred tenants to look after.

He rode back slowly. There was no gallop and jump left in him. Edward Lenton was a cad. A man who'd try that on a young girl who was in his care . . . *loco parentis*. What a life Livvy must have led with him, but never a word out of her till now. He'd changed his mind about going to Mortal. He was too old to horsewhip the chap. And a scandal would only make things worse for Livvy. But how he hated men like Lenton, who took advantage of their position to abuse others less fortunate than themselves.

Chrysanthemums and Michaelmas daisies. The trees turning brown. Cub-hunting had begun a month ago. The shooting was good this year, and winter well on its way.

The vicar arrived at Mortal the following Tuesday. A dear old, pink-faced man, with a battered Gladstone bag. As soon as he had said, "How do you do, Mrs. Lenton," he had asked for news of Ellen.

How was she going to tell him the truth, even part of it? At luncheon she said: "It's a long story," and introduced him to Edward.

"This is Ellen's father, Edward," she said. "My husband, Mr. Lenton." They sat down.

Mr. Pickford said grace. The talk was desultory. The vicar spoke of his parish in the shires. He'd hunted in his youth. "I was better off, then. That's why Ellen wanted to be a governess, to save me money for her clothes and food. She even sent me her salary to help out. We are in very straitened circumstances," he said, "but God sustains us."

Lavinia could see her husband was feeling the strain. The vicar was a poor man but a man with connections, with powerful friends. Young men who'd been at Oxford with him were now political powers. The names fell quite unself-consciously from his lips.

After lunch Lavinia took him to her boudoir and told him the tale. He sat quite still, a plump little figure in black, his hands on his lap, finger to finger.

When he had done, he closed his eyes. She saw his lips moving. When he opened his eyes he looked at her and said: "I do not see how you could have acted otherwise in the circumstances. It is always the circumstances. Pilate did not wish to condemn Our Lord. But He was condemned owing to circumstances, died, and rose again. By dying, Mrs. Lenton, He saved us. God will protect Ellen and she may yet be the cause of great events, very great events."

"We are looking for her, Mr. Pickford."

"I think you will find her, Madam. Now, if you will forgive me, I will say goodbye. I do not wish to sleep under the same roof as the man you have been unfortunate enough to marry."

He took her hand. She sent Charles to order the dogcart.

Upstairs at Mortal, May settled nicely into Lavinia Lenton's room— a sweet, clean, nice-tempered girl for whom nothing was too much trouble. The bedroom had always smelled of *potpourri*—roses. Now it smelled of dog as well.

"Fair stinks of dog, Madam," May had said one day.

"We'll wash him."

"Wash him, Madam? He's bigger nor me. An' where'll I wash him?"

"In my bath."

They had both laughed hysterically as she helped May the first time. But now the big dog was used to it, and stood quietly while he was being soaped. There was still a smell of dog in the bedroom, but the roses predominated.

And God help Edward—or anyone else—who came into the room at night. Mac followed her about the house, and went with her when she rode Nestor.

Nestor was a changed horse and his temper had become uncertain. He'd lash out and even chop, more like a stud horse than a gelding, if a man he did not know came near him, and his mouth was ruined. Lavinia rode him about the park and to a couple of nearby meets, but she controlled him more by her voice than the reins. He'd never hunt again but she rode him to see her friends and let them see the scars on his barrel, where the new hair had grown in quite white. No one ever mentioned the scars. No one even said anything, when she said she'd not hunt this season.

There were shooting parties. There was Christmas. The servants' dance. Dinner. Turkey, mince pies, plum pudding with half-crowns, florins, and shillings that had lain in its black richness since the previous winter. Presents. A seed pearl necklace for Eva. A blue-eyed, yellow-haired doll from Paris, that closed its eyes when laid down for Betty. A French doll. Lavinia had not realized it came from there till after she had bought it. Ellen. Delphine. Everything she wanted to forget. Three pairs of black kid gloves for Delphine—she had to give her something. Nimrod's *Conditioning of Hunters,* bound in red calf and gold, for Edward. A Paisley shawl for Parker, a dress for May. A gold watch fob for James, a set of razors—one for every day—for the bailiff. A gold-mounted riding crop for Blackburn, a silver teapot for Mrs. Fawcett. A twelve-bore for Joliffe. Pipes, tobacco, and shawls for the tenants and their wives. Toys for all the children on the estate. No one was forgotten, from the old granfers who had served her father when he was a boy, to babies a month old. They were her people. Edward they might call the squire, but she was the Mortalon. She was Mortal. The Madam was the mistress. The men touched their forelocks to her. The women bobbed. The children waved.

But Christmas for the household servants was haunted by Ellen's absence. The servants spoke about it to each other. "Poor bloody girl," Charles said. "A bloody fine Christmas she'll have, I'll bet."

Upstairs there was silence, Lavinia wondering and thinking of the girl whom Edward had betrayed. Thinking of the old parson conducting his services, and praying for his daughter.

10 : The Season

Edward continued to make love to Delphine. He insisted on candlelight so that he could enjoy her beauty. It was unbelievable that this glorious creature was the dowdy woman he saw about the house. What an actress she was! What a mistress! He had got over his pique about Lavinia and gave her the money she asked for without question. If she left him alone, he would leave her alone.

After all, there was more than enough money to go round, and he had the laugh on her with Ellen waiting for him in Paris. Let her play her games with her lawyer and her French detectives. On his visits to

London, Mrs. Caramine assured him that all was well. There was just the spring and the season to get through, when the household moved to his house in Berkeley Square. This, at least, was his own.

Life at Mortal had settled down again like a pond that has been stirred up—the mud sank and the surface cleared, as autumn gave way to winter, and winter to spring. First the snowdrops, then crocus and daffodils—the forsythia bushes were heaps of gold. Apple blossom, honeysuckle, and wild hedgerow roses—the Tudor roses of England. The season of love, of gambolling lambs, birds singing, of courting couples, had come again.

The rhododendrons that lined the drive came out in a glory of mauve, pink, red, and white. The hunters were stripped of their shoes and turned out to grass. God was certainly in His heaven, that must look like England in a good summer. The garden was filled with the hum of bees. And butterflies—red admirals, peacocks, and tortoise-shells —adorned the purple buddleias.

But where was Ellen? There had been no news from France, John said. No news of Ellen, that is, but plenty of other news. Brothel after brothel had been visited. The detectives had contacts everywhere.

What a strange job this was for them! English gold for looking at girls. And writing reports. Reports that curdled John Longbeach's blood.

Every Sunday Mademoiselle brought the children down to the dining room. First church, and then luncheon, dressed in their best. They always walked to church because horses were never used on Sunday. Mr. and Mrs. Lenton led the way, then Mademoiselle and the children, and the servants not on duty. The horses still got their tidbits between church and luncheon. But Mr. Lenton never went with the others.

Mademoiselle always looked her usual dowdy self. It was really impossible to believe she was what she was. If I had not seen it with my own eyes, Lavinia thought. But she seemed to be a good governess. The children were well, though somewhat subdued. They could chatter in French now, which Edward could not understand but could hardly check since it was at his insistence they were learning it.

The only time, other than Sunday lunch, their mother saw the children was for an hour after tea, when they were brought into the drawing room and sat there reading or looking at pictures through the stereoscope. Sometimes Lavinia was shocked at how little she knew about them. They were pretty, well-behaved children, but seemed to have little to do with her. Perhaps a mother's relationship with her children depended on her affection for their father. These babies had not been conceived in love, neither had most of the children of her friends, who felt much the same about them as she did. In babyhood they had had wet nurses, farm girls who suckled them. Then a sequence of nannies, nursery governesses, governesses. Perhaps in the holidays after the London season, when they all want to the sea, she would get to know them better. She must try. They were sweet children. Pretty, obedient, well brought up. It was just that they had somehow escaped her. After all, Evangeline would be presented soon and probably married, as she had been, in her first season.

She had no further trouble with Edward when she asked for money, even large sums. He gave her a check at once. Delphine apparently kept him satisfied. But he still went up to London as usual, once a month, saying he needed a change. A change of what?

She always said: "Of course, you need a change, Edward."

Most of their conversation had a double meaning now. But something was going on in Edward's mind, some obscure and probably horrible plan was being hatched.

Mrs. Caramine knew where Ellen was and Edward had bought her. She was being reserved for his pleasure. Instead of going to Scotland for the grouse in August, he was going to Paris. It would be hot, but to make up for it no one would be there. There was no chance of meeting an acquaintance. He would write a couple of noncommittal letters about the moors that one of his friends, who understood such capers, would post to Lavinia. In the meantime, he had Delphine and the little blonde in black with whom he had danced at Mrs. Caramine's when he had gone to London to see Ellen.

At the beginning of May, the household moved. The servants, horses, and carriages, went down in advance. A skeleton staff was left at Mortal. For a week the family lived a simple, butler-less and footman-less life, and then took the train to London—Edward, Lavinia, Delphine, the girls, May, Parker, and Edward's valet.

This was the first stage of the trip to Paris, where he was going to have his revenge, not merely on Ellen but on Lavinia, who so disloyally had taken her part against him. By now he believed his own story. The girl had led him on and then rebuffed him. This was the final version, the one he was going to stick to. In humiliating Ellen, he was humiliating his wife. Indifference toward Lavinia had turned to hatred, that was masked in acid politeness. God knew he had never enjoyed her, but had never given up the hope of begetting an heir—a Lenton. But with locked doors, May, and the dog sleeping in her room, there was no chance of it now. She was defrauding him of his legal marital rights. But till he got his package back, she had the whip hand of him. How quick that lawyer of hers had been! How suspicious and under-handed! He must have moved it the moment he got home, only a couple of hours before he himself reached the office.

The London season was like every other London season. *Levées,* balls, theater parties, luncheon and dinner parties. The Eton and Harrow match, the boat race, Ascot. Rounds of calls and teas—visits to the dentist. Theater parties, at-homes. A woman's world of twirling parasols and feather boas, of ostrich plumes, of fans, of dressmakers, *modistes.* There were shoes, corsets, and underthings to be bought. Ten months of gossip to be exchanged with friends. Children to be shown off and admired. Drives in the Park. Books to be exchanged at Mudie's lending library. All the corners of a bucolic existence to be rubbed off with the abrasive of metropolitan intercourse.

London to Lavinia Lenton was no longer what it had been. Edward had pulled the scales from her eyes. She began to see the poor, who before had been invisible. She saw the prostitutes in Piccadilly and the Haymarket, some of them children of fourteen or even less. She discovered more facts of life.

In bleaching factories, young girls worked for eighteen hours a day, when the temperature might touch more than a hundred degrees. Children, too, were worked, and sometimes went three days without sleep. Then there was the "slop system," when contracts for needlework were let, sublet, and re-sublet, girls working seven days a week from dawn to midnight, and earning one and threepence halfpenny a week. Lavinia discovered that some needlewomen received sevenpence for stitching one hundred and forty-four collar bands. No wonder girls went wrong, as it was termed. And all this had been going on all the time. Was going on. She wondered how she could have been so blind.

Her mind at this time was divided into a number of compartments. Her social life, her entertaining. Her friends. The life of London in the season—brilliant, multicolored as a film of oil on water. London, the center of the world. Carriages, fine riding horses. Soldiers in scarlet. The occasional excitement of a red fire engine, its gray horses galloping through the streets, one of the firemen ringing a big, brass bell. The traffic held up by a fallen horse. Beggars, roughs, barefooted children.

Chimney sweeps, black with soot, followed by the little boys they drove up the chimneys to clean them. She heard of their becoming stuck, and being suffocated.

Then there were Edward and the other men like him, so well groomed, so well mannered. Other women seemed to accept them. Men were like that. But wickedness was still new to her. And Ellen —what had become of her?

So when the end of July approached, she was glad to leave London. She had seen all her friends, particularly Maud Fortall—the Hon. Mrs. Harold Fortall—with whom, though she was considerably younger, she had a lot in common. Maud was childless, unhappily married, a little wild—some people said fast—but she was very pretty, and she was amusing. They often rode together in the Row, with their grooms riding behind them. A striking couple of beauties. The dark and the fair of it, men called them. A lot of people had names like that. Beauty and the Beast—that was Lord Jenlain, the ugliest man in England, and his third wife, a girl of eighteen, who looked like an angel but would be the death of him, they said. They said this, and that. Gossip. Scandal.

Lavinia went to Covent Garden. She went to see *The Mikado* at the Savoy. She went to the flower show. She took the children to see the cart-horse parade in the Park. Horses as big as elephants, with their polished harness, the brass ornaments glistening in the June sun, their coats as bright as mirrors, their manes, tails and forelocks plaited up with ribbon. She went to the Eton and Harrow match, the boat race; Ascot, the Derby. Went to see the daughters of friends, dressed in white silk and satin with ostrich plumes and tiaras on their hair, nervous as kittens while they waited for the carriages that would take them to Buckingham Palace to be presented to the Queen; white, virginal, ignorant, all of them sure they would not be able to walk backward, doing practice kicks to their trains. Lavinia went everywhere and enjoyed nothing.

She bought clothes for herself and the children. The best evening dresses and summer frocks were packed in big, round-topped trunks to go back to Mortal. More holiday frocks were shopped for. Linens, cottons, sailor dresses with round straw hats for the children. Winter clothes had to be made. They were chosen from wax dolls dressed up in the latest fashions. She bought a purple velvet dolman, frogged with black braid; an ermine cloak, a peacock-feather hat with the bird's head embodied in it, and a feather muff to match—brilliant blues and greens. Shoes, buttoned boots, stockings, underwear. New evening dresses of velvet, shot silk, satin, lace, organdy. Afternoon dresses of cashmere, merino, poplin, plush, tarlatan. Kid gloves that reached to the armpit, short gloves for daily use. Maud gave her a kid fan with a hunting scene painted on it.

That was London in the season. But this year it was all different. Last year she had been almost as ignorant as the girls who were coming out. Coming out like chicks from the egglike security of home and school-room into the world. A world in which almost everyone who was any-body lived in the country most of the year, and opened their town houses in the early summer. By July they had made their plans. The women and children to the seaside, the men to the moors in Scotland or Yorkshire. By September they would be home again in the country for the partridge shooting that began on the first.

Lavinia, with Mademoiselle, May, and the girls, was going to Folke-stone to a hotel on the Lees that she had patronized before. It would be good to get away, she said. She meant to be free of Edward's com-pany for a month. His smugness annoyed her. What had he to be smug about? The affair with Delphine was too difficult in the London house, but he was not a man to deprive himself of his pleasures, and she had no doubt he was a regular customer at Mrs. Caramine's. She was as-tonished at her lack of resentment of Delphine, possibly because it was impossible to reconcile her appearance by day with her role by night. She took the carriage and pair with her to Folkestone. There were some nice drives over the Downs. They would have picnics. She would really get to know her children. A curious situation of tacit acceptance now existed between her and Delphine—this Mademoiselle who hid her beauty so well that friends asked Lavinia how she could stand so plain a woman about the place, a real frump. But they also said: "But per-haps you are wise, after all. A pretty governess can be such a nuisance." They had all heard tales of governesses who were a nuisance. These things should not go on at home.

Folkestone was beautiful, the air on the Lees a pleasant change from the stuffiness and smells of London. They bathed, wearing what amounted to a full set of clothes in navy blue piped with white: a cap, a sort of long-sleeved jumper with a sailor collar, bloomers, black stock-ings, and canvas shoes. To carry privacy still further, the bathing cabins were dragged by an old horse right into the water.

They paddled; they bought shrimping nets and pushed them along the edge of the sea, and took their transparent catch to be cooked at the hotel for tea. Fresh shrimps, pink as lobsters in death. Lovely.

Sometimes Lavinia went down to the front alone with May and sat on a rug watching the sea and listening to the pebbles being washed up and rolling back with every wave. The sound soothed her. She liked to watch the sea-gulls and the fishing boats with their dark sails. If only they could stay here forever—for a long time, anyway. Away from Edward, away from Mortal where she was continuously being reminded of Ellen and the dreadful mistake she had made.

She recognized her feelings about Delphine—Mademoiselle. She loathed her, but she was her greatest asset against Edward. For a man to seduce a governess was one thing; for him to introduce a harlot into his home was another. More than even his friends would countenance. Not because it was wicked or immoral, but because it was in bad taste. As a governess she left nothing to be desired, except that the children did not like her. But even that was a good thing because it had brought them closer to her. She was charmed by them. Sweet, intelligent, bubbling over with high spirits when they were alone with her or May. She had managed to put Ellen out of her head, and was really enjoying herself.

Then the telegram came, brought by a page boy on a silver salver: "Have important news. Must see you. Will call at Berkeley Square 11 A.M. Wednesday. John Longbeach."

They were having tea by the open window in their suite when it came. A large sailing ship was visible on the horizon, a sea-gull swept past, screaming, as she wired her reply.

"I'll have to go up to London the day after tomorrow," Mrs. Lenton said. "I'll only be away one night."

"Yes, Madame," Mademoiselle said.

"I'm sure the children will be safe with you."

"Of course, Madame. Madame is taking her maid?"

"Yes, I shall take May."

When one forgot the other thing, Delphine was really a responsible person who kept the girls beautifully. They had never been so well groomed before. Sometimes she thought she must be mistaken, that she must have misread the letter May had pasted together. Anyway, twenty-four hours was not long to leave the children. And John—how she wanted to see John and talk to him!

On Tuesday the girls and Mademoiselle went to see her off at the station. They all waved their white handkerchiefs as the train pulled out.

Once it had gone, Delphine took Betty's hand. "Now we will do something exciting," she said. "We will go and look at the channel steamer."

There she lay, her big paddles, one on either side, at rest in their white-painted housings. It sailed at midday.

At the gangway, Delphine handed over her tickets. She had bought them when she wrote to Mrs. Caramine telling her to send the telegram from London in John's name. Mrs. Lenton had taken the bait. Twenty-four hours in London to see her lover. Edward had spoken about John to her several times. He did not believe it himself. She was too cold a fish. But it sounded good and seemed to please Delphine.

Evangeline said: "Do we have to have tickets to get on board?"

"Of course, *chérie,* or everyone would come swarming onto the ship. Come! We must see everything." They were still seeing everything when the ship hooted a couple of times and cast off.

"Oh!" cried Evangeline, "we're off! What shall we do?"

"Nothing, darling," Delphine said. "What an adventure we shall have. Just enjoy the voyage and we'll take the next boat back."

The girls had never seen her so gay.

John Longbeach was in London. As usual he went to see his friend William Stead, the editor of the *Pall Mall Gazette.*

William Stead looked up from his desk and put his blue pencil down. He was always glad to see John.

"Come in, John. Sit down!"

John Longbeach came up once a month. Business and pleasure. Got to keep track of things. But Stead knew what he came for. A woman. Why didn't he get married? Stead, happily married himself, believed everyone should get married. He watched John lower himself rather carefully into a chair and laughed.

"You won't break that one."

"I hope not. But I don't believe in taking chances."

"That's the lawyer in you, John. Care, safety, precedent."

They both laughed.

"I had a bit of time to spare so I thought I'd pop in to see you."

"Thanks, John. There's nothing an editor likes better than being disturbed."

"I thought we might have a chop together at Simpson's."

"Something is worrying you?"

"Yes, it is. I've got some bad news from Mrs. Lenton."

Stead knew about the Lentons of Mortal. Clients, and the biggest landowners in John Longbeach's county.

"What's it about?"

"Her husband."

"Where is she?"

Longbeach took a match from a little silver box in his pocket and lit a cigar. "Folkestone. She's down there with the children and the governess."

Stead tidied his desk. That is to say, he pushed the papers about—letters, copy, bills, telegrams—and weighted down the heaps with a horseshoe, a round glass letterweight that produced a snowstorm in its interior when moved, and a flat piece of green malachite.

"Come on, then. Let's get some lunch, John."

They picked up their top hats and went out into the summer heat. Not that it was hotter outside than in. It simply seemed hotter in the glare amid the roar of the traffic. Vans, drays, four-wheelers, hansoms. The horses were sweating under their harnesses.

The people were sweating too, wiping their foreheads with handkerchiefs; the women dark under the armpits. There was a smell of sweat in the air, and horse manure. It felt like thunder. According to the papers, 1885 was the hottest summer England had experienced for twenty years.

The two men walked through the crowd, a swirling river that ran both ways at once as if unable to make up its mind between banks lined with shops and offices.

John Longbeach was thinking of Lavinia. Mrs. Edward Lenton. Lavinia was in his mind. She was at the seaside with the children. He hoped she was having a good time. No one was in London. Mayfair and Belgravia were empty. The houses had their blinds drawn as if each contained a corpse. Everyone was at the seaside or in the country or on the Continent. The masses that pressed round them were not people in the accepted sense. Clerks, shopkeepers, merchants, workingmen, ragamuffins, children—some with bare feet.

Longbeach had been fifteen when Lavinia's mother had called on his mother about some charity affair. His mother had said: "Take Lavinia out and show her your rabbits." He remembered being ashamed at having rabbits. Fifteen was too old for rabbits. He had some ferrets too, and that in a way canceled out the rabbits. Ferrets were manly. He used them for rabbitting and ratting. But he loved his rabbits. He had always had rabbits. How did one get rid of them? Of course he gave quite a few away, but more always kept coming.

The little girl—she must have been ten—danced along beside him, her long fair hair bobbing loose on her shoulders. They had gone through the stable yard and into the kitchen garden.

"Here they are," he said. "And the ferrets too."

"How lovely! The rabbits, I mean," she'd said. "White rabbits with black noses and ears. I've never seen those before."

"They're Polish," he'd said.

"Can I have one? Oh"—she'd put her hand to her mouth—"I shouldn't have said that! I'm not supposed to ask for things."

"Of course you can have one. I'll pick you a nice one." He meant a male. There were too many of them and when they grew up they fought.

He remembered how he had asked her to go and pull up some carrots for them while he chose the rabbit. They weren't easy to sex, especially in front of a little girl. You had to turn them on their backs and press them between their hindlegs, while they kicked and struggled. He had one picked out by the time she came back. They put it in a small wooden box. And then he'd shown her the ferrets—two white ones—and a polecat.

Lavinia. Mrs. Lenton. She'd grown up, been presented to the Queen, married. He'd been to her father's funeral, and now that he was a qualified partner in his father's firm he did a great deal of the Mortal business. With Mr. Lenton, naturally. Edward. A man he loathed. But he got glimpses of her. Sometimes at Mortal when he went there with papers, she'd give him tea or a glass of sherry. He saw her in church and at garden parties. His little Lavinia was a great lady, the mother of two children—the elder almost a woman. But she had not changed for him. She was still the little girl who'd asked him for a white rabbit.

The dark girl he'd picked up at the Empire Promenade was entirely forgotten. A pretty thing, eighteen years old. Jean, Jeanette, Jane—something like that. There must have been more than a hundred of them there. All young, all pretty, the pick of London parading their charms. He'd spent the night with her and she'd given him breakfast— two boiled eggs that she had overcooked. That was what he remembered best about her—the hard-boiled eggs. He was not a woman's man. When it became a nuisance, he had one. Once a month or so was enough.

William Stead was thinking about a divorce scandal that had shaken London society. He wondered if he had handled it well. How terrible it was that a divorced woman should be *déclassée,* beyond the pale, utterly ruined, if she was caught in adultery. What hypocrisy and injustice there was here! Women were chattels. They had no rights.

In London Lavinia was waiting impatiently for John Longbeach. The heat in London was intolerable. Someone a few houses away was ill. The street was filled with golden wheat-straw two feet deep to muffle the sound of the traffic, the horses' hooves and the grinding iron tires of the vans. The great plane trees in the Square carried their leaves despondently, as if they, too, were hot; as if they were clothes they wanted to discard. Lavinia was nervous. She snapped at May and made her cry. For some reason she had taken particular care with her clothes, and thank goodness her hair had gone up right at last. May was not as good at hair dressing as Parker, but she was learning. I ought to be more patient, Lavinia thought. But her impatience was growing. He had said eleven and it was twelve. At once she decided to send two telegrams—one to John to say she was waiting for him in London, and one to Mademoiselle to say she was staying another night. She was furious at herself for having taken such pains with her appearance. In a white *broderie anglaise* dress, she looked cool and self-possessed, but she was neither. She was angry with disappointment and heat.

Why did women put up with it? Chemise, knickers, corset from bust to hips, corset cover, camisole, four petticoats. What madness in this weather! She sent May out with the telegrams.

When she came back, she said: "Come into the bedroom and undress me." She had a lukewarm, perfumed bath and dressed again. When May picked up the corset, she said: "Put that thing down."

"Shall I get Madam's dressing gown?"

"No. The pink sprigged dress and only one petticoat. We are all mad, May. All women. I do not think I am ever going to wear a corset again, except at night."

"But Madam . . ."

"I know, May. I know everyone wears corsets, but I'm not everyone."

In the pink sprigged muslin, she settled down to read a novel by Mrs. Humphrey Ward. How quiet the house was with no one in it! A footman and one of the kitchen girls, who had some knowledge of cooking, had been left in charge of the house, and were just able to take care of anyone who wanted to spend the night in London between trains. The rest were on holiday or had gone back to Mortal.

No one could have been more surprised than John Longbeach when he got back to the office and found two wires from Lavinia. One sent from Folkestone and one from London. She had been there waiting for him and he had not known. What in God's name could have happened?

"I'm going back to London, governor," he said.

The old man nodded. Harum scarum, no peace with this damn Lenton business. Just back and off again. All these letters from France lately. Detectives, he snorted.

John decided to take the afternoon train and spend the night at his club. He looked at the wire again. "Have been waiting Berkeley Square since 11. Come at once. Lavinia Lenton." What could it mean? He had been wondering how he could get in touch with her. He had news for her. Horrible news. How was he going to break it?

He had had an idea that Edward might go to Paris in August. He always stayed at the Meurice, and he had described him to the detective agency. He had been seen and followed. The report ran:

> *Cher* Monsieur Longbeach,
> The individual in question arrived at the Hotel Meurice at 5 P.M. with a valise. After dinner at 9 P.M. he took a *fiacre* to No. 10 Rue St. Briquier, a house notorious for the ill treatment of the girls. All foreign, and therefore not under the protection of the law. By various means (cost 2,000 francs, please see detailed account attached) it has been discovered that the girl, Mlle. Ellen, is there. Now arrives the question of extraction. It would appear best to have a personal conversation on the subject and Monsieur is anxiously awaited by us. We remain, with compliments and felicitations, the servants of Monsieur.

It had come ten days ago. By God, he thought, how right I was about that man. I just got the papers away in time. He thought of the manila envelope pinned with thumbtacks to the back of his tie drawer. He had been convinced that Edward would not give Ellen up and that Paris was the place to watch. So easy to get to.

Lavinia, watching from the window, saw John Longbeach cross the Square and opened the door to him herself. "What is it?" she said. "I got your wire and came up to London at once."

"My wire?" he said. "What wire?"

"The one which said you have news and had to see me in London at eleven o'clock yesterday. I was here. You didn't come. It was sent from London but I thought you might have gone back. That is why I telegraphed to you at Mortal Major."

"I sent no wire, Lavinia." Her name had slipped out. She let it pass.

"You sent no wire?" she repeated. "Then who did?"

"Someone who wanted to get you out of the way."

"Then I must go back. Come to Folkestone with me, John." So she had heard, and had accepted a Christian-name basis.

"May," she called. "Get ready. We are going back to Folkestone. Mr. Longbeach is coming with us."

Something was very wrong. They both felt it. He put his hand on her shoulder. It dropped to her waist—supple, smooth, uncorseted—and he pulled her to him. Lavinia did not resist. It seemed so natural, inevitable. Why had something like this not happened long ago? Why had no one ever kissed her properly? Or was it improperly? The answer came to her as he let her go. John loved her. No one had ever loved her before. How terrible it was, now, at this juncture! But how wonderful it might have been. . . .

"John," she said, staring into his eyes, "we should not have done that."

She was taking equal blame. "No," he said, "but we have." He went to the sideboard and poured out two glasses of Madeira. As if the scene had been rehearsed, they half raised their glasses in a gesture that was almost a toast, to something that should not have happened.

May was ready and called a four-wheeler. A hansom would not take three people. They were lucky to find a train almost ready to leave. They had a compartment to themselves. Lavinia and John sat facing each other, May in another corner, and England, lush with summer, flowed past them. Cows in deep pasture, rabbits in the hedgerows, a pheasant here and there, a great wain loaded with hay in a country lane. Neither voiced their fears. It was impossible to believe in evil. Not in England, not today in the summer of 1885.

When the cab drew up at the hotel, Lavinia went to the desk for the key and ran upstairs, followed by May. The sitting room and two bedrooms were empty. On the round sitting-room table near the window, beside a bowl of fading pink roses that she had put there before she left, was her telegram to Delphine. It was unopened.

Longbeach, who had been paying the cab, came into the room. She threw herself into his arms.

"John! Oh, John!" she sobbed. "Where are they?"

"Stay here. Get her some tea, May—and smelling salts," he added, as Lavinia collapsed in a faint.

"She never uses them, sir," May said, "but I'll get feathers." She ran into the bedroom and came back with some cock's plumes torn from a feather boa. "Matches, sir."

John gave her a box of wax vestas. She lit the feathers and held them under her mistress' nose. The room smelled like a farrier's shop. But it brought Lavinia to.

"Stay here," John said. "I'm going out. I'll be back in an hour. Take care of her, May. Put her to bed."

There was very little doubt in Longbeach's mind about what had happened. The French girl had abducted the children—kidnapped was the word. He went straight to the docks.

"Had a woman in black, a governess, gone on board on Tuesday with two blonde girls—one about fifteen and a young child?" Three sovereigns distributed gave him the answer he had feared.

"Yes sir. To Boulogne."

"And they have not come back?"

"Not yet, sir. But the stewardess heard her say they were going to Paris."

They, too, he thought, as he walked slowly back up the steep hill to the Lees.

When he went into the suite Lavinia was up, waiting for him. She was wearing a lace dressing gown, her long fair hair down, tied with a white ribbon.

"I've wired to Edward," she said. "He is responsible for this. We both are, but he brought that woman into the house. He insisted on her being employed."

"What for?"

"To sleep with. She was his mistress."

"That woman?"

"She was beautiful, John." She told her story.

"Did you say you had wired to Edward?"

"Of course. To Rundle, in Perthshire. That's where he's shooting."

"My God!" John said.

"What is it now?"

"He's not there, Lavinia. I suppose he told you he was going there."

"I've had two letters from him." She put them into his hand. He read them to pass the time and arrange his thoughts.

Dear Lavinia,
A line to tell you I am well. I am assuming my health interests you. And that the shooting is very good this year—200 brace yesterday to four guns. I am glad I brought my own retriever, easily the best here. So far the weather has been fair. Only one really wet day. Wonderful for Scotland . . .

etc. etc. The second letter resembled the first.

"He says nothing."

"He never does. He only writes so that people will see his letters with the others that go out. It would look funny if he did not write."

"Sit down. I've news for you. I've been wanting to see you for ten days but did not know where to write. Edward is in Paris. At the Meurice. These people I put on to look for Ellen have informed me. I felt he would go to Paris. They followed him and have found Ellen."

"By following him?"

"Exactly."

"My God, John!" Only now did she dare ask him where he had been.

"To the docks, Lavinia." He gripped her wrist hard. "That woman took them to France an hour after you left for London. She must have got someone to send you the telegram in my name."

"Mrs. Caramine?"

"I should think so."

"And now what shall we do? Wire Edward at the Meurice?"

"No, darling. Confront him. We'll take the night boat and be in Paris in the morning. May will chaperone you."

"I will go," Lavinia said. But she still could not believe Edward was in Paris . . .

11 : A Sea Trip

Delphine had no trouble with the girls. They were obedient. She had seen to that. They were seasick and exhausted with worry by the time she had them on the Paris Express. When Evangeline said: "What will *Maman* say?" Delphine just said: "Leave it to me, and don't ask questions. You know what happens to little girls who ask too many questions." She did. But her anxiety communicated itself to Betty, who cried quietly for the whole train journey. But in the rush of cross-channel arrivals at the Gare du Nord, who was to notice a white-faced girl with blonde pigtails, holding her baby sister by the hand, accompanied by their governess? Children often cried. Just tired and seasick. The Channel had been choppy. So they were lost, anonymous in the seething crowd that milled about them—tourists, visitors, people returning home from their holidays, with other tired children carrying shrimping nets, leading dogs, carrying birds in cages. People were being met, were shouting, crying, laughing. And through the crowd the blue-bloused porters moved, purposeful and unseeing, carrying luggage fastened to straps over their shoulders.

"Cheer up!" Delphine said, "You are seeing my country, *ma patrie.*" She felt it, she felt France seeping up through the soles of her sensible shoes. Another hour or so and Delphine Le Grand would disappear. A myth, a *revenant,* someone who in reality never existed. She had clothes stored with a friend. Chic, shapely, corseted, smart once again, men would turn their heads to look at her. She was back in the world she loved, in the city she loved, with money in her pocket. Her salary, the money Edward had given her, and more money—a much larger sum—almost in her grasp. Hers was the half-world, where crime rubbed shoulders with art, and art, in the form of dancers and actresses, mixed in bedroom intimacy with aristocrats and millionaires, a perfumed twilight of gaslight, candles and lamps turned low; of gold and kisses enlivened by an occasional woman's scream or the slash of an apache knife. Perfumed with patchouli, tuberose, and violet, and all to the music of violins and pianos played in a haze of cigar smoke. This world had a certain decadent beauty that attracted both the young bloods and old roués. Painters, in velvet bérets and baggy trousers, fondled their mistress-models. The sound of champagne corks exploding was like a battle, not on the field of Mars, but Venus.

As the cab drove through Paris—her Paris—the trees on the *grands boulevards* caught the light on their lower leaves. There were the smells of Paris: smells of drains, of flowers, of coffee, of fresh bread baking. The shuffling patter of a thousand feet, all going nowhere. The feet of men called to the boulevards by the attractions they had to offer, that of the sauntering women who came to be seen. This was life, keyed up, palpitating. The people circulated in the wide streets like blood in an artery, pumped through it by the heart of France. Paris— the City of Light. As restless as blood, clotting here and there if there was a fight or an accident, recovering and driving on, round and round through the veins and blood vessels that nourished the shuttered, secret houses. The houses that were the body, the flesh of the city.

All this was in Delphine's mind as she sat with the two children in the *fiacre,* and the coachman—a thickset, heavy man, the father of a family, his white, patent leather top hat cocked over an eye—drove to the address she had given him. He knew it well. It was infamous. It was the business of a *cocher* to know where his patrons could obtain their pleasures. What his present fare was going to do there was none of his affair. The world was a bad, sad place, but often the worst people gave the best *pourboire.* After all, one had to have a philosophy, and this was his.

Betty slept in Delphine's arms, a sweet child. Evangeline stared at the strange city, so different from London.

Their destination was not Madame Fifi's establishment in Brussels. Madame Fifi was all but bankrupt. She had taken to the tables in Ostende. This was common knowledge among the fraternity of her peers, so Carrie Caramine had arranged another sale to an equally well-known speciality house in the Rue du Pot d'Etin. The Street of the Tin Pot. It ran into the Rue St. Honoré behind the church, forked, and ended in a *cul-de-sac*. It was easy to drive past it, for this prong of the fork was narrow and scarcely lit at all, neither by the sun by day nor gas lamps by night. A street of no importance, leading nowhere.

The establishment to which they were proceeding was owned and run by Madame Jumelle, Veuve Jumelle, a widow of fifty who was never tired of explaining how lucky she had been to find this house. The windows facing the street had been bricked up, the others looked out onto the back of the church, which was at this time derelict, abandoned by both man and God. As a rule she kept about a dozen children there, but needed continual replacements for which she paid most generously in cash. Only virgins interested her. They were reserved for the men who had paid to deflower them and continued their visits. They were, as she often said, as pure as wives. More pure, in fact, since they had no chance for incontinence.

It's an ill wind that blows no one any good, Mrs. Caramine had said when she heard of Madame Fifi's ill fortune at roulette. How much more subtle her revenge could now become by sending Edward's two daughters to the same house as Ellen, carefully warning Hortense Jumelle to keep them out of his sight!

The cab stopped.

"We get out here," Delphine said.

"How dark it is," Eva complained.

"Paris, *chérie,* is not London. People are more economical here." She suddenly felt an immense affection for them, as in her mind she was already spending the money they would bring her. It occurred to her a peasant might also feel affection for the fat calf he handed over to the butcher.

The door opened as they climbed the steps. There was never any need to ring here. Someone was always watching. Pushing the children in front of her, Delphine went in. The narrow hall smelled of cooking cabbage. The luxury began on the third floor. Down here it was the residence of a bourgeoise, a widow woman in poor circumstances.

They were led by a good-looking woman of early middle age into a room facing the back of the house. Here Madame Jumelle greeted them. She kissed Delphine.

Delphine said: "My aunt." The woman bent to kiss them. Eva backed away.

"The little one is shy," La Jumelle said laughing. "So many girls are shy, but it cures itself. Come children, Julie will show you to your room." The woman had been waiting at the door. "Take them up," Madame Jumelle said.

"Go with her, girls. We're spending the night here."

Julie herded them out of the door to the foot of the stairs.

"I don't want to go!"

"Do what you're told, Eva," Delphine said.

"Take them up, Julie," Madame said.

There was the sound of a slap. It was so quick that Delphine had not seen the woman's hand move. Eva screamed and looked wide-eyed with fright at her governess.

"Mademoiselle . . ." she said.

Julie twisted her arm and went upstairs, driving both children before her.

"The first lesson," Madame Jumelle said, sitting back in her arm-chair. "An *apéritif,* Mademoiselle, and then business. I will pay you half now and half tomorrow morning." She pointed to a covered cage hanging in the window. "When you come tomorrow you will hear him sing." She got a bundle of notes from a drawer in the dresser, unlocking it with a key from a chain on her waist. "Five thousand francs, Mademoiselle. Five thousand more tomorrow."

"That was for one, Madame, the big one."

The woman laughed, her big breasts shaking. "You drive a good bargain," she said, "but I have a reputation for fair dealing. Another five thousand for the baby. She will not last long but I shall make a profit."

Delphine tucked the five thousand-franc notes into her stocking top. "Then ten thousand tomorrow, Madame?"

"But certainly in the morning, and you will hear Henri sing. I hope it is fine. If the sun shines he sings better, but he always sings. He's German, and fifteen years old. A German officer gave him to me. His father sent all the way to Germany for him during the occupation in 1870. And now an Absinthe?"

She got out two glasses, poured in the greenish-yellow cordial, put a perforated contrivance over each glass with a lump of sugar on it, and added water from a carafe, pouring it on the sugar a little at a time.

The mixture became opalescent, cloudy. The smell of aniseed filled the room. "Now sit down, Mademoiselle, and drink to our bargain."

Delphine knew La Jumelle was thinking how ugly she must look, and smiled. Well, she would be surprised tomorrow.

"You smile, Mademoiselle?"

"At my thoughts, Madame." The old cow would soon see. She would dine by herself, a cheap meal, since she would have to pay for it. Tomorrow would be different. The minute she sat at a table some man would join her.

"This is a hard life, Mademoiselle," the widow said. "It is hard to get the goods and they do not last, these tender little flowers. But that is true of all flowers, Mademoiselle. *Boutonnières* cut from the parent plant and worn for an evening. I have had some hardy ones but never from good families, and yet that is what I must have for my clientele— hothouse blooms. But delicate." She raised her ringed hands in a gesture of despair.

Delphine made her excuses. "*À demain,* Madame," she said.

"*À demain,* Mademoiselle."

The cab was still waiting. The driver had put a nose bag on the old gray horse. She decided to pay the driver and walk to a *brasserie* in the Place du Théâtre, where she dined on onion soup, a sole—it was Friday; she had reverted to Catholicism—and drank half a bottle of Graves. Now that like a butterfly she was about to emerge from the sooty chrysalis of her professional disguise, she was able to appreciate the humor of her position. She stared openly at men who, had she been differently dressed, a glance would have brought to her side. Through her heavy skirt, unbelievably hot for the season, she felt the notes in her stocking top. What if they knew, "those persons there," that not only was she beautiful but also rich? Tomorrow everything would be safely banked at the Crédit Lyonnais. For a day or two she would roam her beloved streets, pick up men, go to the theater and amuse herself. And then back to work. Back to the Coq d'Or where she could get an engagement to sing and dance any time she wanted. She had a pleasant voice and liked singing popular songs, doing a few dance steps, and showing her legs and a great deal of her body to an audience composed almost entirely of men. That was her plan for the immediate future.

Having drunk her coffee, she went out, crossed the Rue de Rivoli, past the Louvre, and over the Seine to the Rue du Bac, where her friend, Denise, lived, and her clothes were stored.

She turned the key in the lock on the third floor. Nothing was changed. Denise, who worked as a mannequin and saleswoman in a dress shop, sprang out of bed.

"*Chérie,* you are back!" She lighted a lamp and burst out laughing. "*Mon Dieu!*" she said, "to imagine it is you under all that!"

"I am back, and to stay for a while. But not like this," Delphine said with a smile. Then she undressed and got into the big bed with her friend. They talked till dawn. Girl talk—of men, of clothes, scandal, political news, the theater, murders, and babies.

12 : The Dormitory

When Julie had driven the two children upstairs to a kind of large dormitory where a dozen girls, aged nine to fourteen, gazed at them wide-eyed, she told them to undress. When they hesitated, she slapped them both.

"Do what you are told."

She turned from the row of black iron bedsteads to the other girls.

"I'll give you ten minutes to see to it. If they are not naked when I come back, you'll all be whipped." She went out and bolted the door behind her.

The girls, even the youngest, fell upon Eva and Betty. In five minutes they were stripped. The eldest child, a very pretty girl, said: "I am Daphne. What are your names?"

"I'm Eva," Evangeline said. "This is my sister, Betty." She held her clasped to her naked body.

"Well, I'll tell you one thing," Daphne said. "It's no good fighting her or anybody. She loves to whip us. Do what she says and you'll get sweets, chocolates, and good food."

"You're English?" Eva said.

"We're all English. We have to be. They can't get little French girls, it's against the law."

"Get? What for? What are we doing here? And what are those awful nightdresses you're all wearing?"

"It's just at night," the girl said. "In the daytime in the playroom upstairs, we wear lovely clothes. A little short, of course. But lovely. Lovely. For the men to see us."

"Men?" Eva said. "What do they come here for?"

"To play with us, darling. They like little girls, even if they are quite old. Funny, isn't it?" She began to giggle and was going to say more when the door opened and Julie came in with two nightdresses, gray with use and bad laundry.

Julie pulled Betty away from her sister and ran her hands over Eva. "You're a beauty," she said. "Tonight you'll sleep with me." She began to drag her off. Betty clung to Eva. Julie knocked her off her feet with a slap. "Hold her, Daphne," she said. Daphne ran forward to obey.

Leaving the girl locked in a room, Julie went downstairs.

Utterly bewildered, Evangeline sat on the bed and burst into tears. What was she doing here? Why had she been separated from her little sister? They had never been parted before.

"Well?" Madame Jumelle said to Julie.

"They are quite something, Madame. The big one ripe as a peach. I have her in my room."

Her mistress laughed. "Always the first fruits, Julie. In the Bible it was for the Lord, here it is for Mademoiselle Julie. You never change, but you will not have her for long. She's just what the Prince has been waiting for. He's getting impatient."

"Tomorrow he will have her, Madame."

"Tomorrow won't be too soon for *Monsieur le Prince*. I have sent a boy with a message. You have clothes for her?"

"Just the thing, Madame. A silk dress, very short. Chemise and lace knickers. I hope he does not tear them."

"He will, Julie. He always does. But I charge him extra—and now a little *coup?*"

"Very voluntarily, Madame. Madame is most amiable."

The two women sipped their Absinthe. Madame Jumelle lit a small cigar. A coal fell from the grate as the fire burnt up. A single lamp, its shade fringed with beads, illuminated the room with its souvenirs of France's departed glory. The bust of the emperor looked like real bronze. He appeared benign. A household god.

Madame Jumelle was thinking of money. By now the boy she had sent with a note should have reached the Prince's establishment in the Faubourg St. Honoré. Julie's mind was occupied with the little virgin Venus she had locked in her bedroom. Under a cover of green baize, the blind canary slept in his cage.

At ten o'clock the next day, Delphine, in a beige silk dress, a red leg-horn straw hat adorned with velvet flowers, high-heeled shoes, and a white parasol, returned to Madame Jumelle's house. Again admitted without ringing, she was shown into the same room. Bourgeois, tasteless, still smelling of cooked cabbage, to which the odor of beeswax and turpentine floor polish had now been added.

She looked at the pictures. Napoleon. Napoleon at Austerlitz. Napoleon at Marengo. Napoleon on his white horse, leading the retreat from Moscow. On the mantelpiece beside the black marble clock was a plaster bust of the emperor. Above it hung a sword and the remains of a flag, torn and stained with what must be old blood. In the window Henri was singing as if his heart would burst.

Madame Jumelle came rustling in. She moved as if she were on wheels, like a child's toy dragged on a string. A smell of mothballs came with her. Naphtha was added, like another condiment, to the smell of cabbage soup and turpentine.

"Ah, Mademoiselle," she said, "how do you do. You are punctual, as I expected. The creditor is always on time; it is the debtor who drags his feet. But my God, how lovely you are!" She was looking at her professionally. "Yesterday?" she said questioningly.

"Yesterday a governess, Madame. Who would employ me in that capacity today?" The women laughed together.

Henri continued to sing.

"You see," Madame Jumelle said, "What a bird! Fifteen years old and so gay. He brings life and light into the heart of a poor widow. He is blind, of course. I had his eyes put out. They sing better that way." She sat down. Her legs were so short that her feet did not touch the ground. So that was why she moved like a toy.

"The footstool, if you will be so kind, Mademoiselle."

Delphine pushed it over. It was mahogany covered in *gros point*.

"You are most amiable, Mademoiselle. I see you are admiring my pictures. My great grandfather served him, an officer of the old guard. Imagine that, Mademoiselle! In those days my family was rich, famous. That is his sword. The battle flag was put into his hands by the emperor himself. What my illustrious ancestor would have thought to see me entertaining German officers, I cannot imagine, but—" she waved her hands and they fluttered like white pigeons over the black silk bulge of her belly and came to rest—"but, after all, one must live, Mademoiselle. And now, here is the money." She had it ready in her reticule. The new notes joined the old, to be warmed between silk stocking top and rounded thigh.

"An Absinthe, Mademoiselle? I insist."

"I shall be charmed, Madame."

The sugar and water ritual was gone through.

"And now goodbye, Mademoiselle. Please remember I am always at your service."

Delphine was standing on the worn red carpet, ready to go, when the door burst open and the children ran in.

"Mademoiselle! Mademoiselle! We heard your voice!" They looked at her in astonishment.

Delphine stared at them. How they had changed in a night! Bedraggled, with tear-stained, dirty faces, wearing chemises that were far from clean—and barefooted. She turned to Madame. "Who are these children, Madame?"

"Two of my little guests, Mademoiselle, whose manners must be corrected."

Eva said: "It's us! You can't go. You can't leave us."

The door closed behind Delphine. She was on the street once more. Her beloved *trottoir*. She stood to watch a great white horse pulling a laden dray, as he struck sparks from the cobbled pavement with his iron shoes.

A man whose shape she recognized was approaching. Edward! Fortunately he had never seen her properly dressed. She turned her back and raised her boa to hide her face. What was he doing in Paris? Here? What would he say if he knew that within two hundred meters his kidnapped children were imprisoned in a *maison de spécialité*?

Upstairs in Julie's room Eva was bewildered. How could it have been Mademoiselle? Not Delphine. This woman who had been so different, so beautiful, so cruel. The way she had looked at them when they had called out to her—as if she had never seen them before. The voice. The eyes. It was Delphine. But why had she brought them here? What would happen to them? That awful Daphne. The other children. Men? The playroom upstairs? The pretty clothes? These dirty nightdresses. She fingered the garment she had on. Coarse cotton. Harsh, dirty, stained.

Betty had been returned to her in the morning. She was clinging to her crying. Would they take her away again? And that woman in whose bed she had spent the night. Julie, who had held her in her arms and said she loved her. . . . She looked round the room. It was comfortable. Not like a servant's room, more like Mrs. Fawcett's room at home. At home at Mortal. She thought of her mother. She knew that her mother did not know where they were. They had been kidnapped.

Edward, as he walked down the street, was thinking he would never smell a cabbage again, or even see one growing in a kitchen garden, without thinking of this time, of Ellen. She was as much his now as a dog or a horse. In a way he enjoyed the sordidness of the approach. The grubby hall, Jumelle, who looked like a *concierge,* the two flights of narrow uncarpeted stairs and then—luxury. A dream, a nightmare, a combination of Eastern harem and medieval torture chamber with Julie, an expressionless woman who was still good looking, in charge.

He had Ellen whipped almost daily. He did not whip her himself. He merely watched. He never whipped anything. He gave orders for it to be done and sacked a keeper or a groom who did not lay it on. The exception was Nestor, and he often thought of it with shame. He had lost his head. Gentlemen gave orders. They did not do things. He thought of the floggings he had watched in the barrack yard, of men lashed to the triangle and beaten till their backs were raw. But there was another reason for his restraint. He knew if he once began he would not be able to stop. If the ride had been a little longer, he would have killed Nestor.

He climbed two flights of stairs and paused to gain his breath and control the wild beating of his heart: then he climbed the third, unbolted a door and said: "Ellen."

She would come to him like a dog.

At Rundle Castle in Scotland the Honorable William Foretallent was explaining to his hostess why he wanted to open the telegram that had come for Edward Lenton. Mrs. Graham was amazed.

"So his wife thinks he is here?"

"Exactly." What a pretty woman she was.

"All right," she said, "on condition you tell me where he is."

"He's in Paris."

"At this time of year?"

"Yes."

"Is it a woman?"

"I don't know, but it seems probable."

"Oh, you men!" Helen Graham shrugged her shoulders. "You certainly stick together." She gave him the wire.

Next day he rode over to the post office three miles away and sent Edward a somewhat cryptic telegram: "Wire from wife. Wants to see you at once. Writing. Billy."

At the Meurice a few hours later, when the *chasseur,* a brass-buttoned child in a pillbox cap, brought Edward the telegram, he was furious. That damn woman! What could she want and why should he cut short his holiday to please her? Writing. A letter from Scotland would take three or four days and would contain nothing, only the full text of his wife's wire.

PART TWO

RESCUE

. . . aiming at the raising of fallen or degraded women.

Shorter Oxford Dictionary

PART TWO

RESCUE

... aiming at the raising of fallen or degraded women.
Shorter Oxford Dictionary

13 : Rescue

For Lavinia Lenton the trip to Paris to find her husband and rescue Ellen was a nightmare. John and May were wonderful, but her thoughts tortured her. It was not only the children. She assumed they had been kidnaped for ransom by an adventuress posing as a governess. With them it would just be a matter of money. Perhaps they should have gone to the police at once. But that would have taken too long. The police would have said: "Where is your husband? Have you informed your husband?" How would she have explained his presence in Paris?

But whatever happened was all her fault. As soon as she had found out about the woman, she should have sent her packing. And why hadn't she? Because Delphine Le Grand could keep her husband satisfied; because while she was there in the house, he would not knock on her door in search of the marital rights to which he was entitled—and he might have done so in spite of May and Mac. That was why. She had fooled herself into thinking the girl was a good teacher, and let it go at that. But that wasn't the real issue. The issue was between right and wrong, and she had taken the easy way.

In Folkestone she had really got to know the children. She had spent more time with them than usual—grown to love them. Betty, adorable. Eva, growing into womanhood, ripening almost visibly.

The crossing was rough and she was not a good sailor, but fortunately May was not sick and had taken good care of her. No trouble at the Customs. Then Paris, the Gare du Nord. The city that she had never liked and now feared. The *fiacre*. The Meurice.

At the desk Lavinia ordered a suite—a double room with a sitting room and a separate single room.

"We only have a room with a double bed, Madame," the clerk said, looking at John.

"Then put in a cot for my maid."

The clerk said: "Of course, Madame," thinking how discreet *ces Anglais* were. Looking at her signature in the register, he said: "We have a gentleman here, also of the same name."

"My husband," Lavinia said. "Is he in?"

"No, Madame."

"Then when he comes in please notify me of his arrival. This gentleman is my notary."

A handsome notary, the clerk thought. A triangle. A murder of passion, perhaps—but not here, if possible not here. He was a man with aspirations. Assistant manager one day, perhaps. Even manager. The Meurice was his life, as sacred to him as a church.

Upstairs when the *chasseurs* had gone and the cot had been installed, May said: "Madam, I feel ill. May I lie down?"

"Of course," Lavinia said. Now she was alone with John, really alone. May would stay in the bedroom till she was called.

John said: "Take off your hat."

She took it off, a straw summer bonnet, trimmed with poppies and cornflowers.

Then he said: "Let down your hair, Lavinia. I want to see it down. I have dreamed of it."

Slowly, almost in a dream herself, Lavinia began to pull out the pins one at a time, holding them bunched in her right hand as she withdrew them. Her long fair hair came loose, sprang from her head in a cascade that fell over her shoulders.

"Thank you," John said, holding a tress in his hand. "How beautiful it is!" Then he took her in his arms. His hand cupped her breast and slid down her flank to her hip. Gently, he kissed her. Gently at first, then passionately, drinking in her lips. He half carried, half led her to the sofa. She thanked God for it, her knees were too weak to hold her erect. All of her was weak, dissolved, liquid with this new sensation. He set her down softly and, putting his hands under her knees, he placed her feet on the couch where she lay, her breasts rising and falling as her heart fluttered.

"I love you," John said.

"I know, John."

"Do you love me?"

"Yes."

"Will you run away with me when this is over?"

"And be divorced?"

"Yes. You'll lose your fortune, but I have some money of my own."

"It will ruin you, John. Your business."

"It will ruin us both."

"A world well lost for love." She thought of the two women she had known who had been divorced. She had always wondered why they had done it, thought they had been fools to be caught in adultery. But perhaps they had not cared. After all, man did not live by bread alone. . . . How ridiculous the thought was in such a context.

"I'll go with you, John, when we have the children."

"It will mean losing them."

"Eva will be married in a few years and Betty will not care."

"We can have others."

"I'll give you a son, John." She knew she could give him a son.

"I'm going now, darling," John said, "to see the detective and find out about Ellen."

When he left her, Lavinia lay still, breathing hard as if she had been running, her mind still unable to grasp the full implication of what John had said, or her own emotions. They shocked her. She shied away from them. What would John find out about Ellen? Where were the children? Where was Delphine Le Grand? When would Edward come in? What would she say to him?

She went into the bedroom. May jumped off the cot. "I'll change," Lavinia said. Clothes were a woman's armor. She must wear it to meet her husband. May was in the bathroom across the passage; she could hear the water running.

When a page boy announced Mr. Lenton's return, she wrote him a note. "Please come up and see me. I have come to Paris to meet you."

When he got his wife's note, Edward Lenton was flabbergasted. He had expected a letter from his friend in Scotland, not a chit from his wife. Particularly now, when things were going so well. What could she want? In a state of great irritation he went to Lavinia's apartment. God damn her, spoiling his fun.

Lavinia met him dressed for dinner. "You are taking me to dinner, Edward. They know I am your wife."

He was due at Jumelle's at nine-thirty. Ellen would be waiting for him, counting the hours. She could not calculate them; she had no clock. She could only guess the time by watching the light fade and the stars come out, through her high barred window.

"What is it, Lavinia? Why are you here? How did you find me?" Now that she had found him, he did not give a damn. What could she do?

"I tried to save your face," he said. "Those letters from Scotland. . . ."

"I know. I got them. And I found you because the detective Mr. Longbeach employed said you were here."

"Longbeach? That counterjumper . . . hiring detectives with my money."

"My money, Edward, as you well know. The money you were spending on women."

He let it pass. "Well, what is it? Why are you here, butting in on my affairs?"

"Affair is the right word. Your affair with Ellen. She's here. We've found that out."

"How?"

"The detective. Do you remember Mr. Longbeach talking about a magnet finding a needle in a haystack? Well, it did. He's gone to see him now."

"He's here?"

"Of course, he's here."

Edward shifted his ground. "Your lover. Even if he isn't, that's what people will say."

"Not with May in my room. She's never left me." She called May in. May came in from the bedroom. "Madam?"

"You have never left me, have you, May?"

"No, Madam."

"Mr. Lenton is suggesting things. Impossible things."

May blushed and looked down. "Oh, Madam," she said.

"You can go, May."

"Thank you, Madam."

"Well, what is it, Lavinia? Why are you here? It's not just Ellen, I suppose? Though why you should be so interested in that little hussy is beyond me."

"Perhaps I am interested in all the ladies you sleep with, Edward. As a wife, that is. But you're right. Ellen is not the reason I am here. It's the children, Edward."

"What about the children?"

"Your mistress, Delphine, has disappeared with them. She has brought them to France. I went to London for the day and when I returned to Folkestone they were gone."

"Good God!"

"I want the story, Edward." Lavinia had full control of herself. "Who knows anything about Delphine Le Grand?" she asked. "Mrs. Caramine?"

"Possibly." He had forgotten she knew about Carmine.

"Then tomorrow we will go back to London to see her. Now you will take me to dinner." She looked at his smoking jacket. "It is a pity you are not properly dressed, but under the circumstances I will accept the sports clothes. Hunting clothes, I suppose they might be called. But we are abroad and it is summer, so not much is expected of one." She picked up her dress and gave him her arm.

She was glad she had dressed so well. The lilac silk poplin was cut very low, the bodice boned and fitted to her body. The cyclamen velvet overskirt was draped up, festooned over a short green and lilac underskirt below which, when she moved, there was a barely perceptible foam of lace—a fine ship in full sail, rustling through the carpet sea.

Quite a picture they made in the dining room. The tall slim blonde woman in a lilac silk poplin dress, and the dapper soldierly looking man in a dinner jacket.

"Champagne, Edward," she said. "There are probably people here whom we know, or people who know people. After all, one only comes to Paris to celebrate something."

What was she celebrating? Her love for John Longbeach, her hatred of her husband? Or just gaining Dutch courage to face a troubled and complicated future with the aid of Veuve Cliquot '75?

Turtle soup, filet of sole meunière, a poulet de Bresse, a baba with cream. Fresh peaches. If this was tragedy, no one watching them would have been able to guess it. The fingers of Lavinia's long white kid gloves were tucked into the wrists. The rings on her hands sparkled. She talked with animation, intensely proud of her self-possession. Money was not the only perquisite of breeding. There was this. The ability of the aristocrat to go to the guillotine with dignity in a tumbril.

The journey back to London would be conducted in the same spirit, with style, always style, *panâche*. She might have taken off one corset but that of her training remained. The *sang-froid anglais* that always astonished foreigners.

The detective agency was in the Avenue de l'Opéra on the third floor over a shoe shop. John Longbeach pushed open the frosted glass door and said in English: "I have come to see Mr. Ferdinand Guitry."

A small stout man left his desk and came to greet him.

"Enchanted, sir, to make your acquaintance," he said. "All is in order. We will proceed at once." He picked up a top hat rather the worse for wear. "*Allons!*" he said, "to Jumelle's establishment. Very *recherché,* I can assure you. Though at the first blow of the eye there is some question."

In the cab he developed his plan. "We will try to frighten her first. *D'abord.* With the magic word police. Before I went into private practice I was with the *Sûreté*. I am well known. Then when she protests, we will offer money. You have money, I hope, Monsieur?"

"Oh yes."

"Gold?"

"Yes."

"Gold is always best, Monsieur. There is something about gold. I acknowledge it myself, and I am a man of culture. The color, the weight. Gold has a beauty of its own. The pieces feel rich, almost greasy in one's hand. You have noticed it, perhaps?"

"I never thought of it, Mr. Guitry."

"But you will. You will now. Perhaps you have never before paid a butcher's bill with gold? The sovereign English? That is what we are about to do. It is an *abattoir* we go to. We are going to purchase a girl as a calf. *Comme un veau.* You must not be embarrassed, Monsieur. You must be calm. Show nothing. Leave all the talking to me as you must, since you speak no French. At first it will go badly. The Jumelle will scream. Shout. I shall continue. I shall ask you for some money. You will give me a handful of gold. I will throw it on the table with a gesture—as one throws wheat to hens. Some will fall on the floor. It will be impossible for one of La Jumelle's temperament to let it lie there. She will pick it up. Once she has touched gold, Monsieur, she is finished. *Amorcée.* You fish, Monsieur? That is what we do in the water—throw in something to attract the fish. . . ."

"Ground bait," John said.

"Ah! That is good." Monsieur Guitry pulled out a little book and made a note of the words.

At last they reached the house and left the cab to wait for them in the dark street. Monsieur Guitry knocked on the door.

It was opened by a woman who, against the light in the cabbage-smelling passage, was no more than a black shape, but a sleek female shape, neat and precise in outline.

"Julie, my love," Monsieur Guitry said.

"Who are you? How do you know my name?"

"The police, *chérie*. We know all. Take us in to *la belle Jumelle.*"

"She is absent."

"I think we will see for ourselves. We have business with her." Guitry pushed his way in. "Madame Jumelle!" he shouted. "Attention, please!" He saw a glimmer of light under a door and turned the handle.

There was no mistaking Madame Jumelle. A fat black spider sitting staring at the glass of absinthe on the table in front of her, as if it was a jewel.

The little man cried: "Madame Jumelle, I am enchanted to see you. I bring good news."

"The police. When do the police bring good news to a poor widow, a descendant of the emperor?" After two absinthes Madame's relationship to Napoleon became much closer.

"We will sit and talk, Madame. Sit, Monsieur," he said to Longbeach as if he was the host. "A little absinthe perhaps, Madame? I will mix it myself, with your permission." He was already doing so. "First a drink, then to business. It is only fools who say business comes before pleasure. Gold," he said. "Midas. Croesus. What is there that gold cannot buy? Happiness, food, wine, women! Give me some gold," he said to Longbeach.

Finding Madame well in her cups, he had decided to change his tactics. He took the handful of sovereigns Longbeach gave him. He flung them on the red velvet cloth of the table. Three fell to the ground, rolling at Madame's feet. She slid off her chair to pick them up, quick as a terrier after rats, as if fearing some would escape her.

"Now what is it?"

"You have a girl we want. The Milord is in search of a mistress. He is alone in Paris and speaks no French. I hear at the *Préfecture* you have an English girl imprisoned here. We want her. We will pay. If not"—his voice became menacing—"we shall make difficulties."

"No law can touch me," Madame Jumelle said. "Her papers to practice as a prostitute in France are in order. She signed them herself. And besides, you are no longer with the police."

"No law, Madame? Of course there is no law. But there are laws about septic tanks. When was yours last emptied? About windows? Are you paying taxes on all your windows? Do you want your clientele disturbed by inspectors of sanitation? Inspectors of this and that?"

"I have protection, Monsieur," Madame Jumelle muttered, half weeping. "I pay the police."

"Well now, you will have to pay the garbage collector, the sanitary inspector . . . Madame, if you do not comply with my generous offer, you will support half of Paris."

"What is your offer?"

"Two hundred *Louis d'or*." Guitry fished in Longbeach's side pocket and piled them on the table. Twenty little piles of ten. Twenty little columns of gold on the red pile of the velvet cloth. La Jumelle could not take her eyes off them. After all, the other English Milord had paid her in advance. She was losing nothing and gaining two hundred English pounds. She would tell him she had had no choice. "The police, Monsieur . . ." She gave in, swept the coins into a pocket in her petticoat and shouted for Julie.

"Julie! Julie! Bring down the English girl of the Milord." She would have one last joke out of it. She had at bottom a humorous nature. "Bring her down as she is," she said. "And now, Messieurs, another drink to seal the bargain, as is my custom."

They were just raising their glasses when Ellen walked in, naked. In a flash the detective ripped off the tablecloth and covered her. Ellen, quite unabashed, smiled into his eyes.

But Ferdinand Guitry was furious. "This is no time for jokes, Madame. Her clothes, if you please."

"Her clothes, Julie," Madame shouted, and went into gales of quivering laughter. "My God, it was funny though," she said. *"Drôle, mon Dieu.* How *drôle."*

"Perhaps, Monsieur Longbeach," Guitry said, "she had better come to my house. My wife is surprised at nothing. In the morning I will bring her to the boat train."

John Longbeach sighed with relief. "I'll find another cab and leave this one for you," he said.

"A thousand thanks, Monsieur. And good night, Madame." Guitry took Ellen's arm. She turned her head to smile at Longbeach. She had not done her hair and it swung between her shoulders like a mane, paler than Lavinia's.

Once in the cab with the detective, Ellen sat back to enjoy the view out of the window. The life of the city. People. Girls. Women. Men. Shops. Cafés . . . Brasseries . . . Restaurants . . . Bright lights. This was freedom. She thought of the way she had changed hands for money. Sold like a horse. She wondered about her new master. What would he be like? Not this one, not this fat little eunuch. But the other. So tall and handsome. She had seen something in his eyes when she had turned her head back, tossing her long fair hair. She wondered, and then let her mind run back, filling in the space between the two cab rides. The first with Harris, and now this one.

Upstairs in the Rue du Pot d'Etin, above the children's dormitory and playroom with its detached and separate bedrooms that were reached through a passage with soundproofed doors, Ellen had led her private, secret life. Days had merged into weeks, weeks into months. She had nothing to do, nothing to read but a dozen beautifully bound and illustrated pornographic books, written in English but printed in Paris. Collectors' items. Limited editions for collectors of erotica. Completely shocked, at first revolted, she came slowly back to them, fearful as a fawn to water. Aware of danger, but drawn by boredom. By the necessity of an educated person to read, no matter what. First a word here and there. A paragraph. A page. A chapter. And finally the book itself. Now she knew them all. They were well and subtly written, their poison cumulative. What she had thought of as vice was presented as pleasure. These were the natural pleasures of man and womankind. The pleasures of the civilized world, before Christianity had stepped in; not to stop them, merely to check them and drive them underground. She learnt of Lesbos, of the Black Mass. She read about pashas, eunuchs, and harems. Of perversions. Of pederasts and Lesbians. Strange, strong food for a vicarage-bred girl, and whenever she moved she saw her own naked body reflected. Mirrors played a great part in the descent to decadence.

For months Ellen saw no one but Julie and Madame—La Jumelle—who visited her every day. She was well fed but only received small quantities of food. They did not want her to get fat. She was being saved for something. Alone, except for these visits, she was able to think, to go back over her life. Julie bathed her from the basin with orange-flower toilet water. The bridal smell lingered on in the room all day. She combed and brushed her hair till it glistened. She murmured compliments, endearments: *Chérie, lapin, choux, belle, adorable, charmante.* There was something revolting in the woman's touch. Ellen had lost her modesty some time ago in London. Modesty had been shed with her clothes. It was something else. Something that oozed out of Julie's prying fingers. They were soft and cold. It was like being touched by a snake. Shivers went down her spine.

But they were skilled. Loneliness, boredom, and her reading slowly changed her point of view. Julie was, in her way, a beautiful woman. She spoke some English. She hated men. She loved Ellen.

"I am 'appy you are 'ere," she said. "It is necessary for a human being to love. I love you, Hélène. *L'amour,*" she said, and spent the night with her.

Madame Jumelle's visits continued to disgust her. She came, she looked, she gloated, and waddled off again. Moving smoothly like a fat duck on skates. Even corsets could not control her haunches. She arrived puffing from the climb and left when she had recovered her breath.

Then one evening Julie had been sent to tell her that she had a visitor. "The rich Milord has come to see Mademoiselle." Her face was distorted with anger.

Rich Milord. To this day Ellen had not discovered what she meant. She did not know that in France every Englishman was a Milord, and rich. A quarter of an hour later Lenton entered the room. Julie was with him. She carried a dog whip.

Every day after that she had only his visit to wait for. Twenty-two or twenty-three hours of fear, of memory, of shame. She was no longer able to leave her body. The whip sting brought it back. Her will was broken. Her mind blank except for Lenton. Now she half feared and half loved him. He was her master. She thought of a whipped bitch lying on her back. God could no longer help her. She was now in the hands of Lucifer, and a different, a devil's protective mechanism was at work. Nature, in an effort to save her sanity, had forced her into pleasure. She was man-ripe. She could have had pleasure from it. But this, this awful desire. This waiting for the door to open so that she could lose herself in pain and ecstasy.

Lenton was delighted with her. With Carmine who had thought of it. With Jumelle, with Julie. It was always the same—a dog, a horse, a man or a woman could be broken, brought round.

Whatever happened Ellen knew she could never go back now. Never become what she had been before. It was like drink or drugs. These feelings possessed her. The impossible had happened. She loved Lenton. Watchless, she tried to measure the hours between his visits. She wondered about other men. What they would be like. Would there be other men? She laughed now when she thought how delighted she had been to go to Paris with Harris. She hated the woman but she had hated Edward Lenton worse. Immobile, dead as a possum in a God-sent trance of escape, she had been able to leave her body in London. But the body, apparently having a life of its own divorced from the spirit, had begun to respond to him even then. Harris told her Mrs. Caramine had found her a job in Paris, that she was sorry about what had happened but Mr. Lenton had a hold over her. She hated him, too, and was going to take a chance and save her, Ellen, from his clutches. Once out of the house Harris' demeanor had changed. She had become obsequious, though she remained watchful. Her behavior was that of a maid in charge of a young lady. The journey after her imprisonment had delighted Ellen. She was almost gay. Both in London and at Dover she had thought of trying to run away. But where would she run? To whom? And how did one run without money? Once in France the chance had gone forever. She knew too little French.

They were met by a friend of Harris'. A small, neat, bearded French-man who spoke excellent English—a Monsieur Gustave Bosquet. He took her to an official who presented her with some papers to sign. "Work papers, Mademoiselle," Bosquet said. " 'Permission is hereby granted for work in France.' It is a necessary formality for a foreigner, no more than that." She had signed.

They had had a meal in the restaurant at the Gare Maritime. Monsieur Bosquet had kissed her hand with grace and said *au revoir* and *bonne chance*. He shook Harris' hand.

Not till she reached the Rue du Pot d'Etin did a suspicion that anything was wrong cross her mind. The kind of work she had assumed she was to do was that of governess to some French children. In the darkened street she had hesitated. Make a run for it? But again, where? And what then? Harris had thrust her into the open door, the bolts slammed into their sockets. Bolts again. Madame Jumelle, a stout spider, ran out of her room into the passage.

"You have the papers?" she asked. Harris handed the work papers over. Another woman, a younger, prettier French version of Harris, appeared. Julie.

"Upstairs," Jumelle said, pointing. Resistance was useless. That lesson she had learnt. She climbed the first bare, uncarpeted flight. She thought she heard children talking. Perhaps she was to teach after all. Another flight, no different from the first. The third flight had a red carpet. There were pictures on the walls. What pictures! The two women forced her on. There was an open door on the left.

"In there," Harris said.

It was luxurious. A thick carpet, a large silk-covered divan flanked by full-length, gilt-framed mirrors, a heavy armchair upholstered in a pink Turkish carpet material. There was no closet, no chest of drawers. In the next room, separated from the first by a curtain, there was a dressing table, a tapestry screen behind which, she found out later, was a washstand and a bidet. This room, too, had a heavy carpet, and one wall was covered with full-length mirrors. In front of the dressing table there was a straight-backed chair.

In both rooms the windows were narrow and long, like stable windows, and too high to see out of. In each, from the center of the ceiling, hung a pink silk shaded lamp.

"Take off your clothes," Harris said.

"But the children . . . my work . . . Mrs. Caramine . . ." she had said.

"My God, girl, did you believe me? She just wanted you out of the house. You were being looked for."

Who was looking for her? Who would look? Who would care? She still wondered. Another lie, no doubt.

"Never you mind. Take off your clothes, or do you want me to do it for you?"

Five minutes later the two women had left with her clothes and once again she was imprisoned naked. But more hopeful. God had seen to it. She had escaped Lenton. Someone was seeking her. Even if they did not find her, the idea of someone looking had encouraged her.

What a long time ago that was!

How she had changed! Her past, her girlhood, the vicarage, Mortal, the children—had lost all reality. Mrs. Green and Mrs. Caramine. Harris, Julie, Jumelle, and Lenton were reality. Julie who loved and whipped her. Lenton who loved her and had her whipped. But something else happened. In some way that she did not understand, she was not only Lenton's mistress, she was also his master. Perhaps there was strength in weakness. In the end it was the ivy that killed the oak. It was the ivy that survived.

She felt Monsieur Guitry's hand on her wrist. The cab had stopped. "We have arrived, Mademoiselle," he said. "I will take you to my wife. In the morning the boat train to England, home, and beauty. Your papa awaits you with anxiety."

Papa? England? She thought as she followed him upstairs. What nonsense! Ellen was dead. She was Hélène, the master of men. She could feel it in her heart.

14 : The Boat Train

At the station with Edward and May, Lavinia saw John standing by himself. Why was he going back to England alone? Had he failed to find Ellen? Then she saw her coming in the company of a small, rotund, silk-hatted man who waved at John. John took off his hat. Ellen bowed. The little fat man took off his hat, smiled, gesticulated, bowed, and continued to bow, like a courting pigeon. Lavinia wished she could hear what they were saying.

May had seen Ellen, too, and could hardly contain herself. Miss Ellen in Paris! All this to-do and the mistress in love with Mr. Longbeach. Where would it all end? She did not want it to end. She only wished she could talk about it to someone. But she wouldn't, not even to Charles when she saw him again at Mortal. Not that she cared for him after that hussy he had taken up with, but she was used to talking to him.

Edward Lenton had seen Ellen too. So they'd got her, by God. Got his girl. Outwardly calm, not a muscle of his face moving, his eyes staring, he took in the scene. He must find her in England. He could not give her up. Carmine would find her for him. Old Carmine. She had ways. Threads wove their way out in a kind of spider's web from No. 23. Meanwhile he must be patient. Play a waiting game. That damn Delphine. She'd ditched him too. He was going to miss her. Miss the paradox of her day and night life. The black chrysalis that turned into a butterfly after dark—a beautiful white and black moth. He supposed she was after a ransom. Rich children were sometimes kidnapped. Pay up, get them back, and it would all blow over.

He did not realize that other people might think in different ways and might have other motives. There was no doubt in his mind that Carmine would have the answer. She would be the intermediary. Through her they would find out whom to pay. He lit a cigar and paced up the length of the train, his hands behind his back. Ellen, here on the same train. Free of him, protected from him. But she would never be free of him. A woman was never free of her first man, particularly when he had possessed her body and soul as he had possessed Ellen. For now he *had* her soul. This was what tied him to her—a psychic bond. Not just that she was good at it. That she had learnt all he had taught her and gone beyond it; but that she had given herself to him. A gift that was a jeweled millstone about his neck. The other virgins in his life had been the young servants and governesses whom he had seduced, and Lavinia of course, but there had been no possession there, not even in the beginning. Lavinia's money, her body, her home —Mortal—but neither her mind nor her heart. They had remained inviolate, beyond penetration. For a man it was different. He could not remember his first woman. A street girl picked up on a corner in fear to prove his manhood, as a boy of fifteen. The others—servants, dancers, chorus girls. Girls in houses like Carmine's. Governesses—Muriel. But he had little memory of them. They blended into a composite whole of young womanhood. Warm, succulent flesh. A kind of human poultry that he had consumed with appetite. They were like all meals, even good ones, soon forgotten. All except for one—Ellen, who possessed him. It was impossible to visualize life without her.

He went back to the carriage where Lavinia and May were sitting. He put some English papers and magazines into Lavinia's lap. Ellen and that damn lawyer alone in another carriage. He might see them in the restaurant car, or on the boat. He might have, but he didn't.

The crossing was choppy. Lavinia dozed all the way to London. The sea always gave her a headache, even under pleasant conditions.

Edward had wired for the carriage that had been sent up from Folke-stone to meet them at Victoria. In the crowd that filled the station, he caught a glimpse of Longbeach—he was a tall man—running. He wondered why he should run.

At the Gare du Nord Longbeach had put Ellen near the window, so that she could look out, and sat beside her. They had a carriage to themselves. He thought how pretty she was. How at ease, which surprised him for he felt extremely awkward in her company. Men with scythes followed by women gleaners were harvesting fields of golden wheat spotted with red poppies. The women were picking up the swaths and tying them with twists of straw into bundles which they stooked.

"You'll soon be home, Ellen," he said at last. "Back in the country. Your father is waiting for you. There'll be no questions. I have told him all he need know. I wrote last night."

Ellen turned from the window and smiled at him. A sweet smile that was half an invitation. She took off her gloves as if she was undressing. Her hand moved to his thigh. He took it and held it.

"Kiss my hand, John," she said. Involuntarily he did so.

"Now me. Kiss me." She was in his arms. "I don't want to go home, John. Keep me. I'll be faithful to you. I'll make you happy. I know how to make a man happy."

This child was not yet nineteen.

"No, Ellen," he said, pushing her back. "That's all over."

How can something that has just begun be over? She touched him again.

He loved Lavinia but this girl affected him. She had struck him below the belt. He almost laughed at the aptness of the phrase that had come to his mind.

"Be good," he said.

"I used to be good, John. Oh so good. But I can't be good now. Shall I tell you about Lenton? He had me whipped like a dog, and I love him."

"You should hate him," Longbeach said in disgust.

"Oh, I do! I love and hate. It's like pleasure and pain. There is a point where they meet and are indistinguishable one from the other."

"Where in God's name did you learn that?"

"In a book, John. I read a lot of books in Paris."

"You had books?"

"Oh yes. Of a kind. Of a kind I had never seen before. Most interesting books about things I never knew existed." She relapsed into silence, her eyes wide and dreamy, her moist lips parted.

My God, how kissable they were! As if she knew what was in his mind, Ellen got up, pulled down the blinds giving on to the corridor and sat on his knee. "Now John," she said, "I want you to."

At Calais, holding her elbow, John led Ellen on to the packet. All the way over they stood side by side at the rail, watching the waves. Watching the water churned up by the great steam-driven paddle wheels. The sea, instead of being the usual pewter gray, was blue, marbled with foam from the whitecaps that the wind whipped into spray.

This girl. What were they going to do with her? What should he tell Lavinia? That the vicar's daughter was a wanton who had seduced him on the boat train? A few weeks ago, lawyer though he was, he had known nothing of life. His occasional adventures in London had been nothing. He had never been in love. But now he was madly, passionately in love with Lavinia. Ellen had got him on a physical rebound. In the sitting room of the Meurice when he had lain Lavinia on the sofa, he had been tempted. He had felt she would not have resisted him. It was Lavinia who had roused the devil that Ellen had assuaged. How ashamed of himself he was.

Between Dover and London they hardly spoke. Ellen had said: "Look at the rabbits," and he had looked at them sitting up to watch the train go by. Her expression had been calm, almost smug. He thought of Lavinia on the train, only a few carriages up, with her husband. She had said she would allow herself to be divorced. She would take the risk and become notorious for his sake.

As a rule, in a year there were less than a dozen divorce cases. So few that they were handled by the Divorce and Admiralty Court. A court that dealt with prize money, piracy on the High Seas, neglect of duty by naval officers. What a mixture! The capture of a slaver in the Red Sea one day, a woman found in the bed of a man who was not her husband, the next.

At Victoria he took his bag down from the rack, got on to the platform, and helped Ellen out. As he turned to call a porter, she ran from him. He ran after her. A man opened his arms and stopped him. He was loudly dressed, one of a group, who looked like bookmakers.

"None of that, Mister," he said. "No chasing girls here. Either they comes willing, or they doesn't come."

Longbeach knew he had lost her and went back for his bag and a porter.

Next day in London, Mr. and Mrs. Lenton went to call on Mrs. Caramine. She would know something, Lavinia was sure of it. If there was a key to these strange events, she held it. After all, it was she who had sent Delphine to Mortal.

The butler knew Edward. They were shown straight in.

"Mr. and Mrs. Lenton," he announced.

The two women looked at each other curiously, taking each other in, swallowing each other with a glance. It was difficult for Lavinia Lenton to believe that this still pretty, apparently well-bred, quietly dressed, and well-mannered middle-aged woman was the famous Mrs. Caramine. She was wearing a dark green costume, buttoned from neck to hemline. It had ruffles of lace at the collar and cuffs. Her only jewelry was a rope of pearls and a diamond ring on her left hand beside her wide wedding band. Her dark hair, dyed of course, was dressed in a fashion that became her. Her brown eyes were magnificent. She had small hands and feet. The diamonds caught the light with their prisms, as she moved her hand. The room was in good taste. The sitting room of a well-off, middle-class woman. A Turkey carpet. A mahogany *chaise longue* of the Regency period. A tallboy. A writing desk with a lot of pigeonholes and a falling front with two retractable supports. A desk she could lock. Two armchairs upholstered in dark red plush. On the mantelpiece a bronze and marble clock with two candlesticks to match and a vase of yellow Maréchal Ney roses. There was no sign of vice here.

Mrs. Caramine came forward. She did not offer her hand. She merely made a gesture with it, as she said: "Please sit down, Mrs. Lenton. This is a great honor. You are, as far as I can recollect, the first lady ever to enter this room." Her smile was sweet, that of a charming hostess welcoming a guest. She did not speak to Edward Lenton. This was a woman's day. One lady calling on another.

As soon as Lavinia had seated herself, Mrs. Caramine sank gracefully onto the sofa, leaning one elbow on its high upholstered end. She was interested to see this beautiful, cold, fair woman. She had never spoken to any of her clients' wives, or even seen them close by before.

She looked a young thirty. She was beautifully and expensively dressed. Under her black summer coat, which she had just taken off after her "Do take your coat off, Mrs. Lenton," she wore an ensemble of red silk that by some accident almost matched the plush armchair in which she sat, the rich texture catching the light that came in from the window, shining with a ruby brilliance. In its shadowed folds, it was nearly black. The tight-fitting bodice was trimmed with jet. She had on black gloves and boots. Her hat was a toque of black straw, trimmed with velvet and ornamented with two small, black, red-winged birds, apparently in flight.

Mrs. Caramine examined her visitor with a professional eye. It was the only way she ever looked at a personable woman. She saw them with the eyes of a man, naked beneath their clothes. What were they worth? How much would they fetch, and in what market? A real beauty. An English beauty of gold, roses, and cream. In her mind she stripped her naked. She would strip well, like a blood horse. There was nothing cuddly here. Just real beauty, class and speed. By God, if a woman like this could ever be stirred, what a lover she would be. But they never were. They were trained the other way, just to put up with it. If by any chance they felt a stir of passion, they held it in check, knowing that their husbands would despise them if they showed any amorous inclinations. Ladies were not supposed to have such feelings. Yet, and this amused her, it was women like this who drove their husbands to warmer beds. It was this cult of virtue and false modesty that created vice. But one thing intrigued her. Lavinia Lenton wore no stays. She had never heard of a woman not wearing stays. Even her girls wore them; only two of them, Daisy and Irene, who had particularly small waists could dispense with them. It was worth trying anyway. She was always on the lookout for something new. A black reticule and a ruffle of black lace that edged her petticoat, almost concealing her boots, completed Mrs. Lenton's ensemble. A picture. Something lovely, like a confection that looked wonderful on the table but was quite tasteless in the mouth. Perhaps it was impossible to get the two. To get this finished, trained perfection and expect it to disappear, to change at sundown.

Edward turned his back on the women and stared out of the window. How often he had been in this cosy little room, for a cup of tea or a glass of wine! He knew every corner of it. Almost unconsciously he turned his head to look at the flowered wallpaper in which the secret door that led to No. 23 was concealed. The door that had led to Ellen. And now he had lost her. Who would have thought she would turn out like that? Never in all his existence had he had a woman like her—and she was his creation, his creature. As he watched the traffic, he heard his wife say:

"I have come about my children, Mrs. Caramine. Where are they?"

"How should I know, Mrs. Lenton? I have never set eyes upon them."

"You sent Delphine Le Grand to Mortal, Mrs. Caramine."

"Only to oblige your husband." Implicit in the way she said it, was the fact that she, Lavinia Lenton, had not been able to oblige him. The word "oblige" took on a new and subtle nuance on her lips.

"She has abducted the children," Lavinia said.

"You have informed the police, I suppose?"

"Not yet. I had to see my husband first. And you. But I shall, of course, as soon as I know a little more. And Le Grand, for instance, who is she?"

"An excellent governess, I understand, Mrs. Lenton. But of light morals."

"And where are my children?"

"Since Mademoiselle Le Grand is French, I should think they are in France. She may have taken them home on a visit."

"You sent her to us. I take it that you have added kidnapping and blackmail to your other activities. I assume you are the intermediary. Tell me how much you want. We will pay it in cash when we get the children back unharmed." Lavinia Lenton's voice was firm. Her manner completely assured. Position, money, and right were on her side.

Mrs. Caramine looked at her speculatively. No longer in the first flush of youth. But well preserved and spiritually a virgin. There were men who would like to get their hands on a piece of stuff like that. Mature, well bred—that would fight back. . . .

She said: "You are quite right, Mrs. Lenton. I did send Le Grand to you but, as I said before, only to oblige your husband—a valued client. The girl you had"—she paused—"the girl you dismissed, Mrs. Lenton, was apparently unsatisfactory. But there is no question of blackmail or ransom."

"Then what is it?" Mrs. Lenton gasped.

Mrs. Caramine laughed and went on. "Don't worry, Mrs. Lenton, I'll tell you all I know. Somehow, I had the feeling you would call. But first I want you to meet someone." She rang. To the maid who came to the door, she said: "Bring Master Frank in."

A moment later the maid was back with a sturdy, fair-haired, blue-eyed boy of seven.

"Mr. Lenton," Mrs. Caramine said, "I want to introduce you to my godson, Frank."

Lenton turned away from the window. The child and the man looked at each other.

"How do you do, sir," the boy said.

"How do you do, Frank." What was this farce?

"All right, you can go now," Mrs. Caramine said. The maid took the child out.

"What's all this nonsense, Carrie?" Lenton said as the door closed.

"Nonsense, Mr. Lenton? Call it sentiment. I feel that a child should have at least one look at his father. That is your son, Edward Lenton, by Muriel. Another governess, Mrs. Lenton—one whom your husband made give notice and sent to me when she was pregnant eight years ago."

"Sent to you! He sent her to you!" Lavinia said, horrified.

"He sent Ellen to me, too, as you know, Mrs. Lenton. The practice of disposing of unwanted mistresses to brothels was not invented by your husband. He sent Ellen to me and he made love to her here, where she was no longer in a position to refuse his attentions. He wrote to warn me of your suspicions so I sent her abroad. To Paris. She was kept there for him. On deposit, as it were, till the grouse shooting began and he had an excuse to go away alone. Though *not* to Scotland, as you imagined. To Paris, Mrs. Lenton, to Ellen who was waiting for him there."

"I know all this, Mrs. Caramine, and Ellen has been rescued. But what about my children?"

"A tissue of lies, my dear. Half truths, exaggerations. You must not believe all you hear." Edward was fiddling with his gold watch chain.

Mrs. Caramine went on. "Please do not be deceived by my appearance, Mrs. Lenton. I am a Madam, a whoremaster, but of course I was not born that way. Whores are made, Mrs. Lenton. They are not born, like poets, with their talents. I'll tell you how it began. My mother was kept by Mr. John Lenton. I called him Uncle Jack. He was your husband's father. When I was fourteen, he raped me and my mother killed herself. That is why I sent Delphine to you. I sent her to steal your children. She has done it several times before. I planned it, or something like it, long long ago. I knew Edward Lenton would come to my house one day. Like father, like son. When he came, I spoilt him. He always had the pick. Then when he sent Muriel to me, I kept her to see if she would have a son to taunt him with. She did. You saw Frank. A beautiful boy, but a bastard. I got her married. They live in the country but the child often spends a few days with me. It was a bit of luck that he was here, because I wanted you to see him. As to your children," Mrs. Caramine continued, "you will not see them again. You will never find Delphine, and you have no evidence against me. But it was you, Madam, who put the weapon I had waited so long for into my hand, when you dismissed Ellen Pickford for misbehavior. And now,"—she rose, made a graceful gesture with her left hand causing the big diamond to flash—"now that I have satisfied your curiosity about your daughters, you would perhaps care to look over the establishment? Meet my own young girls? Edward can wait for us. There is nothing he has not seen."

"The girls," Lavinia said. "My God, they are just children! Betty rising five."

"Five is not too young, Mrs. Lenton. A pretty child. Your husband has shown me photographs of them both."

Suddenly she seemed to relent. "I'll give you a tip, Mrs. Lenton. If I had lost my children, I'd try Jumelle's. They are her speciality." She smiled sympathetically. The damn stuck-up bitch, she thought. That would bring her down a peg. To find them might be a greater punishment than not finding them.

Outside in the street, Edward stopped a passing hansom. Lavinia refused to get into it. She said: "Get a four-wheeler."

It would be slower but she could not sit in the close intimacy of a hansom with this monster who called himself, and was in law, her husband. A growler was bigger. There would be a small leather-upholstered no-man's-land between them. How many meals had they eaten together in sixteen years? How often had she slept with him on those terrible pain-begetting nights? Rapes, that was what they had been, legal rapes. For if a woman was not ready, it was rape. With John in Paris, when he had held her, it would have been different. He had awakened feelings she had never felt before. A melting softness and desire. As he had lain her on the big sofa in the sitting room, she had hoped he would go on. She had been ready for him, even with May in the next room. May pretending she did not feel well, and must lie down. May had known about it before she had, and had got out of the way so that it could happen. It would, one day. The idea was no longer hateful and never would be, with him. That was with one part of her mind. She was using it to stifle her worry about the children. She could not bear to think of them yet. . . .

They sat at opposite corners of the cab. By tacit consent they had not used the carriage. No one wanted a crested carriage and pair, with a cockaded coachman and footman waiting outside so notorious a house.

"We will go back to Paris tomorrow night, Edward," Mrs. Lenton said as they got out of the cab. "Please order the carriage and see to the tickets."

"Of course, my dear." What a kettle of fish this was. What a bloody muddle. Jumelle's of all places. There, right under his nose. He had known her reputation, of course—a house for children. But he had not known his girls were missing.

15 : The Runaway

When Ellen escaped John Longbeach and felt herself safe in the crowd, she was laughing. Fancy someone stopping him as if he was after her! He was, of course, but not in the way the man had thought. She was crying, too. Near hysteria, the excitement of the past months culminating in this runaway. She had had to escape him. Escape. Escape had rung like a bell in her mind since she had first found herself imprisoned in the Chintz Room in Coak Street. For a while God had helped her. Prayer had helped her. She had used it like an anaesthetic. The next escape had been with Harris. For a few hours she had felt God had sent Harris. Then she had been betrayed and found herself imprisoned again. But the knowledge that she was being looked for had sustained her. But that, too, only for a while. Julie had seen to that. Julie with her endearments, her ministrations, massages, frictions of eau de Cologne and orange blossom, her soft teasing fingers and, finally, her dog whip. It was one of those small, plaited leather whips that are part whip, part lead, with a spring catch for the dog's collar in the butt.

Julie was still in her mind. The beautiful, passionate, cruel, olive-skinned woman, whose mistress she had become. She had told her her story. Seduced as a young girl, brutalized, handed over from man to man, she had at last come into the hands of an actress. Her personal maid. "That was a joke," Julie said. "But we had things in common—our looks. She was a beauty. Our hatred of men and, after a short time, our love for each other. She died. My mistress died. Murdered, I well know, by a man she had teased to his ruin. But I was supposed to be his accomplice. I went to prison, Hélène, and there I learnt about La Jumelle. I felt it was best to disappear, and where could I bury myself better than here? I, who love women. Girls. Children. The men who come, I hate. If I could, I would kill them all. Beasts. Assassins."

Then she would cover Ellen's body with kisses. Always one thing or the other. Kisses, or the whip, depending on her mood. A strange woman. Ellen did not hate her.

And then Lenton, the abominable Lenton. It was he who stopped the pain. Said: "Stop!" and Julie stopped. Then he had loved her. It might not be love but it stopped pain, and ended it in a wild convulsion that racked her body, never reaching her mind, leaving nothing to remember but a delicious agony.

She walked slowly down Victoria Street. Lost, merged in a crowd, she did not see. What now? She had some money. A sovereign, two half-crowns, a shilling, a sixpence, and some coppers that John Longbeach had given her. "You'd better have some money," he had said, pressing the sovereign from his gold sovereign-case into her hand and emptying his pocket of loose change. A cheap hotel for a night or two. A couple of days living on farthing buns and tea, and then what? Always what. Suddenly she made up her mind. She went into a public house and ordered a port and brandy. She had learnt to drink in Paris. The warmth of the drink bit into her throat, her chest, her belly, and ran on into her veins. A man sat himself down beside her.

"Want another, dearie?"

She looked at him with cold eyes. "No," she said. It was the first time she had said "no" for months.

He gave her a surprised look. He said: "You might say 'no, thank you' Miss," and left her.

But that was it. That was the answer. Men. That was "what." She ordered a second brandy, paid for it and, stopping a passing hansom, said: "23 Coak Street."

She was going to make a different kind of entrance to Carmine's establishment. She'd learnt the address and something about the place and the girls from Harris en route to France. Last time she had gone to No. 22—the adjoining house—as an innocent girl. Now she was no longer a virgin. No longer a girl. The months since Mrs. Green had taken her there seemed like years. Now she was strong. Carefree. With nothing to lose, how brave one could be.

She rang the bell. To the fat butler who answered the door, she said; "Mrs. Caramine." She did not hesitate on the doorstep but came in.

"Who shall I say, Miss?"

"Miss Ellen Pickford. She'll see me, I know."

"It's late," the man said.

"Early for this knocking shop, my man," she snapped. "Take me to her at once." She followed him.

"Miss Pickford," the butler said.

Mrs. Caramine looked up from her desk. "Good God!" she said. "But what are you doing here? I heard you had been rescued."

From the look of it downstairs, there must be worse places. She had never seen No. 23, only No. 22 where Mrs. Green had left her. No. 22 and the Chintz Room.

"Yes, I was rescued," Ellen said. "Such a nice man. We made love in the train this morning." She laughed. It had been amusing. So quick, and the chance that someone might come in. With the blinds down, like honeymooners. John Longbeach was only her second man but it had shown her the power she had. Even the fat little detective had felt it. "An aura of sensuality surrounds Mademoiselle," he had said. Lenton had done it, and Julie, and the books and the mirrors and the hours and hours of nakedness, waiting alone. She supposed her father would be expecting to hear from her. But he wouldn't. Suppose nothing had ever happened and she'd just gone on being a governess all her life, getting older and older. . . .

Mrs. Caramine's sharp voice interrupted her thoughts.

"Well, what do you want? It's no use trying to blackmail me. It's been tried before."

"I want to work here but I'm not the girl I was, Carrie Caramine. Just you ask Lenton. I sent him mad."

"Work?"

"As one of the girls. But no bloody nonsense, Mrs. C. I want half the money I make and I'll make a lot. Any nonsense and I'll kill a man. Pull or no pull, if a gentleman is killed here, you'll be finished. Girls have died here, I know, and children in the other house. But a gentleman, with his friends for witnesses, is something else."

"You've certainly changed."

"I've had lessons, Mrs. C. Lots of lessons. But I can't be a governess any more, nor do I want to be. So what is left? I want money now. Real money."

"You're in, my girl. On your own terms. Fifty-fifty. I can do with something with a bit of life in her. I've a lot of pretty little tits, well trained, but their hearts are not in it. A girl's heart's only in it when she wants money and likes men."

"Like men? I hate 'em!"

"It's the same thing, my dear. You only hate them because you cannot do without them."

Ellen laughed. "You did not ask how I was rescued."

"How were you?"

"By a man called Longbeach. A friend of Mrs. Lenton's. Came with a French detective. He wanted to take me back to my father. The prodigal daughter returns. Can you see it? The bowed head. The looks. The whispers. The gossip. By God, Mrs. Caramine, you made me a whore, but I seem to have a talent for it. They say lots of parsons' daughters do. But they'll know where I am—my friends, the do-gooders. They'll save me again if I lift a finger." Let Mrs. C. put that in her pipe and smoke it. Of course they didn't know where she was.

"Why did you leave this Longbeach man, Ellen?" Mrs. Caramine asked.

"I told you. He wanted me to go home. Had prepared the ground he said."

"But why did he let you go?"

"I ran away. Then I had a couple of drinks in a pub and wrote him a letter, telling him I was coming to you. I said: 'Once a whore, always a whore. No one should know that better than you.' The 'that' referred to the incident in the train. I think it'll upset him," she added.

"What about a cup of tea, Ellen? You must be tired. I'll show you to your room, and then you can pick your clothes from the dresser. Tomorrow you can start work."

Ellen had given Mrs. Caramine more to think about than she realized. A French detective had traced her to Jumelle's. This Longbeach was a friend of Mrs. Lenton's. But the children were there too. They had all been under the same roof and he'd never known. Nor had Ellen, of course. But they were going back. Mr. and Mrs. Lenton. That was a real revenge. He'd been there, making love to Ellen only a few yards from his own daughters. Still, there were aspects she didn't like. That damned Mrs. Lenton, for instance. How much did she know? She shrugged her shoulders. What did it matter, anyway? Even if she knew the lot, she couldn't do anything.

That evening alone in her room after a cold collation and half a bottle of burgundy served by the butler, now very obsequious, in Mrs. Caramine's sitting room, Ellen reviewed the day. It had gone very well. She had made a sensible decision.

Her room was large and beautifully furnished. It had, like all Mrs. Caramine's rooms, a private bathroom. She wondered if there was another house in London with quite so many. It had a large double bed with a gilt, heavily carved headboard. A big dressing table laden with pots and bottles—perfumes, cosmetics, creams, and lotions. A thick carpet with a pink design on a pale ochre ground covered the floor. There was a large chest of drawers and armoire, both gilt like the bed but ornamented with painted panels of an erotic nature. Above the bed was a large picture that looked as if it was based on Rosa Bonheur's Horse Fair, with naked girls taking the place of horses and goat-legged satyrs that of the men. Opposite the bed, on either side of the dressing table, were pictures of nude girls bathing. The two side walls were covered with full-length mirrors, fitted to the armoire on one side and to the chest of drawers on the other. On the ceiling, also heavily ornamented with gilt, was a large painting of a recumbent Venus, nude and in great detail, apparently glued to a cloud since she was upside down. It was a beautiful room. Vulgar, ornate, but exactly expressing its purpose. When she walked across the carpet after her bath, she saw a dozen Ellens reflected and counter-reflected in the mirrors. The gaslights were held by half-women finished in dull gold. The shades were pink silk. The light, a rosy, voluptuous glow, was reflected upward and turned to salmon by the yellow carpet.

Ellen lay on the bed and sighed with contentment. After all, this too was a career. The Pompadour, Nell Gwyn, Madame de Maintenon. . . . She had served her apprenticeship and was beginning at the top in what was recognized to be the best whore house in London, perhaps in the world.

There would be no more force. All friends, Mrs. Caramine said. The pick of society, and this was where she would entertain them.

When John Longbeach had told her about the abduction of Eva and Betty, she had been upset. But not for long. That was another world, one in which someone called Ellen Pickford had once been a governess. Words came to her mind: whore, harlot, daughter of the horse leech, fornication, adultery. Wicked words, that had lost their meaning. It had been made obvious to her that women served only one purpose— to give pleasure to men and be rewarded by them according to the satisfaction that their service gave. Lenton was the only man she really knew, but she was curious about others. How would they act? How would they look? What would they do and say? Tomorrow she would begin to learn. John Longbeach was already forgotten.

She thought of the clothes hanging in the closet. Day clothes, clothes for out of doors. Evening dresses. What a variety to choose from. The dresser said that Mrs. Caramine bought them from ladies' maids to whom their mistresses gave their discards. Many of them had only been worn once. How funny it would be to entertain a man in a dress that had once belonged to his wife, his sister, or even his daughter! It was curious how, once a certain point had been reached, amusement replaced disgust. She had heard her father talk of men taking to drink and apparently enjoying their degradation. This must be a parallel. First to avoid dirt and finally to roll in it. If people were disgusted, censorious, why not give them the real thing? After all, one might as well be hung for a sheep as a lamb. Mrs. Lenton had thought her a wanton. Had believed her husband's lies and by doing so had turned her into one.

She got out of bed and turned out the gas. Tomorrow she would meet the girls and Ada Prettyman. See Harris again. She was surprised now that she had ever feared her.

16 : The Detective

The return to Paris with May and her husband was a nightmare. Lavinia could not bear to look at her husband, yet kept glancing at him. This man she had married and lived with for so long, was a monster; but what made it even worse, a man little different from his peers. From all their friends. Those men who came to stay at Mortal for the shooting. Clean, well-bred, polite men. All whited sepulchres. All beasts, all devils. And that woman, Mrs. Caramine, who could have passed almost anywhere as a lady. What had she called herself? A whoremaster. A peddler of human flesh, of young girls. And yet she was able to operate within the law. As it now stood, no one could touch her. Brothels, houses of ill fame, were legally permissible provided they created no disturbance. Girls could be abducted without a finger being raised to stop it.

She had been to the police, to the commissioner himself. A most polite and urbane man.

"My dear lady, if your children have been taken abroad, I can do very little. Notify the Consuls in the large towns. But I am not optimistic. It is, of course, a matter of blackmail, of ransom, no matter what you have been told."

She felt he was calming her. That he knew more than he said.

"Inquiries will be set on foot at once, at the ports—Dover, Folkestone, New Haven."

"Mr. Fawnley Jones," she'd said, "they left from Folkestone. We know that."

"Nevertheless, we will inquire, Madam. Officially. Rest assured no stone will be left unturned. Most serious. Blackmail, kidnapping, ransom." He dropped the words like coins into a slot, unctuous to the last.

What was to be done must be done by her and the detective in Paris whom John had employed. Luckily she had his address. Off the Avenue de l'Opéra—a Monsieur Guitry.

At the Meurice again there was a slight *contretemps* when a double room and a single room were taken, and Lavinia asked for a cot in her room for her maid, as she had before. The desk clerk could scarcely control his astonishment. Madame and her maid in one room! The husband in another! With a kind of perverse Gallic humor, he gave Edward No. 310, the same room that the lover-advocate had occupied.

Once in her suite, Lavinia wrote a note to Monsieur Ferdinand Guitry, telling him who she was and asking him to call at once as the affair was most urgent, and to ask for her, not Monsieur Lenton. The letter was given to a *chasseur,* who was told to hurry and deliver it in person. If Monsieur Guitry was not at the office, he was to go to his home. She gave the boy two *Louis* and told him to take cabs.

She had just finished dressing for dinner when Monsieur Guitry was shown into her apartment. She introduced herself. He was enchanted to meet her. He hoped Mlle. Hélène was now safe in England, and of what further service could he be to Madame? He was, as she must know, entirely at her disposition and it was a pleasure to work for so beautiful a client. He would do his utmost. . . .

At first Lavinia was disappointed in this fat little man with a tiny imperial, whom she had seen in the distance with Ellen at the Gare du Nord. Then, as she watched his quick black eyes roam over the sitting room, saw the way he stood—his legs slightly apart as if he was on the deck of a ship—she began to take to him. He was like a stoat or a ferret. A fat little stoat that has just gorged itself on a rabbit. She sent May for her husband. He came in. Tails, white tie, white waistcoat, white kid gloves, a carnation in his buttonhole.

"My husband, Monsieur. Edward, this is Monsieur Guitry, the detective."

Guitry then showed his form. He seemed to grow a little. He bowed, but he was not enchanted. He did not put out his hand.

"I know Monsieur Lenton," he said. "I had the dubious pleasure of shadowing him to the *Maison* Jumelle where I found the English Mademoiselle."

"We will sit down," Lavinia said. "I am a little tired with all this traveling. I do not care for the sea."

"Ah, *le mal de mer!* How terrible it is!"

Lavinia almost smiled. She was right about him. A stoat. A ferret.

"And what is it this time, Madame?" he asked.

"My two daughters have been abducted by their governess. I have reason to believe that they are at Madame Jumelle's. It is, I imagine, a matter of ransom. I wish you to go there and negotiate." She still could not believe it was anything else.

"Mon Dieu, Madame, if it was only that. . . ."

"Only what, Monsieur?"

"Only a matter of money, of ransom, Madame. I fear worse things."

"What things?"

"First, the question of kidnapping for ransom, blackmail. A most serious offence. But if there is no demand for money, there is no offence. You follow me, Madame?"

"No, Monsieur." Lavinia could feel herself losing color. "Please explain."

"The young ladies are pretty, Madame?"

"Very."

"And aged?"

"Fifteen and five."

"And well brought up, naturally, being your daughters. Such girls are in great demand, Madame. Young, well brought-up virgins of the upper classes."

"Why? What for?"

"Yes, what for, you bloody frog?" Edward said, his fists clenched.

"Monsieur will please keep out of this discussion," Guitry said in a cold hard voice. "Madame is my client."

He turned to Lavinia, laid his hand on her gloved wrist, and said: "How can I tell you, Madame? If you cannot guess? They are girls, are they not?"

"You mean for that . . . ?" Lavinia whispered. So Caramine had meant what she said.

"For that, Madame. I can only pray we are in time. When did they disappear?"

"Almost a week ago."

"You permit me to get up, Madame? To walk about? I must think. I am possessed by rage. *Mon Dieu! Mon Dieu!"* He almost wept. "The innocents, and that *diable!* That ogress who panders to the most debauched men in Paris." He strode up and down the apartment like a caged animal. He stopped suddenly in mid-stride.

"Will Madame be good enough to order a small dinner up here?

Room service. Two soles, four chops, a salad, a bottle of Pommard, and coffee of course."

When the order had been given, Monsieur Guitry said: "We will eat and will act at once. Tonight. I know you are tired, Madame, but eat well. Drink some of the wine of Burgundy. It will give you strength. You are about to face an ordeal that makes a man—even a man like me, an ex-police officer accustomed to blood, bodies, murder. . . . My God, I blanch. I fear for my sanity when things like this come up. And in France, Madame. In my country."

When the food came, he flung himself on it, his napkin tucked into his high collar. He gulped his coffee. He said: "Come, Madame, we'll go."

"I'll get my cape," Edward said. He had stood watching them eat. He had not been invited to join them.

"Do not *dérange* yourself, Monsieur. You are a client of Jumelle's. We do not need you. You have money, Madame?" Guitry asked.

Lavinia told May to bring in her bag with the money. She gave it to the detective.

"Our only weapon, Madame," he said as he held the door open for her, leaving Edward and May to stare after them.

When the cab had gone a little way, Guitry stopped it.

"We will talk here, Madame. I must prepare you. A cab after all is a little room, and more private than most. Yes," he said, "a little secret room on wheels. For lovers, for conspirators. A place of secrets. But now, before I begin"—he fished in his pocket—"if you feel faint, I have both brandy and smelling salts ready though I do not think you will. Still, one should be prepared in my profession. First, Jumelle. I have her dossier. Maiden name: Hortense Thérèse Dupont. Born in La Villette, near the *abattoirs* of Paris. Father: Jean Baptiste Dupont. A butcher. Mother: a prostitute, known as La Poule. No other name. Age of the woman in question, sixty-one years. Married a sergeant of Zouaves, Alphonse Jumelle, January 10, 1844, at Casablanca in Algeria. Six years with him. He died suddenly in circumstances that pointed to murder. Arsenic, but there was no proof. Next Paris and the *banlieue*. Ran two baby farms. Twice imprisoned—too many of the children died. Malnutrition is not murder, Madame. Then she took to her present occupation. Bought a large house in the first *arrondissement*. Financed by God knows who. There she procures children for rich men with those tastes. Children aged from nine to sixteen. Virgins, therefore chiefly of the middle and upper classes. And all, Madame, are English. To steal French children is too dangerous, but there are no laws in France to protect foreigners." He handed Lavinia the smelling salts.

"You perceive the reason for my anxiety and anger," he went on. "She also sells children to ladies who want them."

"Why do they?" Lavinia asked.

"It is better not to ask. But you will pose as such a woman. You will act. All women are actresses. You will leave the talking to me. If you see your children, you will try to make them ignore you. Give them some sign of silence. The finger to the lips, *par exemple.*"

"It might work with Eva, but not with Betty. She is too young," Mrs. Lenton said.

"We will see when the time comes—and there is always the money. But of course a child would come dearer to its mother than to a stranger."

As if I cared, Lavinia thought.

"A mouthful of cognac, Madame? Fine champagne of the first quality." He unscrewed the flask, waited for Lavinia to gulp it, and told the driver to go on.

Madame Jumelle was in a good mood. The Prince of Orsinac Lichet had just left. He had been more than satisfied. "With you, Madame," he had said, "it is always worthwhile waiting." He had rented Eva three times for two hours. A man of Madame's own age, the Prince was well known throughout Europe for his perversions. Immensely, fabulously rich, he did not care what he paid for his pleasures. The girl had much more than paid for herself already for though the Prince did not know it, there had been other men. And the little one had gone to Germany; drugged, in a small white coffin with a wreath of artificial flowers fastened to it, effectively masking the holes bored for ventilation. It had been accompanied by a man dressed as an undertaker, in black with a crêpe-bound top hat. Under nine, children were too much trouble. They never lived for long, but in Germany, Austria, and Rumania, there were fewer problems. These countries were wild, with mountains and forests. Sparsely inhabited. Anything could take place there in an isolated castle or country estate.

Julie, of course, was in a temper. She always was when she lost a little friend. First that Milord's girl, and now Eva who, she said, was no more use to her, so badly was she damaged. The usual midwife was coming to repair her, but Julie was right—they were never the same afterward. She had told her there would be others—there always were—but she was never satisfied. No servant ever was.

Jumelle was in this mood when Monsieur Guitry and Lavinia walked in. He had just pushed the door open without knocking.

"Well, Mr. Policeman, what is it this time? And Madame? Pray be seated, Madame. Coffee? A glass of absinthe?"

"Madame Jumelle," Guitry said. "Madame is a client. She wants to adopt a girl whom she can train as a maid. A girl of fifteen or sixteen. She will pay well."

"The children are all in bed, Monsieur."

"We can see them there?"

"Oh no . . . I will get them up. A little minute and you shall see them. Julie! Julie!" she called.

"Madame?"

"We have a lady here who wants a dear little girl to train. Get them dressed and into the playroom."

"But certainly, Madame."

They heard the woman going upstairs. Monsieur Guitry talked of Napoleon, a safe subject here. Lavinia tried to contain her horror. Fancy being in a room with such a creature. And this was where Edward had come to see Ellen, with his children, all unknown to him, under the same roof. It was here Ellen had been kept for him, like a pheasant ripening in a larder. It seemed to her that she could still smell the stale smoke of his cigars.

The maid, a handsome, olive-skinned woman, came in and said the children were ready. She led the way upstairs. Madame Jumelle excused herself. "My heart," she said, touching her breast. "If you find what you want, bring her down."

The playroom was large, well lighted with gas from wall brackets. It was well carpeted. There were a number of armchairs and sofas. There was a spotted rocking horse, two doll houses, and several large dolls. But it was the children who held Lavinia's attention. A dozen lovely little long-haired girls playing on the floor and on the chairs. One was on the rocking horse. They were all beautifully and expensively dressed in white, pink, blue, and tartan frocks; very short, barely reaching to mid-thigh. They wore kid slippers with white socks. They played but they looked as if they had been told to play. They had been in bed. They looked frightened, sleepy, and bewildered. There were two bigger girls sitting together on a sofa. One of them was Eva.

Lavinia approached her and put her finger to her lips. Eva looked straight at her and gave no sign of recognition. What an actress the child was! She looked for Betty. Perhaps she was hiding. She was fond of hiding behind furniture. But she was not there.

Monsieur Guitry came forward. The children shrank away. Men frightened them. All except the big girl with Eva, who got up, curtsied and said: "I am Daphne. Do you like me?"

It was the detective's turn to recoil.

Lavinia pointed to Eva. "I'll take that one," she said. The maid took Eva by the arm.

"We're going downstairs, Mademoiselle," she said.

"Non, non!" Evangeline cried.

"Downstairs and no nonsense." She led the girl down. Lavinia and Guitry followed.

They all stood grouped in Madame Jumelle's sitting room.

"Ah," she said, "you have found one who will do? I am glad. We will now discuss the price. Is a thousand *Louis* too much?" she asked. Whatever she got would be clear profit, and the girl was going to be a nuisance. The fight and fun were out of her, Julie said.

"Much too much, Madame. Five hundred is more like it," Guitry said.

"Five hundred! You must be mad! For a girl like that? Though no longer a virgin of course."

Lavinia sat back in her chair, wishing she had the smelling salts.

"But new," Madame said. "Quite fresh."

"Seven hundred and fifty is the last word." Guitry got up. "Come, Madame," he said to Lavinia. "There are other places."

"Seven hundred and fifty *Louis* I'll take. Because you are an old friend. And now an apéritif. A little absinthe to seal the bargain."

"We regret we have not the time, Madame."

With Eva between them, they went out to the waiting cab.

"But Betty," Lavinia said. "Where is my baby?"

"Thank God we have one, Madame. I will try to trace the other."

In the morning they would all go back to London. A family party. A woman, her husband, her daughter, and her maid. What a return! It would all look so normal, so ordinary, but nothing would ever be normal again. Ever.

There was no one up at the hotel except the night clerk, who hardly gave them a glance. Monsieur Guitry left them at the door, saying he would write. In the apartment Edward was asleep on the sofa.

My sofa, Lavinia thought. Mine and John's. In some way it was now defiled. He had smoked a cigar. The room stank of smoke, stank like Jumelle's. Like Carmine's.

"Wake up," she said.

Edward put his feet to the floor and ran his hands through his hair.

"Where's Betty?" he asked. So Carmine had been right as usual. But where was the baby?

"God knows," Lavinia said. "Or the devil. Look what you have done to her! Look at your daughter. She doesn't even know us. Stand up, Edward Lenton, and get out of my suite. We shall go back to London tomorrow. Please see to it."

"Betty?" he said again.

"The detective is going to try to find her. Now get out."

Edward left the room without a word. There was nothing to say. It was impossible to reason with women. What bad luck the whole thing was. But he must find Ellen. Of course Eva had had a shock. All right, all girls got a shock the first time. She'd get over it.

Her mother and May undressed Eva. When they had finished, they were both in tears. Eva had not spoken. She seemed to recognize neither of them.

"We must get her to Mortal," Lavinia said. "To Doctor Jarvis."

"Oh Madam, Madam," May sobbed.

Alone with Julie, Madame Jumelle sighed as she sipped her drink. "Three girls gone in less than a week. C'est la guerre," she said. "But we did not do too badly."

"Too badly, Madame? To get seven hundred and fifty Louis for a living corpse? That Prince! That assassin!" she spat.

"So they take your little birds and pluck the feathers of their virginity. And you hate them for it. You hate all men. But I get you new ones. Pretty ones, young ones, fresh ones. That's why you stay with me, my girl, to satisfy your lusts. You are a vicious woman, Julie." Madame Jumelle laughed. "C'est la guerre," she said again. "In war there are casualties. There is blood. You would keep them all as pets, ma fille. But me, I run a pet shop. Now get them to bed again and turn in yourself."

Madame Jumelle opened her desk and began to write the letters that would bring replacements.

17 : The Button

The journey back from Paris seemed endless. The cab to the station, sitting with Edward. May and Eva, blank-faced, on the jump seat in front of them with their backs to the driver. Calais. A rough crossing.

Dover. London again. The carriage—Edward had wired for it to meet them. The last time they had been met by the carriage they had come back to see Mrs. Caramine.

On the ship, Edward had left them alone. Both she and May had tried to talk to Eva. To whatever they said, she either said "yes," nodding her head like a doll, or did not reply at all. She was dressed in one of May's uniforms that had been shortened and pinned up at the back with safety pins. Over it she wore one of her mother's coats that was far too big. A silk scarf was tied over her hair. The girl was completely passive. An automaton. A doll, that was the only word for it. Well, she'd be safe at Mortal. Perhaps the familiar faces . . . the house, the surroundings she had known since birth would bring something back. Paint some picture on the blank canvas of her mind.

Lavinia stared out of the window of the carriage. Beyond the glass, all London pulsed as the bright day faded into the dusk. This was England's heart. The heart of the Empire. It was not yet time for the lamplighters but they would soon be along with their tall sticks, flicking on the yellow gas that would stain the streets with patches of gold. Pools through which people, busy on their affairs, passed like fish; bright with it and dull again, almost invisible, gray between the posts that stood like iron trees along the curb. Trees: landmarks for dogs by day and whores by night. Girls plying their ancient trade. Common prostitutes, invisible to virtue that swept by with raised skirts. Meat to woman-hungry men, hosts to the parasites who lived upon them. Each in her appointed place. Pavement flowers, temporary nosegays who knew no parlor vase. Spaced, plumed, garlanded with delight; daughters of nocturnal joy, sharing the night with prowling cats; not people. A social need winked at, for they blunted the knife of vice. It was the whores who saved the virgins, or so they said. So as night fell, they bloomed, spotting the streets, the corners, with color. Contemptible public women, some of them still children, delicate as kittens. Some, hardened into stone, fighting their solitary battles against time and disease.

For the first time in her life, Lavinia got the feel of London. The feel of her time—of its immense prosperity, of the silken garments that hid festering wounds in its underlying poverty. The facts of life. She had asked for them. But not this. Dear God, not this. Not all of them in one long poisonous draught.

In the great houses maids were carrying hot water upstairs. Maids were combing out the long hair of ladies who were dressing for dinner. Soup, fish, a bird, a joint, sweets, dessert, savories, and fruit were being readied in dark basement kitchens by fat cooks, furious with heat. Each kitchen stove a hell of glowing coal.

In the palace, the old Queen, who had left Balmoral early this year, was being dressed in her evening black, with a clean white lace cap upon her white hair. An old woman, a widow. Empress. Through the open windows of the palace, the stamp of the scarlet bear-skinned guards could be heard as they turned about; like the whores, they had their beat. For this was an ordered world, where each man had his place. The women of the great were private women, the property of one man, or supposed to be, and joyless in it. But the men ran in free rut and had their tumbling fun with maids, shop girls, and harlots. Kept their strumpets in neat-gardened houses, their horses in mews that had once held hawks. Lords they were, the lot of them, if rich. Their golden sovereigns jingled as they slipped them, one after another, like kenneled dogs out of their cases, divided into two. One springed niche for the pounds, a smaller one for half sovereigns. Each with the Queen's head upon it, so long had she reigned, and on the other side the bold Saint George spearing his dragon. A pukkah pig-sticker. They folded big crinkling fivers into their pocketbooks. A lot of gold was too heavy to carry, and who knew what adventure the evening would bring forth? Rich—how rich England was in gold, in men, in skills, in blood! How secure, an island afloat on an impregnable ice-gray sea! The gold poured in from every corner of the globe; from an Empire which never knew the night for, as the flag came down with the sun in one dependency, it went up as day dawned in another.

In every street in Mayfair and Belgravia, the whistles blew. Two for a rattling hansom with a blood horse between the shafts, one for a four-wheeler. Carriage horses, glossy with grooming, were put in. Carriage lamps, each with a candle, were lit. The varnished wheels spun as freshly blackened horse hooves struck cobbled sparks.

The summer was about over. London would soon be on the move—to dinners, to receptions, balls, dances, card parties, and the less estimable pastimes of opulence. White ties and tails, carnation buttonholes. Malacca canes. Ladies, in silk and satin, girdled with whale-boned armor, smelling of violets and tuberose, lifted their trailing lace to sit on the dark leather of their cushioned carriages. Thinking of their clothes, their jewels, the lovers they would like to have, as they adjusted their long skirts about sleek, rounded thighs. Petulant as spoilt children, they leaned back, always careful of their hair.

There were layers of society. It was like a pyramid cake whose working base lived in filth and penury, their only avenue of escape a bottle —gin, port, brandy, beer, and stout—which flowed in rivers—Lethe —that led them bemused to the dark and final Styx. At the top was the Queen, balanced like a red cherry on the white icing of established custom. Then came the dukes, viscounts, marquises, earls and barons, the aristocracy, the landed gentry. Burke's peerage. Debrett. The Services, the Law, the Church. Doctors still came to the back door. Businessmen and Merchants, Clerks and Shopkeepers were all classes apart. The streets were bright with uniforms, with liveries, gay with fashion in the West End; and drab, smelling of stale sweat and liquor when the boundary of wealth was crossed.

All this was not in Lavinia's mind. Not all London. Not the Empire. Not the Queen. But she knew she was in it, part of its ebb and flow. She felt it, as a fish must feel the water through which it swims. Her children were in her mind. The full horror of what she had seen had not yet penetrated the depths of her consciousness; she was still numb with her firsthand experience of this evil that she must attack. . . . Women, the weaker sex, the fair sex. The cant, clichés, that were used, nominally to protect women, but only the women of her class, and actually served to blinker them, to hide reality from them. Reality— the dreadful, awful facts of life.

She thought of Maud. Lovely, scatterbrained, who had told her she was in love with Geoffrey Horner, a Grenadier. She could hardly blame her. Harold Fortall, her husband, was a crony of Edward's, and she had detested him even before Maud's confidences. A very handsome, sardonic, young-looking man, who was only being kept by his creditors because his father, Lord Cockshott, was eighty-six and said to be one of the ten richest men in England. It was Maud who, six months before, had told her some of the things that went on in London. She had not believed her then. Maud said she had slept with her lover. At the time she had been appalled, not merely at the risks Maud was taking, but that a woman as well brought up as she could have done such a thing. "I suppose he made you," she had said. Geoffrey was a powerful man. She saw him, having got Maud into a compromising position, taking advantage of her.

"Made me, Lavinia? How could he? I wanted him to." Her big blue eyes had darkened with recollection.

Now she understood. If John had . . . She did not finish the sentence in her mind, but she saw the sitting room at the Meurice again. She felt his arms under her knees. His fingers had touched her flesh. Maud said they were going to run away. Geoffrey had a brother farming ostriches in South Africa. A place called Oudtshoorn out in the wilds somewhere. They were going to join him one day. "How could you?" she'd said. But John and she had thought of the same thing. They were still thinking it. Once the children were safe . . . once she had got Betty back. Her mind alternated. Partly she believed, or tried to pretend, she would get Betty back unharmed. At other times she hoped the child was dead, safe in the arms of Jesus.

But what, after all, were the alternatives for a married woman who did not love her husband? Love. That was a new word, too. To stick it out with a "you have made your bed" attitude, to take the risk of having a succession of lovers, or to bolt. . . .

Edward, his back half turned to Lavinia, was staring out of the window, still unable to get over the fact that he had lost Ellen. It was like having a favorite dog stolen. That bloody lawyer was probably sleeping with her now. Feeling outraged, cuckolded, he recognized a pair of horses. That was the Fortall carriage. He must get hold of Harold. Get his mind off things. They'd make a night of it. . . .

Bowling along behind two bright bays, shiny as fresh horse chestnuts, a cockaded coachman, and a footman with folded arms on the box, the Hon. Harold Fortall M.P. was well content. The old man was going to die at last. What a time he'd had to wait! He was almost sympathetic with his creditors for their patience.

He looked at his wife, a pretty creature plucked from the schoolroom. Three years of marriage had changed her; she was harder to manage now. He wondered about her lover. He was sure she had one, but who was he? He knew him, of course. Maud Fernley would never move out of her own circle. It was an amusing idea in a way. That a man who dined with them should have seen the secret beauties that were denied to him. But he had done the same with the wives of other men.

A curious day. After leaving his father's bedroom, he had walked home. A little tart in black, dark as his wife, had spoken to him. A neat little tit. He'd given her a sovereign and chucked her under the chin. Just a girl. He wondered how many men she'd had. How many a day? How long they stayed? At what age she'd begun?

"A quid?" she'd said indignantly. "Think I'd do it for a quid?"

"No, darling. A fiver, I'd say."

"That's better, me lord," she said, all smiles and dimples. "For a fiver you get the lot."

"It's a present, my dear," he said.

Her mouth had opened. Round, with wet soft lips. Her little tongue had shot out at him in mockery. "Thank you, sir," she had laughed, and dropped him a tiny curtsey, like a little girl bobbing down in a drawing room.

He knew she thought he was a nice gentleman. A man with a good heart and a loving wife who had no need for the likes of her. She would never guess that she got five pounds because he was happy, or that he was happy because his father was going to die and he'd be Lord Cockshott in a day or two. An hour or two.

"He's going to die, Maud," he said, suddenly breaking the silence. "Lady Cockshott—you'll like that, I expect."

She smiled at him. He knew it was the emeralds she was thinking of. They were famous. They'd be hers soon. Not hers, still his, but hers to wear. He understood her kind.

After he had left the street girl, he had run into a Salvation Army Band. A girl there too. Tall, slim, red-haired. Even the bonnet and the uniform had not been able to disguise it all. His cup of tea all right. A clinker. He wondered what she was doing with that crew. She got a sovereign too—dropped into her tambourine. They were just packing up to go home. She'd smiled at him with big brown eyes, soft as a Jersey cow's. But he knew they could flash with anger. There was life in her. Money, by God. That was what brought a smile to 'em all. Whores and Salvation Army lasses. A quid here and a quid there. A fiver for the lot, the little dark doxie had said. And more of course for the Mauds. Marriage, jewels—emeralds. She'd get her emeralds. But he'd see her this time, and how she'd hate him for it. But she'd do it. Not just the emerald necklace. The diamond collar and earrings, the bracelets, the ropes of pearls that would hang down over the smooth, flat belly, known only to his hands. How lovely she would look— pink, white, and ebony. He wondered if any of the bracelets would fit her ankles. He might have one altered. She'd have to do it before he let her wear them at all. Then once she'd worn them in public, she'd do it every time he told her to, because people would say: "Where are the emeralds, Maud?" He could hear them in his mind. She could hardly say: "Harold won't give them to me." Hardly say why. Say: "I have to wear them with nothing else on, or he won't get them out of the safe." What a hold he'd have over the little bitch at last, after the dance she'd led him with her "yes" and "no" and "perhaps"!

He was sick of being a nincompoop. Harold Fortall thought of himself as a buck, and prided himself on his eighteenth-century vocabulary. He was a quick one, always ready for a flurry. That would be a flicker.

By God, he'd do that to her, too, one day. Rumple his Lady Maud in all her finery.

What made him laugh was that since she had a lover, she'd do almost anything to please him. But the jewels would save her face. What bloody fools men were! No mistress was as good as an unfaithful wife and, by God, he'd sooner have a buttered bun than a dry one. The future opened before him, spreading its wings like a butterfly in the sun. Settle his debts, buy some new horses. See what old Caramine would do for him in a special way. Some rum goods. There was nothing you could not get for money. Horses, women. Even your own wife with jewels, by God. It would be fun to unrig Maud.

"I hope the champagne is cold," he said, thinking the old devil may be dead by now. He smashed his right fist into his left hand. His father was just staying alive to spite him, to see if he could survive him. And he damn nearly had with a couple of hunting accidents, and a duel he'd gone to France to fight.

"Cold?" Maud said. "It's always cold."

"I mean really cold."

She did not answer him. She knew he thought she was away in some dream of luxury. Jewels, clothes. Another carriage, big parties in the Grosvenor Square house and at the Castle in the country. But that was the old Maud, not the new one. Not the Geoffrey-Maud. Perhaps he'll leave me alone now, she thought. He'll have plenty of others. What a brute the man was! Women. God knew, everyone had to put up with that. But little girls, little crying girls. She wondered how many people knew about it. Half London, probably. It was Geoffrey who had told her when she had hesitated. How handsome he was! How cleverly they avoided each other! How superficial their conversation when they met in public! She moved on the soft, dark leather upholstery of the carriage with a rustle of silk and taffeta.

When would the old man die? When would Geoffrey lie in her arms again? In the darkness, she blushed, thinking of the things he'd said. The Song of Solomon, indeed. But when she got home she'd looked it up. It was all there, just as he had said it would be. But it looked different in print on India paper. And it wasn't all there, not all of what he had said—and nothing about what he had done.

Jenny, the street girl, slipped the coins the gentleman had given her into a little purse fastened to her left garter. I'll keep it, she thought. I did not take him back. It's mine, mine! But she knew she would not keep it. She would not dare. She'd tried it once. Never again. Christ, how Fred had licked her and sent her out into the street again at four in the morning! Hardly stand, she couldn't. The bastard. The bloody bastard. He took her money, Fred did, and that of the other girls, and split it with Solferino. That was the threat that kept them all in line. She'd seen girls cut, disfigured, by Jack Solferino. Seen them disappear into houses on the docks. Five hundred men a week. That killed them, that did. That was the end of them. There were no flies on Jenny Pim. She knew. They all knew.

The last tune the Salvation Army Band played was "Onward Christian Soldiers." A funny world, with toffs giving girls a fiver for nothing and Salvation Army Bands playing hymns and jingling tambourines, while the whores stood waiting for randy men. All in one street. All at one time.

One of the Salvation Army men was coming toward her. A big, fair-headed chap. That was a laugh, that was. She stood, her heels together, her skirt, gathered in her left hand, raised to show her petticoats and calf above her neat, black kid buttoned boot.

She smiled at him. "Want to come back with me, darling? Think I've got something you'd like? Is that it? Don't be shy, ducks." She put her hand on the man's arm. A small hand in a white kid glove.

"Me? I'm in the Army."

"I know," she said. "Salvation. And you'll not be the first what tried to save sweet Jenny Pim."

She had black hair and a high color. Her eyes were big, gray, blank doll's eyes, like water in a saucer with no depth to them.

What had brought him to her? They had been playing for an hour. They'd just finished "Onward Christian Soldiers." He had been watching her out of the corner of his eye. A trim little figure in black, rooted to the pavement. She knew what she looked like.

"You're just a kid," he said.

"Big enough, darling." She tried to pull him. It had begun to drizzle. Suddenly she laughed.

"What's the joke?" he said.

"You, ducks. You and your bloody uniform. Don't you know you're all the same, the bloody lot of you, when you take it off? Just men. Bastards that want it." She shivered and began to cry. "Come on," she said. "Come on . . ." Red lobster. Blue lobster. All the same. Just looking for a cooking kettle. The April sun broke through her tears.

"You've got no money?" she said, looking up and rolling her handkerchief into a ball.

Money? Of course he had no money. But what was he doing here?

Had God pointed to her? Had God sent him to save her? How did you save a girl? Was it God moving in his loins? God, or the devil?

"I've got no money," he said. That was the way out. She'd let him go when she found he had no money; but she didn't. Her hand burnt into his arm, annealed to it. Soldered.

"I can't," he said. "It's wrong. It's wicked. The flesh, the lusts of the flesh."

She raised her tear-stained face to his. She was going to take a chance on it. Fred or no Fred. This was a straw to cling to. The money was a sign. She did not believe in God. She had no reason to, but she was not going to let him go. She knew that he was not bad, that he was fighting the man in him. She had never met a man like that. Never a man who wanted anything else. Never a man who fought it. Something had taken place in Curzon Street, some mystery in the cold drizzle. Some bond, akin to both, had been forged. This was not an accident but the first link in a chain of events. Both knew it and both were afraid.

"Come on," she said. "God damn the money! I'll do it for a button."

Before he knew what had happened, she turned to face him and ripped a button from his dark blue, frogged tunic.

18 : A Gun Shot

Edward had paid little attention to his daughter on the journey home. If she did not speak to him, he did not really care. The cause of her silence he ignored. If Lavinia did not choose to discuss it, she could hardly claim his interest. But under this crust of calm, he was seething. He had been made a fool of by that lawyer of Lavinia's; by Ellen's escaping him; by the theft of his letters, documents and pictures that were now hidden God knew where; by Delphine's running away. No woman had ever run away from him before. By what had happened to his daughters—obviously something had happened to one girl and Betty had disappeared. They were his. Someone had dared to touch his property. But all this was in the back of his mind; it was the background, the scenery. The real play was Ellen, who had set his blood on fire. Against this, the abduction of his daughters faded into insignificance; he had never really cared for them.

Almost unconsciously he saw the women into the house at Berkeley

Square, waited till evening at the club, and then drove to Coak Street. Carrie might know something. Anyway, he'd find solace there in the arms of Daisy, the little blonde tart he'd taken a fancy to. She reminded him of a half-bred Arab mare he'd once had. Sleek, pretty, always in rather high condition, but prettier that way with her rounded quarters and long, switching nervous tail. And there might be news. He'd ask first.

He gave his hat, cane and gloves to the footman and went into the ballroom where Mrs. Caramine entertained. By God, he thought. By God! What luck he'd had! There was Ellen in a low-cut blue dress, dancing with a man he knew by sight.

Mrs. Caramine took both his hands in hers. "You must have second sight. Your little doll is here, Mr. Lenton. But no longer entirely yours, I'm afraid. She's quite grown up. You must have given her a real education. But girls do grow up fast nowadays."

"I want her, Carrie. I want her now."

"You'll have to ask her yourself, Mr. Lenton. She's here on a different basis from the others. Calls herself Hélène and is all frenchified. Made her own terms. But she's put some life into the place already. My God, I was at my wits' end. Like a bloody morgue it was. And by the way," she went on, "I trust Mrs. Lenton is well? Such a pleasure meeting her. And the girls? I hope you found them?"

Lenton had not waited for her to finish talking. The music had ceased. Ellen was talking to her partner.

"Excuse me, sir," Lenton said. "May I speak to Ellen for a moment?"

"Of course, my dear chap. But I've booked her first, haven't I, darling?"

"You have," Ellen said. "Of course, Mr. Lenton, if you are willing to wait a couple of hours. . . ." She looked at him, her big gray eyes as innocent as a child's.

"Wait? You expect me to wait for you? I never have," he said.

"But you will now, Mr. Lenton. Hours, Mr. Lenton, according to my pleasure." She swept past him to the stairs, on the arm of the man she had been dancing with.

Carrie Caramine returned to the attack. "How about Daisy, Edward? Daisy, come here!" she called. "I can give her orders, Mr. Lenton. . . ."

But Lenton had gone. This was the last straw, the final insult. That little bitch! *His* little bitch, making him wait. He still saw her going off upstairs beside that proud, black back, her long fair hair swaying as she walked, her croup switching her blue silk bustle, her train held up in her hand. The world, his world, had really collapsed. He would go home to Mortal, and the partridges.

He slept at the club and got home in time for luncheon, ate it quickly and sent a stableboy to the head keeper, telling him he wanted to see him at once and to bring a brace of pointers and a retriever. By three o'clock, accompanied by the head keeper, he was in the roots, the two liver and white pointers working with lashing tails among the swedes and gold wheat stubble. Spot and Flirt were good dogs. They quartered the ground methodically, backing each. When one froze, cataleptic with the excitement of scented birds, the other stopped too, both immobile as statues while Edward walked up to the partridges—little families still, not yet big coveys, so wary that they had to be driven. They crouched, flattened below the wide leaves of the root crops, or invisible in the stubble, to rise with a whirr of wings exploding at his feet, upward into the wind, the old birds leading the young.

A right and left. Two birds fell, pitched down, thudding, for Bess the retriever to pick up.

"Hi lorst! Hi lorst!" the keeper shouted, the dog ran forward, big, black, curly-coated, and brought the dead birds back in her soft mouth, not a feather out of place.

Kill, kill—it was good to kill. Neatly and cleanly. Left and right. He nearly always got two birds. When he had shot eight brace and tramped five miles, Edward turned back. A good afternoon. The pointers had not run in. Bess had not lost a bird.

They put up a hare. He rolled it over, screaming as it died. "Puss," he said, "poor puss." The retriever brought it back. A big one, its ears and hindlegs dragging on the ground as the bitch held it, her head high. A good afternoon, he thought. Funny how women could not stand a hare's scream. Women. God damn them! All of them. Lavinia, Carmine, Delphine, Ellen—the bloody lot. Why couldn't a man do without them? Some men could. For the first time in his life, he was envious of them. That man Ellen had gone off with, whom he knew by sight. His name came back to him. Hawthorn. Ellen, his woman, whom no one but he had ever touched. The exercise and the partridge shooting had made him forget for a while, but now it was back. I should have waited, he thought. I should have had Daisy, and made her jealous. What a lot of things a man knew he should have done when it was too late!

Once they were back in London, Lavinia put the channel crossings out of her mind. Four crossings in a week. One with John, three with

Edward. All of them horrible. She concentrated on Eva. They put her to bed. A couple of days rest and they would go down to Mortal. The country would cure her. Peace . . . time . . . Edward had gone to his club as soon as they arrived and she'd heard nothing from him. Nor did she want to.

Up to the time they left for Mortal, Eva had not spoken. She did what she was told, seemed to understand the words, but there was no recognition or change of expression in her face. It never changed.

Lavinia, Eva, and May arrived at Mortal by the afternoon train. She met her husband at dinner. She asked him what he had been doing. It was like speaking to a stranger. An unwanted guest, to whom one had to be polite because of the presence of the servants. She found herself wondering how he had ever got to Mortal.

In Paris Monsieur Guitry was still looking for Betty. There was nothing more she could do except pray and think of John Longbeach. Where was he? Where was Ellen? When would she hear from him?

She sent a groom to his office at Mortal Major. He returned to tell her that Mr. Longbeach was still away.

Dr. Jarvis was attending Eva. He sent a woman to take care of her. Part of the story had been told him. He seemed to accept it. Certainly at this time, Lavinia was in no condition to explain anything further. There were so many things she was trying to understand. Among them was herself. She had never really thought about herself before. Her character. She had been born into an upper-class rut and had followed it without question all her life. Puppy-blind, she had grown up, run a great establishment, borne children, done everything people did without a real shock of any kind. Marriage had, of course, been an unpleasant surprise. But even that had been somewhat expected. Her aunt had told her she would not like it but that she must put up with it, and she had. As all women did. It was a cross to bear and she had borne it with fortitude. Bored and disgusted by Edward's attentions, she knew from what her friends suggested, rather than what they said, that her fate was no worse than theirs.

Mill-pond smooth, her life had followed the pattern of the London season. The holidays by the sea with the children and their nurses, when young, and with their governesses when older. Four summer holidays with Muriel, a quiet, refined, red-haired girl, with never a glimpse of what lay beneath her well-groomed, ladylike exterior. Then came the partridge and pheasant shooting in the autumn. Fox hunting. The first snowdrop. The carpets of crocuses, yellow, purple, and white. Daffodils, narcissus. Fruit blossom and may. Roses in the early summer, and London again. Neat as the hands of a clock, her life had moved in the circle of the seasons. Her movements, the unthinking product of centuries of stereotyped behavior. Women like her did not think. And then the bombshell of Delphine's nude beauty, followed by the exploration of her own. The picture-puzzle letters that had been the key to it all.

But it was Edward's insistence that Ellen be given notice that had really begun the sequence of events, just as Mrs. Caramine had pointed out. Started a snowball that had turned into an avalanche. And now? She had lost one child, and could only hope that she was dead. The other was irreparably damaged in mind and body. Her young flesh torn by a royal monster. And she herself was in love, really in love, passionately desirous of one man while married to another.

What was there to do now? Nothing but wait till she heard from John. Two days later the butler said Mr. Longbeach wished to see her. The very sound of his name put new life into her. She rang the bell for tea and went to meet him.

She came into the room and closed the door.

"Lavinia!" he said. They embraced with their eyes.

"Ellen?" Lavinia said. "Where is she now? You got her out safely?"

"The children, Lavinia?"

It was difficult to remember that he knew nothing. That he had left her to go and see Monsieur Guitry and find Ellen.

Her lips began to tremble and she sat down quickly. "We've got Evangeline, John. I don't think she'll ever be right. The doctor was here again today. But Betty's gone."

"Gone?"

"To Germany, Guitry thinks. Oh! That awful woman. And they were there all the time in the same house. Oh, John! John! To think, when you went there for Ellen, they were there, under the same roof, within a few yards of you."

"Jumelle's? At Jumelle's?"

"Yes. The detectives, your people, are looking for Betty. We brought Eva back. I went there with Monsieur Guitry. It was awful. That frightful playroom. The dappled rocking horse. The clothes they were wearing. We found out where they were from Mrs. Caramine. You were there, John. Quite close to them, when you got Ellen. So was Edward. Imagine it! And you never knew. You might have been in time to save them. I saw Ellen on the station. Where is she, John?"

"Monsieur Guitry took her home to his wife for the night. He brought her to the boat train. We saw you and Edward."

"I know," Lavinia said. "It was awful, not being able to speak to you. But Edward . . . with Edward there . . ."

John thought of the journey back with Ellen. That was something he could never forget, and never tell Lavinia. It was impossible to believe, as he sat looking at Lavinia, that he had made love to Ellen in a first-class carriage of the boat train.

"I told her I was taking her home to the vicarage. That I had written to her father. He was waiting for her there. . . ." How could he go on? "Then at Victoria, I lost her. She just picked up her skirts and ran. I ran after her. A man stopped me. Thought I was chasing her, and she got away. She's in London somewhere. No money. No place to go. She's being looked for, but I don't believe we'll find her. She does not want to come back. She's changed. She's taken to it, taken to the life. I never would have believed it. Utterly debauched, depraved. Says she understands life now. She's lost all she had and can make more money this way. 'More money than I ever dreamed of, Mr. Longbeach,' she said. I could never have believed it possible."

The door opened and Charles brought in the tea on a big silver tray. Lavinia poured. A ritual. He was reminded of Madame Jumelle and her absinthe. Of standing drinking it with the detective, to seal the bargain of Ellen's release. On all levels there was ritual, custom, formality. And at that very moment the little girls had been there, both of them probably, in some room above his head. The blind canary, the sword and flag. The Napoleonic pictures. Madame raising her glass to the bronze painted plaster bust, and saying: "The Emperor . . ."

He sat silent, wrapped in horror, sipping China tea from Crown Derby cups. Caught in a mesh of love. The net that had fallen over them, caught them like fish. Seeing each other, knowing each other, but unable to reach each other. John did not even dare to take Lavinia's hand.

The silence, that may have lasted a minute but seemed an hour, was broken by Lavinia.

"John," she said, "I'm going to stop this traffic in women." She spoke quietly but firmly. Her jaw was set, her eyes cold.

"What are you going to do, Lavinia?" She only knew the half of it. Nothing of the extent of the trade and its ramifications. Nor of the vested interests that protected it.

"It's all covered up, John. I'm going to rip the cover off and expose it."

"It will ruin you, Lavinia."

"Ruin me? What is there to ruin? I have lost everything. My husband, my children. Are you with me, John?"

"To the end. But what are we going to do?"

"It will ruin you, too. People will talk about me. They will be certain that a woman who is prepared to discuss so unpleasant a subject, even if they have no proof, must be immoral. You'll lose your clients."

"I can live without them, and I shan't lose them all. But how will you begin, Lavinia?"

"By talking. By telling the truth. It will be like throwing a stone into a pool. There will be rings round it. Ripples. Little waves of horror, of emotion, of revulsion. Other people will talk. More pebbles and some big stones, perhaps. Ones that'll splash. . . ."

How sensible she was! "Go on," he said.

"It can't be done in a week or a year. I think it may take me all my life, John. But someone must do it and I don't know anyone, any woman that is, who is better equipped. Look what Florence Nightingale did. A woman against the world. That was woman's work, too."

"The Lady with the Lamp."

"We need light here, John. Oh God, how we need light. Publicity is light. If we could only get something into the papers. They write about crimes, about murders. This is slow murder. Murder for money, for the sale of young girls' bodies."

They had collected themselves now. The harness of their upbringing was back in place. As John took her hand to say goodbye, everything was correct except the expression of their eyes.

When he had gone, Lavinia sank back into her chair. Henry came in to light the lamps. She sent him back. She could think better in the dark.

Upstairs in the nursery wing, Eva sat dreaming. She had a doll in her lap. An old doll that she had loved as a child and seemed to remember. Grubby, its fair hair thin with use, she cradled it like a baby. She was lost in a world of Grimm and Hans Andersen, of dragons and princesses, of wicked stepmothers, of wolves, gnomes, trolls and fairies. But she had her work to do. Work or a whipping, and no supper and no pretty clothes. Emma, the woman the doctor had sent to take care of her, was busy in the next room. She crept out and down the stairs. She saw Charles. He was no good. Last time she had seen him, he had run away as if she frightened him. Well, there was another man here. Well-dressed and more like the men in Paris. She knew where to find him. She had watched him from the top of the stairs. She had no idea he was her father. She had no recollection of the house, only that she could find her way about it without difficulty.

She opened the door of the study. Yes, there he was. Sitting at a desk. She hoped he would like her dress. It was so pretty.

She smiled sweetly at the man, dropped a curtsy, and lay down on the sofa. Tonight she would get chocolate and no whipping.

Ever since their return from France, Edward Lenton had spent his time in the study, raging. That bloody Carmine. How she had tricked him! There was no honesty left in the world, no straight dealing. Thousands she'd had out of him. Thousands of pounds—and then to hoist him with his own petard. His girls. Not that he gave a damn about them really. Girls were nothing to him. Just property. Not like a boy. And things had been going so well with Ellen till Lavinia had burst the bubble of his happiness. A cuckold, that was what he was. If only he could prove it. But they'd been too clever for him. You could never catch a lawyer. May had never left her side, day or night. So she said, anyway. He'd tried to bribe her. Promised her a monkey if she'd talk—say what he wanted her to say. But she had laughed in his face. A servant! No respect.

He had not heard the door open, but feeling someone in the room he looked up. Eva was there on the sofa, her dress disordered. She felt his eyes on her, smiled and said: "I am ready, sir."

Good God! They had done this to her. Evangeline, his daughter! How they had fooled him. Caramine, Delphine, Jumelle, Lavinia—the bloody lot of them. He sprang up and almost ran into the gun room.

The soft evening light, still faintly rose with the sunset, shone on the blued gun barrels in their glass cases, turning them mauve. Shotguns, rifles.

Betrayed all around. Muriel fooling him with a son. *My heir*. Ellen. Lavinia. He, Edward Pardaine John Charles Lenton—a cuckold. Evangeline . . . his hands shook as he turned the key standing in the lock of a glass-fronted case. . . .

In the drawing room Lavinia heard a shot. There was no one staying at Mortal who might have taken a stroll with a gun. But there was nothing extraordinary about a shot. A keeper killing vermin—a crow, a magpie, a hawk. A hundred reasons for a shot. She dreamed on. Part of her mind occupied with what might have been, part with what she was going to do. Another Lady with a Lamp.

Finding her charge gone, Emma ran downstairs. Seeing the study door ajar, she peeped in. There she was on the sofa, crying her heart out. She went in but no one else was there. Just the sobbing child. Emma pulled down her dress and dragged her to her feet.

"Don't whip me," the girl wept. "I tried. I tried so hard."

How was she going to tell Madam? But she must be told. This was not the first time—and with her father, too. Thank God, he was not there. She could not have faced him. She must get the girl back up-stairs and into bed. She'd tell Doctor Jarvis when he came tomorrow.

It was only when Edward did not come in to dinner that Lavinia thought of him.

"See if you can find the master," she said to the butler. "Ask Benton if he has changed." She hoped Edward had decided to eat by himself. These meals, silent except for banalities, meant to deceive the servants, were becoming a greater and greater strain.

The butler returned. "There has been an accident, Madam. A gun accident. I have sent for the doctor."

The shot! She remembered the shot. She heard hooves hammering down the drive in a wild gallop, and then she fainted. The day had been too much for Lavinia Lenton.

Doctor Jarvis, telling a stableboy to take his sweating horse out of the dogcart and bait him, went into the house, bag in hand. A gun accident so early in the season? He'd attended several in his life, but they had all been at big parties. The stable yard and house were fully lit. Everyone was up, no one wanted to miss anything.

The butler took him into the library. They had made up the big sofa there as a bed, not wanting to move the wounded man. Some attempt had been made to bandage him with linen sheets torn into strips.

"It's his face, doctor," the butler said. "Must have been messing about with a gun." No servant was going to suggest his master's suicide or suicide attempt, or be able to recall any possible reason for such an act.

"Send someone for a basin of warm water and some towels," the doctor said, as he bent over the patient and unwound him from a cocoon of bloody bandages.

Edward Lenton was conscious, his eyes open. He seemed to recognize the doctor but could not speak. When he had cleaned the wound and disinfected it with a carbolic solution, the doctor bandaged him again. A professional job in a criss-cross of absorbent bandages over moist pink lint. The butler, who had been assisting him, was very white and sweating.

"A drink, sir?" he said.

"I think so. For both of us. You look as if you need one."

"Bit shaky, sir. Not used to blood. And the shock . . . the master . . ." Leaving the sentence unfinished, he went to the dining room. When he returned with a decanter, two glasses and a syphon of soda water, he looked better. The doctor poured the drinks.

"Now," he said, "we'll go to the gun room. That's where it hap-pened, isn't it?"

"Yes sir. In there." The butler pointed to the open door. They went in together. The gun, a deer-stalking rifle, lay on the floor in a pool of blood, now coagulated and almost black.

"You'd better have that mess cleaned up," Dr. Jarvis said. "And the rifle, too. If it had been a shotgun, he'd have blown his head off. Now where's Mrs. Lenton?"

"Here I am!" Lavinia stood in the doorway. "I fainted, Dr. Jarvis. They put me to bed and I fell asleep. When you came, they woke me." She looked beautiful in a white satin dressing gown with lace insertion that trailed out on the floor behind her. Her long hair was down, loose and unconfined. "We'll go into the drawing room," Mrs. Lenton said, leading the way.

"Sit down, my dear," the doctor said. "I'm going to give you a drink. A brandy and soda. Medicinally, of course. My favorite prescription."

"Don't let's beat about the bush, Dr. Jarvis. How badly is he hurt? Will he die?"

"I don't think so. It might be better if he did. As far as I can see, he'll never speak or move again."

"An operation?"

"I don't know. I don't think it would do any good. And drink your drink. Doctor's orders." He smiled at her. She was a beautiful woman. It had occurred to him that pretty women and children were always met with smiles. Theirs was a world decorated with smiles, as the world of Royalties was decorated with flags.

"Eva?" Lavinia said.

"I'll look in before I go. And I'll be back tomorrow." He took out a big gold hunter and snapped it open. "Today," he corrected himself, "at ten."

When he had gone, Lavinia told Benton to fix himself up a bed in the library and call her if there was any change. She told the butler a stableboy must stay on duty and a horse be kept saddled. Then she went upstairs to her room where May was waiting, wide-eyed. The master had shot himself; she was hoping he would die.

But she got no news from her mistress. All Lavinia said was: "Thank you, May. You can go to bed now."

"A cup of tea," the girl said.

"All right, my dear. A cup of tea. Bring two cups."

If Edward had killed himself, she could have married John after a year's mourning. Black—mauve—gray. She saw the mourning colors in her mind. But she could not leave a cripple. A mentally defective daughter was bad enough. She could have left Evangeline. The girl did not know her. But this was different. Till death does them part. And how nearly death had parted them! But he was going to be helpless. Perhaps God had punished them this way. It would be worse than death for a man like Edward. A hunting, sporting, womanizing man. He could not speak. He could not write. Her fortune was back in her hands. He could not divorce her. Suddenly she made up her mind: she would become John's mistress. Not openly, of course. Just his occasional and very discreet mistress.

May came in with the tea.

"Pour it out, May."

The maid drank hers sitting on the edge of her chair. Thank God for May, a girl she could trust.

At ten the doctor came, changed the dressing and confirmed his diagnosis. No operation. And he'd sent to London for two male nurses. Three nurses at Mortal, Lavinia thought.

"I'm going to see Evangeline now," he said. When he came back, he looked upset. "Let's go into your boudoir, Lavinia"—he'd known her since childhood—"I have bad news for you."

"More bad news? What is it this time?"

"It's shocking. Now I know why Edward shot himself. Of course we'll call it an accident, but God knows he had reason."

"You didn't get it from Eva?"

"No, from Emma. And I want the truth about Eva. You said she'd had a shock. Had been raped. But there's more than that. Tell me all of it." Then he told her what Emma had said. The effect a man had on Eva. "Ghastly," he said. "They must have trained her there to lie down and lift up her clothes whenever a man approached her. Whipped her if she didn't. Given her chocolate if she was a good girl. Good . . ." he said. "By God! I got a little out of Eva, too. No wonder she was so damaged. Multiple rape, I thought it was. But it wasn't. It was man after man, day after day. A child like that. . . ."

"I'm going to fight it, Dr. Jarvis. The whole abominable traffic. Eva is not an isolated case. Hundreds, thousands of girls are treated like her." Lavinia was walking up and down the room. "Will you give evidence when the time comes? Of her physical and mental condition, I mean?"

"I will, Lavinia. It's an abomination. I had heard things, of course."

"Well, I know them. I've seen some of it. But John Longbeach knows more, and he's going to help me."

"You'll run into trouble," he said. He did not just mean opposition.

He meant the trouble that comes to a pretty woman when she associates herself with a handsome, brilliant, young man. The doctor said he would be back tomorrow, and said goodbye.

A dozen people called to inquire about Edward in the afternoon. The news had spread like a fire in the dry tinder of a county that was always short of gossip. John was among them. When they were alone between two callers, he said:

"I've had an answer from my friend, Stead, of the *Gazette*. He's game for a crusade even if it ruins him. He's what I said—a real Christian."

"We'll win, John. In the end, right and the truth must triumph."

"I hope so." He did hope so, but he was a lawyer. Justice did not always come out on top, and because he was her lawyer no one took exception at finding him with Lavinia in a crisis like this.

19 : The Gazette

It did not take long for the news of Edward Lenton's accident to reach the London papers. "A regrettable gun accident at Mortal, the country seat of Mr. Edward Lenton . . . severely injured . . . the well known sportsman . . ."

"Poor old Edward," Sir John Froman said, looking up from his armchair at Hart's.

"And bang goes the pheasant shooting at Mortal," Jack Brag, sitting next to him, said. "What about a glass of Madeira, John?" And he rang the little bell on the small table beside him. "Nasty things, guns. Hard to understand it, though. Been shooting since he was twelve."

"Accidents will happen, Jack. But he's a bad man to be pinned down. Very active chap, Edward was. Liked the girls, too, I understand. Never knew him well, but I liked him."

"I liked him, too. And some of the best pheasant shooting in England. Wonder how it happened? We'll never know, I suppose."

"Some people say it wasn't an accident. What do you make of that?"

"Nonsense, old boy. He had everything. Health, a rich wife—a beauty, too—and plenty of interests."

"Well, you never know, do you? My wife sat next to him at dinner once. Didn't like the chap."

"Why?"

"No reason. You know how women are. She just didn't. Suggested having them down once, but she wouldn't ask them."

At No. 23 the affair took on a different aspect. Mrs. Caramine, having a cosy tea with Ada Prettyman, pushed a newspaper into her hand. "That's what I call a judgment, Ada. It almost makes me believe in God." Of course Ada knew nothing about Delphine and the girls.

"He was a good client," she said.

"We don't need him, my dear. A bad hat, taking him all around. Arrogant."

"You always made a big fuss of him, Carrie."

"I know I did. And I had my reasons. But they're over now."

When the news seeped through to the girls, they were mildly amused. No more fun and games for him, eh? They had little feeling for their clients. Some were better than others, or less bad. None of them treated the girls as human beings.

"Like a lot of bloody horses," Flossie said. "When they want a good ride, they come here. Well, from the look of it, he's had his last." There was no particular venom in her voice. It was all quite matter-of-fact.

Flossie and Millie were sitting in Daisy's room. They were all in varying states of undress. A maid was lacing Millie's corset, pulling on the woven silk tapes.

Daisy suddenly began to sob. "The bastard," she said. "The bloody bastard. He always hurt me."

"Then what the hell are you crying for?"

"Because I'm so 'appy, that's why." She flung herself face downwards on the bed. "I'm glad," she said. "I'm glad. Glad. Glad."

Flossie sat down beside her and stroked her hair. Daisy was a kind of pet to them all. She was the baby, the doll. She was the only real Cockney among them, and they thought her intensely funny. They were all middle-class girls who had gone wrong. Their stories were almost identical. Daughters of shopkeepers, of auctioneers, of clerks. They had been seduced, become pregnant and either had been thrown out of their homes, or run away with a man who had later abandoned them or sold them into a brothel. Daisy's tale was different. She had seen a drunken harridan selling her daughter to a woman in an East End slum, and had said: "Take me with you, too." Anything would be better than the life she was leading at home.

"How old are you girl?" the woman said.

"Thirteen, Ma'am, and big for it, ain't I."

"Thirteen and you want to come, kid? Come and welcome."

She had not known thirteen was the legal age of consent, because she had never consented to what had been done to her since the age of ten, when her tubercular mother had died and left her to an aunt whose husband had abused her. Because she was pretty, and funny, and had character, Mrs. Caramine had bought her for the other house. Then she had been promoted to No. 23. She had no complaints. Even the men were gentle with her. All except Lenton, and now he'd bother her no more.

Daisy turned and rested her head on her elbow, her fair hair hung over her face and bare shoulders.

Flossie lifted her petticoat and gave her a slap. "Silly little bitch," she said, and pulled her head onto her breast. "It's over, ducks. He's the one to cry. No more greens for him, not at 23 nor anywhere. Funny," she said to Millie, "how they want it. Randy lot of bastards, though you'd never think it when they come in, dressed up to the nines."

Riding Nestor in the park, Lavinia pulled up to look at the house. How beautiful it was! Mortal. Mort Hall. The Domesday Book house. Castle, manor, hall. What changes it had seen! The Keep was Norman. The castle sacked by Cromwell. A single crenellated tower and a portion of the wall was all that remained of it. And the great arched gateway with its carved armorial bearings—its motto MORT. Death. Dead. Part of the house was black-beamed Tudor, part Queen Anne. There was a bow-windowed Georgian wing. No one except Cromwell had ever destroyed any of it. Each generation seemed to have added something. The vast estate had dwindled to some ten thousand acres of farms and woodland. The revenue was not large. Most of her money came from the banking business her great grandfather had founded with money made during his service with the old John Company.

Always beautiful, today the beauty of the old house—a history of England, its pages stone—tore at her heart. The autumn foliage stained the woods with gold and russet brown. The red copper beeches were almost black. Tall French poplars were slim, gold pencils, sharp in the blue cloudless sky. The woods, the spinneys, the coverts. The cultivated fields, rich brown ploughland, now green with young winter corn and blue-gray roots. Hedges neatly cut and laid—dark strings climbing the rolling land. She heard a cock pheasant and smiled sadly. That bird would live till he died in a fight, or of old age, or a fox got him. There would be no more shooting at Mortal while she lived. She had always hated it.

Beautiful, all so beautiful. But so tragic. Poor Edward. She could afford to be sorry for him now. And Eva. But a place as old as Mortal had seen tragedy before. There were dungeons with rusted chains masoned into the wall beneath the Keep. There had been strange and brutal doings here. Tortures, executions. There was at least one good thing. Eva remembered nothing. Her mind was blank. She had even forgotten how to read.

She patted Nestor's neck. He'd never be the same horse again. But she'd never hunt again, so what did it matter? He made a good hack even if he couldn't jump. Tomorrow was going to be a big day. She was meeting John Longbeach in London and he was taking her to see Mr. Stead. If he did what she wanted, the fat would be in the fire. John had not told him the whole story, only part of it. Even John did not know it all. It would be wonderful to see John again. She had only seen him once since the accident. She would keep the house in Berkeley Square open now that she was going to spend more time in London. Her life had changed. No longer the *châtelaine* of a house famous for its parties. Mortal was asleep again, the way it had been in her parents' time. Country houses could do that. Sleep, rest, doze. And come alive again, gay with children and young people and then, as if exhausted, lie back for a generation and rest in the arms of the great trees that surrounded them. Fold their wings like butterflies, concealing their glory.

She took May to London with her. First class, not in a third-class carriage, which was the way so many maids travelled. May had changed too. Travel, her Madam's unhappiness, extra wages, the new clothes Madam had bought her—all this had turned her from a country girl into a young woman of some style. A real lady's maid and companion. She spoke better, her vocabulary was larger. She carried herself straighter, she was no longer shy.

There was a man in their carriage who got out at the first stop. When they were alone, Lavinia said:

"May, we are going to see Mr. Longbeach in London."

"I'm glad, Madam."

"So am I, May, but it's not what you think. We are going to see a newspaperman, a friend of his, a Mr. Stead. I'm going to tell him the story and see if he'll publish it."

"Oh Madam, not about Miss Eva and Miss Betty?" The girl began to cry. "In the papers?" she said. "Oh, oh! What will people say?"

"That's what I want to see."

"Oh Madam, don't. Don't, please! There's things that should not be talked about."

"That's why those things happened, May."

"Oh Madam, but you . . . they'll talk about you, Madam. My Madam." The girl flung herself on her knees and pressed her face into Lavinia's lap.

"I know what they'll say, dear," Lavinia said. "And I'm ready for it. But if it's too difficult for you, I'll find you another place. I'll give you a wonderful character . . ." Lavinia paused. The last time the word had been mentioned was when she had refused to give one to Ellen, and driven her on to the streets.

May jumped up, swaying with the motion of the train. "No, Madam. No never. Not if you was to commit murder."

Lavinia pulled her down into her arms and kissed her. Servant, maid, this girl was more like a daughter or a sister.

"Thank you," she said. "I'd hoped you'd feel like that. Now dry your eyes and listen to me. This is a dirty business, a horrible business. You are going to hear and find out things you never dreamed of, but there's only one way to stop it and that's my way. I'll lose my friends, I know that. But I'll make others. There are good people in the world and we've got to find them, even if we wade up to our necks in muck. It may be dangerous, too. You're not afraid?"

"Not with Madam. I'm not afraid of ought. Not May Springer, whose dad worked for the old master, and granddad too."

Lavinia took her hand. They were still holding hands when the train pulled into Paddington. They took a cab to Berkeley Square. May helped Lavinia change from country tweeds into a navy blue coat and skirt. The coat was frogged, Hussar fashion, with black silk cord. She put on a small black hat with a veil, a boa of black cock plumes iridescent with green and purple, black gloves and black button boots.

"Madam looks lovely," May said. She thought: That's what he'll think. Mr. John. If only the master would die and she could marry Mr. John! As usual, she had tried to make her mistress wear a corset.

"A black one, Madam. A black evening corset. It would go so well."

"Who's to see it but you and me?"

"Yes, Madam," May said.

But Lavinia knew what was in her mind. She almost laughed. She felt like that too. Like a girl going to meet her lover, only she'd never felt like that when she was a girl. She'd never been in love before.

John Longbeach met the women at the offices of the *Gazette* in Northumberland Avenue. He seemed surprised to see May.

"She's in it with us, John," Lavinia said.

"They were my young ladies, sir," May said.

"You're just a girl, May. You'll hear things." He stumbled over the words. "I mean you're not married, May. Things . . ." He gave up.

"I'm a country girl, sir. I've seen things. Bulls, horses. Men and girls in the haycocks. I may not be married, sir, but there's nought I don't know about the likes of that, and worse too."

"Very well," John said. "Come along in." He took them through an office where a lot of men were working at desks, and opened a door of mahogany and frosted glass. A small, thick-set man in heavy glasses got up.

"This is Mrs. Lenton, Will," John said. "Mrs. Lenton and Miss May . . ." He looked at the girl.

"May Springer, sir," she said. "Like a spaniel. It's easy to remember."

"Lavinia—Mr. William Stead," John said. "I've told him the story." They shook hands.

"If what John says is true, you are a brave woman, Mrs. Lenton. You realize the consequences?"

"I do. But I think you are a brave man, Mr. Stead."

"Not as brave as all that. The *Gazette*'s a crusading paper. We like to lift stones and see what's underneath."

"You won't like what you're going to find, Mr. Stead."

"I know a lot, Madam. Your children are not the first to be abducted. Not even the first upper-class children, though perhaps none of the real aristocracy has been taken before."

"Then why have we not heard about it?"

"Because the parents were afraid of the scandal. The girls were gone. I'm not sure even if they wanted them back once they had gone."

"Do you mean that?"

"I do, Mrs. Lenton. And now let us get something clear. To discuss this matter, we must be frank. There can be no euphemisms. Are you prepared for that?"

"We are," Lavinia said.

"Very well. In the age in which we live, hypocrisy has reached its apogee. It's a swing of the pendulum, away from the ribaldry of the Regency, when well-bred women showed their breasts and talked like stableboys. Now we pretend that as long as a subject is not mentioned, it doesn't exist."

"I know. That's why we are here."

"Did you know, Madam, that the age of consent for a girl is only thirteen? And *that,* only after a tremendous fight in the Commons who wanted it kept to twelve? Did you know that parents whose children have been abducted, even if they know where they are and the uses to which they are being put, cannot get them out by any process of the common law of England? There was a case not long ago in Hull," he went on, "where a man kept a children's brothel. It was known as the Infant School. Fourteen girls and the oldest was only fifteen."

Only fifteen, Lavinia thought. Just Eva's age.

"Some were only twelve," Mr. Stead went on. "When their mothers went there to try to get them back, the man cursed them. They had no redress, no power to get them back or see them. In the end he was convicted, Mrs. Lenton, but not for running a children's brothel or stealing children. They got him for selling drink without a license. When I heard this story, I went to Sir James Ingham, Chief Magistrate of the Metropolitan District, and asked him about it. 'Suppose,' I said, 'I brought you an affidavit that a girl was being detained in a house of prostitution, is there any law that can enforce her release?'

" 'Not that I know of,' he said. 'No law in England to protect a girl unless she has property.'

"Then," he went on, "there was the debate in the House of Commons with respect to at what age a girl should be responsible for her own ruin. The Member suggested the age should be raised to fourteen. Another said that it should be reduced to ten. Because, Mrs. Lenton, he said it was hard for a man, having a charge brought against him, not to be able to plead the consent of the child. Mr. Benjamin Waugh and I, and others, are trying to get a bill passed for the abolition of the oath for children of tender years. A case was reported in the *Times* where the counsel for the defense objected to the girl's evidence because she was not old enough to understand the nature of an oath. The judge called the child up to him and asked her what she knew about the Supreme Being—they had put her on the table just under his head—and she burst into tears. The counsel for the prosecution, hoping to make the question simpler, asked her: 'Now my dear, who is God?' More tears. The judge said he could not accept her evidence. She was five, Mrs. Lenton. A prison chaplain told me that he visited a home for fallen children near Newport. Fifty girls under ten, all of whom had been violated. In another home at Farnham, there were forty children under twelve years of age in the same condition. Only in four instances, John"—he turned to Longbeach—"have the perpetrators been punished. In London, two men were shown in court to have outraged, respectively, sixteen and twelve children. And only one was convicted. It was pleaded that those under that age did not understand the nature of an oath. In eight weeks, thirty cases involving injury to forty-three girls aged from three to sixteen, have been brought before the Law Courts. Can you imagine this in England? Do you realize the magnitude of these crimes, Mrs. Lenton?" William Stead was trembling with indignation when he sat down. "Did you know all this, Mrs. Lenton?" he asked. "You have suffered a frightful loss, but you are only one of hundreds of suffering mothers."

"I did not realize there was so much of it going on. That it was so . . ."—she searched for a word—"so common. How terrible it is!"

"That is the kind of fact we are going to bring out. Nobody knows it. No nice people. Only the pimps, the procurers, the madams and their customers. Babies too," he went on. "Baby farmers. There's no end to it. No end to the vice in London. But you're the first woman to come to me, ready to see her name in print. Rape," he said. "How many women report a rape? The scandal, their good name. What good can it do, they say? It's over. They want to forget it. Did you know that you have only to go to the slums to find mothers who will sell their daughters for the price of a bottle of gin?"

"Then it's worse than I thought," Lavinia said.

"And the export trade. Hundreds of English girls sold in France and Belgium every year. Sent to Germany, Rumania, to the Argentine, and Asia Minor. Now," he said, "we will have a cup of tea, and then you will tell me your story if you want to."

May was crying quietly. Mr. Stead patted her shoulder.

When they had finished their tea and a boy had taken away the heavy white cups and saucers, Lavinia told him about Delphine and her two girls. Mr. Stead listened, fingertip to fingertip. When she had done, she handed him the letter Dr. Jarvis had given her.

"That's the doctor's certificate," she said. "He agrees to publication. He says so in the letter."

"Now," Mr. Stead said, "you are really sure? You know, Mrs. Lenton, once the cat is out of the bag, it's out."

"I know."

"Very well then. I'll write the piece myself. Banner headlines." Again he said: "You are sure? Once this is out, you are ruined socially."

"I have never cared for a social life."

"What do you say, John? She's your client."

"If she is willing, she should do it. I'll stand by her."

"We are going through with this, Mr. Stead," Lavinia said. "No one is better qualified than I to stand it." Almost objectively, she went on: "There is even plenty of money when we need it."

"We'll need it, Mrs. Lenton. But not now." Stead got up. The interview was over.

That night John took Lavinia and May to dinner at the Trocadero. "I'm never going to be seen in public with you alone, John," Lavinia said.

"You are very wise. With what is going to happen, your reputation is of the greatest importance." He looked at May and raised his glass.

"Here's to the brave Mrs. Lenton and her Springer." May laughed. Poor kid, John was thinking, she was in deep waters. They all were.

Next day the *Gazette* came out.

FAMOUS HOSTESS HAS DAUGHTERS ABDUCTED BY
FRENCH GOVERNESS

Mrs. Edward Lenton of Mortal in Gloucestershire . . . The younger child, Elizabeth, is still being searched for. The eldest, Evangeline, was found in a Paris *bordello*. She has been physically damaged and her mind is deranged.

Dr. Jarvis' medical certificate followed. After that came an editorial on the subject of child prostitution.

By ten o'clock the edition was sold out and two more editions were printed.

At No. 23 Coak Street, Mrs. Caramine was livid. That bloody woman! Who'd have thought it to look at her? That she'd have dared to do this? Changing the age of consent from twelve to thirteen was bad enough, but all this publicity. . . . Now she had set the pattern, other people would be going to the papers. Had they no feelings any more? No sense of shame? For the first time she regretted Edward's accident. He'd never have allowed this to happen. His name spread over the papers. His daughter publicly called a whore by her own mother.

In the clubs the reaction was much the same. If Edward Lenton had not been incapacitated, she would not have dared to do it. An unnatural mother. What was the good of washing dirty linen in public? Of course there were child prostitutes. There always had been. That had all been gone into only a few years ago, when the age of consent had been raised. Bloody nonsense. A bloody scandal, that's what it was. . . .

There were some indignant letters to the *Gazette* for publishing such filth. Their general tone was that sleeping dogs should be let lie.

Since Lavinia saw no one but her own servants, there had been no social repercussions. Three days after the paper had come out, she went to see Mr. Stead again.

"What do we do now?" she asked.

"Nothing," he said. "Nothing. It's a dead horse, Mrs. Lenton. It's no use flogging a dead horse."

"Then it was for nothing," she said. "Just a nine-day wonder?"

"No, Madam. Just the first shot in the battle we are going to fight." He pushed a pile of letters towards her. "Friends," he said. "People on our side."

"Why didn't you publish them too?"

"I don't want controversy. Let this soak into the public conscience. We must form a committee, get more evidence and fire another salvo. Do you know the real enemy, Mrs. Lenton?"

"Vice?"

"No, Madam. It is apathy."

The thing was to interest other people. Lavinia Lenton soon found how hard it was going to be. They did not want to listen. She spoke first to her friend, Dorothy Ventnor. If she could interest her husband. . . . He was an M.P.

"He wouldn't touch it with a barge pole, my dear," she said. Dorothy was an attractive woman of her own age. She and Lavinia had come out together. A small pert brunette, with a common nose—was how her enemies described her. The right kind of nose was Roman or Greek. Norman, high-bridged. *Retroussé,* tip-tilted, was common but, by God, it was attractive. Dorothy was what people called a *jolie laide.* Feature by feature, nothing much. But put the lot together, assemble it, the big brown eyes, the arched eyebrows, long lashes, large full mouth, ears like rose petals, the small heart-shaped face set on a beautiful neck rising out of a pair of creamy shoulders, and you had a charmer. Her hair was dark brown, very fine and thick. A real shawl when it was down.

"And what about you, Dorothy?" Lavinia asked. "Will you help me?"

The brown eyes blazed. "I'll help you, darling. The men, God bless them, are such cowards and, do you know, I think the biggest cowards of all are the M.P.'s. They want to please everybody. This is woman's business. It's women they are sending abroad. Bad enough the way they send shiploads of old horses to be slaughtered on the Continent, but girls . . ."

"My girls," Lavinia said. "I don't think we shall ever find baby."

How Betty had hated being called "baby," but that was what she was to Lavinia. More now than ever, as the full horror of it all clouded her every act.

"And Evangeline? Is she better?"

Lavinia ignored the remark. By-passed it. "Do you know, Dorothy, we're going to have to be very open about all this. Say things and write things no woman has ever said or written before. I'm going to start with you. You asked about Eva. Well, the conventional answer would be: 'She's better. Happily convalescing in the country down at Mortal. Needs rest and quiet. The doctor says it's just a matter of time.' Time, Dorothy. A lifetime won't put her together again."

"Not all the King's horses," Dorothy said.

"Not all the King's horses, not the Queen herself. And beautiful . . . The girl wrings my heart with her beauty. In a few months she has matured physically. Bloomed, grown, filled out. She has a nurse, as if she was a child, who loves her. Changes her clothes three or four times a day. She loves clothes. New clothes seem to take her mind off things. And Mac, the deerhound, never leaves her. But her mind has gone. She cannot think. And thank God she cannot remember. She just sits and stares."

"Then what is it?" Dorothy said, going over to the big mirror over the fireplace to fiddle with her hair. It would be easier for Lavinia if she could not see her face. Poor Lavinia. Her poor friend. She'd feel better when she got it off her chest. Eva was her goddaughter. She went back in her mind to the christening. The baby in long clothes. The two nurses. The guests. The toasts at luncheon afterward.

"Dorothy," Lavinia said, "Eva cannot be left alone for one instant. If she sees a man—her father, a visitor, a footman—she lies down and pulls up her dress."

"My God, Lavinia!" Dorothy swirled around, a dark blue wave of petticoat and skirt.

"You're the first person I've told," Lavinia said. "Of course the county has the usual garbled version of servants' gossip." How well she knew the talk that seeped upward, by a kind of capillary action, to the long, horse-faced women who made the social rules. She realized they were the enemy. The patina of convention must not crack. The women would fight her, try to muzzle her. They were the ones who condemned divorce, no matter what the cause or the man's offense. And God only knew how close she had come to it herself. . . .

"So that was why Edward . . ."

"Shot himself. Of course. He introduced the woman who stole them into the house as his mistress. He insisted on it. They must learn French, from a French woman. . . . Then when his own daughter lay down on the sofa in front of him, it was too much—even for him. He went straight to the gun room."

"Pity he missed," Dorothy said.

"Perhaps. Perhaps for me. I'm laying my cards on the table, Dorothy. I am beyond shame, beyond caring. I was going to run away with John Longbeach. We are in love. . . ." Dorothy opened her mouth to speak. "Nothing like that. Not yet, but it may come. If it does, we shall be discreet. I always have a chaperone. May. My darling May. What would I do without her? But what I mean is, if we had run away and Edward had divorced me, no one would have listened to a word I said. A divorced woman to them is no better than a whore. But now . . . now I am still Lavinia Mortalland and of Mortal. I still stand for something. For the county, the country, for England. We've been there more than eight hundred years. The lot of them are newcomers compared to us. They'll have to listen. I'll stuff it down their throats."

"How wonderful!" Dorothy said.

"What is?"

"Love, darling. To feel like that about a man. Ready to throw your cap over a windmill. Lose your fortune."

"We spoke of that. John has some means. But now everything is changed. I can't leave Edward when he is helpless."

"Means? Means are not wealth."

"And what has wealth brought me? A husband who married my money and had me thrown in like a pound of tea. A man who has never been faithful to me, who kept one mistress—another governess —in my house for four years. A man who has lost me my children. It's only a few months ago he told me I was thirty-three and old enough to know the facts of life. I said: 'Tell me. I want to know.' Well, now I know. I have eaten of the fruit, Dolly. Oh God, how I have eaten." Lavinia burst into tears.

Dorothy let her cry. That, at least, was one advantage women had over men. The relief of tears. The torrential downpours that washed their spirits clean. Tears did for a woman what a drink did for a man. When Lavinia had cried herself out and dried her eyes, Dorothy said:

"What are we going to do?"

"Form a committee. You, me, Mr. Stead, John, and we'll get others. John knows some people and so does Mr. Stead."

"Professional people?"

"Yes. Lawyers, doctors. A manufacturer or two, but most important of all is the journalist—William Stead. John knew him at Oxford. He is an extraordinary man. I went to see him and give him the story."

"I never knew they went to Oxford."

"He didn't, but John met him when he was there. And he's a Christian. Oh, Dolly—do you know what I mean? A real one—not like us."

"We go to church."

"And why do we? Because it's the thing to do. The gentry must set an example. But they don't believe in Jesus. This man does. That's what's so extraordinary. Do you think Edward's a Christian? Do you think men who use little girls can be Christians, Dolly?"

20 : The Tea Party

"We have to get the facts," Mr. Stead said. "We'll begin with a British Consul. Boulogne, Calais, Antwerp, Brussels, Paris . . ."

"Who's going?" Lavinia asked.

"Mr. Portal and John Longbeach."

"Do they talk French?"

"No, but they'll get an interpreter."

"I'm going," Lavinia said. "I'm going with May. The interpreter would be bribed. They'd get nothing out of him."

"It may be dangerous."

"I think the whole thing is dangerous, Mr. Stead."

"There are immense interests involved. Hundreds of thousands of pounds. And they are people who will stop at nothing. Murder is nothing to them—we know that already. And you still want to go? I must say I'm glad. Because you're right about the interpreter. They won't get the evidence if they can't talk French."

"When do we go?"

"Next month. Mr. Portal can't get away till then."

"November? In Northern Europe?" Lavinia said.

"It may be a good time, Mrs. Lenton. They will be less on their guard. So will you make your plans? Be ready to leave about the twenty-fifth of November and in the meantime see if you can interest any of your friends. We have got to interest people, thousands of people, before we can get Parliament to move. Big people, little people. Lords, ladies, tinkers, tailors. The whole country has to be roused. You've no idea of the job ahead, Mrs. Lenton. Getting the evidence is the least part of it. That's just the crowbar we're going to use to turn the stone of public complacency. But how they will scream! Muck-raker. Dirty linen. The Law of the Land. They'll even talk about Freedom. . . ."

In spite of so many people living in the country, there were still a lot of people in London. Members of Parliament when the House was in session. Civil servants. Officers at the War Office and in the London Command. Barristers. Judges. Parsons. Sailors. Widows who preferred London to the country. And, of course, businessmen by the thousands. Stockbrokers. Newly rich South African mine magnates. Merchants.

Lavinia made a list of twenty names and sent them each a note, ask-ing them to tea the following Thursday to discuss her campaign against child prostitution and the prostitution of women in general.

There were five polite refusals, regretting previous engagements, and one irate letter from Lettice Hawkes saying she must be mad if she thought that she, Lettice, was going to soil her hands and her mind with such things. Of course the loss of her children had been tragic, but surely the least said the soonest mended. What was the good of making a scandal? And who would want to marry Evangeline now that it was all public? Even if she was not quite all there, a marriage would have been possible with a big enough settlement. *Bien entendu,* had everyone not known the story? Really, my dear Lavinia, the sooner you give up these wild plans, the better for everyone. These things should be left to men who understand them better. As to Eng-lish girls being taken abroad, she had spoken to her husband about it and he had made some inquiries at the Foreign Office and the Police Commissioner's Office. No girls except her two had been reported miss-ing for more than a year, and the Consuls abroad reported that though there were some English girls in *those places,* they had gone there of their own free will and had signed papers to that effect. . . .

This was what Lavinia wanted to see for herself. The girls, the papers. Could they speak, much less read, French? And that fool, Urquart Hawkes, M.P. A friend of Edward's and quite obviously on the other side of the fence. The P.S. proved it. After Lettice had remained her affectionate friend, with much love—"and I do hope dear Edward is better"—her husband had written in his own hand: "I trust you will take Letty's advice or you may find yourself in serious trouble. You will not be the first who has put his finger in this pie and regretted it afterwards."

Dear, dear. Almost a threat. Mr. Stead would be interested in this letter.

On Thursday afternoon between four-thirty and five o'clock, fourteen ladies came to Berkeley Square to tea. Pretty women in their thirties and early forties. Lavinia's closest friends and near contemporaries. All married, all rich, all socially prominent, several of them titled. They fluttered upstairs to the big drawing room overlooking the square, like hens going up to roost. Beautiful, brightly colored, perfumed hens; befurred, rustling in silk and taffeta, richly smooth in Lyons velvet. Some came in pairs. Their carriages dropped them and drove on to wait in a side street with the horses rugged.

The women chattered like birds. Oh darling! My dear! Did you know? Did you see? Did you hear? Each scattered her own gossip as if it was grain for the others to peck at. Dear Lavinia, of course we came but I am not sure if you are being very wise. After all, we are only women. And men—a shrug of a green velvet shoulder, a toss of a head that sent the short black ostrich plumes of a bonnet dancing—men are different. And, to be brutal—this was young Lady Portlavish, well known for her outspokenness—they have to get it somewhere and at least it saves us a lot of embarrassment. . . . Mary Portlavish was a dashing redhead with a lovely hourglass figure, and had had a reputation for being on the fast side, as well as a hard rider to hounds, before her marriage. She now lived in London because her husband was in the Cabinet. She was smiling and everyone was nodding their heads. Ostrich plumes, exotic birds, bits of fur trimming, were bobbing up and down as the other women agreed with her. They hoped Mary'd go on and say something really spicy, that they could repeat but would never have dared to say themselves. Something about men and beds. About why they wanted prostitutes; because they could do with them things no lady . . .

Lavinia cut Mary short. "We are all married," she said. "We all know what men do. What they are driven by nature to do. But I am going to stop their doing it to children, and I am going to stop the export of women abroad for immoral purposes."

There was nothing tentative about her speech. The women were shocked. It was so unfeminine to speak like this. To lay down the law. The only old woman in the room—Serena, Dowager Duchess of Saltcombe, a friend of Lavinia's mother—gave a loud, rather vulgar laugh.

"That's it, my girl. Give it to 'em," she said. "Time someone stood up to the men."

She was a tall woman of eighty who still stood like a Grenadier. Her face was painted in the old-fashioned way, her hair blatantly dyed. If she had not been a Duchess, she might have been a madam herself. There was no third choice.

"Mealy-mouthed little bitches," she said, "that lie whimpering on your backs, waiting to be served!" She glared around the room. "And not a vixen in the lot of you. No wonder the men go elsewhere to get a live tit. You should have seen my Mama. Madam, I called her. By God, she kept him at it. Can't get blood out of a stone, that was her recipe. When she was in Brussels, they left the dance early and they had to get him out of her bed to go and fight. Waterloo or no Waterloo, the day after it was over she was back in his tent. Never even took his spurs off, she said."

The old lady sat down, the jet bugles on her purple dress shimmering and rustling like black leaves in a storm.

Lavinia said: "Thank you, Aunt Serena"—she had always called her Aunt—and went on, "There must be some checking at the ports. No English girl must be . . ."

The Duchess of Saltcombe was on her feet again. "That's it, my girl. No girls. No old horses. Nothing should leave these shores but Redcoats. Soldiers. That's all we ought ever to send over the sea." She raised her lorgnette and stared round to see if anyone was going to have the hardihood to contradict her.

The tea being brought in created a diversion. The big silver tray, the Queen Anne silver teapot, milk jug and sugar basin. The silver kettle, on its little stand above a spirit lamp, boiling away. Hot muffins and buttered toast under silver covers. Thin triangular sandwiches cut from a cottage loaf. Small cakes. A hunting cake, rich and dark with fruit as a plum pudding. The tea Earl Grey. The footman in Mortal livery of dark red with dark green breeches, a hooded hawk on the oxidized silver buttons.

Talk buzzed like bees. Pretty mouths, pretty lips, white teeth closed over mustard and cress sandwiches. Melted butter ran down ivory chins and was mopped up with tiny, lace-edged napkins. Cups were raised and put back with a little click into the waiting saucers. Ringlets bobbed. Hats, what a variety! Fur bonnets, a kind of shako, a velvet turban, a hat made entirely of pheasant hackles; a red exotic finch fluttered in full flight over a hat made of ermine.

Tea talk. Table talk. Much ado about less than nothing. This was the interval during which the play was being discussed without actually being mentioned. When they had finished, Lavinia would put on the final act and see how much applause she got. Thank God for Serena, the old war horse.

At last the end was reached, of both cake and conversation. Only crumbs remained. And Lavinia, standing with her back to the marble Adam fireplace, feeling the warmth of the coals on her legs and back, said: "Next week I am going to the Continent with some friends—our committee. We are going to see what we can find out there. There will be more articles in the *Gazette*. There will be speeches. You will be able to hear the truth at last."

"Straight from the horse's mouth," the Duchess said.

"And then," Lavinia went on, "you will have to make up your minds. Decide whether you are women or chattels. It won't be an easy decision. Mine was forced upon me. Now all I ask you to do is to talk. Talk to each other and to others. Say what you like about me. But whatever you or anyone else may say, I, we, are going on with it. This is a slave trade. A white slave trade in the flesh of English girls, and we are going to attack it as Wilberforce attacked the slave trade and smashed it fifty years ago."

She could say no more. If she went on, she would break down. The women began their protracted goodbyes. They said how brave she was. How sorry for her they were. None of them but the Duchess offered help.

"You can use my name, girl," she said. "It'll annoy the Duke." She did not care for her son, "a bloody nincompoop." But her name, when they came to printing some broadsheets, would help. As for the other women, they would talk. They seldom got their pearly teeth into anything so juicy as this. . . .

One thing stuck in their minds. Lavinia was going to the Continent with some men. Of course she was taking her maid. They raised their arched eyebrows. What had happened to her children was terrible, but it should be accepted as God's will. Something sent to try her. What good had all this publicity done? What infinite harm could come of it. Calling attention to things that were supposed to be hidden, and ruining her reputation. People of her class did not do good. Not much beyond being Lady Bountiful and looking after their tenants when they were sick. . . .

The women stopped in the hall, waiting for each other. Watching each other come downstairs. They moved, circling in a rustle of rich materials, an aura of perfume, of furs, of reticules, dangling from their arms as they pulled on their tight kid gloves, working them on finger by tight finger, their hats bobbing like the combs of exotic birds. They chattered, excited by thoughts they would never mention. Thoughts of girls being taken by force, here in London, only a few streets away. Of Lavinia going to the Continent on business of this kind. They imagined the conversation. They knew where it must lead. It was impossible to touch pitch without being defiled. And there was another thing, she did not wear a corset. . . . When had that started?

In Mortal Major, John Longbeach was looking at his home. Soon he was going to leave it. His great adventure and his life's work would begin with Lavinia, his love, and their attack on organized vice. On what was now called the white slave trade—the export of English girls to the brothels of Europe and South America, and to the harems of North Africa and the East.

The house, half-timbered Tudor with later additions, stood back from the road. Once, a hundred years ago, it had been a farm. Some apple and pear trees, gnarled and mossed with age, were all that remained of the orchards. The farm buildings had been torn down or converted into stables, and the house itself had settled back, its roof tree slightly arched, its walls out of the plumb, into comfortable retirement. Old James Longbeach, not old then, had bought the place when he married for its settled beauty, for its privacy and its stables. He was a hunting man. Mortal Major, since then, had crept out toward it. No rushing development scheme, just a slow pushing out from the cobbled market place as if the town, like a man in age, was putting on weight and, corpulent with prosperity, had slacked its belt and spread. But Tidworth still remained relatively isolated, surrounded by paddocks that, had the place been a little larger or more pretentious, could easily have been called a Park. There were some notable trees in the grassland—two great copper beeches, some sculptured elms, old oaks and a giant ash. It was what people called a gentleman's property. Big enough for half a dozen guests with stabling for eight horses and able to supply a little rough shooting. Rabbits, a hare or two, a covey of partridges and perhaps a pheasant. Not shooting in the full sense of the term, but with enough game to make a walk with a gun and a cocker worthwhile for a little sport or something for the pot.

This was the home James Longbeach had brought his young wife to, and John's mother after her death. The house John had been born in, almost an extension of his mother's womb in its warm security. It was part of him, with its clipped yews and holly hedges, its honeysuckle arbor, its herbaceous borders of delphinium, foxglove, hollyhock, Michaelmas daisy, and chrysanthemum, standing like soldiers among the smaller plants—borage, marguerites, iris, Christmas roses, salvias, pinks, and primulas, bare now but a sight in summer.

There was a flagged herb garden and a small rose garden. There were kennels and the hutches where, as a boy, he had kept his rabbits, guinea pigs, and ferrets. About it all was a sense of habitation. The walls seemed to echo history. Other boys had kept their pets here, bright little girls had come out to see them and had been kissed. He had kissed Lavinia here once, when she was a child. Older lovers had walked hand in hand on the flags. Mothers and wives had stood by the sundial as if they could change time, as they waited for their men at the wars. For hundreds of years pigeons had bowed and cooed on the roofs, and bantams had crowed in the stable yard. It was a piece of England's slow, green country heart.

Inside, it was the same. The brick and stone floors worn with a thousand boots in their passing. The wooden floors upstairs listed slightly like a ship to port or starboard. The furniture was all solid mahogany that glowed with care, like the hide of a well-groomed horse. Regency, early Victorian, Queen Anne. Stuff that had belonged to the governor's father and grandfather. To his mother's people. There were some family portraits of red-faced men and their plump ladies. Sporting prints, Morland's, Herring, a small Landseer of a collie herding sheep in a snowstorm. Black silhouettes of relatives, their names written on the backs of their bird's-eye maple frames. And everywhere fox masks mounted on little oaken shields, and white-tipped brushes hanging from nails. In the hall there was a rack for crops and whips. Staghorn and bone-handled, their plaited thongs wound around them, their tasselled lashes dangling against the plain paper of the wall.

It was difficult to believe that a place like this had been Ellen's background, too. Less opulent, perhaps, because this house was opulent in its solid comfort, but the same in principle. She had lived the same way, had listened to the blackbirds sing and watched the thrushes tug their breakfast worms from summer lawns. Continually, John's mind went back to her, and to the Mortal girls. There could be no turning back now. He owed it to England, to this house, to history and to himself. Only a few hours away in London, these things were going on. If only he could comfort Lavinia. Could jump on his mare and gallop over and take her in his arms. In his mind he felt her body, soft and supple in his hands. He felt her crying for him, her woman's body. How was it that men who had this could want the other? How could Edward have done what he did? Take by force, enjoy mastering a woman—a child even—as if she were a wild horse to be conquered only by whip and spur. There must be some inexplicable pleasure in brutality that he did not understand. He supposed men like Edward

Lenton had been brought up with brutality. How lucky he had been with his parents! The governor, irascible but kind, his mother the gentlest of women. And he had not been to boarding school. The Army, where they still flogged men for having a dirty button. Forty less one. Thirty-nine strokes of the cat laid on by the drummers. The young officers vying with each other for toughness and hardness of heart. That was it, he supposed. They learnt to show nothing, to feel nothing. To brag about their seductions. To drink and to whore-monger.

There would not be many more nights at home before they were off to the Continent to get the evidence Stead wanted. He and Portal, with Lavinia and May for companions. They were going to see the British Consuls first. Then visit the Police. What a thing for a woman like Lavinia to do! Out of Mortal into a cesspit. He thought of Jumelle, the slave trader, again; and the others he was soon to meet.

Mrs. Longbeach looked at her husband. Something was the matter. Something serious. "What is it, Mr. Longbeach?" she said. She had always called him "Mr. Longbeach."

"What is it, my dear? It's John. He's riding for a fall in this business."

"What business?"

"This girl business. Houses of ill-fame. Abductions and so on."

"I still don't understand, Mr. Longbeach."

"You are not supposed to understand, Mrs. Longbeach. No woman can understand. Not even the Queen, particularly not the Queen."

"But if it's girls and women, sir, it is woman's business."

"It may be. But it will ruin John. That and Lavinia Lenton. He's in love with her. Can't you understand that? Moony, that's what he is. A moony lawyer."

"But she's married."

"To a cripple and a bad hat at that. And she's a woman, a beautiful woman. By God, there ought to be no pretty women," old Longbeach said. "There's talk now. There're a lot of them like you with this 'woman's business,' putting their pretty fingers into the pie. There'll be no end to it once it begins."

Mrs. Longbeach said no more. She'd talk to John, he'd tell her. Risks? What did risks matter if it was for women? She'd been lucky, one of the lucky ones. Old James, clean as a nut and straight as a die. Kind, considerate. But she'd heard stories. She knew things. That was the trouble. Men refused to believe that women knew anything, or had brains. And Lavinia? Lavinia was a good woman. She would do nothing wrong. Lenton would not last, she was sure of that. Then . . . She let her mind run on. John had never married. Perhaps he had always been in love with Lavinia. He'd known her since childhood. But what could he have done? A country lawyer's son and a great heiress. But now she was no longer a girl. She was a grown woman, and still young enough. In her mind she saw the children, heard their laughter. She knew in her heart that if it was not Lavinia, there would be no grandchildren. He was that kind of man. The fires were burnt down. The wild, wild-oat fires that ripped young men to pieces. She smiled. How surprised James would be if he knew what she knew! What she thought. John's love would be stronger now than a boy's. More steadfast and, curiously enough, probably more passionate. She knew what was in his mind because she was his mother. She could read his brooding eyes. She had picked up odd bits of talk. This was a Cause, a Christian Cause. His love for Lavinia was only a part of it. Everyone knew about the girls being gone. Everyone knew where they had gone. Why they had gone. Everyone was thinking about the position of women. Instruments of men's pleasure, breeders of sons. Heiresses who were married for it. How times had changed! In her mother's time, women had suffered too. But they had stood up for themselves. Hearty, earthy times those were, when a spade was called a spade. When she got John alone, she'd talk to him. Say she was on his side. Of course people knew about this traffic in women, but it had had to be brought out into the open. She could help. Women like her—mothers, grandmothers in their sixties, could do a lot. We have power, she thought. Power in the home, and there are a lot of us.

John had gone for a walk. He walked and rode a lot now. He could not bear to keep still. This was even bigger than he had thought it was. The money involved was unbelievable, and what would people not do for money? The thing was an octopus. In the middle of it, its body as it were, were the Caramines, the brothel keepers. Then the arms ran out. The tentacles of supply—the pimps, the seducers, the bullies, the informers, the keepers, the abortionists, the immoral doctors, the midwives, the innkeepers. Even the whores themselves, intent on reducing others to their own status, and then the demanders, crying for their supply. This was where they were going to run into trouble. Some of the richest and most powerful men in England. Generals, Cabinet Ministers, M.P.s, peers of the realm. Flesh eaters. Cannibals. How completely shocking it was. He thought of Lavinia's girls. The horror that had deranged Eva's mind. And little Betty? Ellen, the virtuous country girl, who had succumbed to vice. If the girls had been recovered well and unhurt, Lavinia would have come to him, because Edward would never have attempted suicide. Well, they might have gone to South Africa too. There were openings in a new country for a good lawyer. But now the dream was over. Eva could not be left and Lavinia was not a woman to leave a husband—even if she hated him—who was so utterly crippled. And besides there could be no stain on the character of a woman leading a crusade. Calumny would finish it. So there it was. There it lay like a body, their love dead, before it had been born. Yet, in another way, it was alive. They acknowledged it with their eyes, with occasional touches of their hands, when they were alone. It had a certain terrible, ascetic beauty, like a blood horse in heavy bit. Its forced restraint were the bonds of convention and will that held them apart. Since he had known Lavinia and learnt the truth about this commerce of love, he had been near no woman except Ellen in that swift affair that had meant nothing beyond proving the vulnerability of men. He had even got over his shame, for the act had been as unself-conscious as that of an animal. It was Ellen who puzzled him. To how much pressure had she been subjected? He knew now that he had loved Lavinia since boyhood.

His mother was up when he came in, which surprised him.

"John!" she called. "John!"

"Mother, what is it?"

"Come and talk to me. Your father is asleep."

He went into the drawing room and kissed his mother's forehead.

"Sit down," she said. "And tell me about this business you are in with Mrs. Lenton. Your father is very upset about it."

"Tell you, Mama? It's not a thing to talk to ladies about."

"Isn't that why it has happened? There has been a lot of talk, John, about Mrs. Lenton's interview with the *Gazette*. A lot of people think she should not have said anything. But they'll come around in time. It's just the shock of it, that such things should go on in England."

"So you know about it?"

"I read the papers and I have plenty of time to think. That's really what I wanted to tell you. That I know, and that I'm with you, John, even if it hurts your career."

"It may."

"You must do what is right. What you feel is right. And I know about Lavinia, too. That you love her."

"I think I have always loved her."

"I think so too. But be patient."

John Longbeach got up and stood with his back to the mantelpiece. "Patient?" he said. "For how long? Edward may live forever."

"Poor man," his mother said. "Poor Lavinia. Poor, poor Lavinia, losing her girls. And poor you. Kiss me goodnight, John, and leave me alone. I'd like to sit here for a while." She picked up her Bible from the table beside her—she must have been reading it while she waited for him—and adjusted her glasses.

21 : The Consuls

The party going to the Continent was oddly assorted. It consisted of two women, Lavinia Lenton and May Springer, and two men, Longbeach and Portal. Lavinia had not met Mr. Montague Portal till Stead introduced them at Charing Cross. Portal was a cadaverous-looking man who seemed ill at ease. Lavinia felt he did not think there should have been any women, particularly youngish and pretty women, concerned with this business. He thought, she felt—despite his knowledge of her story—that she looked frivolous. It was a frightful and frightening mission they were going on. But she was with John again; legitimately, on business.

Longbeach was careful to pay her no more than the usual attention of a man to a woman. He was equally solicitous of May. Lavinia dreaded the crossing. She hated the sea but, to her surprise, found she was getting used to it. But she dreaded, even more than the channel, what they would find out. She wished she had wired to Monsieur Guitry to meet them. There had been reports from him about Betty. All negative so far.

That night they went to a hotel in Ostend. Next day they went to Brussels to see Her Majesty's Pro-Consul there, Thomas Edward Jeffes, a nice-looking man in his fifties, who seemed surprised to see so many people in his office. They introduced themselves.

"And what may I do for you, sir?" he asked Longbeach.

"A lot, Mr. Jeffes. We are investigating the export of English girls to the Continent for immoral purposes."

"And what brings you to me?" Mr. Jeffes' voice was less genial.

"We came to you," Portal said, "because you should know what British subjects are here."

"I do, sir. I do indeed, and so I ought to. Not only is it my duty, but

I am a member of a charitable organization that helps poor English people in this city. And I must say that I have also heard stories of this nature. I was most indignant too. To think English girls could be brought to a city like this and held against their will. But"—he rubbed his hands together—"when I went into it I came to the conclusion that the girls were not telling the truth."

"They were lying?" Longbeach said.

"Exactly. I think the whole thing is a myth. There is no white slave traffic, Mrs. Lenton. I don't believe it is possible for a virtuous girl to be admitted to a"—he hesitated, looked at Mrs. Lenton and said—"to one of those houses."

Longbeach said: "We believe that there are cases of English girls being taken to brothels and being forced to submit against their will."

"I have heard the same tales," Mr. Jeffes said, "but I don't believe them. I believe that if they expressed a wish to leave they would have been allowed to go. I'll give you a case that I took up. A pretty little girl, who looked about fifteen, Lucy Nash. Yes," he said, "that was her name. Lucy Nash. I heard about her and visited her in hospital. Here was a chance to get at the truth. I said: 'I hope you didn't sign the register with the wrong name, Lucy?' She said: 'No, I didn't.' Then I said: 'How is it the Police have got your name down as Maud Mure? Why did you do that?' 'I didn't do it,' she said. 'I just made a mark and pretended I couldn't write.' They have to have a birth certificate for the police, Mr. Longbeach."

"But it wasn't her own certificate?"

"Apparently not," Jeffes said, as if that explained everything.

"Did she want to get away," Mr. Portal asked, "when you saw her in hospital?"

"She wanted to get out of hospital very badly. But she did not say she wanted to go back to England."

"Did she make a statement of any kind, Mr. Jeffes?"

"Yes, indeed." Mr. Jeffes took a file from his desk. "I'll read you part of it:

When I was sent to hospital I was treated for the cruel lust of which I had been a victim. When I began to recover, fresh horrors were in store for me, and they commenced to operate on me for the purpose of making me capable of prostitution. They did not even give me chloroform, but the students held my hands and feet whilst the operator seemed to cut and tear away my living flesh, inflicting on me agonies I can never describe, besides the intolerable shame. This was repeated at intervals about seven times; and during the operations my screams and appeals to my tormentors were heard, as the other patients told me, over the whole building, and the other girls there used to cry at the sight of my sufferings. The principal doctor seemed to hate me and take a pleasure in prolonging my torments. He would delay the operation, and stop to explain to the surrounding students what was being done, and took no heed of my cries for mercy. When I had been in hospital some time, I begged my tormentor to take pity on me and let me go, as he did other girls, but he would not, and I believe if I had not soon escaped from his hands, he would have tormented me to death or madness.

"Why do you think she told you all that if it was not true?" Portal asked.

"I think she had been coached. Some people"—he looked at them meaningfully—"want to make a lot of such things. Sensation," he said. "Mountains out of molehills."

"Out of torture," Lavinia said.

"How was she made to work in the brothel?" Longbeach asked. "Was she intimidated . . . ill-used?"

"Her story, Mr. Longbeach, was that she was in the house for some days before she was introduced to a man. She said if she hadn't been beaten, she never would have done it. She said she was then brutally raped by several men in succession." He looked at Lavinia apologetically. "But I don't entirely believe her story. It was not corroborated by what I know from the other girls."

"I don't understand the police not acting," Lavinia said. "Are they corrupt?"

Mr. Jeffes smiled. "They say one brothel keeper gave a hundred thousand francs to a Commissioner of Police. I suppose one could call that corruption."

"I see," Mr. Portal said. "And that's how they get over the birth certificate. They'll accept anything. Even one for a woman of thirty if the child is obviously only fifteen."

Mr. Jeffes nodded.

Portal went on, addressing the whole group: "I went into it in London," he said. "Anyone can search the Index at Somerset House for a shilling and obtain a certified copy of a birth certificate for a further two and sixpence. The girls are forced to sign them. Later on they are told that entering France or Belgium under a false name is a crime, so they live in a constant state of terror of the police and naturally don't complain to them."

Her Majesty's Pro-Consul made no comment. It was obvious that as far as he was concerned, the interview was over.

"I am afraid," he said, "that you have come on a wild goose chase. There is no doubt that there are English prostitutes here, and in other European cities, but my own feeling is that they come willingly and are under no restraint."

"That is your considered opinion?" Longbeach said.

"It is."

Quite obviously, there was nothing more to be got out of him. "Well," Portal said, "we can only note your report. And"—he looked at the others—"I think I am speaking for all of us when I say you do not seem to have gone into this question very deeply. I imagine the subject is distasteful to you."

"Most distasteful. What else could it be?"

"Yet these girls are British subjects," Longbeach said.

"Nothing to be proud of, Mr. Longbeach. My own feeling is that the country is well rid of them."

Their next visit was to the police. Here Lavinia's French came in. Longbeach asked the questions and she translated them. To begin with, the police laughed at her.

"White slave traffic, Madame? How could there be? There is no such thing in Belgium. We have a very rigid code of laws governing every aspect of prostitution."

"We believe you, of course, *Monsieur le Préfet,* but perhaps there are isolated cases that have escaped your attention?"

"Perhaps, Madame," he conceded, "but very few."

"Could we see the records?" Longbeach asked.

Lavinia translating, said: "If there are any records of interest, we would pay for copies. Pay very well indeed."

"That would be most irregular, Madame," the *Préfet* said.

"Then it is of no matter," Lavinia said, as she took a bundle of thousand-franc notes from her reticule, looked at them and put them back. She got up to go. The others followed her example. As she reached the door, she turned back.

"We are at the *Splendide,* Monsieur, should anything occur to you that might interest us, and you are passing that way. . . ."

"But certainly, Madame." The *Préfet de Police* smiled politely. He would certainly pass that way. Why not? The records he would give them were old anyway. Letters from Klyberg, a trafficker who had been arrested in Antwerp seven years ago. No one would ever miss them, or care if they were lost. The case was over and done with. It would be nice to make such a pretty lady happy. Though why, in God's name, a woman like her should be mixed up in such an affair as this was beyond him. And then there was the money. Above all, there was the money. She seemed to have plenty of it.

At six-thirty precisely, Monsieur Delbeck, the *Préfet de Police,* was shown into Lavinia's sitting room where she and Longbeach sat sipping a glass of port. They were feeling the cold. Mr. Portal was an abstainer. May was in the bedroom.

The men got up to greet the police officer. He bent over Lavinia's hand.

"A glass of *Porto* to keep out the cold, Monsieur?" she said.

"Certainly, Madame. A thousand thanks." He blew on his hands to warm them.

"You have something for us, I see," Lavinia said.

"A little something, Madame. An old case, but perhaps it gives a picture. Some letters," he said, giving her the manila envelope he had in his hand.

Lavinia glanced at the contents, went to the writing desk, put a thousand-franc note into an envelope and gave it to the policeman.

"*Merci,* Madame," he said.

"It is almost Christmas," Lavinia said. "Shall we say we have exchanged *cadeaux de Noël?*"

"What a charming idea, Madame!" He drank his port and said: "If there is anything more I can do . . ."

"We will write to you," Longbeach said.

Monsieur Delbeck looked at Lavinia.

"He says that we will write to you, Monsieur."

Monsieur Delbeck bowed to Longbeach and Portal. "Enchanted," he said. He kissed Lavinia's hand again and went out.

As soon as the door closed, they looked at the letters. There were three of them. Their meaning was unequivocal:

London, 10 April 1876

My Dear Xavier,

I have just had a visit from your friend Louis who has asked me if I would find two English girls for you. I told him yes. If you can come on Monday next I shall have them all ready, so that you will not lose time. I arranged for Alen of Frascarti, so that he arrived at noon, and at six o'clock left again for Ostend with two packages for which he paid me 300 francs, as Lemoine and everyone pay me now.—Your friend, Klyberg.

P.S. I have two very pretty packages who will suit you very well; two good girls.

The other two were to a different man:

Middlesex Hospital
26 July 1876

My Dear Quoilin,
  My wife has written to you that an accident happened to me on board that boat when leaving Rotterdam. I beg you therefore to do me the service of coming on Monday next to fetch the packages. Come straight to me and you can take them away the same evening. I have a fine tall dark girl, beautiful teeth, fine bust, in a word a handsome woman and a good girl. My wife has kept her with herself for three weeks today. I also have a tall fair girl if you have room for her. I must regret that I cannot go over as I have business in Holland. They have offered me a house at Leyden. Sarah, the woman who keeps the house at Amsterdam, has also asked me for two packages, so that as soon as I can travel I shall make money, and if I take this house at Leyden I shall be my own agent. Awaiting the pleasure of seeing you again, I am, your devoted friend, Klyberg.

London, 4 September 1876

My Dear Quoilin, I do not wish you to miss this fine opportunity. One does not find such a package every six months. She is taller than I am. There is no comparison with the other fair girl who is at the Hague. She is quite healthy, well clad and very ladylike, in a word the very thing for you. 800 francs settle the business for you either in one way or the other. It is "a find," so answer my telegram at once saying at what hour I may expect you. I wish you to have the handsomest woman at the Hague, and even in Holland. If I keep her some days longer with me I run the risk of losing her and that is why I am leaving. If you cannot take her, you can place her for me with Madame Elsie until tomorrow. Always yours, Klyberg.

  The name "Madame Elsie" struck Lavinia. Her own dressmaker. And the word "package," *colis,* described girls as packages to be sent or delivered.
  In addition to the letters, there were some notes giving the names of some English procurers. Dandy Courtney and Carroty Jack, and also the addresses of two clearing houses on the Continent: *Maison Charles,* 18 Canal an Haren in Antwerp, and 42 Rue St. Jean Népomucène in Brussels, and one in London at 39 Dean Street, Soho.
  These revelations in black and white were too much for Lavinia. She felt she could not go down to dinner and had something sent up on a tray for herself and May. The two men dined alone. They had nothing but their mission in common.

Portal said: "We might as well go back." He did not like the Continent. The rich food did not agree with him, the water was not safe and he didn't drink wine.

"All right," Longbeach said, "but I think we'll stay on for a day or two." He had an idea Lavinia would not like it, but it would really clinch things. He'd get into a brothel and try to get out an English girl if he could find one.

22 : The Paradise

"There is only one way to find the truth, Lavinia," Longbeach said. "I am going into one of those houses."

"How, John? They'll never let you in."

"They will as a client."

"No!" Lavinia was revolted at the idea. She was in love with John. He had held her in his arms. Kissed her. It was more than she could bear. The girls were young, trained. Some of them must be pretty. Just suppose . . . but she couldn't suppose. . . .

"You can't do it," she said. "You must not."

"I've got to. And be ready. If I can, I'm going to get a girl out."

"And bring her here?"

"Where else? Get her back to England. I've got a couple of men to help me. A couple of Englishmen. They know a place where there is an English girl."

"They've been there?"

"Yes. And they are only too ready to help. I'm going in and they are going to wait for me."

Lavinia twisted her handkerchief into a knot. Where would it all end? And this was only the beginning. . . .

The house was in the Rue Benoît, a respectable neighborhood and well known to the cab driver who leered at Longbeach when he got out.

"Bon séjour!" he said. *"Amusez-vous bien,* Monsieur!" The street light shone on his white varnished top hat. He wore a coachman's coat with a shawl over his shoulders. His legs were wrapped in a horse blanket.

Longbeach went up the steps and pulled the bell. The door was opened by a swarthy man in shirt sleeves. An ugly customer. Behind him was a thickset woman dressed in black bombazine, white-faced, her dark, oiled hair done in a chignon on the top of her head. Her small eyes were like currants pushed into a ball of dough. Her mouth was a knife slit below a blob of a nose. The madam, without a doubt.

"Madame Picard?" John said.

"At your service, Monsieur."

He could feel her assessing him. His age. His clothes. His possible wealth. His desires. He knew he looked the part. A well-off Englishman in search of an evening's pleasure. He handed his deerstalker cap to the shirt-sleeved man and slipped off his ulster. He was wearing a black velvet smoking jacket, frogged with braid.

"*Entrez,* Monsieur," the woman said, indicating a door to her left.

"*Je ne parle pas français,*" John said.

"Of English I have a little, Monsieur." Madame's slit of a mouth opened a fraction in a slight smile that showed her teeth. They were large and very white; the grin of a wolf. She flung open the door.

"I 'ave a girl English," she said. "Pretty, young. Very docile. Amiable," she said. "Blonde. You like them blonde, Monsieur? Brunette, too. *Rouge.* All colors. Even a black one from the *Côte d'Ivoire.*" She showed her fangs again.

The salon was a long room, the center bare of furniture, the floor polished parquet. Against the walls chairs and sofas were arranged in groups, each with a small table separated from its neighbor by palms in decorative ceramic pots. The room smelt of beeswax and turpentine, with an overlay of perfume and tobacco.

"The paradise of Picard," she said. "The idea"—she waved a ringed hand at the palms that embowered each cubicle—"is from the Orient, Monsieur. Ten years in Indo-China with my husband, a businessman. Now in the arms of God. He died of fever, Monsieur. The vases and pots I brought back. My only souvenirs." Her tone changed.

"Wine, Monsieur?" she said. "The girls will be down in a moment. You have good fortune. You are the first. First come, first served—is that not what you say? The pick, Monsieur. In an hour, ten men will be here—*dix, douze,* who knows? Mumm? Veuve Cliquot? Ayala? Pommery? Cordon Rouge?"

"Mumm, Madame," Longbeach said. "Perhaps you will join me in a glass?"

Picard rang the bell by the fireplace. A neatly dressed maid came in, a blank-faced, high-cheek-boned peasant.

"Mumm, Marie. The ice bucket and three glasses." She smiled at Longbeach. "One for you, one for me and one for your little friend when she arrives." She saw him glance at the grand piano at the far end of the room.

"*La musique?*" she said. "*La danse?*" She raised her skirt and pirouetted. "That is life, is it not? *Les filles, la musique, le vin et la danse.* Is that not paradise, Monsieur?"

The wine was brought in, the bottle lying sideways on its bed of ice in the silver bucket. The glasses were good ones, fine glass with thin stems. Looking at the champagne bottle, Longbeach thought of it for the first time as a weapon. A champagne bottle was heavy. It had to be to withstand the pressure. It was, when you came to think of it, shaped like an Indian club.

Two girls came in, their high-heeled shoes clicking on the parquet. Both brunette, both young—not twenty to look at them. Their long hair hung down their backs. They were in evening dress, one red and one canary yellow, cut low enough to glimpse their nipples. Their bustles were enormous. When they got nearer he saw that the dresses were split, divided up the front to show their long, slim, silk-stockinged legs and wide, red satin ruffled garters, with a flash of white thigh. Madame Picard knew her business. The champagne cork went off like a pistol shot as Picard loosened the wires. The girl in red danced off like a retriever to pick it up.

"They think it is the *bonne chance,*" Picard said. "The good luck." She laughed. "They are 'appy, my girls. This is a 'ouse of the first quality, Monsieur."

Two men in dinner jackets were ushered in. They were followed by an older man in tails. And more girls, in dresses like the first two, also in bright colors: peacock blue, violet, green, pale blue, rose. They disposed themselves in couples on the sofas. The men went over to talk to them. More champagne was brought in by the flat-faced maid. A young man with long hair walked down the room, looking neither to the left nor right and, seating himself at the piano, began to play.

"The musician," Picard said. "Now it is complete. The soirée has begun!" She put down her glass, got up and said: "I will fetch the little English. If she gives you no pleasure, there are others." She showed Longbeach her teeth again, crossed the room and spoke to the fair girl in the rose dress.

So that was her. Longbeach filled his glass and emptied it into a potted palm. Well, he was in. In a minute he'd meet the girl. Carrington, one of the young men, had said that they had been thinking of trying to get the girl out themselves. They thought the only way to do it was to act drunk and say he wanted a breath of air before he took her upstairs. She might let the girl go into the street with him for a moment.

Picard came back, followed by the girl. "Your *compatriote*, Monsieur," she said. "Though love, *l'amour*, has a language universal."

John Longbeach got up. "Sit down," he said to the girl. "And more wine, Madame." He lifted the bottle. "*Du vin.*"

"It comes, Monsieur, on the instant." She put her hand on the girl's bare shoulder. "'Er name is Mollee."

"Molly," the girl said, sitting down and trying to arrange her skirt.

Madame pulled it open. "So modest, my girls," she said. "But that is good, is it not, Monsieur? The paradox." She swept off.

The man at the piano was playing a polka. Another bottle of wine was being opened at Longbeach's elbow. The maid filled both glasses and put the bottle in the ice bucket. The girl raised her eyes and looked at Longbeach.

"There were two Englishmen here last week," she said. She had a nice voice. Her eyes were blue, shadowed with purple; they looked enormous. She rearranged her dress again, covering her thighs.

"I met them, Molly," Longbeach said.

"And they told you about me?"

"They did."

"They said . . ." Tears came into the big blue eyes, her lips trembled. She pulled herself together. "Can you get me out of here?"

"I'm going to try, Molly."

"If you try and fail, I'm finished," the girl said. "She'll send me to Germany. That's what she does if girls are difficult, and that's the end of them."

"We shan't fail," he said. "But we've got to be gay. I'm going to pretend to get drunk. You just do what I tell you."

"Oh yes, I will." The girl's face brightened. She almost smiled.

"How old are you?" Longbeach asked.

"Eighteen."

"How long have you been here?"

"Six months."

"Shall we dance, Molly? We've got to put on a show." He stood up. It was a waltz. She was like a feather in his arms.

More men had come in. Most of the palm alcoves were occupied. Some of the girls were sitting on the men's knees. The dresses were off their shoulders, their skirts had parted. There was the sound of laughter, squeals, giggles. One couple left the salon and went up the curved staircase that led off it. More corks popped.

"I'm going to make a fuss over you, Molly," Longbeach said. "Kiss you, pet you. Can you stand it?"

"What choice have I? You can do what you like to me."

"My God, I don't mean that. I mean we've got to put on a good show. I'm going to begin to act a bit drunk."

She laughed. "It's the palm that will be drunk," she said, as he pulled her onto his knees.

My God, he thought, if Lavinia could see me now. Molly was warm, pliant, soft as a kitten in his arms. He kissed her. How easy it was for a man to lose his head! You can do anything you like to me. . . . How many men had done what they liked with her? He thought of Ellen in the first-class carriage; of how she had seduced him. How long would it be before Molly became an Ellen? An animal, or died of it? Those were the alternatives.

Molly was whispering in his ear. "Those Englishmen," she said. "Carrington. Denis Carrington. He took me. We went up to my room and he didn't do anything. I slept," she said. "I slept all night. He just lay beside me, holding me. And he'd paid, too."

Longbeach had pulled down her dress. Her breasts were exposed. He cupped one of them in his hand. He felt it harden and gain weight.

Picard looked in on them. "Ah," she said. "It goes well, I see. *Ça va mieux, ma petite,*" she added. Turning to Longbeach, she said: "That will be one hundred francs."

"For how long?"

"All night, Monsieur. And if she gives you any trouble just let me know. At first . . ." she shrugged her shoulders—"but that is all over now. *Pour commencer c'est quelquefois difficile. N'est-ce pas,* Mollee?"

Longbeach felt the girl tremble in his arms. He understood enough French to get the gist of what was said, though it was a long way from "the pen of my aunt" that he had learnt at school. But the implication was clear enough. He pushed Molly away from him so that she sat perched like a bird on his knees, her bodice sagging, as he felt for his pocketbook. He pulled out two one-hundred-franc notes.

"Only a hundred, Monsieur, unless you want specialities."

"I think Molly is worth two hundred, Madame. To find an English girl and spend the whole night."

"But certainly, Monsieur. And a *petit déjeuner* thrown in."

"And another bottle now." Longbeach put a further hundred francs into her hand. "I am having a good time," he said. "I like to drink. I do not wish to be bothered further."

Madame pocketed the money. "Drink all you wish, Monsieur. From now on it is gratis. On the 'ouse. And you will not be disturbed. *Mais non. . . .*"

Madame Picard was delighted. The English were all rich. Without doubt, they recommended her house to each other. Those two last week, and now this one. She must get more English girls. It was evident that they liked their compatriots. How well her life had turned out! Born in the old quarter of Marseilles, accustomed to men since the age of eleven, she had soon learnt how to profit by their passions. At twenty she had met Picard, a businessman who had paid her fare to Saigon where she had run a house, first as his partner, and then as his wife. Women, narcotics, even some illicit dealing in arms, had built them a modest fortune, now all invested in this house. No, *mon Dieu,* she had no complaints. Life had been good to her. What a change from the garrets, passages and dark doorways where she had begun. Sailors. *Légionnaires.* Dock workers. Then in Indo-China, officers who wanted a change from their slim Chinese girls. What beauties they were! But breastless. Still, there was no getting away from the charm of those lissom yellow fruits. At sixteen she had killed a man in the old port. Knifed him in the guts when he had got her down on the *pavé* and tried to rape her. But what was one more body found in the old port in those days? The police never caught her. But other people knew. She had a name as a hard one. A good one, if you paid her. One hundred *sous* in those days, but hard. There were men who liked to sleep with a pretty killer. *Mon Dieu,* she thought, I was pretty then. A slim flashing girl, with laughing dangerous eyes. Big-breasted with switching buttocks under the short skirts of a fishwife. It was that that had got Picard. "They say you killed a man, *chérie,*" he said.

"Is that all you come to me for?" she had laughed at him. "Any woman can kill a man on her back. I am insatiable, a veritable man eater."

"You are *dûre,*" he said. "A hard one, a pretty one. You are what I am looking for."

"If I was not hard, how do you think I should have lived? I have no illusions. I know what men want. I give it to them."

"And you?" he'd asked. "What do you want?"

"A man and money." It was then he had told her his plan.

"I will pay your fare to Indo-China. You will make money and we will set up a house together."

"I will make money, *mon brave,*" she said. "But it will be for me. I do not need a pimp. *Pas de maquereau.*" To this day she remembered his face when she had turned on him. "All right," she had said. "I killed a man and I'll kill you if you try any tricks." She had drawn her knife from her stocking top.

He had sailed the following week and a month later she had gone after him. How she wished he had lived to see this establishment in Brussels. But perhaps he saw it from up there. She raised her eyes to the ceiling. Jean François Picard had been a good man. And how well things were going tonight! She felt someone at her elbow. It was the *Anglais* with his girl. He was staggering a little. Molly was holding him up.

"Air," he said. *"Promenade, Madame, avec* Molly. Five minutes, then . . ."* He pointed to the stairs.

"Très bien," she said. "But it makes cold. She 'ave not much on as I have no doubt Monsieur 'ave discover. Jacques!" she called and the shirt-sleeved man, now in the yellow and black-striped waistcoat of a *valet de chambre,* came in.

"The Monsieur wants air. He is going to take Mademoiselle Mollee into the street for an instant."

"Mais oui, Madame," the man said, taking Longbeach's shoulder to hold him up. He led him to the front door with Molly supporting him on the other side. The three of them went down the steps into the street. Longbeach drew in several deep breaths. Then he straightened up, turned and hit Jacques on the point of the jaw as hard as he could.

"Come on, Molly," he said. "We'll run for it. They'll be after us in a minute." Seizing her hand, they ran together. A moment later Carrington and his friend stepped out of a doorway. They held out a big dark cloak with a hood that Molly slipped over her pink dress. Up the street a cab was waiting. They bundled the girl in as heavy footsteps pounded after them. There were some shouts. The cabby cracked his whip and the horse set off at a hand gallop.

"I picked a good one," Carrington said complacently, as Molly burst into paroxysms of sobs.

In her hotel suite Lavinia went over the last few days. The Consul's smugness. The Police Chief's obvious corruption. And John. Exposed not merely to temptation but to danger. She knew that they would stop at nothing. There was too much at stake. May, sewing in a corner under the gas bracket, watched her mistress. She had an idea of what was in her mind, particularly with reference to Mr. John. If only the master had killed himself, or would die. A married woman could not go on forever manless. She had the habit of it. May's temperament was romantic. She had held Charles off, but that was because she was a virgin and in no great hurry to change her condition. When Madam got settled again, she might think of it once more, though not with Charles. Next time—if there was a next time—she would fly higher. But the gentry were different. Her mistress was so lovely. It seemed such waste. All she could do was to leave them together as much as she could and let nature, as she called it, take its course.

Lavinia kept looking at the clock. Ten, ten-thirty, eleven, twelve. Surely he would get back soon. She wondered about the two young Englishmen who had been to that place and told John about the English girl. Been there for the usual purpose, she assumed. How lucky women were not to be driven so hard. Lucky one way, perhaps, but not in another; forced in wedlock and out of it, like these poor girls. And what, after all, could they do? Even with men like Stead and the others to help them. It was like trying to empty the sea with a tablespoon. There were so many interests involved, so much money. The whole array of procurers and Madams. Their clients—among them some of the highest in the land. It was inconceivable that men, honored in every walk of life . . . fathers of daughters themselves. . . . And John, John. Where in God's name was he? A physical longing for him overcame her. Her mental pictures of the brothel, the half-naked girls, the emanations of lust that must permeate the place, induced a longing for John in her. John as man to her woman. Feelings she had thought, only a few months ago, no respectable woman could entertain. She wanted his kisses, his hands on her body.

And then the door burst open and he came in, pushing a young fair girl, wrapped in what looked like a military cloak, in front of him. The hood had fallen back from her heart-shaped face. Her eyes were wide with fear, her long, pale blonde hair hung over her shoulders. Behind the girl were two young men she had never seen before. The Englishmen.

"You're safe? You're not hurt, John?"

"I'm all right, Lavinia."

She ran forward and took the girl in her arms. "My dear! My dear!" she said. "It's all over now. You're safe. You'll soon be back in England."

"Oh Ma'am," the girl said, bursting into sobs on her shoulders. "Thank God, thank God, your husband came!"

Her husband. In her heart he was her husband, and had been since that day at the Meurice in Paris.

John was introducing the two men. "Mr. Carrington. Mr. James," he said. "Mrs. Lenton, my client." He smiled at the young men's surprise. "I am a lawyer, you know."

May was staring at the group in astonishment.

"Drinks, May," Longbeach said. "Brandy. Brandy for everyone. And by God we need it. I had to knock a chap out." He looked down at his knuckles. "I hope I haven't broken anything. He had a jaw like a rock. Sit down. Sit down," he said to the two men. "I'll pour." He took the bottle, put two fingers of brandy in each glass and squirted in the soda water from a blue siphon.

"Lavinia," he said, turning to her, "do you think May can find something of yours that'll fit this child?"

"Of course, John."

May came forward. "Take her into the bedroom," Lavinia said. "Go with her, dear." Molly hesitated. She did not want to leave her rescuers.

"You'll let me stay here?" she asked. "They'll be after me. I owe her money. A lot," she said.

"You'll stay, dear. And you're safe. Just go with May. But drink this first." Lavinia put her own glass into the girl's hand. "You look as if you needed it."

In the bedroom May took the girl's cloak. "Oh," she said, when she saw the pink dress that fell open to the waist when Molly moved. Her breasts were fully exposed; she had had no time to adjust her bodice.

"It's what they make us wear," Molly said in tears.

So this child was a scarlet woman, used and abused, and only a little older than Miss Eva. From what Madam said, there were hundreds of them, thousands. Children, kids. May found herself crying, too, and holding the girl to her. Only now did she realize the full enormity of what was going on under their noses. Before, it had just been words—except for Miss Eva—but somehow she had felt that to be an exception. A bit of terrible luck, a misfortune, a kind of accident. But with this half-naked girl in her arms, she saw that it was more. It was terrible, as if the devil had suddenly revealed himself to her. She undid the few hooks and eyes that held the pink dress on, letting it fall to the ground. The girl stood statue-still, quite naked. A statue of white tipped with pubic gold. May threw one of her mistress' dressing gowns over her and led her to the bedroom.

"Lie down, dear, while I run in a bath."

Molly hesitated by the bed. Beds to her were no longer to rest on.

"Come along, dear. Lie down," May said.

Still frightened as if there was some catch in it, Molly lay down and listened to the water running. A few moments later it stopped and May came back.

"It's just right," she said. "You lie and soak while I find something for you to put on."

She found a simple white wool morning dress and she took underclothes from the chest of drawers—a chemise, a camisole, knickers. She would have to wear the same stockings and shoes. When everything was laid out on the bed, she went back to the bathroom.

"Get out now and I'll dry you." She wrapped a big towel around the girl and rubbed her dry.

"Feel better?" she asked.

"Ever so much better. I feel clean again."

"What! Didn't you have a bath there?"

"Oh yes! But I couldn't get clean, not ever. How could I?"

May dressed her. She did her hair, piling it upon her head. "There, dear," she said. "Now we'll go back."

"Must I?" Molly suddenly felt shy. The men had seen her naked, or worse than naked. And the beautiful lady? What would she think, seeing her in one of her dresses? She had told May to find her something to wear but now that Molly had put it on she might not feel the same about it. May took her arm and led her into the sitting room. The men got up when she came in. Lavinia came over to her, kissed her and stood beside her with her arm around her waist.

"Feeling better?" she asked. "I've sent down for something to eat. We're all hungry. Some cold chicken or something. They said they could find something," she said vaguely, pushing Molly into an armchair near the fire.

What a beauty she was—she wondered how John had resisted her. What a temptation! The French had a word for it—*jolie à croquer*— pretty enough to eat, to devour. She shuddered at the thought.

"Molly," she said, "I want you to be brave and tell us the whole story. Get it over once and for all tonight, and then forget it."

"Oh, I couldn't, Ma'am, Mrs. Lenton." She looked appealingly at Longbeach.

"I think Mrs. Lenton's right," he said. "Tell us. Put it into words. It will only fester in your mind. Besides, we need it, Molly. We're going to try and stop this traffic in women. You can help us to save other girls."

"It's too horrible," Molly said, blushing and covering her face with her hands.

A waiter came in with a tray of sandwiches, two bottles of wine and some glasses.

"Tea. That's what she wants," May said, lighting a small spirit stove and putting on a kettle. "There's nothing like tea, is there, dear?"

"Tea?" Molly said. "I haven't had a cup of tea since . . . since . . ." and she burst into floods of tears.

23 : Encounter at the Zoo

When she had eaten a couple of chicken sandwiches and drunk three cups of tea, Molly stood up.

"All right, Mrs. Lenton," she said. "I'll tell you how it happened." She looked very pretty, standing arrow-slim in the white wool dress. Longbeach thought she might have been Lavinia's sister. Both tall, slim and fair. Ellen was fair, too. All English types. These were the women he had become involved with; he'd slept with one, held another all but naked on his knees as he fondled her, and Lavinia . . . he felt his passion grow as he looked at her. He thought of the evening in Paris, of the silk softness of her flesh, of her supple unconfined body in his arms. He knew he could have had her then, just as he knew that Ellen had caught him at the psychological moment. A year ago he had never thought of a woman at all except on his occasional visits to London. A client of the very trade he was now devoting his life to checking. Not that he had ever had a young girl, but the women he had had, how had they begun—like this child? Some had been lower-class girls, seduced servants, but there had been one or two who were educated, almost ladies. And now he was going to hear about this girl he had rescued. Carrington and James both looked awkward, as if they shared some of his feelings.

Lavinia said: "Smoke if you like, gentlemen." Longbeach offered them cigars.

Now that she had made up her mind, Molly seemed at ease. One foot in its pink satin high-heeled shoe peeped out like a rosy mouse from the hem of her dress, as she tapped the floor with impatience. She wanted to get it over. Lavinia poured herself a glass of Bordeaux.

Molly looked around, catching their eyes in turn, and said:

"I'm a good girl. High-spirited, that's what they said I was. My Dad is a chemist at Oxford—that's where we live—and he was against it—high spirits, I mean. No dancing, no parties, no fun. That's all I wanted,

Mrs. Lenton"—she looked at Lavinia—"just fun, a bit of life. I went out a few times with boys. Undergraduates. No harm at all," she said. "There were a lot of us girls. We went on the river in punts, nothing at all. Not even a kiss in it. But he found out, my Dad, and took a strap to me. I was seventeen then, and too big for it. That's what's worrying me now, Mrs. Lenton. He'll never have me back after all this. 'A fallen woman, a whore of Babylon,' that's what he called me when I had done nothing." Tears collected in the corners of her blue eyes. "What'll I do now, Mrs. Lenton?" she asked. "I don't know how to do anything. I can't even cook. Not an egg." She went on: "My mother's different— she loves me, but she never told me anything. None of us girls knew anything about men, about getting married and all that." Molly made a helpless gesture with her hands. "I know now. By Christ, what don't I know. . . . I'm sorry," she said. "I didn't mean to swear, but you pick things up—swearing, drinking, smoking."

Lavinia gave her a cigarette from her case. "I smoke," she said. "And I drink. I swear, too, sometimes."

Molly smoked in silence for a few minutes. "It's hard to go on," she said, wringing her hands. But she did, her eyes fixed on the wall as if she were looking through it into the distance, into the past.

"It was a fine day. Very fine. Lovely. The sky was blue with little clouds like white feathers. The larks were singing, going up and down like they do, fluttering their wings as if they were on strings. I was happy. My father and mother had gone off for the day to visit friends and I thought"—she hesitated—"I thought it would be fun to go to London all by myself to see the crowds. Go to Madame Tussaud's, perhaps, or the zoo. I had a pound I'd saved up. All shillings and sixpences— pocket money, Christmas money. I had one half crown. I felt rich. So I bought a return ticket and went up to London. I did go to the zoo," she said. "I rode on an elephant. I saw the lions and tigers and then, all of a sudden, I thought about going home. I'd be caught, all right. I hadn't done the things I was meant to do at home and I was no good at lying. Not then, I wasn't. My Dad would take a strap to me. I couldn't bear it and I began to cry. There I was, all alone in London, all the fun was over and my Dad waiting for me. Then a nice woman came up to me. Rather stout, old, like my grandma—mother's mother, that is.

" 'Crying, dearie?' the woman said. 'On a nice day like this? Come and have a nice cup of tea with me, and tell me all about it.' So I went with her and she gave me tea. There's a place there they serve tea in thick cups and a Bath bun. Two Bath buns," Molly said.

"I told the lady about my Dad and how he'd beat me and shut me up in my room for two or three days with just bread and water, and nothing to read except the Bible.

" 'Well dear,' she said, 'what about coming home with me for dinner and the night? And I'll take you back in the morning and tell your father some story about me being taken faint near your house and you bringing me home to London, and so on.' She put her hand on my wrist and said: 'Don't cry, dear. We'll think of something between now and tomorrow.' So when she said: 'Come along, dear,' again, I went with her.

"Outside the zoo she called a hansom. I'd never been in one before and I was so excited. It had a pretty brown horse. I'd gone in a bus with two white horses—I'd sat on top so I could see more—but I'd done that before. This was different. We went to a house in Denton Street. I did not notice the number, but I'd know the house again, I'm sure."

"Her name?" Longbeach said.

"She said her name was Mrs. Jacks. But it may not have been. I didn't know then that people often give their wrong names. I didn't believe Mr. Carrington when he told me his name." She looked at Carrington. "Denis Carrington," she repeated. "So I don't suppose her name's much good. But I'll know the house. There was a crack in the front step shaped like an M. M for Molly, I thought. It was a comfortable house and we had a lovely meal, a sort of flat fish that Mrs. Jacks arranged for me. She took the bones out. Steak-and-kidney pie and a custard. I had a nice room, but I hardly slept I was so worried. And in the morning she said she thought the best thing to do was to take me abroad. She had a friend who could give me work there and she had been going to visit her next week and a few days one way or the other would not matter. What did I think about it? Well, I was more frightened than ever now. Being away a whole night and so on. So I said: 'Yes, I'll go.' 'You'll like it in Belgium,' she said 'My friend likes young girls. She'll give you pretty clothes.' She showed me a lovely dress she was taking over for her friend's daughter. 'What will I do?' I asked. 'Be a companion to her daughter and talk English to her. It's really a bit of luck meeting you because she'd asked me to find a young girl but I haven't been able to. Not a nice, respectable, well-brought-up young lady like you.'

"That's what she said, Mrs. Lenton, and I believed her. We went to Charing Cross Station and she bought tickets to Ostend. When we got there, Madame Picard was there to meet us. Mrs. Jacks said she was the mother of the girl I was going to be companion to. 'An only child, dear,' she said. She kissed me and said goodbye. I said: 'What about the pretty dress for Miss Picard?' She said that in all the excitement she had forgotten to bring it but would post it as soon as she got back. So I went with Madame Picard who, Mrs. Jacks said, kept a small hotel in Brussels.

"We took a train and it was dark when we got there. But I was nervous. It didn't look right somehow. All the windows were barred. 'For burglars,' Madame Picard said. *'Cambrioleurs.'* I didn't know any French then but I got the idea. Once inside, she showed me to my room, and before I had looked around she was out and had bolted the door on the outside. I banged on the door with my fists. I think I became hysterical. A prisoner. I suddenly remembered what Mrs. Jacks' little maid had said to me when we were alone for a moment. 'Run away from 'ere, Miss,' she said. 'If you've no money, I've got two bob I'll give you.' She had pushed it into my hand and then before I could ask what she meant Mrs. Jacks was back. I left the two shillings on the table in the bedroom when we left, and a shilling of my own. My last shilling. All I had left in my purse was my return ticket to Oxford. But now I knew what she had been trying to tell me, and I lay down on the bed and cried.

"I don't know how long I lay there but it was some time, and then two of the girls came in. They brought me something to eat on a tray. They wore dressing gowns but they left a dress for me. A proper evening dress. They made it clear that I was to put it on, which I did when I had eaten my supper. Then Madame Picard came in and took me downstairs. It was then I saw the other girls in those awful dresses. Dresses?" she said. "Could you call them that? They were worse than being naked. And men came in. You saw it," she said to the men. "It was like that every night. A man came and sat next to me. I spoke no French, he spoke no English. After a while he said something to Madame and she said I could go to bed. I must be tired.

"I was only too pleased to get away. Shocked?" Molly said. "I don't know if I was shocked. It was worse than anything I had imagined. I told you I knew nothing. I had never seen another girl naked, and with those dresses they were worse than naked and shameless. They tried to show themselves. They sat on the men's knees. I don't know what I thought. I don't think I thought. It was a nightmare. So I went to bed. An hour or so later, the man came into my room. The door had no key. And"—she hesitated—"he forced me. I screamed. I cried. He only laughed. He hurt me," she said. "Two days later he came back, but now I knew what he was going to do. I fought him off. I'm a strong girl. I fought and fought. I screamed and hit him. I hit him and he went away. I was quite exhausted and thought I'd won. How silly I was! Five minutes later he was back, and did what he wanted—I could not fight any more. He must have told Madame Picard. There were ten other men that night. After that I was broken in, as they call it. She gave me two nights' rest and then I was given one of those dresses and told to go down with the other girls. I refused, and that man whom you hit, Mr. Longbeach, beat me, had me, made me dress, and practically threw me downstairs. That's the story, Mrs. Lenton." She sank to the floor, covering her face with her hands. May was crying bitterly.

"How could they?" she said. "Oh Madam, how could they? She's just a girl."

"Take her to bed, May," Lavinia said. "She can sleep with me."

When the two girls had left the room, the men poured themselves more brandy.

"Well gentlemen," Lavinia said. "Now you know her story—and she's only one of dozens, of hundreds."

"We never knew," Carrington said. "We just thought some girls were like that."

"Perhaps some are, but very few, Mr. Carrington. Most of them are slaves. White slaves."

"My God!" James said. "Why does nobody know about this?"

"They don't want to know," Lavinia said. "But they are going to. Did Mr. Longbeach tell you that they stole my daughters? We got one back. She was only fifteen and is now mentally deranged. The other, a baby of five, we cannot trace."

"So that's why . . ." Carrington said.

"That's why, Mr. Carrington." Lavinia was calm, her face stony.

Carrington said: "We'll go now. I'm glad we could help. If we can do anything else . . ."

"Mr. Longbeach will give you his address. If you want to help us we shall be glad. We need help to smash this evil thing."

They shook hands. "I could not have managed without you," Longbeach said.

"Glad we were here. I only wish we could have pitched into that swine, too."

Longbeach went to the door and downstairs with them. When he came back he found Lavinia in tears.

"Just one," she said. "We've saved just one."

"It's a beginning, darling." He sat down beside her. "It's an opening wedge. Now we've got to get her back and see Stead. Give him the evidence, the Consul's story. The story about the police. The details. My God," he said, "now we know how it's done. We have some names, some addresses." He kissed her.

"Good night, Lavinia," he said from the door.

"It's not good night, John. Not tonight. I'm coming with you. I must." This had been too much to bear alone. She must talk. They could talk in his room. It was only two doors down the passage. Talk. She knew it was not talk she wanted. It might begin that way. But that was not the way it would end. And the end would be a beginning.

It was four o'clock when Lavinia got back to her suite, undressed quietly and got into the double bed beside Molly. Not to sleep. To think, to remember, or rather to try to remember. That was the curious part of it. She could remember no details, only the immense relief. The relief of the act. The relief of her decision to be John Longbeach's mistress. They would have to be careful—not because of Edward now, but because of their mission. People would be only too ready to accuse her, to discredit her. They would do it anyway but, and this was the important point, there must be no evidence. Then she slept. Deeply, profoundly, beside the girl who had, in a sense, been responsible for her downfall.

Before she slept there were thoughts of the brothel, of John there, of the girl herself, the child who had, in the last six months, lived through a hundred nights of horror. She had thought of Edward as she lay with John in her arms, of the difference between the only two men she had ever known. How was it that one had left her taut, strung as a violin, and the other free, almost happy for the first time in her life? The girls. Eva was safe at Mortal, lost in a world of fantasy. Betty—she was sure she was dead. Another human sacrifice to the gods of lust. She had lost one child, but they had saved another. She woke once, crying, and drew Molly to her.

In the morning when May took the coffee and *croissants* from the *valet de chambre,* she held up three fingers and pointed to Molly still asleep beside her mistress. The waiter nodded and was back in a few minutes with another *petit déjeuner.*

How pretty they looked asleep, the two fair heads on the pillows. May hesitated to wake them, but if she didn't the coffee would get cold. It was a fine day. The winter sun streamed into the room. She touched her mistress' shoulder. Lavinia sat up. May put a bed jacket over her shoulders.

"Your breakfast, Madam."

Lavinia smiled at her. She looked different. Younger, in spite of her shadowed eyes.

The girl woke, rubbing her eyes like a child and looked round lost, half frightened as if she did not know where she was.

May put her tray in her hands and said: "Good morning, Molly."

"Good morning, May." Molly turned to Lavinia and said: "I couldn't believe it when I woke. I thought it was all a dream."

"It's no dream, dear. You'll soon be home now."

"I can't go home, Mrs. Lenton."

"Very well, if you can't go home you can stay with us. You can help us. Now drink your coffee and don't worry."

Lavinia ate her *croissant* and thought of John. The man who had become her life. Did he still love her? Would he respect her after what had happened last night? This morning, only a few hours ago. How shameless she had been! She had heard that once a man had possessed a woman, he no longer cared for her. But this was just another lie. Look at Maud and her lover. Maud had told her it got worse. Worse or better. Love was a kind of pain, an ache, a delicious agony. Now they must get back to England. To Stead, to reality. The girl must stay in the room till John got the tickets. They would get the two young men to go to the boat with them. She had a feeling that Madame Picard was not going to take this lying down.

24 : London Again

There were no repercussions from the abduction of Molly. Escorted by Longbeach and the two Englishmen, the women took the train to Ostend and boarded the English packet. It was a silent journey. All were occupied with their own thoughts. Thoughts of love or sex in its various manifestations. Lavinia wondered how what had taken place between her and John could be reconciled with the horrors of Madame Picard's establishment. And yet they were related. Both based on desire, and desire was life, the force of creation, the urge for reproduction common to all human beings which, if thwarted in one direction, changed its course, put on a mask of bestiality and went off in another. The question, as she saw it, was less of morality than of willingness. If both were willing, the picture changed. She and John were, according to the accepted custom, immoral. This she found impossible to believe, no matter what people would think or say if they were found out. It was much more moral than her relations with Edward had ever been, though they had been justified by the bonds of marriage. They had been without any spiritual significance. There had been no giving on her part and only a taking on his. She had been used as an instrument, if not of pleasure, at least of temporary satisfaction. In this her sensations must have been, up to a point, very like those of Molly Hastings—in principle at least if not in fact. A married man had his rights. He could no more be denied than the man who paid his hundred francs at Madame Picard's.

May was still dazed by the experiences of the previous night. The girl, Molly. The awful dress. She had tried it on before the others woke. It had been impossible to hide herself in it, to cover herself. When she walked, the dress opened like a door. A door—the word came to her mind—the door to the woman, to the girl who wore it. To her secrets, to the heart of her womanhood, exposing it all.

And Madam. Madam was changed. She saw the looks she and Mr. Longbeach exchanged. This, too, was impossible to believe. She had wanted it for her, hoped for it. But now that it had happened, she was at a loss. Her Madam . . .

Longbeach himself was confused, his mind a mixture of pride and shame. Had he taken advantage of Lavinia? Had he, excited by the events of the evening, by the girls, by Molly on his knee, lost his self-control? Was this a repetition of the Ellen story? Then it had been Lavinia who had stirred him and Ellen who had taken advantage of him. Now it was Molly and the other girls who had moved him to make love to Lavinia, though she had come to his room, ready to offer herself to him. Coming into his arms without words. Kissing him and pressing her body into his. He thought of Edward. Edward might live for years. He thought of their campaign—that a scandal would ruin. They would have to be careful. They would have to show nothing. He must find a place where they could meet occasionally. Lavinia might know of a place, hear of it from some of her friends. She knew people in London who moved in a fast set where these things went on. There must be such places—houses of accommodation, he believed they were called. He looked at her sitting in the railway carriage. Lavinia. His Lavinia, now. He knew her body, he knew her desires and needs. He knew Molly's body, too. It was hard to believe that only a few hours ago she had sat almost naked on his knee.

Molly's mind was concerned with the future. Mrs. Lenton had said she would take care of her. But for how long? She knew nothing. There was nothing she could do. Except one thing. Would she slip back into that? She shuddered at the thought but she had heard stories about girls who tried to go straight and failed. Mrs. Lenton had said she was going to see her father but that, she knew, would be useless. Her father, in spite of his protestations and his religion, was not a good man. She knew him. Her recent experiences told her that he was evil. That he was one of those men who liked being cruel to girls. Even his own daughter. He liked to hurt me, she thought. Mrs. Lenton was her only hope. She would think of something, have her taught something. Dressmaking, perhaps. Hat making. There must be something that a girl could do to make a living.

The voyage had been moderately calm. England seemed very secure as it fled past the railway carriage window. The trim fields, the cattle grazing, the hedgerows bordered with rabbits. The farm houses, the towns the express roared through. Secure, but only in appearance. If it was secure, how was it that English girls were taken abroad in such numbers and for such purposes? John Longbeach had come across evidence of crowned heads who spent eighteen hundred pounds a year buying young English girls. It was Ferdinand Guitry who had given him the information in a report a couple of weeks ago.

Once in London, Longbeach said goodbye to the women and they took a cab to Berkeley Square. He went to his club for the night.

"You're safe now, Molly," Lavinia said.

"Thank you, Mrs. Lenton," said Molly, looking around the comfortable spare room. "But what am I going to do? You can't just keep me here. I'm not a relation or anything. . . ."

"You're a sister, dear. All women are sisters. Tomorrow we'll buy you some clothes and then I'm going to see your father. If nothing comes of it, I'll take you down to Mortal, our place in Gloucestershire, and we'll spend Christmas there." She left May with her. "Find Molly everything she needs, May," she said, "and tell her the story."

"Story, Madam?"

"Yes. Why we went to the Continent, and about Miss Eva. . . ." Lavinia left them—she could not tell that story again—and unpacked for herself. She looked at the dress she had worn last night. That she had taken off in John's room. I'll never part with it, she thought, as she hung it on a hanger. The other things she left piled on the bed for May. She knew that was why she had opened her valise—to get out the cyclamen dress herself.

Shopping for Molly was a pleasure. The girl was happy and so easy to please, always saying she had enough. That she had never had so many clothes in her life. Lavinia bought her lingerie, stockings, shoes, a coat and skirt, and two dresses off the peg. She took her to Madame Elsie, her own dressmaker, and ordered more clothes to be made. Madame Elsie attended to them herself, measuring Molly and calling out the figures to her assistant. Bust thirty-two, waist eighteen, hips thirty. Molly thought she looked at her in a funny way.

"A young niece, Mrs. Lenton?" she said. "How charming! Light colors for a young girl, don't you think, Madam? White? Rose? Beige? Pink?"

"Not rose," Molly said. "Please not rose or pink."

There was a kind of appraisal about Madame Elsie's looks and remarks, as if she was a piece of merchandise, that Molly did not like. Though of course it was a silly idea and she dismissed it from her mind. Still, it stayed there, recessed in the depths of her unconscious. When the fitting was over, they went home in the carriage.

Next day Lavinia said she was going down to Oxford to see Molly's father.

"Don't let him have me," Molly implored.

"I've got to try, dear," Lavinia said. "I've got to see him." She took the ten o'clock train and a cab at the station to the address Molly had given her.

Molly's parents lived in a neat detached house a mile or so out of Oxford, where the shop was.

When Lavinia had introduced herself, Mr. Hastings had been polite, astonished at being called upon by a woman he did not know. He said he had just come back from Chapel. He was a small, rather well-built man, dressed in Sunday black. Lavinia had chosen lunchtime to be sure he would be at home. His eyes were gray and cold. His hands were hairy. Coldness seemed to ooze out of him.

"I have come to see you about your daughter," Lavinia said.

"I have no daughter, Madam."

"How odd, Mr. Hastings!" she said. "Molly is staying with me in London."

"I had a daughter once, Mrs. Lenton," he said. "She disgraced me. I consider her dead. Indeed, Madam, I wish she were. Then we could put flowers on her grave."

At that moment Mrs. Hastings had come into the room. She must have been listening outside the door. A small motherly woman, with bright brown eyes.

"Molly?" she said. "You have news of Molly?"

"I was just telling Mr. Hastings that she is staying with me. I rescued her."

"Rescued?" Mrs. Hastings gasped.

"From the pit there is no rescue," Mr. Hastings said. "And please keep out of this. We have no daughter, and you know it. I did what I could, Mrs. Lenton, to keep her on the straight and narrow."

"With a strap. She told me," Lavinia snapped.

"With a strap, Madam. And perhaps I was too sparing with it. 'Spare the rod and spoil the child,' " he quoted.

Mrs. Hastings was crying quietly. "Molly," she said. "Our little Molly. Thank God she is safe."

"Defiled," Mr. Hastings said. "Worse than dead. Every day I pray for her soul. But I have no regrets. I did my best for her, but the devil claims his own."

That had been the end of it. She did not even say goodbye. She got into the waiting cab and drove off. In the cab she made up her mind. When she got out she asked the driver if he could give the lady of the house he had just been to, her card. "But the man," she said, "must not know." She gave the cabby a sovereign.

"I'll see to it, lady," he said. "The butcher boy will give it to 'er when he delivers the meat."

When she got back to London and told Molly, the girl was not surprised. "I knew it," she said. "I knew I could never go back, and I didn't want to. All he'd do would be to take a strap to me again."

Though she did not say so, this was Lavinia's own impression of Molly's father. "Well you're not going. You'll stay with me and we'll all go down to Mortal. But I've arranged for your mother to have my address. I'm sure we shall hear from her."

"Oh mother," the girl said, "she's different." Tears came into her eyes. "But how did you manage it? Without him seeing?"

"The cab driver, dear. He's going to give my card to the butcher boy to deliver with the meat. We were lucky enough to see his trap at the door. And the cab driver knows him. Jones, the name is. Jones."

"Amos Jones," Molly said, enraptured. "Yes, he's our butcher."

Lavinia laughed at her. "You should have your clothes in a week and then we'll go down to the country. I'm looking forward to showing you our home. May told you about the children. Eva . . ." she said, leaving the sentence unfinished.

"Oh yes, Mrs. Lenton. How dreadful." She flung herself on her knees and buried her face in Lavinia's lap. "Dreadful, dreadful," she said. "The poor child." As if she, who had had a similar experience, was a much older woman.

Lavinia stroked the girl's hair. What a strange life it was! If her girls had not been stolen, Molly would still be in a Brussels house of ill fame. Edward would have been well and John no more than her husband's lawyer. It was her children who had started this avalanche, not only in her personal affairs, but in those of the nation. What a scandal there would be when Stead broke the news they had brought back in the *Pall Mall Gazette*. She must see Maud again before she went to the country. Give a little dinner party, perhaps. If everyone was not too booked up.

Everyone was too booked up, so she postponed the party and decided as soon as Molly's clothes came, to take her down to Mortal. She thought it best for her to see no one till Molly was more settled, and she had thought out a way to explain her presence. She did not even see Mr. Stead, but wrote to tell him she was going to the country and would see him next month. Anyway she knew John had given him their news.

She had just given the letter to the footman to post when John Longbeach called. She had not seen him since he had left them at the station.

"Well, Mrs. Lenton," he said. "I saw Stead and gave him our report. Then I went home and squared things with the old man. He's not taking kindly to the campaign. I'm just a country lawyer . . . sticking my nose into things that don't concern me . . . thin ice . . . where angels fear to tread . . . all the old *clichés* and platitudes. But I said I was committed and that I had no choice. Of course I'll still be down at Mortal Major most of the time so the office won't be neglected. But this comes first. The governor is sure it will ruin me. Dirty linen and so on. But once one knows the truth, how can one ignore it?

"Is Molly about?" he asked. "I want her to sign a statement. I've written it all out. It will be easier for her than telling the whole story again to Stead. And then I want to take her to Denton Street and let her show me the house she was taken to. I found out a little about Mrs. Jacks. Stead knew about her. He has been quite busy the last few days. But I want confirmation."

"I'll send for Molly, Mr. Longbeach," Lavinia said, thinking how curious all this was. Mrs. Lenton, Mr. Longbeach—instead of dearest and darling. She rang the bell.

The difference was that of day and night, of privacy, of public and social life. Her lawyer and collaborator in the one. Her lover in the other. Molly came in.

"Good morning, dear," Longbeach said. "You're looking very well."

"Thank you," she said.

"I've come to see you, Molly, because I want two things. I want you to sign these papers. It's a statement of your experience. It's accurate,

I made it myself. And then I want to take you to Denton Street. You said you thought you could recognize the house."

"Oh yes, Mr. Longbeach," she said. "I'll know it by the steps."

Longbeach got up. "Then go and get your hat and coat. We shall not be more than a couple of hours, Mrs. Lenton."

Molly came back wearing one of Mrs. Lenton's coats and a little fur hat they had bought on their shopping tour. Lavinia went over to the girl and put her arm around her shoulders. "You're not afraid, dear?"

"Not now. Not here. Not with you and Mr. Longbeach."

They had got her in time. The rest, the security and the natural resilience of youth had saved her. They had not been able to save Eva. Two years made a lot of difference. The younger the girl, the easier she was to break. Molly had been a woman, though only seventeen, when she had been kidnaped. Eva only a child of fifteen, and young and undeveloped for her age.

Once in the street, Longbeach said: "Shall we walk?"

"Yes," she said. "It's not far, is it?"

"No, it's not far." That was what was so extraordinary. A mile or so separated Berkeley Square from the slums and stews of Soho. They walked up Piccadilly to the Circus. Through the crowds of busy people. We look like a father and his daughter, an uncle and his niece, Longbeach thought.

He looked at the showily dressed, loitering women. If he had been alone, they would have accosted him. At the Eros statue there were two young girls standing. Children in short skirts and white button boots, with smart light-colored velvet coats of exaggerated cut. Molly saw them too. She squeezed his arm and said: "Are they?"

"Yes, dear," he said.

"How awful," Molly said. "How awful, and can no one do anything to help them?"

"That's what we're trying to do now. That's why we are here."

They went up Shaftesbury Avenue, turned left up Wardour Street and found themselves in a market full of carters' barrows, piled with cabbages, cauliflowers, carrots, turnips, and sprouts. Some barrows had hunks of meat on them. A pearly was shouting: "Cats' Meat! Nice fresh cats' meat!" There were stray cats rubbing themselves against his legs.

They found themselves in Denton Street, outwardly respectable, but the people who passed them were a mixed lot. Italians, Greeks, a few Negroes. A sly, shifty-looking lot.

"It's on the right," Molly said. She walked with her head down, looking at all the steps. When they had gone a couple of hundred yards, she stopped and pointed. "That's it! Look at the third step." There it was, a crack shaped like the letter M.

"You're sure, Molly?"

"I'm sure. I recognize the lace curtains, too."

Longbeach noted the number. It was a neat house of four stories. Well kept, and probably built about one hundred and fifty years ago. How many girls like Molly had been decoyed into it? They walked back to Piccadilly and picked up a hansom.

Mr. Joseph Hastings had been well aware of the new trend. Not that it was a trend yet, but without doubt a fissure was appearing in the solid rock of established custom. There were new women, like the one who had just left the house, this Mrs. Lenton; and not only new women but men too—even ministers—who supported them. Take that Reverend Theodore Parker of Boston who, thirty years ago, had attacked woman's role of housekeeper, wife and mother, calling it monstrous. Waste of the most precious material God ever made. Reverend, indeed. A devil's advocate. But the seed had been sown in the fertile ground of woman's concupiscence. The idea of freedom. What an idea! One had only to look at St. Paul . . . "the head of every woman is a man . . . and if they would learn anything let them ask their husbands . . . ye wives be in subjection to your husbands."

What these women could not see was that their safety lay in their dependence, in the weakness which God had given them for their own protection. This was what he had tried to instill into his daughter. To root out ideas she had obtained somehow, with a whip if need be. Yes, with a whip, a strap. For to spare the rod was to spoil the child. Not that she was a child any longer . . .

Even the dear Queen was on his side. He had it pat, had learnt it by heart. She was most anxious to enlist everyone who could write or speak to join in checking this mad wicked folly of Women's Rights with all its attendant horrors. It was a subject that made the Queen furious. God created men and women different—let them therefore remain each in their own position. She had said that some time ago but it had made a great impression on him. This was the Queen Empress speaking. A woman, a mother. So she knew what she was talking about.

Thank God there was no nonsense like this about his wife. She took orders, did what she was told. Of course when he had sent Molly upstairs and went up to punish her, she cried and besought him not to.

Said she was not a little girl now. Exactly—that was just it. She was almost a woman, with a woman's temptation. He could feel it himself when he was up there alone with her. All the more reason. The Eve must be whipped out of her. It must, it must. . . . He wiped the saliva from the corner of his mouth at the thought of it. But he had failed. She had sunk into the pit. In spite of him, the devil had claimed his own. And now this woman had had the audacity to rescue her, to save her from the just punishment of her sins. Of course she was under-age and he could have claimed her. If he had got her back he would have tried to save her soul—if she still had one after such contamination. But he couldn't do that. He had told everyone she was dead.

It could not be said that Mr. Hastings despised his wife. She existed for his convenience. To attend to his house and comfort. When he had married her—a young, pretty, dark, vivacious girl, rather on the plump side with a light soprano voice—he had almost hated her, blaming her for the lust she aroused in him, by her willing acquiescence to his insatiable demands. There was evil in all women. Each carried the fruit of knowledge between her soft thighs, modestly concealed but mystically apparent to man, drawing him to it, offering the Eden of her beauty, the soft garden of her flesh where he could lose himself. Even good women who, in all innocence, knew not what they did. Trained to subordination, they carried their weakness to such depths that by some strange reversal it became strength. The lascivious weakness of a woman's love could sap a man of all vitality. Only by keeping them pregnant could he survive. But Mrs. Hastings—Martha—had borne him only one child, and that a daughter, whose budding beauty and willful behavior was a threat to mankind, or would be if he could not break her spirit. What shocked and astonished him was the fact that he was not immune to her and, worse still, that she knew it. She knew he liked to punish her. If only she had been different—a boy, or ugly and misshapen. God did not create pretty young girls, they were the devil's work. But he would have none of it. He would not be tricked by her golden hair, big gray eyes, and long slim legs; not by her budding breasts with rose-tipped nipples; not by any of it, any of the devil's tricks that drew a man's hands to a girl's body as if they were on strings.

He looked back in horror at the early years of his marriage when, uxorious to the extreme, he had hardly been able to tear himself away from his wife's arms. Then religion had come to his aid and given him the strength to resist her. To put Satan—in this warm, plump form—behind him. And then this new temptation had arisen to plague him, to test him. Still he had not been able to get Molly out of his mind as he waited on his customers. Castor oil, paregoric . . . Certainly Madam, excellent, I can assure you . . . Cod Liver Oil, Elliman's embrocation, maccassar oil. Pills, draughts, cough mixtures, prescriptions.

He had kept wondering what she was doing. Before long she would get married and some man would . . . some man. In the back of his mind was this amorphous young man she would meet one day. She was not a light to remain hidden beneath a bushel, but he'd dim it for her. She would no longer flame like the daughter of a horse leech. Molly was the daughter of a respectable, chapel-going apothecary. A man of substance who had succeeded by his own industry. But how did a man bring himself to part with a pretty daughter? However, the question had not arisen. She had run away—a wicked and ungrateful girl.

Molly's mother was under no illusions about her husband. A whited sepulchre, a bitter, cruel man without any capacity for love. He'd taken her youth and consumed it. And now he had tried to do the same thing to her beloved daughter. To whip the joy out of her, hoping to make her cringe before him. She knew he was attracted by her beauty, and hated her for it. Just as he had hated *her* when she was young and pretty. He had beaten her, too, and she had never cried out. People thought it was only working-class men who got drunk and beat their wives, but it was not true. She had found that out long ago from other women. Mr. Hastings used his religion as an excuse for his brutality. He quoted the Scriptures. How shocked he would be if he knew that every night she prayed that he would die and release them both from the bondage of his capricious will.

Apart from Molly, her only pleasure had been her potted plants—her three aspidistras, her five geraniums, her cactus that had red flowers every summer, and her ferns. She wished they had a real garden but gardens did not interest Mr. Hastings. He did not care for flowers and it was cheaper to buy vegetables. And he would not have a dog or cat.

And then Molly had gone. Dead. Lost, strayed like a dog. And he would make no inquiries. But God had taken care of her baby. This lady had said she was safe and that she would take care of her. Mrs. Lenton. If only she had told them where she lived. . . .

25 : The End of the Road

William Harold Faulkner Ponsonby Fortall, Lord Cockshott, had been preparing himself for death for a long time. A lifetime of twenty-four years had gone by since he had had his seventieth birthday—the threescore and ten Biblical allotment to which men felt themselves entitled by the dispensation of God. He attributed the length of his life to drinking only the best wines, riding only the best horses and making love to only the most attractive women; and all in moderation. Never more than a bottle of port and a bottle of claret a day. Never hunting more than three days a week. Never sleeping with more than one woman at a time. Moderation, that was the secret of longevity.

He took a silver penknife from the table by his bed and prepared a new goose quill, cutting it to a blunt point and then splitting it neatly upward for a quarter of an inch. He had the feathers sent down from the Castle, where he kept a small flock of gray lags specially for the purpose. Their pinion feathers had once been used to fletch the arrows of England's archers. He was engaged in writing, not his reminiscences, but a kind of *aide mémoire,* intelligible only to himself, of the most notable horses and women in his life. It was typical of him that the horses came first.

Lying propped up in the great tester bed, with four pillows and a portable desk on his lap, he wrote and dreamed. Orator, Hector, Bess—what a mare she had been! John Peel, a big gray. Bloodstain, Starlight, Jack, Ranger, Roman, Countess. . . . And the girls. By God, they were harder to remember because they were more alike, and romantic adventures very similar one to another. Evenings and nights with soft perfumed flesh that quenched desire, but did not have the glory of a long point or a great leap. Timber, stone walls, bullfinches, water. Lord, the variety of it! And scenery. The wide fields of plough and grass, the five-barred gates. The spinneys and coverts—how much better they looked from the back of a good horse! The smell of gorse, the bare winter trees all black bones against the sky. The music of the hounds. The sweet smell of horse sweat, the pull of reins in his hands.

He looked down at them. Frail now, and blotched with the liver-colored spots of age. The horses they had patted and held, the women they had loved. Polly, Lily, Phillipa, Margaret, Denise—the French girl he had kept for five years. But they were hard to place, to isolate and keep apart. Not like the horses. Fifteen-three. Sixteen-two. That was old Roman, an Irish horse, the biggest he had ever hunted. But you saw horses in the daylight, that was it. In the winter sunshine. Cubbing in the golden woods of autumn.

With girls it was by lamplight mostly. Candlelight and in the dark. Love was a dark thing, really. Most men were conceived in the dark, and born in it; like animals in a cave.

He'd had some good children, though. Bastards, that he'd done well by. That was a curious thing. That his only son should be such a bastard and the bastards have turned out so well. It was probably because he'd always been such a good judge of both women and horses. Always picked good ones, brave ones, gentle ones with big hearts as well as pretty bodies. They had been chosen for their looks and natures. Araminta, Harold's mother, had been a good match. A fine-looking girl with a big estate. But there had been no juice in her. No blood, no milk.

He stared into the glowing coals of the banked-up fire. Hot. Everyone said the room was hot, but he didn't feel it. And what a jumble the room was. He'd had a lot of things moved into it from other parts of the house and from the country. Fox masks and brushes. Whips. His favorite pair of guns. A stuffed spaniel in a glass case. Pictures of horses and dogs and women. Oil paintings, daguerreotypes—all valueless and all priceless in terms of memory. With them and the lists he was compiling, he had 'em pinned down. His memory was good enough, but it slipped. He needed these things so that he could lie there dreaming and remembering.

Waterloo, by God! How many men were there alive who could remember Waterloo? The farm at Quatre Bras. The Duke. The Guards. The Frenchies charging. Heavy cavalry coming at them in great cuirassed waves. The smell of powder, the cries of the wounded. The blood. By God, it had been bloody! And if old Blücher had not turned up in time, they'd have lost the day.

He allowed no one to come and see him now, or at least as few people as possible. His valet, Crabtree, his doctor, his lawyer. And his son—because he could not keep him out. Liked the boy's wife, though. What the hell was her name? A small dark piece. Maud—that was it. Maud. She'd been a Fernley. Good blood there. Too good for the boy by half, and he'd never bred from her. He wondered whose fault it was.

Araminta had been his second wife. Caroline had died without issue. But she'd been a good wife. A looker, too. Red-haired. Chestnut. He'd always had a weakness for red-haired women, chestnut horses, and

Irish setters. All wild, all hot, all nervous—but full of blood and fire. Caroline's death had been a great blow to him. He had married Araminta in 1840, fifteen years later, largely at the instigation of her mother. Ysolde Worlake, a beautiful woman, who had once been his mistress. The Worlake estate marched with his own. Araminta was an only child. There had been something rather humorous about marrying this beautiful cold young woman who, both by age and accident, might so easily have been his daughter. This sardonic sense of humor, and his physical courage, were about the only characteristics his son had inherited from him. "Why don't you marry her?" Ysolde had said one day. Breed a son and tie up the two places? Indeed, why not? And he had, to his perpetual regret. As a sort of joke to please Ysolde, of whom he was still fond, and to breed himself heirs. Heirs. Just one had come of it—and what a beauty. A young man, a boy—he still thought of him as a boy—who thought of himself as a buck, a rake, a dandy. As if it was still the Regency. Gambler, womanizer, duellist. A man who associated with common pugs. Whose best friend had been Lenton, a man of his own ilk. . . .

The boy was forty now. Well, he'd made him wait for it. It had been his intention to live to a hundred, but he was not going to make it. The end was pretty near. But what a life he'd had! Horses, women, friends, soldiers, war and love. He'd been on the Duke's staff in the Peninsula. The Iron Duke. Copenhagen, his chestnut charger. The things he'd seen—atrocities by the Spaniards, by the Frenchies. Men flogged and hanged. The regiment. Her Majesty's first regiment of Foot Guards. The Grenadiers. Bearskins, scarlet. . . . The band playing them into battle, the drummer boys no more than fourteen, some of them.

He rang the silver bell by his bed. Crabtree, his man, came in.

"You rang, my lud?"

"Candles, Crabtree."

"The lamp, my lud."

"Candles, God damn it! When I say candles, I mean candles."

They were lit. The room came to life, little pools of it around the silver candlesticks reflected by the big Queen Anne silver rose bowl. It was empty now. No more roses for me, he thought. That was interesting.

"I've seen my last rose, Crabtree," he said.

"No, my lud."

"Don't argue with me."

The man went out and was back a few minutes later with a bunch of yellow roses.

"Your last roses, my lud, if you want it that way."

"Want it? Who the hell wants the last of anything?" First it was women. Then horses, and now roses. "I shan't live till summer, Crabtree."

"Don't say it, my lud." The man rubbed his eyes with his knuckles.

"Stop piping your eye, you bloody fool. You've nothing to worry about. I've left you enough to buy a pub. That's what you always said you wanted. A pub in the country, and a plump partridge of a wife. Always liked them plump, didn't you Crabtree?" They did not have many secrets from each other, the old lord and his man.

"I don't want a bloody pub, my lud. I want to go on taking care of you. Forty years of it, man and boy."

"Like a bloody nursemaid. Now get out and do something about the bloody row in the streets."

Neither his sight nor his hearing had gone. But the sound of the traffic in Grosvenor Square, which was never very heavy, had become intolerable to him.

"Yes, my lud," Crabtree said. "Straw."

"Aye, my boy. Bedded down with wheat straw like a bloody horse in a box."

Box . . . coffin . . . and dying in bed like a woman. He'd never expected it. Box to box. Cradle to coffin. Bed. He'd made Harold in this bed. Araminta had given birth to him in it. He'd loved Caroline in it. In this room. By God, she'd turn in her grave if she saw the room now! Fox masks. Pictures of his girls and horses and dogs in her bedroom. There had been no need for girls with her about.

Downstairs Crabtree was crying openly. "The old bugger," he said. "Bedding himself down."

"I'll see to it," the butler said. "I'll go myself."

Who'd sent the roses? He'd forgotten to ask. Lord Cockshott rang his silver bell again. Crabtree, who had gone back to doze in his chair outside the bedroom door, came in.

"Who sent them, Crabtree?" The old man pointed to the vase.

"The Honorable Mrs. Fortall, my lud. With best wishes. She brought them herself and I'm to let her know when you need more. Hothouse, my lud."

"She's a good 'un, Crabtree. Too good for him. But they'll be the last. The last," he said. "And I wonder how many roses I've seen. Roses and thorns. Like women, Crabtree. Never a rose without a thorn."

Why was it women were always associated with roses? That was a pleasant subject to dream about. Emma, Lady Hamilton. Why the hell should he think about her? Of course he had known her. She had run to fat though. But in her young days in Italy. . . . He had never liked full-fleshed women. Not like Crabtree. He liked 'em herring-gutted. Like race horses, greyhounds, with no hair on their heels. Nelson, the cock sparrow, with a patch on his eye. England expects . . . His "Kiss me, Hardy," on the deck of the *Victory* when he was dying. Nelson and the Duke. What a pair! They didn't breed 'em like that today. Nor like me either, he thought. The country was going to the dogs. Bound to. Too many new-fangled things. Take railways. Just take them. Puffing up and down England, stinking the place up and scaring the horses. And the men. Men like his son. What a pity everything was entailed. He'd have cut him off if he could. Women, too. Mealy-mouthed now. Didn't even call a spade an implement for digging. They had limbs instead of legs. God damn it, as if God hadn't made 'em all over! As if God had just made their faces and the devil had fabricated the other bits. And this chap, Charles Darwin. By God, he might well be right! Descended from monkeys, and going back to 'em. . . .

Funny the way his mind jumped, and refused to jump. Like a balking horse, jibbing, refusing. He'd been thinking about roses and then Emma and Horatio Nelson had come into it. Trafalgar. Ships of the line. Tall troop ships as full of redcoats as an egg was full of meat. Eggs. By God, he'd like an egg! He rang his bell.

"My lud?"

"Bring me an egg."

"A boiled egg, my lud?"

"What the hell else? Do you think I'd eat a fried egg in the afternoon? It's not breakfast. Make it two. Two brown ones and half a bottle of claret."

"The doctor said . . ."

"Damn the doctor. If I want a bloody egg—two eggs—and some claret, I'll have 'em."

Masterful to the end. Dying game. Damning and bloodying and to hell with everyone. Crabtree smiled. There was still life in him. He might yet see roses again. The old bugger—the old dear. . . . Lord, he'd seen him! Still pinching the girls if they came too near his bed. Would only have pretty housemaids. That was something the male staff liked, even the butler. A house full of pretty girls. Not that they kept the place very clean, but you couldn't have everything.

He sent a footman down for the eggs. ". . . and toast. And see they're brown. Three and a half minutes." The butler was decanting the claret. Tasting it too, he bet—a half-bottle taste. But what was it the old man always said? " 'Muzzle not the ox that treadeth out the corn'— from the Bible, that is, Crabtree. . . ." Full of quips like that, he was. A pleasure to serve. "Take a glass yourself, Crabtree," one minute, and a jack boot at your head the next. But he'd know no more boots, more's the pity. That was certain. It would be a dull world without him, and no pub or plump partridge of a woman would make up for his loss.

26 : Blueskin Reports

The Honorable Mrs. Harold Fortall was looking her best. Obviously, a woman in love. She managed one way or another—and never the same way—to see Geoffrey Horner at least once a week. But each time the result was the same. An attack, that was almost a rape, by her husband when she got home. How could he know? How did he guess? It must be guesswork because they were so careful. She had even tried seeing Geoffrey in the morning. Who ever heard of anyone committing adultery before ten? But there he was, waiting for her when she came back for lunch. It was the indignity of it that upset her. If he knew, why in God's name didn't he divorce her, name Geoffrey as corespondent, instead of this cat and mouse game that he played? It was going to happen. It had to happen. Why did they hesitate themselves? They had made up their minds to go to South Africa. Geoffrey was going to send in his papers. Why could they not set a date, make up their minds? At least, she couldn't. She was trapped by the pattern of her social life. Afraid of becoming a pariah. In her heart she knew she half enjoyed the intrigue, even the indignities of Harold's attentions. Fresh from the arms of the man she loved into those of a husband she hated. But it was so much easier than it had ever been before. Sometimes she almost laughed at him. Possess her? That was what he thought. Or did he not? Did he, too, get some perverse pleasure out of the situation? Was she as depraved as he? Only Lavinia understood her. Lavinia with her tragedy and her absurd crusade. She wondered about her and that lawyer. Of course what went on was awful, but why not let sleeping dogs lie? Particularly such dangerous dogs. Already there was talk about her. People were calling her one of those new women, independent. They said if Edward had not been helpless, he would have stopped her long ago. All this muckraking and washing of dirty linen in public. And the people she was mixed up with now. Longbeach, Stead, Mrs. Butler, and others like them. Tilters at windmills. She was making herself ridiculous. But how complicated life was: Maud looked at the little enamel watch pinned to her breast. Eleven o'clock. She was meeting Geoffrey at twelve. They were going to have lunch at a house just off the Bayswater Road that catered to people like themselves. A retired butler and his wife ran it most discreetly. Excellent food, service and privacy in a small flat on the second floor. She had a round cardboard hatbox in her hand. In it was a black cloak and a heavy veil. She would put them on in the hansom. If anyone saw her get out, they would never recognize her.

It was still early but she wanted to get there first. She did not want to meet Geoffrey wrapped up like a mummy. She stopped a passing hansom and got in. She had no idea she was being followed by a man of color. Negroes and half-castes were rare in London but they somehow remained invisible.

Blueskin stopped another hansom and said: "Follow that cab!" to the driver. "There is a quid in it if you don't lose it."

"Ten bob now," the driver said.

Blueskin handed half a sovereign up through the trapdoor in the roof and sat back. He liked riding in hansom cabs. After driving for fifteen minutes, the trapdoor opened and the cabby looked down.

"'E's slowing up."

"Look at the number," Blueskin said. "I don't want 'er to see me. And drive on."

They passed the stationary hansom. A hundred yards beyond it Blueskin banged on the roof. The door opened.

"Number fifteen," the cabby said. "Shall I stop 'ere?"

"This'll do. And here's the other half quid." He handed up the small gold coin.

"Thanks, guv'nor."

Blueskin got out and sauntered off to wait for the gentleman. Lord, he thought, what a lot of bloody fuss these toffs made of it. Just to block some other chap's wife. As if it mattered who it was when you wanted it. Not much difference in 'em really, though some was better than others. Like horses.

He sat on the pavement and took off his left shoe, staring at it, poking it with his finger. Christ, he said to himself, here I am opposite No. 15, but e'll never spot me. A darkie trying to mend his shoe on the pavement. He did not have to wait long for the second hansom. When the man went in he strolled over to it. The cabby was just going to put a nose bag on the horse.

"You want to take a cab?" he asked incredulously. "Can you pay for it?"

Blueskin pulled a handful of silver out of his pocket.

"Jump in, guv'nor. The bloody horse'll have to wait for 'is lunch."

In the house Maud was watching for her lover through the lace curtains. She wondered how many women, and men too, had stood like that, watching for love to come behind a trotting horse. She saw the cab, watched Geoffrey get down and pay the driver. How handsome he was! In a minute he would kiss her, hold her. After lunch . . . Well, after lunch they would make love. The whole afternoon was spread like a carpet of delight before her. And then Harold, almost certainly Harold. If only she could find out how he knew. But already, while contemplating her lover's arrival, she was thinking of her husband. The beast. Two men in a day. She wondered how many of her friends had that. She knew she would be almost disappointed if he was not waiting for her when she got home.

Naturally she had not noticed the colored man fixing his shoe on the opposite side of the road.

Geoffrey was entranced by the sight of Maud. She had on a black cloth coat and skirt, a black pillbox hat with a short veil that reached to her mouth. The jacket of her suit was fitted close to her body. It had a high black fur collar that came to her ears. Out of it, her oval face, bright in excitement, blushed with anticipation. Her eyes, even through her veil, sparkled. She had on black kid gloves and one arm was thrust through a black fur muff.

"My God, you are lovely!" he said. "Take off your hat." He went to kiss her. She clung to him, fragrant of violets, her favorite perfume. Her lips were soft, moist as he always remembered them, but each kiss was a new experience. He lifted her off her feet with his embrace. She struggled with him, half in anger at his urgency.

"Wait, darling," she said. "Wait till after luncheon." She went to the mirror to straighten her little black hat. She raised her veil to see her face better. Geoffrey was right. She was, as the French said, *en beauté,* one of her very good days. There was no beautifier like a lover and there was no love better than this adventurous illicit kind. Like the stolen apples of childhood that were so much sweeter than those you were given. How lucky Geoffrey was to have her! She was looking forward to luncheon, to watching him pick at his food, too excited to eat properly. Men could never wait. They were like children. After luncheon . . . after coffee . . . the curtain would go up in the bedroom and the play begin.

"Take off your hat, darling. Your gloves. Let down your hair." She would not hurry. She would savor it. Stand at the mirror, look back at him, her red mouth full of hairpins. When her hair was down, he would fondle it and stroke it. Kneel at her feet and take off her shoes, her jacket, her skirt. Her stockings. Her corset—a new one with white satin panels. How clumsy his fingers were! Knickers. She would stand in front of him in her chemise, and then pull it up over her head. Then he would kneel at her feet again before he undressed. All this in her mind before luncheon, during luncheon. An undress rehearsal, so that when the delicious meal was over—though it seemed to come naturally —each moment would be a studied perfection, complete in itself, an incitement.

Blueskin drove to Coak Street. Mrs. Caramine saw him at once.
"Well?" she said.
"You can tell the guv'nor they met. They're at it now. 'Ammer and tongs, I bet."
Fortall didn't want to know where they met; he didn't care. Only when.
"I'll tell him," Mrs. Caramine said. "I'll send a boy."
Harold Fortall was a good customer, one of the best, and he would be a lord any day now. Ellen would be amused at the Blueskin story. She had not met Fortall yet. It was some time since he'd visited the establishment, but he'd be back. In the short time Ellen had been with her a kind of friendship had sprung up between them. One of my own sort, Mrs. Caramine thought. When a well bred 'un went wrong, really wrong, and did not break, they were special.

Take Ellen, or Hélène as she called herself now. She had style, she was educated. She even talked French, picked it up in Paris. That, and a lot of other things. By God, she'd have Fortall by the short hairs! The man would go mad for her. All that ever kept him away was this wife business. How he loved and hated her! What a bastard he was! But she'd suck him dry, Ellen would. He hated his wife because he had her and couldn't possess her. Because she came to him hot from her lover and was complaisant to all his desires just to keep him quiet and keep him off the scent. If she knew the truth . . . but come to that, if anyone knew the truth. . . .

Ellen hated all men but was insatiable for them. Her mind hated them, her body craved them. That was the way fortunes were made. A good-looking girl who was good in bed and had ice in her heart. The trouble with most of them was that they had to have love, even the imitation love of the pimp who exploited them. Or they just gave up. Lost all feeling, neither giving nor getting pleasure. Having no interest in anything, not even in money.

Crabtree had sent for the doctor. Lord Cockshott was sinking fast. There was deep straw outside the house in Grosvenor Square. The old man listened to the traffic in the distance, heard the noise fade as it passed and start again when the horses got out of the knee-deep golden bed that covered the street. This time it was the end. Ninety-four years of it, a good and varied life. The old Queen's coronation in Westminster Abbey. A young girl, then. By God, what a lot he'd seen! Friends—men, women, children—horses, dogs. Servants—good and faithful servants. Well, he'd provided for them. But what a pity it was the bloody place was entailed. If I could have done it, he thought, I'd have left that young pup nothing. Not a bloody penny. Funny that the place and title should go to such a wastrel. He liked the girl, though. That Maud. She'd probably cuckolded him and serve him right too. He saw the doctor talking to his lawyer. In at the death, he thought. A lot of bloody vultures. Jackals. Dogs. Christ, he was feeling weak. It was seeping out of him. Life—whatever it was—was slipping away. Well, he didn't give a damn. He'd had about enough of it.

The door opened and that young bastard came in. By God, he thought, I wonder if he is! That would account for a lot of things. He gave a kind of chuckle. The doctor took his wrist and pulled out his watch. Bloody fools, he thought, going through the drill.

His son leant over the bed to stare at him. A bastard, he thought. By God, that was funny to think that Araminta had tricked him and he'd only guessed it on his deathbed!

"You bastard," he said, as he raised himself on skinny elbows. What a pity the little filly wasn't with him. He'd have liked her to hear him call his son a bastard. He fell back with a gurgling chuckle. His eyes glazed, his mouth fell open, exposing a few blackened teeth. Old Lord Cockshott was dead.

The new Lord Cockshott turned away from the bed. The doctor looked shocked.

"I've never seen a man die laughing before," he said. "And he wouldn't have a parson near him, my lord. I said: 'What about a parson?' And he said: 'I've lived without 'em and I'll die without 'em.'"

"The old bastard," his son said, going to the big dressing table and picking up a bunch of keys.

Mr. Rodwell, the solicitor, said: "What are you going to do, my lord?"

"Open the safe, get out the jewels and go home. I've got something important to do at home that won't wait."

He took the jewels out of the velvet- and satin-lined leather cases, where they had lain resting since his mother's death, and slipped them into his pockets. A couple of hundred thousand pounds worth of sparkling beauty, waiting for soft necks, bosoms, slim wrists and fingers. Some of the jewels were old, the emeralds the oldest, with a pedigree of death and torture hidden in their green fire. Wars had been fought for them by rajahs and princes. Men had been murdered. Women, who wore them, poisoned by jealous harem rivals. Every big stone had a story of death or potential death. Each had been the reward offered by a man to beauty in return for pleasure. They were a reward. With jewels there was always a *quid pro quo.*

Crabtree could have killed him. Arrogant. Brutal. Thoughtless. So obviously delighted at his father's death.

Harold Cockshott patted his breast pocket. It held Mrs. Caramine's note that had been delivered by one of her runners just before he got the doctor's message.

"See to it all, Rodwell," he said. "The papers, the obsequies and so on. Send him down to the Castle. Just let me know when to turn up."

He felt very well; very content. The old bugger was dead at last, and he was going home to his sweet, pretty, obedient, and faithless little wife. No emeralds for her today, though. He'd just lock them up and give them to her later. He burst into a roar of laughter as the footman opened the front door.

The bastard, the footman thought. The bloody bastard.

At home in Wilton Crescent, Maud, safely back from her adventure, was reading a French novel. Where was Harold? She was both relieved and disappointed by his absence. The butler told her that he had gone out just before she came in. "A message, Madam," he said, "from his lordship, I gathered."

The yellow-backed-paper novel was really very dull after the reality. No one could write about love. The excitement of it, the satisfaction, the euphoric daze that followed it. She got up to look at herself in the mirror. How lovely she looked! Geoffrey had told her so. She had taken infinite trouble with her toilette before going to meet him. But now she glowed with a kind of inner light. There was a new bloom to her beauty. Her shadowed eyes looked bigger, her lips fuller, softer and more red. Ripe as cherries. That was what a man could do for a woman.

When she'd come in, she'd had a bath. Hot as she could bear it, with half a jar of violet-scented bath salts in it. Her maid, Louise, had smiled knowingly as she unlaced her corset. The knot was not the one she had tied. Fortunately, being French, she liked intrigue as much as her mistress. A blind eye and a silent tongue she had always found to be productive of presents. After all, she had her fun too. So why begrudge the upper classes their *amours?*

Maud enjoyed her bath. Usually, if Harold was in when she came back, there was no time for one. He took her straight to the bedroom. The first time she'd said: "Do let me have a bath first, Harold. I feel so grubby." And he'd said: "No, darling. I like you that way."

Lying luxuriously in the warm water, she'd wondered what he meant exactly. Anyway she had never suggested a bath again. He never even gave her time to, going at her like a bull at a gate. What a man he was! What a beast! And what on earth was he doing at his father's house now? Was he worse? Perhaps she had been wrong after all. Perhaps he did not know when she had seen Geoffrey. But how could there be so many coincidences?

When Louise had dried her, she told her to get out her beige silk *chiné* that had designs of flowers and leaves—all rather big but muted colors—that blended softly into each other. She wore it over three petticoats—one of lawn edged with wide lace, one of white silk and a top one of cream taffeta. She put on cream satin slippers and Louise did her hair in the somewhat old-fashioned Empress Eugénie style, with drooping curls that suited her so well, and went into the drawing room.

God damn Harold! What did he know? What did he guess? Either way she was looking pretty enough to upset him. This time she would not make it easy. She would be firm. She had just picked up her novel again when she heard the front door close. He was back. He came into the drawing room, looking triumphant.

"And how has your ladyship spent the day, may I ask?"

She felt herself blushing. He knew. He could not know.

"Shopping," she said. "And where have you been?"

"In at the death," he said. "The old boy's gone at last, Lady Cockshott." He bowed to her, making a leg in mockery.

She jumped up and ran toward him, her skirts rustling. Lady Cockshott. What a fool she was ever to have thought of running away to an ostrich farm in the wilds of Africa! It was just that the old man had taken so long over it. She had been so bored. That was why. No other reason. It had looked as if it would go on forever. How clever she had been to refuse to set a date for their elopement. Lady Cockshott, or the mistress of an ex-officer of the Guards.

Her husband had her by the waist. "Upstairs, your ladyship," he said.

She went in front of him, her heels clicking, her petticoats rustling, her bustle moving provocatively as she climbed the stairs. And she had been going to be difficult. To be firm. She was smiling as she opened the bedroom door.

Louise gave them a curious look as she went out of the room.

27 : The Actor

The day after his father's death, Harold Cockshott presented himself at Mrs. Caramine's.

"Well, my lord," she said, dropping him a curtsey. "What an honor!"

He laughed at her. "What do I owe you, Carrie? You're the first I'll pay."

"A monkey will cover it, my lord."

"I should say it would, my dear. But you've been very patient. No duns. No rude letters—and I've got quite a collection of them." He took out his checkbook and wrote a check for five hundred pounds.

"It's more than a year," Mrs. Caramine said. "Works out at a tenner a week, and you've had good value, my lord. I wanted to keep you on a string"—and she smiled sweetly—"but the price is up now."

"Up eh, Carrie? That's all right, but I want more for it. I want something special."

"And I've got it. As it happens she's in my room now. Come up and meet her." She opened the door to let Lord Cockshott precede her. "Hélène," she said, "this is Lord Cockshott. If she doesn't like you, my lord, it's a no go. Hélène picks and chooses like a lady, don't you, darling?"

The girl on the low red plush chair got up gracefully in a single motion.

"Christ!" Cockshott said.

"I beg your pardon, Lord Cockshott," Ellen said, extending a kid-gloved hand.

"You're a lady."

"I was, Lord Cockshott. Now I'm a harlot and, to tell you the truth, I rather like it. It's much better than being a governess."

Wearing gloves in the house was now a habit with Ellen—part of the

Hélène personality and a trick taught her by Edward Lenton, who loved leather gloves, high-buttoned leggings, boots, belts. . . . She put her arm around Carrie Caramine's waist for an instant and then sank into her chair again.

"Do sit down," she said. "Pour yourself a drink." She waved at the decanters and syphons on the small sideboard. "And smoke if you want to. I have theories, Lord Cockshott. Theories about comfort and manners."

Lord Cockshott looked around for Mrs. Caramine, but she had slipped away.

"I suppose you wanted to ask her how much," Ellen said. "Well, I can tell you. You see I handle these goods myself on a commission basis. It's twenty-five guineas, take it or leave it. And all refreshments, except for the wine, are free." She smiled up at him.

Harold's hand shook as he poured out a brandy. A clinker, by God! A lady with a tongue in her head and a body like a mermaid, a bifurcated mermaid.

As if she read his mind, Ellen stood up and turned around slowly on her high heels, with a swish of skirts. Her dress was her own design, an indigo satin, cut low and close to her figure. But the closeness did not stop at the tiny waist—it went on clinging to her, molding her thighs almost to her knees, where it fanned out in a wide arc of accordion pleats like the petals of a dark flower. An inverted bell, out of which she rose in slim perfection.

She saw his eyes light up. "Will I do?" she said, "or do you want one of the kids downstairs?" She looked him in the eye, then looked down, letting her long lashes lie over her cheeks, and raised her skirt and petticoats to show her ankles and calves.

Cockshott gulped his brandy and soda. Ellen sat down again. She knew she had him nailed. He was an Edward Lenton all over again. About the same age, the same type. Just for fun she asked him.

"Do you know Mr. Edward Lenton?"

"Poor Edward," Cockshott said.

"Yes indeed, Lord Cockshott. Poor Mr. Lenton. No more fun and games for him, I understand."

"You know him, Hélène?"

"Oh yes, Lord Cockshott. I was governess to his children, and he seduced me. Such a charming man. Quite a ladies' man."

"His children were abducted. You heard about that?"

"I did, indeed. But that was by my successor, a young French lady."

Cockshott took her hand. "Do you always wear gloves?" he said.

"Generally. It keeps my hands white and small. A hundred years ago ladies always wore gloves in the house. But I'll take them off if you tell me to. I'll do anything you tell me, Lord Cockshott," she said, sticking out a satin-shod foot from under her skirt and examining it as if she had never seen it before. Then she looked up and smiled. "Anything you want, if I want it too. But no rough stuff, my lord"—her face hardened for an instant—"if you want that, pick one downstairs."

Four hours later, when Lord Cockshott picked up his opera cloak and stick, he was a changed man. He was in love. Not real love, but real lust. The girl had sent him mad. He knew he would not be able to keep away from her. And with Lady Maud, as he called her, so willing after she had been with her lover, he had as much on his plate as he could deal with.

Lady Cockshott was lunching with Lavinia Lenton, a simple luncheon *à deux*. Lobster bisque, roast pheasant, and that the head keeper had sent from Mortal—he sent three brace a week—a *soufflé*, a caramel custard and a bottle of hock.

Maud looked her best. In black, of course. A black cloth costume trimmed with sealskin. The tight-fitting jacket had sealskin collar and cuffs, the skirt a sealskin hem. Two lines of sealskin came down the front, parted company below the waist and went round her hips.

While the servants were in the dining room, the conversation had revolved about the death of her father-in-law. About the title. About what a character he had been—a man who had fought in the Peninsula under Wellington and at Waterloo. A kind of human bracket that joined the modern world with the past.

"Poor old man," Lavinia said.

"A happy release," Maud said. "He was in no pain. His light, which had been burning dimmer and dimmer, just went out. He liked me, but they never let me know. I'd like to have seen him again with Harold."

"Lord Cockshott?"

"Yes, I often tried, my dear, but I couldn't bring them together." A suspicion of a smile flitted over Maud's full lips.

It was extraordinary what love did to a woman, Lavinia thought. Maud's lips were fuller, more moist, redder than they used to be. Her blue eyes had greater depth. There was a kind of wonder in them, an excitement like that of a girl. Lavinia guessed she was going to meet Geoffrey.

Alone in the drawing room at last, Lavinia said: "Now tell me."

"Tell you, darling? There was a scene at the deathbed, I understand. The old boy died game, like a fighting cock. Pecking and striking to the end. Not that Harold told me much. He never does. But that's what I gathered."

Maud touched her sealskin toque. "Do I look nice?" she asked.

"Lovely."

"I'm glad. Because I'm going to meet Geoffrey at three."

So that accounted for her scarcely suppressed excitement. It was just what Lavinia had thought.

Maud continued: "I wonder how he always finds out. . . ."

"Don't tell me he knows! He's not said anything, has he?" Harold Fortall—Lord Cockshott—had never struck Lavinia as a *mari complaisant,* not a man who would allow himself to be cuckolded in silence.

"It's not what he says; it's what he does," Maud said, her eyes darkening. "That's what I can't understand, but he never misses. Every time I see Geoffrey, he's there, waiting for me at home. Or he comes in soon afterward."

"And he doesn't say anything?"

"Not a word. He just tells me to go to the bedroom. Even in the mornings. I thought the morning would be safe enough. How can he guess, Lavinia? Or, if he doesn't guess, how can he know?"

"Geoffrey doesn't know that Harold guesses?"

"Oh no. Though I did tell him what happened sometimes when I got in. I didn't say always. And it is always. That's what frightens me. But it's exciting, too, in a way. In a horrible way. I think of it all the way home in the hansom. Of him waiting, guessing. Being in Wilton Crescent. So what can I do? I don't want to argue, to talk. He hardly even bothers to ask me where I've been. I always have some parcels—I do some shopping on the way home. And that girl of mine knows. Louise, my maid. How could she not know? And so I suppose the other servants too. . . ."

"Oh my dear, how awful!" Lavinia put her hand on her friend's knee. "If you're going to run off with him, why don't you do it and get it over?"

"But I'm not, Lavinia. Not now. I was a fool ever to think of it."

"You mean since . . ."

"Yes, of course. I like being Lady Cockshott. And then there are the jewels. Magnificent," she said. "There's not an emerald necklace like it in England. Diamonds, too. Rubies, sapphires. He'll have to let me wear them, won't he?"

"Poor Geoffrey," Lavinia said. "He loves you, you know."

"And I love him, and I'm not going to give him up. Not yet at any rate. You see if Harold knows—and I think he does—he'd have done something about it before if he was going to. Do you know what I think, Lavinia?"

"No." What explanation could there be?

"I'll tell you. I think he likes it. It gives him power over me. I have to do what he says. And he's a beast, Lavinia. He goes to that place."

"You don't mean Caramine's?" Lavinia had difficulty in saying the name.

"Yes, darling. From there to me and from me to there. He's boasted about it. There's a new girl there. Hélène. A blonde."

Hélène. Ellen. John had said she had gone back there. Life was extraordinary. Quite inexplicable.

The gilt clock on the Adams fireplace chimed the quarter.

"A quarter to three. I must fly, Lavinia, and thank you for the luncheon." Lady Cockshott put on her black kid gloves, finger by finger. When she took them off it would be with Geoffrey. She picked up the sealskin muff from the carpet beside her. She bent over to kiss Lavinia and went out.

A minute later Lavinia heard the footman whistling for a hansom. Maud was off to her lover. Lavinia, alone in her drawing room, began to think of John and the terrible things that were being done in the name of love. Love sacred and profane. Free and bond. Of girls, hundreds of them, trapped and imprisoned at this very moment as she sat here.

She thought of Harold Cockshott taking advantage of his wife's infidelities, of him being sardonically amused by them. Of Maud, half hating and half enjoying the indignities he forced upon her. Of young Geoffrey being deceived, still thinking she would run off with him. Of Maud's maid, Louise, an untrustworthy little piece if ever there was one.

She wondered what John was doing. What Stead was doing. How were their plans progressing? How very circumspect they had been! She looked at the clock. It was four. She found herself jealous of Maud. Maud was braver than she, or more reckless. Certainly not more in love. What Maud felt for Geoffrey was not love. It was a mixture of desire for him because he was so attractive, and hatred for Harold. A way of getting back at him. But for her there was too much at stake. She'd go down to Mortal for Christmas. There had been some nice "Dear Mrs. Lenton" letters from Molly. She was happy, she said. She loved Eva. She loved the country. She had never lived in the country before.

It was six when Maud got home. "Any messages?" she asked.
"None, your ladyship."

She went upstairs to bathe and change. Louise undressed her. Their
eyes met conspiratorially. But Harold had not been here to meet her.
She had just finished dressing when a footman brought her a note from
him on Hart's Club notepaper. "Please do not wait dinner. I shall be
late. Cockshott." The swine. But he had been diddled this time. And
her ladyship dined alone.

She thought of Lavinia and her affair with that lawyer. It was hard to
believe. She was such a serious woman. And she wouldn't talk about it.
Said it was sacred. As if a bed were sacred. And this other business she
was mixed up in. This girl business. As if you could change things or
stop men. . . . Look at her own husband before the accident. Look at
Harold. At Geoffrey . . . her Geoffrey. Why, even he had been to
Caramine's, and other houses, though he said hers was the best and that
she was a power in the half-world of London. The *demi monde*. And
he'd hinted at other things. Cruelties. Of girls being whipped, tied up,
and tortured. Of course it was all wrong and she'd help Lavinia if she
could, after her terrible experience with Eva and Betty. Betty, her own
godchild, lost somewhere, suffering God knew what. She had met the
French governess. What was her name? Delphine. A very ordinary-
looking girl. Even now she could not believe that she had ever been
Edward Lenton's mistress. Certainly she had magnificent eyes. But she
had been so dowdy, so old fashioned. Yet suppose . . . suppose it was
all a trick, a kind of disguise. If, under that dowdy black, there had
been a body to match the eyes. Lavinia had said there was. That she
had surprised her naked once. A beauty, with black hair that came
down to her waist. . . .

The more you saw of life, the more extraordinary it was.

28 : *The Festive Season*

Lavinia had just read the description of Lord Cockshott's funeral in
the *Times*. A eulogy about this old man who had been such a character, who had served under the Iron Duke and known Horatio Nelson.
A link with England's past . . . a human bracket that had joined the
eighteenth and nineteenth centuries . . . The Castle in Warwickshire,
his country seat . . . The house in Grosvenor Square . . . The family
jewels . . . famous emeralds . . . spoils from India in the days of the

John Company. All were mentioned. His two wives, his son. But nothing of his other loves or his life. Lavinia wondered about them. He was so old. He must have seen and done so much in almost a century. A hundred years—the overlap of memory of nine such old men would go back to the Conquest, to William of Normandy. Everyone had two lives—the visible one, like the clothes you wore for all to see, and the secret one, the nakedness that lay beneath them that could only be guessed at, ignored, or not thought about at all.

This was the problem she was faced with: no one was ready to believe evil of the handsome, prosperous, well-dressed men they met at dinners and balls. Their clothes were a complete disguise. And equally, no one seeing the street girls or hearing—and they did hear, even when they covered their ears with their hands—about houses of ill fame, was ready to believe that these girls were human. That under their tawdry clothes and finery they were just girls, just women like themselves.

She thought of the Cockshott emeralds. The great necklace, bracelets and earrings to match. They were supposed to be unlucky. But bad luck had never stopped a woman from wearing them. According to the stories one heard, Caroline, Cockshott's first wife, had died in great pain after a long illness. Araminta had suffered, too. Some feminine complaint that had prevented her from having a second child and was said to have soured her nature.

What stories there must be about all old jewels! And Maud was such a superstitious little thing. But she would wear the emeralds now and they, and all that went with them, would end her affair with Geoffrey.

Lavinia was sorry for him. He was in love with Maud, madly in love. And she had been wrong about her, thinking her different, brave enough to throw her cap over a windmill. It had just been talk. What she liked was admiration, the adventure and intrigue of it, and getting her own back on her husband in a way that she enjoyed. She had once thought she and Maud were alike, but they weren't. She was a one-man woman and that man was John Longbeach. Maud? Well, Maud was different. That was the kindest thing one could say about her. Yet she still loved her in a way.

A footman brought in the mail on a silver salver. Nothing of interest. Some bills, some invitations and then, at the bottom of the pile, the letter she had been waiting for from Molly's mother.

Dear Mrs. Lenton, I cannot tell you how grateful I am for your interest in Molly. I have tried and tried to get my husband to forgive her but he will not do so. He still says he has no daughter. But I have one and I shall be able to get up to town in the spring. I come up every year to see the dentist. I will let you know the date later but it will be about Easter. Please do not write to me—he looks at all my letters in case Molly writes. Please give her all my love, her mother's love, and the enclosed letter. The butcher brought the card with your address between two mutton chops. It was all bloody. I did not write at once because I was too upset. I have had a kind of breakdown. But don't let Molly worry. I am quite well now, and if he can make up his mind so can I. Again thanking you for your Christian help—I sometimes wonder if he is really a Christian at all. For did not St. Paul say: "And the greatest of these is Charity?" There is no Charity in his heart, or forgiveness.

Yours very sincerely and gratefully,
Martha Hastings.

The letter confirmed Lavinia's intention of going down to Mortal for Christmas. She would stay a month. Two months. Stay till the spring perhaps. She had seen Mr. Stead. He was working on things, he said. But he seemed to have lost some of his enthusiasm, to be nervous.

"I don't know how the public will take it, Mrs. Lenton. I do not know if they are ready for it yet."

Anyway she needed a rest and a change. She wanted to see Eva and Molly. Parker and the other servants. And Edward . . . she did not look forward to seeing him.

London had been a great strain. Now that she was aware of it she could go nowhere without seeing examples of the evil she was fighting. The Haymarket. Piccadilly. Women and girls. Children in boots that buttoned up to the thigh, short frilly petticoats, long hair loose on their backs, large feathered hats, furred bonnets, a tight polonaise often edged with fur or high-collared, frogged, military-looking coats.

And there was love. Frantic meetings with John. Outwardly cool; a lady going somewhere accompanied by her maid. Somewhere. Always somewhere new. Strange rooms in houses of accommodation. In apartments with strange furniture. Chairs, sofas, beds. Steel engravings on the walls. Outward respectability, but each had an aura of illicit love, of passion. There was something revolting in it. In her own urgency, and John's restraint that was not restraint. And it was not as if they were young. People of their age should not go on like this. Yet once they had parted, she did nothing but go over it all in her mind, remembering every word, every movement, every act, feeling in retrospect his hands on her body. She wondered what May really thought when she dressed her like a bride. Happy for her happiness but ashamed, too, of her madam. She thought of May waiting for them to be done. What went on in her mind?

Well, there would be none of this at Mortal. It would be impossible there. She knew she was running away. She said she wanted to rest. To see Nestor and Mac. To see her old home again.

There were a number of different lives going on at Mortal. The life of the great house went on of its own volition. The life of the servants in the house, of the stables and the gardens all proceeded serenely on their way. There were no changes except that Charles was now courting a new housemaid. He had given May up.

Then there was the life of Evangeline and Emma and the deerhound. A tight little nursery circle with Molly on its periphery.

And finally that of Edward, his valet, and two male nurses, also utterly separate from the others. The big house contained them as a pond might contain three children's boats. Sailing, drifting, or aground, but each irrelevant to the other.

The county gossip had died down. The nine-day wonder of the children's abduction and Edward's accident was over. Its residue had changed in form. It was now concerned with Lavinia Lenton—that unwomanly woman, who was washing England's dirty linen in public. It was said that the Queen was most displeased. The tragedy of the past was lost in the scandal of the present and the astonishment that a lady should be mixed up in such muckraking.

There had been few visitors to Mortal. Fred Holiday came down once to see poor Edward. He took a look at him and went off by the next train. At Hart's the following day, he said:

"I went down to Mortal yesterday to see Eddy Lenton. Quite upset me. Ought to put him down, poor chap. Port? Yes, I'd like another glass of port." And that was the end of Lenton at Hart's. There'd be no more talk of him till he died. Then there'd be wreaths, a special train to Mortal Major to see him buried, and letters of condolence to that bloody woman who certainly ought to have known better than to try to change the morals of the country. Things were as they always had been, and always would be. It was no good trying to change them.

Lavinia did not want to see Edward but he could not be left entirely to his attendants. She would see John, of course. And she wanted to ride Nestor again, to be in the country where she had her roots; and get some of the things she had seen and done out of her mind for a while if she could.

Last Christmas she had been living with Edward. The mother of two beautiful children, the mistress of a house that was always full of people. A wife, mother, and hostess. Now everything was changed. She was a grass widow married to a helpless, speechless man for whom she had no feeling at all—not even hate—but for whom she felt responsible. She was the mistress of John Longbeach. A woman deeply engaged in a crusade against vice. The mother of only one daughter, one who had lost her mind and retreated into the security of her doll-playing childhood. Responsible for Molly Hastings whom she had rescued. . . . All this in a few months. Now she smoked cigarettes; she drank a brandy when she felt like it, and, above all, she knew the facts of life. This was another thing she must attack. The ignorance and hypocrisy that sent girls to their marriage beds, into life, completely ignorant of sex. An education that ignored physiology in the name of decency. A religion that made men disown their own daughters if they erred. She would never forget the scene she had had with Mr. Joseph Hastings, the Oxford chemist.

A year ago Nestor had been a splendid hunter. Now he was a broken-winded hack. In a way he seemed symbolic to her. Nestor, Eva, Betty, Molly, herself, even Edward. For years all their lives had gone on unchanging, and then the wheel had turned, bringing disaster, cruelty, and death—for Betty was dead, she was sure of it.

But once at Mortal her mood changed. Molly greeted her. Eva recognized her, not as a mother but as someone she knew and was not afraid of. There was still peace and security in the old house. And John was only ten miles away.

There was no change in Edward. That he knew her she could tell from his eyes. He looked at her with contempt and hatred. A human log in a wheelchair, with active brains and no means of expressing a thought or a desire. She felt he blamed her for his predicament, perhaps even for keeping him alive.

She spoke to all the servants. She went over the house touching the furniture—stroking pieces as if they were alive. Most of the furniture at Mortal was a comfortable mixture of the great English eighteenth-century designers. Mayhew, Chippendale, Robert Adam, Mainwaring, Hepplewhite, Kent, Johnson, George Smith, Lock, and Sheraton. But there were older things. Tapestries, statues and, in the hall, a pair of great oak fifteenth-century armchairs, each arm and the back supported by beautifully turned spindles. The back was decorated with an inlaid design of ivory, the arms carved duck heads, their necks extended in flight. Between them was a mahogany semi-circular card table by Hepplewhite and a chair to match, the back carved with a honeysuckle design, the seat caned, the legs beautifully turned, the back ones splayed out for support. There was some more modern Regency and early Victorian furniture, painted with birds and inlaid with mother-of-pearl.

And the pictures—Rubens, Turner, Van Dyke, Peter Lely, Constable, Titian, Lawrence, Landseer, Morland, Davis . . . ancestors . . . landscapes . . . animals—farm and hunting scenes. But all familiar, all friends of her childhood, each with memories, each a part of her life. Her own portrait as a girl, by Winterhalter.

A collection of comfort and beauty brought together by a family over the centuries. Ivories, jades, red and black lacquer pieces ornamented with gold. China. The Orient. India. Armor, weapons, carpets—all rich with craftsmanship, all with the patina of time and loving care. Room after room of it.

Mac, the deerhound, abandoned Eva and followed at her heels. She went to the stables to see the horses. She had Nestor saddled and rode him over the park and into the woodlands. In a day or two she would drive over to Mortal Major and drop in at John's office. What a good thing he was a lawyer! A woman of property like herself could always have business to transact with her solicitors. She laughed. It was Christmas but the spring was already in her blood, John Longbeach in her mind. The snowdrops were out, nodding their heads. Her depression had vanished.

Molly, who went walking with her, was a different girl. But it was curious that such experiences should have such a variety of results. For Molly, a nightmare that was over. For Eva there had been an escape into the past—a rejection of everything that had happened after early childhood. And then there was the acceptance of a life of vice. That was the way Ellen had taken it.

"I'm quite well, now, Mrs. Lenton," Molly said. "What shall I do?"

"Stay here for a bit longer. I think I have found a job for you. Would you like to help other girls who. . . ." She could not say "have fallen" —what a word! "Rescue work," she said vaguely. "They wouldn't be afraid of a gay, pretty girl like you. We are doing things. Mr. Longbeach, Mr. Stead, Mr. Booth, Mrs. Butler—there are a lot of us."

"I'd like to, Mrs. Lenton. I was rescued; I'd like to help others."

And that was the way Lavinia left it. They went on to talk of Eva. "She reads again now," Molly said. "And she has almost stopped playing with her dolls."

"She doesn't remember?"

"Oh no. I'm sure she doesn't. She's like a happy child. She'll grow up again, I think."

They walked through the woods, the dead leaves a soft brown carpet beneath their feet.

"I'm so glad you came for Christmas; I hoped you would," Molly said. "Can I help to get everything ready? The tree, the holly, the mistletoe—everything?"

Mistletoe meant kissing—not that there would be anyone to kiss her. But it proved something—that Molly was no longer afraid of men.

"Father didn't approve of Christmas," Molly said. "Not dancing and being happy."

"I heard from your mother, Molly. I'll give you the letter when we get in. She enclosed one for you. She thinks she can get up to London for the day in the spring."

"And I'll be there?"

"If you're not, I'll come down to fetch you."

What a charming girl she was! When they got back they went to the stables. She found Blackburn working on a new double bridle with yolk of egg and apricot jam. "What on earth are you doing?" Lavinia asked.

"Nothing like apricot jam and yolk of egg to get new leather a nice color. I couldn't let Madam go out with a yellow bridle, like a shop-keeper out hunting for the first time with everything new—yellow bridle, yellow saddle, yellow tops to his boots. . . ." Blackburn had the greatest contempt for the *parvenu* and *nouveau riche*.

"But I'm not hunting any more."

"Well, hacking, Madam. And old Nestor wouldn't like it. Never wore anything that wasn't broken in, and never will," the old man said.

Lavinia laughed, as he picked up a deer's shinbone to put a final polish on the reins, setting them out flat on the tack-room table. It wasn't his job, but he loved leather and would not let a groom near any new stuff till he had got it to his liking. No excuses after that. There were a dozen or more double bridles hanging on the walls but he had wanted her to have a new one with reins the master's hands had never touched. Nothing was said but Lavinia knew what was in Black-burn's mind.

The two men Dr. Jarvis got to look after Edward Lenton as soon as his wound healed, were not pleased to see Mrs. Lenton. They were male nurses trained in a lunatic asylum. Lenton was too heavy a man for a woman to handle and he had to be carried about, fed and bathed like a baby.

Both Fred Harper and Joe Crawley were happy enough at Mortal. They were well paid, got good food, and had plenty of maid servants for company. They thought it queer that Mrs. Lenton paid so little attention to her husband. Always in London she was. But they were glad of it. And a mad daughter. Like a bloody princess, but mad as a March hare. And that big dog always with her.

To save trouble, and having no idea of his likes and dislikes, they fed Lenton what they liked themselves. Steaks, chops, bacon and eggs—washed down with beer and tea. No more game, no soups, no soufflés, no claret, no port, no brandy.

"Wot's good enough for us, Joe," Fred Harper said, "is good enough for 'im."

Not that they could not have had anything they wanted. But they were men of fixed habits, though they did like a nice bit of roast beef and Yorkshire pudding for Sunday dinner. But soup, fish, game, vegetables—other than potatoes and cabbage—were not fit for human consumption in their opinion.

Benton, Edward's man, had stayed on too, and no one knew his master's tastes better, but he had no love for the man he served and so did nothing for his comfort. He merely drew his wages, kept his master's room and clothes tidy and lived like a fighting cock.

Edward often regretted he had made such a mess of his suicide attempt and, to pass the time, fell back on his memories. He found that with some effort, some mental digging, he had almost total recall. So he went back, like a dog on a trail, retrieving the lost days and nights. Girls, women. He brought them back, soft-mouthed in memory as a retriever. Horses, hunters, hunts, shoots. Spectacular shots that he had made. He read, too. Benton had rigged a bookstand for him—that was about all he had done—and whoever was on duty came and turned a page every now and again. So he had his memories and his books; and his hatred for Lavinia and her lover to keep him warm. Then there was the girl. His girl. He could not get over it. How pretty Eva was! And she'd lain there. Here, in this very room that had been turned into a bedroom for him. That was what had driven him to it. The shock of seeing her waiting. Saying: "I am ready, sir." Ready for what? Good God! What a fool he'd been not to use a twelve-bore and blow his bloody head off. And yet he was glad in a way. If he could not do things with his body, he could still do them in his head. Ellen and that bastard Hawthorn. Telling him to wait. His Ellen. Lavinia. Daisy, plump little Daisy. . . .

Christmas presents had been bought in London for the staff, the tenants, and their children. For Eva there was a large, fully furnished doll's house and two illustrated books of fairy stories.

For the last week before Christmas the whole household was on tip-toe with excitement. The maids' faces pink from scrubbing in the cold frosty weather. Everyone said there would be snow. Two trees were brought in from one of the spinneys—one for the servants' hall and one for the drawing room. Molly helped to decorate them with candles. Buckets of sand and water were placed near them in case they caught fire. Presents were wrapped, labels written. Holly cut and hung behind pictures. Mistletoe brought in from the apple orchard.

The cook got down the plum puddings that had been hanging, in their white pudding basins wrapped in the cloths they had been cooked in, from the beams of the stillroom, and made new puddings for the following year. To be good, a pudding had to be a year old. She made mince pies; she pinched the breasts of the turkeys in the meat safe and said they were not as good as last year, and what was the world coming to? But she said that every year.

The laundry maids put extra starch into everything so that the servants' aprons and petticoats rustled like taffeta when they moved.

Christmas came but once a year. But it came with its presents, its Christmas cards, and calendars. With the servants' ball and the tenants' dance, with carols sung by the village children and a service in the little church. All by rote, by custom, unchanged for years. By magic almost.

For once the weather prophets had been right. It snowed on Christmas Eve. But Christmas Day was lovely, a real Christmas-card Christmas. The fir trees and pines and rhododendrons piled with shining snow. The black branches of the oaks and beeches and elms tipped with it, as if it was sugar icing.

It all went well. There was no hitch. But the dinner was a strange one. Just the three of them. Lavinia, Molly, and Eva, at the decorated table. All women. The butler carved the turkey because there was no man to do it.

Lavinia thought of John at home with his parents. Would they ever have Christmas together?

No one could have been more astonished than Lavinia when, on New Year's Eve, Mrs. Murgatroyd was shown into the drawing room.

"Muriel!" she said. "What brings you back here, may I ask?"

"Oh Madam, I thought of writing but I knew you would not see me. So I came."

"So I see."

"It's him, Mrs. Lenton. It's Edward."

Lavinia experienced quite a shock to hear Muriel refer to her husband as "Edward." But how she had changed! The girl she had employed as a governess had turned into a voluptuous woman. Pretty still, with her brown eyes and dark red hair, but assured now. And this was the mother of Edward's son. It amazed her to think of the experiences they had shared. The man and the children they had borne him.

"Sit down," she said.

Muriel sat down.

"And now what about Edward?"

"I love him, Mrs. Lenton. You don't, do you? You never have."

"No, I don't."

"He told me, Mrs. Lenton. He said . . ."

"I don't want to know what my husband said." She could imagine Edward discussing her with his mistress. "Just tell me what you want, Muriel."

"I want to stay here and take care of him. As soon as I heard, I came."

"It happened so long ago. His accident, I mean." And so many other things had happened since then. She wondered why it had taken Muriel so long to find out. "How did you find out?" she asked. "You said you heard, but why did it take so long?"

"My sister-in-law keeps birds. Canaries. She breeds them," Muriel said. "And she lives with us."

The explanation was still not clear.

"I was cleaning their cages because she was ill," Muriel went on. "I saw his name and all about a gun accident. She uses newspapers, old papers, in the bottoms of the cages," Muriel said weakly. "That's how."

So that was how. What a chance! What a way to find out! If Muriel's sister-in-law had not been ill that day . . . if she had not kept canaries.

"She'll take care of the boy and my husband. There was never much between us. Mrs. Caramine gave him a thousand pounds to marry me. But he loves the boy even if he's not his own."

Lavinia looked at Muriel with renewed interest. She saw Delphine. She saw the girls she had seen on the streets. And after having been seduced and betrayed by Edward, this woman still loved him. No wonder there was no difficulty in finding girls for the brothels. Once a girl was in love with a man they seemed to do whatever he told them.

"He's helpless, Muriel. He can't speak or move. He's like a baby." A horribly disfigured baby, she thought.

"I know, Mrs. Lenton."

"I'll take you to see him. But you're sure your husband . . ."

"My husband understands."

"Well, at any rate he'll have no cause for jealousy." It was a cruel thing to say but she could not resist it.

They both stood up. Muriel drew back to let Mrs. Lenton pass her. In the library Lavinia dismissed the man on duty. "I'll call you when we go," she said. "There he is, Muriel." Lavinia watched her face. Would she be revolted? She wasn't. She ran forward, knelt beside the bed and, taking his face in her hands, kissed him.

"Oh Edward," she said. "Oh Edward. I came as soon as I heard."

Edward knew her all right. His eyes brightened. He gave a sort of inarticulate grunt. It was an extraordinary scene. The broken man, the kneeling woman. Lavinia noticed that the heels of Muriel's boots were run over.

Back in the drawing room Lavinia rang for tea. When they had had it she said: "You know about the girls, I suppose?"

"Yes, I do. But I only knew Eva."

"He was responsible for it," Lavinia said. "He brought that woman into the house."

"He couldn't help it, Mrs. Lenton. He was that kind of man. He needed women." Then, as if she suddenly realized that she was talking to his wife, she said: "Women like me. If only I could make you understand, Mrs. Lenton. He had to own a woman."

"Well, what do you want to do, Muriel, now that you have seen him?"

"I want to stay here, Mrs. Lenton, and take care of him. I don't want any money. Just a room and some food. You need never see me. Oh please, please!" She flung herself down on her knees at Lavinia's feet.

Of all the impertinence. His ex-mistress wanting to come back to Mortal. And yet . . . it would be a Christian thing to do. She often felt guilty about Edward. This was a solution and she supposed in a way it was her fault, the way Muriel had said. If she had been common. . . . But if she had been common, she would not have been an heiress and it was the money Edward had wanted. The money and Mortal. And he had spent her money on other women. . . .

That was how the new year came in at Mortal—January 1, 1885.

29 : The Do-Gooders

Mrs. Caramine knew all about the do-gooders. About Alfred Dyer, one of two brothers who published moral tracts and religious books for old maids. It was he who had started the trouble with his investigations in 1880. Then there was Ben Scott with his ridiculous "London Committee for the Exposure and Suppression of the Traffic in English Girls for the Purposes of Continental Prostitution." Benjamin Waugh was another of them, and so was Josephine Butler. But they were barking up the wrong tree. As long as there was a demand for anything there would be a supply, and the demand for girls would cease only when men stopped being men. No one knew the figures better than she. The demand was always greater than the supply.

"Crumpets, Ada," she said, lifting the silver lid off the dish on the tea tray. She wondered what Ada Prettyman felt about this latest thing they'd thought up.

"What do you think of it?" she asked.

"Of what?"

"This Society for the Protection of Children. Lord Shaftesbury, Lord Dalhousie, Cardinal Manning, and Dr. Barnado are mixed up with it."

"First the export trade and now its the kids," Prettyman said, licking the butter off her fingers. She liked having tea with Carmine. Cosy, that's what it was.

"Lords," Carmine said, thinking of Shaftesbury and Dalhousie. "Why, we've got twenty lords to their one." She laughed. "Lords are men, Ada. They want their greens like everybody else, and some of 'em like them tender."

A week later she was less complacent. Ada Prettyman found her raging.

"The bastards," she said. "They're going to try and summons me. A warrant. But I've sent the boys out. Everyone knows it's dangerous to fool with Carmine. And I've told some of our clients. By God," she said, "if that list of names came out in Court, it'd set all England by the ears. Lords, Generals—half the bloody aristocracy."

Things had not been easy for the Committee. The strings Mrs. Caramine pulled led to some very high and some very low places. The first setback had been with Jeremiah Minahan, the ex-Inspector of Police who, when he placed his dossier on Mrs. Caramine's activities before the Assistant Commissioner, was told it was all most improper. Brothels for the nobility indeed—what were things coming to?

The next thing was an attempt to prosecute Mrs. Caramine for keeping a disorderly house. For this two ratepayers had to furnish evidence that she caused a nuisance. But they found no ratepayers willing to go to court. No one had noticed any disorder in Coak Street. A lot of hansom cabs and carriages could hardly be described as disorder. There was no noise. A little dance music, perhaps, but nothing else. And never on Sunday. Privately, everyone knew what went on at Nos. 22 and 23. Publicly, no one was ready to acknowledge it. No respectable person, that is. But at last two workingmen agreed to testify. Poor men, jealous of the rich man's pleasures with their girls. Minahan had evidence. Mrs. Caramine had tried to bribe him; when that failed, she had tried to frighten him with great names. The star exhibit was a letter written to Mrs. Caramine that had been received in error by a Miss Maud Caramine, also a resident of Chelsea. Written in Italian and obviously intended for Mrs. Caramine, it was a demand for "a lively young girl of sixteen with a nice complexion and a pretty throat to live with me as my mistress. . . . The King gave me your address. . . ."

Carrie Caramine believed in style and she drove to court in style. Charming, ladylike, dressed in the height of fashion, she made the charges seem ridiculous, though everyone knew that they were true. She arrived in a brougham, which had been given to her by a peer, behind her pair of dashing chestnuts, their silver mounted harness glittering. As soon as the footman opened the carriage door and Mrs. Caramine stepped onto the pavement, the reporters surrounded her. She greeted them with a smiling: "Nothing can be done with me, gentlemen. I have too many friends." The men laughed. They knew who her friends were but were not likely to mention them in print after Erny Parke, the editor of *The Star,* had been jailed for a year for libeling Lord Euston. This whole subject was a hot potato and Carrie was right about her friends in high places. Friends, clients, patrons, gentlemen. Jimmy Clarke of *The Standard* said she ought to hang out a sign in Church Street: "By Appointment to the King of the Belgians, to His Royal Highness and the Duke of that. . . ."

"She's still a looker," the man next to him said. "Must have been a beauty in her time."

The helmeted policemen stood impassive as statues. They knew all about it. Everyone knew all about it. But no one was going to say a word, or write a word, more than they need.

Then Mrs. Caramine's barrister for the defense, Mr. Leslie Morgan, black-robed, white-wigged, and impressive, said that his client had lived in Chelsea for twenty years and that until the present time no complaint had ever been made against her by any inhabitant of the borough. He glared about him and repeated his remark. No complaint of any kind. He agreed that Mrs. Caramine had technically broken the law. To this indictment she had pleaded guilty, but to no more. As to the charge of deporting young women to the Continent—it was frivolous. There was not a particle of supporting evidence. Because she had pleaded guilty, no evidence for the prosecution was called.

The case ended with a fine of two hundred pounds and a deposit of a further two hundred as a security of good behavior. Since the action was not fought, the testimony of witnesses was not required and the case against her, so painstakingly built up, was stillborn. The bonfire, that should have alerted England, had fizzled out. There was not even enough smoke to make the public aware of the existence of a fire. The newspaper reports were cursory. Not only was this a dangerous subject, it was also an unpleasant one. Indecent, something that should be kept from the knowledge of all pure women.

In court, Carrie Caramine accepted the verdict with grace. She looked rather sad, put upon. A woman who, while performing a somewhat unpleasant public service, had been trapped by a legal technicality. She opened her velvet reticule, paid the fine in cash, gave the name of an officer in the Guards as a guarantor of the security and swept out of the building.

The case of the Queen versus Caramine was over. A tea-cup storm that should have been a hurricane. The ridiculous committee was silenced, made a fool of. Both the business and pleasures of the night would continue as before.

Stead went back to his office and wrote up the trial. It caused no stir. Who cared about prostitutes? They were a necessary evil. If there weren't any, men would turn to respectable women—the wives and daughters of middle-class ratepayers—and no woman would be safe.

Now only one hope was left. The Criminal Law Amendment Act that had first been introduced in 1883 and was up before the House again. It raised the age of consent to sixteen. It allowed police to apply for search warrants in cases where girls were believed to be detained and provided summary powers for the suppression of clearing houses for girls sent abroad. This was the hope. But it was Whitsuntide—

holiday time. The newspapers were filled with the story of Victor Hugo's death. W. G. Grace, the cricketer, had been caught out, having made only five runs, and the ducks on the Serpentine had been stoned by some small boys—vandals. A terrible affair.

Summer had come softly—a slow burgeoning of blossom. Carpets of crocuses appeared, fragile chalices of mauve, white, and yellow. Yellow daffodils unwrapped themselves from their paper coverings and burst out, exploding into sunshine on the lawns and in the woods. Bluebells. Fruit blossom. White almond, wild cherry, pink apple, rose peach, one after the other. The birds in the Park built their nests and sang for the joy of it. But for the street girls of England, the daughters of the night, there was no change. People were working for it. But what people? God-fearing men and women without power except for their belief in God and justice.

Mrs. Josephine Butler had been tilting at this windmill for years. In 1881 she had presented the Cabinet with a petition signed by a thousand ladies, suggesting that "such changes should be made in the Law as shall make it impossible for a young girl or child in our country to be deprived of her liberty by force or fraud and kept in a foreign city for the basest purposes. . . ."

Lord Shaftesbury had declared that to stop the traffic "it would be necessary to lay bare as many horrors and cruelties as had ever been exhibited in the history of the world." But they had not been laid bare. No one was ready to raise the carpet of hypocrisy and expose the filth that lay beneath it.

Mrs. Josephine Butler had taken disgraced women into her own house. How stupid could people be! Of course her father, John Grey, had been an associate of Clarkson, who had successfully agitated for the release of Negro slaves. It was said that she could remember sitting on John Wesley's knee. And she had married George Butler, a parson—now Canon of Winchester. But her daughter's death—falling over the banisters at her home—had deranged her mind. That was a good enough excuse for her strange behavior. She had attacked the Contagious Diseases Act of the sixties. This Act permitted the medical examination of prostitutes, and some respectable women were picked up on suspicion—an iniquitous piece of legislation.

She had visited Europe and picked up diseased and broken English girls who had been thrown out of brothels there. Attempts had been made on her life by procurers.

When the second reading of the Law Amendment Bill took place, there were less than forty members in the House of Commons. Holiday time. A wet day. And a pretty unsavory business—this public discussion about the traffic in young girls sent abroad, and the prevention of the prostitution of children. Everyone in the House was for the measure, or said they were. They were all against sin. But too many views were aired. Nothing had been decided by six-thirty when the debate ended. The Bill had been talked out by Mr. Cavendish Bentinck.

Thirteen remained the age of consent. The evidence of small children could still not be accepted because they did not understand the nature of an oath.

Nothing was changed. The first round had, without question, gone to the madams.

30 : Birds of a Feather

Well, that was that, Mrs. Caramine thought as she drove away from the Court with her escort of Guards Officers. The honors were hers. The prosecution had really been on her side—so had the court, the public, the reporters. But nevertheless, it was a straw in the wind. That she had been prosecuted at all meant something.

By the time the carriage pulled up with a flourish at No. 23, Mrs. Caramine had made up her mind. She'd have a party, a meeting. See what the views of some of the others were.

Her face was a charming mask. All smiles, her great eyes tender as she spoke to the two officers in her carriage. Business was less good with the Scots Guards in Egypt, but she could not complain. The officers of Her Majesty's household and the Cavalry of the Line were among her best customers and still here. Young men, handsome, rich, vigorous. What a lot of them she had slept with in her time.

"You will come in, gentlemen, for a glass of wine?" she said to her two companions. "It is perhaps a little early in the day for anything else, but should you want it, it is there."

"We'll come in," Major Stewart Grant said. "A glass of Madeira to drink your health, Carrie. And we might pop in this evening for a couple of hours."

They followed her upstairs to her cosy private room.

Three days later the party was convened. Ada Prettyman, Ellen—who was now all but one of the staff—Madame Elsie, Mrs. Shaw-Kimble, Madame Mourez, the Baron, Jack Solferino, Mrs. Hopewell. The very cream of the trade.

They had had refreshments—tea, sandwiches, cake—and three bottles of champagne had been opened when Mrs. Caramine, standing with her back to the window, said: "Well, what do you make of it?"

"Nothing," Madame Elsie said. She was very elegant in apple-green and rose, with a Leghorn hat trimmed with flowers and a parasol edged with lace. A walking, or rather driving, advertisement to her establishment of *haute couture*.

"Nothing, Carrie. The do-gooders have too much against them. All the big guns and human nature. It's a man's world, as no one knows better than us who cater to it." She paused and then said: "There was a beautiful piece in my place in the autumn. A relative of Mrs. Lenton's, that I'd like to get hold of. I can't get her out of my head."

"That woman. She's a bloody nuisance. Not like the others either. She's got money behind her." Mrs. Caramine was beginning to wonder if her revenge might not be backfiring. Who the hell would have guessed it? A well-brought-up woman like that. You'd have thought she'd be ashamed to bring her children into it.

"I took her measurements," Madame Elsie went on. "Handled her myself instead of letting one of the girls do it. Of course, Mrs. Lenton's a good customer. Wanted a whole lot of stuff in a hurry. A regular trousseau. You'd have thought the girl had nothing to wear."

"How are things going?" Mrs. Caramine asked.

"Not bad, Carrie."

Not bad at all. In six months she'd had one hundred and forty girls through her hands. At work by six-thirty, breakfast at eight. Work till dinner at one. Then work till nine, when the girls had a snack, and then on, plying their needles till midnight or later; all night sometimes, in the season—with balls, drawing rooms, and receptions going on almost every day. In the workroom there were sixty-two women and girls with an allowance of one hundred and fifty cubic feet of air. They worked from fifteen to twenty-four hours and then went to bed in small cubicles, two girls to each, that were almost as airless as the workroom.

No wonder they were ready to go abroad "to gain experience" in dressmaking establishments in Paris or Brussels. But they never got there. Not to the dress houses.

No. Madame Elsie could well say business was not bad. She rearranged her skirt with a white-kid-gloved hand. Carrie was being stupid. There was nothing to be nervous about.

There was a real Madame Elsie who had a dressmaking establishment in Regent Street. In 1859 one of her girls died of overwork. The scandal ended her business with the aristocracy.

"What do you think, Mr. Solferino?" A man she disliked very much. Common. Italian. She was prejudiced against all Italians. Short, thick-set, hirsute, with beetling eyebrows that met over his nose. A Neopolitan, who ran Soho. Quick, like all his kind, with a knife that he delighted in using. He ran a gang of roughs, toughs, pimps, thugs, burglars, and assassins. Madame Elsie wrinkled her nose in distaste. She had asked him what he thought—if such an animal could think—just to see what he would say. Her mind was on a new house of assignation that she had arranged for her clients. Couples like Maud Fortall and her lover, for instance. She must find more cosy nooks in various parts of the West End.

"We got to make example," Solferino said. He hissed like a snake.

"No killing," Mrs. Caramine said. "Not just for fun."

"An example . . ."

Mrs. Caramine raised her hand to stop him.

"Must be strong, signora." He raised his arm and flexed his muscle. "Strong . . . example. Fear. Like dogs."

"Don't worry, Solferino. I may have work for you before long."

"I ready. You say. My boys ready. Knife. Blackjack. What you say, signora?"

Through it all the Baron had sat silent. What a collection of scum—panderers, murderers. Purveyors of flesh, wholesalers and retailers of vice. Beautifully dressed in a morning coat and striped trousers with a moss rose in his buttonhole, he smiled benignly.

Mrs. Caramine said, "And what do you think, my dear Baron?"

"Nothing, dear lady. Only that business will go on as usual. We live in the world, in a great metropolis. Not in heaven or utopia."

How calm he always was, acting as if he was still a real aristocrat. She looked around the room at them. All there save for Harris, who had had the day off.

Something had upset Harris. She felt herself changing. For one thing she had turned from the Old Testament to the New. In the Gospel of St. John, when a woman was taken in adultery, in the very act, Jesus had said: "He that is without sin among you, let him cast the first stone." Who was without sin?

Her mind went back to Ellen. Hélène now. Frenchified and bad as they came. A Jezebel. Well, she had been whipped, but it had not driven the devil out. Quite the reverse.

She thought of La Jumelle's house in Paris where she had taken Ellen. Of going downstairs and finding Madame preparing drinks. Everything was an excuse for a little *apéritif* with her.

"*Eh bien?*" she had said when Julie came in.

"A picture, Madame," Julie had said. "Fresh, ripe as a plum."

"And a virgin, near as damn it," she had added in her mixture of English and execrable French. "Only one man." How long ago it seemed!

"Unbelievable!" Madame had said. "If I could climb so high more than once a day, I would go and have a look at her. As it is, she will keep." She had laughed. The laughter shook her big breasts and was lost, as it sank into the restriction of her corset.

What an *affaire,* though, to keep this *colis* here till the milord came from England to visit her.

"How romantic!" They had raised their glasses.

"And profitable, Madame, I imagine," Harris had said.

"Of course, Mademoiselle, girls are always profitable, and when he has done with her he may leave her with us." La Jumelle had put down her glass and rubbed her fat little hands together.

Harris went on thinking of Ellen. Hélène indeed, with her airs. A lot of good chastising had done her. Julie had whipped her and what had happened? There she was—a queen among the sinners. Lording it over everyone. "Spare the rod," the Lord said. Well, she had never spared it, not on the likes of them. Her long legs ate up the miles as she walked. She liked to tire herself, to torture the flesh and exhaust it.

She had made a couple of trips to France since she had taken Ellen over. Miss Hélène, indeed. That Ellen. Once with two more children for Jumelle and once to bring back three French girls. Beauties too, who spoke no English. Prime sinners no doubt, like all French girls—and there were a lot of them in England now—and Belgians and Dagos. Solferino went in for them foreign tarts. Easier to manage since they couldn't speak the language—like English girls in France and Germany.

Harris was dressed in a tweed suit with a man's cap on her short cropped hair. Marching, with swinging arms like a Grenadier, down the street. Harris caused stares, laughter and jeers from the barefooted urchins who dodged in and out of the traffic. She liked to walk, to observe life which she classified as sin. Everything was sin, and the most sinful things were women. Girls. Veritable destroyers. "Lions seeking whom they might devour," she muttered.

Just look at them. Look at the painted, loitering hussies. Some of them climbing into the trees in the parks at night to sleep like monkeys in the branches, and the police did nothing to stop them. Turned a blind eye to them because they had no place to sleep but the parks and the trees where they hid from the law—as if that was a reason.

She walked up the King's Road to Sloane Street and up Sloane Street to Knightsbridge. Always girls hanging about the barracks there, waiting for innocent young soldier boys. Through the Albert Gate and across the Park to Oxford Street. Then the Charing Cross Road, Piccadilly Circus, and via the Haymarket to Shaftesbury Avenue, and home again. That was her usual walk. And a good walk for sin. No better in all England comprising, as it did, Leicester Square and the warrens of Soho that were Jack Solferino's territory.

Then she heard music, the clash of tambourines, and a brass band playing "Home Sweet Home." She deviated from her usual course and went toward the sound.

She liked music. Bands, hymns. That was why she liked going to church to praise God and sing to Him. Hymns like "Onward Christian Soldiers," "There Is a Green Hill," and the like. Rousing hymns that you could sing loudly.

She turned the corner and there they were, blowing their guts out and singing to beat the band. Men in uniform and caps, and women in blue poke bonnets trimmed with dark red. As if they knew it was her favorite, they began to play "Onward Christian Soldiers." "With the Cross of Jesus, marching as to war," she sang, and joined them.

This was nice, this was. Singing outside like this.

One of the men carried a placard on which was printed in big black letters:

SALVATION ARMY. GREAT DOINGS BY THE HALLELUJAH
CLERGYMAN . . . FIRING BY GREAT GUNS . . .

"What's it mean?" Harris asked a man standing near her.

"They've gone off their bloody heads," he said. "It makes them act strange."

A queer lot. In uniforms and poke bonnets. Caps like soldiers. The man she had spoken to showed her a paper, *The War Cry*. "They sell it for tuppence," he said.

The moon was full. High in the sky. She followed the band down Piccadilly, surrounded by a mass of half-drunk women bedaubed with paint and smelling of patchouli and drink; and sporting men—their companions. All making ribald jokes, swearing and cursing. Jokes, swearing, and cursing Harris did not hold with.

It was "Home Sweet Home" again now . . . "No place like

home. . . ." The police tried to keep the crowd moving but they milled about like cattle. Harris saw a Salvationist give a slip of paper to a pretty girl dressed in bright red, a sinner if ever there was one. Sinners belonged in houses, not on the streets to tempt passing men into evil. Jezebels. The men who went to houses knew what they were doing.

"Here," she said, "let me look at that."

"Who're you?" the girl asked.

"I'm Harris," she said, as if that meant anything as she took the paper from her hand. *The Deliverer,* a tiny slip of paper, easy to conceal, that urged the girls to call on the Salvation Army who would welcome anyone who was willing to accept their help.

"Wot's it say?" the girl asked. "I can't read."

"If you go to them, they'll help you."

"Nobody'll 'elp us," the girl said. "Not even God."

"Where're they going?" Harris asked, as the crowd moved slowly down the street, the brazen music almost drowned out by shouts of derision and abuse. Vegetable refuse from Covent Garden was thrown at them. Some swells in red-lined opera cloaks attacked them with their malacca canes.

"Goin'?" the girl repeated. "They're goin' to the rink, of course." It was an old skating rink in Oxford Street that the Army had taken over.

Caught up in the crowd, in the excitement, in the pleasure of being able to sing as loudly as she liked, Harris moved with them. Tickets were being passed out to all who wanted to go into the rink. "Fall in and follow us . . . follow us to Jesus. . . ." A hundred girls at least were in the crowd. A bright tail of sin and color.

They marched into the building, Harris in the van on the heels of the bandsmen. A man in uniform stood up and spoke as if they could be saved. As if there were hope, as if it were possible. Some of the girls jeered and heckled. Some were in tears.

"Who is he?" Harris asked. The whole evening had been astounding. She should have been back long ago.

"Bramwell Booth," a girl said. "He wants to save us. And what the hell are you doing 'ere? You don't look like a tart to me."

What was she doing exactly? Looking for God . . . for Jesus. For years she'd been trying to save girls. Beating them up, whipping them. Never sparing the rod, the dirty little bitches . . . yet they were necessary, a necessary evil. It was in the Book. Babylon. Daughters of the horse leech . . . Jezebels . . . Delilahs. All she had done was to make them suffer for their sins. Whipped them with whips. But here was another way. And who was she to cast the first stone? She followed a pretty little dark girl to the penitents' bench, to God . . . to salvation. That's what it was—the Salvation Army. She had been due back hours ago. As she knelt she gave a hoarse laugh. Go back? She'd never go back. She had *arrived* at last.

"Welcome, sister," an oldish woman in uniform said, taking her hand. "I am Rebecca Jarrett."

Harris had heard of her, a well known old-time procuress who had been saved. A welcome ally. That was one thing about these Salvationists—they knew the enemy. They were all traitors to Evil, renegades from it, safe in the arms of Jesus, of God. She and Rebecca must have a lot in common. What a job they could do together if ever they teamed up.

"So you were at Caramine's?" Rebecca said.

"I was trying to do God's work there. To punish since I could not save. But this is better. Better to snatch the brand from the burning. . . ."

A pair of us, Jarrett thought. Harris was her own kind, a captain of the street, not cannon fodder. A director. And physically a big, powerful woman, built almost like a man, with great hands and bony wrists, who could stand up to anybody. A singing voice like a musical bull that could be heard over any amount of talk and shouting. Looking at the big gaunt woman beside her, Rebecca recalled her own past. Seduced at the age of twelve, she had been kept by a series of men, run brothels of her own in London and Manchester. In one of them, a small four-girl operation, one of her girls had died of pneumonia. This had made a deep impression as she had been fond of her. Then she had run into the Army. Almost by accident she had drifted into a meeting. She remembered her feelings. Funny-looking people in uniforms, the women with bonnets and tambourines. She had been saved. Then she had felt it was too much for her and she decided to go back to the old life. Drink, men, girls, music, late hours. But the officers had reasoned with her. Miss Sapworth, Mrs. Bramwell Booth, Mrs. Josephine Butler. They had saved her from herself. She had been ill and in a hospital. But everyone had been so kind to her. Then she had gone to Winchester where she had helped girls who had lost their way . . . a home for them there. It was bright, with gay-colored rooms and no bolts on the doors.

She was going back tomorrow. She saw the dear Canon or Mrs. Butler almost every day. Imagine a woman like me with the Canon of Winchester, or his wife! Even now she could not believe it. But she was glad she had met Harris. She might be able to persuade her to come down for a visit. Anyway, one way or the other she was sure she would see more of her.

31 : The Interlude

They had always left Mortal in May for the house in Berkeley Square. This was when the drawing rooms began and the new crop of débutantes were presented at Court. Balls, dinner parties, riding in the Row in the morning, drives in Hyde Park in the afternoon. Calls to be made or received between three and six in the evening. The whole routine of it—two cards left if no one was at home, with one corner turned down to show it had been left in person, and then on to the next house where Lavinia might stay to a tea of muffins, sandwiches, and cakes.

Then came Ascot, Henley, Lord's, Goodwood, and finally the Cowes Regatta in early August before the grouse shooting opened on the twelfth. This was followed by the partridge shooting that began on September 1st and pheasants on October the 10th. Duck shooting began in August for those who liked it. In the late summer there was cubbing, followed by fox hunting.

Edward had always left for the grouse moors before the shooting opened in August. He was a first-class shot and much in demand with his pair of Holland & Hollands. He had reciprocated by having large shooting parties for the pheasants in October. Mortal was famous for its pheasants and had raised as many as four thousand in a good year.

The six Noah's Arks, as the big domed trunks were called, were sent on in advance to London. Everything would still go on as it always had—just the same, but utterly different. The purpose was no longer amusement. There would be no invitations to shoot at Mortal. All this was in the back of Lavinia's mind when a footman came into the rose garden where she, Molly, and Eva were enjoying the sunshine, to say that there was a lady from London in the drawing room. Lavinia left the others and followed him.

A lady to see her? Surely not another of Edward's mistresses. The woman was standing by the window looking out when she came in. Well dressed and, when she turned round, obviously a lady. Not a person, as people who were not ladies were often described by the servants who announced them. Well, but not fashionably dressed, in her fifties. She came forward, hand outstretched.

"I must apologize for this intrusion, Mrs. Lenton, but William Stead thought it might be a good idea to call on you as I was down here with friends. I am Josephine Butler—Mrs. Josephine Butler—and we have interests in common and one common tragedy in our lives. I, too, lost a daughter."

"Not . . ." Lavinia said.

"Oh no. In an accident, Mrs. Lenton. She fell over the banisters in our house and was killed as I came in at the front door."

"How dreadful."

"It was dreadful. And time has done nothing to heal the wound. But it is the living dead we must speak about, Mrs. Lenton. The whole problem of prostitution to which I have given so much of my life."

What ramifications there were to this awful business, Lavinia thought! How many people were involved! Enemies, allies.

"I hear you have a girl here whom you rescued in Belgium," Mrs. Butler said.

"Yes, I have."

"I've seen them there. The ones they throw out into the street. Sick, diseased, broken. I've brought some back, too. I've rescued girls in London with the help of the Booths and the Salvation Army. We've got homes for them—but not enough. I thought . . ."

"What did you think?"

"That you might help me, Mrs. Lenton. And I wanted to meet you."

"I'll help you, Mrs. Butler, and so will Molly. She's the girl I brought back. I'll introduce you to her."

They went out to the rose garden together.

Lavinia and John now met in the Mortal woods, first by accident, then by a tacit, never mentioned agreement, almost every day. She rode after luncheon and he came when he could get away from the office.

She looked very well in a sweeping riding habit of dark green, brown, or black, with neat-fitted jackets, a black tricorne hat, and a starched stock at her neck fastened with a gold pin made in the shape of a horse's head. Even when John didn't turn up she enjoyed riding Nestor along the bridle paths that ran through the coverts. The early summer green of the trees—oak, ash, elm, beech, hornbeam—with a ground cover of mauve rhododendrons, was a fairyland to a woman in love going to meet her lover; or riding slowly just thinking about him.

On the edge of the woods there were masses of more ornamental rarer rhododendrons—rose, red, white, blush pink. Great trusses of blooms that almost hid the foliage of the bushes.

In all this time since Christmas—all winter, spring and this early summer—they had made love only once. And that like country bumpkins amid the flowering gorse. In a space, the size of a room, grazed smooth by rabbits. The grass for a bed, the sky for a ceiling; the friendly horses tied nose to nose in a copse, the deerhound standing guard. The scent of the yellow gorse—sweet, almost sickly—remained in her nostrils. She had only to see some of it, for it all to come back. The strangeness of it. The peasant commonness of it. A lust born of the season, that had possessed them both. Coupling like foxes in a covert. After that they did not, as a rule, even kiss. Sometimes riding on her near side, John would lean over and touch her thigh. Sometimes, on the off side, he would take her gloved hand, turn back the gauntlet, and kiss her wrist.

Sometimes he brought news from Stead with whom he kept up a correspondence. Poor Stead was of two minds—with them heart and soul, yet afraid of the public, of the reputation of his paper. Waiting for time, as if this horror would ripen like a fruit. They talked of Molly, of Eva, and Muriel. The two girls got on well with Muriel. So did everyone at Mortal except the men who looked after poor Edward. She was constant in her supervision of them. Her love for the man who had ruined and betrayed her was hard to understand—except that he had been the first man in her life. Edward had been the first man in Lavinia's life, too, but she had never loved him. That must be the difference. She had some idea about how Muriel felt because of John.

When she saw him riding over the fields toward her on his gray mare, she pulled Nestor up and waited at the edge of the woods. A prince on a white horse . . . a lawyer on a gray . . . a princess held prisoner by her cause, her sense of duty, in Mortal, her castle. But there was no fairy godmother. Only the witches whom God would help her to defeat. At least she was no longer alone. There was Josephine, General Booth, and the Salvation Army, and the others. Many more than she had at first believed, and one of these days Stead would move. There was an Act before Parliament now, the Criminal Amendment Act had come up again. If they passed it . . .

John pulled up his horse beside her.

"My darling," he said.

Words of tenderness and endearment. They had to live on words and touches of the hand, with an occasional kiss, cut off before it carried them away. The birds of the air, the rabbits of the hedgerows, the foxes in their earths were luckier than they. But the time would come when everything would change. It had to, and she would bear this man a son.

They rode side by side. The bits jingled as the horses snapped playfully with nibbling lips at each other. They rode silent, slowly, in the beauty of it—the early summer woods and their attachment to each other.

Fancy his having loved her since she had been a little girl. How could a boy fall in love with a baby? But he said he had and she believed him. Except for her, there had been no woman in his life. Women, yes. He had told her about them. An extraordinary conversation, but she had understood him. This business they were in together had helped her. Even good men . . . But there had been nothing like that for a long time, and there never would be again.

"What have you been doing, John?" she asked.

"Today? Making a will, arranging a mortgage. The usual things, Lavinia. I had another letter from Stead. Something is coming up. They have a lot of evidence."

That name took the brightness out of the day.

"And I have another bit of news for you, darling. I heard from Guitry. Betty is dead. She was unhurt, untouched. You can take my word for it"—he was going to give her no details—"so you were right, you see, when you said you felt it."

Lavinia did not reply. She put her heel into Nestor and cantered homeward. She had to get home, to be alone to cry.

The interlude at Mortal was over.

32 : Berkeley Square

Lavinia took Molly with her to London, leaving Evangeline and Muriel in the country. Parker, her old maid, had been promoted to housekeeper, Mrs. Fernley having been pensioned off. May was with her; part maid, part companion, almost a daughter. What a household of women she had! Women and girls—as temperamental as the English weather. All sunny smiles one minute and floods of reasonless tears the next. Of course there was a reason—women and girls could not live without the company of men. The authority and security of their presence. Girls needed young men. Not Eva. She had got over the first and terrible phase of her relationship with men, and was now only timid of them, and that, Lavinia hoped, would pass and a good man, a man like Stead or John, who would ignore her past, come into her life one day. There was, after all, plenty of time for it. Though unfortunately it would not be possible to present her at court or bring her out properly.

Berkeley Square was beautiful, the great plane trees in full and voluptuous foliage. The Derby, to be run on the third, was in everyone's mind. From Duke to Tailor they were thinking of the Epsom Downs; Tattenham Corner, the straight, the finishing post where the wins and losses were decided. Magnificent thoroughbreds were being strapped and groomed and exercised. Jockeys were putting on their new silks, saddlery being gone over for the last time. Bets were being laid and the chicks of success spent by the reckless before the race was hatched.

The house was in good order. The servants, awaiting their mistress' arrival, greeted her with smiles, bobs, and curtsies. The maids capped and aproned, the men in Mortal uniform, except the butler, in black with striped trousers, who looked as if he might be a Foreign Office official. She had been away some months but felt as if she had never left London. At Mortal it was the same when she went back. There it seemed to her she had never been away. She was going to miss her rides with John, but she was going to ride. She'd had Nestor and a couple of other riding horses sent up. These, with the carriage horses, made five in the mews to be looked after by the coachman, a groom, and a strapper.

She was eager to see William Stead again. He had something cooking. He had written, saying he was about to take a very serious step and would like her help. That was one of the reasons she had come up to London. The season was the other. If she wanted to carry out her scheme of rousing the women of society, it was no good rusticating in the country.

Then there was darling, silly little Maud to see. She was still as flighty as a girl, which was dangerous when combined with her woman's instincts for intrigue, and—one had to face it—for passion. She was a woman who wanted both the flattery of love and the satisfaction of it. She understood her need for a man's kisses, his arms, his body against hers. But Maud did not love Geoffrey, and would certainly not be ready to lose her title and position by running away with him. Before, bored and in debt, he had been an escape. Something to play with. A great big beautiful man doll to take to bed and pet and think about.

Still, it would be interesting to see her and hear what she had to say. She must see Serena and the others. She must invite people to tea, to dinner, get back into the swing of it—a rich grass widow, still young and beautiful, with a crippled husband and a ruined daughter in the country. She knew what people would say, what they would be watching for. And she must be doubly careful about meeting John. But meet him she would. Meet being a euphemism for making love. Thank God, she could trust May and use her as a chaperone. Maids always knew. There were the obvious signs of love: the underclothes, the corset differently laced, the expression of the face, the glow of the complexion. She knew the signs now and recognized women fresh from their lovers, or in love with their husbands. There were some who were. Some delicately raised and bred who still could not do without it, natural as mares in season. Their whole training was against it, but with some women it could not be stifled. Common people were different. No one ever checked them, although in service they had to behave.

Life was really very strange, and often horrible. She wondered what Mr. Stead would have to say. Tomorrow she would go to his office. In the afternoon she'd take Molly to Madame Elsie for some summer clothes. Chiffons, muslins . . .

In the afternoon after looking at Madame Elsie's little wax dolls— mannequins dressed in the latest fashion—and choosing some models, Lavinia left Molly and went to do some other shopping, saying she would be back and pick her up in an hour.

Madame Elsie was sure that Molly was not a relation of Mrs. Lenton, not upper class at all. A middle-class protégé of some kind. She'd measured and handled enough girls and women to know. Molly did not have the arrogance, the assurance of the aristocracy, of one who'd been born rich. This was her opportunity. She used the excuse of dressmaking to get her almost totally undressed. It showed here too, in the lines of her body.

"If you ever want a job, Miss Molly, you let me know. I can get you a good position as a nursery governess. I'm sure you like little children?"

"Oh, I do, but . . ."

"Oh, I don't mean now. But one never knows, does one? Circumstances change, and I want you to know you have a friend in me."

What a luscious little piece she was! Nicely rounded and as appetizing as an apple. And one never knew. She might get her hands on her one day. Mrs. Lenton might get tired of her. They might quarrel. A thousand things could happen.

Alone in Regent Street something kept worrying Mrs. Lenton. The name Elsie. Madame Elsie. When had she heard it? At last it came to her. In Paris. The detective had mentioned it. A Madame Elsie, the London dressmaker who procured so many girls. But how? What girls? Sewing girls of course, what others? Something else came to her —advertisements that she had seen in the papers:

> Wanted: Young apprentices. Must be under 20.
> Madame Elsie, Modes, Regent Street. . . .

There was a way to find out, at least to prove the possibility. She must get into the workrooms on the third and fourth floors. There must be a door. No one would stop her—they would not dare. Retracing her steps, she found the tradesmen's entrance—a shabby door on a side street. It was open. She went in and climbed the dirty stairs. There was no one about. The fitting rooms were on the first floor. She climbed another flight. There was a green door on the landing. She pushed it open. There must have been fifty girls sewing at tables. Young girls, all white as sheets, working as if they were possessed. Three forewomen paraded up and down the aisles between the tables. Anything would be better than this, or appear to be better. No one seemed to have noticed her. She went out and up the next flight of stairs. Here was where they slept—little airless cubicles for two. This was slavery. She went back into the street and into the shop—carpeted, smelling of riches, perfumes, furs.

Molly seemed embarrassed when she found her. Madame Elsie had worried Molly. The way she had looked at her, the way her hands had run over her. The talk about a job abroad. But she was not going to tell Mrs. Lenton. What had she to tell? And besides her mother was coming up to London tomorrow.

33 : The Prodigal

It was summer and Oxford looked more lovely than usual. The trees in fresh green leaf. Or perhaps it was just because she was going up to London. Mrs. Hastings looked down at her plate as her husband pronounced grace. He was now asking for a blessing.

"Bless, Our Lord, this food to our use and us to Thy service and make us ever mindful of the needs of others in Jesus' name. Amen."

The words in her husband's mouth didn't mean what they said. *His service* meant interference in the lives of others. Meant criticism. And as to *the needs of others*—the needs of his own daughter, for instance. Their Molly.

When Joseph Hastings had done he paused for an instant, his eyes closed, his hands folded on the tablecloth. Then he attacked his breakfast, slicing through the eggs with his knife so that the yolks ran out like thick yellow blood over the bacon.

Mrs. Hastings watched him with distaste. This small, clean-shaven, pasty-faced chemist was her husband. But was he the man she had married? Had he changed or had she, as a girl, not realized his cold and even vicious nature? Even his virtue was a kind of vice. He was suspicious of all happiness, and was after it like a ferret down a rabbit hole to seek its source. The sources of happiness were evil. Women, drink, good fare, convivial friends, the singing of songs other than hymns, the wearing of bright or pretty clothes and the body, particularly the body of a woman.

He looked up, wiping the egg from his mouth, and said: "So you're going up to town today, Martha? Your yearly jaunt to the dentist. If you ate less sweets and cakes you'd have no trouble with your teeth."

Sweets and cakes were sinful. Sins of the flesh. Lusts of the belly. "Look at me," he said.

She was looking at him with new eyes. Each day, ever since Molly had disappeared, she had looked at him with new eyes. Hundreds of eyes. Looked at the Adam's apple in that scraggy throat. Like a plucked chicken, she thought.

"Yes, dear," she said. "I will try to eat less chocolates. But I love them so."

"Self-control, Martha. You have no self-control. No will power. Why," he said with his mouth full, "I believe you still think of Molly."

Martha could not resist saying: "I thought you were never going to mention her name again."

"I speak of her as one speaks of the dead. Once, Martha, we had a sweet child. Let her live in our memory that way."

Think of Molly, indeed. Why, she was on her way to meet her and that wonderful Mrs. Lenton. She had certainly given Joseph what for. Stood up to him. Well, she'd stand up to him too, one of these days. She'd had about enough of it. In a few hours she'd see her darling lamb. Hear the story. And it was he—she glared at her husband—who had driven her to it.

A girl had to have a bit of fun. Dances, picnics, They'd had her taught music at Miss Harthill's Academy for Young Ladies. But just to play hymns. He'd taken the strap to her when she played other things. Suppose she refused to go to chapel with him? Suppose she said: "Cook your own breakfast!" Perhaps he'd take the strap to her too. But she'd not take it like Molly, who was so brave. She'd scream. Bring in the neighbors. Oh, there were ways. Why had she never thought of them before? Courage was coming into her, rising like a tide with her anger. He'd driven Molly away. He had refused to have her back when Mrs. Lenton had pleaded with him. He'd stop her now, or try to, if he knew where she was going. Let him try. Let him just try. Her hand tightened on the handle of the butter knife. I'd stick him, she thought. I'd stick it into him. That I would.

She was all dressed up and ready. Her brown dress, her black bonnet. Her Paisley shawl in case it turned cold, her umbrella in case it rained. Gloves, purse, everything. She had ordered a cab to take her to the station. The train, another cab to Berkeley Square, and Molly would be in her arms. By ten o'clock. Yes, by ten o'clock certainly. She looked at the grandfather clock in the corner of the dining room. That was hers, that was. It had come from her home. It had stood in the big farmhouse kitchen.

Outside a blackbird sang. Outside it was pretty, summerlike. Birds, animals, the beasts of the field, and men and maids were courting. She had been raised on a farm. This house was never bright, not even when the sun shone into it. It had an air, an odor of sanctity. Of mothballs, beeswax and beefstew. Cheap cuts. He insisted on that. Good eating was a sin. How well they had eaten at home! Home-grown hams, poultry, cream, game.

She heard the cab pull up. Time to go.

"Goodbye, Joseph," she said. She did not kiss him. She had given up kissing him long ago. A parchment cheek, bloodless and cold as fish.

In the cab she thought about the visiting card that had come pressed like a flower between two chops. Bloody. She had said so in her letter to Mrs. Lenton. An engraved card. You could feel it with your fingers. Not printed, and beautiful pasteboard. She had washed it under the tap, dried it and hidden it between the pages of her prayer book. If Joseph found it, she'd lie about it. Say she found it when Mrs. Lenton had left. Say she must have dropped it. I should have burnt it, she thought, but she couldn't. Suppose she forgot the address? That was impossible—she knew it as well as her own name. But just suppose. Besides, it would have been unlucky to burn it. So valuable—the most valuable thing she had ever had.

She hated her home. She hated her husband. There—at last it was out in the open. She felt better. A hypocrite who talked of God and played into the devil's hands. The devil was very real to Martha. Horns, forked tail, pitchfork, and all. More real than God. Joseph had spoilt God for her.

The train running over the ties seemed to say: "Molly . . . Molly . . ." England fled past her. Green. The hedges bright with bridal blossom. Laburnum dripped gold in cottage gardens. Rabbits, big and little, ran with lolloping white scuts across the fields. She looked at the grazing cattle with the eyes of a farmer's daughter. Shorthorns, Herefords. Some Alderneys. The houses came thick now. Then slums, dark with soot, sordid, frightening. Factory chimneys. Streets. London. London and Molly.

In his shop behind the big bottles filled with colored water in the window, Mr. Hastings made out prescriptions and chased the boy who swept up the floor and delivered parcels.

"You'd think 'e wanted to eat his bloody dinner off it," the boy muttered.

Waste of money going to a London dentist. There were dentists in Oxford, weren't there? But no. She had to go to London. Her father had taken the family to London every year to see the dentist and go to the theater. Abomination, anathema. A farmer, no more than a working man, indulging in such extravagance. But he sold stuff to Smithfield and Covent Garden. Business and pleasure, and the dentist. A soft man, her father. Spoilt his children.

"Yes, Madam?" he said to a customer. "What can I do for you?"

Prescriptions to be weighed out on the scales in their glass cases; the tiny weights picked up with tweezers. A thermometer . . . castor oil . . . Epsom salts. He felt like a doctor in his long white coat. A man of probity and distinction, an elder of the chapel.

He had said he'd never mention the girl, or think of her, but he did. She was in his mind a great deal. Living a life of sin and pleasure. Men . . . dancing . . . drinking . . . fornicating. I should have killed her, he thought. She would be better dead. Aye, lying dead at my feet rather than in bed with some man she had picked up in the street. There were women like that in Oxford. Young women. Pretty women, some of them. Who spoke to him as he passed them. They made him think of her. Better dead.

Mrs. Hastings went up the steps of the house in Berkeley Square. It was on the corner of Charles Street. The square was beautiful with its fountain and great plane trees in full leaf, their blotched peeling trunks patterned with gray and yellowish white. Behind the railings there were uniformed nurses and children playing on the grass. Beautiful. Peaceful. She looked at the lovely houses, the equipages. Pairs and single horses swept by. A groom passed her leading two horses—a brown and a bay—with side saddles. This was the world of the rich. Now that she was here, she hesitated, half afraid, half savoring the pleasure of the moment.

Then the door opened all by itself and Molly was in her arms. Just the way she had thought she would be. Molly, laughing and crying, and Mrs. Lenton standing behind her in the hall.

What with the gloom of the hall after the bright sunlight outside and her own tears, Mrs. Hastings stood bemused, her arm round Molly, till Mrs. Lenton came forward. "I'm so glad you managed to come, Mrs. Hastings," she said. "We saw you from upstairs. Now what about a glass of wine and a biscuit? Then we can go upstairs and talk."

The Madeira and her happiness went to Mrs. Hastings' head. How wonderful it was! How wonderful and how well Molly looked! She'd grown. She had roses in her cheeks, and how beautifully she was dressed.

Mrs. Lenton put her arm over the girl's shoulders. "She's like a daughter to me, Mrs. Hastings. Aren't you, darling?"

"I'd like to be. Oh, I'd like to have two such wonderful mothers."

Martha Hastings began to cry. Molly ran to her side and kissed her. "Don't cry, Mother. Don't cry."

"I'm so happy, Molly. But I'll get you back home somehow. That I will." And she would. She would. Her mind was made up. Somehow, anyhow.

Mrs. Lenton had left them alone in the drawing room. How kind she was! But before she left for Oxford again they had arranged for Molly to write to Mr. Jones, the butcher, on the first of every month. "And he'll see I get the letters. I saw him before I left."

On the way home she realized she had not been to the dentist. She had forgotten all about him. Well, she'd lie. She'd say she had one filling put in. She could not remember ever having told a lie before—at least not since she had been a little girl. She smiled out at the countryside. She supposed one had to begin sometime. And she'd get Molly back.

34 : The Filibuster

Lucy Stead looked at her husband when he came in. He was even later than usual tonight. How well she knew him! They had been childhood playmates in the North of England. She knew his every mood and he was in a bad one now. Something was up. She felt a kind of premonition. They had been so happy here in Wimbledon. In Cambridge House with their children, the pony trap, and the tennis courts. Found a way of life that was perfect. A big house, a big garden, a nice conservatory full of palms and potted flowers. Azaleas, cineraria. The editorship of the *Pall Mall Gazette*. The most influential paper in England. Before that it had been the *Northern Echo,* the little yellow halfpenny sheet that he'd built into a great newspaper that was read by the Prime Minister himself, and often quoted in the House of Commons. Yellow, because it was printed on cheap paper, as if the paper mattered. At that time he used to ride a pony to the office in Darlington every day. He got back at three A.M. A crusader. Always a crusader. Slum clearance. The truth about the Navy. A series of articles that had been instrumental in sending an expedition to the relief of General Gordon in Khartoum. Then prostitution. That had been on his mind for a long time. He'd thought of writing a novel about it. That had been in 1876 when he had received a letter from Mrs. Josephine Butler. He had given it to her to read. He was not the kind of man who believed women should go through life blindfolded. It was something she never forgot.

Then, last year, there had been the Lenton business. He had published the story of how Lavinia Lenton's two girls had been abducted and sold into prostitution in France. Next, there had been the attempt to prosecute the notorious Mrs. Caramine. He had reported that, too.

It had ended in a fiasco. But she knew he had not given up. He never gave up. In time he would tell her what was on his mind. She brought him a cup of tea—he drank no liquor except an occasional glass of stout.

Stead drank his tea. What a day it had been! It had started so well. He had been up early and petted Polly, the children's black pony. A lovely day. Even the three rather grim-looking houses in Northumberland Street, just off the Strand, that were the offices of the *Gazette,* had looked bright in the sunshine. He had said "Good morning" to the porter who sat in his cubicle at the foot of the bare rickety wooden stairs. The building vibrated to the rumble of the presses. His presses. His paper. One of the voices that spoke to England.

The front page consisted of two leaders. The second page was a first-person interview with someone who had a story to tell. Then came occasional notes, short leaders of a controversial nature. They were followed by sports news, a travel piece, and other oddments. The writing was good, much of it Stead's own. Racy, ironic. He felt a paper should lead opinion, create discussion, and give factual news.

It was May 23rd. He had been correcting some copy when the office boy brought in a card. Mr. Benjamin Scott. There had been a letter from him in the morning mail, so he was not surprised. "Ask him to come in," he said.

An old gentleman appeared in the doorway.

"You're following up your letter, sir, I presume," Stead said. "What do you want me to do? Please amplify the situation."

The old man rested his chin on the hands that held his walking stick and looked round the small room—the old chairs, the safe with a bottle of stout and a glass on top of it.

"Clarify it, eh?" he said. "Very well I will, and you're the only man who can help us. I want you to stop the white slave traffic. You're the only man who can do it."

"How?"

"With your paper."

"Me? I can't do it. The only thing that could do it is the Criminal Law Amendment Act—and it's dead. Dead as the dodo." He thought of the piece he had written.

"You weren't in the House yesterday, Mr. Stead?"

"No, I was here. But its end was obvious. Only twenty members there and all of them wanting to get away. Holidays, Mr. Scott, that's what count. Not women."

"You know, Mr. Stead," Scott said, "it was us—Alfred Dwyer and I and some others—who brought proceedings against Mrs. Caramine, the worst white slaver of the lot. And we lost. And she drove away in triumph, Mr. Stead, behind as fine a pair of chestnuts as there are in London. Horses bought with the flesh and blood of girls."

"I know, Mr. Scott. I reported the case. You will probably also remember that I reported the abduction of Mrs. Lenton's children by their French governess. Only one has been recovered. I have been in touch with Mrs. Josephine Butler for some years. I have the reports of an investigation conducted by my friends in Brussels and Ostend. They succeeded in rescuing a girl. One girl. I'm doing what I can. Collecting ammunition. It's on my mind. My God!" he said, "it's preying on my mind. It's a nightmare. I've been thinking about it for almost ten years —since Mrs. Butler first called it to my attention."

Scott looked at him dejectedly. "If you can't help us, we're beaten."

"There's no interest in Parliament," Stead said. "Just apathy. Nothing but apathy."

"If they knew the facts . . ." Scott said.

"They do."

"Not them, the people of England." Mr. Scott's voice rose. "Tell the people of England, William Stead. In the name of God, tell the people of England. Parliament is no good. Did you know Mrs. Caramine sends the members circulars, advertising new attractions?"

"To the members of the House?"

"She circularizes them. It's the people who must be told. The people who elect them. No one else will. No one else has the courage. You might be able to force the bill through. And this might help to convince you." Scott handed him a circular.

Stead glanced at it. "Accomplished, slim, red-haired. Only eighteen and fresh from the country . . . Mrs. Caramine extends her welcome. . . ." He dropped the paper as if it were red hot.

"*Now* will you?" Scott asked.

"I don't know. I don't know if the public could stand it."

"You have daughters, Mr. Stead," Scott said. "Not long ago at one of her houses a girl of thirteen was flogged unconscious before she was debauched."

Stead did not answer him. The old man got up.

"Thank you for seeing me, Mr. Stead. I am afraid I have wasted a lot of your time."

Stead shook his hand. "Goodbye, Mr. Scott." He felt himself hardly able to speak.

When Scott had gone, Stead told his staff to get him copies of all the debates on the Criminal Law Amendment Bill. Then he went to see his friend Howard Vincent, ex-Chief of the C.I.D. From him he got more details, more chapter and verse. He had had Mrs. Lenton's story. He had the report John Longbeach had given him. But still, with all this, he had not been able to believe it was as bad as it now turned out to be.

"And all this is going on now," Vincent said. "It's going on, and it will go on. Tonight and every night."

Having left Vincent, Stead went to see the President of the Council for the Protection of Women and Children. He spoke of the child who had been flogged in Mrs. Caramine's house.

"Suppose," he said, "I asked you to take over her case?"

"We should refuse. She was over thirteen and probably consented to be whipped. It is not our affair."

"Not your affair?"

"Not our sphere."

At Scotland Yard there was the same story, the same obstruction. The Home Secretary, Sir William Harcourt, refused to allow the police to put such evidence as they had into his hands. Leave the white slave traffic alone. It was more than advice. It was almost an order. So this was the view they took in high places.

It was late when he got back to his office, much later by the time he got home. Stead did not go to bed that night. He went through the pamphlets Scott had brought him. He knew—he had known—for years. He'd even sent Portal and John Longbeach to investigate. And still there had not been enough to risk his reputation and that of his paper.

But unless someone did something the bill was lost. Someone? Who was that someone but himself? Lucy in a dressing gown, her long hair down her back, brought him more tea and begged him to come to bed. She picked up a pamphlet and he snatched it from her. He believed that women should not be kept in ignorance, but this was too much, too strong. Yet this was what he was going to publicize. His mind was made up suddenly. "All right," he said. "Read it, Lucy."

She sat by the lamp reading, as he strode up and down the room. Tears rolled down her cheeks.

"You see," he said. "You see. And what am I to do, Lucy?"

"You must do what you feel is right, William." That was what he had always done, what she admired about him.

Next day he got out Mrs. Butler's letter again. It had been written in 1876. "Dear Sir," it began—she had not known him then—"I could wish for the sake of justice and virtue that your paper were the most important in the kingdom." Then, after alluding to the brothels in Brussels and Paris, she went on:

> Here is slavery and tragedy enough; but how would a book here be read which contained the ghastly truth? But it will have to be made known in some way. For surely God will arise one day; and the tormented creatures which He created and cares for will be avenged.

Her letter concluded with a sentence that had fallen like a thunderbolt on the sensitive young editor's heart: "In the grandest house of the kind in Paris, I saw the portraits of all the great men who had frequented it—diplomats, generals, and English lords. Oh, it was terrible to see them! The brothel keepers put a cross underneath the portrait to mark the number of visits made to the place by these great men! Pictures notched like the butt of a gun."

This morning, years later, he had told his staff to collect all reports on the Criminal Law Amendment Act. By lunch time he had them, the whole history of the Criminal Law Amendment Bill. He looked at the mass of papers and reports his men had left, neatly clipped together, on his desk. First came the Report of the Select Committee of July 1882, which proved the existence of the white slave traffic—as if it needed proof. Some recommendations were made. It had begun its work in May 1881 and its purpose was to inquire into the state of the Law relative to the Protection of Young Girls from Artifices to Induce Them to Lead a Corrupt Life, and into the means of amending same. The members were the Marquis of Salisbury, the Earl of Mount Edgecumbe, the Earl of Belmore, Earl Cairns, the Bishop of London, Lord Leigh, Lord Penzance, Lord Aberdare, Lord Dalhousie, Lord Tollemache, Lord Norton, and Lord Mount Temple. They recommended that it be made a serious misdemeanor for any person to solicit any woman to leave the United Kingdom for the purpose of entering a brothel overseas; that the age up to which it shall be an offence to indecently assault a girl shall be raised from thirteen to sixteen; that the age of unlawful abduction shall be raised from sixteen to twenty-one; that it shall be a misdemeanor for any person to receive into any house or into any premises occupied by him any girl under the age of sixteen years for the purpose of her having sexual intercourse with any person.

In debate Lord Shaftesbury had said: "Nothing more cruel, appalling, or detestable can be found in the history of crime all over the world," and Lord Dalhousie had added: "I would fail if I were to attempt to give your lordships an adequate description of the life of shame, degradation, and wretchedness which the vile, iniquitous traffic has inflicted on our countrywomen. In my opinion no time should be lost in putting a stop to a practice which, in arrant villainy and rascality, surpasses all that we know of any other trade in human beings in any part of the world in ancient or modern times."

Only three newspapers had come out with the facts. In each the editors apologized, regretting to raise such a "disgusting" subject. On the 13th of December 1882, the *Daily Telegraph* editor stated:

> My attention has been drawn to a nefarious practice, similar to that disclosed in Brussels, which if suffered to continue unchecked will be productive of much mischief. Young girls are, it appears, decoyed to Paris from their homes in England by means of advertisements most plausibly worded, and on their arrival find to their dismay that the situation which they expected to obtain is a mere myth, and that, on the other hand, temptations of every kind are deliberately placed in their way. Cases have been brought to my notice in which the unfortunate victims have been induced to sign documents, of the true character of which they had absolutely no idea.

On the 11th of January 1883, the *London Echo* wrote:

> English men and women are not likely to forget in a hurry the consternation and righteous wrath with which the first revelations concerning the iniquitous traffic were received, nor the attempts at official denial. Every effort must still be made to warn and instruct the ignorant and inexperienced against accepting any specious offer of employment on the Continent without the fullest inquiry.

The Roman Catholic *Tablet* went further:

> It is clear that a new anti-slave agitation is clearly needed. Horrible and revolting as have been the revelations as to the export of English girls to Brussels and Paris, that trade is trivial compared with the vast organised system which prevails in Germany, Austria and Roumania for the sale of young women to dealers in human wares all over the world. When once they pass into the hands of their purchasers, their doom is sealed.

In May 1883, about a year later, a bill was introduced in Parliament. An act to make further provision for the protection of women and girls, and for the suppression of brothels. It was known as the Criminal Law Amendment Act. It raised the age of consent to sixteen, gave the police powers to apply for search warrants when girls were thought to be detained and authorized the suppression of brothels and clearing houses for continental white slave traffic. It passed the Lords but died of apathy and indifference in the Lower House.

In March 1884, Lord Dalhousie introduced a second act that resembled the first in almost every particular. And again it passed the Lords but failed in the Commons.

In 1885 Dalhousie introduced a third bill. This was the one that was before the House now. In it the age of consent was reduced to fifteen, as if this would make it more palatable. On May 22nd, the Friday before the Whitsun weekend, it had come up for its second reading. Less than forty members were present—the rest were already on holiday in the country. Some members thought it a good measure while others said no man would be safe if it became law. One member suggested that they should discuss it with their constituents before voting. Mr. Cavendish Bentinck who spoke last, spoke at such length that he was still at it when the debate came to an end at six-fifty P.M. He had talked it out. A filibuster, as they called it in America.

The last clipping was Stead's own piece:

> Once more we regret to see that the protection of our young girls has been sacrificed to the loquacity of our legislators. Mr. Bentinck talked out the Criminal Law Amendment Bill yesterday afternoon, and we fear that the chances of proceeding with this measure before the general election are of the slightest. Everyone agrees with the principle of the Bill, but no consideration, divine or human, could induce members to hold their tongues on the second reading, leaving the consideration of details to the Committee. The result is that the second reading could not be taken; the Bill, it is feared, is lost, and that although the Home Secretary left the age up to which protection should be given as an open question. *A House of Commons in which women were represented would not display such indifference to a question which is really one of life and death to immense numbers of poor girls.*

Then, as if this was not enough, Benjamin Waugh—whom he knew fairly well—was shown into the office, and regaled him with more stories of children who had been abducted and raped. It was too much. There was a limit, a saturation point to horror, and he turned on Waugh in anger.

"Talk . . . talk . . . talk. . . . What about facts? Can I see these children with my own eyes? I've been to the societies—they fluff me off. They are afraid of it themselves. Scotland Yard shut me up. Show me, I say, and I'm your man."

"All right," Waugh said.

"When?"

"Now, at once. Get your hat."

"There's not much time if the Act is going to be passed. But if what you tell me is true,"—and in his heart he knew it was—"I'll raise all England. I'll . . ."

Their first stop was a shelter in Hapur Street. Here there were two little girls who had been abducted and raped—one was seven and the other almost five. When the children had been taken away, Waugh said that of the twelve men who had misused them, only one had been convicted.

". . . since the girls were too young to understand the nature of an oath, William." So their evidence had been valueless. Because of their terror of strange men, it was only with infinite pains that Stead had been able to coax the baby onto his knee, and she had sat there trembling with fright.

"By God!" Stead said. "I'll do this if it's the last thing I do." There were tears in his eyes.

They went next to the Salvation Army headquarters where, with Mr. Bramwell Booth, he took notes on what the girls who were brought in said.

"The papers will report none of this," Booth said. "The cases are too revolting."

"I was as bad as the rest," Stead said. "I wanted to try but every instinct of self-preservation and prudence restrained me. The very horror of these crimes has been their protection."

"I've been in children's brothels," Booth said, "and found middle-aged men in bed with two or three children in every room. I went with a police superintendent and they just laughed at me. There is no law to stop them, Stead. No law in England."

"I'll form a secret commission, Bramwell. We'll get the evidence and when I have it my paper will publish it *in toto*." The title came to him in a flash. "I shall call the series: *The Maiden Tribute of Modern Babylon*."

"You can count on us, William," Booth said. "I'm speaking for the whole Army. You see that is our mission—salvation."

He thought he'd known everything. Years ago it had been brought to his attention. Then there had been Mrs. Lenton's story and the report John Longbeach brought back. But this . . . this no words could describe. But they must. And he must find the words. No one else in England would do it. Or could do it.

In twenty-four hours Stead had aged. As usual Lucy had waited up for him in Wimbledon.

"You're ill, darling," she said.

"Yes, I'm ill, Lucy."

"What is it?" She knelt beside his chair.

"My heart," he said. "I'm sick at heart. I've made up my mind. I'm going to do it, Lucy. But I shall never be the same man again."

When Mrs. Lenton got Stead's note she went to see him. It must be something important.

"Well, Mrs. Lenton," he said when she came into his office, "I have news for you and I'm going to want your help. I am so glad you are back in London."

She thought he looked tired, even exhausted. His eyes were sunk into his face, his mouth despondent.

"You have no idea what I have been through," he said. "What I have seen. Horror piled on horror. I have been into bordellos in disguise. They have taken me for one of themselves, a rich client in search of debauchery. I have been offered a score of girls to do what I liked with. What do they like, these men? These whited sepulchres. So depraved are they that their lust is only aroused by cruelty. Alone in padded, soundproofed rooms, they delight in the terrified screams of their victims. Ratepayers, voters, rich men, churchgoers. . . ." He paused for breath. "I have it all. Statements, witnesses—the whole chapter and verse of it. But this will not be enough. To expose it fully, I have decided to buy a young girl myself."

"You're what?" Lavinia gasped.

"I'm going to buy a certified virgin. Oh yes, they are certified like horses in a catalogue. Sound in wind and limb. Used to ladies. Quiet too. Ride and drive. They even have catalogues. My God!" he said, "I've seen these girls listed: age, coloring, weight, measurements, aptitudes and remarks. Broken like horses, Mrs. Lenton; raped, whipped and starved into submission. So tame, so frightened that they can even be sent to the Continent alone and unescorted. Put on the ship at one end and met at the other." He ran his hands through his hair. "Mrs. Butler knows a woman who, a couple of years ago, was a procuress. She has been saved by the Army and works for her with fallen girls in Winchester. With great difficulty she has persuaded her to return to her old haunts, find a suitable child and buy her from her parents. It's impossible to believe, isn't it? And it's this very impossibility which has given the business its protection. No one wants to believe it so they don't. But they will. I'll raise England, Mrs. Lenton. I'll create such a scandal as has never been seen before."

Lavinia was crying quietly. May, who was standing beside her chair, patted her shoulder. Lavinia raised her tearstained face and said: "Tell me when you want me and what you want me to do. You can count on me, Mr. Stead."

"I know," he said. "Thank God for my friends. I've written to Lord Salisbury and Cardinal Manning, informing them of my plan. I don't know what will come of it, Mrs. Lenton. I may ruin my paper and ruin myself, but I must do it. I must."

PART THREE

THE PRICE
OF VIRTUE

Virtue in distress and vice in triumph renders
atheists of mankind.

Cleomenes

35 : The Price of Virtue

Charles Street, Lissom-Grove, was a mean street. And No. 32 a mean house—diseased, mangy with soot and peeling plaster. Eliza Armstrong sat on the worn steps nursing her baby brother. Jane, her eldest sister of seventeen, was already in service. She supposed she would go into service herself before long, but she did not want to leave the baby. Her two young brothers and other sister she did not care for. She could hardly remember ever seeing her father sober—Basher, as he was called—but she was skillful in avoiding him. Her mother drank too. But so did everyone in Lissom-Grove. Her father was looking for another boy, small but wiry enough to climb up chimneys to clean them. Her brother Johnny had died. Aye, he'd been took sick and died. Lots of sweeps' boys died. It was soot in the lungs, they said, and being beaten up when they weren't sharp enough. He'd told her how frightened he was sometimes. Afraid of getting stuck. "And who'd get me out, Eliza," he'd said. Boys had been stuck in the chimneys of the great London houses before now. Regular black rabbit warrens, they was. Twisty, with curves and elbow bends built into 'em, and six storeys or more up.

There were lots of children in the street. Boys, girls—barefoot, half-naked, with lice in their hair. A dead dog lay in the gutter not far from Eliza. Cabbage stalks, rats, and the cats that lived on them, fish heads and garbage. But this was her world. She knew no other.

Eliza cuddled the baby and thought about the swarthy man. A Dago he was, who'd spoken to her a couple of times. He'd spoken to other little girls, too, and their mothers. She hadn't liked the looks of him. Slimy-like, with sweets in his pockets for the kids. And she'd seen him go into The Sailor with her Dad. Why would that be, she wondered.

The facts of life had never been explained to Eliza. There had been no need. She'd seen them all. Heard her baby brother being conceived and seen him born. Seen men, and girls with their skirts raised, standing against walls in dark passages. Boys, young louts, had tried to get their hands on her but she fought them off. She'd seen drunks reeling home, her own Dad among them. Heard women screaming when they were beaten. Watched women fight, tearing each other's hair, and then lying passed out in the garbage of the gutters. She'd seen girls disappear too; girls not much older than herself. Some younger. Here today playing in the street, and gone tomorrow.

In Winchester Mrs. Butler was talking to Rebecca Jarrett and Harris, who had joined her at the Cottage, helping her to take care of the girls they'd rescued, and going into the pubs and dives to look for others. Young kids who had got into it and couldn't find their way out, drowning in vice like puppies thrown into a well.

To both of them Mrs. Josephine Butler was a kind of angel. The Army had sent Harris to her when they heard she had met Rebecca.

Mrs. Butler said: "I'm going to ask you to do something very difficult, Rebecca."

"Yes, Ma'am."

"I want you to go back to London and buy a young girl from her parents."

"Oh no! No, Ma'am, I could not do that. Not get mixed up in it again. I'm saved; I belong to Jesus now."

"This is for Jesus. For God. To save the child and hundreds more besides. So listen to me. But you know how to do it, don't you? You have friends?"

"Friends, Ma'am? Not now, not any more."

"But you do know people?"

"Oh yes, Ma'am." Rebecca thought of Nance Broughton. She'd been a procuress, was still one, no doubt. She had known her very well. They had even been in service together at Claridge's Hotel at one time.

"Then do it for me." Mrs. Butler looked at her imploringly. "We have helped you, Rebecca. Now help us to help others."

Mrs. Butler wrote to Stead:

I've found a woman who will do what you want. Pray for her. She is reformed and only with the greatest difficulty did I persuade her to return to her old haunts. She will stay with the Army and will call on you in a few days.

Two days later Mrs. Jarrett called on Stead at the office. A respectable but ravaged-looking woman in her fifties. She sat on a chair, picking at her black cotton gloves and staring at him out of dark, sunken eyes.

"I don't understand, sir," she said. "Mrs. Butler says you want a young girl, sir." He did not look like a man who wanted a young girl. "To buy one, I mean," she said.

"That's right."

"What for, sir? If it's to . . ." She could not say "sleep with," she couldn't—not now. She plucked at her gloves in desperation.

"I'll begin at the beginning," Stead said. "You know that young girls—children—are being sold in London by their parents. Sold into slavery, into prostitution?"

"Yes, sir."

"Very well. I and my committee—of which Mrs. Butler is a member —want to stop it."

"Yes, sir." But if he wanted to stop it, why was he going into it himself?

Stead looked at the woman in front of him. He knew something of her history. Josephine Butler had told him about her. Seduced and prostituted as a child in the Cremorne Gardens, a park on the river dedicated to venery, that had been closed up a few years ago. Encouraged by her mother, who was also a woman of easy virtue, she had been kept by a series of men until, at the age of sixteen, she was running a brothel of her own. She had become ill, been hospitalized and her children, illegitimate of course, had been taken from her and she had lost track of them. Then she had gone downhill fast till, by a lucky accident, she had fallen into the hands of the Salvation Army and been saved. Now he was throwing her to the wolves once more, exposing her to the dangers she had escaped.

"I want a girl," he said. "A young girl. I want her certified a virgin. I want to send her to Paris in charge of the Army, just to prove that it can be done. Mrs. Jarrett," he said, "till I do this and prove it, no one will believe the truth. Will you do it?" he asked. "Will you help us save the girls of England from being exported like cattle?"

Overcome with emotion, Rebecca began to cry. At last she recovered herself and said: "Yes, sir. I'll do it. I'll go this very afternoon to see my friend, Nance Broughton. I'll tell her I want a girl to help in the house. That I'll pay the mother and don't want no questions asked." She knew Nance wouldn't believe her. She knew the child's mother wouldn't believe her. That was the usual story when a procuress bought a child. Help in the house. What kind of house? What kind of help? To them there was only one possible answer, especially as only pretty girls, young ones—kid leather—were wanted.

"How much do you want?" Stead asked. "I mean"—how hard it was to say the words—"will she cost?"

"Two pounds, sir," Mrs. Jarrett said. "Five at the most for a little beauty."

He gave her the money. So the price of virtue ran between two and five pounds for a girl bought off the streets. But this was the only way to do it. Buy one himself and expose the racket. Show how easy it was. God help them all.

Stead got up and shook Mrs. Jarrett's hand. "Bring her to Poland Street at tea time, the day after tomorrow," he said, giving her the address.

36 : The Midwife

Madame Mourez, *sage femme*, had been first the maid, then the mistress and finally the assistant of Doctor Chantfort, the Paris abortionist. When he was imprisoned she escaped the country and came to England where, posing as a midwife *diplômée*, she learnt her new trade by trial and error. She was deft and quick and relatively successful. Then, meeting some compatriots engaged in prostitution, she put her services at their disposal and soon became known in that world as a valuable acquisition to the fraternity.

She was a small woman of fifty, who dressed very respectably, did not drink, and was always ready on call. A midwife with her little black leather doctor's bag. She had no feelings. She remembered vaguely a passionate girlhood, but her experiences had been unfortunate. Betrayed by man after man, her heart—except as an organ of the body—had ceased to function. It had atrophied. It was difficult to imagine that her breasts had ever held milk or that she had raised a son at them, a young man who was now a bus conductor on a line that ran from the *Place du Théâtre* to the *Porte de Neuilly;* married, and the father of a fat little girl with gold locks that were done up in screws of newspaper every evening.

Abortionist, examiner of virgins, repairer of broken children, surgeon, and factotum in general to the pimps and madams of the West End— that was Louise Mourez. Torn and flogged bodies she took calmly, mending children and young women, as if they were china cups, to render them serviceable again.

It was on this woman at her home, a whore house in Albany Street, that Rebecca Jarrett had called. They were old acquaintances. Her presence now nauseated the reformed Jarrett, but she had given her word to her benefactor, Mrs. Butler, to go through with it. The parlor in which they sat was that of an ordinary middle-class home. Shiny, black-covered horsehair furniture, a red and green carpet laid over linoleum, a ticking cuckoo clock, the pendulum swinging through its arcs and marking off invisible hours, days, months and years of horror. It was strange to think of Madame Mourez living in this homelike place, with its china dogs on the mantelpiece, its dyed pampas grass in a tall vase, when she went to do her butcher's work. Still stranger to think that none of this had occurred to her before. Jarrett had been here often enough in the old days, less than two years ago.

"A virgin of twelve or thirteen years to certify?" Madame Mourez said. "What could be simpler? The matter of a moment only." She laughed. "Another young girl for the delectation of some old roué who likes a doll to play with. Strange, is it not, that so many men—even educated men—believe that the use of a virgin will cure them of venereal disease? What an illusion! But such sicknesses are the wages of sin—also the price of avarice. Men go to cheap houses, pick up cheap girls, *et voilà*. . . ."

"Then," Rebecca said, "at six in the evening."

"I will attend you." Madame Mourez bowed Rebecca out.

She had also seen Nance Broughton. They had talked about the time they had been in service at Claridge's together, and both engaged in prostitution. It was a good way to find clients—men who were only too glad to find a complacent chambermaid who could put them on to a good thing. She had had a nice house of her own then too—orderly, with clean, pretty girls whom she treated well.

"Nance," she'd said, "I'm married now to Mr. Sullivan, a commercial gentleman and I need a girl to help me. I can't get on my knees and scrub like I used to."

"Why come here?" Nance said. "Aren't there any girls in Wimbledon?" That was where she had said her six-roomed house was. "Why come to Lissom-Grove, Becky?"

"I wanted to see you and I thought you'd know a likely kid. I wanted to give some poor kid a chance to better herself."

"Girls. There's plenty of girls here." She had introduced her to a couple. Sixteen and seventeen they were.

"Too old," she said, "and not pretty enough. I want a kid of twelve or thirteen. These teeners are after men already and they won't stay put. They'll try to bring men into their rooms. They'll get pregnant."

"There's one kid," Nance had said. "Eliza Armstrong. She'd clean up nice. We'll go and see her ma. She lives down the street and she drinks."

"I want no nonsense," Rebecca had said. "I'll pay two pounds down and three after she's certified."

"What do you want her certified for?" Nance had looked at her sideways. "Pretty and certified—for scrubbing floors?"

"I want a clean girl, not a little harlot. Same reason as I want her young."

'You mean you want to buy her, Becky?"

"Yes. That's not difficult, is it? It never used to be."

"Difficult? There's a dozen you could buy for a fiver, and no questions asked. Five bloody quid. How do you think their mothers would ever get a fiver any other way all at one time?"

And that was how it had been. She'd pick her up tomorrow. Pretty she was, pretty as a picture. But dirty. Grubby with street dirt and the soot her father brought into the house. He was a sweep, Nance said.

Mrs. Armstrong was a woman of forty, nursing a snotty-nosed baby at her dirty breast. Her hair was stringy. She reeked of gin.

"I'll not let Eliza go," she said. "Who's to mind the kid if she goes? Besides, she's got no proper clothes."

"I'll buy her some clothes," Rebecca said.

"And how much will you give me?"

"A fiver. Two pounds down and three more when I find she's a good girl."

"She's a good girl, all right," Mrs. Armstrong flared. "And better be. No boy's had his hand on her, much less more."

"Then you've nothing to worry about. I'll be back for her tomorrow."

"I want a quid now."

"All right," she'd said. "Here's a pound."

Mrs. Armstrong had bitten the gold coin with blackened teeth. "And the other quid tomorrow and three more next day?"

"I'll give them to Nance," she'd said.

Lord, no inquiries as to where she lived or what she wanted the child for. And this was a mother and Nance said there were plenty like her down here. This part of London was new to Rebecca. She'd never dealt with children before, only with big girls who'd sooner lie down than work, sweatshopped in factories.

Well, everything was arranged now. She went slowly back to the Army headquarters, where she was spending the night, to report to Mr. Booth, the general.

Lissom-Grove, off Shoreditch High Street, was an area of tumble-down houses, factories, and warehouses. Over everything lay an aura of disease and despair, a miasma. Liverpool Street Station and Spittal-fields Market were not far away. The Goods Station was even closer. There was no green anywhere. The children ran here like wild things. Little girls, clad in only one nightdresslike garment, played in garbaged gutters. Green metallic flies were busy about the body of a black cat that the boys had stoned to death for the sport of it. Slatternly mothers gossiped, their bodices undone in the summer heat. Drunken men and women reeled into and out of the public houses. Small children dodged them with the mugs and bottles they had been sent to fetch. Rubbish putrefied in heaps. There were boxes of fermenting ordure, fecal matter. Rats, half the size of cats, dodged in and out of piled packing cases black with soot. Rebecca saw it all with new eyes. Evil was born in dirt and poverty. What chance had virtue here? But no one insulted her as she strode through the filth. She was too big a woman, too powerful. Besides, what was the point of it? No sport could be had with so ugly a creature, who would certainly refuse to be intimidated. There were no prostitutes. No one had the money for one and why pay for what could be taken? The women knew too much to resist men who would beat them into submission anyway, while the crowd looked on and laughed. This was a subhuman world of pickpockets and thieves. Nance Broughton had told her her husband was a handyman. Rebecca almost laughed —she knew he was a burglar. But of course a man had to be pretty handy for that.

At Mortal, with Mrs. Lenton and Molly gone, Muriel had fallen into her old position of Eva's governess. The old schoolbooks were there, mixed up with the new ones. Molly had taught her to read again and she picked up where Molly had left off. But mainly she went back to the simple books she had used herself in teaching Eva nine years ago. She felt this would bring Eva back, lead her up step by step again into the present. She had always loved Eva and was heartbroken at her state. To cheer her up and add more light and laughter to the house, she got her husband to bring Frank down for a while so that she could teach the two of them together, Frank at nine being fully the equal of the now retarded Evangeline. Muriel had written to Mrs. Lenton for permission, told her that she had begun teaching Eva again and said she was progressing slowly. The big girl and little boy got on together. They seemed mentally to be almost as much of an age in games and play as they were in class.

Muriel had no idea that Edward had ever seen Frank, or knew him to be his son. He knew he was her boy but she thought he must believe him to be the result of her marriage. She supposed he would think their child was dead, had been aborted or disposed of, as was usual in such cases, by Mrs. Caramine.

Frank did not recognize this human log, wrapped up like a sausage in a Stuart plaid. He bore no resemblance to the dashing, well-dressed man he had met in his godmother's parlor.

For Edward the situation was hellish. A torture of Tantalus. Rage and regret tormented him. Not regret for any acts that might have been regarded as sins, but regret that he could no longer have women. Have Muriel. He watched her moving about his room. She was a woman now—ripe, in her full sensual prime. He knew the body under those tight-boned, sweeping clothes. He'd known it young and virginal and could guess at the changes. The warm soft contours of flesh that nine years and motherhood had given her. He yearned to touch her heavy mane of dark red liver-chestnut colored hair, that was piled in a great twisted chignon on her head. Above all he raged at the boy. Running and shouting as he played with Mac and Eva. His bastard. The by-blow who should have been his heir. How Lavinia must hate him to have done this to him. To taunt him. Here he lay, the last of the Lentons, able to move nothing but his eyes. The eyes with which he watched his son and lusted after his son's mother. The men who took care of him looked at her like that too. By God, he ought to know the look. Appraising. He wondered if either of them was sleeping with her. They gave no sign of it, but she needed someone. There was a feeling of desire about her. He was too cynical to believe it was for him—that she loved him and only him. It was all a trick, some deep-laid plot hatched by the pair of them. The bitches. Lavinia and Muriel. Women he had had and who now conspired to betray him. His eroticism was now a kind of madness. Girls and women were all he thought of. Ellen. Those delicious days of power in Paris, at Jumelle's. And she had betrayed him too.

37 : Derby Day

Basher Armstrong was a big man, an ex-soldier. A barrel on legs, who had been a second-class pug once. One of the fancy, as he put it. But he hadn't the bottom for it, couldn't take punishment. And that was the end of it. He'd become a chimney sweep then. But there'd been a brash charm to him once, and he got jobs. And he'd got a wife, too. Betty Morden, a quick little trick of a girl. Till she'd had all them kids. Then a slut, and a drunken one at that. But he was still a man. Men got out of his way and the women looked at him. Clean-shaven, except for his mustache, when he remembered to shave. Dark, hairy. Hair ran from his throat over his chest to his loins. Hair on his back. On his arms to his fingertips. His bloodshot eyes were gray, his hair a grizzled black, his eyebrows bushy. Formidable. An ugly customer rolling down the street. Boys. Christ, he'd had a lot of boys, but they ran away or died on him, or got too big for the work. Betty said he'd starved their Johnny but he hadn't. He just tried to keep him small enough for the chimneys. That was all. Cut down his food and given him gin. That stunted 'em. Of course he'd licked him. How the hell did you get a kid up a chimney if you didn't lick him? Afraid, they was. The only way was to make them more afraid of not climbing. Against the law now. But there were still people who preferred climbing boys to them new-fangled brushes. Less mess, they said.

But he was on a new line now. Scouting for girls. A quid a time and drink money. That was what Mr. Solferino had said. Take the parents into a pub and treat 'em. Tell 'em they'll go to good homes. Nice homes. Meet nice people—gentlemen. He'd laughed, Solferino had, when he said that. "And see that they are clean girls. Not touched. I only want the best; nothing secondhand."

That was when he'd said: "I got one myself, Mister. Rising thirteen, a neat trick and clean as a whistle." Eliza had been in the street and he'd called her. Solferino had looked her over.

"A fiver," he'd said when she'd gone back to play in the gutter. "I'll tell you when. And find me some more."

"How many?" he'd said.

"As many as you like as long as they're not cross-eyed or crippled."

That had been a big day. A new future had opened for him. Nice work, easy money, and a fight or two on occasion, Mr. Solferino had said. A real gentleman. That had been a month or more ago. He'd be hearing from him soon. He had some pretty kids lined up.

This evening Basher was feeling pretty good. He'd seen Solferino again. "Next week I'll send for the kid, Basher. You got the names of some others?"

"Yes," he said. "And their dads is willing. Mums, too. Glad to get rid of 'em before they gets into trouble." A fiver for his and a quid each for the others for making the arrangements. Wot could be fairer than that? Might even go into the business himself. Solferino had hinted as much. Basher by name and basher by nature.

"I can do with one or two more hard boys," he said. "A dust-up when there's trouble, putting the screw on them as makes trouble. Do-gooders and the like what pokes their noses into affairs that ain't none of their bloody business."

"Well, that 'ud suit me." And a fiver for Eliza was a good price. Just an expense she was, another mouth to feed. He'd break it to Betty when he'd had a pint or two, and if she kicked up he'd know what to do. Master of his own house, he was. Make no mistake about that.

He downed a couple of pints at The Sailor. Half a dollar, Solferino had given him. On account, mind.

"That's only four pounds, seventeen and six I owe you now," he said. But that was all my eye. When he got the kid he'd give him a fiver all right. A real gent he was. Basher wiped the foam from his mustache and went home.

Betty was nursing the kid, her bodice open, and her big tit in its mouth. Like a bloody cow she was now, but a neat little trick when he'd married her. Neat and good tempered.

"Where's Eliza?" he said.

"Out."

"Well, Betts, I've passed her on to Solferino for a fiver, and I'll give you a quid of it for yourself. And no questions asked as to how you spend it."

Elizabeth Armstrong laughed. "You're too late, Basher," she said. "She's gone."

"Gone where?"

"To Wimbledon, in service."

"Christ!" he said. "And not a word to me, her father!"

"A fine father you are. What were you doing selling her to that pimp?"

"A businessman he is, is Mr. Solferino. An' you keep a civil tongue in your mouth when you're talking about me friends."

"Aye. And a fine business with girls on the streets and watchers and all. Well, he won't get our Eliza, he won't, because she's gone. That's what."

"That's what, eh?" And he hauled off and hit her. The baby fell screaming on the floor. Then he took his belt to her. He'd show her, he would. Show her who was boss. And what a bloody fool he'd look when Solferino sent for the girl. Snatched from under his bloody nose. What did he care what he did with the little bitch? That's what they were for, wasn't it? Money for jam, that was. Little bitches, the place was full of 'em. But clean. Fresh stuff, that was what he wanted. And now this. He knocked his wife down again and belted her.

"You bloody interfering fool!" he shouted. "Service. God damn service. She's mine, ain't she? Mine to do what I like with. And I'm going to take the hide off you. I'll place me own bloody girls," he said.

Bet Armstrong struggled screaming in his grip. "You let me go, you bastard, or I'll tell on you. Who killed little Johnny? Who beat 'im and starved 'im 'cos he wouldn't climb? Was afeared of it." A blow on the mouth silenced her.

The bitch. What would he tell Solferino? What a fool it would make him look when he couldn't deliver the goods.

"You let up, you big bastard, or I'll tell the police on you. Tell 'em about little Johnny. That's what I'll do."

"You keep your trap shut. Dead, ain't he? And none of my fault."

"Not your fault? Taking the hide off the kid and starving him? Do you think a kid can live on gin?"

That's when he left her lying on the floor, her mouth bleeding. Bloody bitch. He'd had enough of her back chat. Right from under his nose. Five shiners. Golden sovereigns. Gone to Wimbledon, gone forever. And him looking a fool. Me, Basher, a fool. And having to explain it to a bloody Dago pimp.

The Epsom Downs were aseethe with people. This was the sport of kings. Bookies shouting odds from their stands, tipsters selling slips that named the winners. "No doubt at all, guv'nor. Every 'orse I mentions will place or win . . ." Sideshows, Aunt Sallies, Bearded Women, brass bands. Vehicles, from four-in-hands with their two yards of brass tooting from the boot, to costers' donkey carts. Pearlies, their clothes almost hidden by white buttons, with clean bright scarves and new caps, and their women in hats high-piled with soiled ostrich feathers. Nippers running in and out between men's legs. Pickpockets, whores, carriages, and coaches—all horseless now, their shafts and poles on the grass—the owners and their guests drinking champagne and eating cold salmon, chicken and eggs in aspic. The ladies' dresses, bright as flowers, petaled with parasols. All eager for life, for a win, for love, for acclaim and compliments. It was summer in England. June 3rd—Derby Day.

In the paddocks and the stables men were putting a final polish on their blood horses. The best in the land, bred to this purpose. To speed, to beauty. Gray top hats, bowlers, morning coats, checks as loud as draught boards. Every kind of dress, of man, of woman. The Prince of Wales was there, portly and cheerful. So was Solferino.

In Lissom-Grove there was no change. The dead cats and cabbage still lay fly-covered in the gutters.

Eliza had left it all without regret, with Rebecca Jarrett, whom she called Mrs. Sullivan. She had taken her to buy some new clothes. A pair of boots at Chandlers, a frock at Davis', a hat and scarf at Thompson's. And then back to put them on at Nancy Broughton's.

Newly dressed, fine as a young lady, and holding Rebecca's hand, they boarded a bus for the Marble Arch. What an adventure! Eliza had never been so far west before. Never seen the wide streets, the emporiums, or the fine houses of London, her native city. They sat on top just behind the driver, looking down on the two big gray horses, harnessed to the pole, as the bus wove its way through the roaring traffic. Carriages, vans, brewers' wains pulled by horses the size of elephants, hansoms, four-wheelers, butchers' traps, mounted policemen. A detachment of Household Cavalry on black chargers—all scarlet, white horsetail plumes and tin bellies, bright as silver in the sun. This was life, this was.

At the Arch—old Tyburn Hill, scene of a thousand public executions—they changed buses and plodded at a slow, ponderous dappled trot to Albany Street, where they got out, walked a short distance and went up the steps of a private house.

Inside the house, Will Stead had said: "They should be here soon," looking at his watch.

Lavinia watched him with admiration. There was no holding up now. He had gone into this in a big way. He looked much older than when she had first met him. She was not surprised. She knew what he had been through. He had told her of the sights he had seen. She had read Ben Scott's pamphlets. Josephine Butler had become her friend. But this thing that they were going to do was in a way incredible. In a few minutes, a woman who had been a prostitute and had kept a brothel, was going to bring them a child that she had bought. Bought from her mother like a pup on a string at a street corner. Then she was going to be vetted like a horse. Not for soundness, not for reasons of health, but for virginity. After that . . . after that she would not think. Stead had told her what he was going to do, but the risk was enormous. He had written to Lord Salisbury, Cardinal Manning, and the Bishop of London about his plan. He had covered himself in every way possible. . . . But no one approved of it.

This evening she was seeing John. He had come up to London. "I can't stand it any longer," he had said. Maud had arranged something. A place to meet, to make love. That was why she had dressed the way she had. To be beautiful for John. She was wearing a flowered Chinese chiffon bound at the waist with a cherry pink sash that fell over her left thigh. The pink motif was carried out in her hat—a wide-brimmed straw decorated with artificial white and red roses and a wide, cherry-colored ribbon that pierced the brim and tied under her chin. She had on half-length white gloves and white kid boots. The effect was very fetching and enchanting. A little girlish, perhaps, but love turned women into girls. Her lingerie was French. Lace-trimmed silk, all threaded with narrow satin ribbon, smelling of lavender sachets, which May kept in the drawers of her dresser. Time, which she had been able to control in Mortal, now weighed on her as if the hours she must wait had actual substance. Maud said she had been there with Geoffrey. It was very comfortable and discreet. A small house in Mallard Street in Chelsea. Madame Elsie had given her the address. Most obliging, Madame Elsie was to her clients. That name again. How it cropped up! Lavinia thought of the girls in her sweatshop sewing their eyes and hearts out. John. She'd take May, of course, as a chaperone. The couple who ran the place also had a milliner's shop. Specialities. "You'll have to buy a hat, of course," Maud had said, "but they are very nice. I've got one on now." It had been a pretty little straw boater trimmed with ribbon and flowers—forget-me-nots and lilies of the valley. Maud had laughed her pretty silvery little laugh that was like the tinkle of glass wind charms.

"They're here," Stead said, breaking in on her dreams. A moment later a gaunt woman, holding a pretty though rather grubby child by the hand, came in. The puppy. The bitch pup bought on the street corner, that could be ill-treated, whipped, and abused—even killed—and no one would give a damn. There was no law in England to protect her.

"This is Mrs. Sullivan," Stead said. "And Eliza," he added. "Eliza Armstrong." The child bobbed, holding her new skirt out in her two hands.

He did not introduce Lavinia. Instead he rang the bell and ordered tea. A beautiful tea. Watercress and cucumber sandwiches. Cakes. A pot of cream as well as milk. Delicious. Eliza's eyes were as round as marbles.

"Now eat nice," Mrs. Sullivan said. "Don't gobble and there's lots of time." When Eliza had done, Mrs. Sullivan said: "I'll take her out now and buy some more clothes. A chemise and drawers. She's got no drawers. Just a petty."

Good God! Lavinia thought. A child this age with no underclothes.

"And when we come back," Mrs. Sullivan went on, "I'll give her a bath."

Stead pointed to a door. "It's through the bedroom," he said, as Mrs. Sullivan led the girl out on their second shopping expedition.

When they had gone, Stead said: "Well, what do you think of her, Mrs. Lenton?"

"I think it's frightful. That it can happen, I mean."

"Happen? My dear Mrs. Lenton, at this very moment there are probably a dozen girls, or even a score, being sold in London. Terrible. Terrible is an understatement. There's no word for it. No words. But I'll find them. God will put the words into my mouth."

Lavinia was drawing on her gloves. For a few hours she must put it out of her head. She was going to John, going to her lover. To meet him in a house of assignation. An adulteress, no matter what the excuse. No matter that it was love and not lust that drew her into his arms. There was no other word for it but adultery.

For Eliza the big store they went into was a fairyland. Things. All kinds of bloody things. China, crockery, luggage, furniture. Clothes on people made of wax or something, with lovely faces and china eyes, like bloody great dolls. They went to the lingerie department. Nighties, chemises, drawers, petticoats—all tucked and frilled with lace. Silk, satin, lawn—some embroidered with lace insertions. Corsets, corset covers, corselets, stockings, garters of ruched satin.

"I want some cotton drawers and a chemise for this little girl," Mrs. Sullivan said. They were brought out from a box under the counter and held against her. Beautiful, white, new. They smelt lovely. Mrs. Sullivan paid for them and, taking the package from the saleslady, they went out of this Aladdin's Cave, back into the street.

When they returned, Mr. Stead was alone.

"I'll take her into the bedroom," Mrs. Sullivan said. "Give her a bath and change her."

Change me, Eliza thought, like a bloody baby. Tears came into her eyes as she thought of her little brother. Ma did not look after him properly. Eliza had never seen a bathroom before, hardly even seen a tap, not in a house, that is. In Charles Street there was a stand tap at the corner that served a dozen houses. People went there with buckets and waited their turn. Hot water was heated on the kitchen stove. She watched the water rushing into the enormous bath edged with a wide border of polished mahogany.

Rebecca felt the water and turned off one faucet. "Too hot," she said. Then she tried it again, swirling the water round with a gigantic sponge, and turned off the cold. "Just right, Eliza," she said, as she undid her frock.

Eliza sat on a stool and removed her boots, black cotton stockings, and garters. Rebecca pulled off her petticoat, her only undergarment.

A lovely little thing, with the makings of a beautiful girl. But skinny now, and grubby. Without a blemish on her skin except for some blue bruises on her slim thighs.

"What's that?" she asked.

"My Dad did that," Eliza said.

"Get in, dear," Rebecca said. She was angry with herself for looking at the girl the way she had. The old instinct. Years and years of looking at girls and women in a certain way could not be washed out as easily as she had thought. Even in Winchester, with the girls they saved, she did it. But she fought it down. Satan. God created women but Satan used their beauty, their young flesh.

"I won't," Eliza said. "I'll drown. I can't swim."

"Get in, you little silly."

Eliza climbed over the wooden edge and put one foot in the water. It was warm, lovely. Then the other foot. Then she stood, a lovely little figure whose breasts were just beginning to form.

"Sit down," Rebecca said. She sat and Rebecca sloshed her back with the big sponge. Her front. Then she soaped her. "Now lie down and soak."

"My hair," Eliza said.

"I'll put it up," Rebecca said and wound it in a knot on the top of her head, fastening it with some of her own hairpins.

When she was dry—the towel was the biggest she had ever seen—Eliza put on her new clothes. Drawers, chemise, petticoat—all new, all smelling of the shop. Then her stockings and garters, her new black boots, new frock, new hat. She felt funny. She had never had underclothes on before. Never worn new clothes right out of a shop. Rebecca combed and brushed her hair. It was clean, it was. She kept it clean, not like some girls on Charles Street.

They went back into the other room where Mr. Stead was waiting. He hardly looked at her. He looked as if he was upset, ashamed, or something. "Take a hansom, Mrs. Sullivan," he said.

"Yes, sir."

"Goodbye, Eliza. I'll be seeing you again before long."

Seeing her again? My God, he thought, this was going to be the worst part. Was he doing right? Was there no other way he could have done it?

In the street Rebecca stopped a passing hansom. Eliza had never been in a hansom. What a day! Rebecca gave the driver an address in Milton Street.

"Dorset Square," the man said.

They got in and closed the double folding doors over their legs. It was a beautiful brown horse that went very fast. At No. 3 they got out and Rebecca rang the bell. A woman in black opened the door. "Ah, Madame," she said. "I was waiting for you. And so this is the little one. Come upstairs." She led the way to a nice sitting room. There were things that looked like feathers in a tall vase. And the furniture was beautiful—all upholstered in black shiny horsehair. "Now," the woman said. "If you will be so good as to wait here, Madame. Come, my child," she said, taking Eliza's hand.

Eliza looked at Mrs. Sullivan, her new mistress. "Go with her, dear."

They went into a room that was bare except for a couch and a table with some things on it, that looked like instruments, standing in glass jars, and a big pile of folded, newly laundered towels.

"Now *chérie*," the woman said, "I won't hurt you." She knelt down beside her, took down her clothes, and touched her.

"You dirty woman!" Eliza screamed, pulling up her drawers and running back to Mrs. Sullivan. "She's a dirty woman," she said. But Mrs. Sullivan paid no attention to her.

"She's fresh," the woman said. "She has not been deflowered."

Mrs. Sullivan gave her some money and they went out.

What an experience! What was it all about? Why had she been taken there? She looked at Mrs. Sullivan's face. It was set hard. Eliza was too embarrassed to say anything.

In the street they picked up another cab and drove to Poland Street. Here, when they got out, Rebecca found she had no change and they went into a ham and beef shop to get it. When the driver was paid they rang the bell at the house next door and were shown into a big room where a woman greeted Mrs. Sullivan and said: "Everything is ready upstairs." They went up to a bedroom. It was a nice room. The bed had brown-red curtains on rods all round it. Mrs. Sullivan said: "Now undress, dear, and go to bed." Eliza was quite ready for bed. She was very tired and took off her clothes.

"Take everything off," Mrs. Sullivan alias Jones said.

Eliza did as she was told, slipped in between the sheets, and fell asleep at once. She was awakened by Mrs. Sullivan holding a handkerchief that smelt funny to her nose, and saying: "Sniff it, dear. Take a good long sniff."

"What is it?" Eliza asked.

"Perfume, dear. It's nice."

"It's horrid," Eliza said, and threw it on the floor. Then she fell asleep again.

Downstairs Mr. Stead—he was known here as Mr. Smith, an obvious alibi—was talking to Mrs. de Vere, the Madam.

"She'll be ready for you now, sir," she said, simpering.

"You gave Mrs. Jones the chloroform?"

"I did, sir. The chloroform and the use of the room, sir. Shall we say five pounds? And glad to accommodate you, Mr. Smith. Any time," she said. "We are always ready to oblige a gentleman, though of course we have our own girls."

So it had been done. He'd bought a girl. Brought her to a brothel and had her chloroformed with an anesthetic bought from the Madam. And God permitted this . . . God and the Law. He would be free now to go up and violate her if this were for real. "Have her," as the saying went. "She is ready for you, sir." Ready, indeed. Another sacrifice to the minotaur.

He went upstairs slowly, with dragging feet.

In Mallard Street, Lavinia lay in John's arms. She was crying. She didn't know why. With the sudden release of tensions that had been building up for months, crying with a kind of unhappy happiness. With fears for the future. How could she go on like this? How could she not go on? Crying with the ambivalence of a good woman in love who knows that she has sinned; crying wtih horror at her own thoughts. How long would Edward live? For years, perhaps. And the little girl she had seen whom Stead had had examined and was with now in a brothel . . . in civilized England, in London in 1885.

Outside a newspaper boy was shouting: "Read all about it . . . All the winners." "Minton," a man shouted. "Minton won by a nose." Another Derby, the one hundred and fourth had been run at Epsom. The crowds would be streaming home. Winners, losers. The horses were safe—strapped and fed, rugged up and bedded down in straw, their legs bandaged, in their boxes. Much safer than the girls of England. Much better cared for. More beloved, for this was the sport of kings.

John sent May for a paper. Minton, belonging to Lord Hastings with Archer up, had beaten Mr. Broderick Cloete's Paradox by a nose. Some said it was a dead heat. But the last year had been a dead heat and the judge appeared to think you could not have one every year, and had given the decision to Minton's favor.

John had sent for the paper to break the spell. To bring them both back to ordinary life, as if that was possible. How extraordinary life was! The Derby just run at Epsom. Stead buying a girl not five miles away, and he sleeping with another man's wife. All these events so utterly different, bound to each other only by the fact that they were happening in England on the same day.

But he had news for Lavinia. The problem of meeting her when he was in London had been solved now by his taking two small furnished apartments in Bayswater. One was being stripped and refurnished as an office for their anti-vice campaign and the other left as it was with the addition of some extra comforts and *objets d'art*. Pictures, bric à brac that he'd picked up here and there. This would be his *pied à terre* in London, and since Lavinia never met him without May and never after nightfall, all possibility of real scandal, though not of talk, would be avoided. Neither of them could stand these houses of assignation; the atmosphere of the rooms, the obsequious manners of the retired servants who ran such discreet establishments inevitably gave them both a feeling of guilt. They differed from the usual clients in that they were hurting no one. Their adultery was technical. Edward had ceased to exist as a man. But still it was there.

"I've taken a place in Bayswater," he said, "for an office. And another flat next door that I can use when I spend the night in London."

Lavinia burst into tears. Whatever the risk, anything was better than this.

38 : The Maiden Tribute to Babylon

Stead came quietly into the bedroom where Rebecca was waiting for him seated on a chair looking at her hands folded in her lap. She was praying. She put her finger to her lips and whispered: "The girl's asleep."

The gas was turned low, giving the room a sickly green underwater color. It stank of chloroform like an operating theater. The whole effect was nauseating. The macabre light effect, the smell, the atmosphere of moral decay. Yet the room was pretty enough—comfortable, almost luxurious. Rebecca pointed to the brown-curtained bed that stood like a box, its head to the wall.

He went over to it carefully and parted the curtains. He must be sure he checked it all carefully, exactly as it might happen. Eliza had kicked off her bedclothes. It was a hot night—a premature tryout of full summer. There she lay—any man's prey. A slim slip of a child, naked and utterly defenseless. A child with budding breasts and a pigeon fluff of golden pubic hair on her belly. To some men—the kind who generally came here—an appetizing morsel of girl flesh. Something to be used without consideration, raped. Whose screams for her mother would bring no aid, bring nothing more than a smile to the lips of the hardened girls and women who heard them. Been through it themselves, they had. And since they had, why not the others? What the hell was one more or less—a girl had to lose her cherry sometime.

As the curtain rings moved on the rod, Eliza woke and cried: "There's a man in the room!" Stead withdrew quickly.

Rebecca went to Eliza's side. "Man, dearie? There's no man here. Why do you think there is?"

"I heard 'im, that's why," Eliza said.

"Look," Rebecca said. "There's no man in the room."

"No," the child said. "I heard him go out, that's why. But he was 'ere."

Mrs. Jarrett left her. When she came back she said: "Get dressed, we're going to leave. There are too many men in the house." And Eliza dressed again.

In the street they picked up a cab and drove a long way to another house where they went to bed again. This time Rebecca went to bed too. She said they would go to her house in Wimbledon in the morning. But next day while they were having breakfast—porridge and a kipper and bread and marmalade, a kind called Dundee and very good, some ladies came.

One of them Eliza knew, though she did not know her name. It was the beautiful lady who had been with Mr. Stead at tea yesterday. The other was a French lady, a Madame Combe. Madame Combe said she had some little children, and had two sons in the Salvation Army. Then Mr. Stead came in and said: "Good morning, Eliza." He went on to tell them the cab was ready and they all went down.

They first visited a doctor who examined Eliza again and said she was undamaged by her experience, and then they drove to Victoria Station. Eliza got into the train with Madame Combe. She was crying bitterly. It was all so queer. New clothes, bus rides, cab rides, the tea party, the awful woman who had mucked her about, getting undressed and going to bed, getting up and going to bed again, and all in the middle of the night. That awful perfume whose smell she couldn't get rid of, and then this wasn't the way to Wimbledon and Madame Combe wasn't the woman she was going to work for.

And then they were off with a crashing of couplings. Eliza had never been in a train before and through her tears she saw Mr. Stead and the beautiful lady waving handkerchiefs to them as the train pulled out. She must try to be brave. She must try, but she cried all the harder. What was going to become of her?

As the tail of the train disappeared, Stead said: "Well, we've done it, Mrs. Lenton. I've bought a certified virgin and sent her to the Continent like a white slaver."

There were tears in Lavinia's eyes. "You're a good man, Mr. Stead," she said. He was a good man and she was an adulteress who, had she dared to do so, would have prayed for her husband's death.

They parted at the station and she got into her carriage. When would she see John again? If only it could be now, at once. Yesterday seemed a long time ago. If only she could fly into his arms for comfort, for love, for everything. When would it happen again? How long could they wait? Illicit love was not bliss—it was torment.

Stead took a cab to his office. Now he would begin his articles. He began writing at white heat the series entitled *The Maiden Tribute to Modern Babylon*. Now he had the proofs, the facts, the witnesses, the reports, exactly as it might have happened. There was no longer any question of hearsay. He wrote a description of a London brothel:

> Flogging or birching goes on in brothels to a much greater extent than is generally believed. One of Mrs. Caramine's rooms was fitted up like a torture chamber—in a street leading off Gray's Inn Road. There were rings in the ceiling for hanging women and children up by the wrists, ladders for strapping them down at any angle, as well as the ordinary stretcher to which the victim is fastened so as to be unable to move. The instruments of flagellation included the ordinary birch, whips, holly branches, and wire-thonged cat-o'-nine tails.

He reproduced the letter of a respected businessman living in Malta that had fallen into his hands:

> Dear Friend, I take pleasure in sending you news of myself, which at the moment is most excellent. I can assure you that I have found a woman the likes of whom you can never find. Without praising her too highly, she is as beautiful as it is possible to find and I hope she may serve your purpose well. As matters stand at the present moment, I can send her by the first mail steamer, so as soon as you get this letter, send me the ticket or the money. You know, dear friend, that for mine and your own personal interest I must keep this matter absolutely quiet. I will send you her photo. Her beautiful teeth alone are worth a million. I will not detain you any longer but will shake hands most cordially. Your friend for life, B.

Stead compared the fate of these girls to those of Ancient Greece, saying:

The foreign traffic is the indefinite prolongation of modern Babylon, with utter and absolute hopelessness of any redemption. When a girl steps over the fatal brink she is at once regarded as fair game for the slaver who collects human "parcels" in the great central mart of London for transmission to the uttermost parts of the earth. They move from stage to stage, from town to town—bought, exchanged, sold—driven on and ever on, like the restless ghosts of the damned, till they too sleep where the wicked cease from troubling them and the weary are at rest.

He quoted another letter that began:

Very dear friend, I have learnt from my friend, B., that you sent him a ticket to have a woman sent to you. It happens at this moment that this woman has failed, and, as I have a woman I am trying to place some-where, I talked with B. and have decided to send her to you. Now, my dear friend, as I know that the woman is going to you, I dressed her without regard to expense, for I knew with you I had nothing to lose. I was also forced to feed her during fifty days. Now I send her to you with all confidence, for the woman is young and pretty, and easy to train, and you must know in your letter to B. how the woman ought to behave. On her arrival, take means to get good offers. Now, my dear friend, I have been forced to dress her from head to foot. I bought her a straw hat with cream-colored roses, a white silk blouse, a marine blue skirt, a green scarf and a pair of shoes. She is a pretty little brunette with a graceful figure. Let me also tell you that her health is good. Thy friend evermore, N.

In the *Pall Mall Gazette* of the following day, Stead described the origin of his title, *The Maiden Tribute:*

A London Minotaur

As in the labyrinth of Crete there was a monster known as the Mino-taur who devoured maidens who were cast into the mazes of that evil place, so in London there is at least one monster who may be said to be an absolute incarnation of brutal lust. The poor maligned brute in the Cretan labyrinth but devoured his toll of seven maids and as many boys every ninth year. Here in London, moving about clad as respectably in broad cloth and fine linen as any bishop, with no foul shape or semblance of brute beast to mark him off from the rest of his fellows, is Dr. ——, now retired from his profession and free to devote his future and his leisure to the ruin of maids. This is the "gentleman" whose quantum of virgins from his procuresses is three per fortnight; all girls who have not previously been seduced. But his devastating passion sinks into insignifi-cance compared with that of Mr. ——, another wealthy man, whose whole life is dedicated to the gratification of lust. During my investiga-tions into the subterranean realm I was constantly coming across his name. This procuress was getting girls for ——, that woman was beating up maids for ——, this girl was waiting for ——, that house was a noted place of ——'s. I ran across his traces so constantly that I began to make inquiries in the upper world of his redoubtable personage. I soon obtained confirmation of the evidence I had gathered at firsthand below as to the reality of the existence of this modern Minotaur, this English Tiberius, whose Capreae is in London. It is no part of my commission to hold up individuals to popular execration, and the name and address of this creature will not appear in these columns. But the fact that he exists ought to be put on record, if only as a striking illustration of the extent to which it is possible for a wealthy man to ruin not merely hundreds but thousands of poor women. It is actually Mr. ——'s boast that he ruined two thousand women in his time. He never has anything to do with girls regularly on the streets, but pays liberally for actresses, shop girls, and the like. Exercise, recreation, everything is subordinated to this supreme end of his life. He has paid his victims, no doubt—never gives a girl less than five pounds—but it is a question whether the lavish outlay of three to five thousand pounds on purchasing the assent of girls to their own dishonor, is not a frightful aggravation of the wrong which he has been for some mysterious purpose permitted to inflict on his kind.

Stead then described an agent who procured a girl for him as "a motherly old lady" whose profession was that of a charwoman. He said she regarded her job with utter complacency. She was a widow with a large family and must do something for the children. Her second justification was the assumption that the girls whom she procured would inevitably be seduced, and she said naïvely, "If a girl is to be seduced it is better that she should be seduced by a gentleman, and get something for it."

He said the procuress trotted out the child for him to see, made her stand up, smile, and generally put her through her paces and showed her points. The motherly fashion in which she put her arm round the girl's neck, and urged her with kisses of encouragement not to be timid, but to please the gentleman, was sickening beyond expression.

He described how he had seen five virgins bought and delivered by appointment. He quoted from Pastor T. Borel of Geneva, who had written the first white slave pamphlet to be published on the Continent in 1875. He also quoted from a pamphlet published by the Dyer brothers, referring to the abuse of small children in which they stated that the presence of these children is unknown to the ordinary visitors to the house. The secret is known to none except the wealthy debauchees who pay large sums for the sacrifice of these infants to their fastidious lusts. Men sunk in vice, diseased, cynical, worn out, old enough often to be the children's grandfathers; men who desire merely a thing to debauch—no longer a human being, but a *thing* in the shape of a woman, out of which all feeling, all hope, all intelligence has been stamped by cruelty and violence. These children often cry and weep and call upon their mother, and it is only when stupified or maddened by successive glasses of champagne that they cease to struggle.

He began publishing on Saturday, July 4th, with a leader that stated:

If Ministers think of allowing the Bill to drop because the public is not keenly alive to its importance, it is necessary to open the eyes of the public, in order that a measure, the urgency of which has been repeatedly admitted, may pass into law this session. WE HAVE, THEREFORE DETERMINED, WITH A FULL SENSE OF THE RESPONSIBILITY ATTACHING TO SUCH A DECISION, TO PUBLISH THE REPORT OF A SPECIAL AND SECRET COMMISSION OF INQUIRY WHICH WE APPOINTED TO EXAMINE INTO THE WHOLE SUBJECT. We say quite frankly today that all those who are squeamish, and all those who are prudish, and all those who prefer to live in a fool's paradise of imaginary innocence and purity, selfishly oblivious of the horrible realities which torment those whose lives are passed in the London inferno, WILL DO WELL NOT TO READ THE *PALL MALL GAZETTE* OF MONDAY AND THE THREE FOLLOWING DAYS. The story of an actual pilgrimage into a real hell is not pleasant reading, and it is not meant to be. It is, however, an authentic record of unimpeachable facts, abominable, unutterable, and worse than fables yet have feigned or few conceived. But it is true and its publication is necessary.

Stead spent a broiling weekend in his office in his shirt sleeves, bathed in sweat and sometimes in tears, as he put the final touches to the first two parts of *The Maiden Tribute of Modern Babylon,* and on Monday he fired his first tremendous broadside against the countless numbers of men and women who were undermining the whole moral structure of the nation. This was a head-on clash between the forces of good and evil. The leader which initiated the Maiden Tribute Campaign was prophetic:

The Report of our Secret Commission will be read today with a shuddering horror that will thrill throughout the world. After this awful picture of the crimes at present committed, as it were, under the very aegis of the law, has been unfolded before the eyes of the public, we need not doubt that the House of Commons will find time to raise the age during which English girls are protected from inexpiable wrong.

There followed a statement of the various matters with which the articles would deal. These were the sale and purchase and violation of children, the procurement of virgins, the entrapping and ruin of women, the international slave trade in girls, the atrocities, brutalities, and un-natural crimes.

Stead dealt first with the procurement of virgins. He quoted an in-terview with Howard Vincent (not mentioned by name) who told him it was an exceedingly common procedure, twenty pounds being the average price charged by a brothel. Then followed a conversation he had had with "a well-known M.P."

The M.P. laughed and said: "I doubt the unwillingness of these virgins. That you can contract for maids at so much a head is true enough. I myself am quite ready to supply you with a hundred maids at twenty-five pounds each, but they'll all know very well what they're about. There're plenty of people among us entirely devoid of moral scruples on the score of chastity, whose daughters are kept straight until they are sixteen or seventeen, not because they love virtue, but solely because their virginity is a realizable asset, with which they are taught they should never part except for value received. They are the girls who can be had at so much per head; but it's nonsense to say it's rape. It's merely the delivery as per contract of the asset virginity in return for cash down."

A brothel keeper stated: "Maids, as you call them—fresh girls as we know them in the trade—are in constant demand, and a keeper who knows his business has his eyes open in all directions." He went on to say that his own method of obtaining maids was to dress up as a clergy-man and entice likely victims into his brothel with promises of spiritual ministration. He added: "Another very simple method of supplying maids is by breeding them. I know a couple of very fine little girls who'll be sold before long." He affirmed that drunken parents often sold their daughters to brothel keepers; in the East End you could pick up as many fresh girls as you wanted—in one street in Dalston you might buy a dozen.

A female brothel keeper, showing Stead round her large country house, answered his query about the inevitable fuss made by a young virgin when she was raped. "In my house," said the lady, "you can enjoy the screams of the girl with the certainty that no one else hears them but yourself. Here's a room where you can be perfectly secure. The walls are thick, there's a double carpet on the floor. You can lock the door and you can do as you please. The girl may scream blue mur-der, but not a sound'll be heard. The servants will be far away in the other end of the house. I only will be about, seeing that all's snug."

"But," Stead remarked, "if you hear the cries of the child, you may yourself interfere, especially if, as may easily happen, I badly hurt and in fact all but kill the girl."

"You will not kill her," she answered. "You have too much sense to kill the girl. Anything short of that, you can do as you please. As for me interfering, do you think I do not know my business?"

Stead continued his narrative:

> In the course of my investigations I heard some strange tales concerning the precautions taken to render escape impossible for the girl whose ruin, with or without her consent, has been resolved upon. To oblige a wealthy customer, a brothel keeper strapped down girls hand and foot to the bedposts so that all resistance save for unavailing screaming would be impossible. Before the strapping down was finally agreed upon, the lady of the house, a stalwart woman and experienced in the trade, had volunteered her services to hold the virgin down by force while her wealthy patron effected his purpose. That was too much even for him, and the alternative of fastening with straps padded on the underside was then agreed upon.

The first article concluded with an account of Eliza Armstrong's purchase and how she had been spirited out of the country without anyone being the wiser. The story was related in a completely impartial manner, but in order to shield the child from any publicity or future embarrassment, Stead gave her the pseudonym of "Lily."

Stead knew that with the prospect of a general election there was every reason to hit hard, and he did. The leader and piece on July 4th were a kind of apéritif, a preparation of what was to follow. Then came broadside after broadside—July 6th, 7th, 8th, 9th, 10th. Broadsides that both stunned and shocked the public. They could not believe their eyes. It was impossible. Untrue. The Home Secretary, fearing riots, wanted the series stopped. Stead replied that he would stop if the Law Amendment Bill was carried through. Sir William Harcourt would not give him the required assurance and the series continued.

W. H. Smith & Sons, who owned all the station bookstalls, banned the *Pall Mall Gazette,* but the street sales were so great that copies were being sold at two and six each instead of a halfpenny. Newsprint ran out with the *Gazette* presses running both day and night, and paper was borrowed from the *Globe.* Newsboys were arrested and charged at the Mansion House on the orders of the City of London Solicitor General, but the charges were dismissed by the Lord Mayor.

In the House, Mr Cavendish Bentinck asked if the attention of the Home Secretary had been directed to a certain paper publishing objectionable matter throughout the metropolis, the proprietors and publishers being the owners of the *Pall Mall Gazette,* and whether any means existed of subjecting the authors and publishers of this objectionable publicity to criminal proceedings.

Bentinck's protest amused the House who knew his predilections and when they saw him they shouted: "Pity the poor old fornicator."

Northumberland Street was mobbed by poor men eager to read the paper and see what the toffs did to their daughters.

The third installment stated that:

> The Report of our Secret Commission, it is now evident, has produced an effect unparalleled in the history of journalism. The excitement yesterday in London was intense. We knew that we had forged a thunderbolt: but even we were hardly prepared for the overwhelming impression which it has produced on the public minds. . . . Before the 12th of August it is a crime to shoot a grouse, lest an immature cheeper should not yet have a fair chance to fly. The sportsman who wishes to follow the partridge through the stubbles, must wait till September 1st, and the close time for pheasants is even later. Admitting that women are as fair game as grouse and partridges, why not let us have a close time for bipeds in petticoats as well as for bipeds in feathers? At present that close time is absurdly low.

Then the temper of the crowd outside the *Gazette* office changed. They were different men. Not the fathers of wronged daughters but toughs, recruited by Solferino. Bricks crashed through the windows and ugly curses echoed through the streets. "Beat the bastards up! Wreck the bloody place!"

There seemed no chance of getting the next edition away. The police refused help in spite of the danger to life caused by the maddened, vicious crowd of pimps, watchers, and murderous roughs. Someone was distributing drink. Bottles of gin passed from hand to hand. Stead, standing by a window, was cut by a piece of flying glass as a brick came crashing in. A dozen men had found a balk of timber and were using it as a battering ram on the door. But it held. Furniture was piled against the doors and windows. The staff, like sailors repulsing pirates, fought hand to hand with men trying to get in. Not a single policeman appeared. There was no sign of the law.

But at last, when things died down, Stead got a messenger through to Bramwell Booth. The man came back and told him Booth had said: "Tell Mr. Stead we'll help him. We'll throw open this building for the sale of his paper. Say I have written him a letter."

There was no *Maiden Tribute* article on Thursday. Instead, Stead wrote:

We are prepared to put every member of our Secret Commission into the box and support their testimony from a vast array of witnesses drawn from every rank, class, and condition of men.

The rest of the press was silent, or muted at best. Only the *British Medical Journal* came out boldly on Stead's side:

Of one thing we feel certain, and that is that a great end will be served by this exposure, undertaken, as we feel assured it was, with intense sincerity, and with an overruling hatred and fierce anger of practices which have too long secretly prevailed in our midst, and have too long passed unscathed by public indignation. Desperate diseases need strong remedies. A cancer such as this, which is eating away the vital morality of whole classes of society, spreading widely, ravaging the unprotected classes, calls for the knife. It has been applied publicly, red-hot, and with an unsparing hand.

On the following day, Friday, July 10th, in the final installment of *The Maiden Tribute,* the police were accused of being utterly corrupt, and in support of the accusations some appalling stories were printed. For instance, it was alleged that one famous brothel in the East End paid out regularly five hundred pounds a year in bribes to detectives. The remainder of the article was devoted to the Continental white slave traffic:

Only last week, before the publication of these articles, a sample lot of three *"colis,"* or parcels left the region of Leicester Square for Belgium. Two of these are now in Antwerp, one in Brussels. A much larger consignment is expected shortly. . . . The bagmen of this international traffic are now in the provinces. They say that London girls have been frightened by the recent exposure of what comes of going abroad. The work of inquiring into the ramifications of this new slave trade was the most dangerous part of the investigations. The traffic is almost entirely in the hands of ex-convicts, who know too well the discomfort of the *maison correctionelle* to stick at any trifles which might remove an inconvenient witness or help them to escape conviction. It was at first a new sensation for me to sit smoking and drinking with men fresh from gaol in the *snug* of a gin palace, and asking as to the precise cost of disposing of girls in foreign brothels. One excellent trader who dwells in such odor of sanctity as can come from having his headquarters within archiepiscopal shade, kindly undertook to dispose of a mistress of whom it was supposed that I wished to rid myself before my approaching marriage, by depositing her without any ado in a house of ill-fame in Brussels. For this considerable service he would only charge ten pounds.

The *Times* said:

> Not by the artillery of the law are the fortresses of vice erected in all great cities to be battered down. Only by moral agencies, slowly operating, by an increased sense of the value of purity in man and woman, by preventing overcrowding and its demoralising concomitants, and by trying to keep alive even in poverty a sense of honest pride, which if not exactly virtue is akin to it, is it possible to contend with an evil which seems to grow mightier, more conspicuous, and less ashamed.

But the provincial press in general was on Stead's side. He was one of them; he came from the provinces and they all hated London. The *Liverpool Echo* in a leader on Saturday, July 11th, said:

> The extent of the feeling created will be found reflected in the proceedings in Parliament last night. A Bill which a few days ago was regarded as a dropped measure, and which was almost universally cold-shouldered by the representatives of the people, has been suddenly taken up by the Government of the day as one thoroughly ripe for discussion and urgently needing immediate attention. . . . Nothing else than loathing and contempt can be bestowed on those who, under the pretense of morality, are anxious to throw a veil of secrecy over these horrid infamies.

They could say what they liked in London. Say it was done for money, that it was pornography, that Stead should be prosecuted, that the *Gazette* would go broke, that no club would take it, that the Prince of Wales had canceled his subscription. . . . They could say it until they were blue in the face, but the country was up. England, the provinces, were enraged. The Salvation Army swung into action with mass meetings in London, Manchester, Hull, Leeds, Sheffield, Newcastle . . .

At Exeter Hall Mrs. Booth, the wife of the General, told an audience of women a story that moved them to tears and fury. She said: "A wealthy family man, respected by the neighbors for his supposed piety and good works, asked a brothel keeper to obtain a girl child for him to ravish on a Sunday evening. The procuress promised to do her best to find the type of girl whom she knew would please him. On the Sunday afternoon, she spotted a beautiful rosy child coming out of Sunday school and at once approached her. With great cunning she managed to entice the girl into the brothel and kept her in a room by herself until the valued client arrived. When the gentleman entered the brothel and was told by the procuress that a little beauty awaited his pleasure, he asked to be taken to her without delay. But a few moments later, his expression of sensuous anticipation changed to one of abject horror and embarrassment when he was confronted by his own daughter."

England was up all right. Parliament would have to act if the members wanted to be returned to the House.

But Mrs. Caramine and her girls continued to drive out behind the high-stepping, heavily curbed and bearing-reined chestnuts, the harness of their silver-mounted collars flecked with foam, and men stood on the Park chairs to see them better, as they did for royalty.

How well she knew men, Carrie Caramine thought! And what was in their minds as, in imagination, they undressed the beauties lolling back on the seat of the open carriage, their faces shaded by big flower-ornamented hats and silken parasols.

The horses were fast and passed every carriage with whirring, shiny, rubber-tired wheels. There was no speed limit as long as the horses did no more than trot. But no one else extended their animals. The very speed of their passing, the rhythm and hammer of their hooves, was enough to attract both attention and censure.

Ladies taking the air in the other carriages behind their tall and stately Cleveland bays turned their faces away from this spectacle of the *demi monde*. But it was prime showmanship. Such beauty adorned in silk and furbelows suggested its very opposite to the lecherous audience of men who dreamed of holding those satined and perfumed creatures in their arms. To see the Caramine girls driving by was one of the sights of London, comparable to the mounting of the Guard or seeing a troop of Household Cavalry trot by.

Like them, her equipage suggested luxury, riches, power—for these were the playthings of powerful men, to be dandled, fondled, dressed and undressed—like dolls by little girls. Carrie Caramine believed in showing the flag, in proving her contempt for the muckraking of the *Gazette*. And what better flag was there than this—"my horses and my girls." The flaunted silks and satins, white kid gloves, parasols. Besides, it would soon be autumn, and she might as well make hay while the sun shone.

As a rule August and September were slow months for Mrs. Caramine. Most of the young men were away in Yorkshire or Scotland, tramping the moors from butt to butt, waiting for the driven grouse.

The old men were on the Continent taking cures at Wiesbaden, Ems, Hamburg, and Marienbad. And, by God, they needed them too, she thought—paunched with the rich food and ten months of debauchery. Of course some men could not get away and they continued to patronize her. Still, there were advantages. There was time to get new clothes for the girls, do up the rooms, replace breakages, and so on. New girls to be broken in.

39 : A Mother's Heart

Martha Hastings had lived for years in terror of her husband. But with Mrs. Lenton helping her daughter, with Molly safe, with letters coming from her—bloody with Mr. Jones's steaks, kidneys and chops—she bought better cuts now, her courage returned. With her daughter gone—lost and worse than dead—what had she had to live for? Now everything was changed. Every day after the first of the month she watched for the butcher's smart two-wheeled trap, a bay pony between the shafts. And he entered into the spirit of it, did Tom the delivery boy in his blue apron and straw boater. Couldn't stand 'im. Not that psalm-singing bastard of a chemist. No one could. And he'd liked the girl. And the mother too, a partridge of a woman that reminded him of his own ma. If there was a letter in the meat he'd wink and say: "Careful, Ma'am. Extra special today. The guv'nor wrapped it hisself." And there'd be tears in her eyes, there would, poor old body.

The letters that came once a month were short, loving, full of Mrs. Lenton and another woman called Muriel and the girl Eva, who was wrong in the head but getting better every day. They ended with rows of childish crosses.

Then there had been letters from London. How wonderful it had been to see her there in the beautiful house in the Square. She could visualize her. Quite the young lady in her lovely clothes. Lovely, that was what they was. And wouldn't that upset him if he knew. Me seeing her and her living like that. If that was the wages of sin it was surprising there was an honest girl left in England. But how lovely she had been! Saved. The hand of God was in it. But not his God. Molly had told her something about her life in Belgium. She knew she had kept a lot from her. "It was too horrible, Mama, to talk about. But she saved me—she and Mr. Longbeach."

Molly wrote about Mr. Longbeach, Mr. Booth, Mrs. Josephine Butler, Mr. Stead, and then she said she was leaving Berkeley Square and going to help Mrs. Booth with her work. Not join the Army exactly, but help with girls. "I can help them, Mama, because they're not afraid of me when I tell them I was like them once." How she had cried over that letter, and then gone up to the bedroom and prayed. Prayed to *her* God, not his. Prayed to Jesus. It was then when she got up from her knees that she made up her mind.

"Joseph," she said at supper, "I'm going to work at the shop."

"You're what?" he said.

"I'm coming to work at the shop. There's nothing to do here alone and I might as well learn something about it. Suppose you were ill? Suppose you died?"

"I'm not going to die, Martha," he said. "But I'll be ready when the Lord calls me."

"Well, I won't be," she said, "not till I know how to run the shop."

"You can't dispense," he said.

"Of course not. But I could hire a young chap if it came to that. What I want is to learn the running of it. Meet the people. Serve them. Help with the books and so on. You said only the other day you needed help because the business was growing."

And he'd given in as she'd known he would. He was a mean man and he'd get her for nothing. It would keep her busy between letters.

It did not take Martha Hastings long to learn her way about the shop. She got on well with the customers. But there had been more in it than that for her. There were medical books in the shop—a pharmacopoeia—and if there were things in the various jars and bottles that would cure people, there were also other things.

Never did this enter her mind. Not in so many words. It just hung there like a mist, seeping into the crannies of her being. Just suppose he was dead and Molly could come home. She could run the business now. She had a good head for figures. People liked her. They asked for her. And little by little, hardly realizing what she was doing, she accumulated a nice little store of arsenic. How harmless it looked! A white powder—what a sense of power it gave her.

Long before she gave him the first dose, she told people she was worried about his health. She told him he wasn't looking well and should do less. She cosseted him. So when finally he became ill, no one was surprised. No one at all. And everyone said how wonderful she was, running the shop and nursing him at the same time. She put an advertisement in the paper and got a young man who could dispense. Henry Blenkensop, a nice young chap; dark, with glasses.

She would have been shocked at the idea of poisoning her husband. What she was doing was getting Molly back. Preparing the way for her return. Destroying the man who had destroyed her daughter, and nursing her husband who was ill. That the two were one and the same man did not really occur to her. Her mind was divided into idea-proof compartments. It was only Molly she thought of.

The letters were more frequent now that she could pick them up at the butcher's herself.

"And 'ow is Mr. 'Astings to-day, Ma'am?" Amos Jones would say.

"Better, thank you, Mr. Jones. Much better. But he's not on his feet yet, poor man. It's his stomach, the doctor says."

Mr. Hastings had visitors from the chapel. They came and prayed over him and sang over him, and read to him from the Bible. She made them tea and gave them cakes.

There were always flowers in the sickroom. She was a wonderful wife and helpmate. Such a pity about the girl having gone wrong. From such a good Christian home, too.

Sometimes Mrs. Hastings got out Molly's baby clothes. Her long christening clothes, her little kid boots with three buttons. Her tiny dresses. She'd saved them for a grandchild. Well, there might be one now. And her book of nursery rhymes and her schoolbooks. All the things she had touched with her soft, baby fingers. My baby. My baby . . . Well, it would not be long now. In her next letter she'd tell her that her father was ill.

But she'd give him a chance.

"Joseph," she said one day when she had given him his tea, "if we could find Molly, wouldn't you like to see her now and tell her you have forgiven her?"

The dark eyes, in a face as white as the pillow, blazed at her.

"Molly?" he said. "Who is Molly?"

"Molly Frances Hastings, Joseph. Your daughter and mine. She's in London, I hear. We could find her."

"My daughter is dead, and worse than dead."

"You mean if I could find her you would not see her?"

"How could I see someone who is not there? A harlot, a daughter of the horse leech, the scarlet woman of Babylon. I have no daughter," he almost screamed, "and I forbid you to mention her name again."

Mrs. Hastings shrugged her plump shoulders and went out to fetch the doctor. "Doctor Morris," she said, "how lucky to find you in. I think my husband is worse. Please come at once."

She returned in his carriage. He stood by the bed. He felt the patient's pulse. He looked very wise in his glasses and long black frock-coat. "You were right to call me. I'll come in again tonight. It's an infection, a flux, an inflammation of the bowels." He nodded his head.

"Be brave, Mrs. Hastings, you have done your best."

"Then he's . . ."

"He's sinking, Mrs. Hastings."

Outside, in the distance, the college bells were chiming. How peaceful it all was! How beautiful Oxford was on a Sunday!

Joseph Hastings died on Monday. An upright man mourned by the community. An elder of the chapel. At the funeral Mrs. Hastings cried. It was over at last. She had not told Molly. There was time enough for that.

And then came the news. The *Maiden Tribute* articles in the *Gazette*, and Mrs. Hastings began to understand what Molly had been through. Tried by fire, she had come out purified. Thank God for that. Her God. Not Joseph's. It was Joseph's God who had thrust Molly into the pit.

40 : The Petition

Now was the time to strike, while the iron was hot, and Lavinia Lenton drove from friend's house to friend's house. Even to the houses of mere acquaintances, getting signatures—upper-class signatures— for the petition that would force Parliament to act.

She began with the Dowager Duchess of Saltcombe, Aunt Serena. The old lady sat in her immense drawing room. It had nothing later than the Regency in it, including herself. Surrounded by her dogs—a brindle mastiff so fat that he could hardly walk, and six pugs; three fawn with black faces that looked like mastiff pups with curly tails, and three black ones. The room smelt of dogs and roses. It reminded her of her bedroom at Mortal. There were roses in every vase. Great pink cabbage roses, red roses, flat *Malmaison* roses that looked as if they had been sat upon.

The Duchess was dressed in stiff black silk embroidered with tiny bunches of moss roses. She looked rather like an old crumpled rose in the black vase of her dress herself.

"Well, my dear," she said, when Lavinia came in. "You're looking very pretty. Do you know what you look like?"

"No," Lavinia said. "Pretty?"

"You look like a woman who has been making love. And don't raise your eyebrows at me, child. By God, I was a goer in my time! My time," she repeated, her eyes dreamy with remembrance. "I just came in the end of it. I'm the same age as the Queen, you know, but I never went her way, nor held with it. I'm one of the last of them. Oh, there may be fifty or so of us left. But I remember old Cockshott in his prime. Cocky and his like. Soldiers. Men, by God. And we made no pretense about not liking it, or them. All this swooning and smelling salts and burnt feathers. Fiddle-de-dee, my dear. Men and women were made for each other, like keys and locks. It takes a key to turn a lock and if it's not used it rusts. It takes a man to make a woman, Lavinia. So don't lie to me and don't tell me either. Just say what you want. You must want something or you wouldn't be here. Ring the bell and we'll have a glass of Madeira or some sweet Constantia wine, and a biscuit."

Lavinia sat down, arranging her flowered silk *chiné* dress about her feet. The mastiff came over and looked into her eyes, his big black muzzle on a level with her face.

"I want you to sign this petition, Aunt Serena," Lavinia said, unrolling a sheet of foolscap. "I want you to head the list."

"Then it's not money you want," the old lady said. "That's a nice change. All most people want signed now are checks."

"It's a petition we're getting up, a round robin that we are going to present to Parliament about the Law Amendment Bill. It's got to be passed."

"You and Stead and the do-gooders," the Duchess said. "Well he certainly sent the balloon up with his articles. Modern Babylon, indeed." She chuckled. "Took the lid off the drains, that did. That's what the Duke liked. 'All open drains in my bloody stables,' he said. 'So I can see what's in 'em.' She paused and opened her lorgnette to look at Lavinia as if she had not seen her before. "Took some doing, my girl," she said. "A lady like you being mixed up in it. I'm proud of you. You've got bottom."

"My children," Lavinia said.

"I know, dear. But even with that, most women would have kept their mouths shut. Stayed in the country, licking their wounds. I'm proud of you, my girl." She closed her glass. "Give me the paper."

Lavinia took it over to her.

"You move well," the Duchess said as she took it.

A blank sheet and old Serena to top the list. "Paper," she said. "Love letters. Death warrants. Soap and paper are the basis of civilization." She looked up at Lavinia and said: "If you haven't got a lover, get one or you won't keep your looks. Women dry up without it. Shrivel. Their mouths get hard, their lips pale." She got up and went to the Chippendale writing desk. She dropped a scarlet quill into a silver inkpot and scrawled her name in letters one inch high: Serena, DOWAGER DUCHESS OF SALTCOMBE. "That'll fox them," she said. "That'll bring the tiddlers in. The doubters and the cowards. They'll swim in the water round a big fish. The big names—and mine's still big. Like the tail of a kite, that's what they are." She returned to her seat and sat down with a metallic rustle of silk petticoats.

"Poor little bastards," she said.

"Who?" Lavinia asked.

"Little girls. Taken before they're ripe for it. It never hurt a grown woman as long as the man was a gentleman—and I've known footmen that were gentlemen. And gentlemen not fit to be footmen, too. No, it never hurt 'em, being tumbled, because it would never happen if they had not put themselves where it could. But children. By God," she said. "I'm glad you did it. Go on and get some more. I'll get some paper and make a list of my own. I'll send for 'em and they'll come here to sign it." She laughed. "Timid," she said. "Timid as a puss slinking away from the hounds. But sheep if you give 'em a bellwether. That's me, me dear. They'll follow me lead, you'll see. Old Queen, eh? My age but older, much older. No blood in her. Not the girl she was in Melbourne's time and the Duke's. Used to ride with 'im in the Row. Equerries. Grooms. Soldiers. Then she married that Albert, and we all became respectable. Us English respectable? A fast lot we are under-neath, dear. Rakish.

"I'll bet," the Duchess said àpropos of nothing, "you wear drawers, Lavinia. When I was a girl no lady wore drawers. My uncle, Lord Cowley, was the ambassador in Paris and I remember a story he told—not to me, naturally—about a lady tripping over her crinoline at a state reception." The old lady laughed coarsely. "He said the King of Italy or Sardinia or someplace turned to the Empress Eugénie and said: 'I am delighted to see your ladies do not wear drawers and that the gates of paradise are always open.'" The Duchess stared at Lavinia through her lorgnette. "Dr. Tile brought them in for health reasons," she said. "But they fought hard, the ladies did. They did not want to wear such masculine appendages. But I got 'em. Tartan knickerbockers —Hunting Stuart—to which I am entitled though perhaps it was a strange place to begin wearing it. And I was no spring chicken then— forty I was, but still a looker, and it amused the Duke. I was a Water-loo baby, born in 1805, a bloody good vintage. But nobody except whores wore drawers when I was a girl."

She sniffed the air. "I must send for some more roses," she said. "I think I can still smell a bit of dog. Like a bloody kennel the place is sometimes, but I've got no one else to talk to now." Tears came into her eyes as Lavinia bent to kiss her goodbye.

Maud Cockshott was next on her list. She, too, was in when she called.

"Sign, darling?" she said. "Of course I'll sign, but what good do you think it will do?" She scribbled her name and said: "Now tell me about John. When did you see him last? The rooms I sent you to were nice, weren't they? Comfortable and pleasantly furnished. I liked the French engravings in the bedroom—so suitable, I thought.

"But I'm breaking with Geoffrey. He's too serious. As if I'd run off now, and that's all he can think about. Do you know what I'll do, Lavinia?" She bubbled, trilling with blackbird laughter. "I'll send him to Caramine. Harold has a girl there he's mad about. Hélène—she pretends to be French, but she's English. Her real name's Ellen and I believe she was a governess who was sacked for sleeping with the master, they say. But a beauty. Blonde as an angel, with a lot of French tricks. Isn't it funny—one never sees a picture of a dark angel—like me?" she said, shaking out her curls. "Oh, must you go, Lavinia? I hoped you'd stay for luncheon."

"I must get on," Lavinia said. "My carriage is waiting. There are so many people to see." She must get out of here quickly.

"Well, good luck, darling." Maud put up her piquant little heart-shaped face to be kissed.

Lettice refused to sign at first. "My husband would not let me. I'd like to please you but I don't know what my husband would say if he found out."

"Do you mean he'll vote against the Bill?"

"I don't know, Lavinia. I really don't. These things aren't for women. Politics," she said vaguely.

"Women," Lavinia said. "What do you think *they* are?"

"Who are? Those girls? Just little tarts. James says we need them like we need sewers and so on."

"Three-year-olds, five-year-olds. Little girls of twelve," Lavinia said.

"Oh, you and that *Gazette*. All that filth of Stead's. An opportunist if ever there was one. A muckraker, who's brought England into disrepute. All vastly exaggerated, James says."

"Well dear," Lavinia said, "he'll lose his seat over it. I'll see to that in the next election."

"You wouldn't. Not to a friend. . . ."

"In this business, Lettice, there are no friends. Only those who are for or against us. There is no middle course. You'd better tell him. His constituents will know by this time tomorrow. I shall send someone down to tell them."

"That damn Salvation Army. Those Booths with their tambourines. And you trust them?"

"With my life," Lavinia said getting up. What a day so far! Maud sending her lover to Ellen at Caramine's—there was no doubt in her mind it was Ellen—Lettice refusing to sign until she was threatened.

"I do believe you mean it," Lettice said.

"Of course I mean it."

"Then give me the paper."

"And you'd better tell James if he doesn't vote for it he'll lose his seat in the House—just tell him, dear."

Lettice shrugged her pretty shoulders. "It's all such a nuisance," she said. "Why couldn't they let sleeping dogs lie? We should have been out of London long ago if all this hadn't come up."

So it went for a week. Visits. Calling on everyone. And because they really had no option, they signed. They had to be against sin, at least publicly. Some willingly, some half-heartedly. A few, like Lettice, only under pressure. When she had visited everyone she knew, Lavinia took her round robin to the Salvation Army headquarters. There they were busy sticking all the lists that had been brought in on to each other. In all there were over three hundred forty-three thousand signatures. This monster petition, two miles long, was coiled up in a gigantic roll and driven to the Houses of Parliament in an open dray drawn by two splendid shires escorted by mounted policemen. It was followed by three Salvation Army bands and Salvation Army member troops, in columns of fours led by their officers. Behind them came a regiment of mothers followed by a crowd that wanted to see the fun.

Eight Salvationists, picked for their strength, carried the petition into the floor of the House and set it down beside the Mace. A testament that England's will could not be ignored.

In Princes Hall, Piccadilly, Mrs. William Booth addressed an audience that listened to her in astounded horror. Among the things she said were the following:

"I read some paragraphs from the report of a debate in the House of Commons which made me doubt my eyesight, with respect to the age at which female children should be responsible for their own ruin. I could not help the blood rushing to my temples with indignant shame. I could not help rubbing my eyes and reading again and saying: 'Could this ever have happened in the House of Commons in England?' Oh, my God, are we to come to this? I did not think we were so low as this —that one member should suggest that the age of these innocents should be heightened to fourteen, and that another suggested that it should not be so high. Another that it should be reduced to ten and, Oh! my God, pleaded that it was hard for a man—*hard,* for a *man!*— having a charge brought against him, not to be able to plead the consent of a child like that.

"Well may the higher classes take care of *their* little girls! Well may they be so careful never to let them go out without efficient protectors. But what is to become of the little girls of the poor? Of the little girls of the working classes? I say I could not have believed that in this country such a discussion amongst so-called gentlemen could have taken place. I am bound to say that I do not believe there could be found twelve roughs in any taproom in England who would be parties to, or tolerate, such a discussion."

This was the kind of thing that was going on all over the country. The clock could not be put back now. A commission had been formed a few days after the last article had been published—to verify the charges Stead had made. It consisted of Samuel Morley, M.P., the Archbishop of Canterbury, Cardinal Manning, the Bishop of London and Mr. R. T. Reid, Q.C., M.P. They found that: "After carefully sifting the evidence of witnesses and the materials before us, and without guaranteeing the accuracy of every particular, we are satisfied that, taken as a whole, THE STATEMENTS IN THE *Pall Mall Gazette* on this question are SUBSTANTIALLY TRUE." Such a report was incontrovertible.

The summer heat increased and, with it, the temper of the people. Members of Parliament were deluged with letters, with delegates from various groups. Riots were feared if there was any delay in passing the Bill through.

Lavinia rode Nestor in the Row, accompanied by a groom, most mornings. The trees, heavy now, dusty and overburdened in their summer foliage, sagged as if exhausted by the heat. She was well known as one of the leading figures behind the movement, and blamed by the wives of members of Parliament who were unable to leave London on their holidays. August came. The talk was of grouse. The twelfth. Would they get away in time for the opening of the season?

She drove around the Park only a couple of times. There were too many stares, and she was passed twice by Caramine's chestnuts at a spanking trot. She knew what people were saying: What chance had she against such beauty and established custom? Thank goodness for the office, she thought, as she drove there with May in the carriage beside her. May faithful and loving, still titillated, dressing her like a bride. Undressing her again in Bayswater. Was she not doing what the pretty horse breakers she saw in the park did in their love nests? Yet she was always in a fever to get to John. A few minutes in the office going over papers, reports, lists of signatures, letters, and then into the apartment next door where May was waiting.

She had never been in London so late. The heat was appalling, the asphalt soft, the ammonia smell of horse manure unbearable as it fermented.

41 : The Enemy Camp

Jack Solferino was taking the air. A small sharply dressed Italian from Napoli, a *Mafia*, he was high in the organization, an aristocrat of crime who specialized in vice. Girls and girl traffic control, pimps, watchers, procurers, everywhere in London and the provinces, particularly the ports—Liverpool, Cardiff, and the like. Neat as a lizard, fast as a snake to strike, with black hooded eyes. His slit of a mouth was at the same time sensual, consisting almost entirely of a full moist lower lip. He dressed like a bookmaker in large checks with tight trousers and cloth-topped buttoned boots. Round his neck he wore a dark blue, white-spotted silken scarf. He'd killed men with it, garrotting them. To half choke a girl was generally enough. His waistcoat was fancy—dark red with gilt buttons, lined with heavy buckram, almost knife-proof. On his hands he wore yellow dogskin gloves. He always carried a gold-topped Malacca sword stick. Small, weasel-quick, an avaricious killer, a woman coper the way some men were horse copers, and dealers. Girls were just salable flesh to him. Something to be trained and peddled in the market place. He had his customers, his sources of supply. It was a shame that that clumsy fool, Basher Armstrong, had let him down. Eliza would have fitted into a special niche. The others could wait. Basher had given him a list of them—girls all under fifteen whose parents were willing to let them go.

But this damn piece in the *Pall Mall Gazette* was going to hurt them all, no doubt about that. And the act being passed. Not that it had made any difference so far but it might in the future. But he had an idea. He was going to see Carmine about it now. He respected her brains and, more than her brains, her connections. It might be possible to turn all this to their advantage. This girl Lily whom Stead had written about corresponded with Eliza Armstrong. Suppose they squared Basher and got him to make a fuss. Suppose . . . There was an angle here. If they could catch those bloody do-gooders out. Bring them to Court for abduction. He laughed. That would fix them.

He was walking through his own territory—Wardour Street, Greek Street, Rupert Street, Brewer Street, Denham Street—the whole maze of passages and side streets that made up Soho. Down to Leicester Square, a wasteland of shabby shops, side shows and heaps of rubbish. He was king here—from Charing Cross to Park Lane. But this was the center of the jungle where ramshackle houses with communicating doors, cellars knocked into each other, back entrances and skylights that led from roof to roof all jostled one another and were inhabited by people as savage and corrupt as himself—and their victims. Once he had a girl here she never got away, nor, once broken in, had she the heart to go. She was finished. Just an instrument of pleasure, no longer a human being. Besides, they were ashamed to go home even if they could. Shame, fear, and money were the weapons he employed on men and women alike to keep them in line.

He'd written to Carrie Caramine and suggested a meeting. Between them they'd cook something up. He had the underworld and the police in his pocket. She had the toffs, the rich world—society, as it was called. And, my God, they didn't want no change. Not them. They had it too easy this way. Too safe. But what bastards some of them were. Lords and Earls as cruel as rat-catchers when they were free of restraint. But he'd get by with his organization. Lord, he had it taped—export and all. Ships' captains grafted, blinded with gold. Gold-blinkered like horses they were, like the police. As long as there was no fuss. No screams. No scenes. Well, that was what the organization was for—to keep things nice and cosylike.

"Morning Fred," he said, as he passed Fred Barnes loitering in a passage. "Girls all right?"

"All right, guv'nor. No more nonsense."

"Have a cigar, Fred?"

"Don't mind if I do." They lit up and strolled on together. Two tomcats on the pavement tiles—scarred, scrappy, and full of themselves. Bright as buttons, sharp as knives. Layabouts of the first order, masters of women.

Mrs. Caramine waited for Solferino impatiently, dressed to the nines. Not for him but for a social engagement, to pay a call on Lord X. A lot of influence he had and queer tastes that only she could satisfy.

Satisfaction guaranteed, was her motto. No matter what if the price was right. She was wearing a high-necked lace blouse and she looked very dignified and grand because, if she lowered her chin, the whalebone stuck into her. The edge of the neck was tucked into a tiny ruffle that also went down the back, covering the hooks and eyes—an inch apart—which fastened the blouse. The blouse was lined, reinforced with boned bast, and tight fitting. She wore it with a beige skirt of ribbed silk, looped with silken cords that could be reefed like the sails of a ship to show the flesh-colored satin underskirt. Beneath that were her three petticoats of white taffeta silk and lawn, all ruffled with gathered lace. Her stockings were white silk, her shoes white satin ballet slippers with ribbons crisscrossing her ankles. At the back the skirt rose into a little pleated bustle from which hung a narrow train.

She walked up and down the big downstairs drawing room with an angry swish of skirts. Those God damned articles! A modern Babylon, indeed! What did they expect, those pussyfooters and blue stockings? Do-gooders. Creeping Jesuses. Dried up old virgins and men—God save the mark. Why, without the likes of us, she thought, civilization would come apart at the seams. Vice was an escape valve. Why pretend there was no vice in the world? And after all, someone had to cater to it. That was what she'd tell old X. (His name was never mentioned. She even pretended to herself she did not know it though he had once been her lover.) Let him get on with things. Act or no act, if the police did not enforce it, and they hadn't so far . . . But that bloody Stead, the sentimentalist. What did it matter what happened to a few little girls picked off the streets? Their mothers were glad enough to let them go. And Solferino, where the hell was that Dago pimp? By the time he came, she was in a fine temper.

"I've been waiting half an hour for you," she said.

"And dressed up, Carrie, like a bloody lady." He bent over her hand with exaggerated grace.

She could have slapped his oily olive face. He stank of violets. "So you have an idea," she said. "That'll be a change. It's generally me that has the ideas." Mrs. Caramine sank gracefully onto a low, armless, velvet-covered chair and arranged her skirts in a fan about her feet.

"But yes, Signora. You know the articles. . . ."

"Know the articles, you bloody fool? Of course I know them."

"Well," he said. "Lily . . ."

"Yes, Lily?"

"Well," he said again, "I know who she is. She's Eliza Armstrong. And suppose we just put it about and then go see the father?"

"What's the good of that? He's sold her, or her mother did. They're just like the rest."

"*Si, si.*" How he loathed this elegant clever woman. She was smarter than he, wickeder, and he resented it. Also her airs and grace and style. Who the hell did she think she was? Just a Madam. "Exactly, Signora. But people do not like such things to be known among their neighbors. Not talked about. I'll have it talked about. That's easy. Then we'll give Basher. . . ."

"Who's Basher?"

"Her father. I was doing business with him. I wanted the girl myself. I had a place for her. A very pretty little piece. Well, as I say, we'll give him a fiver. . . ."

"Who will?"

"You will, Signora. I am a poor man. And tell him to go to the police with his story."

"They won't do anything. They never do. Why, they'd spend all their time looking for lost girls if they listened to all these people."

"They'll do something if you tip the wink in the right quarter."

Lord X, Mrs. Caramine thought. He was a Duke, really. X was his nom de plume. His alias. He could do it. Be glad to. Tell them to follow it up. Implicate Stead. What a joke.

Solferino went on: "If we could get Stead. Prove he had the girl, that those articles in the *Gazette* were just a blind. I can get coves to swear to it, and girls too. They'll swear to anything."

"By God, you've got an idea, Solferino," Mrs. Caramine said.

"I am a man of ideas, Signora," he said smugly. "And I do not like other people to pick my flowers. *Arrivederci,* Signora," he said, kissing her hand and bowing. "I will see to Basher and leave the police to you. How amusing to have them working for us in this way!"

Amusing, that was the word all right, Carrie thought. Hoist that bugger Stead by his own petard.

It was nearly teatime when Solferino left Coak Street. And she had not even offered him a glass of wine. Dressed up like that. As if she had been expecting someone and had wanted him out of the way. Still, he had her fiver folded in his pocket. That was a matter of principle. Why the hell should he pay for it?

Basher would be at The Sailor or one of the other public houses. He laughed at the idea of him going to the police about his missing daughter. He looked at the girls in the streets as he walked home. His girls. Directly or indirectly. They moved like bright flowers between the lampposts, or stood talking together. Flowers temporarily rooted in old pavements, and then moved on.

If only one could really move on. Go somewhere, Jennie thought as she watched him go by. The bastard. That was the difference between the girls and the other pavement users. She looked at a man coming toward her. In less than a minute he would be near enough to speak to. She wondered if he knew there were thirty-two stones in the curb. That the fifteenth from the corner of Piccadilly was cracked across its center. How well she knew this street! Her beat. "It passes the time," one of the girls had told her. "You've got to look at something in between." The brick walls were different too. Some were softer than others, showed more wear. And corners. The corner where she generally stood was rounded, smoothed off by the backs of girls who'd stood against it for a hundred years, leaning their flesh against the brick, against the stone. Flesh that wore them down the way shoe leather wore the steps of the houses, and the iron-shod hooves of the horses wore down the cobbles of the road.

As soon as Solferino had gone, Mrs. Caramine ordered the carriage to come round. The brougham with a single good but unspectacular bay. Unspectacular, that is, among the other splendid bays of the West End. She was going out as the Countess de Gruchy, an alias she sometimes assumed. The flashing chestnut three-quarter breds were only used by the famous and infamous Mrs. Caramine—a snook cocked to respectability and an advertisement of her establishment. She liked to send her girls driving in it. A pair of 'em, pretty as the geldings and as fast. All furbelow, lace petty, and parasol—bright as birds, decoys that brought in plump pigeons for the plucking.

But not today. This was *grande dame* day. Respectable and no mistake about it. A lady of fashion going to call on a Duke—Lord X as it was his fancy to be called. Ferdinand when they were alone together. He'd known and had her in his prime. Lover, friend, patron and now, in age, a customer, needing the aphrodisiac of young virgin things. Fresh stuff. The bud rather than the dewy rose.

"Through the Park, John," she said, and the horse stepped out into the summer sun. Up Sloane Street to Knightsbridge, through the Albert Gate, through the Park—and how beautiful it was—out of the Grosvenor Gate and down Brook Street. Mrs. Caramine loved the Park in the afternoon. The carriages—lacquered, polished, their wheels spinning, the spokes catching the light, reflecting it like steel. The uniformed coachmen, their long holly whips held at an angle over the near horse. The footmen. The toilettes of the women—organdy, chiffon, muslin, flowered silk. The parasols bursting like blossoms over the lovely occupants of the open carriages. Women. Young mothers grooming their daughters as if they were fillies for the matrimonial stakes. Getting them ready to come out, hatched like chickens after their presentation into the barnyard of society. Christ, she knew girls and women. She knew what they wanted, what they would do. What they could be made to do, and the kind men liked. Two kinds sent them mad: the hot ones like Ellen whom each man thought he alone could satisfy, and the cold ones each man was convinced that he alone could melt. Ellen had been that kind, too, in the beginning, till that bastard Lenton had broken her in Paris. But satisfy? Poor fools—a girl like that could exhaust a dozen men. Could kill one too, if he was no longer young, by playing on his vanity.

The flowers in the beds were no brighter than the driving and strolling women. No more fragrant. No more useful. Just decorations for vase and bed. There were less carriages now—people had gone home for tea. She would drive here tomorrow with the chestnuts and show the flag again.

In Grosvenor Square, not six doors away from Cocky's house the carriage pulled up. A powdered footman opened the door. His silken calves were so good she was sure they must be padded. A butler, who could have doubled for a bishop in his portly dignity, took her visiting card, holding it in front of him on a gold-plated tray as if he were going to eat it.

"His Grace is expecting your ladyship," he said.

Good God, Carmine thought, he knows who I am as well as I do myself. What a game it was! What a charade! What an Arabian thousand and one nights she controlled. A genie with a magic house. A widow's cruse that was always full of pleasure for those who could afford to pay for it.

She followed the broad black back of this great servile insect, a pasha no doubt among the female staff of this big house. A man. But also a worm. A super flunky, obsequious to wealth and authority. They went up the wide carpeted stairs, past immense canvases of battles, gods, goddesses, nymphs, and fauns, down a wide passage at the end of which the bishop-butler flung open a door—through which a man mounted on a cart horse could have ridden—and announced: "The Countess de Gruchy, your Grace."

She went in and curtsied—a mocking, graceful tribute to royalty. The ornate carved, gold-leaf decorated and paneled door closed behind her.

"Sit down, Carrie my dear."

"Thank you, Ferdinand."

"By God," the Duke said, "you look pretty! Got up to kill."

"To love, my lord."

"I wish I had it in me, me dear. But I ain't the man I was." He chuckled. "And what a man I was, wasn't I, Carrie?"

"You were, indeed. One of the best."

"And so were you."

She laughed. "We ought to know, oughtn't we, Ferdinand?"

"Damn me!" the Duke said. "You're like port, you improve with age."

"A long time in the wood, my lord."

"Well, I wish I could, but I can't. Can't get blood out of a stone, can you?"

"I can't," she said. "But I could arrange for something that might."

The old man's eyes lighted up.

"But there are going to be difficulties, your Grace," Mrs. Caramine said.

"Difficulties?"

"The Act, my lord."

"No one's going to pay much attention to it, Carrie."

"I think they are unless we do something," Mrs. Caramine said.

"What can we do?"

"We are going to start a case against the abductor of an innocent young girl."

"Lord," he said, "no one will take any action. People been going to the police about missing girls for years. You know that?"

"But suppose you tip 'em the wink, Ferdy." She laid her hand on his bulging thigh.

"But why, Carrie?"

"Because it's Stead. You remember the *Maiden Tribute* articles?"

The Duke turned almost purple with rage. "The scoundrel. Washing all that dirty linen in public. Muckraking. Dragging England through the mud. . . ."

She let him rail on. "Lily," she said. "That was the girl he wrote about. We've found her parents. Her real name is Eliza Armstrong. Thirteen. A real little beauty, I'm told. Funny how they grow on the muck heap, isn't it, Ferdy? The way we find you little lovelies from the slums?"

"Well?" he said.

"Well Ferdy, they are going to complain to the magistrate at Marylebone. Suppose you said there might be something in it for him if he took it up?"

"Honors list?"

"Something like that. If we could discredit Stead it would be in the bag. Discredit those bloody do-gooders. Show 'em up. Show that they are men like everyone else, that they want their greens and that all this publicity was just to sell the paper."

"By God, I'll do it, Carrie." He got up. Every inch a lord, a duke, an aristocrat. A man of privilege. He put his hand to his gray silk ascot tie. He smoothed the bulge of his fawn waistcoat, fiddled with the fob that hung from its pocket, looked down at his striped trousers that were strapped under the instep of his highly polished black boots, at the pattern on the Aubusson carpet on which he stood. All as if he expected to find some answer to some question that had not been asked.

"If we can discredit them, things will go on as before," he said half in query, half in assertion.

"Exactly, my lord."

"Bentinck did his best at the House," he said.

"The Lords passed it," Carrie countered.

"God Almighty, what else could they do, Carrie? Got to be against sin, you know."

"So I've noticed," Mrs. Caramine said. "That's why I'm so poor." She laughed. "You bloody old hypocrite, Ferdy."

"You'll get me something nice?"

"I've never failed you. Just give me a week or two. Something to look forward to, your Grace." She swept him another deep curtsey, sinking to the carpet—a lovely rustling flower in the wind.

She had remained slim and graceful, her eyes were the same magnificent dark orbs he had always admired. Her hair was the same—dyed now, of course—but the same. Even her face, piquant. By God, there was something about age—when your sight went a bit, as long as they kept their shape, women still looked good. But what a girl she had been in her prime! One of the best and, as she said, he ought to know. But now he needed them young, needed the titillation of youth and reluctance. But she'd get it for him. She alway had. He was too old to go to the Continent now. It was too much trouble. He rang the bell.

Carrie held out her hand. He kissed it. By God, he thought, I've kissed her all over. He'd kept her once for a year. What a year it had been! Then he had helped her to get on her feet. Introduced men to her and so on. Twenty years ago. Nearer thirty, really. How time did fly. . . .

Mrs. Caramine drove home, well enough content. The seeds were sown, both on the high ground of the aristocracy and in the muck of the slums. Now she could relax and wait. Silly fools, those do-gooders.

Bloody fools if they thought human nature could be changed by an Act of Parliament. A word here, a word there. A little more money to the police possibly, but she'd put her prices up to cover it. She'd talk to Prettyman about it when she got back and wrapped the countess up again. Poor Countess de Gruchy, she did not get many airings. Anyway, everything was *en train,* as the French said. It was now in the hands of God. And tomorrow she and Ellen would take a drive in the Park behind the jingling, high-stepping, frothing chestnuts. Dressed to the nines, they'd cock a snook at the parasoled ladies they swept past. It always amused her to see their raised eyebrows. Caramine, the notorious madam, and one of her girls behind the finest and showiest pair in London. How amusing it was to think that the first prosecution under the new act would be against William Stead, the author of the *Maiden Tribute.* Everyone would believe he had bought the kid to use himself, because that was human nature, to believe the worst.

She laughed and went to see if the girls were ready for the drawing room. Friends might be arriving any time.

42 : The Young Captain

Maud Cockshott adjusted her small high hat—it was like a child's topper—of fawn beaver, in front of the mirror. She looked very pretty today, all in autumn beige, sparkling bright as an autumn leaf caught in the zephyr of anticipation. The princess-style dress fitted tightly over her hips, swathing them, and flared out in a peplum supported by petticoats. Moving lightly as a dancer, the motion of her legs invisible, she seemed to slide gracefully over the floor, her skirt rising and falling like a flag in a breeze. An aura of femininity emanated from her, the perfume blending with the near-metallic rustling of her clothes. She would take off her hat in a minute. She wanted Geoffrey to appreciate the full beauty of her ensemble. Later she would take off her hat, let down her mane of night-black hair, a silken shawl over her back, a frame for her face and masking her lovely firm little breasts.

Satisfied with her appearance, she turned to Geoffrey. "This is the last time," she said. "It's over, Geoff. He knows. There's no doubt about it now." She knew he'd be there waiting for her when she got back to Grosvenor Square. Though how the hell he found out was beyond her. Damn him and love him, the beast. But the risks were becoming too great—besides she was tired of Geoffrey, of these discreet houses of accommodation. Never the same one, but still he knew. They were in London only because Harold's affairs kept them there. Affairs was probably the right word.

Geoffrey came up behind her. He annoyed her. He always began this way. There was no variety in it and variety was the spice of life, or so they said. "The last time, darling? You mean here? Like this? You've made up your mind at last?"

"Yes, darling. But not the way you think. I am going to be a good wife after today." She wasn't going to be, not really. But she was sick of a liaison that was as dull as marriage. The excitement had gone out of it. If it was only satisfaction, Harold could give her that, and more of it than Geoffrey. He was a more experienced lover—though she was careful not to let him know the pleasure he gave her. This affair, which without question he knew about, excited him. There was something wicked about him, something decadent that appealed to her against her will and judgment. Even his *amours* at Caramine's had an effect on her that must parallel his interest in her since she had taken a lover. How curious it would be if, when she became a good and faithful wife, he lost interest in her.

All this was in her mind as Geoffrey fiddled with her clothes. Why did he take so long? Surely he knew how to undress a woman by this time. Already in her mind she was home with Harold's hands tearing at her. How she wished she knew what Louise thought about it all. Did he have her too? God knows, she was pretty enough. At last it was done and she found herself in Geoffrey's arms. She responded to him because she was made that way and enjoyed his ardor—an enjoyable proof of her power as a woman. But she was thinking of ceilings. How many there had been! A fine thing if that was all one could think about. At least the ceiling of the big bedroom in Grosvenor Square was beautifully ornate—old Cockshott's ceiling, the one Harold's mother had looked at. Scrolled, gold-leafed.

She turned on her elbow and said: "I mean it, Geoff. It's too risky now."

He was flabbergasted. His jaw dropped. If he slapped me, she thought —and God knows she was in the right position—she might have gone on with it. But there was none of that in him, none of Harold's exciting brutality. He was weak. Vacillating. Stupid. He was a bore, that was it.

"You can't, Maud. Not after all this time and all our plans."

That was just it. All this time—but she could not tell him so. "It's not fair," she said. "Not fair that a woman can't do what a man can do." At this moment she was all for women's rights, a single standard. Tears came into her big dark eyes.

Geoffrey kissed them away. "Salt tears," he said, as if he expected to find them made of ice cream. But he was taking it better than she had thought he would, or she thought so till he said:

"I do not think I can stand losing you, my darling. I'm going to shoot myself."

What a bore the man was! But suppose he really did. . . . Fancy a man shooting himself because he had lost you. She just said: "Don't be so silly. What do you get from me, Geoff? Just someone to sleep with. You can get that at Caramine's. There's a girl there called Hélène—French—who Harold goes to."

"You mean you know that he goes from you to her and from her to you? What a revolting idea!"

"She's very good, I understand."

"Christ!" he said. "That man. It was bad enough before, but to know this. Why in God's name did you tell me?"

"I thought you knew. Everyone knows Harold Cockshott's reputation. And there's my maid as well. . . ." She might as well be hung for a sheep as a lamb. "She's French, too. They seem to have something, these French girls."

To Maud's great surprise, Geoffrey burst into tears, the wracking sobs of a man whose heart is broken, whose world has collapsed about him. She got up and dressed slowly. Glad she had worn a corselet that she could put on by herself. Fully dressed, she returned to the mirror. That was one thing these people always had—a full-length mirror so that a woman could see that there was nothing out of place when she left. She adjusted her child's topper and smoothed her dress over her hips. She raised her skirt to show her petticoats in a half turn. Pretty—pretty as a picture, abloom with love and anticipation as she swept out of the room with a swish of skirts and petties, a click of heels on the parquet. Utterly satisfied with herself, with life, and relieved that a situation that had begun to bore her should have ended so easily. She detested scenes. So vulgar, so common. At the door she turned. "Don't forget the name, Geoffrey. It's Hélène." She dropped her lover a full court curtsey, her body erect, to the floor, and went out. She hoped she would have no trouble picking up a hansom.

Geoffrey sat on alone for an hour. The comfortable room with its big rumpled bed was an empty shell. Dead. But Maud was still there in a way. The bed was still rumpled from her lovely little body. She had dropped her handkerchief—a tiny piece of lace and lawn—that smelt of her. Of her tuberose perfume and the woman herself, as if it were a part of her skin. He put it into his pocket. In his rooms he had one of her gloves and a lock of her dark hair.

Well, that was that. The dream was over. Life was over, And, by God, he'd take her advice and go to Caramine's and ask for the French girl. Then he'd have had two of Harold Cockshott's women. In some obscure way he felt it would bring him nearer to Maud. She had told him to go to her. What a thing for a woman to tell the man who loved her. He'd go tonight.

"Quite a stranger, Captain," Mrs. Caramine said. "But it has happened before and will happen again. Why take a cab when you have a carriage of your own? But there's one thing about a long absence. We've a new lot of girls—young beauties, the best in England. I have to," she went on. "That's my reputation—only the best at Caramine's."

Geoffrey did not beat about the bush. "You have a French girl," he said. "Cockshott's friend."

"He recommended her?"

"In a way," Geoffrey said.

"Come this way, Captain. Hélène is not with the others. If she likes you, well. . . ." She smiled into his eyes. "Then, after that it's just a matter of terms."

A week later he called on Lavinia.

"Is Mrs. Lenton at home?" he asked the butler.

"She's at home, sir."

By great good fortune Lavinia was alone when he went in. "Captain Horner," she said, "how nice of you to call."

He took her hand. "I do not know, Mrs. Lenton," he said. "I am in despair."

"It's about Maud?"

"So you know?"

"I am her greatest friend."

"She's thrown me over."

"Sit down," Lavinia said. This was not going to be easy.

"She won't run away to South Africa with me."

"Do you think she'd have been happy as a farmer's wife?"

"I'd have made her happy."

"And in between? Before she was your wife?"

"I'd have made her happy," he repeated.

"She loved you, I know," Lavinia said, thinking of what Maud had once told her and how surprised she had been. Acting like a lovesick housemaid, she had thought. That had been before John. Who was lovesick now?

"I think she found it impossible to give up her position, Captain Horner. She's Lady Cockshott now."

"I have never been allowed to forget it. She changed as soon as old Cockshott died. And do you know what she did, Mrs. Lenton?"

"No, I don't."

"Well, I can't tell you." Captain Horner blushed.

"If you have read the papers, you should know you can tell me anything. I am unshockable."

"Well . . ." he said.

"Well, go on."

"When she told me it was over, she said I should go to Mrs. Caramine's and ask for a girl there, a girl called Hélène."

Mrs. Lenton, who had been leaning against the mantelpiece, sat down. This was too much. The Criminal Amendment Bill had been passed but there had not been a single prosecution. Caramine, like a gigantic spider, still sat in the center of her web. Hélène. Ellen. Madame Elsie. Nothing had changed. Could it all have been for nothing? She composed herself and asked, "What is she like?"

"Who, Hélène?"

"Of course."

"I could not tell you. How could one talk to a lady about such things? I should never have come, I must have been mad. It's just Maud. I had to know about her."

"Tell me," Lavinia said. "I've spent the last year trying to get places like Mrs. Caramine's shut down. Did you know, Captain Horner, that it was through her I lost my daughters? They were sold through her. One is dead and the other mentally deranged."

"My God!" Geoffrey said.

"So you can tell me. What is she like, this famous Hélène, the new attraction at No. 23? Hélène . . ." She laughed bitterly. "Ellen Pickford, who was once my children's governess and was seduced by Edward Lenton, my husband. You see, Captain Horner, you need mince no words." Mince words? She wasn't going to mince them either. But she was surprised to find herself saying, "About this Hélène, Captain Horner. Is she really so good in bed?"

Geoffrey snapped open his gold half-hunter and said: "Excuse me, Mrs. Lenton. I had no idea it was so late. Goodbye, Mrs. Lenton." He almost ran out of the room.

What a pity he could not stay for tea. My God, the warp and woof of it—the whole disgusting pattern. This tapestry of evil was still completely intact. She began to laugh. How funny it was, dear God, how funny. Funny that neither God, nor His heaven, nor the laws of England could do anything for the children and women of the land. When she was able to control her laughter, she rang the bell.

When the footman answered it, she said: "Charles, I am not at home if anyone calls." As soon as the man left, she went upstairs, called May to run a bath, and prepared for bed. Even this. Even bed and preparing for it now filled her with horror.

43 : The Continent

For a change Basher Armstrong found himself in the right. A wronged man, with the law on his side. The father of an abducted daughter. Things were going well at last, and about time, too. England was recognizing his worth as a solid citizen. Solferino had put enough money into his pocket to keep him well oiled, and in a few days he was off to the "continong" to bring the little bitch back, accompanied by a detective. 'Ow about that? A copper. And all expenses paid. He'd heard things about the frogs, he had. Booze. Tarts. Over the sea, by God, he who'd not even been in a train since he left the army—troop trains. Ten years in the militia. A corporal with a good conduct discharge. This was going to be different. A bloody passenger. Going abroad to see to his rights, that was what he was going to do. And a right proper tale he'd have to tell them when he came home with the kid he was going to rescue from one of them foreign knocking shops.

Me own flesh and blood, mark you. He flexed the bulging muscles of his hairy, tattooed arms. My kid. My little Liza. Beery tears seeped from his eyes. Solferino'd get her yet, but by God she'd nearly slipped through his fingers. Christ, he'd told 'em all about it at The Black Man, The Sailor, The Anglesey, and The Phoenix. A bloody 'ero, he was.

Then came a letter from the kid. And he and the inspector of police went to see Mr. Bramwell Booth. A finger in the pie, them do-gooders had.

Mr. Booth, very neat in his uniform, as if he was a real soldier. A fine thing, masquerading like that in front of him with ten years of service.

Basher pulled in his belly and straightened his back. Soldier, hell! "Where's me girl?" he said.

"With some friends of mine in France. She is in a very good situation. It would be a shame for her mother to have her back again."

"We'll see about that," Basher said. "I've got the law on me side. Coppers," he said. "They'll fix you. Pinching people's kids."

"I'll apply to have her made a ward in chancery."

"Like hell you will."

"Mind your language," the inspector said. Whatever the game was, these Army people were all right.

"Come on," Basher said, "we'll 'op it. But we'll be back. The law," he muttered darkly and stamped out into Queen Victoria Street.

Next day the officer took Mrs. Armstrong to see Mr. Booth.

"Are you her mother?" he asked, looking at the bedraggled, not entirely sober slattern in front of him.

"I am," she said.

"Well, you can't have your child back."

"Why not?"

"Have you got a hundred pounds?"

"I'm a poor woman. I haven't got a hundred pence."

"Well, that's what it cost me to send her away. But I'll give you her wages."

"I don't want her bloody wages. I want me kid. I'm scared, sir, after wot I seen in the *Gazette*. I want ter show me friends and neighbors I ain't sold me daughter for a bloody fiver. Me own flesh and blood. Bone of me bone. Lies, that's what it is. All lies. 'I 'ear you sold your kid, Bet Armstrong,' that's wot they say. But I'll show 'em. Bloody lot of liars."

"I can tell you this, Mrs. Armstrong. When I received your daughter she was pure. No one had touched her. Not the way they did Lily in the *Pall Mall Gazette*."

"You'd better give Mrs. Armstrong her address," the officer said.

Mr. Booth produced the address from a drawer and said: "Go away now and talk to your husband. If you really want Eliza back, you shall have her." He offered the officer the medical certificate.

"I'll take your word for it, sir," he said. With that they left.

And a few days later Mrs. Armstrong wrote Mr. Booth a letter to say she had talked to her husband and they wanted Eliza back. Mr. Armstrong was going to France to fetch her with a police officer.

Things are going all right, Basher assured Solferino. "I'll get 'er back for you. No bloody error about that, guv'nor." And he was paid for the other girls he had procured, or rather tipped Solferino off about. What a joke going to Paris with Inspector von Tornow of Scotland Yard!

But the kid wasn't at the address they'd been given—the Salvation Army headquarters on the Quai Valmy. Done a bunk, she had.

But what a time Basher had in the stews of Paris with the money he'd got from Solferino. Tarts. Booze. . . . And hot. Did he sweat—never seen anything like it. Like a bloody oven. Trees on the pavement and little round tin houses to have a leak every few hundred yards. Chaps coming out buttoning up their flies as bold as brass and no one turning a hair. Women everywhere—neat little dark-eyed tits what looked you up and down. No modesty 'ere. Just what he'd thought it would be. Frogs. Toads more like—kissing and cuddling in the streets. Proper shocking it was to a respectable Englishman.

And Fifine . . . that was the girl he'd picked up. A real hot piece. Taken 'im 'ome, she had, and her friend had come in—a yellow-haired girl with a big bottom, called *Merde*. That was all she could say, just her name. Whatever you said to her. But he'd had 'em both and they was better than English tarts in some ways, which was more than you could say for the food. What muck! And the beer . . . slops. So he'd drunk brandy and the girls had wine. Bottles of it. And they sang and danced and high-kicked, laughing fit to bust because he was English and so funny. Bloody frogs. *Merde* had given him quite a bite on the shoulder. But they'd liked the tattoos, especially the snake on his stomach.

It took von Tornow two days to find him with the help of the French police.

Meanwhile, the Steads were in Lausanne having a holiday. Walking, climbing, boating on the lake. How beautiful and peaceful it was after the horrors they had been through! The sordid scenes, the horrible procedures that had been necessary to obtain proof, the files of revolting evidence—all were forgotten in the clean mountain air among the wooden chalets and the sweet-smelling pinewoods, as they picknicked and listened to the birds and the sound of distant cow bells.

Then Bramwell Booth's letter came. The chase was up. They were after him who had done nothing more than save a girl; remove her from a slum environment and place her in safety. But he had made one mistake—he had not got her father's consent. If he'd agreed, not a word would have been said. Over thirteen, wasn't she? Over the age of consent. But if abducted without parental authority while she was a minor, a crime had been committed.

"You had better come back," Booth wrote. "I'll send her to you at Wimbledon."

So they packed up. The big trunk, the baskets, hampers, rolls of rugs. And they went home, where Eliza—who had grown a lot and looked well and happy—was delivered to them. There was no legal way to keep her from her parents, no matter how they treated her. There was no protection for a child over thirteen unless she was an heiress—would come into money or property or, in the case of being abducted from her parents, only if they could prove financial loss. That she was useful and necessary. This was the line they would take. Doing house-work and looking after the baby.

When Basher and the detective got back to London after their wild-goose chase, they found that Mr. Thicknesse, Secretary of the Minors Protection Society, had taken a hand in the proceedings. He had dis-covered that the child was with Mr. Stead's family in Wimbledon. He had been to see him. "You'll have to give Eliza up, Mr. Stead," he said.

"I don't want to do that. She's well and happy."

"Well, you'll have to write to her parents and see what they want to do."

He sat down at once and wrote:

Dear Mrs. Armstrong, Your child is well taken care of and very happy, but of course if you and Mr. Armstrong really wish to have her returned to you, I am and always have been perfectly ready to comply with your request. I would however suggest that if you only wish to satisfy yourself that Eliza is all right and safe, you and Mr. Armstrong should see her for yourselves and that then she should retain her situa-tion where she is giving great satisfaction and doing very well.

"Ha!" Basher said. "Want ter keep 'er, do they? Well, I got other plans." He struck his right fist into the palm of his left hand. Bash! Bash! By God, he had to bash something.

His wife drew away from him. The baby began to whimper.

"You go there tomorrow, Bet. And bring 'er back. You hear?" he shouted. "I'll 'ave no more bloody nonsense with the kid—my property, that's what she is. That's what the law says. So you tell 'em."

44 : Cambridge House

When she left England in June, Eliza had been too tired and bewil-dered to pay much attention to anything. Madame Combe had a basket of food—bread and butter, hard-boiled eggs, ham, and cold tea in a bottle—that they ate on the train.

The country went whizzing by. Hedges and more hedges, farms, cottages, cows in the fields, towns; then Folkestone and the sea. She had never seen the sea before, had not even heard much talk of it.

A porter in a blue sweater took the luggage. Sailors. Screaming gulls. The great white paddle-wheeler. Waves with white on top of them, like bits of paper. The ship going up and down very nicely and the wind so strong she had to hold onto her new hat. The paddle wheels turned, churning up the water.

Then she saw France. Madame Combe had tears in her eyes. More porters in blue jumpers this time, all shouting. Another train. More country but different looking. She cried a bit with loneliness and being so tired. Too much had happened. What was it all about? What a long way she was from home, from Lissom-Grove and Charles Street.

Madame Combe was very kind. She talked about her five little children and her two big sons in the Army.

"Soldiers?" Eliza said.

"*Mais oui,* soldiers of Jesus. The Salvation Army."

They had taken a *fiacre* and gone rattling over the cobbles to the Army headquarters on the Quai Valmy.

Eliza was given food—thick soup—and told she might soak her bread in it. A stew. Cheese, coffee—all different, all strange. It was clean too and they set her to work—housework and polishing, scrubbing the white wood floors. That was all homelike enough. And they prayed and sang hymns—in French though—so she went "la la" because the tunes were the same.

In Paris her homesickness was somewhat allayed by the excitement of travel and the strange sights of foreign parts, with everyone gesticulating and talking at once. Teams of great white horses with red and blue sheepskins on their collars, dragged enormous blocks of white building stone through the city. Soldiers—*cuirassiers*—with long black horse tails hanging from their helmets. Dragoons dragging their sabers on the pavement. Girls and women—smarter than at home. And the poor, much the same, wrapped in black shawls with kids in their arms and kids dragging at their skirts. Dogs, cats—like at home—but the people were different because they spoke French. The houses were taller, thinner somehow. The streets wider, some of them, and planted with trees.

Then just as she was getting used to it—in July—Lieutenant Combe, a nice young man and one of Madame Combe's two sons, took her by train to a place called l'Oriole in the Department of Drôme in the South of France. Hundreds of miles through country with no hedges and filled with vineyards. He told her they were for making wine. And there were mountains. She cried a lot because she missed Madame Combe and she wasn't used to being alone with a man. Not that he wasn't nice to her.

At l'Oriole she stayed with the family of a Monsieur Bérard. It was real country and he had a lot of children. Cocks crowing in the morning woke her up, like they did in the Bible, but they crowed more than three times and they started before it was light. There was a nice fat baby here, too, and he made her cry too because he reminded her of her little brother. But she wrote here—they said she could—to say she was well and happy.

My dear mother, I daresay you are thinking of me very much. I should like to know how you are getting on. I am in a very good place in the country. I hope I shall come and see you very soon, and I hope I shall see my sisters and little brother. I love him very much. I am not with the lady who brought me here. She left me at a place and was a very long time fetching me again. Give Mrs. Sullivan my love. I did go to a meeting every night to hear them speak about God. They has got a little baby here. I nurse it every day. I has good food to eat and all I want. Mother, you know I love you very much and the little baby. I hope he can walk now. I have asked the Lord to bless you. Where I am the people talk French and I am learning to talk it. Goodbye. God bless you and my brothers and sisters. A hundred kisses when we meet. From your Eliza.

She was pretty proud of her letter—neat and not a blot on it. She was pretty pleased with herself, too. Nice clothes, good boots with buttons, black cotton stockings. Petticoat, chemise, and drawers. And a red-and-white-check gingham dress. And she'd grown. Filled out and was brown with the summer sun of France. Fine day followed fine day, with pale blue, burnt out skies.

They had mules on the farms instead of horses. She'd never seen a mule before. Half horse and half moke, it was. Donkeys she'd seen in the costers' carts in London. Pretty, gray, mouselike things, with long ears. But except for their long ears and mousy noses, mules weren't at all like donkeys. And so much bigger.

And all the people drinking wine. Singing and laughing. Black-eyed, black-haired people, lively as crickets. If she hadn't missed her baby brother, she'd have been quite happy here. And how they would have liked it! She thought of the baby's running nose. Always a cold he had. Soon get rid of it here. If she were here, and Johnny . . . Johnny, playing in the sun. French babies weren't the same. They even smelt different.

Then she was moved to a new place, the Plaines de Bas in the mountains. Getting fed up with being moved, she was. But the Plaines wasn't the end of it. A Captain Raby of the Army arrived to take her back to Paris and then to London once again. Back to good old England. But not home. Not yet. He took her to Mr. Stead's house in Wimbledon.

She thought about the South of France and of how hot it was. And the way everyone went to sleep after lunch. And the mules and the goats and the vineyards. And the noise of the cicadas. How they sang! Only it wasn't singing really. Not like birds. She had plenty to think about, not 'alf she 'adn't—people, adventures, trains, boats, children, dogs, cats, mules. Seagulls, rabbits.

But she was glad to be back in England. And she liked it here in this big house with Mr. and Mrs. Stead and the kids, and the dog and the pony. But she wasn't the girl she had been, not by a long chalk. She'd been over the water, she had. To abroad. Paris and all. And she had friends now, lots of friends. In the Army. English friends, French friends. Rebecca Jarrett and others besides. And clothes. She knew how to behave and some French words, and all about Jesus. It was very nice to think about gentle Jesus, meek and mild.

Not that she understood all the goings on and all that she had been made to do. But no one had hurt her or cursed her. No one had been drunk, and if the work had been hard it had not been too hard. She missed the baby. But she'd see him soon now, she was sure. He'd 'ave growed. Babies growed fast. But she was stronger, too. She'd still be able to lug him around.

She went over it in her mind. Mr. Stead and the pretty lady waving their handkerchiefs as the train pulled out of the station and her leaning out of the window with Madame hanging on to her. The green fields and the country and the dear little rabbits and then the sea. And the waves going up and down with little white feathers on the tops of them, the gulls swooping and crying and sailors in blue jerseys with tattooed arms. Then France and Madame Combe chattering away in French. Paris, a big town, but not at all like London. Not even the smell or sound of it.

It was August now and she had left England in June, just after the Derby.

Mrs. Stead came into the room and said: "Will you clean the table silver now, Eliza?"

"Yes, Ma'am."

A nice lady. Soft-spoken and gentle.

These were not the mills of God but those of the devil that were grinding so irrevocably. The beginning had been the arrival of Mrs. Armstrong and her daughter at Cambridge House.

Although it was only ten o'clock, Mrs. Armstrong did not appear to be entirely sober. Hung-over, perhaps, and bedraggled. A bonnet with broken ostrich feathers was set rather to one side on her gray hair. Her eyes were bloodshot. Her black dress had a ragged hem and though it was summer she wore a jet-beaded cape over her shoulders that was green with age, its ornamentation incomplete.

The girl with her, her daughter Jane, looked about seventeen. She was neatly dressed, embarrassed by her mother's bellicosity, and tried to restrain her by plucking at her sleeve. They had taken a cab to Waterloo Station and from there had come by train to Wimbledon. Real country, it was.

Lucy Stead met them in the dining room. So this was the woman who had sold her daughter. How strange she looked in this comfortable mahogany-furnished room with its Landseer prints, *Dignity and Impudence. The Stag at Bay,* with the vase of flowers fresh from the garden on the table. Mrs. Armstrong had brought a public-house smell with her. Stale beer and gin and smoke. There were even traces of sawdust on her boots. She'd stopped for a quick one to give her courage in this great moment of her life. Was she not a mother fighting for her daughter? Bone of me bone. Blood of me blood.

Mrs. Stead made no attempt to take her hand. "You are Mrs. Armstrong?"

"I am that, an' I've come for me girl."

"So I understand. I suppose you'd like to see her alone?"

"That's what I came for. To see what you done to 'er. Blood of me blood. Bone of me bone," she repeated. The refrain had been in her mind all the way in from Lissom-Grove. Me daughter, me little girl.

"I'll send her in." Mrs. Stead turned away with a swish of skirts, holding them up in her left hand as if to avoid contamination. She supposed the dining room could be aired but at that moment it seemed to her it would never again be the same.

Mrs. Armstrong heard her calling Eliza in the hall. A moment later the girl came in looking very well. Almost pretty. Clean and well dressed. She'd growed, she had. Filled out like.

"Liza!"

"Ma!" Eliza ran to her mother.

"You all right, my love?"

"I'm fine."

"They treated you right?"

"Oh yes. An' how's the baby? I bet he's growed."

"I'm going to get you out of 'ere. Me and your Dad wants you 'ome. We've got the law on 'em, we 'ave," Mrs. Armstrong said darkly. She kissed Eliza.

Then Mrs. Stead came in and they all went to lunch. Mr. Thicknesse, Mr. Jacques, Miss Green—they had been waiting for them outside. Lunch at a pub. The Star it was, a homelike place. Steak and kidney pudding with two vegetables, greens and spuds and a nice rice pudding. And a pint of bitter with it. Right in the middle of it, Mr. Jacques asked Mrs. Armstrong how she thought her daughter looked.

"She looks pretty well and I think she's growed."

That seemed a safe thing to say but they weren't going to soft-soap her. Not 'arf they weren't.

Then he said: "You won't take her away with you? Don't you think it's much better for her to stay and I'll get her a good situation?"

But Mrs. Armstrong wasn't having any of that. "No, I'll take her away. I'll get her a job near home."

Then Mr. Thicknesse said: "Let the woman think it over."

Woman, indeed! Me! A lady!

"In two or three days, she may consent."

Consent! Did they see any green in her eye, that Mr. Jack and Thicknesse? Thick ear she'd give 'em, if she had half a chance.

Then they took her to a room and Mr. Jacques said: "I will pay you her wages. I'll double them as you've had so much trouble." He put two pound ten down on the table and she picked it up. Then he read out a paper he had written:

August 24, 1885
I have received my daughter, Eliza, safe and sound together with double wages for all the time she has been away. My daughter tells me she has been very happy and comfortable and that the people she was with have been very kind to her. I am quite satisfied that she has been subjected to no outrage or bad usage.

Mrs. Armstrong signed the document. It was witnessed by Ralph Thicknesse, Honorary Secretary of the Minors' Protection Society.

Then Mr. Jacques said: "Do you want the child examined, Mrs. Armstrong?"

"I don't want her messed about no more."

"So you are satisfied with what the child told you?"

"Yes, I am. An' all I want is to 'ave the kid back 'ome."

Two days later Eliza was back in Charles Street. Back to living in a room on the first floor of No. 32 with her father and mother and five sisters and brothers—all cooking, sleeping and eating in the same room. Back to taking the baby out into the street to get the air—fetid, but still fresher than it was in the room. Eliza fell back into it as if she'd never been away. It was all like a dream. The adventure was over, or so she thought.

Basher looked at his daughter with new eyes. She was bigger, filled out. The kid had tits now, and a bit of a bottom. They must have fed her well over there. Let things simmer down and he'd get his fiver for her all right. Just a matter of a week or two for things to blow over a bit. Solferino might even up the price a little.

Solferino and the madams. Now they had that bastard, Stead, the do-gooder muckraker, where they wanted him. They'd have him in the dock, they would. The whole damn crew of 'em, and fix them for good. A lot of bloody whiners, telling free Englishmen what they could do with their own property, and if a girl wasn't property what was? Christ, he ought to know, oughtn't he?

"I'll tell you something, Basher," Mrs. Armstrong said. "Do you know what I said to that Thicknesse bastard? I said 'I 'opes as 'ow Jesus'll give you your true reward for 'elping me get back me little girl.' That's wot I said, 'im being one of them Bible bangers."

"Amen to that," Basher said. "Aye. Amen," jingling the coins in his trouser pocket. Not coppers, now, nor tanners. Dollars and half dollars, that's wot they were. That was what came from working for a chap like Solferino. "Got work for you Basher, I have," he says. "Don't mind a bit of fighting, do you?" "Basher's me name, ain't it? An' I've earned it."

But things were no longer the same for the Steads. No one called at Cambridge House now; people cut Mrs. Stead in the street, people whom she had considered friends. A mob broke into the grounds, destroying the garden, and stood about throwing stones and jeering till dispersed by the police. They had been led by a big rough they called Basher. They came from the slums—from Whitechapel, Paddington and Marylebone—out-of-works, toughs, burglars, street Arabs. Some of them little more than children.

When her husband came home and looked at the devastation, he said: "Someone paid for this. They came by train and were put up to it. I suppose the police made no arrests, Lucy?"

"No. They didn't even try. They just told them to move along."

"That's it," said Stead. "They've been told not to. There's too much in this dirty business for them. It's us they hate for having taken the lid off this cesspool and letting out the stink."

"Everyone hates us," Lucy said, beginning to cry. "But I'm glad you did it. I'm proud of you, William."

Stead put his arm round his wife's waist. "Thank you, darling. I couldn't have done it without you and I'll see it through. But you've got to remember that this is the age of hypocrisy. They say there is no dirt in England because it's all swept under the carpet. It's not so long ago people were upholding slavery, even churchmen. Child labor, pregnant women, and children working in the coal mines." And before he could control himself, he was crying too.

45 : The End of a Summer

After the Bill had been passed, Lavinia had gone back to Mortal with relief, where a peaceful country summer was already merging—though it was only August—into a promise of autumn. The great elms looked tired, as if carrying all that weight of sculptured foliage was really too much for them. The beeches, too, had lost their freshness. The rowans were in full orange berry—great bunches that looked like grapes.

In the herbaceous borders the phlox and flags were over and the Michaelmas daisies, marguerites, and chrysanthemums in bud and flower. They'd go on for a long time. The roses were still good in their second flowering. A few would hang on till Christmas.

Her husband's friends were in Scotland for the grouse shooting. She thought of last year, of how Edward had been supposed to be there while she and the girls had been to the seaside. Partridge shooting would begin in a couple of weeks, but not at Mortal. There would be no more regular shoots. Just a few killed by the keepers for the pot and to keep them down a little. If too many were left, they died.

But she hated it. She flinched now every time she heard a shot. She loved partridges. Loved to put them up in neat little family coveys when she rode through the roots.

She was seeing as much of John as she could without causing talk. After all, he was her man of affairs and the very difference in their positions was a safeguard. No one could think that there would ever be more than business between them. Sometimes he came to Mortal for lunch or tea, driving over with bundles of papers tied with red legal ribbon. And they often met out riding; picking up the old habit. She missed what she called in her mind "the office" in London. But once in John's arms, everything was forgotten. She hardly recognized herself in this voluptuous creature who, between seeing him, relived the hours they spent together.

If only it could have been open, if only she could have run away with him. Of course Edward could not divorce her—speechless and unable to communicate. And she felt a sense of responsibility toward him. Not personal. She hardly saw him now that Muriel had taken him off her hands. But the house—Mortal—Eva, Muriel, the staff. They could not be left.

Her relationship with Muriel was curious. She had become quite fond of her, and how extraordinary that was. Partly she was sorry for her—loving this cripple who had betrayed her; partly she was grateful for her help. Then there was the way she got on with Eva. Often she thought of the lot of them—the women with whom she was so closely associated—all of whom had relations of various kinds with men. Eva and Molly forced. Muriel seduced and betrayed. She herself—well, what about her? There had been no seduction. At least it was mutual if there had been. A meeting of a magnet and the iron filings. And then there was Maud Cockshott, with her adulteries and teasings; her trick of playing with fire. Any fire. Lighting it in a man and warming herself at it. And her husband's curious way of revenging himself on her. Forcing himself on her. Indignities to which she had to submit in a mixture of hate and enjoyment. Yet she still loved Maud. She was so pretty, so dainty—only French words expressed her. *Coquine, coquette,* words like that, which could not be translated.

Soon after she got back to Mortal there had been a letter, sent on from Berkeley Square, from Mrs. Hastings saying that Mr. Hastings had died after a long illness. She asked Lavinia not to tell Molly yet. "I have not written to her," Mrs. Hasting said, "because I want time to settle down and Molly seems very happy in her work. Just knowing she can come now makes me very happy." And a lot about being so grateful to her and so on.

So that horrible man was dead. It was impossible to regret him. It was almost a kind of judgment. But the letter had made her think about Mr. Stead and Josephine Butler, the good people she met. Bramwell Booth. How shocked they would be if they knew about her! They would not be able to understand at all. How could a woman, dedicated to their cause of upholding chastity, of saving young girls, herself behave so loosely? There was no other word for it. Love, to them, would be no excuse.

Day after hot summer day, all this went round in her mind. Men and women. Their relationship with each other. What did one know of the people one saw, even of the people one knew? Who would be able to guess the past—and even the present—of the women in her household, including herself?

There had been a postcard from Stead at Lausanne, showing a picture of the castle at Chillon. They were having a lovely holiday. Everything was going very well. Eliza was in the South of France.

Then a week later there was a telegram from him sent from London. "Can I come and see you. Important. Stead." She wired back. "Come for the weekend."

Something was wrong. She'd ask John. With Stead in the house, he could stay the night. Affairs. He and Stead were known to be associated. Perhaps they'd manage something.

She was shocked at her own thoughts. Here was Stead in difficulties of some kind, and she was going to take advantage of the situation if she could. At dinner she told Muriel and Eva in front of the servants that Mr. Stead was coming down to stay next day, and that she was asking Mr. Longbeach too as there was a great deal to discuss. Then she turned to the butler and told him to see that the dogcart met the afternoon train from London.

Tomorrow there would be two men here, one of them John. She thought how strange the table was, with three women—or rather two women and a girl—sitting down every night in evening dress to be waited on by a butler and two footmen. Strange and unnatural.

When Stead arrived, John Longbeach was already there—the man of affairs—standing a pace behind and to the right of the chatelaine of Mortal, to greet her guest. These two would be the first to stay since the accident.

"Come in! Come in!" Lavinia said.

"How good of you to ask me, Mrs. Lenton," Stead said, taking her hand. A footman took his hat and light coat.

"We'll go into my room," Lavinia said, leading the way upstairs to her boudoir and ringing the bell for tea.

"Milk and sugar, Mr. Stead?" she asked.

"Yes, please."

"You're the same, aren't you, Mr. Longbeach, if I remember rightly?"

If she remembered. She must have poured him a hundred cups. How beautiful she looked! How gracious, pouring tea from the silver teapot.

She was dressed in pale blue with ruffles of lace at her throat and wrist. Her face was very pale, her hair pale gold—an aura lit by the sunlight behind her.

When Henry had left the crumpets in their silver-covered dish, the sandwiches and cakes on their three-tiered stand, Lavinia said: "And now what is it, Mr. Stead?"

"We had to give Eliza back. Her parents went to the police. They even sent a detective to Paris with Mr. Armstrong to find her."

Then his voice changed. "It's a put-up job," he said. "Someone is behind it."

"They are," John Longbeach said. "Caramine and her crew. I've heard rumors. I think they'll take you to court."

"For what?"

"For abduction."

"Me! When she's suffered no harm and they allow thousands of others . . ."

"I know," John said. "But they want to discredit you. If they can do that it will discount all we've done. All you have done. All the *Maiden Tribute* articles have done—all of it. We'll be worse off than we were before. We can't cry wolf twice. And they've got a lot of people on their side, the whole vice ring. Madams, procurers, watchers, pimps. There's a lot of money at stake. I don't think even we really know the profits they make. That's the money side. Then there's the pleasure side —the men like Cavendish Bentinck who want things to go on as they are."

This was the lawyer speaking. Lavinia liked this side of him. Serious, intelligent, unemotional.

Tonight she'd wear the cream merino—its bodice had long sleeves edged with embroidery—that suited her very well. Or the green, with deep kilting that reached to the ground. Then there was the dark red, with a basque bodice, pleated overskirt and a waterfall back. Or the blue pleated underskirt with a flowered silk skirt and a beige bodice. . . .

Somehow what she would wear tonight seemed very important. She'd talk it over with May. But how extraordinary it was to be thinking about clothes when Stead was in such trouble. Women. She suddenly detested herself and all her sex. It was the way they were brought up. To please men, at least to look beautiful for them. And what a disappointment they must be to them. Because if they were trained in deportment and to attract, to use their fans, to archness, to the rustling of taffeta petticoats and the flash of lace, they were also trained to restraint, to accept their husbands passively as a duty. Love? They knew nothing of love.

Blushing at her thoughts, Lavinia rose. "I'll leave you gentlemen to talk business," she said. "If I can help in any way, please let me know." The only help she could give them was financial.

The men got up and bowed. She walked down the passage to her bedroom to bathe and to discuss what she should wear with May.

Bathed and perfumed, her hair glistening from the brush and wearing the dark red basque bodice with pleated overskirt and a train that dragged on the carpet behind her, Lavinia went into the drawing room where the others were waiting for her, the two men in white ties and tails. Muriel in a pale green dress that Lavinia had bought for her because it set off her dark auburn hair, and Eva looking very charming and girlish in pale blue silk. It was Eva's first party. Lavinia was glad to see her so composed. All the women wore long white kid gloves.

The butler announced dinner as she came into the room.

The dining room, illuminated by candelabra, looked beautiful—the snow white cloth, the heavy glistening silver, the cut Waterford glass whose prism caught the candlelight. The *épergne* of dark red roses, that matched Lavinia's dress, perfumed the whole room. It was curious that dark red roses smelt better than those of any other color.

Muriel and Eva in their light colored evening dresses stood out, as did the white shirts and ties of the men, and the gloved arms of the women. Lavinia's dress disappeared against the darkness of the room, only flashing a rich ruby red as she moved and the silk moiré caught the light. It was low-cut and off the shoulder, to show her splendid arms and breast.

The dinner was simple—a clear bouillon followed by boiled salmon served with a white sauce garnished with slices of lemon and sprigs of parsley. Then came three roast chickens, carved by Mr. Longbeach, with mashed potatoes, carrots, and turnips as vegetables. The sweet was strawberry ice cream with an alternative savory of deviled marrow-bones on toast. The wines were a dry Sherry with the soup, and white Bordeaux—or Pommard for the men if they preferred it—with the en-trée. A bottle of Veuve Cliquot popped its cork festively for the sweet. Then came coffee and liqueurs.

The conversation was general—the health of the Queen, the size of the partridge coveys, the price of wheat, public education, corruption in the police force. It was mainly the men who talked. All Lavinia did was to guide the conversation, to throw the ball of subject into the pool of any silence that occurred. Muriel hardly spoke except to Eva, who said nothing but simply sat still, observant and flower pretty. Though she looked completely composed, Lavinia's mind was in a turmoil. Seeing John opposite her, looking so handsome in evening dress, affected her deeply.

Later, in the early hours, he would come to her room for the first time at Mortal. The room she had shared so long with Edward. One day she hoped he would always share it with her. One day. But how long would it be?

Lavinia rose and the other women followed her.

When they were alone, Stead said: "I feel better about things. Mrs. Lenton is a wonderful woman. Beautiful, calm, courageous."

"You've a stiff fight, Stead," Longbeach said, "but we're behind you. I can speak for Mrs. Lenton. Funds," he said vaguely, "and so on . . ."

"I know. And it's been wonderful to be here for an evening. Out of it all. So peaceful." They went into the smoking room and lit their cigars. "They've got money behind them," Stead said. "Influence. And the police are on their side, too."

"Naturally. The police were doing very well out of it—and still are. Law or no law, the madams aren't worried from what I hear. They think it will just cost them more. Golden bribes instead of silver ones."

"We'll bring it all out," Stead said. "We'll defeat them once the public really knows what's going on."

"I think you will, Stead. But they'll make you pay for it. I think I have an idea. I'll ask Mrs. Lenton to go to London and do some entertaining. It's not the season, of course, but while the trial is on, people will be only too ready to come up to London—a nine-day wonder."

"It will be more than that, Longbeach. It will be the end of an era."

Alone in his room, waiting for the time to pass, John Longbeach wondered what was the cause, the reason, for this cruelty and perversity. The bored satiety of the rich and powerful, able to take what they wanted from women, buy it from them with money, or the promise of favors or the fear of losing a job? Then the act itself—was this all that could be achieved? Was this all, this instant of release after so great an effort, plans, expenses, negotiations? There must be more. Was there more when it was taken by force from a screaming girl in a padded room? Was it the unwillingness of the victim, her resistance, her punishment, her being brought to heel like a whipped dog, lying pleading on her back? Did cruelty become an aim? Was the primary object to be made to feel great through the inspiration of fear?

Then there was hatred for the women of their own kind. Wives, often sickly, who granted men their rights as a duty. Of their mothers who had never loved them. All cumulative; bursting the dam of restraint in houses of ill fame, such as Caramine's, that catered to their wants.

How lucky he was with Lavinia, an exception to the frigid rule. Ashamed of her complacence, yet happy in it with a kind of perverse pleasure in the fact that it was sin. Surprised at her own body, delighted in his appreciation of it. Always at once hesitant and eager, diffident and bold. Brought up, schooled and trained to a code in which love such as theirs was considered as something for the lower classes alone, she had tried to fight it, confusing their passion at times with Maud's lust and mischief. But Maud was incapable of love. She had lovers to satisfy herself, her bodily demands, her vanity, her hatred of her husband—a man whose name was a byword even in London. Always there were reasons. Always cause and effect no matter how abominable they might be. If there had been no demand for the amenities Mrs. Caramine offered, there would be no Mrs. Caramines. In a way the good women produced the bad. His own life had not been blameless but he was no whoremaster, no skirt-chaser. As the occasion demanded, he had fulfilled his needs, quite expeditiously and without any memory of them afterward. But he could see how a rich and idle man was led, step by step, into debauchery.

He looked at the carriage clock on the mantelpiece. It was two. He put on his dressing gown and went into the passage that led to the main bedroom. Lavinia would be waiting for him.

THE LAW

The highest law is often the greatest roguery.

Terence

PART FOUR

THE LAW

The highest law is often the greatest roguery.

Terence

46 : Justice

At John's suggestion, Lavinia went back to London taking one of the carriages and more staff. She wanted to attend the trial of her friend. She wanted to be in on it, to see it, to suffer with Stead; after all she had been, in a way, instrumental in bringing the situation about. She was going to get up new petitions, pull all the strings she could with John's advice and help.

John was in her mind as much as Stead. Love was really a shocking thing, and she was more in love with him than ever.

Molly had rejoined her for a few days. She took her out to buy mourning. Her mother had at last told her about her father's death and she was going home to Oxford.

"You know, Mrs. Lenton, I can't be sorry about it. Is that wrong of me? Wicked, I mean?"

"What a question! I don't think so, dear."

"I'm glad you don't think so, because I value what you say and I hated him. Hated, hated, hated . . ."

Lavinia had never heard her so vehement. "I'll miss you, Molly," she said.

"I'll come and see you. Can I come and stay from time to time? And then there's my work, too. I must go to Mother now because she needs me, but I am going to try to get her to sell the house and business and come up to London and join in the work. Perhaps we could run a home for girls."

"That would be a good idea," Lavinia said. But at the moment her mind was full of the trial and the extraordinary course the events of the last few months were taking. And John. She was meeting him at the office at three—accompanied, of course, by May. The trial would begin tomorrow. But between now with Molly and tomorrow with Stead, was the afternoon. Would he like the dark blue? Should she wear her red hat with it, or would that be too gay?

Very quietly dressed, she took her place in the magistrate's court and was quickly aware that the tide of opinion had turned. It was running against Stead. There was a burning desire on the part of many people in court to see him discredited. Many people wanted the *Maiden Tribute to Modern Babylon* disproved because the accusations were so awful.

There were others—the white slavers and their clients—who wanted no change in the established customs. There was money in it; unbelievable sums. There was pleasure in it; unbelievable and unpublishable pleasures.

When the prisoner, Jarrett, was first placed in the dock, no one knew exactly what was coming, though the alleged abduction of Eliza Armstrong had been common gossip for months—since July, in fact. It was now September the 8th.

It had been arranged that the whole day should be devoted to the Armstrong case, the night cases being heard in the smaller court that was sometimes used for this purpose.

The court was crowded. Full, and still more people pushed their way in. Counsels, counsels' clerks, solicitors, solicitors' clerks. Reporters, the artists who would draw the protagonists—the accused in the dock or held in readiness for it, the accusers. In one group Mrs. Josephine Butler, Mrs. Stead, Mrs. Bramwell Booth.

Then the curious, crowding the court as if it were a theater, some well dressed, respectable, some too well dressed, flashy, and others just loafers, roughs who had pushed their way in. The legal profession in their robes looked like gray-wigged crows, pasty-faced as their parchments, or red-faced and flushed with port wine and good living. And over all, over the crowd, hung the lion and unicorn of England, on fumed oak paneling. The odor of justice was rank with stale sweat, the stale perfume of prostitutes and stale beer, all delicately blended with a mixture of disinfectant—Jeyes Fluid from the cells—touched with urine. Fear left a smell, lies and perjury had an odor, tears rotted like leaves into an invisible humus.

Death, defeat, victory, revenge—all had an atmosphere, a color, from dung to blood. From fumed oak yellow, to policeman blue. Stolid with precedent. Justice was performed here like an operation without anesthesia, and the crowd—always the Roman circus, thumbs-down crowd —crying for a victim, shouting: "Crucify him!" in their hearts. They had come to see the fun, to see the do-gooders hoisted with their own petard. To see the defamers of England's womanhood shown up. To see Stead who, for publicity, to boost the sale of his *Gazette,* had invented a tissue of salacious lies that had forced the paper's sale at the height of the *Maiden Tribute* series to a florin or more at the hands of scalping newsboys shouting pornography.

Rebecca Jarrett, tall and ravaged, came in between two jailers. She was dressed in a brown ulster with an umbrageous straw hat trimmed with green as if she needed shade in the courtroom. Stead, Bramwell

Booth, Jacques, Mesdames Combe and Mourez came, in single file, into the narrow strip that fronted the dock. Booth, in his blue Salvation Army uniform, looked like a policeman. Behind Jarrett were the Hallelujah Lassies in their neat serge dresses and poke bonnets. Pretty, some of them, and clean now in mind and body, purified souls saved from the burning pits of hell.

There was a buzz of talk: "Which is Stead? Is he the General? A pretty little tit. That's the bloody midwife." Coarse laughter. This was going to be quite a show, this was.

Mr. Poland, appearing for the prosecution, looked keen, sharp as a terrier out for rats. What an array of talent! Sir A. K. Stephenson, Solicitor to the Treasury. Mr. Charles Russell, Q.C., M.P., defending Mrs. Jarrett. Mr. Williams for Mr. Sampson Jacques, Mr. Waddy, Q.C., and Mr. Suthherst for Booth and Combe of the Army. Mr. Overend for Madame Mourez. Stead was conducting his own defense, aided by Mr. Lickfold of Lewis & Lewis.

At five minutes to eleven Mr. Vaughan, the presiding magistrate, entered the court and Mr. Poland launched his attack. He could hardly wait.

"Sir," Mr. Poland began, his hands clasped behind his back, "I do not propose to refer in detail to the various charges. The child, Eliza Armstrong, is the subject of this inquiry. She is the daughter of Charles and Elizabeth Armstrong. Charles Armstrong is a sweep and has lived with his family for a considerable time at Charles Street, Lissom-Grove in the parish of Marylebone. This girl is a little over thirteen years of age and appears to have been regularly sent to the board school and to have been well educated, having regard to her class. At the time when this matter commences—it commences with the second of June, the day before the Derby Day—there was living in the same street a married woman by the name of Mrs. Broughton, who was well known to the Armstrong family."

He paused and went on: "You will find beyond all controversy that Mrs. Broughton and Rebecca Jarrett had, in former years, been on very friendly terms, both indeed having been servants at Claridge's Hotel in Brook Street."

Mr. Poland paused again and went on: "On Tuesday, June second, Mrs. Jarrett called on Mrs. Broughton and told her she was married and needed a young girl to help her as she could no longer scrub floors herself.

"Mrs. Broughton mentioned two girls—one aged seventeen and one sixteen. They were too old. Why"—he glared round the court—"were they too old? Mrs. Jarrett insisted that the girl must be between thirteen and fourteen. Mrs. Broughton suggested Eliza. But her mother refused to let her go. She helped with the baby. But at last, being persuaded that Mrs. Jarrett was a respectable woman and being told that she would buy Eliza new clothes, she agreed on condition that she wrote home once a week and came to visit her parents once a month." Poland drank a glass of water. "The child," he said, "was now in the custody of the prisoner. And what did she do?"

"Well, what did she do?" a fat man shouted.

"Silence! Or I'll clear the court," Mr. Vaughan thundered, rapping the desk with his gavel.

"What did she do?" Poland asked, as if he were cross-examining himself, "She took her by omnibus—by two omnibuses—to a house in Albany Street, Regent's Park, where she met Mr. Stead and another lady, whose name we do not know or she would be a defendant before you, and they all had tea together. Eliza, Jarrett, Stead, and this unknown lady. Some articles of clothing were kept in a cupboard—a chemise and drawers—and the child was told to put them on.

"Then the child was taken in a hansom cab by Jarrett to No. 3 Milton Street, Dorset Square, the home of Madame Louise Mourez. After some conversation between the women, Eliza was left with the French midwife, who examined her. She screamed and when she went back to the other room said the French lady was a dirty woman.

"Leaving the house, the party took another cab and drove to Poland Street, Oxford Street, and on to a house that Mr. Stead himself has described as a brothel. Here the child was made to undress and go to bed. And something in a bottle was held to her nose by Jarrett who told her to have a good sniff. Mr. Stead himself has said that the material was chloroform. Mr. Stead then went into the room and the child screamed that there was a man in the room. Under the partial influence of the chloroform, she did not recognize him. Jarrett told her not to be frightened but to get up and dress again, as they were going somewhere else.

"They went by cab to another house and the girl was put to bed again. The following morning the unknown lady, Mrs. Combe, who is connected with the Salvation Army, and Jarrett took Eliza to Victoria Station where Mrs. Combe took charge of the child and carried her out of the country. Out of England, without the knowledge of her parents. Mr. Stead and the unknown lady were on the platform to see them off —destination, the Paris headquarters of the Salvation Army in France. This was on June fourth, the Eton holiday, and Jarrett wrote to Mrs.

Armstrong from Winchester to say the child was well and happy with her—a complete and utter fabrication. Eliza was in Paris, the sin capital of Europe.

"Then on June sixth Mr. Stead, the editor of the *Pall Mall Gazette,* brought out an article with the headlines: "CHILD OF THIRTEEN BOUGHT FOR FIVE POUNDS, giving a full account of all that had taken place on the third of June. No detail is omitted—the taking of the child from the mother, going to A—— Street (that is Albany), to P—— Street (Poland Street), even of examining the child as to her purity. He states the child had been bought from the mother for three pounds down and two pounds more after the certificate of virginity had been given. Lies," Mr. Poland shouted. "Lies. A vile fabrication from beginning to end.

"Other parts of the article in this newspaper I cannot read in public. It is too filthy almost to be referred to, but it alarmed the mother most terribly, because the description given led her to think something too terrible to think of had happened to the child." He paused dramatically and again stared round the courtroom before going on. "This girl was examined by a French midwife—intimately examined—taken to a brothel, drugged there and then taken abroad to the Continent.

"I do not say she was outraged," Mr. Poland continued, "when she was taken out of this country to France on Thursday, the fourth of June. But she had been outraged in this way, when she had been falsely and improperly detained and imprisoned, kept away from her mother and her family; and the feelings of the father and mother outraged.

"I will now read from the account which Mr. Stead gave of this matter on the twenty-first of August at St. James Hall.

" 'That we took the child from a place that was steeped in vice from a mother who was well aware she was going to a brothel, as she thought.' " Mr. Poland looked up from the paper he was reading and said: "If the mother's statement is true, this is a vile falsehood. To have printed it is a foul libel.

" 'And instead of taking her to a brothel,' " Mr. Poland again looked up and said: "Mark this!—'we placed her in good and Christian guardianship. We did take the girl to a brothel for about half an hour, but she did not know it was a brothel; she thought it was a hotel. No suspicion that anything was wrong crossed the girl's mind and when we took her away we placed her in the hands of the Salvation Army, who had absolutely nothing to do with taking her away from her mother's house or taking her to the brothel afterward. . . . As long as these crimes can be committed in secret places, they will go on being done. They are being done—I say that I know, not as a matter of hearsay but of absolute fact, that these deeds which we have exposed have been going on and are going on at this very moment.'

"And what happens next?" Mr. Poland asked, inserting his thumbs into the armholes of his waistcoat, swinging back his robes like a bird folding its wings and sticking out his belligerent head, the terrier again about to snap. "Mr. Stead, having abandoned this wretched child to the Salvation Army, goes to Switzerland for a holiday in the Alps." He made it sound like a crime. "So you see," Mr. Poland went on, "there is no doubt about the part of the chief director in this matter." He picked up the paper again and read:

" 'It was no part of our original intention to mention any names. But it has now become necessary to do so. At the outset of our inquiry we were informed that children of twelve and thirteen were procured by brothel keepers and decoy girls, examined by midwives, taken to brothels and there drugged or intoxicated before being violently outraged. One case in particular of a child just under thirteen who was ruined by force in a certain brothel—she shrieking in vain the while for her mother and crying to be taken home—came before us, but it was a matter of evidence, not of knowledge. In order to verify the possibility and the facility with which such crimes could be committed, I was, at the early stages of the inquiry, to employ an agent, in whose present integrity I firmly believe, but who had at one time kept a brothel in Marylebone.'

"I assume," Mr. Poland said, looking up, "that is Jarrett." He continued to read: " 'And who was believed by her friends to be still living a life of sin. If it were to be done again, I should have no need to use an agent—I could tomorrow buy a child twelve years of age direct from her mother for four pounds, and get a written receipt certifying she was being sold for prostitution. In this case the bargain was three pounds down and two after examination by a midwife had proved her to be all right. I was told that the bargain was not made with the mother but through the intermediary of a neighbor. As I only wanted the child in order to enable me to verify the facts already reported to me of the ease of procurement, certification, drugging, and rape, and then to rescue her from what appeared to be most demoralizing surroundings, I paid three pounds down on the day of delivery and subsequently gave two for transmission to Charles Street.' "

Mr. Poland now put the newspaper down and in a calm, penetrating voice, said: "I should consider Mr. Stead a very credulous man indeed if he believes that there is an English mother, even in poor circumstances, who would sell her child for prostitution and give a receipt certifying what she had done. They might trick the mother, as they did in this case, but as to there being any mothers who are prepared to sell their children for that purpose, I decline to believe."

He now raised his voice and went on: "I have some experience of vice in this city, and I believe it is a foul libel to say and to print that any English mother would sell her child into slavery and prostitution." He glared about him, the terrier turned bulldog and then, lowering his voice to a confidential tone, said: "And to prove my contention I will tell you what the mother did. What did she do? She was poor and the father was poor. They had a family to support"—sympathy oozed from Mr. Poland's lips—"the child was in the hands of the Salvation Army in Paris. What could the mother do against such an organization? Nothing." He folded his hands as if in prayer and looked upward at the ceiling of the court and went on: "Thank God there are people in this country who interest themselves on behalf of poor people. I do not mention their names but there were those who interfered on behalf of this woman. They advised her to go to Mr. Cooke of the Marylebone police court and make an application in regard to her child for the purpose of ascertaining whether these terrible suggestions were true or not. This was about the ninth or tenth of July, the article in the *Pall Mall Gazette* having appeared on the sixth. Mrs. Broughton was communicated with. She showed letters from Jarrett that upheld her contention of respectability. She was married to a commercial traveler named Sullivan. She lived in a six-room house. She was, in fact, a respectable householder. All lies. In another letter she said the child was well and in Winchester. There was no child in Winchester. Eliza Armstrong was in Paris. There was no child with Jarrett. Fraud upon fraud.

"And again I return to Mr. Stead's statement that except for the momentary surprise of the midwife's examination—'which was necessary to prove that a little harlot had not been palmed off on us'—she experienced not the slightest inconvenience. No inconvenience, indeed!

" 'No inconvenience,' Mr. Stead reiterated. 'Eliza was not the Lily of my article. But we took her over the same ground up to the very point where Lily had been outraged. . . .' "

Mr. Poland's pale face became suffused with the blood of righteous rage as he thundered: "The law deals with such conduct. The Treasury has taken up the case because Mr. and Mrs. Armstrong did not do what persons in a higher class of life would have done, that is take out a *habeas corpus*. I fail to see any possible excuse for this behavior, this shocking sequence of events.

" 'In no other way,' Stead said calmly, 'could we have proved by our own personal knowledge that a midwife would certify for immoral purposes, would sell chloroform for drugging the victim or that a brothel keeper would allow a child so young to be admitted to the premises for purposes of violation. I may say that I kept personal watch over the girl from the time she left the midwife until she was safely housed for the night, and that nothing could exceed the care which was taken to avoid imparting any impure thought to the child's mind. She has now been returned to her mother safe and sound and much improved in health and condition.' "

Mr. Poland appeared conciliatory as he said: "No one imputes misconduct toward the child when she was sent out of the country. They sent her to the Salvation Army and made her do housework because they thought it better for her than to be with her father and mother. But the fact remains that the child, Eliza Armstrong, was taken from her mother, taken out of the country, out of England. Picture it yourselves,"—he looked at the crowded court—"a young girl of thirteen subjected to such treatment and then carried away among strange people abroad. Mr. Stead has a great deal to answer for and I shall proceed to the evidence of the facts I have brought before you. Call Eliza Armstrong."

Lavinia Lenton, sitting next to her friends, Josephine Butler and Mrs. Stead, was appalled at the prosecution's line. Mr. Stead was being attacked for showing up evil. Attacked for the abduction of a child who had been returned unharmed when thousands of children, including her own, had been unprotected by the very laws which were now being invoked. This was a parody of justice, a mockery. Vast forces were behind this. The same that had delayed the passing of the Law Amendment Act for years, and would have stopped its passing again but for Stead's revelations, the Salvation Army's two-mile-long petition and other help.

"Call Eliza Armstrong!"

There she stood, her little friend, dressed in the grayish brown cape and the Duchess of Devonshire flower-trimmed hat Jarrett had bought her in June. A woolen muffler was the only addition to her dress. A whole summer had gone by since then, a whole London season. The partridge shooting had opened a week ago. This evening she was meeting John again at the office; she wondered what Mr. Poland would think if he knew she was the unknown woman.

47 : *A Good Little Scrubber*

"And how old are you, Eliza? I can't hear you, my dear. Bring the child a chair."

A chair was set in the well of the court facing the counsel, reporters and her friend, Rebecca Jarrett, who smiled at her.

Eliza adjusted the big hat that made her look like a mushroom.

Mr. Poland began again. "And now, my dear, how old are you?"

"Thirteen, sir."

"And until recently you were living at 32 Charles Street, Lissom-Grove, with your father, Charles, and mother, Elizabeth Armstrong. And your brothers and sisters. . . ."

The rigmarole that everyone knew; the recapitulations so dear to lawyers, pinning facts down like butterflies.

Mr. Poland said, "Did your mother bid you goodbye?"

"She kissed me beside the door before I went out."

"Then you and Mrs. Jarrett, whom you knew as Mrs. Sullivan, went to have tea in Albany Street?"

"Yes. With Mr. Stead and a lady."

"Then you went out to buy some clothes?"

"Mrs. Sullivan took me out to buy a chemise, a pair of drawers and a frock."

"Then you went back to Albany Street to put them on?"

"Yes. After that we went to a house in Milton Street in a cab. And Mrs. Sullivan asked for Madame."

"When Madame came what did Jarrett say?"

Eliza did not answer the question.

"Then Madame took you into another room, yes? And what took place then?"

"She lifted my clothes and touched me."

"Where were you when this took place?"

"I was standing beside her."

"Did you call out?"

"No, sir."

"Did she hurt you?"

"No, sir."

"Then your clothes were let down?"

"Yes, sir."

"And Jarrett was in the next room. Did you say anything to Jarrett?"

"I said: 'Madame was a dirty woman.'"

"Then you were driven to Poland Street?"

"Yes, sir. That's when Mrs. Sullivan got change at a ham and beef shop to pay the cabman. And we went into the house next door. Upstairs, into a front room—a bedroom."

"And after a little while Jarrett told you to go to bed?"

"Yes, sir."

"So you undressed and went to bed?"

"Yes, sir."

"Did Mrs. Jarrett do anything to you?"

"She put something on a handkerchief and put it on my nose and said: 'Give it a good sniff.'"

"Did you smell anything?"

"Yes. A funny smell. She said it was scent."

"What did you do then?"

"I threw the handkerchief away."

"Did anybody come in?"

"Yes."

"Did you see who came in?"

"I could not see, there were curtains all round the bed."

"What did you do?"

"I heard a voice, a man's voice, so I screamed out, 'There's a man in the room!' and I heard him go out. Mrs. Sullivan said: 'What's the matter, Eliza?' I said: 'There's a man in the room.' She put the curtain up and said: 'There's no man in the room.' And I said: 'No, because he's gone out of the room.'"

"What happened then?"

"Next day some ladies came—Mrs. Combe and the lady who had tea with us in Albany Street—and we went to the station with Mr. Stead."

"You don't know what station?"

"No, sir."

"And you were taken away in the train by Jarrett and Madame Combe?"

"Yes, sir."

"Who saw you off?"

"Mr. Stead and the lady."

Then followed the story of her sojourn in France—in Paris and at l'Oriole.

For Eliza the day in court had been no great ordeal. Nuffin' at all after what I been through, she thought. Traveled, that's what she was. Seen the world and abroad. But she did not like Mr. Poland. It struck her as strange that his name should be the same as the street where she had gone to bed and the man had come into her room after she had smelt the scent. Mr. Poland of Poland Street, Dorset Square. No, she didn't like 'im. Like a bloody ferret, he was. She'd seen ferrets often enough. Bert Toller, a rat-catcher up the street, had 'em, and terriers too. That Poland was like a terrier in some ways. A terrier, a ferret, and a rat. White-faced. She'd have sworn his eyes was pink if you'd asked her, which no one did. Just these silly questions. Yes sir. No sir. Did you undress when you went to bed? What did he think? Did he go to bed in his bats' wings and white wig and all? Gray it was, and looked as if it needed a good wash.

But it was rather nice sitting there with Rebecca in front of her, smiling at her. Dear Rebecca. Didn't she love her—not 'alf she didn't. And here she was sitting in the Queen's court like a queen herself, the center of everything with everyone listening to what she said.

She was a woman now, or just about, and women liked to be in the middle of things. Like an egg-cup under the crust in the middle of a pie.

The beautiful lady was there too, but she wasn't going to say she knew her. No bloody fear, she wasn't. And what were they saying about the Army and nice Mr. Booth? And dear Madame Combe who'd been so good to her? She was glad to be 'ome in dear old England again where she understood the lingo, but them people abroad hadn't been 'alf nice to her, they hadn't. And clean. Everybody was clean, and the houses and beds. Everything all clean. Spitted and polished. It was 'er baby brother she'd missed. If she could have had him with her she'd have stayed forever an' no complaints. Wot a little duck—runnin' nose and all.

But it was really hard to remember everything—what came first, what she had done when and with whom. Bloody inquisitive he was, that Mr. Poland. And what was all this fuss about Rebecca and Mr. Stead, as if they'd done something wrong? And her ma. They'd given her ma two quid and she'd gone to the pub with it. The Sailor. Of course she'd sold her. That is, having got the money she didn't give a damn no more. She'd seen the same thing happen to other girls in Lissom-Grove, and sometimes they'd come back later with babies, or sick. Like little old women, they was. But they'd been unlucky and not like her. In good 'ands, she'd been. New clothes and all. And a lovely big 'at that Rebecca had trimmed with her own hands. A real straw 'at it was, not a bonnet.

She turned away from Mr. Poland and the magistrate and looked at the body of the court. Mrs. Stead—how happy she had been at Cambridge House, playing with the children and dogs and stroking the pony's nose.

"Now Eliza, pay attention."

There he was at it again. What did you do then? Who was there? Then someone said: "Recess for lunch." Grub. Hungry she was. A nice steak and kidney pudding, perhaps, and a mug of beer—that would set her up. She suddenly felt weak and tired.

"Come on," her mother said, taking her wrist. She shook herself free. She wasn't going to be messed about by anyone no more. Not Ma, nor anyone. She wanted to be with Rebecca but they marched her out between two warders.

They had recessed for lunch but Stead's party had not gone out of the court. The crowd was hostile, provoked by agents of the opposition. Toughs organized by Solferino and his fraternity. It was hard to believe after the success of the *Maiden Tribute* articles and the passing of the act that the prosecution should take the line it was. Trying to discredit the Salvation Army, pillorying Stead. So far Lavinia's name had not come out—the unknown woman who had been with Stead at Albany Street.

John Longbeach tried to comfort her with his talk of British justice. Justice! This travesty . . . Lavinia's attention wandered. What would be the outcome of this trial?

The mother, Mrs. Armstrong, was now put on the stand. A pale haggard woman, wearing a shabby bonnet, with a gray woolen shawl thrown over her shoulders.

Mr. Poland addressed her: "Are you Elizabeth Armstrong? You live at 32 Charles Street? Is your husband a chimney sweep? You have six children—three boys and three girls? Was Eliza thirteen on April the eighteenth of this year?"

"Now," he continued, "were you at home on Tuesday, June second?"
"Yes."

"Was your little girl, Eliza, on the street nursing the baby?"
"Yes."

"Did she come and tell you about Mrs. Broughton's request and you went to see her? Did you find Jarrett there?"

"Yes. And I said: 'You can't have my child.'"

"And next day—Derby Day—did Mrs. Broughton come to you?"

"Yes, and I said: 'Nance, what kind of a woman is she? Do you think she is a generous woman?'"

"'Oh yes,' she said. 'Do you think I'd recommend her if she wasn't? I lived as a fellow servant with her, so I know. Come in and see her.' And I did."

"What did she say?"

"She said she was a cripple and wanted a girl who could kneel and clean about."

"'She's a good little scrubber,' I said. 'But she ain't very well off for clothes.' 'I'll buy her some,' she says. And she took the child away."

"Had she told you what her name was?"

"She said it was Sullivan."

"Had you consulted your husband before you let the child go into service?"

"No, and he was very angry when he found her gone."

"Did Mrs. Jarrett give you any money?"

"She gave me a shilling for the baby I had in my arms."

"Is that all the money you had from her?"

"Every farthing."

Mr. Poland looked round the court triumphantly. "And you did not hear from your daughter or know what had become of her?"

"Not till Nance Broughton showed me a letter from Mrs. Jarrett at Winchester, speaking of the child."

"And then your neighbors called your attention to the account in the *Pall Mall Gazette* of a girl being sold for five pounds?"

"Yes."

"And you went to the magistrate at the Marylebone police court?"

"Yes."

The hearing was now adjourned and bail was granted. The court would reconvene next day, Tuesday, Saturday, and the following Monday.

The defendants marched in single file from their pew and into the street, where the crowd, ill-tempered from the rain, was waiting to jeer them as they drove off in cabs that were standing ready.

48 : Three Women

Alone at Mortal with only Eva and her son, Frankie, for company, Muriel had plenty of time to think. The routine of the house was broken, its rhythm gone; with Mrs. Lenton away it just ran down like an unwound watch.

Muriel supervised Mr. Lenton's needs and the care his attendants took of him. There was little else she could do for him. His eyes haunted her—tortured, filled with hate, lust, and intelligence. He knew everything that was going on. There had unfortunately been no damage done to his brain. It seemed to live on in an entity incapable of expressing anything.

Her feelings about him were curious—those of a mother for an injured child. Those of a mistress for her lover. In her mind he was still that, particularly at Mortal where every room and passage had its own particular memory. Somehow his betrayal had never seemed real to her. Something due only to her pregnancy.

When Mrs. Lenton had agreed to Frankie's coming to stay with her, neither of them had considered the effect his arrival might have on his father. This heir who was no heir. This boy he could not claim as a son even if he wanted to.

The man who had made love to Muriel bore no relation to this cripple. That was on the one hand; on the other he had an immense claim on her and was always in her mind.

She missed Molly, who had now gone back to her mother after working for Mrs. Booth. They had been very close to each other but had exchanged no confidences. Molly knew Mrs. Lenton had told Muriel her story and left it at that. Nothing Mrs. Lenton said about Carrie Caramine was believed by Muriel. She had done her no harm. She had taken care of her and all but adopted Frankie. The stories were due to mischief makers. It was no use Lavinia asking her how she thought Mrs. Caramine lived on the scale she did. It was impossible to believe that a woman who had been so kind to her could be a monster trading in the flesh of girls. She refused to accept it because, had she believed it, she would have had to believe that Edward Lenton had sent her to Mrs. Caramine with orders to dispose of her. Naturally Carrie denied any such possibility the moment she had found out that she was pregnant.

"That's why he sent you to me, dear. To take care of you. He's such an old friend. All his family." So what possible reason was there to believe anything else? Then he had lost touch with her. . . . Mrs. Caramine said it was best that way. "Forget him, my dear. I'll find a nice respectable man for you to marry." If it had not been for that, Edward would have set her up in a little house once the baby had been born. She was sure of that. She bore Edward no grudge. She could believe no evil of this man who had loved her so passionately. Nor could she understand Lavinia's coldness. She did not look cold. Yet Edward had told her of his difficulties with her—of her lack of affection, of her repulsing him time and time again. Then there were Lavinia's stories of Ellen whom, she said, he had also sent to Mrs. Caramine. "Just the way he did you, Muriel." And of Delphine, who had abducted the children. He certainly could have had no part in any of this, not with his own daughters. Poor, poor Edward, how misunderstood he had always been!

But it made her happy to be in the same house with him again. Mortal, that held so many beautiful memories for her. And to be teaching Evangeline once more, to see her mind growing, to see her taking hold of life again and coming out of the cocoon of infancy into which she had retreated.

Nothing Lavinia had told her about Mrs. Caramine or the houses she kept, or white slavery, had made any real impression on her. Even Molly's story was as unreal as a horrible fairy tale.

And now she was alone with them, with the people she loved most. Edward, Eva, Frankie. She was grateful to Lavinia for letting her stay and have the boy, but there was a barrier between them, despite shared confidences, that she knew could not be broken down. It was not merely one of station, of class, of money. It was not due to their both having had children by the same man. It was one of temperament: The oil of her hot heart could not mix with the water of Lavinia's cold one. It was impossible for her to imagine Lavinia ever being in love.

Eva was beginning to lead a normal life. Muriel had taken over where she had left off as a governess all those years ago. Even with the same books. And Eva had recovered, except that she was young for her age. Back to ten or eleven, with no signs of growing maturity. Nature had buried the past but had lost much more than a year in the process. This was not a young woman; it was a charming child, very well grown for her age. Indeed physically, Eva looked nineteen while her interests remained those of a child just beyond the doll-playing stage. Emma was still her nurse. Dr. Jarvis still visited her every week or so when he dropped in to see Edward. Mac never left Eva's side except when Mrs. Lenton was at Mortal. She used to walk about the garden with her hand on his neck. A pretty picture—sentimental. A tall fair girl and a great shaggy hound.

Dr. Jarvis questioned her about dreams.

"Oh no, doctor, I never dream."

"That's right, sir," Emma said. "Sleeps like a baby. Never moves. I ought to know because I sleep in the same room."

No dreams. That was good. But there was still something that worried the doctor. Not in her face. Calm, beautiful, completely unworried, almost expressionless. It was in the eyes and only there for flashing seconds. He could not even be sure that he had really seen it. Eva had no recollection of such moments, none at all. She was happy. She loved Muriel. She missed Molly but Molly had become more Muriel's friend than hers though they had spent much time together.

One thing she did not do but nobody seemed to notice it. She never went near the library. She enjoyed being with Frankie, her unknown half-brother. They had sympathy for each other—the girl who was so young for her age, the little boy who was already something of a man, protective toward her.

With no idea of how he tortured him, Frankie spent a great deal of time with Edward Lenton, walking beside his bathchair when one of his men pushed him along the garden paths. It was he who took Eva to him one afternoon.

"Come on, Eva," he said. "Come and walk with the Master. You can push him if you like." Lenton was still the master—inert, silent.

"No Frankie!" she said. "No! No!"

Then something came over her. The light that Dr. Jarvis had seen flashed for an instant in her eyes. She extended her hands to Frankie and sprang up from the grass. "Yes! Yes!" she said. "Let's do it."

"Do it?" he said. "Do what?"

Do what? Eva did not seem to understand the question. Then she said: "Walk with him, of course—push his chair."

For half an hour they pushed the chair up the long grass walk that ran between the wide herbaceous borders. Up and down, up and down. Frankie pushing in front of her, her arms on the outside of his on the metal bar. Behind them one of the male nurses walked in boredom.

Christ Almighty, what a place! Fancy living here—just trees and grass and bloody flowers. If it hadn't been for a girl in the village he couldn't have stuck it—money or no money, good food or no good food. And that little bitch pushing the bloody chair—a nice bit of stuff she was. Still, greens was greens and things might be worse on that score.

After that Eva pushed her father about the garden every day it did not rain, and that was most days. It was a fine summer with corn-crakes in the fields sounding like a thumbnail run along a comb. With yellow hammers in the hedges, saying "A little bit of bread and no cheese." With cock pheasants calling, rooks in the trees and jackdaws in the chimneys. It was beautiful. Hot, with just a taste of autumn in the morning mists that were flung like a blanket over the water meadows.

Oh, she was happy! Happy, singing-happy. Everything was going to come right, she could feel it in her heart. Oh yes, she was singing all over. But she was not going to let anyone know.

In Oxford Molly was sitting in the little garden at the back of the house. It was Saturday and her mother would be out in a moment. Her dear Mama. How extraordinary it was without Papa. The house, which had always seemed like a prison, was now a home. And Mama had made no changes. It was just that . . . well, that's what it was but she didn't want to say so. Even to think it. She was sorry now about what she had said to Mrs. Lenton when she had heard about her father's death. So she put it away from her with all the other awful things and thought about Mortal and Muriel and Eva and Mrs. Lenton, and how kind everyone had been to her.

She pulled down the hem of her dress, one of Madame Elsie's, and a shiver went through her. Those hands on her. . . . And something must have happened because Mrs. Lenton had said: "We'll never go back there again, Molly."

Mrs. Hastings came into the garden, her small, quick feet moving like a mechanical toy. Clockwork. Wound up by her own happiness. Her child, her darling, her baby. Molly sitting there good as gold, pretty as a calendar, on a wicker chair under the laburnum. What a shame it was over—she would have looked so beautiful under those long golden blooms.

"Molly!" she cried.

"Mama!" Molly jumped up and came to her arms. "You must sit down, Mama," she said. "I'll go and squeeze a lemon and make a nice lemonade."

"Yes, darling." How wonderful—lemonade! He had always been against things like that. Against anything nice. Lemonade, ice cream, cakes, trifle with a bit of sherry in it. Well, she'd given him his chance, that she had. And it had been a wonderful funeral. Even if nobody had loved Joseph Hastings, he had been much respected. There had been customers there, her friends now. His chapel people, of course. And some wholesalers, salesmen. Yes, a good funeral. No expense spared. A two-horse hearse. And where's Molly, people had asked. Very few of them believed she was dead. If she had been dead there would have been a bit in the paper. That was what people like them did, respectable, middle-class people. "Abroad," she'd said. "My Molly's abroad. He"—she'd nodded at the grave—"didn't hold with abroad, so he cut us off from her. But she's coming back. Quite a young lady now, you'll see. Got work in Paris as a companion to an old lady. A countess," she'd added, "with a castle." Might as well be hung for a sheep as a lamb. Hung, indeed. For a second she'd blanched. That could have happened. . . .

But she'd get married now, with her looks and the finish that nice Mrs. Lenton had given her. Marry a nice young chap, in trade say, and have babies. She settled down in her chair flecked by the sun shining through the laburnum, and cradled an imaginary grandchild in her arms.

49 : The Old Bailey

Lavinia, John, and the others no longer went to the magistrate's court. It was the Old Bailey now, the greatest and most sinister court in England. Pompous with death, with obloquy. No one left this court unscathed. Even the innocent were tarred with publicity. "Had up, wasn't he? Got off. Yes. But there ain't no fire without smoke."

The snowball that had grown from the first letter Josephine Butler had written to Stead to this avalanche that would rock England, that had already changed the law and that would, in the end, have world-wide repercussions.

The trial began on October 23rd, a beautiful autumn day, the park trees stained with brown and gold, the flower shops full of chrysanthemums. The flower women by the Eros statue in Piccadilly—how apt a place to put them—old whores sitting by their baskets of flowers watching with bleary, cynical, gin-soaked eyes the efforts of the young women of today to seduce the passersby. Anything in trousers that had a few bob in their pockets. Christ, what they didn't know wasn't worth knowing. Lord, in their time they'd walked and stood in the streets. They nodded their bonnets. "Buy some nice vi'lets, Mister! Vi'lets! A carnation, real 'ot 'ouse, for your buttonhole." Laugh—you couldn't 'alf laugh to think of it! Like bloody flowers they'd been themselves once!

For twenty-three days the pheasants had been falling to the guns. High birds—rocketers—driven over elms and beeches, the loaders passing the second gun, the black retrievers bringing in the birds, their mouths as gentle as baby fingers. England, October the 23rd, 1885.

But at the Old Bailey there was majesty. Wigs, robes. Not a judge here who had not at some time in his life put on a black cap to condemn some miscreant to die, to be hanged by the neck. It was all here—a miasma, the usual odor of disinfectant, of urine, of sweat, of parchment—the gloom of the great court, the anterooms, and passages reminiscent of prison. Like God, in every courtroom the lion and unicorn of England stood rampant on their shields. And what the hell had they got to do with justice or England? There had never been lions in England, and the unicorn did not exist.

Mr. Justice Lopez was the judge. Sir Richard Webster conducted the prosecution, curiously enough, since it was he who had put the frills onto the Criminal Law Amendment Act. Charles Russell, Q.C., M.P., defended Jarrett. Waddy defended Bramwell Booth. Stead had continued to conduct his own defense. What an affair, with Virtue in the dock and Justice suitably blindfolded! Lopez, thin and bearded, entered the court surrounded by aldermen, sheriffs, and all the pomp of medieval England. The Clerk of Arraigns read out the charges.

The defendants had on divers days between June 3rd and August 24th feloniously by force and fraud taken away and detained Eliza Armstrong, a child under fourteen, with intent to deprive her parents of the possession of her, etcetera, etcetera. The voice droned on. The crowded court was silent.

A second charge was made against the defendants for indecently assaulting the child. The charges and the procedure resembled those of the previous trial. This was simply an echo, but louder and grander than the original sound. Everything, like the court itself, was on a bigger scale.

Eliza was called first. Neat and clean and self-possessed, she made a good impression.

"Of course I thought I was going into service when Mrs. Jarrett took me away. Mrs. Jarrett was very kind to me."

Things looked good for the defense. This was not a child who had been raped and abused. Mrs. Armstrong came next, her face pasty and blotched, her double chin running into an enormous bosom. Her friend, Mrs. Broughton, said that her friend, Mrs. Jarrett, had worked with her at Claridge's Hotel. "Quite a respectable place, I understand, m'lud." And that was why she had changed her mind and let Eliza go. Then came the story about the row with her husband for letting the kid go.

"And when was that?"

"Between eight and nine."

"And when were you taken into custody?"

"About ten o'clock."

"What were you taken into custody for, Mrs. Armstrong? You have been in trouble before, have you not?"

Mrs. Armstrong glared at the lawyer. "Trouble for what? I've never bin a tart or a thief."

"Have you been charged with assault?"

"Yes, by my sister-in-law."

"Have you ever been charged with drunkenness?"

"Yes, but I've never bin in jug."

"Were you drunk on June third?"

"That's wot they say."

"Had you your infant in your arms?"

"Well, if I was drunk I don't remember."

Things still looked good. Mrs. Armstrong was obviously a woman of doubtful character. The trial dragged on. The court was always crowded. Lavinia Lenton and John Longbeach went every day.

The defense now began. Mr. Russell said that the act, which now protected hitherto unprotected persons, was entirely due to the efforts of the defendants. Waddy, for Booth, said that his client had done nothing but take care of the child.

Then Stead spoke: "I propose to set forth my case as briefly as I can by telling you a plain, straightforward story, not as a counsel who acts as a mouthpiece for a client, but as one who speaks on his own behalf, and says to you not what he is instructed to say but what he believes." He then explained his motives for planning the alleged abduction of Eliza, but was interrupted by the judge:

"I wish to give you every possible reasonable latitude that I can," said Lopez, "but you must recollect—as I've already said firmly, and I shall say very firmly again when the time arrives—that the motive has nothing whatever to do with the crime which is charged in this indictment."

Stead continued: "I am not here to advocate any liberties being taken with the children of anyone, least of all with the children of the poor, but I'm prepared to call witnesses—the secretary of the Society for the

Prevention of Cruelty to Children, Dr. Barnado, and others if I'm allowed—to prove to you that the detaining of children from parents, who have a legal right to them but who have forfeited all moral right, is one of the practices most familiar to charitable and philanthropic persons in this country. You have got to take some risk to save a girl from ruin; I believe that in doing what I was doing with Eliza Armstrong, I was standing between her and ruin. I hope and believe that when you have heard the evidence I shall call, and when you can realize—however imperfectly—as I had had to realize, for months and months, the full significance of that infernal system known as the white slave traffic, you will find that no body of Englishmen should return a verdict against me."

The judge interrupted several times but still the tide of feeling was in Stead's favor. Lavinia was thinking how well things were going and was allowing herself to go over in her mind the details of the dinner party she was giving that night.

There were big crowds outside in the Strand. Ugly crowds. White slavers, runners, pimps, toughs. Basher was there with a gang he had collected. Solferino, very smartly dressed, was on the outskirts, on the fringe of it, when Mrs. Caramine drove up in her carriage with two baskets of rotten eggs that she handed out.

"You'll know what to do with 'em, boys," she said. The crowd cheered her. One of the old kind, she was, with no bloody nonsense, spoiling people's fun and washing dirty linen in public.

Rebecca Jarrett had found the first trial almost more than she could bear. When she was released on bail she found her name in big letters outside a waxworks show. She paid threepence and went in to see a harridan in wax. Her mind went back to the beginning of it all when Mr. Stead had asked Josephine Butler if she could help him to buy a little girl. She remembered Mrs. Butler's horror at having to ask her if she would undertake the job. "You can do it, Rebecca, but I couldn't. You know the people, they'll trust you."

That was the awful part of it—she did. She was known as a brothel keeper; that was what she had been before she was saved. A whore and a brothel keeper. Anyone who sold her a child would be under no illusions about the use she would be put to. How she had prayed to God to give her the strength to go back to her old companions. And she did it. She did everything Josephine had asked her to do. And now she was going to pay for it. Funny it was, having been a whore and a madam—and no trouble at all—to find herself, now that she was saved, in it up to the bloody neck.

At the luncheon recess Stead was confident about the way things were going. True, coming out of the court, they had been jeered at and had some rotten eggs thrown at them. But none had hit their mark. Stead, Booth, Mrs. Lenton, and John Longbeach had chump chops and coffee for lunch. "Nothing to worry about, Mrs. Lenton," Stead said. And she agreed with him, her mind on the dinner and on John. So near to her always and yet so unapproachable in public.

In the afternoon things changed. The Attorney General examined Jarrett: "In the past, before you were employed at Claridge's, you kept gay houses?"

"Please, sir, don't go into my past. I've been saved."

But he went on. He destroyed her. She was not going to betray her old friends, bad though they might be. She lost her head. She contradicted herself, perjured herself. She burst into tears. But Sir Richard Webster drove on. When he asked her about Lily in the *Pall Mall Gazette* article, she shouted: "Lies! All lies!" Then, almost hysterically, she cried: "I think Mr. Stead made a mistake . . ."

The court gasped. Here was a turn they had not expected. There were shouts of "Muckrakers!" The judge threatened to clear the court.

The Attorney General attacked again: "Do you mean that, having had your attention called to all the details in the article, you now deny that it is about Eliza?"

Rebecca beat the edge of the box with her fists. "Let me speak. I want to tell the truth."

"You are on oath. Do you mean you have not been telling the truth?"

"No. Yes. But there's another little girl I think is Lily."

"What made you think that?" the judge asked.

"The child told me herself."

Sir Richard returned to the attack. "Do you mean someone has told you that there's another little girl?"

"There is another little girl. Her name is Grace, and it's all lies the Lily stuff."

Stead now examined her. He could not believe that she had done this to him. Had destroyed him.

"I heard you say, sir," she said, "that Lily was not Eliza but that she was made up of two little girls, Eliza and Grace, who were actually had in a brothel."

Josephine Butler was called to the stand. She told of her relationship with Jarrett and of her work in the rescue home.

Stead returned. He gave in great detail an account of his investigations of the vice ring and the white slave traffic in London, tracing his interest in the subject back to the letter he had received ten years ago, while still on the *Northern Echo,* from Josephine Butler.

"Did you ever communicate with the police about the awful cases you discovered?" the judge asked.

"No."

"Why not?"

"Because ninety-nine out of every hundred of them could have escaped unpunished. There was then no law to protect their victims. No Criminal Amendment Act had been passed." He glared round him. They had brought him to bay.

"Did it occur to you that in pursuing this course you were tempting poor parents to commit crimes?"

"No," Stead said. "I only wanted to buy girls who were already in the market; girls who, if I hadn't bought them, would have been seduced."

"Do you mean," the judge said, "that Eliza Armstrong was in the market?"

Every eye shifted to Eliza. That sentence had changed her from an almost impersonal witness to her own abduction to a victim or a prize. They suddenly saw her as a slave on the block.

The Archbishop of Canterbury was called next. Never before had a British Primate been asked to appear at a criminal prosecution. His presence was objected to by the Attorney General. The judge sustained his objection and Stead protested. "M'lud, unless the whole nature of my operation is placed before the jury, how are they to decide?"

"The only question we are trying, Mr. Stead," the judge said, "is whether the child was taken away against the will of her father."

"Then, my lord, I am not allowed to show the true cause and nature of my operation. That it was inconsistent with any intent to abduct for any criminal purpose."

"Intention has nothing to do with it. The only question is the unlawful taking away of the child. Motive is not for the jury to consider."

The Attorney General said: "The question is, whether in your attempt to do good, you have not overstepped the law."

That was the end of the matter for that day. Now it was obvious which way the case was going. The law which Stead had forced through with his *Maiden Tribute* pieces was being turned upon him.

He thought of the forces against him—not merely the slavers and the men they pandered to, but the police to whom vice was a source of profit. A blind eye cost money, but given money enough they were ready to go blind. But worse than that was the Government's intention of discrediting him and whitewashing the frightful facts he had unearthed. For the sake of England, of her prestige, trade relations, and diplomacy, it was essential that the whole thing should be proved to be a *canard*. A bit of yellow journalism by an editor who knew that pornography would sell.

Justice. Where was Justice? At this moment, law or no law, girls were being sold on the streets of London, raped, debauched, and sent abroad as if they were cattle.

50 : The Necklace

Maud Cockshott was happy to have ended the affair with Geoffrey. It had become tedious. Lord, what a scene there had almost been when he'd said he'd shoot himself, and she'd told him to go to Caramine's, to the French girl there everyone was talking about. And Harold had been home waiting for her. My God, the indignity of it and her not able to protest. But when you tricked a man—and he knew of it—he had you, a lamb to the slaughter. All this was in the back of her mind, like the backdrop of a play, as Louise did her dark hair, brushing it with long, soothing strokes.

"And what will Madame wear tonight?" As if there was any question about it—the new gray satin from Madame Elsie. Their first dinner party since Cockshott's death. Everything had been black till now. Black, then gray, white, mauve, purple. Mourning, the compliment of the survivors to the dead. She should have worn black longer. It was very soon to go to a big dinner party but Cockshott had been so old. Dead socially for so long. Ill so long, a recluse, that nobody would mind. Besides, he'd have to let her wear the jewels now. Tonight. The famous Cockshott emeralds. She had not even seen them, she only knew of them by hearsay. Third-hand from her friends, whose dead grandmothers had told them of their green glory. The diamonds, too.

They had come up to London for a few days and were going to dine with Lavinia. What a good performance she was putting up with her friend, Stead, in the dock on a charge of abduction. How sordid it all was and what a pity she had ever got mixed up in it.

Harold did not really like the country and managed to find excuses to get away from it, and she generally came with him. Business, indeed. She knew his business. Most of it was conducted in Coak Street.

She wondered how Lavinia was getting on with her lawyer. A most extraordinary affair. But she had been very discreet. There was never a word of gossip about her. She hoped they would manage a word or two in private tonight. Or perhaps they would be able to arrange a luncheon. How nice it was to be back in London and mistress of the big house in Grosvenor Square. What a pity the old man had lived so long, doing them out of the place. She thought of Geoffrey. Poor Geoffrey! But what a bore he had become. She had not replaced him and her heart was free. That was a bore too. She enjoyed intrigue and missed it. But the trial was exciting. It was wonderful being on the spot rather than getting the news hot off the presses.

When Harold came in, her maid bobbed him a curtsey and left the room. He had a large leather case in his hand. The jewels. But she pretended to ignore it.

"I suppose you want to wear the emeralds, Maud," he said.

"It would look funny if I didn't. People might think you'd sold them."

He laughed. "I would if they weren't entailed, but they are. You can wear them, Maud, but I want to see you first."

"See me?"

"Yes, darling. See you in them and nothing else. See you the way your lovers have seen you."

"How common you are, Harold. Haven't you seen enough naked women at Carrie Caramine's?"

"I see we have no secrets from each other, darling. But either you do what I say or you don't wear them."

He opened the case and poured the jewels out onto the bed—a shining heap of green and ruby red, of blue and flashing white. He held up a rope of pearls. "That will go around your waist," he said. He dropped it and showed her a pair of diamond bracelets. "These will fit your ankles. You have lovely ankles."

"No," Maud said. "Certainly not."

Then she changed her mind. Why not? She was his wife. How beautiful she would look nude and bejewelled. The diamond collar, the great emerald pendant and earrings. Bracelets, anklets. A harem houri. She wished she could be painted that way. She began to laugh.

He wanted her to resist him. That was the mistake she had always made. Well, she wouldn't. By God, she thought, I'll make him fall in love with me.

"You must help me put them on," she said, as she began to undress.

In Berkeley Square Lavinia Lenton was dressing too. All over London women were dressing for dinner. What a terrible day it had been in court. Mrs. Caramine had again appeared in her carriage and distributed rotten eggs and fruit. And then the climax—Rebecca Jarrett breaking down under cross-examination and the whole defense collapsing like a house of cards. How sorry she was for Stead—for what he had already gone through and what was still to come.

But whatever happened, he had done it. The Law Amendment Act was on the statute books. For a few hours she'd put it out of her mind. The tide would turn and she wanted people to see that she was not afraid of being associated with Stead. She stared at herself in the glass as May brushed out her hair. She knew she was *en beauté* tonight. Love had made her bloom. The anxiety of the trial and the proximity of her lover had shadowed her eyes so that they looked enormous. She looked and felt voluptuous. A woman. Slim still, but a slim Venus who might one day, in ten years or so, turn into a Juno. She supposed John was dressing too. She wished she could watch him tie his white tie. She wondered if he would wear a buttonhole. She wondered . . . No, that would be impossible tonight. Tomorrow, perhaps. Always a tomorrow to look forward to, to wait for. She knew Maud would try to get her alone to exchange confidences.

"And what will Madam wear?" May asked.

"What shall I wear?"

"The pale blue, Madam."

"All right, the pale blue." It was a beautiful dress of ribbed silk embroidered with tiny bouquets of flowers and cut very low off the shoulder in front. It had a tiny bustle of braided basketwork that formed a shelf for a cascade of lace that descended to the floor in a trailing train. The bustle was fastened around the waist with a tape. She would wear two taffeta petticoats; one white, and over it a blue one, slightly paler than the dress which had two hanging panels of lace in the sides that matched the train. The whole effect was one of water, of fluidity, pale blue and foaming white, the rustle of her petticoats around her legs like the bubbling of a trout stream.

She was profoundly shocked at her own feelings. Here she was, happy because she was going to be beautiful for her lover. Because she was giving her first dinner party in London in order to interest people in the cause that was so near her heart—and yet disaster had struck her friend, Stead. Of course she was sorry, but she could not really feel it.

May brought out her jewel box. Diamonds and sapphires tonight to match her dress, her eyes, her mood. Things would come right, she was sure of it. Molly was safe at home and happy. Muriel was content at Mortal with Edward and their son. This business of Stead's would come right too. She felt it. She put her hand to her breast. And I? Me and John? Us? That, too, would come right. Look at what had happened already, look how her life had changed! Eva was better—almost well, Doctor Jarvis said. There was only her loss of Betty. Betty seemed a long way off now, with Molly almost a daughter.

She pulled on her long white gloves, working them over her fingers one at a time, almost as tight as her skin. A formal look in the long glass, a twitch to her train from the kneeling May who, looking up, said: "Madam looks beautiful tonight." She went down the stairs, one hand on the polished mahogany rail. Poured down it like a rustling waterfall to find John Longbeach waiting for her at the bottom of the stairs. He had just arrived. Another good sign.

By eight-thirty all the guests had assembled in the drawing room. The windows were open onto Berkeley Square. Carriages and pairs were driving around it, taking people to dinner. There was the sharp clip-clop of well-bred, well-fed horses. The street lights caught their shining flanks and the top hats of the coachmen. From the distance came the drone of the Piccadilly traffic. There were flowers in all the vases—roses, chrysanthemums. Potted palms and ferns stood in the fireplace.

Lavinia thought she had never seen Maud look so beautiful, or Cockshott more attentive. They might have been lovers. So those were the famous emeralds—they were indeed magnificent. Green, blue, red, black, purple—the women moved chattering and rustling, using their fans. The men in tails, their white starched shirts touched with yellow by the lamplight.

The butler announced dinner. Lavinia went down on the arm of Lord Taudel. Pair by pair, the bright and the dark, in a wave of perfume and laughter to find their place names at the table. It was a big dinner, formal in the sense that everything and everyone was decorated to their fullest extent. Informal in that they were well known to each other—some since childhood.

The ladies were extracting their fingers from their gloves and tucking them into their wrists. Maud, eating her turtle soup, could not help looking down at the emerald pendant. It hung rather low on its golden chain. But who would have imagined the chain was long enough to span her waist? She caught her husband's eye further down the other side of the table. What a beast he was! She smiled at him.

The conversation with the butler and two footmen in the room was banal—pheasant shooting, cubbing, gardens, the health of the Queen. After the *chaud-froid* sweet—ice cream with a hot chocolate sauce— Lavinia gave her signal and the ladies rose like a flock of brightly colored birds frightened by a shot, their petticoats rustling like wings, and the men were left to their port. Cockshott took a cigar case out of his pocket, opened it, looked at the cigars and put it back. The other men laughed.

"A lot to be said for dinner at Carrie's, isn't there, Harold?" No one smoked at decent houses except in smoking rooms dedicated to the weed, and then only when wearing velvet smoking jackets and caps so that no odor was carried into other parts of the house.

They talked about horses, women, hunting, shooting and fishing, until Lord Taudel said: "I suppose we'd better join the ladies."

"The bitch pack," Cockshott said.

"Well, you should know about that," Martindale said.

"I do, Marty. I do, indeed." And they went out laughing, chaffing each other. Rich men at ease in any company, without a care in the world. No one had mentioned the trial except Cockshott, who said: "That muckraker, Stead, is going to get it in the neck."

"What a fool he's been to bring up all that stuff, as if anything could be changed," someone said.

"Do you want it changed?" Cockshott asked, as they went upstairs to their ladies. Ladies of their own flesh, their own kind. Not the sort you bought for pleasure.

51 : Solferino

Upstairs at Carrie Caramine's another party was going on. Very small, very select. Carrie herself, Ada, Solferino, Ellen, Madame Elsie and Captain Glover of the Merchant Service. Solferino, very dashing and smart in a long skirted buff-colored coat and tight trousers, with a blue and white spotted Ascot tie pierced by a large horseshoe pin of diamonds, held the floor. He had a glass of port in his hand. He looked flushed with drink and excitement.

"By God, we've got 'em by the short hair, Carrie," he said. "What happened at the Old Bailey today has settled their hash. And once it's done, it's done. They can't start it over again. They've blown the bloody gaff." He took a gulp of wine. "And the crowd was nasty too. 'Ad enough of them do-gooders. Spoil sports that's wot they are, and out to ruin business." He began to laugh. "Good, them rotten eggs was. They liked throwin' 'em. Funny thing a crowd, Carrie. They like to chuck things. No one can say you done anything to anyone, not if it's throwing. Not like a cosh."

"Sit down," Carrie said. "I think you're right." She looked round the group with cold, dark eyes.

Extraordinary eyes, that woman had. Like black stones. Unnatural-like.

"We've got the Government on our side." She laughed. "Dirty, that's what it is, and they don't want it public. But we've got to be careful. Go steady for a bit. A scandal now could really ruin us."

"Go slow?" Solferino said, "when I've got five little tits lined up for you? Beauties, fresh as butter!"

"Then you can break 'em in yourself, Solferino. No more young ones for me for a bit. That's what I told a certain personage"—everyone knew whom she meant—"who sent for me to say he felt like one. 'No, my lord,' I said, 'you'll have to manage with big girls for a bit.' Quite broke him up, that did; he's no good with big girls, got out of the way of them, I suppose. But I said: 'It's that or nothing, my lord.'"

She looked at Captain Glover. "That's why the Captain's here, Solferino. I'm clearing out my girls—in the other houses, that is."

"But . . . " Solferino said.

"That's it. Things are going well in court, but there'll be a swing-back, you wait and see. The Salvation Army, Doctor Barnado, the lot of them, they'll not rest. . . ."

Madame Elsie said: "Well, we've had a good run for our money."

Ellen laughed. "Getting respectable, aren't we?"

"No, darling," Mrs. Caramine said, "we're just going to steer clear of the law."

Solferino gave himself another glass of port.

Downstairs the evening had begun. Business, up to a point, was going on as usual.

Solferino, with his beige billycock hat pushed back on his head and swinging his loaded stick, had plenty to think about as he walked home through the streets that he regarded as his property. Girls were his business; he had begun life pimping for his big sister in Malta. Sailors, mostly. Then by the time he was twelve he had a stable of kids working for him. He had style, Solferino did, and he knew it. He knocked 'em cold. Girls and women fell for him. Men he could deal with. A mean, below-the-belt fighter in no way averse to using his feet. And even as a boy he'd hired bullies, big bruisers, who for a few pints and free greens would take care of him. He was quick with a knife and had used acid. That soon brought them to heel. What else had they but their looks and their backs? After the first couple of times the threat of it was enough. But it was a bugger about the kids. That was a good business that was, or had been. Basher'd be upset, too. Still, there might be a way around it.

He greeted his girls and his watchers with a nod as he passed them. Keep 'em on the job.

The women, now that they were alone, let their hair down. Solferino got on their nerves—the arrogance of him!

"I hate that bastard," Ellen said. She hadn't liked the way he had looked at her, undressing her with his eyes. But not the way other men did, not with lust. He saw her as a salable product. She thought about her new friend, Geoffrey. A laugh that was. Really a joke. He was in love with her. Then there'd been a letter from her father. She'd better see him and finish it once and for all. In a way she was glad about all this fuss. Glad some check was being put on the traffic in young girls. As far as she was concerned she had no complaints. But she knew she was one in a thousand. How many girls saved their money? She hated men but she used them and she made them pay. She also loved men. Not only men, but the excitement of it, the power she had over them. The peace she felt after it. She was a hot one, there was no doubt about that. And she might have been a governess all her life, never knowing a thing.

She excused herself. "I must go and change," she said.

The other women looked at her. Whores the lot of them, but past it. Her life was still in front of her. She swept them a smiling curtsey and went out of the room.

"That's a one," Madame Elsie said.

"Reminds me of myself when I was her age. She saves her money and she'll go far."

"One of us," Madame Elsie said.

"I'm not sure. I think she plans to get out of it. When she's got enough, she'll go off somewhere and say she's a widow. Husband killed in India, something like that. She's a lady. Educated. She'll go far."

As she bathed and changed the Ellen of her private life into the Hélène of her public life, into the garments of it, she thought, Carrie Caramine was right. The case was going against Stead. If he lost and was sent to prison the public, that now clamored for his hide, would change sides. He would become a martyr and his cause reap renewed publicity. And add to this the power of the Salvation Army, whose ramifications were not merely nationwide but worldwide.

Solferino was a fool, of course, though his street girls, provided they were over age, could continue to solicit. Of course Carrie would be able to carry on in some hole-and-corner way. But the industry as a whole would be broken. The girls would have to be willing. They would no longer be bought and sold like cattle, at least not in a big way. And she? What would she do? Continue quietly on her own for a few years —she had a figure in mind—go on till she had twenty thousand pounds invested? She had some good financial advisers. With that she would be free and she'd change her personality again. She laughed. A respectable widow with no children and a nice jointure. Quite a catch she'd be.

There was still her father. She'd have to see him and tell him what had happened. They could meet at a hotel. Say Claridge's in Brook Street. There was also Geoffrey. Why did he stay in her mind?

Sitting in the anteroom of the mess, Geoffrey opened his brother's letter without much interest. He tore off the Cape Colony stamp because the commissionaire at the club collected stamps for his son from all the members who could be bothered to save them. The South African ostrich farming dream with Maud was over. He realized now, when he saw her name in the court news and social notes of the *Times* almost daily, that it would not have worked. But he was annoyed at how well her advice about Carrie's girl, Hélène, had worked out. She had told him her story and he believed he was one of the few people, other than Caramine, to know it. He liked her. Hélène, or Ellen, as he now called her. And not just making love to her either. He liked to talk to her. He was, he even acknowledged to himself, more than half in love with her. Liking was a part of love and, looking back on his affair with Maud, he discovered that he had not been fond of her. That had been an obsession, an infatuation. Even the illicit part of it. The intrigue had had a bearing on it. Well, in that sense, there was nothing illicit about Ellen. She had a number of regular lovers, most of whom knew each other. Cockshott was mad about her, spending a fortune on her. So were the others; all but himself. "You get a discount, Geoff," she'd said. "And do you know why?" He'd said he did not know why. "Then I'll tell you, my boy. You talk to me. You make me feel like a woman." What an extraordinary remark from a girl whose whole life and profession was based on her sexual charms! A woman. She was also a lady.

He took the letter out of its envelope. His brother, who had also been a soldier, had been mauled by a lion in the Transvaal. "I'm all right," he wrote, "but I can't get about like I used to, and I want you to send in your papers and come out as soon as you can. I'm sorry your affair went wrong, but there are some nice girls here and you'll probably be better off with a colonial. As I say, come out. Because, as things are, I shall not be able to continue you the allowance I make you as I'll have to cut down all around, which would be a shame as I have built up a good farm and am running nearly a thousand birds. . . ."

My God, Geoffrey thought, without the allowance of five hundred a year he could not stay on in the regiment. His brother Jack had been the oldest son, inheriting everything, and had sunk the lot in his farm. But he'd been jolly decent helping him, though always with the understanding that if he did not marry money he would come out and help him. Jack was a confirmed bachelor, and never even in his youth much of a ladies' man. Poodle-faking and all that had not interested him. Horses, hunting, fishing, and shooting had been his line.

Well, this certainly changed the picture. He'd send in his papers today, see the Colonel and get away within a month. He looked around the anteroom. The pictures, the trophies. Captured colors and weapons. He looked at his brother officers—alone reading the papers, or in groups, a glass of sherry in their hands. Leave it all? Well, why not? In a way he was sick of it, of London, of guard duty—Buck House, St. James's Palace, the Bank of England. Lining the streets, parades. Parties, dinners, balls. A lot of bloody nonsense, really. His mind slipped a cog and went back to the time, the very short time ago, when he had been going to run away with Maud. He'd looked forward to it then. The wilds. The big game. A bit of polo, perhaps. Plenty of dogs. Dress the way you wanted. The sunshine. Nothing had changed. He'd just let it all go when the dream had faded. Now it all came back—a free life in the colonies. And Ellen? It was going to be very difficult to leave her. But why leave her? By God, he thought, I'll take her with me. I'll marry her. What an idea! It would have been impossible in England, even if he left the regiment. Too much talk. Too many men he knew had slept with her. But in Africa, in the wilds of Oudtshoorn.

. . . Make a new start, both of them. Get married secretly in a registry office and meet at Tilbury. Meet on the boat. He ordered a glass of sherry from a passing steward. By God, he said, I'll marry her if she'll have me.

52 : The Judgment

It was now November. The court was filled with coughing, sniffling people. The pea soup fog seeped into the chamber smelling of soot and sulphur. Stead was in a bad way—exhausted and depressed. Listless, his eyes dull. He seemed to be paying little attention to what was going on.

There was one outburst from him when he said: "My lord, I am here charged with breaking the law of England. I went to a lawyer to find out what the law was and now I am not allowed to call him or use the advice he gave me."

Russell spoke in the defense of Jarrett: "The charge is that Rebecca Jarrett unlawfully took the girl, under the age of sixteen,* out of the possession and against the will of her father or mother or any other person having lawful care or charge of her. Was Rebecca Jarrett guilty or not guilty of that offense? I have submitted to m'lord that it is necessary to prove that the father did not assent . . ."

The judge interrupted him: "I'm very clear that in this case it is the father's will that is necessary to deal with it. I must at once say that I feel very strongly upon the subject."

Russell answered: "Yes, m'lord, I recognize that it's the father who has domain over his child. What I'm suggesting is that it isn't a criminal offense to take a child out of the possession of the family with the assent of the mother, unless the person so taking is aware that a fraud or imposition is being practiced upon the father."

"I shall tell the jury that if there is a father alive, and that the child is in his possession, the person who takes her does so at his peril," the judge said.

"Rebecca Jarrett does not, I admit," Russell said, "come under your notice in circumstances to recommend her to you. Her antecedents have a tendency to discredit her. Her conduct in the box would also have a tendency in that direction; so does her reluctance to give the

---

* An ironic charge since Stead had been responsible for raising the age of consent from 13 to 16 by forcing through the criminal amendment act.

names of the places where she lived because that would introduce the names of her former friends. Gentlemen, I ask you to believe that the true state of this case is that until the neighbors had noticed the disappearance of the child, Mrs. Armstrong did not busy herself about the child, but acted finally upon the pressure put upon her by the neighbors."

The Attorney General summed up the case for the prosecution: "What are the facts of the case? A child who is sent to Sunday School is taken out of the possession of its parents, is taken to brothels, drugged, examined by a procuress, has been taken away to a foreign country, and her address concealed. And because these facts have been brought to the knowledge of the Government on sworn testimony, we're told that this is a prosecution as unjustifiable as it is cruel, that the Government is hunting out Mr. Stead instead of the villains who betray these girls. The case is not to be decided as to whether one or two ignorant women have told stories that slightly vary. I ask you to look at the broad facts. I ask you, then, whether you can come to any other conclusion than that this child was unlawfully taken away from the father against his will."

Here was the letter of the law at its worst. What use was logic or common sense, against such a statement of facts? Stead was in a state of near collapse and at the end of his tether when he got Bramwell Booth's note:

> Your reputation at this moment is such as you never dreamed of. Your name is as well known as any living man's—and known not in connection with some old party cry and doctrine, but with the rising tide of a great new movement amongst the whole English-speaking population of the earth, in favor of right and purity and freedom. This court, this jury, cannot harm you in the end—the *worst* they can do is to make you fight a little harder.
>
> Don't go talking about offering yourself up. God, I tell you, is above all this chatter. I have more to fear than you from the Attorney and the Judge—you have a house-top from which to answer in the P.M.G. and *when all their lies are forgotten God's truth will go marching on.*

Galvanized into action, Stead drew on his last reserves of energy and stood up to speak. The court was silent but for coughs and stifled sneezes, every eye on the victim of this arena. A man making his last stand, now no longer at bay but on the attack.

"Gentlemen of the jury, rising to address you at this supreme moment of my life, I have to speak to you from a very full heart, with very intense conviction, and with feelings which I am afraid may sometimes shake or impede my utterance . . ."

The first point he made was that he had no pecuniary interest in the *Pall Mall Gazette,* and then he went on to defend both Rebecca Jarrett and Bramwell Booth. Of the former, he said: "She may have got muddled up in the witness box but I still believe in her." Of the latter, he said: "I have seen modern miracles wrought by his organization. . . . Although I know men, as a journalist, from kings to harlots—I know few men I would more willingly trust with my own soul than Mr. Bramwell Booth."

After defending his colleagues, he described the achievements of the *Pall Mall Gazette:* "Wherever the English tongue is spoken, *The Maiden Tribute* has strengthened public sentiment in favor of protecting young girls. Within a few days of the time when the P.M.G. containing the story of 'Lily,' arrived in Australia, an act raising the age of protection to sixteen, which for two years had been waterlogged and blocked, was revised and passed through Parliament without any difficulty. For here was a story, a simple story, that the common people could read and understand, which I wrote as it were with my very life's blood before the eyes of all men."

He then pointed out that almost half the clauses in Britain's Criminal Law Amendment Act had been traced to suggestions made in *The Maiden Tribute,* whilst in two of the clauses direct reference was made to the case of Eliza Armstrong. A newly introduced clause stated that if it was proved that parents assented to the sale of their children for an immoral purpose, the law had power to step in and deprive that parent of the custody of the child.

He paused briefly before making his final plea: "Now, I have to say this to you before sitting down: I do not say I am any authority about the law; but this I know, that again and again, twelve men in the jury box have stood between the perpetration of a great iniquity in the name of the law and the destined victim. And I appeal to you, gentlemen, *you* who are the fathers of families, to ask yourselves in your conscience: I ask you whether you think you can or cannot return a verdict of guilty against any of us.

"What I tried to do was not to abduct a girl, but to raise up sufficient sentiment in this country to make abductions and all allied offenses more dangerous. *That* was my purpose! You know now how I succeeded. But whether I succeeded or not, I admit I made many blunders—many mistakes. All men are fallible. I only ask you to judge me as a fellow man. You know what it has cost me, and *must* have cost me—reared as I was, and trained as I have been—to go down there; and all for what?

"Mr. Attorney General said, 'We must protect the children of the poor.' Was not this the object which I did all this for? You *know* it was! You know that was why Rebecca did it—and Jacques did it—and Booth did it—and we *all* did it! It was not in order to abduct a girl, but to rescue a girl from what we believed to be her inevitable doom. And, gentlemen, if in the exercise of your judgment, you come to the conclusion that you can take *no* note of motive—*no* note of character—*no* note of interest—*no* note of the scope of the operations—all I have to say, gentlemen, is that when you return your verdict I shall make no appeal to any other tribunal.

"M'lord has told me that the question of motive can be considered afterward if so be you return me guilty. Gentlemen, by your verdict I stand or fall. And if in the opinion of twelve men—twelve Englishmen born of English mothers—with English fathers—and possibly fathers of English girls—if they say to me 'you are guilty,' I take my punishment."

When he sat down the court was silent, aware that something unusual had occurred. They had listened to an historic defense. And then there was a roar of applause. It might have been a theater rather than a court of law. The jury was out for three hours and when it returned it was still not in agreement. They felt the responsibilities of the defendants were not equal.

The judge answered: "That is not a matter for you but for me to deal with. It's a question of law. I tell you most distinctly that if the child was in the possession of the father, it is the will of the father that must prevail, and his will only."

The Attorney General said that the jury wished to distinguish between Jarrett and Stead.

"Our difficulty," the foreman said, "is that if Jarrett obtained the child by fake pretenses, we feel it was directly contrary to Stead's directions. We find it, therefore, difficult as businessmen to hold him criminally responsible for that which, if he had known it, he would have repudiated.

"The question is did Stead and Jarrett, or either of them, take Eliza Armstrong out of the possession and against the will of the father."

The jury now retired again and was absent for a further three hours, by which time it was nearly seven P.M. On their return, the Clerk of the Court asked them: "Are you all agreed?"

"Yes," answered the foreman, but this did not appear to be the case.

The Clerk then repeated: "Did Stead and Jarrett, or either of them, take Eliza Armstrong out of the possession and against the will of the father?"

"Yes, Stead did. Stead did not have the consent of the father to the use to which he put the child."

There was no doubt what the verdict would be. When the judge said: "I will tell you at once that I find Stead and Jarrett guilty," no one was surprised. Shocked, perhaps, at so great a miscarriage of justice, of the spirit of the law being lost like a child in the forest of procedure.

Branch, the foreman of the jury, now defied the judge and said: "We find Stead did not have the consent of the father for the use of the child to which he put her, but we feel that Stead was misled by Jarrett and we further recommend—we trust that the Government will secure —the efficient administration of the Act recently passed for the protection of children."

This brought a roar of applause from the court for this was the first trial under the new Act, and in it an innocent man was being prosecuted on a technicality while the vice rings remained untouched.

"That is desirable," Judge Lopez said, "and I take it you return a verdict of guilty against Stead and Jarrett as instructed."

The foreman nodded agreement. He had no choice in law.

Samson, Jacques and Madame Mourez were also found guilty. Booth was acquitted. Madame Combe had been discharged early in the proceedings.

The judge then pronounced sentence: "William Thomas Stead, it will be convenient that I shall deal with your case first. I regret to say that you thought fit to publish in the *Pall Mall Gazette* a distorted account of the case of Eliza Armstrong; and you deluged some months ago our streets and the whole country with an amount of filth which has, I fear, tainted the minds of the children you were so anxious to protect; and which has been—and I don't hesitate to say, ever will be— a disgrace to journalism.

"An irreparable injury has been done to the parents of this child. They have been subjected to the unutterable scandal and ignominy of having been charged with having sold their child for violation. I have come to the conclusion that I cannot pass anything but a substantial sentence, and that is that you must be imprisoned without hard labor for three calendar months.

"I now come to the case of Rebecca Jarrett. I think you were pressed into service. I do not think that you volunteered it. Under the circumstances, the sentence that I pass on to you is that you must be imprisoned without hard labor for six calendar months."

Jacques was sentenced to one month, and Madame Mourez to six months.

The trial was over but England was roused to fury. The police did not dare resist public pressure and the courts all over the country were filled with pimps, traffickers, and procurers. Cardiff, London, Manchester, Bristol, Liverpool cleaned themselves up. The Salvation Army launched a new drive, a national scheme for the deliverance of the unprotected girl and the rescue of the fallen, setting up offices and homes all over the country for fallen girls in need of help.

But the London papers continued to attack Stead, now muzzled in prison. *The Times* was comparatively restrained:

> In the weighty words which he addressed to Mr. Stead, Mr. Justice Lopez touched the essential facts of the case in a manner which exactly appraised itself to the public conscience. We are satisfied that the ends of justice would not have been served by the passing of any lighter sentence than has been passed. It is a matter of rejoicing that a test case has shown that one of the gravest charges against the English populace—the charge of selling their children for infamous purposes—cannot be substantiated. And, in another direction, it is also a matter for rejoicing that the law has sternly shown that all things are not permissible even to those who believe themselves to be engaged in saving souls.

The *Morning Post* actually called for a heavier sentence against Stead. Only the *Daily Chronicle* expressed the opposite view, suggesting that: "The exercise of the Queen's prerogative for shortening the term of imprisonment would not establish a precedent."

The provincial papers took a completely different line. With hardly a single exception they were solidly behind Stead. The comment of the *Bristol Mercury* was representative of the whole:

> Mr. Stead can afford to treat with contempt the interested howls of the London editors who, while shedding crocodile's tears over the wrongs of Eliza Armstrong, have done their utmost to blast the reputation of a journalist, the latchet of whose shoes they are hardly worthy to unloose.

The *Newcastle Daily Leader* struck a prophetic note:

> The public of this country who look matters straight in the face will hear with a sense of shame and outrage that Mr. Stead has been sentenced to undergo three months imprisonment. . . . Men and women throughout broad England, with the sense of justice in them and the lamp of human love in their souls, will take the matter up and not rest until Mr. Stead is free.

But Stead did not go free, *despite* the countless petitions which were received by the Home Secretary from all over Britain—*despite* huge mass-protest meetings held in most of the great cities—*despite* the agitation caused by conscience-stricken James Branch who declared that Mr. Justice Lopez had forced the verdict on the jury—*despite* powerful sermons and weighty pronouncements delivered by the Archbishops of Canterbury and York. Nor did he appeal against his sentence.

In Holloway Prison he wrote to his friend, Benjamin Waugh:

> Goodbye, my dear friend. I am going to gaol with joy in my heart, and a peace which is very rare to me. Now I am inactive, and am still at peace. It is a new experience—possibly only a transient one—but very pleasant and heavenly while it lasts.
>
> I have a kind of dread of the relapse when this trial is over, and I am left all alone in a cell. But God will be there. Perhaps He wants a quiet talk with me, and has not had time hitherto, and so we are to be alone.
>
> God bless you, dear Mr. Waugh. You have loved me with a love passing the love of woman, and I am deeply grateful to you for it all.
>
> But now we must part for a season, take one parting word from me. Pray do moderate your wrath against those who have been prosecuting me. Remember that we must be as charitable to a judge as to a harlot, and that we must be just even to those we judge to have been unjust.
>
> Pardon this liberty, dear Benjamin, and believe me to be nonetheless thankful to you for your sympathy and helpful inspiring love, which I feel you have heaped upon me far more than I deserve.
>
> I am yours in brotherly love,
>
> W.T.S.

So Stead went to prison, but not to suffer. On November the 13th the Home Secretary gave orders that he should be treated as a first-class misdemeanant; in practice, this meant that he was to be treated as a "political prisoner" of the Government. To quote his own words:

> "Never had I a pleasanter holiday, a more charming season of repose. I had been trying in vain to get rest and at last it had come. I had sought it in vain in Switzerland, but I found it in Holloway. Here, as in an enchanted castle, jealously guarded by liveried retainers, I was kept secure from the strife of tongues, and afforded the rare luxury of journalistic leisure. From the Governor, Colonel Milman, to the poor fellow who scrubbed out my room, everyone was as kind as could be. From all parts of the Empire, even from a distant Fiji, rained down upon me every morning the benedictions of men and women who had felt in the midst of their life-long labors for the outcast the unexpected lift of the great outburst of compassion and indignation which followed the publication of *The Maiden Tribute*. I had papers, books, letters, flowers, everything that

the heart could wish. Twice a week, my wife brought the sunlight of her presence into the pretty room, all hung with Christmas greetings from absent friends, and twice a week she brought with her one of the children. On the day after Christmas, the whole family came, excepting the little two-year-old, and what high jinks we had in the old gaol with all the bairns! The room was rather small for blind man's buff, but we managed it somehow and never was there a merrier little party than that which met in Cell No. 2 on the ground floor of the E Wing of Holloway Gaol."

But Rebecca Jarrett did not fare so well in her cell in Millbank Prison. She found it hard to get used to the beady eyes of the rats that had made themselves quite at home. But she had plenty of books to read and a stocking to knit. It was over anyway, and the prison chaplain told her that she had done a good work for God and wasn't to be anxious. Everyone was very kind to her, but Oh! when Christmas came, she didn't even get a cup of tea but just the usual tin of skilly and the dry loaf of black bread. The wardresses had fastened the prisoners well in while they spent Christmas down in their own parts. The dinner was the same as usual—one potato, and there was no need for a knife to cut the meat. That was how she passed her Christmas Day in prison. But when she left she found over two hundred letters from all over the world waiting for her, six lovely shawls, and four lovely rugs for her bed.

Mrs. Bramwell Booth met her at Westminster Bridge and took her to get a cup of tea—the first in six months.

John Longbeach had clipped out all the newspaper reports. The *Western Daily Mercury* attacked the *Times*. Nothing, it asserted, could possibly be more unfair than the *Times* report. All the points in Mr. Russell's cross-examination of Mrs. Armstrong were either slurred over or missed altogether, while the defendant's case was made absurdly prominent. The *Rock* asked whether "at a time when the nation had been shocked at the discovery of crimes of the foulest description, that have been allowed to go unpunished, is the Public Prosecutor going to content himself with placing in the dock those who have exposed the evil while the criminals go scot free? Shame on such protection of vice!"

The *Methodist Times* said:

Do the Government intend to prosecute the *Pall Mall Gazette* and no one else? Are the public money and all the resources of the state to be used in attacking those who have exposed this infamous traffic, while those who engage in the traffic, and their base pleasure in the traffic, go free? Is this the way to fill the guilty with terror and encourage the virtuous?

Longbeach thought how like the situation was in many ways to that of eighty years ago when the Abolitionists—Wilberforce and his colleagues—had been attacked by the same powerful and influential quarters. The men with vested interests—the slave-ship owners, the planters, the slave dealers, and middlemen. The traders on the coast with their barracoons filled to overflowing with black ivory. How hard it was to stop men dealing in men, turning flesh and blood into gold; black men then, white girls today. The rich seekers of these horrible pleasures would not cease demanding them. Demand created supply. The river of this traffic in women might be checked but it would go on in rivulets, in seepages of vice. The price would go up, become commensurate with the dangers and difficulties of production. There could be no relaxation of vigilance. More houses for fallen girls were required. Rest houses where they could be rehabilitated. More girls must be warned of their danger. The ports and railway stations must be watched for procurers.

But in all this they would only be attacking an effect—not the cause. The cause was the low wages paid to women and girls in the mills and sweatshops, which made any other fate seem preferable. Even the fire was a change from the frying pan. But education—even education in sex—would come one day. The ignorance of upper- and middle-class girls was appalling. They knew nothing except that certain things happened in marriage that must be put up with. Something unclean. Most men never saw their wives naked, nor did the women see their husbands. The most they had ever seen was a nude statue by some accident, if they had been at school abroad or on a tour of the Continent—as if a passive marble Apollo bore any resemblance to man in rut. Some people even went so far as to have pierced nightgowns so that flesh should have a minimum contact with flesh. Love in the sense of passion was considered indecent for a woman of the upper class. Yet it was there in many of them—hidden and secret.

Lavinia was a passionate woman. She had been surprised to shocked tears at the discovery of her hidden desires. At the joy of it. At the relief, the release. She was a changed woman—years younger in appearance and with the movements and carriage of a girl.

And Ellen. Longbeach was able to consider his seduction by Ellen more objectively now. Ellen was a lady, a parson's daughter, brought up in a remote country village. But once her inhibitions had been brutally broken down, she had reveled in the use of her body. "Lenton?" she had said. "I love him, and I hate him. With Edward I was like a whipped dog that licks the hand of its master and yet may, if the occasion ever offers, turn upon him. One hears of it," she'd said, "of a dog savaging its master. I never used to understand it, but I do now." She'd laughed. "But I owe Edward a lot," she'd gone on. "If it had not been for him, I might have died a governess."

But in a way Ellen had been lucky. She had only been used and abused by one man till, finding her power over him, she had used it on others, becoming, as she was now, one of the most successful courtesans in London. Except in this first instance, she had always been able to pick and choose as men did. It boiled down to this: If a woman was not coerced, if no force was used, there was no reason, other than a moral one, why she should not live as she wished. Only two people were involved in the act and if both were willing there was nothing legally wrong in it. Morals and taste were involved, but no human rights. It was human rights that interested him as a lawyer.

With children it was a different story. The procurers wanted children for two reasons: First, to satisfy the wants of their perverted clients and secondly, because, physically weak and friendless, they were so easy to train. A few whippings, a little starvation, some glasses of champagne—and it was all over, their unformed characters set in this new mold.

Older girls had to be seduced with promises of marriage or employment abroad where, lost and unable to speak the language, raped successively by a dozen men, they, too, were finally brought to heel and became docile as cattle, quite unable to fend for themselves. They could not get home and if they did, as likely as not their parents would disown them. Here, again, it was a matter of education—not merely of children but of parents, of changing public opinion. A girl who had been seduced was not necessarily evil. Molly, for instance. Her father, Lavinia had said, denied her very existence. "I have no daughter," he had said. How lucky he had died, although of course Lavinia would have provided for her.

He thought of his talk with Ellen's father, the old vicar. A dear old man, as innocent as a child. Plenty of village girls became pregnant before marriage. In the country men had to have children and, without consciously knowing it, wanted to prove a girl's fertility. Children were the only insurance the poor man had, children to take care of their parents when they were past work. How impossible it had been to explain that Ellen had chosen a life of sin and luxury! "She can

come back, Mr. Longbeach. This is her home and I am her father."
That was when he had been to see her at Mrs. Caramine's. She had
laughed at him. "Poor father," she'd said. "There are plenty of whores
and harlots and scarlet women in the Bible, but I don't suppose he ever
thought he'd breed one. How long ago was that, John? Four thousand
years or so?" she'd continued. "Well, men haven't changed much in
all that time. Sodom and Gomorrah are still with us. London, Paris,
Brussels, Antwerp, Berlin. Men still want young women to lie with—
the bastards," she'd said, turning venomous. "But don't worry about
me, John. My head's screwed on right. I have plans. I'm very lucky,
you see, in having some education. Not like most of these poor bitches."

And it was difficult to believe that Caramine was the most famous
Madam and procuress in London, with a worldwide reputation and
octopus tentacles that led outward in every direction—to the Continent,
to South America, to the United States and Asia Minor; that this well-
dressed, quiet, ladylike woman was one of the powerful forces that
had quashed the Criminal Law Amendment Act at its previous read-
ings and that could have succeeded in doing so again in July if it had
not been for Stead's revelations—the *Maiden Tribute* series that had
rocked Victorian England back on its smug heels.

He went over the case again in his mind. What a travesty of justice
it had been! The letter of the law with no thought of its spirit. This
had been the first prosecution under the new Act. How hypocritical
people were! He thought of himself and Lavinia—Lavinia who was,
in all but fact, a widow. Her husband could scarcely be called alive,
incapable as he was of speech or movement. Neither of them had any
feeling of sin about their surreptitious meetings in London. But in the
eyes of the world they were adulterers. How hard right and wrong
were to define! Justice. The law. The law had been right to condemn
Stead, if breaking the law was the criterion of justice. But it was not.

John Longbeach's mind was on the Armstrong Case, the miscarriage of justice, the rescue of fallen women and the protection of others.
On wages and that this new belief in the survival of the fittest was
contrary to all Christian principles. Also on his mind was Lavinia. The
sweetness of her nature, his boyhood dreams of her—his fairy princess.
The warmth and beauty of her body. He saw her with her arms raised,
doing her hair. He remembered the first time she had let it down for
him at the Meurice in Paris. How love had come to them both then,
suddenly. The French *coup de foudre*. The feelings that had flooded
him when he had picked her up in his arms and carried her to the
couch.

When would he see her again in the little flat he had taken and furnished in London? She would arrive in a hansom, heavily veiled and accompanied by May—maid, friend, and accomplice. It was Maud Cockshott who had put her up to these tricks of evading detection. She would return to Berkeley Square a few hours later in another hansom laden with cardboard hatboxes and parcels which he had ready for them to take home. Or she would come openly in her carriage, ostensibly to assist in their work at the office, which she did, but the work was only a prelude. It was May who dressed her and did her hair again, occupying herself in the flat with needlework in his study and leaving them the bedroom and sitting room; or cooking a simple lunch in his tiny kitchen. They never met in the evenings or after dark.

How absurd it all was! Official meetings and discussions at his office, chance encounters—carefully planned beforehand. Their rides over the Mortal lands, surreptitious assignations—instants only, as time flowed by, utterly wasted for them both, when they were apart.

53 : The Doctor

John Longbeach missed Lavinia when he went back to Gloucestershire; he had no excuse to stay on though he understood her desire to remain in London and do what she could for Stead. Since the trial and the judgment, events had taken the turn he had predicted. Stead was a martyr, and the law, as if it were ashamed at its betrayal of justice, was at last moving in on the slavers. There were prosecutions now. Houses were being closed, pimps and madams were in jail. The business, as far as the export of English girls and children was concerned, was all but over.

It would go on, of course. There would be exceptions, a trickle as it were, but the mainstream of this infamous traffic had ceased to run. The hundred varied strings that had culminated in the *Maiden Tribute* series had now woven a net that was unbreakable. Mrs. Butler, the Dyers, the Booths, Dr. Barnado and Stead had done it. Above all, Stead. And Lavinia, the loss of whose children had brought at least some upper-class attention to bear on the subject.

Meanwhile their affair was going no better. They met publicly, as a man of business and his client. Privately, in the London office, as lovers. Then, for a few hours, he saw life as it might have been. Between these meetings there was only his work and the bucolic amusements of shooting and fox hunting, which no longer gave him much satisfaction though it served at least to exhaust him. To some extent he confided in his mother. She knew he met Lavinia in London. She did not know about the flat there but no doubt, being a wise woman, she was quite capable of putting two and two together without going into details that would have shocked her. He knew she prayed for them both. He knew that her ideas of sin were not the conventional ones. He knew from hints she had let drop that she understood the feelings of a woman like Mrs. Lenton, deprived of what she euphemistically called masculine companionship.

He rode over to Mortal twice a week to keep an eye on the place, see the bailiff and so on. It was also part of his plan to keep people accustomed to seeing him there whether Mrs. Lenton was in residence or not. He saw quite a lot of Eva and Muriel, and often had tea with them. It was after one of these meetings that, seeing Dr. Jarvis driving by in his dogcart, he signaled to him to pull up.

"Well, John, been up to Mortal?"

"Yes doctor, and there's something I don't like. Eva is not so well again."

"She was all right a couple of days ago. Making very satisfactory progress, I thought."

"Well, today she was in a dream. A bad one. She didn't say a word. She just stared and stared. Looked right through me, right through the wall. And then she burst into tears and ran away. Muriel says she's been upset since yesterday, but refuses to speak about it."

"I'll look in tomorrow, John."

"Thanks, doctor. With Mrs. Lenton away, I feel responsible."

"Tomorrow," Dr. Jarvis said, with a flick of his whip, and was off on high, spinning wheels. He always drove good horses.

In London at The Black Man, Basher and Solferino were doing business. "Changed a bit it 'as, Basher," Solferino said, "with them Jesus bastards stickin' their noses in. But I can get over it, that I can."

" 'Ow?" Basher asked, wiping the foam of his fourth pint away from his lips.

"I've spoke to me lawyer," Solferino said. "No 'ouses. Can't send 'em to the knocking shops or overseas, like we did, my boy. But we can place 'em. Domestics, that's what they are now. I'm opening me own agency. Young domestic servants," he said. "All square and above-board, but they'll end up the same bloody way."

"Well, Eliza's ready, guv'nor, when you wants 'er. Nice little piece she is."

"Next week, Basher, next week. And 'ere's a quid on account."

But it didn't work out quite that way. When he got back to Charles Street, Mr. Trumper of the Child's Rescue Association was waiting for him. "I've been talking to Eliza and her mother," he said. "I've got a nice place for her in the Bayswater Road."

"You 'ave, 'ave you? Well, I've got a place for 'er myself, and it's none of your bloody business."

"I'm sorry, Mr. Armstrong, but it is. You see she's under our wing now. Someone will come to see her every month and report on her progress. Very proud of her we are. Quite a little lady."

Basher raised an enormous fist. He'd flatten this mealy-mouthed bastard, that's what he'd do. This, just after 'e'd seen Solferino and got everything all fixed up.

"Don't do it, Mr. Armstrong. Hit me and they'll put you inside for obstructing the law."

"She's my kid, ain't she? My property?"

"Not quite, Mr. Armstrong. You see we're not quite happy about all this. There are things we are looking into. Young girls around here. And you with money to spend and doing no work . . ."

"Well, that's a fine kettle of fish," Basher said. "Me own daughter, wot I saved from worse than death in a Paris knocking shop. Wot's England coming to? That's wot I'd like ter know."

"I'll tell you, Mr. Armstrong. England's going to put people like your friend, Mr. Solferino, in gaol if there's any more funny business with little girls."

With that he turned on his heel and walked away up Charles Street to Lissom-Grove.

And Basher went into the house to beat his wife. No law against that yet unless she lodged a complaint, and she'd never dare 'cos he'd be after 'er the moment she came out. Rights, he had. A free Englishman with ten years in the militia.

At Carrie Caramine's Ellen was smoking a cigarette and sipping a brandy and soda. She was not looking forward to this meeting with her father. But it was something she'd have to get over sometime. He knew the story. John Longbeach had given him a rough outline of it to pave the way for her return last year. Of her present way of life he could have no inkling, except that she was living in London. A job in London. Oh dear, the poor old bastard—what a shock he'd have! She still loved him, but he had become unreal to her. He knew so little about life that he was like a child. A child of seventy. Claridge's at four. They'd talk and have tea, and somehow she'd break it to him.

She ordered her carriage for two-thirty. It was a miniature phaeton, with two coal-black, high-stepping ponies that Cockshott had given her and which must have set him back the best part of a thousand pounds. You could not buy a pair like hers for less. She'd drive around the Park for an hour. The ponies needed exercise and she knew what a picture she made, driving fast in the paletot she had had made by Poole, with Tim, her little uniformed tiger, sitting with his back to her, his arms folded over his chest. Somehow she always thought best when she was driving or riding. It seemed to clear her mind. Here at least no one could get at her. No demands, no talk. No hands fiddling with her. Lord, how she loathed the bastards. Choose? Yes, she chose; she had the best, but they were the best of a bad lot, and she bled them. All except Geoffrey. He was always so polite, so gentle, so grateful. Sometimes he even brought her flowers, as if he were courting her. By Christ, she thought, if I'm not careful I'll find myself falling in love with the little bugger.

She drew the lash of her whip gently over the flank of the near pony. The ponies increased their speed. She did not use a bearing rein but drove them up to their bits, the reins in the middle bar of the Liverpool. Their knees came up to their noses and shot out in a flying trot. The red-spoked wheels span below her. Men greeted her, raising their top hats and she replied with a nod or a gesture of her whip. The women in the carriages she passed were unable to meet the bold look of her eyes and looked away. Twice around and then out up Park Lane and into Brook Street.

At Claridge's the commissionaire came to meet her. Tim jumped down and came to the ponies' heads. They would be baited in the neighboring mews until she was ready for them. She watched Tim lead them off, went into the hotel and found a table for two partially screened by potted palms. She sat down to wait for her father, her mind still toying with her memories of Geoffrey. Her only man friend. That was a kind of joke, too, considering the circumstances. . . .

At last she saw her father coming. White-haired in shabby black, but completely at ease. She rose to meet him. Kissed him on both cheeks and said: "Sit down, Father, and we'll have some tea."

"I'm glad to see you looking so well, Ellen."

Poor man. He did not know that she looked well because she was made love to, flattered, petted, and had almost five hundred pounds worth of clothes on her back.

Tea came, brought by a uniformed flunky in a purple plush coat and white silk stockings. Sandwiches, cakes. She poured. She knew how well she looked, pouring tea from a silver teapot in these luxurious surroundings. She asked about home, about the pony, about Colonel Hawley. And then suddenly she said: "Let's stop beating about the bush, Father. I'm no longer the girl I was. Mr. Longbeach gave you my story, or part of it. But I'll fill it in for you.

"Mr. Lenton tried to seduce me. When he failed, he had me sacked saying I had made improper advances to him. Betrayed me into the house of a procuress in London who sent me to Paris, where I was kept for him, hanging like a pheasant in the larder for his pleasures, which he took in August—the August before last, August of eighty-four. I escaped thanks to Mrs. Lenton, whom you have read about in the papers, and returned to London. Then, since I had been ruined,"—she smiled sweetly at her father—"I decided that I might as well go the whole hog and I took to it as a profession. I am now, my dear father, one of the best known and most notorious women in London. My rise to fame has been meteoric; due partly to my looks, partly to the fact that I am still a lady, and finally because I no longer have a heart or feelings of any kind."

Her father had closed his eyes. She could see his lips moving. He was praying. Praying in the Palm Court of Claridge's Hotel. At last he opened his eyes and looked at her. "I am not surprised, Ellen. I heard rumors. Even in the country one hears things. I put two and two together. That's why I had to see you."

"To save me?" she smiled.

"No, Ellen. Only God can do that, and I think He will. One day a good man will come into your life who will say: 'Who am I to cast the first stone?' In my heart I know this, Ellen; and when he comes don't turn him away because he will be an answer to my prayers." He stood up, laid his hands on her forehead under her beaver hat, said: "God bless you, Ellen," and left her, a small black, rather shabby figure walking over the thick carpets, weaving his way between fashionable women, and couples, reducing them in stature by his passing.

God damn him, God damn him, but he'd upset her. No pleas, no recriminations. She had forgotten what a good man he was.

54 : A New Leaf

Delphine returned to London as Yvette Pichon. Her first visit, after she had deposited her valise at a small hotel near Victoria Station, was to Coak Street. She was glad to be back in England and on her own again. Things had not gone well with her. In Paris she had had some small engagements in various *boîtes—cafés chantants* that were also gambling dens and houses of ill-fame. She had made money—honestly on her back, and dishonestly stealing from drunken clients. Never everything, just a few large notes from each and anything she could blackmail others with. Then, as with so many women, in the race between heart and head, her heart had won and she had fallen in love with a man who had begun as a client, continued as her husband and ended as a pimp who prostituted her.

Mrs. Caramine was not surprised to see her. Nothing could surprise her. Even Delphine's story, when she told it, was an old one. The only amusing thing about it was that a girl like Delphine—Yvette now—should have been taken in as easily as a simple country bumpkin. It merely went to prove that all women were the same in the hands of a certain kind of man. One, that is, who knew women.

"And now?" she asked.

"Now I will work for you. I am still beautiful."

"First, my dear, you will see the doctor. My doctor. Then, if all is well, you are welcome. But things, as you may have heard, have changed in England. We have reformed," she laughed bitterly. "I am giving up this house, the others have already gone. I am going into what might be called private practice, with a dozen selected young ladies. I will find the flats, Yvette, furnish them, dress the girls and have half the takings. I will also arrange for clients—my old clients and any new ones whom I select."

"Certainly, Madame," Yvette said. "I have no choice, have I?"

"Not much, my dear, unless you want the streets and Solferino."

All these years, this work and risks she had taken. And here she was back almost where she had begun. Her money, her savings gone. Her lovely clothes. Just what she had in her battered valise. Still, with hard work and courage, she could arrive again. A protector, a man to keep her. Edward Lenton, perhaps.

"Mr. Lenton?" she said. She could talk her way out of that. Say she had been abducted herself and had come back to find him. He had been mad about her.

"He is at Mortal," Mrs. Caramine said. "Why not go and see him? I am sure he will do nothing to harm you. He spoke of you so often and you broke his heart running away like that. Mrs. Lenton is in London most of the time."

Mrs. Caramine gave her ten pounds—two fivers—and the address of her doctor on a slip of paper. When Yvette had gone, Mrs. Caramine poured herself out a glass of Madeira. It was amazing the way she had retained her sense of humor. She wished she could see the encounter between Muriel and Delphine, or Yvette as she now called herself. And Eva? What would Eva do?

All the way to Gloucestershire Delphine rehearsed the story of how she and the children had been abducted. Of how she had escaped from a house in Paris and searched for them in vain. The servants were a problem but with luck she could get into the library unobserved and wait for him there. He was bound to come in; he always spent so much time there.

It was strange being back. Almost as if she had never been away. Everything was the same. She left her valise and took a cab to Mortal. She stopped it before she reached the drive, saying she would take a short cut over the fields where there was a right of way. How beautiful it was! How peaceful! She climbed the stile that led into the park and walked around the house to the French windows of the library, hoping that on a day like this, even if it was winter, they would be open. They were and she went in. The room looked empty and it was different. It seemed to have been changed into a bedroom. There was a figure in it. A man. He might know where Edward was.

"Where's Mr. Lenton?" she asked.

There was no reply. She went closer. It was difficult to see coming in out of the sunshine. She leant forward. *Mon Dieu, Edouard!*" she cried. Only the burning eyes moved. "What has happened to you?"

A horrible cry, like that of an animal, burst from his lips. His eyes blazed with hatred. For an instant she thought she would faint. Then, gathering up her skirts in both hands, she ran from the room. That woman! Carrie Caramine, who had sent her to him, had said he'll do nothing. What could he do but cry like a beast, immobilized like a log of wood? She ran out into the garden along the wide grass path with its herbaceous borders aflame with late autumn fire. The last chrysanthemums—bronze, purple, white, yellow. Michaelmas daisies, heleniums, dying dahlias tied to green stakes. Mulleins with furry, rabbit-skin leaves. And there, coming toward her, with the deerhound at her side, was Eva. The dog recognized her and came forward, wagging his tail. Eva, white as a ghost, walked past her quite unseeing, her blue eyes dead as stones.

Somehow she had forgotten Eva. It had never occurred to her that Eva would be at Mortal, that she could have escaped from Paris. That she could even survive. Delphine ran on. She had missed Muriel; she did not even know of her existence. Before reaching the cab, she slowed down and put her appearance to rights. Straightened her hat and smoothed her skirt. "Back!" she said to the driver. And he turned his old brown horse. She even remembered the horse.

She slept at the hotel. Next day she visited the doctor and with his report in an envelope returned to Mrs. Caramine, who greeted her with a smile.

"I thought you'd better see him for yourself, my dear. Now you can forget him and the past. Bury him with Delphine, the French governess. I have a nice place ready for you," she said, "in Curzon Street. With a good maid and several men dying to meet my new importation from Paris. A new leaf, my dear, for all of us."

If it had not been for Jack Lenton raping her and being responsible for her mother's death, she would never have sent Delphine to steal Edward's children. If she had not done that, Mrs. Lenton would never have joined the do-gooders with her money and influence and Eddie Lenton would still have been a customer.

The wheels of fate took some strange turns, stopped at some odd numbers. Who the hell would have thought, even a few months ago, that Solferino, whom she'd always despised as a huckster in the retail instead of the wholesale trade, as it were, would end up better off than she was, with his street girls?

Mrs. Caramine sent for Miss Hélène. When she came in, she said: "Well, my dear, this business is over. No more whore houses, knocking shops, cat houses, bordellos, houses of ill-fame in England. What a lot of names they've given us, my dear! But who'd have thought that when we put that bastard, Stead, inside, and proved he'd abducted a girl, there'd be this bloody row about it? I thought we had it all sewn up and now that scum, Solferino, is the only survivor."

"What are your plans, Carrie?" Ellen asked.

"Put the girls into flats with a good maid, and let Ada supervise the money side. Do you want one, darling? I'll set them up well with clothes and all of course."

"Not me, Carrie. I liked it here—the fun of it." She laughed. "The parties, the other girls, the men in evening dress. I liked the style."

"I know," Caramine said. "And you were a sort of queen here. I always thought you'd take over from me one day. Ada could never do it. She doesn't know anything about men."

"What are *you* going to do, Carrie?"

"Retire. Buy a place in the country, near Bath I think, and live like a lady. And if you don't want one of my flats, darling, what are *you* going to do? Set up on your own? You've got enough money to, and you've got the name. You've slept with some of the best in England. And that's a queer thing—they only want women other men they know have had."

"No flat, Carrie. Not yours or on my own. It's too dangerous being alone with men like that. Might get my pretty throat cut. The sharp boys might try to take me over. Solferino, for instance. Do you think he'll leave girls alone in their flats?"

"Well, what then?"

"I might go to the colonies."

"There are good pickings there, from what I hear. Sidney, Melbourne, Cape Town, Jo'burg, Kimberley . . ."

"No, Carrie. Out of the game. There's a man who'd marry me if I lead him on a bit. Going to join his brother breeding ostriches in South Africa."

Carrie began to laugh. "Christ!" she said, "it would be funny to see the feathers on the birds for a change."

If Eva knew her father, she gave no sign of it. She spent much time with him, allowing Muriel to go off on long walks with her son. She read her fairy tales to him. She pushed his bath chair about the garden: She liked to stroll up the slope of the inclined plane of the wall that led to the turret tower, as it was called—gutted by Cromwellian fire—the inside a ruin, but still intact. There was a stone sentry box slit for arrows, where she sat looking out over the great weald, glancing at her father as he dozed wrapped in his red and green tartan rug in the garden below. The head gardener had warned her about the wooden railing.

"Keep away, Miss Eva. It's not safe. I'll have it mended one of these days, but you know what the estate carpenters are. A roof to be repaired here, a barn to be done there. But I'll see to it and in the meantime you be careful, Miss." He'd touched his cap and walked off, spud stick in hand, poking at the weeds in the lawn as he passed. Dandelions, by God! How he hated dandelions and daisies. . . .

Eva was careful. Very. She always stood away from the rail and shook it a little to see how loose it was when she was up there alone, and after every shake it was a little looser. The weakest place was at the foot of the rotting, white-painted posts, where the buried parts met the air. Soon it would be holding by a thread, by the very paint itself. Oh, it all looked sound enough. White and neat. Post and rails. But one good shove . . .

Somehow Eva herself did not exactly know how she realized that Lavinia was her mother. Possibly her brain was slowly rebuilding itself. Putting two and two together; the man in the wheelchair she did not know, but he reminded her of someone, something, some incident. And dear Ellen, their governess, where was she? Where was Betty? Things were coming back. Frightful things. But she was not going to let anyone know. Not even her mother. There was some reason for not letting people know what she knew. Some cause for this deception. She did not know what it was—only that it was essential, vital. No one must guess. She must go on acting simple. Like a child, playing with Frankie as an equal. But there was something deep here, something going on in her mind that she did not understand. All she knew was that she must wait like a fisherman watching his float in the pool of memory.

Then it came. A mist that slowly cleared, a curtain raised on a terrible play. Act after act of it. Mademoiselle Delphine Le Grand, who had taken them to Paris and sold them like slaves. The new Delphine the next day, unbelievably beautiful so that it had taken her some moments to recognize her—her voice, her eyes, her hair—and she had denied them the way Judas had denied Christ for thirty pieces of silver. That was partly how it had come back. Muriel had read that piece from the New Testament at family prayers, which she had taken over when her mother was in London. And then she had seen Delphine here in the garden. Mac had recognized her and she had run away. It was after this that things had become much clearer to her.

But still she would say nothing as she fished in the horrible pool of memory. It was Julie who had told her something. Julie, the snake who had charmed and whipped her. Who had tried to protect her from that man who had . . . No! Not that. That memory she could not face yet. Later, when she was stronger, when she had the rest of it clear. All the memories strung, like evil beads, on the string of those forgotten days. Days that were rising like fish from the depths of her unconscious.

Julie had said her father came to see Ellen who was imprisoned there at his orders. Ellen, dearest Ellen, who certainly never did anything wrong. . . . An old man. Revolting, hairy. Smelling of sweat and perfume—even that memory was coming back too. . . .

It was her father who had made mother sack Ellen. Dear Ellen. And they had not even been able to say goodbye to her. They had not been allowed to. And Betty? Where was Betty . . . ?

It was all clear in her mind now but she covered it up once more. There was a reason. She did not know the reason. There was more, much more. It would come later. It was just a matter of waiting. It was all over now. She was safe, she was home. Mother and Muriel would take care of her. She loved Muriel; Muriel was beautiful. Ellen had been beautiful. Delphine, as she had last seen her, had been beautiful. But ugly here at home. Why had she been ugly? Why had all their governesses been so beautiful? Some she hardly remembered. They had not stayed long—the ones between Muriel and Ellen—but they had all been pretty girls. . . .

Evangeline had grown more beautiful. Though taller, she looked no older than she had a year ago. With her slim neck and straight gold hair that she wore long and unbound—an Alice in Wonderland, wandering wide-eyed about the Mortal parklands, paddocks, and gardens, with Mac, the tall, shaggy Scots deerhound beside her. She still read her books of fairy tales and played with dolls. But new clothes were the greatest pleasure. Every time Lavinia went away she sent her new dresses from London, or brought them when she came down. Part of Eva's youthful appearance was due to her refusal to wear grown-up shoes. Just little-girl slippers with a strap across the instep, and short white socks. This, with her long hair, gave the impression of a very tall, graceful girl of ten, with a remarkable bust for her age. Not that she had big breasts. They were normal, softly rounded, but gave her a look of local maturity as if one part of her body had raced ahead into womanhood, trailing a little girl behind it. You wondered when one part would catch up with the other. When the big, softly expressionless gray eyes would see; when the full, rose-colored lips would kiss and the delicate long-fingered hands drop the dolls they held and reach out for love.

Eva's mind had stood still; nature had buried the horrors of the past so hurriedly, so deeply, that everything else in her life had also gone into the grave. Her sanity had been saved. She had merely forgotten everything. She was content to exist, to wear pretty clothes, walk with her dog, and play childish games—pick flowers, sit in the sun when it was fine and by the fire when it was cold. Always dreaming, always far away, her eyes blank as a sailor's searching the horizon for a landfall. At least that is what people thought though it was not quite true now. Now she could pierce the veil of memory at will. Then her expression changed. Her eyes, her mouth. But she did not do it often. What she saw was too horrible.

Dr. Jarvis was on the whole satisfied with her progress. The man-business at least had ceased; after her father's accident there had been no further incidents. But behind this calm and beautiful façade another life, which had forgotten nothing, was going on. It was like the life of a tree behind the bark; nourishing the flowers and the leaves, quite unperceived, the sap flowed and ebbed. Here a game of consequences was taking place—the checkers of cause and effect being moved about on the squares of memory and time. But both were confused, tele-scoped, expanded, and changed to avoid the unbearable and fitted to the present. In Eva's mind, Edward had become the Prince, and he had scorned her. Not only was there the insult of his refusal but there was the consequence—her punishment. There was no regret, no pain, no unhappiness, as she led her peaceful country life. But behind the curtain, the backdrop of this bucolic stage, a ferment was taking place. Day after day going about her affairs, her walks, her doll playing, her skipping, her flower picking, she observed Edward's every move. Or rather that of his keepers, for these servants were his masters. He could neither instruct, order nor dismiss them. Imprisoned in silence and immobility. This was perhaps the worst of it for him. He could see what went on, hear what was said, but could neither speak nor write. He was tortured by the sight of his daughter staring at him, spy-ing on him. Tortured by her looks, by his thoughts about the men who had debauched her. He felt little hate for them now. That had gone when he had ceased to be able to own anything. A speechless cripple had no possessions, not even his own body. You only owned the things you could use and handle. So his feelings about those men were ones of curiosity, of near-envy as he imagined the scene. So the two, father and daughter, had a hidden thought in common. The girl who thought in her unconscious that her father was the Prince and he, as he lay in his wheelchair, almost wished he had been.

Today his keepers, as he called them in his mind, had left his chair against the south wall of the rose garden that Lavinia's mother had planted in the Tudor courtyard. The perfume of the last roses was soporific; sometimes they lasted till Christmas. The hum of the bees and insects. The sounds and smells of summer had gone. He had not heard his daughter come on her thin-soled children's shoes. The first thing he noticed was that he was moving, that she was leaning over him, her long golden hair—bleached almost white—falling onto his shoulders as she pushed his chair. She often gave him rides around the garden and talked to him about the flowers.

Now she was pushing him up the ramp, an easy gradient that had been made along the ruined castle walls and led to the east tower's crenellated top where a great vine had established itself and been trained, suitably supported, into a pleasant summer house. Edward remembered meeting Muriel here—that must have been ten years ago—while Lavinia had been ill with a miscarriage.

He looked out over the rose garden he had just left, at the Keep that rose like a tall salt cellar behind the red-tiled Tudor roof. At the big Queen Anne addition to the house and the trees of the great wood through which the rhododendrons lining the drive ran. By God, he'd had some good shooting in that wood. The driven birds came over very high, flying across the park to the oval spinney.

Eva had left him rather near the edge of the wall. The wooden guard rail looked as if it should be repaired. He must tell someone about it. He was always thinking he must tell someone something, and he couldn't even tell those two oafs who took care of him when he wanted a drink.

But here she was back again. He saw Eva's hands on either side of his body. She would just pull him back a couple of feet and he would be fine, still in the sun but partly shaded, dappled by the dead, autumn-tinted vine leaves overhead. But he was not going backward. The chair was going forward. She was pushing him toward the edge. A foot, six inches. The edges of the wheels were over. The chair tipped and he fell out of it. Falling, he managed to scream. Eva screamed too. High and shrill, so that the peacocks answered her as she ran, her hair streaming behind her, toward the house, the big dog galloping beside her.

APPENDIX

APPENDIX

INTRODUCTION TO THE APPENDIX

The following newspaper clippings and extracts will show that white slavery is still going on. The means of subjugation remain the same—the classic pattern of beating, starving, and raping until a girl's spirit is broken and she becomes an automaton doing precisely as she is told by her master.

Some of the tricks are new—the use of air transport, and promises of good jobs in foreign countries. Another device is to tempt or force girls into drug addiction.

As the law stands, it is difficult to obtain convictions and the penalties are light when the immense profits from this business are taken into account.

The whole question of prostitution is so repulsive that we tend to wash our hands of it and sweep it under the carpet.

The fact remains, however, that at this moment there are thousands of girls who are forced to sell their bodies for the benefit of the parasites who have enslaved them.

It is the fashion today to decry sensationalism and melodrama, but they exist. Strange and terrible things are taking place in the dim-lighted corners of the stage where the human comedy is played. Feminine equality and women's rights are, under certain conditions, no guarantee of their personal safety.

I should like to take this opportunity to thank the librarian of the Josephine Butler Society for her help, the librarian of the Salvation Army for the loan of *Pall Mall Gazettes* reporting the Stead Trial in 1885, the Anti-Slavery Society for their assistance, and to state that I have relied heavily on Mr. Charles Terrot's "Traffic in Innocents" to fill in gaps left by other research.

STUART CLOETE

Member of: The Anti-Slavery Society
The Josephine Butler Society
The American Social Health Association

Extracts and material relevant to the white slave traffic
1880–1965. A proof, not only of its past existence, but also
of its presence among us today.

In any society, at any time, the lone woman without a male protector—husband, father, or brother—has always been in danger of sexual
exploitation, of annoyance, even of rape or murder. White slavery and
enforced prostitution are shocking examples of this phenomenon.

Sexual equality, unless backed up by force, is a myth. It is only the
law that compensates the woman for her lack of physical strength; that
equalizes her. Chivalry, the cry of "Women and children first," is a
product of established custom and social order.

A first vote on woman's suffrage took place in Parliament, in 1870,
and it failed to pass because of Gladstone's opposition. Next vote was in
1885; it did not get past a second reading. Defeated again in 1892 and
again in 1897. Suffrage given to certain groups of women in 1918. Extended to all in 1928.

Sir Edward Coke in the 16th century was responsible for twisting the
English common law against the rights of women (his Institutes of
the Laws of England), and also Sir William Blackstone in the 18th
century, with his four-volume commentaries on the laws of England.

The highwater mark in the legal disenfranchisement of women came
in with the Reform Bill of 1832, which restricted the enlarged franchise of male persons. In English law such flat restrictions had never
been seen, and the Courts held that the word "man" included woman.
From the Reform Bill, dates the public agitation that served to alter
woman's position.

Women's rights, primarily those relating to the disposition of their
own bodies, are dependent on law and order. If this goes and there is a
complete breakdown they become once again servants and playthings.

There is no way of controlling the movement of girls who are of age
no matter what is known about their companions. Any man can take
any woman abroad. They may even depart or arrive separately, without
any apparent connection with each other.

There is nothing to prevent a man marrying a girl and taking her
abroad to dispose of her. He can do this over and over again, for who
is to discover it or accuse him of bigamy?

As to breaking the girls in, the methods remain classic—as they do
in the breaking in of horses—the old techniques of brutal beatings,
burnings and other tortures, multiple rape, being imprisoned nude
and starved till their spirit is broken. Their character destroyed by

drugs and alcohol, and completely intimidated by fear of further brutality, disfigurement, and even murder, the girls soon become the passive instruments of their masters.

Promises of marriage, or of employment abroad as dancers or entertainers are the usual bait offered to the young women who finally end in the brothels, or on the streets working for their owners.

It has always been easy to trick girls with promises of marriage or of lucrative employment abroad, particularly if connected with the theater. Bright lights, pretty clothes, and admiration all tempt them.

The advertisements on pages 414 and 415 are legitimate examples of the kind of thing which will always evoke a response among attractive and adventurous young women.

Officially, white slave traffic has ceased to exist in Europe. But it still goes on under many guises. One example being the producer who sends out a small band of chorus girls to Algiers or Beirut and conveniently leaves them stranded. While trying to get their passage home from the Consul, another producer arrives and offers them a part in a "show" that often turns out to be in a fifth-rate bar-cum-brothel.

It is known that a number of rich Arabs still have white women in their harems. How they are recruited is anybody's guess.

Prostitutes are lured from waterfront bars in France and taken to North Africa. Some are drugged. One reason prostitutes are so often chosen is that nobody notices that they are missing—and if their absence is noticed, it is seldom reported to the police.

A relatively new twist in the abduction of respectable girls and their reduction to chattel status is getting them to become drug addicts. A junky requires a minimum of 50 dollars per day to satisfy her craving. The man who supplies her is her master, and to obtain her "fix" she will do whatever she is told.

Girls and women are highly negotiable articles. Traded like animals, they are passed from hand to hand and from country to country.

The Girl That Disappears

General Theodore H. Bingham, former Police Commissioner of New York
Richard Badger. Gorham Press, Boston, 1911

Fairly established prices are maintained for women and they are referred to in letters that have been found as "stock." A few of these girls are starved or clubbed into submission after they reach the United States. London is known throughout the underworld as "the great breaking-in ground" for white slaves.

Girls who fail in their auditions and are
down on their luck could be picked up
and offered spurious contracts at the exits.

[421]

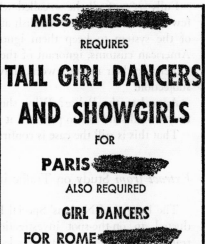

Advertisements taken from "Stage and Television Today," October 11, 1962; all quite legitimate, but indicating the possibilities of trickery.

The majority of the men engaged in the traffic are also foreigners. A Frenchman, Alphonse Dufaur, living in Chicago, made $100,000 a year as an importer, according to his books.

I [General Theodore H. Bingham, former Police Commissioner of New York] would stake my reputation on my ability to take half a dozen conscientious investigators and within a year show five hundred cases of women lured from their homes in France, Hungary or some other European countries, taken first to London and there subjected to terrible forms of cruelty, and then brought to this country—slaves in every sense of the word.

At least 2,000 of them are brought into this country every year. Brought in like cattle, used far worse than cattle and disposed of like cattle for money.

Fully 95% of all the so-called white slaves are foreigners. . . . Very few of them understand English at all. This is necessarily so. It is part of the system to keep them ignorant of the language, ignorant of American customs, ignorant of their rights under the American Law. Otherwise their masters would have difficulty in keeping them under subjection.

Appeal to the Police? Why, she has been terrorised into believing they would send her to prison if it were not for her master.

That this is still the case is confirmed by a United Nations study.

Extract from Study on Traffic in Persons and Prostitution. *U.N.*

The League of Nations' Special Body of Experts, which in 1927 conducted an on-the-spot investigation into conditions relating to the traffic in persons in twenty-six selected countries of the American continent, Europe and the Middle East, reported that:

> . . . reliable information has been obtained from certain countries which justifies the belief that a traffic of considerable dimensions is being carried on. Many hundreds of women and girls—some of them very young—are transported each year from one country to another for purposes of prostitution. In some countries, where the number of registered prostitutes is very high, 70 per cent are foreign women and it may safely be inferred that the class of clandestine prostitutes in these countries also includes a large percentage of foreigners.

Moreover, in recent years, the traffickers have been giving nominally legal forms to their illicit activities so as to circumvent the provisions of the law. This means that the new pattern in which the traffic is carried on may not be easily detected or reflected in the statistics of offences reported.[1]

In November, 1964, Col. Patrick Montgomery, M.C. of the Anti-Slavery Society in London wrote to me that he did hear in an off-the-record conversation the other day that Interpol's estimate of the annual traffic in white girls abducted from Europe for prostitution is 20,000. This estimate, though coming from a semi-official source, cannot be regarded as authoritative.

This figure seems excessive, but remains fantastic even if divided by ten.

It is impossible to obtain figures for girls between the ages of 15 to 25 who disappear. No records appear to be kept of missing girls. Many, of course, just run away from home. But what happens to them?

Extract from Slavery To-day

Commander T. Fox-Pitt, O.B.E.

Anti-Slavery Society

. . . It is, however, about the form of slavery where men, women and children are liable to be bought and sold that I wish to write here. It is a matter which particularly concerns women and children, because they are far more vulnerable than men.

With the wealth that has come to the oil royalty owners of Saudi Arabia and Kuwait, the demand has increased and the net is flung farther afield than ever before. The prices offered for girl slaves for the harems of the Arabian princes have risen steadily.

In 1947, when the oil revenues were beginning to be effective, Wilfred Thesiger, the great traveller, reported that a woman slave was worth £175 to £225.

In 1953, the Ambassador of France in Arabia reported to his Government that a girl of 15 years of age could cost as much as £400.

In 1955 a French woman doctor on a medical mission to the Yemen reported the offer of £700 for a fair-skinned girl. The deal was to be subject to a medical examination by the doctor. She found the girl terrified at being sold away from her family and friends, and she refused to give the certificate. She felt the mere request for such a thing most deeply wounding to her integrity as a doctor.

In 1959, a friend of mine, who was English tutor to an Arabian prince, said that his employer had paid the price of a luxury American

[1] Pp. 4–5.

car for a 13-year-old Syrian dancing girl. Rich princes, he said, would buy two new girls for their harems every year.

From other sources come reports of a traffic in women kidnapped, or tricked, or beguiled, into Arabian harems from the Lebanon, Turkey and even from Europe. To bear this out we have evidence from the courts of Cairo in which a wife prosecuted her husband for selling her to an Arabian prince. She was a beautiful woman, with the fashionable and exciting beauty of Queen Soraya of Persia, and her husband had received £3,300 for her. In the court, evidence came out of this husband having sold 65 ex-wives in this way over a course of years. For most he was prepared to accept £2,000.

But prices still mount, and our latest informants say that no slave, man or woman, can be bought for less than £1,000 and almost any young woman is worth £3,000. . . . A Swedish traveller on a Sudanese plane from Sudan to Arabia, noticed a number of African children from near Kano in Northern Nigeria. The adults in the party had return tickets; the children, however, had singles—for the good reason that they were not to return. All wear the traditional white robes of the pilgrim to the holy city of Mecca and the children would not know, until the journey was over, that they were to be sold as slaves.

Reports of this slave traffic, in the guise of pilgrimages, come from many places. They are part of the evidence on which the Anti-Slavery Society bases its demand that the slavery conventions of the United Nations be more effectively put into action.

At present there is no one who holds the personal responsibility for collating the information which Member States are obliged to give to the Secretary-General about slavery practices.

Extract from Cape Times Weekend Magazine. *June 20, 1964*

Ibn Saud's Harem by Richard Whitby

. . . Official French sources revealed that hundreds of girls under 15, from the French Cameroons, are sold annually to Saudi Arabia. Similar reports come from Germany. The Bonn Government has undertaken a top secret intelligence investigation that may explode the sex traffic in the Middle East. Countless German girls, under 21, seeking male companionship have gone to "friendship clubs," bars and cafés and been persuaded by debonair gentlemen to seek romantic adventures in Beirut and Damascus. When they arrive in these cities, they soon journey southward into the Middle East and become part of a potentate's harem.

Girls between 15 and 20 are preferred and undergo extensive training in the art of love before acceptance. Many do not realise that they are slaves and have been sold for a price. A fair haired, well-shaped buxom beauty has brought as much as £8,000 in the white slave market! A sizeable number of Swedish, English and Danish girls, travelling in Europe, reportedly [vanish]. . . .

The story that follows is a detailed account of an actual case.

The Tragedy of Micheline Pierre
Folder Published by the Association for Moral & Social Hygiene

In 1952, Micheline Pierre, a pretty 17-year-old brunette from Normandie, gave up the humdrum life on a small farm for what she believed to be the more exciting experiences of living in Paris. Having landed a job as housemaid, she used to spend her evenings off in one or the other of the big city's innumerable dance halls.

In one of these, on May 2nd 1953, Micheline made the acquaintance of a portly middle-aged individual who called himself Leon-Joseph Abiteboul, and who impressed her as being a man of considerable means. The Algerian, who posed as a wealthy businessman, not only showered the girl with gifts, but he also before long proposed marriage.

After the betrothal, Abiteboul suggested to his fiancée a trip to Oran, Algeria, where the girl could stay with one of his aunts, he said. Micheline accepted and on May 13th the couple went to Le Bourget to board an Air France direct plane to Oran.

On arrival at the airport, they were met by a cousin of Abiteboul, a taxi driver named Marcel. The fiancé having excused himself, Marcel took charge of the girl. He put her into his cab (No. 14) and drove her straight to the brothel "Chez Rosette" (1 Rue Sainte-Thérèse).

When Micheline realised that she had fallen into a trap, she tried to escape, but each time she was recaptured and subjected to a severe beating. After a few weeks at "Chez Rosette," she was transferred to another licensed house, "Nana" (17, Rue de l'Aqueduc), operated by a man named Georges Sadok and his common-law wife, Adèle Barreau. It was this couple of notorious procurers who had "bought" Micheline from Abiteboul, it was later learned.

On July 10th, the girl, after having undergone another brutal beating, made a desperate dash for freedom which succeeded. Bruised and suffering from multiple internal injuries, she managed to drag herself to the State Hospital (Hôpital Civil) where she was admitted.

At this stage, you would think, the hapless victim of ruthless white slavers was safe. Surely, in a state hospital, she would be given not only care but protection. And, once the sad case had come to public knowledge, some social welfare agency undoubtedly would take charge and afford the girl an opportunity to return to a normal life.

The truth is far different. While at the hospital, Micheline received the visit of her tormentors, Georges Sadok and Marcel, the cousin of Abiteboul (who in the meantime had returned to Paris). The two men harshly told her to get out of there quick or take the consequences.

Micheline balked and asked that the police be informed but nobody came to her rescue. On September 13 she was discharged from the hospital. At the very gates she was met by the same gangsters and whisked away in a taxi to a secret hideout in the small town of Arzew. From there she was subsequently transferred to a brothel at Sidi-bel-Abbès, headquarters of the Foreign Legion.

What aggravates this scandalous case even more, is that the Oran police not only failed to take action to save the young woman, but did so in spite of a published report on the matter.

Indeed, in mid-October 1953, a Reuter dispatch from Paris told the story of Micheline's abduction and her subsequent misfortunes up to the point of her successful escape and admission to the hospital. The dispatch disclosed that Abiteboul had been arrested in Paris. Investigation disclosed that he was a regular supplier of Sadok's establishment and had already made delivery of a substantial number of young women at a price of 100,000 francs per head.

At Abiteboul's place, detectives found a number of telegrams which the Algerian had received from his business friend in Oran.

Some of these wires read: "Violets received. Smell good. Congratulations. Georgette." This message indicated that Sadok had approved the shipment and was sending the money as arranged.

On the other hand, if he was not satisfied, Sadok used to wire Abiteboul: "Violets Arrived Faded." That meant rejection of the "Goods," and no payment.

Thus, it seems that the Paris police were in possession of all the facts yet, amazingly, its opposite number in Oran took no action to save Micheline.

So serious are these dangers to young women that in 1913 the British Government caused to be issued to all telephone girls at the London exchanges an extraordinary warning against white slavers and their despicable devices. Included with the Government circular was this Girls' Friendly Society leaflet.

A Circular Issued by The Girls' Friendly Society
Warning to Girls—Forewarned is Forearmed

Girls should never speak to strangers, either men or women, in the streets, in shops, in stations, in trains, in lonely country roads, or in places of amusement.

Girls should never ask the way of any but officials on duty such as policemen, railway officials, or postmen.

Girls should never loiter or stand about alone in the street and, if accosted by a stranger (whether man or woman) should walk as quickly as possible to the nearest policeman.

Girls should never stay to help a woman who apparently faints at their feet in the street, but should immediately call a policeman to her aid.

Girls should never accept an invitation to join a Sunday School or Bible Class given them by strangers, even if they are wearing the dress of a Sister or a Nun, or are in Clerical dress.

Girls should never accept a lift offered by a stranger in a motor, taxicab or vehicle of any description.

Girls should never go to an address given to them by a stranger (even if dressed as a hospital nurse), or believe stories of their relatives having suffered from an accident, or being suddenly taken ill, as this is a common device to kidnap girls.

Girls should never accept sweets, food, a glass of water or smell flowers offered them by a stranger. Neither should they buy scents or other articles at their door as so many things may contain drugs.

Girls should never take a situation through an advertisement or in a strange registry office, whether in England or abroad, without first making enquiries from the society to which they belong.

Girls should never go to London or any large town for even one night without knowing of some safe lodging.

Extract from News of the World Apr. 21, 1963

South to Danger by Charles Sandell

Hundreds of young girls pouring into London from Britain's jobless areas are heightening the vice problem. Lonely and friendless, they are easy prey for the touts who draw them into their web.

They arrive at King's Cross and Euston from the North-East, Merseyside, Scotland and Northern Ireland. Some follow husbands and boyfriends in the big trek South for work. But most of them are alone, without a job, without accommodation.

... Many spend their first day hanging around cafés near the stations, miserable and willing victims of evil men.

Mr. G. J. Morley Jacob, magistrate at a London juvenile court and chairman of the London Haven for Women and Girls, told me: "These girls are in grave moral danger. . . ."

Last year the hostel gave temporary accommodation to 464 women and girls. Miss S. A. Shepherd said: "We get girls from all parts of Britain and from Eire, Cyprus, Holland, Italy, Malta and the West Indies. It is amazing how many young girls still come to London expecting, if not to find the streets paved with gold, something very similar. Their stories of poverty, cruelty and foolishness make tragic listening."

Extract from Cape Times May 29, 1965

MILAN. The head of the Milan detective squad, Mr. Gianni Grappone, yesterday said his men were on the trail of a vast white slave ring and that International Police (Interpol) had been asked to help.

Mr. Grappone told a news conference that the ring appeared to be active throughout Europe, seeking beautiful girls for shipment to Africa. Italian newspapers said the ring also sent girls to the Middle East and even Nevada, in the United States. The detective squad chief said the ring had sent an undetermined number of Italian and other European women to Africa over the past two years. He said they were forced to work as prostitutes.

Mr. Grappone gave these details: About a month ago an advertisement appeared in a Milan newspaper saying: "Beautiful girls sought for work as bar attendants at a sea resort."

Police investigated and said the advertisement had been inserted by the owner of a café in Liberia. Hundreds of girls answered, but only the really beautiful ones were given any serious consideration. Once, while checking on the advertisement, police tapped a telephone conversation and heard a man say: "Either she leaves, or we will take her by force."

Two days ago police moved. They took a man and two beautiful girls into custody at the Milan airport as the girls were preparing to board an aircraft leaving for Sierra Leone.

ROME. Interpol—the international police organization—ordered a worldwide search to-day for a plane chartered in Milan yesterday and believed carrying nearly 100 young, blonde European women bound for Arabian harems or African brothels. White slave traffickers were alleged to have chartered the aircraft. . . .

It was disclosed that the planeload of girls left Milan earlier on a chartered flight for Monrovia with stopoffs in Lebanon, Saudi Arabia and Nigeria.

Italian police said girls were recruited through newspaper ads in Rome and Milan. The ads asked for attractive, young girls to work abroad as dancers, hostesses and waitresses. The organisation recruited girls with contracts for nightclub work, but once they arrived abroad they were forced to enter harems or brothels, the police said.

BONN. Dec. 3, 1964. A 34-year-old German worker was sentenced at Nuremberg to 10 years for raping six women whom he had anaesthetized with an ether-soaked glove before the attack.

Georg Rotschka, the court said, assaulted his prey in dark alleys of suburban settlements and clamped his left hand, wearing a glove, over the victim's face. The woollen glove was soaked with ether before the attack.

He raped his victims while they were unconscious.

Extracts from The Last Days of the British Raj
Leonard Mosley

But not all India celebrated with such harmless ecstasy on Independence Day. That morning, in the bazaar quarter of Amritsar, the Sikhs rounded up a large group of Muslim girls and women, stripped them of their clothes, and then forced them to parade in a circle before the jeering crowd. Then a number of the choicest and youngest were dragged off and raped repeatedly.[2]

. . . 600,000 dead. 14,000,000 driven from their homes. 100,000 young girls kidnapped by both sides, forcibly converted or sold on the auction block.[3]

[2] P. 242.

[3] P. 244. A combined Pakistani-Indian Commission to trace these young women was formed but its efforts petered out; principally, according to the Pakistanis, because the Hindus refused to have their wives and daughters back—they had been defiled.

A further example proving that the position of women is dependent on law and order, is what has taken place recently in the Congo. Not only were white women raped and abused by the rebels, but also hundreds of black women suffered the same fate at the hands of the rebels, the *Jeunesse,* the Congolese forces, and finally the troops of the United Nations, particularly those of Ethiopia.

Loot and rape have always gone together, women being regarded as a major part of the booty.

Extract from News of the World *dated Dec. 27, 1964*

Smooth Talk Lures Au Pair Girls

Detectives have uncovered a vice ring which lures au pair girls into a life of crime and prostitution. Dozens of Swedish and German girls are believed to have fallen into the gang's clutches. . . .

Allegations have frequently been made in Continental newspapers that many au pair girls who come to Britain quickly fall into moral danger. In one year, 61 unmarried German girls gave birth to babies in Britain. Another 437 pregnant German girls were sent home so that their children wouldn't become British. In a language club in the West End of London I spoke to several au pair girls who claim they narrowly escaped being enticed into vice dens in Notting Hill. [One girl], a 21-year-old German, told me: "Social welfare organisations are continually warning girls who come over here. But through lack of money or because they've overstayed their work permit, many girls are tempted by the touts that frequent the West End offering good homes to au pair girls."

Another girl said: "The touts say: 'If you have a girl friend back home who wants to stay in a good home and earn a big salary we can arrange it.'" It is only after they succumb to such smooth talk and accept the offer, that girls find most of these homes are no more than call-girl establishments run by a madam. At first the girls are given a luxurious room with modern fittings and furniture. In return they are asked to do simple domestic work. After a few days the girl is invited to a party and introduced to young men. These men have just one purpose, to get a hold over the girl by any method available, not excluding drugs and blackmail. Once the ring gets a hold on the girl, she is smartly moved from her luxury quarters, and the trap is prepared for another gullible girl. The girls, trapped in an embarrassing situation, are often too ashamed to tell their parents and afraid to go to the police.

Embassy officials are constantly warning au pair girls to stay out of dingy drinking clubs. But the vice touts are now moving into social "language" clubs with their evil offers.

The National Council of Women are pressing Sir Frank Soskice, the Home Secretary, to bring in legislation which will give au pair girls better conditions, and better terms of employment and make them less vulnerable to tempting offers from touts.

MEXICO CITY. Oct. 7, 1964. Secret police are checking an 11-year-old kidnap victim's story that a man is abducting young Mexican girls and selling them abroad.

Maria F. Lopez Mendoza says she escaped from the gang after being held prisoner for nine days. She told police at least eight other girls were kidnapped while she was in captivity.

Maria quoted one of her captors as saying, "We'll take these kids out of the country in a few days. We ought to clean up on this cargo."

TO: Parker Latam

FM: Lozano, Mexcity   Rec'd Jan. 17, 1964   (condensed)

. . . Delfina and Maria de Jesus Gonzalez 55 and 40 years old sisters . . . [were white slavers who] not only furnished [girls] to all well known non-santa houses in States of Jalisco and Guanajuato, but had their own "houses" and a concentration camp with private cemetery and crematory furnace to get rid of [those] that were useless to them when they got sick or refused to work as prostitutes any longer. Concentration camp was a ranch called "Lomas de San Angel" about 9 miles from the city of Leon in Guanajuato.

. . . The police received denunciation from three women of Guadalajara saying that their daughters had been kidnapped by two sisters well known as Madams and white slavery operators. After five days investigation [the ranch was raided.] . . . [One] of the police noticed [a] soft spot in the ground [and] decided to investigate . . . and discovered a young woman's arm. [After] investigation [they] found 5 bodies of young women buried in the ranch, and remains of 16 others. Inside the house [they] found 19 young women among them the 3 girls from Guadalajara. . . . The girls at first refused to talk. They were scared to death. After the police fed them and assured them that there would be nothing to be scared of they started to talk, and the horrible truth came out.

The Lomas de San Angel ranch was a prison and concentration camp owned by two sisters Delfina and Maria de Jesus Gonzalez, who were the leaders of white slavery ring, operating in center part of Mexico covering the States of Guanajuato [and] Jalisco. These two women . . . operated brothels in [the] town of San Francisco del Rincón and León in Guanajuato and in Largos de Moreno [in the] State of Jalisco. Police learned also that Delfina and Maria de Jesus Gonzalez were "Suppliers" for the brothels of Chihuahua, Guadalajara, Tijuana, Torreón, Tampico, Durango and Juárez.

Their operation included drivers, women helpers, grave diggers and protection men. They needed the drivers to transport the girls from one place to another, the women helpers to take care of their girls, prisoners in the camp of Lomas de San Angel.

Soon as any girl refused to work as [a] prostitute she was taken to the ranch and subject[ed] to tortures by the women helpers. Many didn't resist the tortures and died, then bodies were burned with kerosene and buried in the ranch.

. . . Once the girl was considered "experienced" she could be sold to Tijuana or to Torreón. The price 1000 pesos. Girls, like in every other brothel in the world, were up to their neck in debt, fancy dresses, shoes, jewelry . . . cigarettes and perfumes were all noted in the Madam's books in the San Francisco del Rincón brothel as debts of the girls.

In Lagos de Moreno the brothel was little tougher—rough *campesinos* and cattlemen were the regular customers. . . . Some of the girls rebelled against the tyranny of the two sisters. When this happened Maria de Jesus ordered the drivers to take girls to the Lomas de San Angel ranch and [keep them] there as prisoners until they either died or promised that they would behave better.

Maria de Jesus and Delfina confessed their white slavery operations [and] agreed with police [guess] of [the] sale of about 2000 girls in ten years of operation.

Extract from Cape Times *June 15, 1963*

White Slave Traffic on Ivory Coast

TOULON. Police here and in Africa's Ivory Coast are investigating a white slave ring which has shipped French girls to West Africa. Several men have already been arrested in Toulon.

One girl from the Toulon area who went to Abidjan, capital of the

Ivory Coast, is reported to have killed herself as the result of her experiences there.

The father of the girl, 21-year-old Marcelle Gernero, has written to the Ivory Coast President M. Felix Houphouet-Boigny, asking for an investigation into his daughter's death.

IN BROTHELS

Several girls have left the Toulon area lately for Abidjan. They told their families that they had been offered good jobs there.

The families fear that the girls were victims of a white slave gang and are in brothels in Abidjan.

Abidjan police informed French authorities that any French girl who wished to return home was free to do so, but that some girls were in such bad physical condition they did not want their families to see them (Sapa-Reuter).

Extract from Time Mar. 16, 1962

ARMED FORCES—Where the Boys Go

Every weekend at the big U.S. naval base in San Diego, the cry goes up: "Let's go down below," or "Let's bug out to T.J." Soon battalions of fuzzy-faced young servicemen are headed across the Mexican border. Since World War II, when the Government cleaned most of them out as a protection to servicemen, U.S. sin centers have been relatively tame, but vice has prospered in the Mexican border towns, and today it is flourishing as never before.

. . . For almost two miles on both sides of Avenida Revolución, Tijuana's main drag, bright yellow, white, red, blue and green neon signs festoon the dirty façades of grubby joints. In front of each stands a swarthy doorman, generally wearing baggy dark pants and a soiled red coat with heavily padded shoulders. He calls in an inviting voice: "Hey, Meester! Want to see nice French movies? Nice exhibition? You want nice girls?"

Each place is liberally supplied with a dozen or more importuning B-girls; some are as young as 15, others are tired strumpets of 45. Invariably, the "Show" lives up to the doorman's guarantee. A girl enters to the tune of an unlikely song such as *Sweet Georgia Brown,* clanked out by an instrumental trio. Slowly she sheds a shoddy evening gown while the audience yells, "Take it off, Baby, take it off!" When she has stripped down to pure buff, she bumps and grinds for a few minutes, then glides around the circle of ringside tables, stopping whenever a clean-cut, brush-topped young man reaches out to touch-test her salient features.

Extract from a Letter from The Anti-Slavery Society July 20, 1964

Dear Mr. Cloete:

. . . A report was published in 1955 by the Movement for Colonial Freedom, in London, written by an American named Joachim Joesten, which dealt with prostitution and white slavery in (then) French North Africa. He estimates that the annual traffic in girls from Europe to N. Africa averaged 10,000 girls, most of whom were abducted and who were destined for the brothels kept for the French soldiers.

I consider that this society has a special duty to discover what became of these white girls when the French troops were withdrawn. Joesten found that the French Govt. could not consider legislating against brothels in N. Africa (1) because their troops "needed" them and (a) because they needed the support of the local potentates, such as the Glaoui of Marrakesh who himself levied a tax of 100 frcs. per day per "prostitute"—of whom there were then 6,000 in Marrakesh.

Joesten said that 60% of the clients were American. Thus it is very unlikely that the demand has fallen drastically, at least in some parts. Even if the demand has fallen it is very doubtful if this would have sufficed to gain the release of the girls.

I shall be most grateful for such information and support on this subject as you can give me.

(signed)
Col. J. R. P. Montgomery, M.C.

This evidence should convince even the most skeptical of the continued existence of white slave traffic, enforced prostitution, and the dangers to which girls are exposed. Young women are easily broken in as prostitutes and are regarded as expendable. The purveyors of Flesh are difficult to catch and still harder to convict. But anyone interested in human rights must be shocked to find these violations on his own doorstep.

Extract from Sunday Times *May* 15, 1966

LONDON. An Arabian office worker, Abdullah Rageh, after making allegations to the police that child brides are being sold in the Midlands for £100 each, has gone into hiding because he fears an attempt on his life.

His claims that the girls, daughters of English and Arab parents, are being sold through a syndicate to Arabs in the Yemen after ostensibly being sent to men in Aden who want wives.

Rageh said: "Sometimes these girls are never heard of again . . . I do not know how much the syndicate gets for the service, but I do know that the mother—who is usually married to an Arab—gets £100."

Rageh said he was beaten after telling Home Office officials in London about the racket.

BIBLIOGRAPHY

BIBLIOGRAPHY

Abandoned Child, The. Bramwell Booth and others.

Age of Extravagance, The. Mary Edes and Dudley Frasier.

Alison Nielands Memorial Lecture. "Moral Standards of To-day." Association for Moral and Social Hygiene.

Armstrong Case, The. W. T. Stead. (pamphlet).

Behind the Veil in Arabia. Jorgen Bisch.

Bernard Shaw. Life and Memories. Hesketh Pearson.

Broken Earthenware. Harold Begbie. (Hodder & Stoughton).

Cast the First Stone. (Judge) John M. Murtagh and Sara Harris.

Chapters on Human Love. Geoffrey Mortimer. (University Press. 1894).

Commercialised Prostitution in New York. (Century Co.).

Commissioner G. S. Railton. Mildred Duff and Eileen Douglas. (S.P. & S.).

Comparative Survey of Laws in force for the Prohibition of Vice, A. Amos Sheldon.

Darkest London. Mrs. Cecil Chesterton.

Darkest Orient. Riza Bey.

Der Salutismus. Dr. P. A. Clasen. (Eugen Diederichs, Jena).

Echoes and Memories. Bramwell Booth. (Hodder & Stoughton).

Elegant Woman, The. Gertrude Aretz.

English Social History. G. M. Trevelyan. (Longmans, Green & Co.).

European Slave Trade in English Girls, The. Alfred S. Dyer. (pamphlet).

Family and the Nation, The. W. C. D. and C. Whethan.

Fire Escape, The. Susan Kole.

General Booth and His Critics. H. Greenwood, M.A., LL.D. (Howe & Co. 1891).

General's Daughter, Soldier's Friend (Mary Murray, O.B.E.). Dora V. Gilliard. (S.P. & S.).

Girl That Disappears, The. General Theodore H. Bingham. (Police Commissioner for Greater New York. 1911).

Girl with the Swansdown Seat, The. Cyril Pearl.

God in the Slums. Hugh Redwood. (Hodder & Stoughton. 1930).

Government Publications:

    League of Nations. *Report of the Special Body of Experts on Traffic in Women and Children:* Part One and Part Two. Geneva. 1927.

    Report and Minutes of Evidence of the Royal Commission on the Administration and Operation of the Contagious Diseases Acts. 1871.

    United Nations: *Department of Economic and Social Affairs Study on Traffic in Persons and Prostitution.* New York. 1959.

Hansard. 1880–1885.

Happy Warrior, The. Humphrey Wallis. (S.P. & S.).

History of Prostitution. William W. Sanger, M.D. 1876.

History of the Salvation Army, Vol. III, The. Robert Sandall. (Nelson).

History of Underclothes, The. Drs. Willet and Phillis Cunnington.

Hotch Potch. Adelaide Cox. (S.P. & S.).

In Darkest England and the Way Out. William Booth.

International Review of Criminal Policy. No. 13. Oct. 1959. U.N.

International Social Council Addresses. 1911 and 1921.

Josephine Butler. Moberly Bell.

Josephine Butler. W. T. Stead. (pamphlet).

Josephine Butler: Her Place in History. E. M. Turner. (pamphlet).

Josephine Butler—Letters (MSS) (In Fawcett Library, Westminster).

Josephine Butler's Printed Works:

    Recollections of George Butler. 1892.

    Salvation Army in Switzerland. 1883.

    The Constitution Violated. 1871.

    The Dawn (periodical). 1888–1896.

    The Hour before the Dawn. 1882.

    Une Voix dans le Désert. 1875.

    Woman's Work and Woman's Culture. (Ed. J. E. B.) 1869.

Josephine Butler—Memoirs:

    Josephine Butler. An Autobiographical Sketch. (Eds. Geo. W. and Lucy A. Johnson). Arrowsmith. 1909.

    Josephine Butler and Her Work for Social Purity. L. Hay-Cooper. SPCK. 1922.

    Josephine Butler. Her Work and Principles and their meaning for the Twentieth Century. Written for the J. B. Centenary 1828–

1928, by Millicent Fawcett and E. M. Turner. Association for Moral and Social Hygiene.

Portrait of Josephine Butler. A. S. G. Butler. (Faber & Faber. 1954).

A State of Iniquity. Its Rise, Extension and Overthrow. A Concise History of the System of State Regulated and Licensed Vice. Benjamin Scott, F.R.A.S. (Kegan Paul. 1890).

A Rough Record of Events and Incidents Connected with the Repeal of the Contagious Diseases Acts. Privately Printed, by Henry J. Wilson of Sheffield, 1907.

Jowett: A Portrait with Background. Sir Geoffrey Faber. (Faber. 1957).

Kingdom-Makers in Shelter, Street and Slum. Brigadier Margaret Allen. (The Warriors' Library No. 6, 1909).

Last Days of the British Raj. Leonard Mosley.

Law Journal Reports. 1885.

Life of Benjamin Waugh, The. Rosa Waugh. (Fisher Unwin).

Life of Catherine Booth, The. F. de L. Booth-Tucker. (S.P. & S.).

Life of W. T. Stead, The. Frederic Whyte. (Jonathan Cape).

Living and Dying by the Needle. Thomas Hood.

Lord Shaftesbury and Social-Industrial Progress. J. Wesley Bready. (George Allen & Unwin).

Love, Marriage and Romance in Old London. C. J. S. Thompson. (Heath Cranton).

Maiden Tribute. Charles Terrot.

Maiden Tribute. Madge Unsworth. (Salvationist Publishing & Supplies Ltd.).

Master Problem, The. James Marchant. (Century Co. 1916).

Mayfair and Montmartre. Ralph Nevill. (Methuen).

Men in My Life, The. Marthe Watts.

Morality Fair. Geoffrey Williamson.

My Father. Estelle Stead. (Heinemann).

My Fifty-eight Years. Commissioner Edward J. Parker. (S.A. New York. 1943).

My Life Story. Mrs. Bramwell Booth. (*Sunday Circle*).

North London White Slave Traffic, Criminal Law Conference 1913.

Official Shorthand Transcriptions, taken at the Central Criminal Court. 1885.

Panders and Their White Slaves. Clifford E. Roe.

Personal Reminiscences of a Great Crusade. Josephine Butler.

Pioneer Policewoman. Commandant Mary Allen.

Problem of the Nations, The. A. Corbett-Smith.

Prostitutes and Their Parasites. J. G. Mancini.

Prostitution. Association for Moral and Social Hygiene. (pamphlet).

Prostitution in Europe. Abraham Flexner. 1914.

Prostitution in Europe and the Western World. Dr. Fernando Henriques.

Prostitution dans le Monde, La. Marcel Sicot.

Psychology of Clothes, The. J. C. Flügel.

Public Morals. Morgan & Scott.

Rebecca Jarrett. Josephine Butler. (Morgan & Scott).

Rebecca Jarrett. W. T. Stead. (pamphlet).

Regeneration. Rider Haggard. 1910.

Review of the 1892 Committee of Inquiry (Harrison & Sons, or Simpkin, Marshall, Hamilton, Kent & Co. Ltd.).

Road to Buenos Aires, The. Albert Londres.

Romance of the Salvation Army, The. Hulda Friedrichs. (Cassell & Co.).

Salvation Army as a Social Force, The. Frederick A. McKenzie. 1900.

Salvation Army Publications:

All the World

The Deliverer

The Quiver

The Revival

Sunday Circle

The War Cry

Salvation Army, The.

Salvation Army Year Book. 1962.

Servants of All. Bramwell Booth. 1900.

Sessional Papers. House of Commons. 1880–1885.

Sessional Papers. House of Lords. 1880–1885.

Sex in History. Rattray Taylor.

Shame of a City, The. John Gosling.

She Avenged Her Father. Gladys Taylor. (S. P. & S.).

Shield, The. Oct. 1961. Nov. 1962.

Sisters of the Night. Jess Stearn.

Six Years' Labour and Sorrow. (4th Report of the London Commission for Suppressing the Traffic in British Girls for Continental Prostitution).

Social Diseases and Worse Remedies. T. H. Huxley, F.R.S. (Macmillan & Co. 1891).

Social Evil, The. (Putnam).

Social Evils the Army Has Challenged. Lieut. Commissioner S. Carvosso Gauntlett. (1946.)

Social Reparation. Bramwell Booth. 1899.

State Regulated Vice. B. Scott (Dyer Brothers).

Street Walker, The. Anon. (Bodley Head).

Study on Traffic in Persons. U.N. 59/IV/5

Three Great Hearts: Commissioner Randolph J. Sturgess, Colonel James Barker and Brigadier Frank Aspinall. Mrs. Colonel Carpenter. 1928.

Times Law Reports, The. 1885.

Tracts on Social and Industrial Questions 1845–86.

Traffic in Innocents. Charles Terrot.

Trial of Stephen Ward, The. Ludovic Kennedy.

Truth about the Armstrong Case and The Salvation Army, The. (pamphlet).

Under the Surface. Mrs. Creighton.

Underworld of a Great City. Alexander Gammie. (Pickering & Inglis Ltd. 1942).

Victorian Vista. James Laver. (Hulton Press).

Vision and Its Fulfillment, A. W. A. Coote.

Vito Genovese, King of Crime. Dom Frasca.

W. T. Stead. A Life for the People. Benjamin Waugh. (pamphlet).

Weakest Link, The. Free Church Council.

Western Men with Eastern Morals. W. N. Willis. 1913.

White Slave Market, The. W. N. Willis. Mrs. Archibald Mackirdy (Stanley Paul & Co.).

White Slavery of Europe, The. Pastor T. Borel. (From the French).

White Slaves of London, The. W. N. Willis.

Why I Went to Prison. W. T. Stead. (pamphlet).

Why We Attacked the "Empire." Mrs. Ormiston Chant.

Woman at Scotland Yard, A. Lilian Wyles, B.E.M. (Faber & Faber Ltd.).

Also Letters, Pamphlets and Books from:

The Association for Moral and Social Hygiene

The International Bureau for the Suppression of Traffic in Persons

The Anti-Slavery Society